Children of the Holocaust

CHILDREN *of the*
HOLOCAUST

ARNOŠT LUSTIG

Translated by Jeanne Němcová
and by George Theiner

NORTHWESTERN UNIVERSITY PRESS

Evanston, Illinois

Northwestern University Press
Evanston, Illinois 60208-4210

Printed in the United States of America

ISBN 0-8101-1279-5

✾

Contents

NIGHT AND HOPE

✻

The Return

No, the relief he had expected to feel did not come. True, it had been pretty bad in the hole. But now that he was out of it, he had nowhere to go. He took an uncertain look along the street and stopped abruptly. Walk, he told himself, as if you were on your way to the tailor. He started out again. Once he used to go like this to his coffeehouse, bowing slightly to acquaintances and knowing that he was one of them. Now he felt his chin trembling. But what could happen to him if he walked along, as he did now, unassumingly treading an empty stretch of pavement? One step—blue paving stones, another step—white. He must not be scared. What was there about him that anyone could notice? He struggled against a constricting feeling of doubt. The pressure in his temples called attention to itself by a violent throbbing. Jew! a voice called somewhere inside him. He was startled, was it his imagination, or did the houses on either side of him give back an echo? His legs carried him involuntarily off the pavement and into the gutter. But no, he admonished himself, that was nonsense. He mounted the pavement once more. One step, blue, another step, white. Did he have his money on him? With a feverish hand he felt his pocket. Was it all there? His white, bony fingers, thickly grown with black hairs, spread out on the coat like a convulsed fan. He sighed with relief, keeping his palm for a moment on the spot where he could feel through the cloth the tough leather of his wallet. He had forgotten something, though—his lips! He must not keep his mouth so tightly compressed. He remembered his moustache. The hand which, by a mere touch, had just conveyed a morsel of tranquillity to the mind of the little man suddenly shot up to his lips, fingering the almost invisible triangle of a moustache.

One step, blue paving stones, another step, white. And now the pavement was at an end. Was he to cross the street? Or should he go back? The echo of that last word reverberated inside him a thousand times and then faded into silence. Back—where? He crossed the street. He tried to visualize his own face, his thoughts again returning to the moustache. The moustache. He had shaved it two days ago, feeling that something would happen unless he did it. He had terrified the owner of the flat. What an idea! "But you can't go out, Mr. Tausig! It's daytime!" That was just why he had to go. The hole stifled him. A living being could not survive so long in the darkness of a hole scooped out of the kitchen wall and concealed by a sideboard. He simply had to go out, and that was why he had shaved. He had shaved deliberately slowly. A smell of marzipan hovered about the room. A round, white, blue-edged clock mechanically and unfeelingly ticked away the time. He washed the white lather off his face and dried himself with his handkerchief because he did not want to bother anyone for a towel. The elderly couple who sheltered him watched him anxiously, horrified by the thought that at that very moment someone would come rushing into their kitchen. They pulled the blinds down; the day changed into a grey semidarkness. "We don't have any children, Mr. Tausig, but we would still like to live to see the end of the war." There was nothing he could say. It seemed to him that, with his moustache gone, he had lost his face. He crept back into his hole and no longer rapped with his knuckles on the back of the sideboard. They would suffer with him, that was the trouble. The end of the war, he thought, when is that coming?

Hynek Tausig stroked his moustache with his fingertips. A car's horn hooted some distance away. There was a smell of marzipan, he recalled, while he had been shaving. And someone had talked about the end of the war. In a car which he could not see, someone was now driving somewhere, someone who knew where he was going. Some people had hope, others had nothing. Nothing at all. One step—blue paving stones, another step—white. His eyes surveyed the familiar patterns of the pavement. As a child he used to pick his way carefully so as to step only on the blue stones. That, he had believed, brought luck. He must not even now tread on the white ones. One step, blue, another step, blue. He must make bigger strides. If he did not step on the white, perhaps everything would turn out well. What about his wallet? He dropped his hands once more, the right pressing his hip. He should not be so scared. Better keep his arm there. But was that not too conspicuous? He let his arms drop alongside his body. Perhaps it would be a good idea to hide part of his money somewhere. But where was he to find a suitable place, a place he could go back to any time he needed? No, he decided, he would not hide it anywhere. If the Gestapo caught him, he would not be returning anywhere, in any case.

The small man was suddenly at a loss what to do with his hands. He tried putting them in his pockets, but was immediately startled by the thought that if he were to meet soldiers they might think he was holding a weapon there. He pulled his hands out abruptly as if they had been licked by some invisible flame. He crossed the street. Careful, he commanded himself, not so fast! Do you want to get into trouble for jaywalking! How stupid of him! He must not do that again.

Someone was walking straight at him. He swerved aside, his eyes diffidently gliding over the stranger's face. The face was unknown to him. Its image, however, remained in front of his eyes even though they were now peering at the ground as if searching for something there. He could see that face all the time, and now he was no longer so sure that it was unknown. A blue stone, a white. There was something familiar about it . . . Not the white. Blue, blue again, and another blue. He must not think about it, that was asking for bad luck. His eyes bored into the pavement. Now, in a flash, he saw that all his fond imaginings of the night before were nothing but a lot of nonsense—the idea that he would feel better in the street than in his hole, that the city was life whereas the hole was death, the street light and the recess in the wall night, and that nobody would recognize him because he had run to seed. Nothing was better. Neither the fact that he had shaved, nor the fact that his moustache had grown slightly again. Neither the hole nor the street. He bent forward over the pavement and walked on in this hunchback fashion. At least no one could see his face. A small, comforting certainty. A man walking in the opposite direction was close to him. They passed. All he saw were black shoes, frayed trouser cuffs of a rough grey material, and dried particles of mud. How was he to judge whether it was someone he knew from a little mud on grey trousers? He badly needed a little certainty. But whatever he did, he must not turn round. He stepped carefully only on the blue stones. Perhaps it was not anybody he knew, after all. But if it were and the man had not recognized him, then he might do so if he were to turn around now. Blue, blue, blue. He would go crazy. His head! But why was he walking along the main avenue all the time? If he did meet anyone he knew, he could easily pretend he was not who he really was, nor even what he was, but—how ridiculously little for twenty thousand!—Alfred Janota, engineer of a boiler-making firm in Hradec Králové. Blue, blue. He had an identity card to prove it. Black on white. Alfred Janota. Blue. His skull was sure to crack with the pain. But he must not turn around.

Blue. He must convince himself in the first place that he no longer had anything in common with Hynek Tausig. Did you say Tausig? Oh, dear me, no. I would not have anything to do with him. It sounds so terribly Jewish! Wasn't he some kind of traveling salesman? He felt like laughing, but only his chin shook. Tausig was Janota. What a comedy! Could he really believe it, though? If they hauled him off to the Petschek Palace, they would soon beat it out of his head, together with his teeth. Blue, blue. But he, Hynek Tausig, really was Alfred Janota. The identity card was genuine. He had paid twenty thousand for it. It bore the rubber stamp of the police headquarters of Prague's third precinct and the signature of a police official. Here was Tausig and here was Janota. A quick exchange. Here was the money and here was an identity card. Blue. What a transaction! How many times in one's life did one do it? For one's own money one became someone else. Blue, blue. He ought to take himself away somewhere and sit down. That man could not have known him or he would have been back a long time ago. Blue. If only there were a lawn somewhere near. Cool, springy grass. He longed to be able to plunge his elbows into it and to rest his head in his hands. Before, he could do this any time he liked. To support his head, before it burst into fragments. He turned away from the main avenue.

A little way off he reached a backwater. A quiet street enveloped in a blue veil of receding mist. There was nobody about. His eyes registered a deserted building site and, in front of him, a pub. A good thing he had come away from the busy thoroughfare. Squirrels carved by Italian stonemasons chased each other on the double stone portal of "The Green Hunter." It was an ancient house, an ancient pub. How about slipping in? The men who were just taking their break inside were doubtless workmen from the building site opposite. What time was it? Ten. The sight of people drove away the serenity of the quiet street. It suddenly seemed to him that the bricklayers inside there did not build apartments. They built nothing but holes, thousands of them. He felt sick. He circled the inn. No curtains in the windows, so that you could see into everyone's stomach, what they were eating and what they were drinking. Who was that leaning against the bar? And whose was the hat with a feather hanging on the wall? Any uniforms? No, no uniforms. "The Green Hunter." What a funny name. Like Janota. But better. A hunter was a hunter. And green at that. Nothing more. No pretense about it. Just a green hunter. What if one of the guests was a Vlajka man? Well, what if he was, Mr. Janota? he heard something say inside him. Why should you care? You have a tongue to speak with, haven't you? How are you? A member of the Vlajka, eh? Oh yes, a meritorious organization, that. It will rid us of the Jewish menace. And, who knows, perhaps sooner than our friends from the Reich. I knew a Jew once, too. Name of Tausig. Hynek Tausig. He sold vacuum cleaners. No, he was quite alone in the world, no relatives. Good, Mr. Janota. You're one of us. One can tell, you know, as soon as you open your mouth. Blue. Well, how about it, would he dare to go in at last, or not? It must look suspicious, hanging about like this. He felt someone looking at him from inside. Someone was looking him over. Two penetrating human telescopes. Serve him right! Why did he have to moon about in front of the door so long? Either he had to go in or go away. But he did not feel in the least decisive. On the contrary, a wave of self-pity surged over him. If only they had curtains there, nobody would have seen him. Everything conspired against him. What good did it do him that he was so down at the mouth and that no one would recognize him? Anyone with his haggard look was sure to be under suspicion these days.

He turned back to the speckled stones bordering the pavement, longing desperately to lie down on one of them. If only he could press his face and forehead against the stone, the weariness that weighed him down would leave him. He would surely go to sleep, and that would be a blessing. The pavement. Suddenly everything he had ever known was narrowed down to the oblong of speckled stone. Here he had been born and here he had lived—forty years already. It had all been but one long day, and now it was evening and he was about to lie down. Heavens! It was only an hour since he had gone out into the streets. Perhaps it would be better to go into the pub, after all. Order an ale and a cucumber, standing up by the bar. But weren't cucumbers rationed now? He forgot to ask in the morning. He saw in his mind's eye the white kitchen clock with its blue border and felt a pang of homesickness. They used to have a similar clock at home. Mother used to wind it and she never forgot. And what about beer—was that rationed or not? He had some ration coupons with him. He pulled out his wallet. Where were they? After he had feverishly fingered through all the compartments, his anxiety turned to certainty: he must have lost them! There, what a blow!

The door creaked and there were voices. Blue jackets smeared with white. The bricklayers came swarming out, their break over. Their questioning glances crushed him. One of them gave him a friendly slap on the shoulder. "Had one too many, pal?" He staggered under the impact of a huge, hard hand. Mustn't fall, he thought desperately, steady! That would be suspicious. The eyes of one of the men seemed hostile, as if he were saying: how come anyone has money for booze nowadays? If only he could do something about it and stop people from looking at him!

Why had he not stayed where he was, in that wretched hole? But how could he? They did not like to see him go out, even at night. Pass the bucket and see that the handle does not rattle, take it back again, and that was all. Why did the guy ask if he had had one too many? What were they thinking about, anyway? Cognac, of course. Maybe it was just a test. Now they would come back, one of them would turn up his lapel and show him the badge, and they would lead him off. And then—he heard the concrete mixer start into action; thank God, they were just bricklayers. Nobody was going to lead him anywhere.

He walked on with a feeling of impending doom. A trap would suddenly be sprung and he would go hurtling down through a trapdoor without even knowing what had happened. He must not enter that inn. He must not enter any public place. Somebody would make a silly remark and they would pick all of them up, him as well. Then perhaps they might even let the others go, but he would be caught. They were good at these things and knew how to do them on a large scale: a whole tramload of people, a whole street, a whole everything.

He was in Karlín. If he carried on like this, neither slow nor fast, he would be in Wenceslas Square within ten minutes. That was something entirely different. There he would not have to walk like a ram with head bent low. The Square, that was his first-aid post; transfusion, density—nobody took any notice of anybody else. Excuse me, or sorry, I'm in a hurry. If it had not been for those three weeks in that hole, he would not be so terrified. He would get over it soon. There, you see, Hynek, old fellow, he said to himself encouragingly, it is better outside, after all. Who on earth would imagine that the little man who would shortly be walking in Wenceslas Square was anybody but Alfred Janota?

Blue, blue. Three weeks spent among suitcases and gazing into the darkness unless he wished to suffocate with the stench of petroleum. And hearing all the time: "For heaven's sake, Mr. Tausig, be careful and don't light it." There was that danger on top of everything else. Blue. He would have burned to death behind the sideboard. Thin wood, piles of paper, cardboard—and he, a mere cinder. The thought of the hole made him feel sick, though at the same time he was conscious of relief at being out in the fresh air. Blue. He would soon be in the center of the city.

Soldiers! That was the end. The trap had been sprung. They were coming toward him, taking up practically the entire width of the pavement. Quickly, to the edge, he commanded himself. How was he to behave? You are Janota, you idiot, Janota, Janota, Janota! Perhaps he should smile. But not too conspicuously. A grimace appeared on his ashen-colored face. The men in the green field uniforms took no notice of him, however. They passed by a nonentity who did not realize that it was enough to remove oneself to the edge of the pavement and that it was not necessary to step right down into the gutter. He breathed with relief. But immediately afterwards he stiffened, the grimace still distorting his face. He heard a voice and felt someone's breathing. "Hey, what's the time?" Here it was. Did Alfred Janota understand German? That was all he could think of. He pushed back his sleeve a little to enable the returned soldier to look at the dial of his watch. But it was not he who was doing it, somebody else inside him was responsible for the action. "Damn," he heard, "a quarter past ten. Bags of time yet." They were walking some way ahead, loud and rowdy, and the last one, the one who had come back to ask him the time, was hurrying to catch up with them. Hynek Tausig was aware only of the variegated pattern of the pavement and of nothing else. The only thing he knew was that he must not stop if he did not want to collapse. Blue.

He met increasingly more people now. There, he assured himself, there will be whole crowds of them in Wenceslas Square. He went alternately faster and again more slowly. He was not used to so much walking. He stopped to rest at the street corner. His eyes sought and found the red board with white lettering. It was pleasant to see that the street was still called Príkopy as it used to be. In a minute he would be at the Koruna. There he would find a buffet and public baths. He had been three weeks without a bath. But that would be dangerous; he would have to hand in everything he had on him— his identity card and his money. He would be given a locker and a key. But what if they had a master key? And anyway, were the baths still there? Again he felt his pocket anxiously. The money was there. Blue.

He should have something to eat, too. Not that he was hungry. But he ought to eat or he would find himself fainting from weakness. He ought to get his change ready in advance. A new anxiety flared up within him—the wallet was there all right, but was the money still in it? He must take a look at once or he would go crazy.

A newsman was standing on the corner of Príkopy and Wenceslas Square, leaning against the wall, his crutch and bag full of newspapers lying on the ground in front of him. He was looking at the passersby in a perfunctory manner, a mere glance here and there. But if someone took his fancy, he would pick him out of the crowd and rivet him with his eyes. The pale man timidly asking for a sports paper seemed very unsure of himself. Why was he speaking in such a low voice? There was something behind it. What other paper, though, could be demanded by an Alfred Janota, whom it would suffice to turn upside down and shake slightly for Hynek Tausig to fall out? Nothing that was noncommittal, nothing political, no news—all that did not interest him. The weight fell off his shoulders; the money was there. But why ever did he fold it in such an impossible way? He had to take out a fifty-crown note. Would the man have change? He felt like leaving him with the whole fifty crowns and walking away. That fellow was scanning him much too closely. Fortunately he did have change. The man saw nothing unusual in being paid with such a high denomination. People needed change and a newsman came in handy. What was the matter with his customer, though? A queer type. The news vendor was counting out the change, his voice slightly ahead of his hands. He could see that the oddball who had bought the newspaper off him was absent-minded. How about giving him a few hellers less? Then he changed his mind; that ashen face with the hint of a moustache did not look at all prosperous. He gave him the correct change: one crown, ten, fifty. As likely as not, thought the news vendor, he is a Jewboy.

Hynek Tausig's hair was bluish-black, but his nose was straight and thin like a Spanish aristocrat's. Perhaps his ancestors had in actual fact come from there, fleeing the auto-da-fé, just as he, their descendant, would like to escape from here. So far, however, he had not done more than cross the threshold. He had only not joined the transport, had not presented himself at the Sample Fair palace, the first stop on the way to the ghetto at Theresienstadt. The knowledge did not give him any satisfaction. Had he gone, it occurred to him, he might now have been left in peace. Whereas now, what were his prospects: getting his teeth knocked out, a bullet or a rope, or, at best, again the ghetto. Why did he not feel admiration for himself for having dared to stay away? He had heard a lot about Hitler even before his troops had marched into Prague. It had never occurred to him to put up any resistance. But for some incomprehensible reason he had thought that his straight nose would enable him to shed what was known as his Jewish origin. That was the only lever he had used to upset it all. He had torn up the small white paper they had sent to summon him to the transport. In the evening he had left his flat— and the transport had left without him.

What an advantage it was, he thought as he patted his pocket once more, what an advantage that he looked like Janota now that it was so essential. Had anyone told him what the news vendor had thought, he would not have believed it possible. He walked on.

Although he considered the money he had to be the sum total of his means of escape, its possession failed to give him a feeling of contentment. There was something that disturbed him, but he could not discern what it was.

At last he reached Wenceslas Square. He was conscious of a certain disappointment that the rectangles of the pavement were exactly the same as in Príkopy. Nor was it as crowded here as he had imagined it would be as he walked along the streets of Karlín. No, no press of people in which to hide. He would like to stop and look round, but he went on without doing either. After all, he had not lost his wits. So many soldiers about! He crossed to the other side of the street, but could not find what he was looking for even there. He fixed desperate eyes on the equestrian statue of St. Wenceslas at the top of the Square—it seemed terribly small and insignificant, and it came to him with sudden force that he had been deceiving himself all the time he was hurrying to get here. And, moreover, had known he was deceiving himself at the very moment he had left the house. He had simply run away from the hole. It's the same everywhere, Hynek Tausig, he whispered to himself, here or there, it's all one. A big mess with a thousand holes. You were bound to step in one of them, you would fall in, and you would never make the fresh air again. The clanging of the trams jarred on his ears, seeming like mockery. "Well, well, Mr. Tausig," the red cars seemed to jeer, "still selling vacuum cleaners? How about boarding a #22 and jumping off at the statue—head first?"

The saint's statue appeared to him somber and hostile. He turned his back on it. He was tired out. Should he try the baths? Who was to decide? It was noon, possibly there would be nobody there. He would go and wash off his fear. Then he would get into the steam, climb up on the plank, lie on his back, and, having sweated profusely, take a lukewarm shower. Then he would give the attendant a little money to let him take a nap. All right, he would go. Come what may. He stepped out faster. But before he was halfway down the Square he had lost most of his courage. Don't tremble, he admonished himself. Tausig would be left behind in the baths, only Janota would come out. However, by the time he had reached the bottom of the Square he knew he would never enter the baths. Yet, in spite of that, he shuffled along right to the entrance. A voice said: "Need any cigarettes?" A pair of inquisitive eyes rested on his face. Cigarettes? He shook his head in negation. No, he did not need any cigarettes, but why did the fellow look at him so searchingly? Tausig in his turn looked harder at the man, to find out what he was like. A clean-shaven face, everything in it pointed: the eyes, the nose, and the ears, even the cheekbones. No, the face did not appeal to him. He ought to say, "Beat it, pal," or "Don't bother me or I'll call a policeman!" But he would say nothing, he would merely walk on. Yet, his feet seemed glued to the spot. That fellow held him in some inexplicable way. Perhaps he should tell him, after all. Perhaps that would drive him away. But what if the man was an *agent provocateur:* perhaps he had picked him as a victim and was trying it out on him. And if he asked: "How much are they?" or "Give me five packets of ten . . ." he would produce a card and take him to headquarters. No, he could not say either the one or the other, for a variety of reasons.

The pointed face had a brain of its own. Taking in the ashen-grey countenance, the haunted eyes and the drooping mouth of the man facing him, he thought that here was a possibility, a definite possibility. This—he thought, appraising the small figure in front of him— was no small minnow, this was likely as not a big fat trout. He came right up to the little man and said: "I won't squeal, never fear. I'm on the run, too."

Should he perhaps fall on his knees now and just beg for mercy, Tausig wondered. Surely he could not end like this? But then, did he, Hynek Tausig, not realize that he could not, the times being what they were, simply up and go for a walk? Just like that. Where would he have gone anyway, had he not met Pointed-face? What was he thinking of, actually, when he left his own flat four weeks ago? The man said he was "on the run" too. What did he mean by it? That he was a "submarine" like him, Hynek Tausig? Or that he had no money? Or did he merely want to pump him? He would have to ask him to let him go, tell him that he was in a hurry. They themselves were forcing him to act like this. But whatever happened, he must not break down now, must not show the man how desperately scared he was. He moved. At last he brushed past Pointed-face, calling out to him "What d'you want?" as he went. What *did* he want? Whatever it was, he was going. If the man wanted him to show his identity card, well, all right, why not? He had his papers in order, and they were made out in the name of Janota.

But Pointed-face caught up with him. "Let me have a hundred, won't you, pal. I'm in the same fix as you."

The two pairs of eyes met: a watery, greyish-green pair with a vigilant gleam in them, with the brown, inquiring, burning, heavy-lidded and seemingly ash-covered, disturbed eyes of Hynek Tausig. If he were certain that a hundred crowns would rid him of Pointed-face, he would give them to him. At forty, Hynek Tausig was fundamentally the same as he had been at fifteen, at twenty, and at thirty: settle everything peacefully. Yes, if he knew it for sure, he would give the money to him and be done with it. But he could not pull out his wallet in front of his eyes, so, in a quiet voice, he said only: "Where would I get them from?"

The tone of his voice betrayed him, however. Pointed-face stepped squarely in front of him. "You miser, leave a pal to stew in his own juice while you make your own getaway, would you?" he hissed.

Good Lord, was it possible that the man could read his thoughts? But Pointed-face did not, of course, think that Hynek Tausig was somebody who ought to be wearing a yellow star, he simply had the impression that this small, pale, and tired-looking fellow was in the same line of business as he and that he was at the moment in difficulties. Otherwise what would he be doing here? Why should he be standing in front of the entrance to the baths—and not go in? And so, if only he could keep up this battle of nerves a few moments longer, Hynek Tausig would win through after all.

All he did now was to whisper: "What d'you want of me? I haven't got anything." Why did that man block his way like this? Damned cheek, anyway. And someone might see them. He said, more loudly this time: "Go away! Don't bother me!" This last in a shrill voice that sounded as if it were forced out of him. He was seized by doubts whether it would not be better to implore, after all.

A policeman came into sight at the bend of the passage. Things were quite different now. Hynek Tausig had to take a step forward in order not to stand directly opposite Pointed-face. "A cop!" he hissed. And Pointed-face vanished with all the speed that Hynek Tausig could have wished for right at the start, when he was meditating about the baths. The policeman was gazing at the receding back of

Pointed-face and he passed Hynek Tausig quietly, taking not the slightest notice of him, walking past with an easy, rolling gait which somehow gave the impression that for all his apparent nonchalance he was alert and ready for action.

So much for the baths, thought Hynek Tausig, trying to center his attention on this and nothing else. The glimpse he had had of the policeman brought back to him the whole hopelessness of his situation. There, on one side of the fence, was the law—what of it that it was a law that would not pass muster in front of any real justice—and there, on the other side of the fence, was he, a human being beyond the pale, an outlaw. If he managed to get into the baths, it would all be different. In his imagination he conjured up the water, almost feeling the soothing warmth of it as it ran over his body. Then it came, suddenly—the realization that he could not possibly go in there. How could he have forgotten! A straight nose was not everything if he did not have his trousers on. He was Alfred Janota only in his clothes. Without them, he was demonstrably Hynek Tausig. He was Alfred Janota only on the outside, not inside. Had he gone in, he might have paid for it very unpleasantly. Come to think of it, it was a good thing that he had been detained by that tramp. He thought of his mother's favorite adage: something bad for something good. But he was annoyed with his parents—by having him circumcised they had spoiled his chances of a bath. Immediately he forgot the reasons that had a minute ago prevented him from going on down, feeling on the contrary sad and sorry for himself that he was now unable to enter the baths at all.

He entered the buffet instead. It was hot inside and the air was bad. The close, sultry atmosphere somehow reminded him of his hole. Two SS men were standing by the shiny beer counter, having drinks poured out for them. At the food stall some soldiers were lunching on schnitzels, standing up. He swallowed. Oh, the swine, he thought, devouring everything. He crossed over to a large board that read "Off the Ration."

Wasn't he conspicuous ordering soup? Decent people were sure to have at least a few food coupons on them. But he was not the only one. One crown twenty. At least this time he would give the correct change. A girl with eyes the color of forget-me-nots and red hands slightly swollen from the steam, was serving; she scooped up the soup out of the pot and, handing him the plate, said, "There you are." Looking at her, he thought she reminded him of a flower, something pure—her voice, however, brought him back to earth. It was irritable, impatient, and rather surly. But why? Could such a girl denounce him? Her eyes no longer seemed so clear and pure, no resemblance to forget-me-nots. I haven't given her the money! it occurred to him. Of course, that was it—he had forgotten to pay. He must put it right immediately. He attempted an apologetic smile, but only a twisted grin appeared on his face. The girl was convinced that the little man had tried to swindle her, and she made no secret of her conviction. She pouted her lips. I know your kind, they seemed to be saying. Hynek Tausig ate his soup, feeling the girl's eyes in the small of his back. Eat it up quickly and get out! He ate hurriedly, scalding his tongue and throat, but he knew he had to be quick. The girl might call someone in the meantime. Better leave the soup unfinished. He left the plate on the high table, at which there were several other patrons. As he pushed his way out, someone caught hold of his arm. So here it was. He had known it was coming. He had felt it in the air. Behind him he heard a dull, embarrassed voice. He turned round slowly. It had all been quite hopeless from the start. He had told the people who had sheltered him that he had friends in the country and in Prague, too, that if he did not manage to get out of town, he would spend the night with them. Did he lie when he said that, or did he believe it himself? He no longer knew. The hand which had grasped hold of him had been relaxed, the voice was saying something. "I'm terribly sorry, I thought it was Ferdinand." The man departed with an apology, leaving Hynek Tausig standing there, wiping the perspiration from his brow. It was moist. Beads of sweat were streaming down his cheeks. He felt sticky all over. He was confronted by the image of someone's life, a troublesome life perhaps, but still a life—the life of someone called Ferdinand, who could meet a friend and the friend would be pleased by the coincidence.

He opened the glass door and emerged into the street. He was possessed by the harassing feeling that unless he immediately, without delay, got out into the suburbs, he would be caught here. Passing a florist's shop with nothing in the window but a single Chinese vase with red roses in it and mirrors in the background, he had a glimpse of himself. God, he could not walk bent like this. He looked at the roses. They were still in the bud. A young couple came out of the shop, the boy not more than eighteen, the girl probably even younger. He, Hynek Tausig, would doubtless be older than the two of them put together. They walked out, seeing no one in the whole Square but each other, the boy carrying a flower pot wrapped in white tissue paper. The girl had her arm around his waist. It looked rather ridiculous because of their overcoats. But the two evidently did not mind this or anything else. He followed them with his eyes until they disappeared from sight in a cluster of people at the corner. They had somewhere to go all right, and they walked along without even thinking about it. Somewhere there was a house with a roof, an entrance and a staircase, a white or blue door with a bell, and a room or some tiny garret with two chairs, a bed and a table. And he had nothing—not even a ghost of anything of the sort.

2

An hour later the caretaker of "The Fountain," a house in Siegfried Street in the Nusle district of Prague, saw Hynek Tausig ring the bell of a third-floor flat. The flat belonged to a childless married couple, he a buyer for a small store and she a cashier in a café. Hynek Tausig was at the end of his rope. He did not notice the caretaker, thinking as he ascended the stairs that it might be best to report to a police station and ask to be included in the next transport. He found it difficult to understand why he had not actually done it already. But he had been busy trying to find a way out. Surely he must have some friends somewhere. Somewhere he must have them. If not, there was only the police station left, or—no, he veered away from the thought, somewhere he *must* have some good friends. Then, when he was passing through Nusle, he had suddenly remembered this house. It rose up in front of him as if it had never been here before and had only just appeared. Something told him, though, that he ought to cross out these people as he had crossed out all the others whom he had thought of. He pressed the brown button of the bell. The buzzing noise had not died down inside and he was already wondering whether he should not go away before anyone came to open the door. Somewhere deep inside him there crouched at the same time the fear that the door would not even be opened on his account. What was he to say? That he was paying them a courtesy visit? Or: "Could you lend me some salt?" Or again: "Thought I'd drop in for a moment." That was what people said. But there was a far worse possibility—that he would have nothing to say.

A man suddenly appeared in the doorway. He had calm grey eyes, slightly distended with surprise. Now his eyes were no longer calm—they darted quickly across the chest of the little man standing outside. And he understood the meaning of that swift glance: they were looking for a yellow star.

The caretaker was dusting the window frames on the landing below. It was only now, as he peered nervously from side to side, that Hynek Tausig caught sight of her. What was he to do, he could not possibly talk in front of her. At the same time he knew that he would hardly be able to confide in those grey eyes. The caretaker was going down, her slippers clacking on the stairs. Some people were lucky—they could come out just like that, in slippers. Hynek Tausig felt that unless he leaned against the doorway he would surely fall. How long had he been standing here? The caretaker was downstairs at last and silence returned to the house.

He stared at the white card on the door with the name of the owner of the flat printed on it. And that man, whose name was tidily set out in the middle of a brass frame, stood in the doorway, still without saying a word. He kept silent and waited. His thoughts were going round like a wheel; if the wheel stopped, he would ask Hynek Tausig to come in. He even felt inclined to say something nice and friendly to him, regardless of the fact that he had been seen by the caretaker and that such visits were dangerous these days. He could see without being told that the visitor needed support. But the wheel did not stop, taking with it all his determination as it revolved down the stairs, down the same stairs the caretaker's slippers had clattered a moment ago. The wheel revolved with increasing speed, revealing something that filled the man in the doorway with horror. His mind focused on the picture of a party of SS men who had beaten him and his wife for a single unfriendly look. That was last May, when they were searching for the perpetrators of the attempt on Heydrich's life. In his own grey eyes the man in the doorway now resembled an empty husk.

"What is it you want?" he asked.

Hynek Tausig went cold all over. Here it was. Though it was also possible that the man did not remember him. He ought to tell him that they had once worked together. That he had once helped him when his wife needed treatment at Franzensbad. That he had had a doctor acquaintance and everything had turned out well. Still, he had known this would happen. Anything would be better than to be standing here like this. Even a bullet in the head. But perhaps those grey eyes were really only looking him over. After all, he was shabby, his moustache a mere halfhearted bristle. Should he himself tell him who he was and what he wanted? His lips could not form the words. Go on, he urged himself, say it. But his tongue seemed wooden. Something emanated from that flat which stunned him and robbed him of the power of speech.

"I am Tausig," he groaned. There, it was out!

"What do you want?" the man demanded. "I'm busy."

Something was pressing Hynek Tausig down, making him one with the dust on the red tiles of the floor. The caretaker would come and wipe him off with a wet rag and squeeze him out into a bucket full of dirty water. Why had he come here? He should not have done it. The door closed, the man with the grey eyes that had lost their tranquillity disappeared, the catch of the patent lock rattled like a thing that fitted perfectly in its place.

He glanced down over the banisters. Taking hold of the rail he shuffled down the stairs. Again he saw those grey eyes in front of him, searching for the star. There was no star, but the door had been closed just the same. Wasn't it really there? Or was it perhaps a star that could not be removed with a penknife?

Out in the street, he was seized by a depressing feeling of uselessness. His head seemed to him like a boiler in which something terribly insipid was being boiled over and over, something that would never taste right again. He still had his identity card. And nothing else. People walked about as if there were no war on. For them, he thought, war meant only marmalade instead of butter, lousy cigarettes, and rotten beer. He had to sit down. He could see himself, a stray dog running about the streets. There was no room anywhere for the likes of him. At the stop outside the park he boarded a tram.

The conductor let the ashen-faced man travel twice across town, from one terminus to the other and back again. When they stopped at one end he offered him coffee out of his thermos flask. "Help yourself," he said nonchalantly. Tired and sleepy, Hynek Tausig looked at him with distrust in his eyes. Coffee? "Thanks." He would take a drink first. The cup was hot. How pleasant to be able to hold it in his fingers like this. Should he trouble his head wondering whether the donor wished to denounce him? Had he bought a ticket this time? No, he hadn't. He had traveled free. He studied the conductor's tranquil face, a wise and at the same time slightly rough face. The conductor. Fiftyish. He gave the impression of belonging in that old red trailer car. Tausig had formerly taken little notice of conductors, one never knew whether they would turn out kind or grumpy. But how could this one have guessed that the best service he could do him, Hynek Tausig, at the present moment was to offer him some coffee? Would he denounce him afterwards? He finished his cup. "Thank you," he said. Should he get off? But where was he to go? The conductor leaned toward him and said something in a confidential tone. Did he hear right? Was the man telling him to sit down in a corner and take a nap? He was on duty till four in the morning. "That's a lot of time, chum, almost all night." "Yes," he replied. He sat down. He was terribly sleepy. Did he intend to denounce him? Sleepier and sleepier. Or didn't he?

The conductor watched the man as he dozed. I guess, he told himself, he's one of those people that the street loudspeakers are always bawling about. Yesterday afternoon he had heard one such announcement right outside the Nusle Park where this man had got on. It was as if a huge glass bowl were being smashed: crash, and then the harsh voice: sentenced to death for giving shelter to . . . No, he checked himself, chasing away thoughts of caution, these people need a helping hand these days.

And thus Hynek Tausig sat huddled in the corner of the tram car, drowsing until four in the morning. Then he got out at the terminus, having been given two large slices of bread and marmalade, a thermos full of tea, and another slice wrapped in newspaper. "Thank you." That was all, he did not even shake hands in his hurry. He walked back along the route of the 19 tram, which he had traveled five times to and fro.

3

The next day Hynek Tausig could be seen strolling about round the Sample Fair palace, bent forward just the same as yesterday, his ashen-colored face a shade darker, whispering: blue. But the meaning of this word had been lost long ago. His bloodshot eyes bore into the concrete cube with its thousand eyes and its huge collar formed by the wooden fence. The Prague quarter of Holešovice. Who would ever have thought that a part of the city would become the bridge over which people who had no business here would send live contingents to the transit point of another world, to the Prague-Bubny railway station?

A few minutes ago he had emerged out of a barbershop. The barber had been a merry fellow, a homespun wit. Still, he was glad he was out of there. The police could come in and pick up a wag like that any time, and the game would be up. No, the barber had not managed to cheer up his early customer who had come to have his moustache shaved off, however much he might have thought the little man needed cheering up. Hynek Tausig had had his moustache shaved off. At least nobody would recognize him now. But he knew very well that after the experience of yesterday it was completely useless to try and convince himself of this.

He came up close to the fence. He could hear quite distinctly the bustle in the warehouse where the Jews were gathering before being taken off to Theresienstadt. He was possessed by the single overpowering wish: to get in among them. To be one of that yellow-branded herd. He would lose his freedom, and *they* would treat him according to their habit, and that—he knew—would be anything but pleasant. In spite of that, there was nothing he craved more at the moment. There were three thousand of them, or even more, behind that fence. He had seen them swarming there from a top-floor window in the passage of the house opposite. He could imagine the smell—they were lying there packed like sardines, on mattresses, and without them, on the floor sprinkled with wood shavings and strewn with straw. And yet he wished he could be lying among them, with his number on a label. As he looked on he also saw the SS beating people when the food was doled out. And yet he envied them, for they had a place of their own. If only he could stand there with them!

He thought only of how to get in there. He had not the slightest doubt that once he was inside, he would somehow manage to get taken along with the others. He saw people coming up to the fence when the policeman had passed by on his way round and talking to someone through the gaps between the planks. He saw an old woman who stood leaning against the fence, perhaps talking to somebody or again perhaps just looking on. Whom might she have there—a husband or a son? But how can she be outside, it occurred to him, if they are in? The woman had red, swollen eyes, which she now dried with a white handkerchief. The policeman had passed by several times, curious rather than zealous. He had not said a word to her as yet, had not chased her away. He stood beside her now and listened. She had not seen him, so he gazed at the gap next to hers, trying to see with whom the woman was conversing. But he could not see anyone, only a thick mass of humanity, people lolling about on the ground and marked with stars and numbers on their luggage. She is probably calling all of them at once, thought the policeman. He must have been right, for until he told her to go away, she kept on weeping and addressing someone who was evidently one of that thousand-headed multitude with numbers.

I must get in there, Hynek Tausig murmured to himself, right in there. There was sweat on the palms of his hands. He was not hungry, not tired. He knew what he wanted. He knew what he was waiting for. And he waited. With the coming of dusk everything grew quiet. A German policeman took the place of the Czech one for the night. But he did not behave with any greater vigilance than his predecessor. Hynek Tausig inspected the uneven top of the fence. I'll simply run up to the fence and jump over, he told himself. No, better climb up and drop down on the other side. And though it looked quite easy in the dark, he knew at once that he would not be able to do it. What was it like in front of the entrance? Of course! He must go and have a look at the wooden staircase. He was taken by a new idea: walk quickly past the guards. They were standing there, lazy and inattentive. On the other hand that would mean he would have to stand here all night. Someone might notice him. He could also go straight to the policeman when he was alone and slip some money in his pocket. But no, policemen probably had all they needed. And then—would a policeman believe him? Could he dare try and spin him such a yarn? What—you didn't feel like it four weeks ago, did you? Here you are—a slap in the face and a bullet to go with it. No, he decided, that was out too.

He moved away from the dark entrance—someone was returning home. He was lucky as it was that no one had come earlier. He shuffled along slowly to the park. It was only a little way from here to the Stromovka. He sat down in the bushes. He would stay here for a few hours, alternately crouching, squatting and sitting, until he got too cold to stay any longer. November, he reflected, was not a suitable month for his attempts at saving himself, even if he was trying to save himself from something that was not altogether his own fault. Why did he get into this fix? The worst that could happen to a man was to be cast out from among the others. To be someone else than they. There was mankind, he thought, the poor, the poorest, the rich, the millionaires, the Jews and the others, Germans and Czechs, nations, castes, classes, groups, and then came he, Hynek Tausig, a nobody whom chance had pushed out of the ranks. He thought of the food queue there behind the fence, twisting and turning, but all the people in it belonging together. Everyone belonged somewhere. Why had he not joined the transport immediately? It occurred to him that the simplest thing to do would be to walk into the police station near here or just hop into the river as he was, all frozen through already. How long could it take? Or simply wait until a policeman came along through the park and stand up in front of him: here I am, officer. I'm not Alfred Janota, and I'm no Aryan either. I am Hynek Tausig, that's who. Would you do me a favor and put me among that crowd there behind the fence? Or take me with you. But if you would be so kind, I'd prefer the first, behind the fence. It won't mean a thing to you, you can just say you found me here and that I belong in this transport and not in the one that has gone. For you it means only a few steps and for me—just now it means everything that is called life.

But no policeman came along. Hynek Tausig felt his body going numb with the cold and prayed silently for the morning. When dawn came at last, he waited a little longer and then he straightened up with difficulty. His bones creaked. He parted the bushes and left the park. After a few hours of walking about in the streets he felt better. He was not alone in the streets. He decided to go and eat some hot soup. He was no longer so frightened as yesterday; he was near the fence. He ate his soup like a well-behaved boy, right down to the last spoonful. He would make it last until ten, then he would go again, and twice more during the day. Unless of course he managed in the meantime to get behind the fence! He licked the spoon. The man who invented buffets and off-the-ration watery soups was a fine fellow, he felt. He was helping him, lending him a hand in these ugly times when people were so terribly estranged from one another. No, he no longer experienced the terrors of yesterday. When one was tired, one probably became more indifferent to hardship, less aware of details, less frightened by everything. But perhaps that could be true the other way round, too.

Get in, only to get in. Get in, he told himself all the time. The very words urged him on to action. He heard some noises behind the fence. No, he could not climb it, that was certain. He must slip in with a new transport. He tapped his forehead with his forefinger. Why did he not think of that before! His eyes flashed with relief. And how about reporting directly at the Jewish congregation center? It was from there, after all, that the call to the transport came. But what if the Gestapo had its people there, too, what then? And even if not, they would hardly be delighted to see him since he had given them so much trouble—they had had to get someone to go in his place when he did not turn up, hadn't they? No, he should not have risked the whole thing. Why did he do it, anyway? Was it meant as a defiant gesture? No, it was not that, a voice said inside him. But the fear he felt now was even worse. All right, he would not do it then. Still, he could do it the other way round—when those people came out from behind the fence, he would join them somehow.

He came to life. No more soup. He again felt the eagerness that had taken hold of him earlier. Something told him that this was well thought out. The dirty planks of the fence suddenly seemed lighter. Now to get a star.

A few minutes later chance sent him a man who could let him have one.

"Excuse me," he stopped him, "would you mind, a moment . . ."

The old man looked at him with black, searching eyes.

"What is it?" he asked.

His deliberately matter-of-fact voice was nevertheless slightly shaky. He was surprised, but at the same time a little relieved, by the unusual request. He was not wrong—the black-haired, ashen-looking little man in front of him did look as though he might have something to do with the Jews. He would hardly want the star as a souvenir. Though even that was possible. He had probably been out somewhere and was now returning home late. But what if he was a *provocateur?*

"What do you want it for?" he asked.

"I've lost mine," Hynek Tausig replied. "I'd get in trouble."

No, no *provocateur* would manage to say it just like that. The old man unbuttoned his overcoat, tore the yellow star off his jacket, and handed it to him. Wait though, did he have a safety pin on him as well? Yes, he had one all right, and he handed that to him, too. "And no good-bye, dear sir, we can't stand her like this forever. You'd better go into the passage over there and pin it on."

As Tausig did not do so, the old man walked away, looking back suspiciously over his shoulder until he reached the corner. Once there, he started to run, hurrying away, his breathing fast and labored.

I am in luck after all, thought Hynek Tausig. This old gentleman was the first link in the chain of his good fortune. He walked on, almost happy. He had a yellow star in his pocket. He felt as if he were carrying not a star but a ton of dynamite, and gradually his tranquillity vanished. What if someone spoke to him? If they asked to see his identity card? How would he then explain that he had a Jewish star in his pocket?

He must not spoil anything. Coward! he swore at himself. Remembering the hole, he thought how wonderful it was to be in the fresh air. Since the moment he had decided to join the people behind the fence he was acting far more sensibly. Now the only thing that troubled him was hunger. But there was no time to eat. Again he stood by the entrance gate and the street was growing dark. He had the feeling that something was going on behind the fence. Today the noise had not ceased with the coming of night. Would they be coming out?

It was almost eleven. If they were taken out to the railway trucks this night, he would reach his destination. He thought of what was to come, and he trembled all over. The minutes became hours and hours an eternity. He waited until two. The noise did not cease. No, he would not return to the park, he would stay right here.

Through holes in the planks he saw the faint flicker of lights. Five past two. At last! The gates were thrown open and the first column came tumbling out. A hot wave flooded his whole body. His chin began to tremble. This is your moment, he told himself, go on! He left the shelter of the house wall, the yellow star in his pocket. He passed along the whole length of the small procession in order to find out who was guarding them. And now a second column was coming out. About a hundred people. A single gendarme accompanied each group. Hynek Tausig quickly approached them. The gendarme shouted something. Was it meant for him? Of course it was—he was told to beat it or he would be taken along with the others! The gendarme chuckled; a good joke, that. "All right, get along with you," he said in a tone that was almost good-natured, "before I change my mind!" This nation would make room for Germany anyway, he thought as he turned away from him. But these here were the first to go. Hynek Tausig, however, did not hurry away. He would consider himself lucky if the gendarme really did it. So he went on in the same direction and at the same pace as before, only having veered slightly to the side. In one pocket he gripped the star, in another the safety pin. Hurriedly he turned the corner and crossed the street to be on the opposite side of the road from the guard. It was now or never. With shaking hands he pinned the star to his coat. There, he said to himself, trying to summon up his courage which seemed to be ebbing all the time, now chuck the identity card into the sewer. The sewer grating grinned at him in the darkness a little way ahead. But he could not make it now, it was too late. The sound of steps. He stopped abruptly and quickly plucked the yellow cloth from his coat. With it he ripped off a piece of the garment. Good thing he had his identity card in his hand—he could show it if necessary. But it was not necessary. The steps caught up with him and overtook him, a man's figure appeared in front of him and was quickly swallowed up in the darkness ahead. The column was drawing near. It began to snow. He turned up his collar and pinned the star on again to hide the rent in his coat. The gendarme was still at the head of the procession. Now—one quick jump, and he was in their midst. The people around him made a humming noise, then whispers could be heard. The gendarme turned around. "Quiet there, or I'll knock your heads off." Hynek Tausig pressed still closer to them, his eyes scanning the row he had joined. An old man, a married couple, two children. A family probably, it occurred to him. "Give me that suitcase," he whispered. The old man could not go on, he had dropped his hat and the column did not wait. "Give me that suitcase," Hynek Tausig repeated. "I'll help you." Then he added: "I have to have something." He did not even have the permitted fifty kilograms. "Don't be afraid, give it to me," he said, swearing and praying under his breath. "Please lend me that bag, grandpa, for a while at least," he murmured. If he had to go on like this another second, it would be too late. But the old man understood at last and passed him the suitcase. The gendarme appeared. "No talking!" Who dared to disturb the silence—wasn't it enough for them that he had told them once already not to talk? "Keep your damned traps shut!" he shouted. The woman could no longer carry her rucksack and her husband offered to help her. "Quiet!" shouted the gendarme again, kicking the woman, whose suitcase dropped out of her hand and fell on the edge of the pavement. "Hurry up, faster!" he yelled, and the column moved ahead at a slightly increased pace. It was snowing steadily. Hynek Tausig was taut with suspense for the gendarme was walking by his side.

Their eyes met. Hynek Tausig dropped his. How old could the boy be? Twenty. And he? A thousand by comparison. He contorted his mouth, on the point of blurting out that he was begging for mercy, that he had done nothing wrong. After all, wasn't he where they wanted him? But the ashen-colored face, whose look made all this abundantly clear, was hidden by the night. The snow gleamed white in the darkness. They were now in a narrow street by the railway station. "How many of you are there?" the gendarme shouted. So things were going to end badly in spite of everything, and so near his destination too. He might as well spill the truth. But before he could own up, before he forced himself to breach the barrier of silence caused by his cramped tongue, someone said, "We didn't count the children." Yes, that was quite likely, thought the gendarme, in the Reich only adults who were capable of work counted as people. "All right, move along you pigs!" he called out. "Move along!" To Hynek Tausig's ears this call meant salvation. Move along, you pigs, move along! The shout dissolved the rigidity of suspense within him and brought relief. Gone was the hole and fear and the cramp of anxiety and the empty square. He was born anew this moment. Who was it who said the children had not been counted? He searched the dark throng which slowly wended its way forward for the man who had understood what was needed. The second link in the chain of his good fortune. Now he was one of the crowd. Move along, you pigs, move along! How nice it sounded when it applied to him as well.

Toward morning Hynek Tausig was loaded into the cattle truck. He was delirious with joy. He had been the eighty-fifth, the last to go in the truck. Full up! The truck was sealed and, together with thirty-seven others, sent off to Theresienstadt.

The clanking noise of the bar on the outside of the truck's sliding door many hours later meant that they had reached their destination—the ghetto. Despite the fact that mere chance ordained that he should be one of the three who fell out of the overcrowded truck as soon as the door was opened by Jewish and German guards—and who were immediately slapped and kicked by Commandant Mönderling by way of welcome—he had the unassailable conviction that the third link in the chain of his good fortune had just been forged. The third and most important, he kept repeating to himself, or—as the saying went—third time lucky.

4

It was evening and he was going to bed. A very different evening from that on which he had felt his courage and resolution ebbing away. But he knew that tonight again he would not be able to sleep properly, for it would be the same as yesterday and tomorrow the same as a week ago. True enough, he woke early. He awoke with the picture of the town interwoven with a thousand threads in front of his eyes.

The ghetto looked emaciated at its star-point ends and swollen in the center like the eruption of a volcano. In spite of the darkness he could feel life there, life in the shadow of death. The fortress resembled an overstuffed body. Through the single window in the ceiling he could see a dark leaden sky. It looked as if it hung very low—in the early morning murk it seemed to be in danger of falling at any moment. It bit into the ground. Rain fell incessantly and heavy fog swirled round the ghetto gates.

At last it was five o'clock. He got up, dressed, went out. Outside, in front of the barracks, his pickax, painstakingly cleaned of every particle of dust, stood leaning against a tree. He picked it up and carried it toward the center of the town.

He worked near the church, digging a well. By merely narrowing his eyes he no longer saw the earth. The same picture kept returning to him with dogged persistence: he was squatting in the Stromovka park, next to him a puddle. His puddle. He drank it dry, feeling the aftertaste of dirt on his tongue. He spat. You are a coward, he reproached himself and went on digging the soft earth. Each time he struck with the pickax he relived it all once more, and again, over and over. Then he would console himself, thinking: what was I to do, everyone left me in the lurch. The earth was yielding and clung to the steel. He busied himself with the cleaning of the pickax.

Toward evening he put on his coat and returned to the barracks.

The barracks he lived in were covered by tons of black, soft earth. The cells were below the ground. Above and beside the barracks towered the ramparts.

He lay down on his cot. He rolled about uneasily for a long time, but again sleep would not come to him. It was not dreams he was afraid of, he was afraid of morning. At long last he fell asleep, a short, fitful sleep, the heavy, noisy breathing betraying the sleeper's disquiet. He was awakened by a sharp whistle. The sound of a whistle did not frighten anyone, it merely disturbed them. Yesterday the room orderly had told them: "There will be a muster tomorrow. I'll wake you up at half past three, so see that you are all in the courtyard by half past four." He looked round him. Yes, that was it now. He climbed out of bed. A muster, he grumbled, what the hell's the use of that. But in his heart of hearts he was glad—that hour between four and five was usually sleepless. He went out. The overcoat, he thought vexedly, embodied everything. Even the incident with Oberscharführer Mönderling, when he had all but kissed his ass in his gratitude that he had been slapped and kicked for something totally different from what he had feared. This listless, taciturn forty-year-old little man had forever been deprived of his peace of mind. The others had all grown used to his taciturnity. He had nothing to say about anything. He paid but scant attention even to the war news. "It'll all be over in six months, what d'you say, Mr. Tausig? Who knows, maybe it'll be next week already. But if not earlier, then in six months for sure." What was he to say? He had heard all this a hundred times before. And it was always "for sure." And yet, if he were not here, where would he have gone? The room orderly was calling him. "Don't you go wandering off anywhere, Tausig. Wait here." He was responsible for having them all present and correct.

And so Hynek Tausig stood, looking up at the ramparts and farther still, at the darkness between the top of the wall and the rocks and the sky. It was going to rain again. After a while he pulled a piece of bread out of his pocket. He ate it slowly. He was one of a crowd. If they perished, he would perish with them. Nevertheless, at the very bottom of his soul a vague discontent was stirring.

The night hovered long over the ghetto. Now at last its cloak began to be torn apart, the wind carrying shreds of darkness to the west. The rain started. But with it came the dawn. Hynek Tausig leaned back against a tree and with a match started to pick his teeth, removing what had remained of the bread. Bread? It was no bread, but rather wood shavings, straw and bad flour with water. From inside the ghetto motley processions of people streamed toward the town gates. Crows circled above the ramparts, their croaking carrying toward the hills. Why do they sing to us, wondered Hynek Tausig, repeating their shrill cries to himself: caw, caw, caw.

"Where is your orderly?" he heard a voice behind him. "We need a dozen men to tend the sick."

Caw, caw. Why pick on me? he said to himself. He did not even turn round. Why must I swallow every bit of dirt they want to slop at themselves in this wretched town?

"He's inside," he said ungraciously. Then he pointed out to the man the strong digger who had made a writing desk of his narrow cot and was now ticking names off on his lists and counting them, unable to reach the required figure. And he was responsible for these people; if they should not all be here, Hynek Tausig told himself, he would be rewarded with a cell in the cellar of the *Kommandatur*, if not with a bullet. That was why they all had to be here, himself included, he told the messenger from the aged people's home, at the same time sending him to the devil in his mind.

After a lengthy argument, the room orderly agreed to release one man from his dormitory, if the gentleman would sign for him. As regards the others, let him kindly visit the other dormitories. "Who is finished?" he asked. Someone told him. Hynek Tausig. "He's outside in the courtyard." Thank you, the messenger knew that himself.

Thus it was that Hynek Tausig became a male nurse for the day, a day which had held out the promise of a rest from his pickax.

They walked side by side without saying a word.

The streets of Theresienstadt intersected the ghetto with the monotony common to all garrison towns. "Well, here we are," said the messenger suddenly. "When you're finished you can go back to your people." With that he left, full of unspoken anxiety that he would not be able to fulfill his mission satisfactorily. But, thought Hynek Tausig, he is probably glad he can go around looking for people to do the job and does not have to lend a hand himself. The thought was immediately followed by the objection that finding people for the job was difficult enough, but he did not turn to look after him.

The house he had just entered was ornamented by three stone bears. He had no need to ask anyone anything. People with sticks and crutches in their hands were carrying down the stairs those of their fellow inmates for whom such aids were no longer enough. Someone was weeping and holding on to the banisters, refusing to vacate the stairs. There were loud cries. "They're killing us!" Hynek Tausig turned that way, but somebody behind him shouted in his ear: "Why don't they do it here?" That's true, he thought. He wanted to turn in the direction of the voice when he heard an unpleasant female contralto crying out in the courtyard: "A cart was to be sent for me!"

He did not report to anyone. He simply took his coat off and began to carry the old people down the stairs. His face assumed an ashen color, the moustache which sprouted on it having a queer hue, neither black nor grey. His hair, too, which kept falling across his forehead, was no longer dark black, but had taken on the ash-grey tint of birds' feathers.

At last they were all downstairs.

Two corpses, shrouded in white sheets, lay by the wall in the courtyard, away from the others. Hynek Tausig's gaze was impelled in their direction. People die, he thought, and have their children about them. When you are eighty, you know that you have not much longer to live. You wait for the end and are not afraid of what is between heaven and earth. Here it was all different. You were all alone when you died. Perhaps these two were both still alive when he carried them down a while ago. Now it was all over for them.

He strolled leisurely out into the street. Turning round, he caught sight of the animals carved in the stone above the entrance.

Should he go back to the barracks? He felt neither a duty to return, nor any compassion for the old men. He was like the stone bears who would be the dead men's only mourners. In the end, however, he came to the conclusion he would do best to go along with the old men. He would help them keep together.

They walked out of the entrance, taking with them the two corpses. They had been told that all of them were required to come out for the muster to be taken.

They trooped out of the house. The muster was to take place on the Common—there was not enough room for all of them anywhere else. But surely it could have been done in the houses and in the streets, reflected Hynek Tausig. To weigh, count, and write down everybody and everything. It would have been like one immense stock-taking. So many people, so many pairs of shoes, hats, laces, and rings. All of a sudden he realized he had parted from those he had wanted to help. He started to push one of the carts which collected the dead every morning and brought the bread every noon. The face of the man limping next to him seemed familiar to him. He racked his brain, wondering who it could be. Was it not the old man whom he helped with his suitcase that night he joined the transport? Was it—or wasn't it? It occurred to him suddenly, as he scanned the faces of all those near him, that they were all exactly the same.

Someone was choking on the highway. He did not turn round. But he should. Certainly he should. All right, he would do it, then. But by this time the sick person was sitting down on the curb and someone was bending over him, hiding his face from view. I am always late for everything, Hynek Tausig thought. He let go of the cart. Better look out for himself. But it was unpleasant to walk along empty-handed, pushed and jostled by the crowd. That conductor on the tram, he recalled, he had helped him, too. He had not asked for his help, and it was doubly nice of him that he helped without being asked. One did not forget such things. He did not even know him. It was hardly likely they would ever meet again. What was he doing—if he was still alive? Lost in his thoughts of the conductor, he glanced involuntarily at another cart, on which there were women. "Water, water!" He raised his eyes and said: "You'll have to wait until we get to the Common. There's no water here." Then, in a louder voice, he asked: "Anybody got anything to drink?" Someone handed him a bottle, which he held up to the sick woman's lips. She drank and repaid him with a grateful smile. He felt he did not deserve it— after all, he had only acted as a mediator. But the look he had received had been worth it. "Whose is the water?" he asked in a husky voice. "Leave it to those people," he heard the reply. No, it occurred to him, people did not always behave like animals. And he thought of himself. Not always. He pushed the cart, repeating to himself: "It's true, people don't always behave like animals." He put his shoulder to the cart and pushed.

It was almost eleven in the morning when they reached the Common.

Hynek Tausig stood in the middle, looking around at the great obedient mass of people. He reproached himself. Why had he, in spite of all his cowardice, not been rendered sufficiently apathetic by all he had seen so far to be able to bear it with indifference? A horse gets a lash of the whip if he does not pull properly, he mused, but a human being does not forget the blows. They still smarted even though the bruise had long disappeared. And it was all the worse for that.

An imperceptible flurry ran through the crowd. He could feel it too. At last he decided to ask. What was happening? Every tenth? He raised his head in surprise. What did that mean? Then someone said it full out, in a whisper: "Every tenth will go to the wall." "Why?" "No particular reason." They said someone was missing. There would be hell to pay. Every tenth, that might be me, Hynek Tausig admitted to himself. But, he added quickly, you can just as well be every fifth or every second. What a fine sight it would be if all the sixty thousand people here on the Common started to run, he thought. They could hardly hope to catch them. But nobody ran. So that was it: every tenth. No trouble, everything nice and quiet. First, second, third—and tenth! Fall out! Nothing for it, he reflected, startled; he would have to fall out. One had sometimes to do it, willy-nilly. Neighbors embraced each other. He had nobody to embrace him. He stood there, a queer, emaciated little man. No wife, no children—come to think of it, he would find it easier to bear than someone for whom the number ten would mean splitting his family. This, then, was also life, these moments of waiting, whether one would be the tenth.

He did not know how long he had been standing there when he heard the SS say: "You on the outside, count off in hundreds. Form columns and divide them off two paces from one another." No more talk of shooting. So it was not true.

He looked up at the sky. From somewhere up there came the roar of a plane. The sky had grown blue and light, perhaps it was beautiful. Man, he reflected, is the king of all creation. He can fly higher than the birds, but he can also fall lower than any other living thing. And again he thought of himself. "Down!" he heard them cry. Why, he wondered. The crowd rumbled, then he heard the whispers: "That's the end, they're going to bomb us!" As if nothing of this concerned him. Hynek Tausig watched all of them lying down, the entire sixty-thousand-strong mass. Unhurriedly he turned and saw a group of people praying, others kissing each other. His eyes returned to the sky. Should he get down, too? But he did not lie down. Now he was the only one standing up. Someone pulled at his trouser leg. He was seized by a sudden impulse to kick the unknown man in the face. The plane had passed. Perhaps it would come back, it occurred to Hynek Tausig, and would drop its bombs. But it did not concern him. Had he then fallen out of the ranks? That frightened him—he must stick with the crowd, otherwise he'd get into trouble again like that other time. But the fear shown by the crowd was repulsive to him. He went on standing. I lack the courage to lie down, he told himself. And when he saw the others getting up from the ground, he did not feel any better. He was pleased neither by having refrained from lying down nor by having remained standing.

Thus it happened that he was the first to see the ghetto commandant, Fritz Mönderling, as he came riding toward them on horseback. Spick and span in his best uniform, he made for the only point of orientation on the Common, greyish-black with its crowd of human bodies. And that point was he, Hynek Tausig.

The SS got busy. They had whips and rifles—in a few moments sixty thousand people were standing in ragged groups of a hundred each. The groups made way for the rider.

Now the commandant was right in the middle. Up to this moment Hynek Tausig watched the ghetto elder pushing toward him, almost simultaneously with the rider on horseback. The elder bore a resemblance to him, to Tausig. The strongest among his mixed feelings was curiosity: what was to happen now?

At last the elder arrived.

"The count today, Herr Kommandant," he reported, hoarse and out of breath, "is fifty-nine thousand, nine hundred and eighty-seven pig Jews."

It looked as if he were reporting to the horse, his eyes being on a level with the horse's mouth. It's like in school, it occurred to Hynek Tausig. Quite a bright pupil, knows the answer pat.

"People missing?" the commandant interrupted the report.

The insignificant man in front of the horse had once been a lecturer at Frankfurt University. He was silent. He had done something wrong and would be caned in front of the class.

"You'll take the consequences!" barked the man on horseback. Then he rode off through the gap which had been formed on his arrival and had remained politely open.

The SS men were shouting. The ghetto was pouring back behind the fortress ramparts. Hynek Tausig was engulfed by the crowd. Was that all? he wondered. Everyone was walking on his own, but he would again push. Those in front had already reached the ghetto gates. He felt that something had been born within him that gave him the sensation of having returned. Yet nothing extraordinary was going on—the hovels were merely being filled up again. The town between the ramparts was being filled, filled in the same way as useless junk was stuffed into the dustbin. Was that a return? Yes, it was: he, too, was a piece of junk.

Next morning he again rolled uneasily on his cot. But this time it had begun already at half past three. That was a fine thing, on top of everything else. He asked himself a strange question. Why do your actions, Hynek Tausig, not correspond to that which every human being, yourself included, longs for? Not to resemble a mouse seeking a way out of the trap. But all of life, he contradicted himself, resembles a cat, mouse, and a trap. And he . . . he was only a mouse, a small, lonely and frightened mouse. Did he, though, really long for anything else? Was he not, if the truth were known, glad that he was what he was?

By the time he got up to collect his pickax and go off to dig the well outside the church, he was more tired and worn than he would be in the evening, after twelve uninterrupted hours of digging, despite the fact that he was a thin, gaunt little man weighing not more than fifty-five kilos.

Yes, that was what he was, a mouse; a mouse that was scared to death by the thought of a cat in its vicinity—or at least a trap.

5

He walked across the ghetto.

He had grown still leaner. His roaming eyes had sunk deep and they had an unpleasant, expectant gleam. They resembled a membrane. He had learned to register the slightest vibrations and pulsations of the town. It had become a subconscious process that went on incessantly. Yes, something was happening. Be careful, Hynek Tausig, he commanded himself. Something was in the air.

At ten in the morning the car from the German *Kommandatur* drove up to the house of the Council of Elders. Nobody was any longer in doubt as to what was in preparation. A transport. Invisible mouths passed the information on to sixty thousand ears.

The information reached him too. He gave a start, but then he thought perhaps he would not be in it. Another piece of news: "Half the ghetto is to go." Why should he, of all people, be left out? He had no one here who would remove his card from the index of the records department, according to which the transport was to be compiled. And even if he had, would that alter anything, if half the ghetto was to be sent away? He had long felt hostility toward the big fortress. He had an antipathy to this town, did not like the stone beak, bent six times, which pecked at the streets and houses, and which let people see that they used to look different. He had lost the sensation of having returned, that relaxing satisfaction he had felt when Mönderling had beaten him, and again when the muster was over.

He walked between the ramparts, from one corner to the other. The well outside the church was finished and he was now working on the railway line, on the Theresienstadt-Bohušovice track. When you have finished the railway line, he told himself, you will ride on it to Poland. Why did he not go back to the barracks and sleep? He had spent the whole night removing the last projecting rock with a pneumatic drill. What was it he was looking for anyway?

The ghetto was narrow, but you could not cross it from end to end even in four hours. Now he had reached the Kavalír barracks. Nothing about them was in keeping with the noble name. Inside, behind the bars, were mental patients. Someone in there was just raising his right arm in the Nazi salute. A nurse came running and took him away to a cell. Something forced Hynek Tausig to give a nasty laugh. What was the difference between that woman and the lunatic? he reflected. She drew attention to herself even more than he did. Whose attention, though? came the disappointing thought. Theirs—the Jews. What did it matter to him, Hynek Tausig? He pressed his forehead against the cool bars. He did not feel like going to the barracks. In his heart of hearts he knew why. He was afraid that on his cot he would find a card with the summons to join the transport. But let him not think about that. He reached the sappers' barracks which had been turned into a hospital. Hospital? Was it not funny, to heal people so that they would be able to go with the transport? In the yard next to the barracks he could see old men praying. They were leaning against the latrine wall, white papers and black prayer books in their hands. The rabbis had come to the conclusion that the ghetto was a stone can. If nothing else, they thought, ancient religious customs would at least be maintained here. But the can was to become a museum, reflected Hynek Tausig. Nothing living would remain here.

He walked faster. Again that unseen whip cracking in his ears. Transport. And somewhere in the background bigger doses of beating. And then the end. A very different end to that which the boys were in the habit of conjuring up after returning from work—according to which a neighbor would one day turn up, saying: "Go on, run along home, you idiots, the war is over." The hope of this kind of end slumbered on in them in spite of everything, despite the fact that they postponed the date of Germany's defeat from day to day and from year to year. The hope lived in him, too, even in moments when he was not actually thinking of it, yes, even when he deliberately tried to avoid it in his thoughts. In spite of it all, he was encouraged by this faint, indistinct mirage. Somewhere something was waiting. And now it was to be spoiled.

The nearer he came to the barracks, the greater his fear that he would be among those included in the transport. He was again hurrying with his head bent forward. You have been like this before, Hynek Tausig, in Prague, on your way between the hole and Wenceslas Square. Should he not stop and straighten up? But he did not slacken speed and he did not turn round. The corners of his narrow mouth drooped. His face was a dark ashen color, distorted by a wild grimace. Suddenly he stopped, as though he had run up against an invisible wall. Why was he rushing so? In order to hold the summons card in his hand twenty seconds earlier? He was almost certain that the white card lay on his cot. But how could he be certain, was he clairvoyant or what? Why cross his bridges before he came to them? He understood then that if man was ever in his life an animal, then it was fear that made him one. Why was he standing here foolishly like this? He realized that he was standing still and people were treading on his toes. Yes, it was fear that did it, every child knew that. Only he did not know it, not he. He started walking again. He was afraid that he would be included in the transport, was he not? But he had been through this before. Nevertheless, in spite of the knowledge he had just gained, fear again predominated. He could only think of the transport, and whether he would be in it. Something told him it was different, but a second voice said, no it wasn't, it was the same. He too. One did not change at forty-one. He had remained the same. A coward, he added in disgust. He had been born only to tremble for his mousy little life.

In the faces of the passersby he saw himself. All of them were cowards, once and for all, he consoled himself, not only he. They trembled for their own sake and concealed it by pretending to be afraid for someone else. But then he thought that even if he did get left out, of it, he would go and beg to be taken along.

He was in front of the barracks. He entered, full of the reserve and excitement of fear. His cot . . . his cot was empty. He felt better. Oh yes, the life of a mouse, but at least it was not over yet. He was not going. He sank wearily on to the cot.

"When did they come with the cards?" he asked the room orderly.

"As soon as you left."

"And what about you?"

"Not me, but my mother is in it."

He nodded, but felt at the same time that this gesture lacked true sympathy. The orderly was thirty. He had been digging on various building sites since the "AK" transport, which had been the first to arrive here and had had most of the hard work. So his mother was going. They would be separated. No, nothing stayed together in this place. At home it was all different, a mother was everything, she had respect and a quiet old age. Not so here. The mother would go and the son would be glad he had been left behind. In a week's time he would go with another transport and would reproach himself that each of them had gone off to die on his own.

"Mother is seventy," said the digger. "I won't let her go alone. I'm going to report with her."

I am a swine, Hynek Tausig said to himself. That is how things are: some men are human beings and some are animals. And some a little of both, and that's me. But most of all I am a swine.

"I guess you're doing the right thing." he said quietly, adding: "I'd do the same myself." This time he was quite sure he really would. This time he was not lying. Still, he was glad he did not have to do it, and he went out again.

It was evening. He returned to the room, which was different from yesterday. It looked like a military camp. The boys were packing their stuff. The gloom of the first moments had gone. His eyes lighted on the digger and he went over to help him. Then he helped his neighbor. He did not say a word the whole time. Finished.

"Lights out, boys," the digger called out when they had all finished. Time to sleep.

But Hynek Tausig could not sleep. He kept thinking that there were a great many things in a human being, something of the animal, too, but that it was up to him to choose; maybe nobody was going to ask him about it after the war. Perhaps he would not have to answer the question: were you in a blue funk, old fellow, or did you not give a damn? After the war, if only he lived to see it, life would be completely different. No one would need to know anything, either about himself or anyone else. One could live without that, just as one did before. Everything would be plain sailing. Good morning and good-bye. Without being kicked and called names. No, he had never imagined that he would carry out a revolution in his life. It was not to be recommended at his age.

Sleep stayed away from him as the night advanced. Bitter thoughts pinned him down on his cot. He could smell the pungent odor of human bodies. He was sure not to sleep any more now. Well then, Hynek Tausig, you are going to live through it all, obedient as ever, helping your pals to the trucks. And if by chance you should stumble under someone's foot, or even into one of the trucks, you will not say a word. No, he would not sleep now, but just lying there was also difficult. He got up, put on his coat, and went to the door. He was not allowed out, but he could look out of the door, could he not?

It was a clear night. The silky blue of the sky was illuminated by the glow of immensely distant diamonds. When you were small, Hynek Tausig, you thought everything was like the stars, pure and beautiful. What would become of man? He could not tear himself away. He stood there for hours, hours and minutes.

The transport left in the morning.

The ashen-looking little man did not move from his place.

Evening came again, and with it night. He would not go to bed. He would remain there, by the door. Today it would be different.

The ghetto lay at his feet. A strange prison, he thought sleepily. Every part of a man was imprisoned separately, broken in pieces. One transport had left. There now remained an invisible time limit for the next. When that ran out, it would all begin anew.

Someone was calling to him: "Don't stand there gaping, man! You'll be as weak as a fly in the morning."

He felt a sudden chill and pulled his coat more closely around him. He forgot to reply.

A moment later he came back to his cot and bent down to look under it. There he had the suitcase he had borrowed. He tore away the paper and pulled out Alfred Janota's identity card. It seemed to him all of a sudden that a man of that name really lived somewhere. He had to find him and give him his life.

Slowly he pushed the identity card into his pocket. He still had some money left. The world seemed huge and free to him now. But that was a deceptive impression, everyone had to find himself a narrow little street. A street of his own. And to walk that street and not turn left or right. Once you did that, you would not be able to go straight again. He could not go to the northwest, where the mountains were. What about the south? No, he must not start doubting, otherwise he would never do it. He went to the door, feeling the snores, the sweaty odors, and the breathed-up air behind his back. He stood there, looking at the sky. The clouds were thick and dark and there were no stars.

A look at his watch. A little after twelve. He looked back at the room he was leaving. They were all asleep now. Should he perhaps stay? He might not be in the next transport, either. He was safely hidden in a crowd. He must not behave recklessly. . . . The echo of the last word did not have time to reverberate through him. No, he must not stop now. He must not undress and get back in bed like a cowardly mouse. By morning he could walk at least twenty kilometers. But if he went to bed now, he would be stronger tomorrow. Take it easy, he admonished himself, take it easy. And don't try to fool yourself! His chin trembled. They might catch him. But wasn't he as good as caught now, this very minute that he was thinking it? That was how it was that time in Prague. He need not look for a gap in the fence. Why not climb into some empty truck at the station and let himself be taken away, far from the ghetto. And then—no, he must not lie to himself.

He stood there a moment longer. Then he left the doorway. But not to return inside.

A little later, concealed by the night, Hynek Tausig stopped on the northern rampart of the ghetto. He caught hold of the bough of a tall cherry tree whose thin trunk grew less than a yard away from the reddish slopes of the ramparts. He clambered down rather clumsily—he was afraid and that hampered him. He scratched his face and hands and coat on the bark of the tree, but at last he felt the damp, yielding earth beneath his feet. He glanced up, murmuring to himself: "I'm leaving." It sounded inside him, however, as if he were trying to convince himself.

And then, slightly bent forward, he ran through the night and the mud, past the gendarmes' post.

Rose Street

The breath of summer blew through the ghetto.

It carried Elizabeth Feiner, known for short as "Auntie," right up to the junk shop on L Avenue. The street, as you could see by looking at the sign on the corner by the barracks, used to be called Rose Street—it had not been an avenue, nor had this town been a ghetto, and the barbershop, "The Sun," shut down long before the war, could hardly have served for the sale of junk and castoffs.

The Star Fort was being smartened up. The German HQ building, where they were expecting a visit from Switzerland, had been whitewashed to resemble the other houses in the ghetto; beneath the scaffolding old women were scrubbing the pavement, and real roses appeared in the earth around the stone fountains.

There were no glass panes in the once wooden door of the shop, and Elizabeth Feiner had covered up the holes with greasy, brownish paper that looked like stretched donkey skin. From the dark interior of the shop she could watch the shadows and the heads flitting past. That was all she saw.

Ever since that morning, which had been hot and stifling, she announced to all comers that she had nothing really worthwhile in stock. Her slightly rasping voice, in which kindness mingled with irritation, suggested that the junk shop, of which she was in charge through no wish of her own, was no less a fake than the roses and the ostentatious L Avenue.

When the door of the shop opened, the old woman's ugly head had dropped down almost onto her chest.

"Good morning, Mrs. Feiner." The words came through the rustle of paper.

The door creaked twice.

The man who came in, ceremoniously taking off his hat, worn low on his forehead even now in summer, slowly placed two boiled potatoes on the counter.

"Perhaps you can use them," he said.

"Oh, Mr. Spiegel," protested Elizabeth Feiner. "What have I done to deserve this?"

Embarrassed, the old man closed his eyes hesitantly. "My dear Mrs. Feiner," he said, "that's a question we might all ask. But of whom?"

His lips, once fleshy, were now coagulated by the bronze-purplish coating of anemia into small, whitish clots; yet his smile was boyishly gentle.

"You are incorrigible," said Elizabeth Feiner.

"I suppose I am," nodded the old man.

She would have liked to stroke his veiny hand. But she only asked almost absent-mindedly: "Do you need anything?"

"No, thank you."

He was ashamed of his husky voice. He must go at once—he had only wanted to look in, anyway.

"Well, I'd better be going."

"Good-bye, Mr. Spiegel."

The familiar creak of the door, and the bent back disappeared behind the greasy paper. Silence. Elizabeth Feiner mutely substituted other, far more friendly, words for the echo of the greeting, wishing herself au revoir soon, as she did every time Joachim Spiegel came, though at the same time she doubted it. How cleverly he passed from the small things to the big ones which she did not understand, she thought to herself.

The shadows were now more sharply outlined. The sun was sailing through a pink sea toward the other side of the town. As soon as it crossed over the beige gable of the house opposite, it would be noon. When it disappeared behind the rock with the eagle beak, the day would be over. If only the sun were more friendly, Elizabeth Feiner thought, it would stay longer in the sky. Or it would sail faster. But anyway, who knew which would be better?

She opened the ledger. She had sold nothing today. But even nothing must be entered, for the Reich was great and strict. It occurred to her that if a thousand Elizabeths decided to mess up their accounts, the war could hardly last so long. Then, however, she waved the thought away with her hand. Nonsense. She pushed aside the potatoes, which to her personified the image of the kind old man, and picked up a blue-and-white pencil.

Nevertheless, she noticed that the greasy paper on the door was again darkened. The door flew open as someone kicked it—she could hear the sharp, dry sound of the kick—from the outside. The paper was torn off and fell slowly into the street. The shop was flooded with light, and she saw the greenish-grey uniform and reddish face of an officer.

He came bursting into the room, shouting: "You damned old Jewish whore!"

Two long strides and he was in front of her and slapped her face.

Werner Binde, the driver from HQ, waddled in with his rolling gait.

It seemed for the moment, as if by slapping her, the officer had given vent to all that raged inside him, as if now he were at a loss what to do and what to say. His eyes traveled around the little shop, until at last they rested on the wooden, shiny top of the counter.

"The account books!" he snarled through his teeth.

He had decided it would be undignified to let the old Jewess witness—however shortly—the indecision of a German officer.

Elizabeth Feiner was, however, aware only of his menacing stare.

"Where's your husband?" he asked suddenly.

"He died," she said.

"How's that?"

She shrugged.

That was too much for Herz.

"Get into the corner!" he roared.

She was so frightened that she failed to do as she was bid. She had not the slightest idea why she had been singled out for this visit; she could not know that, at approximately the same time when she was deliberating whether Joachim Spiegel could become her partner in her old age and death, Herz had been called to see the newly appointed commandant of the town, Albert Ritsche. Somebody had reported to him that they had seen someone in the ghetto smoking. What had the First Officer to say to that?

"Into the corner with you, Jewish swine!" shouted Herz, irritated by her apathy. "At once, and be quick about it!"

Werner Binde was looking on with the same cold interest with which he had earlier scanned the shelves on the walls of the shop. If Herz had not told him outright to follow him, he would quite probably have stayed behind in the car. He transferred his weight from one foot to the other, rocking nonchalantly on his heels. Ever since the old commandant, Wolf Seidl, had left and the new one arrived without Berlin having appointed anyone of those who had served here longer, the HQ resembled a stirred-up wasps' nest, with everyone maneuvering for the best positions. Old sympathies had been disrupted and the officers were in no hurry to establish new ones. They were waiting to see what Ritsche was like. And Binde had only a while ago heard him telling Herz off. The old woman, whom Herz had picked on to work off his rage, repelled Binde by her ugliness. If not she, he thought, someone else would have caught it instead. Nothing of this showed on Binde's face, however. On the contrary, it looked rather as if he were merely dividing up the shoddy things on the shelves in his mind, choosing the ones he had a use for and discarding those he did not want.

Herz turned to him suddenly, taking him by surprise, but Binde retained his composure. He brought his heels together with a loud click and said the first thing that came to his mind: "There's no water in the tank, sir. Shall I go get some?"

"No, stay here," said Herz, adding sibilantly, "Ass!"

It did not occur to him in the least that he was being unjust, having told Binde earlier that he would not need the car any more today. Nor did it occur to Binde himself, or so it seemed by the look in his cool, unconcerned, fishlike eyes.

Then Herz turned again to Elizabeth Feiner. Raising his hand, he made a threatening gesture right under her nose, the taut skin of his grey buckskin glove emphasizing the outlines of his clenched fist.

What a revolting hook of a nose, he thought with distaste, and said: "We'll soon knock rebellion out of your heads. As for you, you scab, you'll get a taste of it right here and now."

All her astonishment was written large in her wrinkled, sinewy and angular face and in the eyes with which she gazed at him. Why had they come here, of all places?

"Don't play the innocent with me," said Herz, as though he had read her thoughts.

"But I really don't know, sir . . ." she said.

"Shut up," Werner Binde hissed at her from the other side of the shop.

Elizabeth Feiner was, however, already sorry she had spoken.

Herz suddenly changed his tone. "Sarah, dear, don't you think your takings are very small?" he said, his voice sweet and coaxing.

And Werner Binde looked on as Herz pulled out of his well-polished black jackboot a length of reed, at whose end there was a dully gleaming lead pellet, doing it slowly and almost imperceptibly, so that the old woman should not see.

Elizabeth Feiner was still standing motionless in a corner of the shop underneath the clergyman's chasubles and the gloomy black-and-white folds of stoles which hung from a round wooden rod. Every now and then they would swing to and fro as they were touched by the wind or by the breath of the two men, and she would feel them quite close to her face. She closed her eyes and breathed in their pungent naphthalene smell. But she did not dare raise her hand and push them aside.

"Come here!" the officer called out to her.

She came back slowly, leaving the surplices to flutter behind her.

"Turn round," said Herz.

Elizabeth Feiner, her chin dropping timorously onto her chest, cast an uncertain glance at Herz's purplish face, at the root of his red nose, and at the cold eyes of Werner Binde, in whose depths she thought she saw a glimmer of mute disagreement.

Binde was leaning against the shelf and examining the old clothes. No, he could not use any of this stuff, his mouth with its slightly raised left corner seemed to indicate. But these sparks went out very quickly. Herz had taken off his cap and was hanging it up with exaggerated care on the peg. The inevitable was about to begin, and Binde's eyes went cold again as before.

Herz prodded Elizabeth Feiner with his elbow. Beneath the surface of his rage there was a gap of tranquillity. And in this gap he found both the impulse and the explanation of what he had come to do, which showed so vividly on his face that Elizabeth Feiner shuddered in fear of her life. For the eyes into which she was gazing and the face which was now frozen in a chilly immobility were the living image of death.

Herz drew his arm back in abhorrence. The figure in front of him was no woman—it was the incarnation of Ritsche's reproof. He was faced with the task of obliterating that which had besmirched his soldierly honor.

He did not speak another word; but when the dirty old Jewish swine collapsed onto the counter at a single shove, as he had wished her to do, he could not help guffawing aloud with merriment.

Binde made no remark now, though he knew well enough that politeness demanded that he should. His mind was preoccupied with the thought that the events of this afternoon were like skittles, knocking each other down, although only one of them had been hit by the bowl. That conceited fool, Herz, had told him off because it had occurred to him to say that he had no water in the tank, yet he could just as easily have said he had no petrol, only because he had himself been given a dressing down earlier. Why? Because someone in this damned town had smoked, or perhaps even no one had smoked at all. Perhaps someone only imagined it. And now this old woman, whose days were numbered in any case, was going to pay for it. In the silence that followed Herz's laugh, Binde realized that if he now let Herz go through with this act without lending a hand, Herz would be sure to ram it down his throat at the most inopportune moment. He therefore responded with a belated sour grin.

But the corners of Herz's mouth were by this time only imperceptibly curved. The surface of his mood had risen in a tempestuous wave, which completely flooded the tranquil gap. The spark which had kindled his smile had now flared up into action.

Herz kicked the motionless feet, shod in old-fashioned galoshes with buckles. It came to his mind that this was not Russia; these bastards obligingly waited until one chose to kick them.

Elizabeth Feiner lay slumped over the wooden counter, the blunt edge of which pressed against her stomach. Her eyes were closed. She could feel all the time how the blood streamed to her head; but it was no longer a head—it was a barrel which seemed to be bursting and yet was completely empty. There was a swoon inside that barrel, and it would claim her as soon as she gave it enough blood. Even thus, with her eyes closed, she saw Joachim Spiegel; he came again and brought her potatoes. Then she had an incredibly silly idea: it occurred to her that all three, the entire phantom of a funeral procession, Joachim Spiegel and both the soldiers who had come in, were from one and the same country. Who would have thought it a little while ago? Lucky they did not notice the potatoes. After all, they were not merely pieces of starch with a few vitamins in them; they secreted within themselves kindness and self-sacrifice. All these thoughts, which took place almost at the very ceiling of her consciousness, rapidly succumbing to a swoon, were responsible for her being able to feel nothing but the blows. It was only when the officer lost his head and started to beat her in a way calculated to make her cry out that she gave up all thought. By that time she was so far gone that she did not utter a sound.

It was half past five, and Herz replaced his whip in his boot. She had got hers all right, even though she didn't make a noise, he thought, looking at the old woman's back.

"Well, Binde, what d'you say?" he asked in a voice of tired satisfaction as he took off his gloves. "Neat work, wasn't it?"

"Very neat, sir . . ." said Binde.

Herz pushed the door open with a vigorous movement and stood on the threshold. Proudly, with a bluishly purple face, bloodshot and covered with sweat, he looked up and down L Avenue. Today, he thought, his pride swelling still further, today they'll be talking about me all over the ghetto.

Werner Binde followed him out of the shop.

But Elizabeth Feiner did not yet know that she was alone.

She lay across the counter in such a way that she could not fall off. She swallowed her tears, and only then did she manage to faint.

2

"It's after half past five, Binde," Herz said when they were back in the car. "Tomorrow's another day."

"Do you wish to go back to HQ, sir, or shall I drive you home?" asked Binde.

"Don't you like boxing?" asked Herz, following a different line of thought. He was no longer thinking of the old woman. And it occurred to him that there had been in the family, on his mother's side, an uncle Helmuth Rinde or Binde or some such name. He felt wonderful. Then he added, "Home."

The driver nodded. Did he like boxing? That, after all, was not boxing. It was a thrashing, and a pretty mean one at that. All right, he thought, they'd put all Jews on the same garbage heap. Well, let them rot there then, but by themselves.

"Do you know something, Binde?" Herz asked him gaily. "Perhaps we are relatives."

Binde saw that Herz's foul mood had been left behind in the town, where he had shaken off the load of abuse piled on him by the new commandant.

"How come?" he asked. "Your name is Herz and mine Binde; you come from Hamburg and I from Berlin."

"Are you free this evening?" Herz began, again on another tack.

"I guess so," replied Binde.

"Come and have dinner with us," said Herz, his voice filled with satisfaction, for he had no doubt that the commandant would find out from the Jewish elder's report how he had dealt with that Jewess.

"Thanks," said Binde.

There was nothing in this reply, however, to tell Herz whether Binde had accepted the invitation or not.

Werner Binde stared with cold eyes at the road ahead, conscious at the same time of Herz's searching gaze upon him. They had once driven together to Berlin like this, at a time when Herz was deputizing for Wolf Seidl. Herz told him, laughingly, that his eyes reminded him of a fish. That was the first time he had taken a dislike to Herz. He really did sometimes concentrate so intently on something that it seemed as though all activity had ceased behind that blunt, low brow of his. And now there was an unexpected invitation inside the limited circle of Werner Binde's cumbrous thought.

Herz stared at Binde's masklike profile. He had been glad at the time that he had been allotted Binde, the best driver at HQ. It was something in the nature of a distinction. Binde was not over-popular—they nicknamed him "kohlrabi" because of his low, foreshortened head—but he was not unpopular, either. His army papers said that his reliable driving had served SS General Erich von Stumpke in the Buchenwald concentration camp, and later the head of the Reich

Winterhilfe for South Germany, Oswald Trautenfelder. He had been transferred from Buchenwald at his own request, which fact, Herz recalled, had at first given rise to all sorts of conjectures. Nevertheless it was possible, and Herz was inclined to take that view himself now, that it had all been a personal matter. Still, there was something slightly fishy about the chap. They'd discussed it with Ritsche when he took up his post, but he had only said:

"One camp or another, what's the difference?"

And the conjectures had ceased.

A little later Binde stopped the car in front of a yellow villa. Herz's wife, Rosemarie Ilse, a stoutish woman of thirty-five with a white skin, light blue, watery eyes, and a head that sat upon her fat shoulders as though she had no neck, was waiting by the gate in front of the garden.

"Maurice," she called out. "At last you're home! Oh, Herr Binde . . . your name is Binde, isn't it?"

The driver nodded.

"You must be tired," Rosemarie Ilse went on. "Come on in, both of you."

The eight-year-old Adolf barred their way as they entered the gate.

"Heil Hitler!" he shouted at his father.

Herz stroked his head, but the little boy drew away, offended.

"I said Heil Hitler, daddy, and you didn't."

"Well, all right then, 'Heil Hitler' . . ."

Little Adolf, however, burst into tears.

"Binde will have dinner with us tonight," said Herz.

That, of course, was more than Rosemarie Ilse had reckoned with. Since when was Maurice inviting noncoms to his house? She had intended to offer Binde a glass of something—after all, he was also a German, and she knew well enough that they had to stick together in this hostile land. But dinner? She stared at her husband in surprise, but a single grimace on his reddish face sufficed to keep her quiet.

Binde did not notice anything. So they were perhaps relatives. What was he to think of that?

They sat down in the drawing room.

Herz's five-year-old daughter came running up to him. She was better behaved than her brother and had waited for her father here. She was called Rosemarie after her mother and grandmother, and Hilde after the mother-in-law.

"Did you annoy Mother today?" asked Herz.

Rosemarie Hilde shook her head.

Ilse smiled happily.

"And Grannie?"

"No."

"They are the nicest children in the world, Maurice," said Rosemarie Ilse.

Just then the maid came in with the dishes.

Rosemarie Ilse still could not understand why Maurice had to drag his subordinates home with him. Surely they were entitled to have a few moments to themselves, just the two of them.

Binde was staring unseeingly into a corner of the room where a vase with artificial flowers was standing. Better be careful about palling up with Herz, he said to himself. But that was only a sidestream of the turgid, muddy flow of thought whose limpid waves conjured up the image of the ugly old woman in the little shop on L Avenue.

He felt the eyes of his hostess resting upon him. His own glided along the white tablecloth, as though running away. Fat lump! he thought.

Rosemarie Ilse's mother then made her appearance, an old lady with a pince-nez on a silver chain, all dressed in black up to her neck, with small yellow pieces of lace on her sleeves.

"Good evening," she said.

All of them replied to the greeting, Werner Binde even getting up from his chair, only Herz nodded silently.

It was evident that the old lady did not feel a great deal of affection for the master of the house. Indeed, she considered Herz a rather rough man. Once she had seen her daughter removing a red stain from the sleeve of his uniform. Since then she was the prey of disturbing notions, but she never plucked up enough courage to ask Ilse what it was.

As for Herz, if it occurred to him that he did not like the old woman, he put the cause down to the relationship. Even a decent woman could be a bad mother-in-law. Her son, Rosemarie Ilse's brother, was at the front as a fairly highly placed Nazi official. He could have been safely somewhere in the rear, but had volunteered to stay in the front line. The old woman was not too proud of it, and her remarks sometimes almost drove him to fury.

The old lady sat down in a spacious armchair in the middle and put a sewing-basket in her lap.

The maid started to serve dinner.

The conversation was sporadic and uneasy, Binde's presence being the obvious cause. Herz admitted it to himself and was vexed. The similarity between the name of the uncle and the driver was all nonsense, he said to himself, and he saw that Rosemarie Ilse's mother was just as annoyed as her daughter. Then Rosemarie Ilse complained that the cinema, where there had been a breakdown yesterday, was still not in order. The talk touched on new films and Rosemarie Ilse commented:

"My God, there's nothing but the war in all of them."

Her mother nodded agreement, now and again looking Werner Binde over from under her pince-nez.

"It's getting quite unbearable at times," added Rosemarie Ilse.

Herz fixed his eyes on her, severe and reproachful. He was watching carefully how Binde was reacting to it all. But the driver was fully occupied in the troublesome business of picking the bone of his leg of chicken.

"Germany is an empire that can wage and survive a ten times bigger war than this one, if need be," said Herz.

Little Adolf agreed eagerly.

"All the same," Rosemarie Ilse went on dreamily, her mouth full of food, "I'd much rather have singing and dancing in my films. Oh, how gay we used to be, Maurice! We had such lovely times."

Herz felt his face suffuse with blood. He'd like to slap the silly cow—why must she talk such drivel?

"Those times are gone," said Binde. "And heaven knows what's in store for us."

"That's right, Binde," said Herz; but he was not sure what exactly the driver meant.

"But surely you're not going to be in the war forever," protested Rosemarie Ilse. "After all, you must get something out of it for yourselves."

"I had a letter from the Hochfellers in Düsseldorf today," said the old lady. "Their house has been wrecked by an English bomb."

"That is the lot of Germany at war," said Herz, replying as it were to his wife's earlier statement (if the cow would only keep her trap shut) and glaring sternly at his mother-in-law.

The old lady rose, offended.

"I am going to bed," she said.

After a while Werner Binde got up, too. He did not feel altogether at his ease with the Herzs. He left his fruit salad untouched, thanked them for the dinner, and said good night. He left full of doubt whether the evening had been good for anything, and even supposing it had, whether things were not bad just the same.

He started the car, switched on the muffled blue lights and, with an uncertain feeling inside him, drove the car along the yellow fence that bordered the ghetto at the place where the road cut through it, to the garage of the HQ.

3

Some ten minutes later that same evening, Herz walked into his study in the upper left wing of the villa. He sat down behind a large mahogany table and carefully got ready his writing utensils. With slow, deliberate movements he took a sheet of glazed paper, a bottle of light blue ink, and a wooden penholder ornamented with burnt stripes. After a short deliberation, having, as he told himself, thought it all out in advance, he wrote a letter to the Third Department of the Berlin Gestapo.

He set his suspicions down in detail, underlining what were sentiments inspired by his fond regard for the welfare of the Third Reich rather than tangible proofs. He put one word down after another with painstaking care, as though they were not words but stones in a building he was erecting. The ideas behind the words took up all his thoughts. It was no longer a letter he was writing, it was a fort he was building, and it was necessary to eliminate all loopholes which might not remain unnoticed, and to strengthen the embrasures in case a hidden enemy should try to squeeze his impudent elbows into them. Finally he expressed quite openly his suspicion that the pre-

sent commandant of the Theresienstadt ghetto was, before the decisive year 1933, a member of a leftist trade union organization, just
like most of the other members of the staff of the Europa Café in
Cologne, in which Heinz Albert Ritsche had worked as a waiter. It
was a daring, indeed a highly dangerous, attack—Herz was fully
aware of that. In fact, an unpleasant comparison came to him as he
thought about it: if someone were to make such an attack against
him, Herz would not know how to defend himself. Words of denun-
ciation were at a great advantage these days: they were invariably the
first. He suppressed a chill which had begun to tingle his spine and,
with the aid of a wave of anger which he always found it easy to
invoke, persuaded himself that all was fair in war. After all, it wasn't
decent of Berlin to send a new man when the old commandant,
Wolf Seidl, left, was it? And if the erstwhile commandant was now at
the front, which offered him the possibility of a hero's death, was
that not chiefly due to his, Herz's, letters and reports? Yes, almost
everything spoke for him. Perhaps it would not then be altogether
ill-considered if the High Command were to appoint him, Maurice
Herz, commandant of the ghetto. He raised his pen for the final full
stop as though it were a spear with which he wished to stab Heinz
Albert Ritsche. Then he signed himself with a flourish. He folded
the letter and put it in the envelope, heated the sealing wax, and
carved his initials, M. H., into the small mound.

He waited a few moments, then pushed the letter underneath a
bronze paper-weight. It was a statuette of Atlas carrying the globe on
his shoulders. To Maurice Herz it was a material symbol of his
dream. He stroked the lifeless bronze with his eyes. Why should he
now believe it completely out of the question that he would gain his
ends? He had once already come so close . . . I have helped to build
this hole, he thought as he gazed out excitedly at the darkened ghetto, this Godforsaken Jewish lair, ever since 'forty-one. At that time
they had meted out punishment not only with their fists, but with
hempen cord. In his mind's eye he saw the number seventeen. That's
how many there were of them, and he had shot the only one to
break loose, without the commandant's orders. It had been a good
joke to appoint a Jewish hangman for the executions. No, he mustn't
allow himself to be pushed around! The time had come to say:
Enough! He started pacing up and down the room. Bringing Binde,

he thought, had not been such a good idea. As for that silly goose, Rosemarie Ilse, she deserved a kick in the pants. Her twaddle was driving him crazy lately, just like the idiotic chatter of her mother, the aristocratic bitch. Between the two of them they'd get him into a concentration camp one of these days, he thought darkly.

The sealing-wax was reflected on the bronze surface of the statuette. It had set some time ago, and the initials M. H. looked like sharp incisions. But still Maurice Herz did not come down to his bedroom on the ground floor. He was gazing at the statuette and at the white envelope, thinking out a plan of action whose tentacles penetrated every nook and cranny in the white building of the HQ, enveloping everything and everyone. He saw himself in a variety of places, behind the commandant's desk and in his villa, at the head of his colleagues sitting round the carved table at the Casino, as well as in Berlin, in new silver epaulettes, making his report which would serve as a model of military brevity and precision: destroyed. Destroyed and annihilated.

It was late in the night before he went to bed.

4

The people who passed by the little shop on L Avenue that evening, trying to look as though the afternoon that had just passed was a normal part of the ghetto's routine, were nevertheless in a hurry. It was clear that no one had the least inclination to wander about in the ghetto. And since they had prudently vanished from the streets at the time of Maurice Herz's and Werner Binde's visit, many of them must have wondered why, on this particular summer evening, the shop, "The Sun," was still open. However, none of those to whom this occurred ventured inside, while Joachim Spiegel, the only one who would certainly have called, did not dare even set foot in Rose Street. The sentry who came on later did not notice, and people had other things to think about than how to enlarge their wardrobe by the addition of torn stockings or stoles. The Jewish sentries paced their beats slowly and with pretended assurance for only short distances from their posts, so that no one came to know about Elizabeth Feiner, who was still lying inside the shop. Thus no report of the incident was included in the Jewish elder's report and was therefore not among the documents which were next day presented to commandant Heinz Albert Ritsche. And Herz's efforts came to nothing.

It was a little before this, at about the time Maurice Herz finally went to sleep, that Elizabeth Feiner came to. It would be an exaggeration to say that after those six hours she completely regained consciousness; everything seemed to give way beneath her and to swim in darkness. An unpleasant whistling noise sounded in her ears, mingling with the shouts of children who called her "Auntie," and changing to the piercing shriek of a locomotive's whistle, then to the wailing of dozens of sirens and, at the same time, to steamrollers which kept running over her forehead with their rough-surfaced, heavy wheels. Suddenly she found it revolting to lie helplessly on the floorboards. When she at last picked herself up and laboriously got to her feet, she did not know for a long time what time it was. All round her there was nothing but silence. It must be time for her to pull down the shutters. It was also dark, which meant that it was after the curfew and thus impossible for any Jew to appear in the streets. Her dazed mind conjured up images of a long-forgotten, distant childhood, of nights when she had been afraid to go out in the dark and frightened when she woke up in her bed in the middle of the night. Now, too, she was afraid, but for different reasons. She wished that the darkness would swallow everything and that the rough, opaque curtain which seemed to hang in front of her eyes would never be raised. And she wished that Joachim Spiegel might be somewhere near at that last moment which would put an end to all the troubles of this world. She immediately rebuked herself, however; she must not link anyone with her misfortune. She realized that she could not stand long on her feet without support, so she sat down on the floor. She longed to be able to close her eyes and sleep off everything that had happened if she was to survive it and to go on living. Thus she sat, her former ideas, according to which a human being could keep his dignity even in this place, shattered and ruined like a wretched pile of debris. Worst of all, an evil thought fought its way through to the surface of her consciousness, searing her brain; had the red-faced officer who had knocked her down not even for a moment seen in her his own mother? The reply which seemed to roar inside her transformed her face so that it now resembled that of an ugly, astonished child. She knew only one thing for certain: that she must not leave the shop in the night. She therefore remained sitting where she was, feeling her legs, her face, and her whole body with her hands. Each touch she felt in the marrow of her bones. But this time, painful though it was, she no longer succeeded in fainting. She had to squat on the cold planks of the floor, alone with the mice and her own, now wide-awake consciousness.

The night passed slowly and heavily. It was like a chilly blanket of darkness retaliating for the hot day. Not even the faint rays of the yet-distant dawn, nor the bluish glow of the stars which she could see through the windows of the shop, could penetrate this blanket.

5

The morning was foggy. From inside the shop the figures, flitting past on the other side of the greasy paper in the window like a grotesque shadow play of L Avenue, appeared only as a monotonous pantomime of heads. It was difficult to make out just how much they were bent under their broad-brimmed hats. The shiny metal or bamboo sticks of umbrellas heralded a wet autumn—the rain and the damp mists, which came early in this region, bringing confirmation. The paper was soon soaked through with rain, and before she pulled down the corrugated iron shutters, Elizabeth Feiner took down the paper and left it to dry overnight on the counter.

Her angular head, even more scarred with bluish veins, large and small, than it was before the end of the summer, looked as though the blood inside it were getting darker. She was racking her brains with a single question, precise and yet ramified at the same time. A few blows were enough to put out what burns in human beings from beginning to end, to become the beacon which we call conscience.

She was now in the habit of sitting motionless on a low stool, as though the contradiction between the depths of her experience and the heights of her resolutions, which had swallowed up everything, had consumed her as well. Thus she would forget that she was not alone.

With her in the shop was Ruth, Joachim Spiegel's niece, who had arrived with the August transport, a month after the SS visit in July, while her parents had remained in Kassel, one of them being an Aryan. She had not heard from them for two whole months. How was Elizabeth Feiner to explain to her why her parents had stayed at home in Kassel while she was here? Would Ruth be able to understand that, according to the Nuremberg laws, there were two kinds of human blood?

She treated Ruth with a curious kind of consideration, which took the form of silence. Now she was staring at the small, thin girl, whose soft dark hair sprouted up from a sallow forehead and whose white teeth were rather widely spaced and almost transparent, as though they were made of ivory. The girl's face with its inquisitive black eyes, such as she once used to have herself, seemed to her to represent a future reproach, because something that not even Elizabeth Feiner was able to give a name to was marking the child's face with the sorrowful expression that Jewish children so frequently have. This reproach at her own constant silence was mixed up with a feeling of gratitude, Ruth being the only one to come these days, as the ghetto was in the throes of an influenza epidemic and many children were ill.

Ruth played with the stoles, straightening them out with her thin, long fingers. After a while she became tired of the silence.

"Auntie Feiner," she said, "why don't you keep the fire going?"

The dark silence which had depressed her but which she herself was unable to break was shattered at last.

"There's nothing to keep it going with," she replied. "I've burned everything."

She couldn't touch the few pieces of furniture that had been left in the place. Where would she put the things if she did? And what if the owner of the barbershop were to return one day?

The little girl was not satisfied, however. She pouted, this childish grimace contrasting strangely with her grave, grown-up eyes; the white expanse of teeth, the two front ones at the top thrusting forward a little, was parted restlessly. She and Auntie Feiner were in the habit of composing verses.

The sun has flown far from our street;
    Now snow is there;

Like slippers white beneath our feet,
  For us to wear.

But they knew this one by heart now. Perhaps they could try to
compose some new lines.

It rained all the time, thought Elizabeth Feiner in an effort to dis-
tract her thoughts in another direction. Winter was coming. But
what were they going to do if the winter came so soon? And why was
she not saying all this out loud?

"I'll tell you a story," she said at last.

Ruth nodded.

"Once upon a time there was an evil man," she began. "He wanted to rule the whole wide world. Nobody loved him, and he was
angry about it and so he sent his subjects to the hangman to be executed, one by one . . ."

She did not realize that she had stopped speaking and there was
silence again.

"But Auntie Feiner," protested Ruth. "It's not finished yet."

"Yes, that's just the trouble, child," said Elizabeth Feiner.

Then she burst out, so suddenly and so urgently that Ruth was
startled and opened her mouth with the small mouselike teeth:

"I'll tell you the rest tomorrow. You must leave me alone now. Go
on, run home, Ruth!"

Her voice was so gritty and unkind and there was so much
urgency in it that it frightened her.

"I know who the evil man is, anyway . . ." said Ruth.

"Go on, run . . ."

Elizabeth Feiner shook all over until the door closed behind the
girl. Her mind was filled with a single question. What would happen
when the door opened again to admit the greenish-grey uniform
with the reddish face? It was not finished yet. That was what troubled her so much. Whatever happened, she had to be alone, she told
herself.

On several occasions during the time when the pale glow of the
sun was obliterated by rain, from the beginning to the end of October, she had thought of going to the Council of Elders to hand over
the keys of the shop to someone else. She did not wish to remain
here any longer. But she hardly ever got farther than halfway up the

stairs. She would like to scrub the pavements as she used to do. There was nothing to be ashamed of in that. It was only when she saw that reddish face with its tight-lipped mouth in front of her that she knew where humiliation came from. Would she succeed in getting away from here before they arrived? She had sixty-two years of life behind her, she did not make hasty decisions. And yet she had changed her mind every time just before she got there. There was something else to be taken into account; someone would have to take her place. Perhaps Joachim Feiner—oh, she admonished herself, how silly of her, that wasn't his name! Both these things were rooted deeply within her, the idiotic desire for human company and sympathy, and the repudiation of this desire. She mustn't tie anyone to herself, and yet, it was so sad to be alone. So she wavered between her resolve to hand over the keys and her repeated last-minute withdrawals. She toyed with the idea, recurrent like the ebb and tide, that if the expected Swiss delegation arrived before the two SS men, it would be composed entirely of young people in whom she would be able to confide. She thought back to that summer morning, the rosy day, and the night when she was unable to get up from the floor. She was glad she had sent Ruth away. It was windy outside, and a slight drizzle wafted from the mountains was washing away the last traces of summer's beauty. It looked as if it was going to start raining in earnest.

She felt tired. Intending to sit down on her white stool, she stopped dead halfway, her shoulders hunched. Someone was standing outside the shop. Now he was about to enter. And although it flashed across her mind for a mere fraction of a second that it might be Joachim Spiegel, she was not surprised to see the green cloth, flecked with countless grey spots. She was not frightened even when Werner Binde carefully closed the door behind him, leaving his hand to rest on the handle for a while. She was only conscious of an uncertain feeling of expectancy.

Werner Binde shook off the rain. He felt none too brave. He was on his way back from the building which housed the Council of Elders and had stopped here, in front of the little shop on L Avenue. "The Sun"—a stone sun with its rays sharply chiseled above the door, that was a barrier beyond which he was reluctant to penetrate. The passersby saw this, and because he had hesitated a little, they immediately vacated his side of the street. He failed to observe this, however, because as soon as he entered the shop and as soon as he left it again and hurried on through the town, he was sure that no one except Elizabeth Feiner had noticed him, since the sidewalks on both sides were again crowded.

"Good day," he said.

She regarded him distrustfully. Was the greeting only a polite ruse? She took off her spectacles, then said: "Good day."

She could not bring herself to ask boldly what it was the soldier wanted, despite the fact that something was impelling her to ask just that question. She was puzzled by his calmness and by the look in his cold, quiet eyes.

Werner Binde was standing face to face with the old woman's angular head, bewhiskered chin, and the red root of her nose.

And Elizabeth Feiner, waiting all the time for what was to come, could not make out what was concealed behind the soldier's fishlike eyes. She had no idea that the very fact that he was here had a certain meaning, that it meant the result of a three months' invisible struggle against Maurice Herz. Werner Binde had come to see the old woman whom Herz had humiliated. This was a climax, the transformation of a wish into action. He did not like Herz, thinking it was because here Herz punctuated every sentence with a slap, while at HQ he acted the perfect gentleman. That, Werner Binde said to himself, is just what I can't stand. He had resented it already in the case of Erich von Stumpke and Oswald Trautenfelder, with whom he used to drive out to inspect the stores supplied by the Mauthausen camp and used for the purposes of the Winterhilfe for South Germany. He was hardly aware that this feeling of distaste dated back to the time when he had met his own stepbrother, Fritz, in Buchenwald. He was not allowed as much as to shake his hand or throw him a handkerchief with which to bandage his wounds. Fritz died in front of his eyes like some animal, and he, Werner, had smiled inanely so that no one would see that he was in any way concerned about the bloody bundle of flesh which had been suspected of a nonsensical offense—listening to foreign radio stations.

Elizabeth Feiner debated with herself: should I ask, or not?

Werner Binde searched his mind to find out whether there was something that drew him to this ugly old woman with the promi-

nent cheekbones and with grey hairs on her chin and under her
nose. He did not dare to dwell on the idea of what the others would
think of him standing here inactive like this.

Elizabeth Feiner was suddenly disturbed by a feeling that the
silence was about to blow up like a load of dynamite. When was it
going to start?

But Werner Binde was thinking of other things. He did not wish
to play with the word *coward,* and yet it was this very word that
haunted him ever since that July evening when he had had dinner
with Maurice Herz and his wife. It had all started with that silly dinner. Nevertheless, Werner Binde knew very well that there was
something that had happened before the dinner. And everything
after it. On the following day the soldiers had each received a tin of
sardines, brought from Portugal via Switzerland. He could not eat
his sardines, even though at the time he had only a vague idea of
what he was going to do with them and did not want to admit it
even to himself. So he carried them around in his pocket, knowing
very well that he intended to give them to this old woman. He had
only been looking for a suitable opportunity. "I feel nothing toward
her," he kept repeating to himself, "absolutely nothing, she is only
old and ugly." Yet, he had never carried out his intention. There was
a barrier in his way, an obstacle that was fully and precisely described
by the word *cowardice.* It was not only that he was afraid of prying
eyes—they could be put off the scent in a number of ways, all of
them foolproof. He could, for instance, pretend to beat the old
woman and then leave the sardines here as if by accident; he could
be at hand in the vicinity of the shop when she went to open up in
the morning. But he rejected them all. They did not afford him
what he was seeking: satisfaction once and for all. That satisfaction,
however, did not come even now that he was finally standing here,
almost feeling her breath upon him. The old woman, he saw clearly,
was afraid of him. She could not look inside his soul. There was no
reason why he should feel anything for her, she was merely a mediator between him and his future peace of mind. All the same, he
could not rid himself of the worrying thought that what he had
dared to do would never be properly appreciated. He stood there in
front of her, quiet and subdued, disappointment staring out of his
eyes; he looked into hers, sunken and old, and read in them a com-

bination of fear and defiance and a profound resignation. She was not as ugly as he had imagined her all this time. And yet—she was ripe for the crematorium. One blow would do the trick. He was furious with himself for thinking like this. He turned quickly to look at the entrance. Nobody there. He looked at his watch, hardly knowing why he did so. He was jumpy, he told himself. Out of the pocket of his greatcoat he pulled the tin and, thinking suddenly that all this fuss was useless, that he should have been rougher, should have simply handed the thing over and nothing more, he left as unexpectedly as he had come, almost without a greeting, perhaps a little nervously, walking out of the shop with his rolling, sailor's gait.

Elizabeth Feiner was left looking at the spot where he had been standing, at the greasy paper that replaced the glass. She stood thus for a long time, uncomprehending. The dynamite did not go off, then. She had, nevertheless, not failed to register the moment when the soldier had been on the point of hitting her. She could not pluck up the courage to touch the sardines in their gaudy yellow wrapping. What if the soldier's shadow appeared again on the paper in the window? And yet, something told her that he would not come back. Had it perhaps been fear that had made him glance at his watch and at the door? But fear was attentiveness intensified and only rarely was it transmuted into action; fear was merely the transformation of one's own thoughts into those of the enemy. She pushed the tin away with loathing, under the stoles hanging down in folds from the ceiling. She was confused. As so often before, it again occurred to her that one had always something to learn, that no final impression was ever accurate, because as long as events were being uncoiled from the spool of life no impression was really final. Who could tell what people were like underneath their shell of coarseness or despair, where only they themselves could see, sometimes not even they. Where then lay the boundaries that divided people? Unthinkingly she reached out for the sardines.

She went out of the shop and pulled down the shutters. Then she opened the old, black silk, man's umbrella, whose great width was quite out of proportion to her emaciated figure, clad in a dark blue dress with grey, opaque buttons. In her shiny alligator handbag with its brass clasps she carried the yellow tin of sardines in oil, that strange gift which she could not as yet comprehend.

Halfway up Rose Street she changed her direction. She felt feverish, as if a flame were burning her up from within, and she was
unable to fight against it. Wasn't the whole thing just a trap? Was it
permissible for a woman who was trained as she was, and as were all
the other people herded together in the ghetto, to accept something
that rightfully belonged to pure-blooded soldiers? But yet another
voice inside her was asking why Binde had been so careful and quiet.
And the first voice answered: that's just a mask! The sardines had
become a source of disquiet, a time bomb planted on her soul.

She saw it all again, as it had been three months ago and as it had
been today. Two men were in the shop, one red-faced and indifferent, his head a little flattened, like a beet-root. The other one had
only acted roughly in one instance, by telling her to shut up. But
perhaps even that was intended to help her. It was all so very complicated. Why, after today's encounter, did she want to think well of
him, as though it were out of the question that there should be a
trick in it somewhere? The red-faced one had beaten her, and he
would have done so even if she had kept quiet. The old proverb
about the dog and the stick came to her mind.

No, she would not go straight to the barracks.

She made for a square building with two crossed horses' heads in
a coat of arms above a stone doorway—the house of the Council of
Elders.

The street, it seemed to her, was not level, it wound itself round
the trees, up and down like a great swing, and the people were laughing at the sight. She touched her head; it was burning. She could not
stand it if Binde were to come to her today, or even tomorrow, she
thought. After all, it was not only the blows and the kicks—there
was something else besides that. She was at the mercy of her own
thoughts, which her brain shot at her heart, and she was helpless to
prevent it. She would tell the Council of Elders that her involuntary
service was at an end. She would hand over the keys. Good-bye to
"The Sun"! Yes, that would rid her of the worry of what would happen if she were unable to go to the shop tomorrow.

She trotted through the town perseveringly, under her huge
umbrella, the tears in which permitted the wind to blow the rain in
and to soak her more than could be healthy for a sick old woman.

At last she reached the house with the coat of arms.

The staircase with its high steps resembled a pyramid. With difficulty she raised one foot and then the other, one foot and the other, and again and again, so that she lost all count of time as she struggled up and up until she stopped in front of the Chief Administrator's desk. She did not even know how she signed the written declaration saying that the shop, The Sun, was in perfect order, nor was she aware of the searching gaze of the man to whom she handed the keys. All she knew was that he was kind and that he agreed with her in everything.

"Just a moment, Mrs. Feiner," he was saying, his voice sounding as if it came from a long way off. "I'll see you to the door."

"Yes. . . ."

"Just a moment, I won't be a minute."

But Elizabeth Feiner did not hear him. She was already walking down the stairs.

The barracks in which she lived were not far—just across the road, standing there along steep slopes that towered up in the twilight and fell on the other side into the depths of a different world which was no longer the ghetto.

She could not remember when she had last felt so ill. Every intake of breath hurt her. Pleurisy, she thought. But it could also be just flu. Notwithstanding the pain, she managed an inward smile. Just. What a silly word!

She was already halfway home before the rain-soaked administrator caught up with her.

"Really, Mrs. Feiner," he was saying. "Why didn't you wait for me?"

She looked at him, puzzled. She couldn't for the life of her think of his name.

She went on taking short steps and not noticing that the man was supporting her.

At the door the Chief Administrator had to leave her.

"Good night . . ."

She thought she nodded her head in farewell. Or at least she wanted to.

She placed the small, shiny tin underneath her pillow, took off her shoes, and lay down. She closed her eyes straightaway, and then pulled the quilt over her head. She wouldn't tell anyone—the other women might be afraid of infection. An indescribable weight was constantly upon her. The end was approaching. That delusive game which she had called life would soon be over. And on just such a remarkable day. The stone frame of the window, with its thin rusty bars set close to one another, was jumping up and down before her closed eyes. On the other side of the room was a real, red-hot stove, surrounded by a swarm of women preparing supper. Room 38, peopled by the evening, full of children and visitors. And from outside she could hear the water swirling in the drainpipe, and thought of Joachim Spiegel's niece, who recited:

The sun has flown far from our street;
Now snow is there. . . .

The arrows kept on coming. Now they came from afar and embedded themselves in the center of her forehead. The autumn and its rains should not have set in. Not yet. She fell asleep, willing herself to sleep so eagerly that an unpleasant, sticky perspiration sprang up all over her body. She was completely covered by the quilt, out of whose torn, ragged end small grey feathers kept fluttering and were then carried upward by the draft, toward the ceiling.

6

That evening Maurice Herz was already at home. Rosemarie Ilse was somewhat excited, and the way she ran about the kitchen made Herz think of everything that he had so successfully brought into play. Events had taken an unexpected turn. Rosemarie Ilse looked at him frequently, her eyes—in contrast to the confused haste with which she hopped round the table—full of gratitude, brilliant and devoted. Maurice had been named Heinz Albert Ritsche's adjutant, to the dismay of all the wives of the other SS officers, who were jealous of her. As far as he was concerned, he was quite content with this new appointment, considering it to be the embryo of his future promotions. True, the Party's special plenipotentiary, who had recently paid a visit to the ghetto to supervise the preparations for the visit from Switzerland, had, in the course of a private talk, made it clear to Herz that the thing with the trade unions and the commandant was unfounded; at the same time, however, he had told Herz that the Third Department commended him on his vigilance. "You are a man who uses his eyes and ears," he said. "That's the kind of man we like." I've undoubtedly strengthened my position, thought Herz. A special plenipotentiary would not have come to tell him if it had been otherwise. It, of course, immediately occurred to him that the fellow in black had not spilled everything he knew. But he at once rejected this idea, which undermined the pillars upon which his satisfaction rested, imparting to him the notion that the plenipotentiary might likewise have told Ritsche everything. They trusted him! That was clear! Well, he would not disappoint them. At the party that was held in the evening the plenipotentiary had honored him with special attention. He was tall and slim, in a black uniform, his personality devoid of the menace which was no doubt inherent in his mission. Herz felt on top of the world. Had it not been for this, he would never have done what he had done just now. His decision was truly born of a momentary impulse: he had, at an opportune moment, invited both the commandant and the plenipotentiary "for a little dinner" to his villa. The plenipotentiary had excused himself with a smile. It looked as if he really regretted his inability to accept the invitation; but he was leaving that very night. Ritsche, however, had accepted. And thus, for the second time in less than a quarter of a year, Maurice Herz had infringed on the unwritten rules of the Nazi hierarchy: the first time from the bottom, by inviting Binde, and now from the top—that was more daring and, it struck him, more dangerous. When he had done it, he had of course had quite a lot of French cognac inside him. But in any case, he told himself as he thought the whole thing over, if you risk nothing you gain nothing.

The lion's share of this evening's success fell to Rosemarie Ilse, who, even though she was not in the least aware of the events that had set into motion the impetuous gesture of invitation, was fully aware of the greatness of the moment. She did not know what to do first. The chickens had not yet arrived from the refrigerator, and she had no time left to distribute the flowers in the vases. She wouldn't make do with artificial ones today, of course! Since the day when she had to let the maidservant, Greta, go because the silly wench had applied to serve on the eastern front, she was continually on the go.

No time to do anything. And even if Maurice did not say much, she could see what high hopes he had of tonight's dinner. He sat by the stove, warming his feet, his reddish, powdered face showing how intensively he was thinking.

Every now and again Maurice Herz would rub his temples with the palms of his hands. He could not make himself out. Were there two personalities in him, one of them daring and enterprising, yes, you might even say rapacious, in its desire to climb to the top, and the other timid and self-effacing, constantly realizing the fact that he was nothing but an unfinished house-painter's apprentice? Both these Herzs were now waiting for the big occasion. To the first it seemed that the drops of water which drizzled persistently from the skies were turning the wheels on his behalf. The second doubted that the commandant would come at all. Perhaps he had not wanted to say anything in front of the plenipotentiary, but now he would show him who was whose superior and who was only an unfinished house-painter. After all, said Herz to himself, an adjutant was only an adjutant. An adjutant must not jump too high or he might slip and fall. But, he rebuked himself, the game was on. Now it was necessary to rake in the trumps.

He gazed into the fire. His disquiet quickly vanished. The plenipotentiary's favor was a card well worth having. And seeing that Rosemarie Ilse kept hopping around the stove like a goat, he said, languidly: "Plenty of time."

When at last the car's brakes were heard in front of the villa, everything was in its place.

Heinz Albert Ritsche was a small, stoutish man wearing gold-rimmed spectacles on a white fleshy nose. Altogether he resembled a businessman rather than a high SS officer. As a matter of fact nobody knew how he had managed to gain his position in the rear. The subject was never mentioned, however, as any undue curiosity would most probably have resulted in the questioners being sent to the front themselves, and that was a possibility that appealed to no one. It was just this, though, that gave Ritsche a flattering aura of mystery, which for others, including Herz, represented an easy target.

They ate in silence. Herz was at a loss to discover the cause of this taciturnity. The dinner over, Ritsche laid aside his napkin and said he had enjoyed the meal.

"Did you really?" asked Rosemarie Ilse, pleased, but slightly disconcerted by the reserved manner of their distinguished guest.

"Yes, really, thank you," said Ritsche.

The children came into the drawing-room.

"Uncle Ritsche," shouted little Adolf, "I want to scalp ten Jewish pigs!"

"You're not old enough yet," Herz told him, smiling.

He turned to the commandant, still a little uneasy: "Children, Herr Kommandant, they're the hope of Germany."

Ritsche nodded his satisfaction. It sounded good: the hope of Germany.

Now it seemed to Herz that the barrier of ice had been breached. He would be damned if he would do it a second time, though. In the next instant, however, he felt a warm glow of satisfaction at having invited the commandant.

Little Hilda asked: "Have Jews got children, too?"

Rosemarie Ilse smiled happily: "Oh, Lord, how clever these children are!"

Herz's satisfaction increased every minute. I was right, after all, he thought. This was the kind of easygoing comradeship he had in mind all along, the kind that as a rule was not without its effect on service relations. He was convinced that this impression was correct. What he needed was to gain Ritsche's confidence, then he would be able to make his weight felt far more than hitherto. He would have an invisible pillar against which to lean. It occurred to him at the same time that in these days, so troublesome for the Reich, personal wrangles were highly undesirable. He would not be disappointed even if the only outcome of his plan were to be a closer friendship between the two of them. It struck him suddenly and pleasurably, that now, as adjutant, he was actually able to view things from a loftier standpoint, on a higher scale.

Rosemarie Ilse, her cheeks full of color, wore a black silk dress and a white apron which she kept taking off and putting on again. She was under the impression that she looked particularly good in that apron, and in the end she left it on. To Ritsche, her neckless body seemed comical. The neck got lost somewhere when she was being born, he thought. After the plenipotentiary had left, he had debated with himself for a long time whether to accept the invitation or not. He had not liked the way those two talked together and could not rid himself of the idea that the red-faced nosy parker had been assigned to spy on him. In the end he had come, but he had not capitulated; he was merely reconnoitering in enemy territory. In order to keep a certain, not too offensive, distance, he had left his wife at home. The devoted glances bestowed on him by Herz's wife he found unpleasant. What an impossible cow, he said to himself. What does she think she is doing, staring at me like that?

Rosemarie Ilse felt that the commandant was looking her over. She leant towards him across the table and, taking courage, blurted out with a girlish giggle:

"You are men, but in your uniforms you look like boys."

The bitch, thought Ritsche.

After a while he said, aloud: "We can well be proud of our women. They're our second reserve."

That was the only thing that occurred to him.

Rosemarie Ilse thought: Mother was right to stay upstairs—every conversation in this house is bound to end with the reserve, the front, and the war. When they had told her who was coming, she had excused herself and had her dinner taken up to her room.

"But, Herr Kommandant," said Rosemarie Ilse, "you'll never let them get as far as this, will you?"

He realized at once what she was driving at.

"Our Führer," he said, irritated. "has several times spoken on the subject, and he has left no room for doubt. It is completely out of the question. If you ask your husband, he is sure to set your mind at rest on that score."

Herz threw a worried look in Ritsche's direction.

The joyful, intoxicated feeling, which had taken hold of Rosemarie Ilse and had made her happy all through the dinner, was gone.

Herz realized that the commandant might think that he was neglecting his wife, or even might wonder why she was still not working as other officers' wives.

"We have already talked about it, haven't we, Ilse?" he said quickly.

She fixed desperate eyes on her husband. What had they already talked about? Oh, God, let her not spoil anything. She couldn't remember. And even she knew very well that these political discussions were no joking matter.

Maurice Herz's reddish face changed its color to blue. The stupid bitch! But he kept his temper and, mistakenly interpreting the commandant's silence as agreement, he said: "Ilse and I have often thought that perhaps she might work on the requisitioning commission . . ."

If the idiot has invited me because of this, thought Ritsche, then he might have saved himself the trouble. Let him send his fat sow where he likes.

Rosemarie Ilse was offended. How silly to lie like that. Surely they didn't have to resort to lies. Was she supposed to go to the Jewesses, like that ginger-haired Herta? Did Maurice think she didn't have enough on her hands as it was? Why were they fighting the war, in that case? She almost started to cry on the spot.

"That is very commendable," said Ritsche. "Your children are growing fast, and anyway, you can always take a Czech maid."

"Never!" cried Rosemarie Ilse. "They're so terribly lazy. And apart from that, I couldn't stand a Jewess in my house. I simply couldn't."

"I'd throw her out, Mummie," put in little Adolf. "You'd let me throw her out, wouldn't you?"

Heinz Albert Ritsche got up suddenly. "It is very pleasant here," he said, "but I must go now."

Herz did not fail to notice how cold, curt, and stiff his words were.

They saw him to the car.

It was Herz's Mercedes-Benz, which he had sent that afternoon to fetch Ritsche. Werner Binde stood by the car's door, and he saluted them with his fishlike eyes.

"It was a great honor, Herr Kommandant," said Herz.

Suddenly he felt terribly small, stupid and vile. No, he should not have played about with that invitation.

Ritsche, on the other hand, lounging comfortably in his seat, did not seem to be thinking along such serious lines as Herz.

Back in the house, Rosemarie Ilse told herself that no one invited Maurice with such a show of politeness. With belated tears in her eyes she flared up at him:

"It's not enough for you that the maid has gone, that I slave away like a nigger from morning till night, is it? What a fool I was to marry you . . ."

"Don't be silly!" Herz replied in irritation. "The requisitioning commission is child's play. And you'll pick up all sorts of useful things for yourself."

He was furious with her, and if it weren't for the children, he would have slapped her. But it was just as well, at least let him have peace and quiet at home. No, Maurice Herz did not have sufficient self-assurance tonight. The meek one inside him was on top. Wasn't it better to be small? He had to think things out.

Rosemarie Ilse came to the conclusion that there was some truth in what Maurice said. She'd take a dog with her to the ghetto. What was she to do with such an impossible husband, in such times, and . . . But she could think of nothing more. She stopped crying, powdered her face, and then went upstairs to talk to her mother and to confide her troubles. After a time she returned downstairs and went to bed.

7

A week later Werner Binde drove the members of the requisitioning commission—generally known under the nickname of "grab-alls"—to the ghetto. Among them was Rosemarie Ilse Herz. He stopped to let them get out at various places according to a plan that had been drawn up beforehand. In the end he was left with the ginger-haired Herta, the gardener's wife, and with Rosemarie Ilse, who recalled that the driver had dined with them last summer, and asked him to be so kind and accompany her everywhere she went. Herta's Alsatian, Rex, sat huddled in a corner of the car, jumping up on to the window and barking all the time.

In accordance with the instructions he had received, Werner Binde stopped the car in front of the Hamburg barracks, in which the women of Theresienstadt lived.

He shambled behind Herta and Rosemarie Ilse along the corridors with the small balconies built in severe military style.

The two women were a long time deciding in which room to start their work, finally making up their minds to begin on the first floor, right in the corner. And so it happened that at about half past nine in the morning they walked into Room 38, the room in which Elizabeth Feiner was lying.

The room was long and high, but the huge and cumbersome three-storey bunks filled it so completely that only a little space was left between the two rows.

Rosemarie Ilse did not feel too well in the stuffy, badly aired room. She kept darting quick glances to one side and another, and turning all the time, afraid that something or somebody might fly out at her. But as nothing happened, she grew used to it in a very short while. The only thing she saw on turning round were the eyes of Werner Binde; he was standing against the wall, almost motionless, staring ahead of himself with a vague expression on his face that might have signified indifference or even superciliousness.

She was ashamed, before herself as well as before the ginger-haired Herta, ashamed of being here and of being so clumsy. Where was she to start? And how was she to do it? Was she perhaps to rummage among those foul-smelling possessions, or in those filthy beds?

Just then she heard Herta give a slight scream.

"Is anybody here?"

Elizabeth Feiner's face took on an almost imperceptible shade of astonishment, so slight that it was gone immediately; only her parchmentlike skin, which had no further layer underneath, became slightly wrinkled around the eyes. For the seventh day running she was being burnt up by high fever. Something was devouring her from within, she was shriveling up, she could resist no longer and was losing her strength.

In those seven days she had not once tried to solve the question that had worried her so much while she was still in the shop: whether she would withstand the onslaught to human dignity that the present time brought with it. The question only cropped up again now, though very feebly.

She lay staring at the yellowish ceiling, her hands under the quilt. It was not the ceiling she saw—it was a stretched-out cloth, with her life parading dimly across it, divided into years, weeks, and seconds. She saw a large blackboard, on which invisible fingers drew the likeness of her father, with his carefully tended ginger moustache, and a little girl rather like Joachim Spiegel's niece. All this was dim and yet somehow extremely clearly outlined. The little girl told her father a lie; instead of doing her homework she had been to visit a friend and then blamed her for her own omission. The father first wanted to strike her, but then he said: "No, I won't beat you, life will give you a worse spanking than I ever could. But don't lie again, ever. A human being should keep himself clean." This picture was rapidly followed by a succession of other scenes faintly remembered from childhood: the girl with the pigtails grows up, and her skin terribly quickly becomes as yellow as the ceiling; her veins become blue and stand out on her forehead, reshaping her face into curious angles; Elizabeth Feiner recognizes herself and opens her eyes.

At this moment Herta called out:

"Damn it all, is anyone here or not?"

Herta, of course, knew there was someone there. But she wanted to hear her own voice.

Elizabeth Feiner again saw in her mind's eye the shapeless and dull days in which she was in charge of the shop, The Sun. Outside it was beautiful weather and inside it was dark. Then Rose Street and the former barbershop were replaced by the moment when she relinquished the keys, that incarnation of a mission which had not led anywhere. Now the pictures grew hazy—all she saw was the ceiling, yellow, dark and depressing. Elizabeth Feiner at last discovered the answer to her question, the question of how to avoid humiliation: the answer was to remain silent.

The echo of Herta's words died away.

Elizabeth Feiner entered upon the threshold of a world which she had hitherto resisted. She no longer had the strength to keep death at bay by thoughts of the little girl; the only thing she knew was that from now on she was not going to speak any more. Reconciled with everything, she lay still, only her eyes roving round the room. From her bunk, low above the ground, she at once caught sight of the German women, the dog, and the soldier in the background. She could not make out his face because of the distance, and she was not altogether sure as to the size of the animal, either. But she had distinctly heard the penetrating voice of the German woman, and she had understood her words. Only now did she make any reply, quite quietly and only to herself, for she did not know how much strength she could spare to lend her voice; and in a way she wished that she alone and no one else might hear it. She narrowed her eyes to mere slits, trying to keep out vision and to prevent daylight from hurting them. The inspection did not concern her, she could still realize that much, for she had nothing at all that might be of interest to the living. She lay still, her head inclined to one side on a none-too-clean pillow, like someone who is losing a struggle that is being waged inside his body but is already out of reach of his spirit.

"You swine!" shrieked Herta. "Are you dumb, or what? What're you doing, wallowing here in bed?"

Elizabeth Feiner did not reply. What was coming next? Why had she feared the fever in the long, cold nights when the wind howled outside? Thinking of the wind was pleasant, so cool and incredible. The rain was rattling on the rusty metal of the drain-pipe; she heard that now very distinctly. The rain!

"These lazy swine!" said Herta again. "Nothing wrong with them, but they don't feel like work."

Herta's voice was coarse and full of hatred. Elizabeth Feiner took no notice of it. Somewhere there were mountain slopes and somewhere there were roses. And elsewhere nothing.

Herta was a child of hatred. Her mother, herself alone in the world, had abandoned her, and later no one had come to take the little girl from the Berlin orphanage. Up to the age of eighteen she had been like a discarded thing that walked, breathed and spoke. Now at last she had found people who were lower than she, upon whom even she might trample. And thus she said what she did calmly and with a feeling of superiority, even though she saw that the woman in front of her had only a few steps to go to the end of her life.

"Frau Ilse," she said. "Go through her things, and you'll see how these bitches can sham."

Although she protested inwardly against this form of address, Rosemarie Ilse Herz nevertheless obediently, but with a feeling of revulsion she found hard to overcome, bent down to the pieces of luggage under the sick woman's bunk, and opened them.

The top suitcase did not belong to Elizabeth Feiner, but to her neighbor. She was one of a numerous family, who kept all they had with their mother; a partly eaten stick of imitation Hungarian salami, two bagfuls of sugar, a cake of soap, and wedding rings in a box that used to hold a watch.

The dog barked, having smelt the meat, and Herta had to hold him back.

"There, you see!" she said.

Rosemarie Ilse threw the salami to the dog. He pounced on it eagerly, but found it too highly seasoned to devour all of it. Rosemarie Ilse was about to put back the things she had taken out of the suitcase, but Herta stopped her, saying:

"Oh, don't bother about that!"

Rosemarie Ilse was still not altogether at ease. She was unable to accustom herself so quickly to her new role, yet she had a feeling that if she were to come again (now she saw how silly she had been not to have come before) she would know what to do and how to do it. She had no doubt that when she was alone without curious eyes watching her, Herta picked up quite a few things that the Winterhilfe never saw! Those two gold wedding rings . . . Rosemarie Ilse was scared to think of it further.

"Frau Ilse," Herta interrupted, "you'd better look under the mattress, too."

Rosemarie Ilse cautiously reached out toward the bunk and, as though she did not even wish to see the sick woman lying on it, gingerly picked up one corner of the pillow between her fingers; she tugged at it sharply, lifted it, and let it fall again.

There was a hollow, crunchy sound as Elizabeth Feiner's head rolled off the pillow and onto the wooden bedstead. Underneath the pillow, on a sheet grey with mold, lay the gaudy yellow tin of sardines.

The stench drove Rosemarie Ilse Herz a step back. She stared at the tin and, with her hand pressed against her mouth, gave a slight scream. Looking at the sardines, carefully wrapped and giving the impression of plentitude, she grew suddenly furious.

"Well, and then we think that they're dying of hunger!" she exclaimed.

"The swine!" said Herta by way of an answer.

She leant toward Rex and, her voice quiet and inciting, urged the dog: "Go on, fetch! Fetch, Rex!"

The animal bounded forward and in one leap reached Elizabeth Feiner's bedside. She was not aware of its presence. Her eyes were already closed. She no longer knew whether anyone was standing next to her, how far away they were, nor if there was anyone in the room at all. She only felt the dog's hot breath on her face, but did not see its open mouth.

All this time Werner Binde had been standing quite still, and it seemed that his eyes penetrated everything with their glassy stare, encompassing everything with a single, greenish-grey look. Suddenly he came alive—before either of the two women realized what was happening he had a pistol in his hand and had fired.

There was a hurt, surprised look in the wounded Alsatian's eyes, and the animal gave out a rattling sound. Finally it fell and remained lying motionless across the open suitcase.

Herta cried out.

Then, screaming and holding hands, she and Rosemarie Ilse Herz ran through the narrow space between the bunks, out on to the veranda, and down the stairs.

Still not a muscle had moved in Werner Binde's flat face. He was still standing where he was, immobile. Then with his usual rolling gait he crossed over to the bunk where only fractions of time divided Elizabeth Feiner from death. But this he did not know. Very gently he moved her head back to the pillow and rearranged her blanket. The old woman's ugly, angular head suddenly seemed to him tender and kind. At that moment she reminded him of his stepbrother, Fritz. It was then he realized that there was more to it than just his personal duel with Maurice Herz. And although his brain immediately started a feverish search for some means of averting the suspicion which his action was sure to arouse, he was aware of something dark at the bottom of his consciousness that would have to be thought out later. Then he bent down, picked the dead animal up by the legs, and, with a single jerk, slung it across his shoulders. Then he waddled out of the room and down the stairs to the car.

"Oh, Herr Binde, what happened?" Rosemarie Ilse's teeth chattered as she spoke.

"Why did you do it?" asked Herta, nervously smoothing her hair under its broad red band.

Werner Binde measured them with his fish-cold eyes, which penetrated Rosemarie Ilse to the marrow of her bones, and before whose stare Herta's eyes swerved away. Then he dumped the dog on the floor of the car.

"Where do we go from here?" he asked, speaking slowly and in a dull voice. After a while, nonchalantly and without deeming it necessary to turn his face toward them, he explained, drawing out the words:

"That dog . . . it was sick . . . I saw it. It had the rabies."

"Oh . . ." said Rosemarie Ilse.

Herta was silent.

When they got in, Rosemarie Ilse loathingly drew her feet away from the dead animal. Binde turned the car round, and then drove along the main L Avenue, along damp mounds of russet-colored leaves, past the shuttered shop underneath the stone sun, and back to the German HQ.

8

Two beautiful sleek limousines stood outside the white house which flew the swastikas on its flagstaffs. They were not painted the dull grey military color, but, on the contrary, shone black like dark mirrors. Each car had a little flag on the radiator, the red cross standing out against the white background.

A clean-shaven, slim gentleman in a pepper-and-salt suit of perfect cut turned—evidently in the name of all the other gentlemen—to Albert Heinz Ritsche, the commandant of the Large Fortress of Theresienstadt, for there was no time left to see the Small Fortress, and said:

"What we have seen so far, Herr Kommandant, is enough for the time being, really. We have a long journey ahead of us."

"Quite, I understand," replied Ritsche politely, without trying by as much as a hint of insistence to prevail upon them to remain longer. "At your service, gentlemen."

The company then slowly climbed into the cars and drove off to the accompaniment of general hand-waving. The officers from the HQ who had accompanied the guests walked unhurriedly back into the building. Werner Binde stopped his car just as the second shining limousine disappeared behind a bend in the road.

Maurice Herz turned round when he heard the sound of the car's brakes, and saw his wife Rosemarie Ilse, Herta, and the driver. He went back to meet them.

"What a coincidence we didn't meet," he said. "We were in the ghetto with them a few moments ago."

Werner Binde muttered something under his breath. Then he lowered his eyes, excused himself, and got back into the car.

He drove at once to a valley between two villages near the town, and threw the dead dog out onto the garbage dump.

9

About three weeks after the morning on which the Swiss health committee paid its visit to the Jewish ghetto in Bohemia, Werner Binde again drove Rosemarie Ilse Herz to town. This time Maurice Herz was with them, his wife having asked him to accompany her.

Rosemarie Ilse started her work of requisitioning in exactly the same way as she had done twenty-one days ago—from Room 38. Werner Binde noticed that in the very corner, underneath the barred window, where Elizabeth Feiner had lain there was an empty bunk.

And then, on their way back, even though they drove very rapidly along L Avenue, he saw quite clearly that the customers in the shop called "The Sun" were being served by a strange man with his hat worn low on his forehead and a black-haired girl.

The Children

Vick stamped his feet impatiently.

If only Jacob were back, he thought, they could go out. Time passed so slowly; they had the whole day. Maybe they'd see a white horse—that meant luck. Or they could slip through into the baths. Or climb a tree on the East Rampart and have a good swing in the wind.

From the courtyard a few feet away he heard a wailing noise. Fifka was standing in the space between two doorposts where a door once stood, holding a cat by the tail and swinging it from side to side, knocking its head against the threshold. This had been going on for half an hour. Occasionally, Vick would hear him mutter: "Go on, die, you bugger!" It was a tricolored cat, probably the only one in the whole ghetto. The boys would roast it like a hare.

There was a triumphant shout from Fifka. Then silence.

Vick was standing on a wet red brick in the middle of a glistening puddle. The brick crumbled with each stamp of Vick's foot. The breeze ruffled the surface of the puddle, the water mirroring Vick's frail body in jerky waves.

Vick's left shoe gaped open at the front, and small dirty toes protruded from the yawning leather. He lifted his big toe—it stuck out over the puddle like a cannon. The brick would fall to pieces. He could only save himself by jumping to dry land. He hesitated: the shoe and his toes would suffer.

He wiped his nose on his sleeve.

What a fool, he thought, standing on a brick in the water. It was because of that silly waiting! Jacob had been down already, but Ginger had sent him back to sweep the corridor. Ginger was the worst of all the prefects in Home Q719. He was sure to meet with an accident one of these days. They all hoped he would. Vick, too. But Vick could not ignore him like Fifka did. Fifka was a half-caste: his mother was Jewish, at present somewhere in Poland, and his father was German, racially absolutely pure! It was said he was in the SS, but no one knew that for certain, and Fifka did not speak about it. Once he said that he was going to kill his father after the war. He took no notice of anything or anybody, and they, Vick and Jacob, would be exactly like him one day.

Vick pulled a string out of his pocket. Casting an expert glance at his toes to see if the mud had dried, he bent forward and tied the shoe together with large knots, from time to time balancing himself on one leg. At last, the loose, flapping sole was fastened to the upper, with only a few rusty nails sticking out.

He leaped across. The last remaining piece of brick slowly sank.

"Victor!"

Vick looked up. It was Berl, Ginger's assistant. He recognized the voice even before his eyes took in the thin narrow face, the bulging green eyes, and the half-smile that Berl never took off.

"What're you jumping about like a goat for?" he called down to Vick. "I bet you haven't even reported for fatigue today."

"Sure I have! I've been going out to the Kavalirka for over a week to dig the ditch for the fence."

There! Berl, as Vick well knew, was taking the boys from Dormitories 16 and 20 today to fell trees. They had been looking for children for this work party since yesterday. Vick glanced at the toes of his shoes, wondering whether the left one would survive if he gave Berl a kick in the pants to take that silly grin off his face. True, Berl was a degree or two better than Ginger. But Berl was just as stuck-up as Ginger, demanding the same show of deference and the same respectful salute from the boys, and Vick was heartily sick of him. Still, he would never have expected Berl to fall so easily for his yarn about the Kavalirka—Vick had not been there for the third day running.

Vick shambled off to a corner, so that in case of an emergency he could hop over the wall. Fifka was probably gone by now—most likely to some dry place, where he was skinning the greyish-black cat with the white spots. Now he understood why Fifka had brought home that old rusty frying pan last night.

It sure took a long time to bash in such a small creature's head.

The puddle which had swallowed up the brick, Vick thought, had been there for over a week. And it would become deeper still.

Above Vick's curly head, capless in every weather, swam light grey clusters of clouds. Vick's grey eyes merged with their shadows and followed them attentively as the wind drove them over the town and beyond. In them Vick could see unattainable things: the rock behind Theresienstadt was like a big ship sailing into the blue. No, the shop was standing still, with only a sea of wind and clouds drifting past.

Vick wrinkled his freckled forehead. He felt sad that he had to stay behind while the sky sailed on to a different world. Then the unseen hand which had shaded his face vanished. Vick, a voice seemed to be saying inside him, if only you could stand right up there and look down on the ghetto and spit right in the middle, on the church spire. Or at least if you could come to the baker's shop on Q Street—and the baker had left the ventilator gates open. Imagine running over to Fifka tomorrow and throwing a loaf of bread on his bunk! Would he be surprised! Just like Jacob was when he, Vick, had nosed out that ventilator, notwithstanding that so many other hungry people came walking past 813 Q Street every day! But a voice cautioned Vick: What if Fifka pinched the bread and polished off the cat meat by himself? He wouldn't put it past him— just the kind of thing Fifka might do.

In his mind's eye, Vick returned to Q Street, where he had discovered a possible entrance to the bread kingdom. The spaces between the steel vanes of the ventilator were narrow, but his snakelike body could get in while Jacob kept watch outside. In a few weeks' time it might be too late, because they were growing! But they would do it, sometime. Sure they would. Sometime in the evening . . . or at night.

He stared at the sky. If they were lucky and the thing came off, he would go the next morning and give his share to Helen. She would open her small mouth in surprise, just as she had done that time when he had climbed down the rampart into the commandant's garden and brought her a yellow rose. He had not been afraid to do it, although Fifka, when he got to know about it, had voiced the opinion that *he* would not dream of troubling himself for such a Princess Wet-Her-Pants. And Helen had told him she would go out for a walk with him, if he wished.

Perhaps one day Helen would be his girl. Really his girl, with everything that went with it. She would not be so thin and sickly then. Vick would get her everything she needed—even meat, perhaps.

Vick stopped taking any notice of what went on in the courtyard.

Before his eyes he had a rose, with thin firm petals which opened of their own accord. Such gentle and fragile things as roses existed, and yet, at the same time, it seemed incredible that they should exist.

Leading the party from Dormitories 16 and 20, Berl passed through the courtyard and out the gate, the boys in the rear clinking their axes. "Quiet there, you stinkers!" Berl shouted. But the next instant he grinned at them to show he wasn't such a bad guy after all.

Vick relived the moment when, holding the rose in his fingers, he had felt an urge to say something nice to Helen or to stroke her hand. He had wanted to say a whole sentence composed of a lot of nice words, but hadn't said a word. He didn't even take her hand as he had intended. Helen kept coughing all the time because she had worn a thin dress. In the end she took the rose and ran home with it. There was no walk, nothing. All that Vick saw was the empty street, the cobblestones and the doorway of the houses: along the whole of Q Street nothing but barracks and houses, barracks and houses.

The cold wind brought Vick back from his dreamworld whose queen was the undernourished Helen with nervous light blue eyes, from the Difficult Children's Home, where they had refused to accept Fifka for fear he would be a bad influence on the other children.

The knots holding his shoe together came undone.

He crossed the courtyard once more, in order not to stand about in one place and thus give Ginger a chance to grab him and send him to work. He also had to do something about that shoe to keep his toes from getting wet.

Just then Jacob appeared at the top of the staircase. Taking three steps at a time, he bounded down in a flash.

"Hiya, Vick!"

"Hiya! About time!"

"Come on, quick! I've got to get out."

They raced through the passageway, out into the stony embrace of the street and the pavement.

"That damned rat Ginger," said Jacob as soon as they were round the corner. "I hope he croaks soon. If only they put him in the first transport out of here."

Vick stopped and took his shoe off.

"Wait a minute. I've got to fix this," he explained.

Jacob handed him a stone.

"Thanks."

"That's a lovely hole," said Jacob, as Vick hammered the nails back into their original holes.

Vick straightened up. "Done," he said.

"He made me clean practically the whole house," Jacob said.

"I was beginning to think he had collared you for the day."

"He wanted some more guys to go cutting down trees."

"Sure," Vick said, "I guess that's why Berl called out to ask me whether I had been detailed for work."

"To hell with all of them!"

"We'll make them pay for it one day, see if we don't."

Jacob nodded.

"One day" meaning a year or two, when they outgrew their unsatisfactory children's size.

"What it needs is just a good pair of fists, that's all," said Jacob.

Across the street a Jewish policeman was pacing his beat in a waterproof coat and a yellow and black cap. In the window above him stood a bottle of thin, bluish milk. The baby ration.

Jacob winked at Vick.

They looked up.

"I guess we could pinch that," Vick suggested.

"That's right, we could. But not now . . . in the evening."

"But it won't be there in the evening," Vick said.

"All right, forget the bottle then. It probably belongs to some sick little kid anyway."

"Sure thing, Jacob."

The policeman turned toward them, and they were careful not to let their eyes stray to the window with the bottle.

We noticed it, that's the main thing, the expression on Jacob's face seemed to say, while Vick thought: We miss nothing in this dump—last week the ventilator and now the milk!

Jacob spat and Vick whistled.

The policeman went on, and only the two of them knew what he had missed. He wore a small moustache. Looks like a stupid beetle, Jacob thought.

They reached the corner of Q and L Street.

"Vick, look!"

A flat-bottomed cart was coming toward them. Vick turned because the man they had just passed reminded him of his father, though he at once discarded the idea as downright silly, since no one knew where his father had been sent.

"Gosh!" he said softly, stunned by the sight of the neatly stacked loaves of bread. The street was offering the young gentleman break-fast on its stone platter.

Jacob distended his nostrils and snorted like a horse. He looked so funny that Vick almost laughed.

Jacob felt the blood rush to his head. What a stroke of luck, he thought. And first thing in the morning, too!

"Where do we start, Vick?" he asked with a drawl. "Would you prefer the bottom or the top ones?"

"Gosh!" Vick repeated. "Aren't we lucky!"

The cart passed by. Jacob crossed the street. Set for a pincer movement, they winked at each other. Vick took deep breaths of the intoxicating smell. Hanging back a little, they strolled inconspicu-ously behind the cart.

The cart rattled and rocked over the cobblestones. A dozen men pulled it, since the only horse in the ghetto had fallen ill.

Vick smiled at Jacob. They were in luck, he thought, although Jacob's morning encounter with Ginger and his own with Berl had not been good omens. Vick would have liked to do something, to jump toward the cart, simply pick up a loaf, then beat it. But that was impossible. They would do it some other way. He did not know how yet. There were too smart for Berl and Ginger! They would not slave away for them at the Kavalirka in return for sweet-sounding promises and half a meal extra. Jacob and he would get their extras elsewhere. Right here, he thought, looking at the cart as it rattled on its way. And then, in a year or two, they would step out along the main avenue, handsome and debonair—Vick with Helen on his arm, and Helen with a genuine alligator handbag. Everybody would turn to look at them and whisper approvingly: "That fellow with the beautiful girl, that's Vick, and the other one is his pal Jacob."

At last the flat-bottomed cart stopped.

"Look, Jakie, you stay here and watch where they put the bread, and I'll go find out where they loaded it."

"And then you'll come back here?"

"Well, sure. . . ."

"Vick," Jacob interrupted suddenly, "look at that house."

"What for?"

"That's the house. . . ."

"What house?"

Vick looked at the cracked plaster of the shabby house in front of them.

Something went dead inside him. He had to recall something that had not been forgotten but merely pushed to the bottom of his consciousness. Now it all came back with a rush.

Vick remembered.

He and Jacob climbed on a ledge and gestured wildly to frighten the inhabitants in the windows. Their walk along the narrow ledge gave them a view of rooms such as they had never seen. The house was a home for the aged, and inside were old women with faces like parchment and ugly, wrinkled skin on their throats. And in a dusty corner which stank of rotting straw and ammonia knelt an old woman. Her yellowish body was swathed in dirty bandages. Jacob snorted. Somebody cried out. There was something in the old woman's eyes which scared them both, but Jacob recovered quickly. "Look!" he told Vick, ashamed of his momentary feeling of compassion. He pulled out of his pocket a piece of bread originally intended to augment their lunch. Vick looked at the bread and said: "What do you want to do with it?" And Jacob, cheerful again, added "Watch!" and flung the crust at the old woman. It must have been a forceful blow, because the old woman clutched her side and fell with a gasp. Vick felt a twinge in his heart. All the old woman's pain stared at Vick. Shocked, he let go of the window and managed just in time to catch hold of a projection on the sill. Something impelled him toward those eyes, making him want to climb inside and stroke the old woman's hair in spite of her filthiness. Perhaps the fact that she didn't touch that crust of bread, which was snapped up by the others, also had something to do with it. But he refrained, held back by his loathing, which not even her aged eyes, empty and extinct and—most of all!—

reproachful, were able to overcome. He hardly knew how he succeeded in getting down from the ledge, those two eyes seeming to stare at him out of every brick and blemish in the plaster.

"That's right, Jacob," he repeated now, "that's the house."

So this was where the bread was being taken.

The two boys stood a little distance away, silent, without looking at each other.

The bread was quickly unloaded from the cart.

Vick no longer cared.

Everything pleasant that Vick had felt as a result of his hope, embodied in the shape and smell of the loaves, was gone.

Jacob was feeling physically sick, staring at the empty cart—a funeral wagon before the wooden enclosure had been taken off so that it could be used for the noon delivery of bread. Its bare and worn wooden boards, over which thin veils of mist were now swirling, formed an open book containing the single dreary word: disappointment.

It occurred to Vick that today it was up to him to be first to recover, and thus even the score with Jacob. Anyway, he thought, all was not yet lost. After all, they did not necessarily need just *these* loaves. At last, he glanced at Jacob. His long face with the almost transparent nose seemed to be saying: Don't kid yourself, Vick.

But why were they standing here for such a long time? And what happened to the guys who pulled the cart?

They appeared a few moments later, followed by a group of old men.

What were they carrying in that white sheet? Suddenly, he knew. A corpse. Vick glanced at Jacob. Jacob, too, realized what the white sheet concealed. Strands of grey hair fell loosely from between the planks and the white coverlet. It was a woman.

Jacob spat.

It flashed across Vick's mind that this was perhaps the old woman Jacob had thrown the bread at. And again the whole scene came back to him. It was disconcerting, the source of something that killed all hope in Vick's heart, a hope that gleamed like the smooth cobblestones over which the day went gliding from morning till sunset, until they were drowned in the dark pool of night. Vick grimaced. He was thinking of the woman's sore-encircled eyes. But he remained silent. What was there for him to do, anyway? There was a catch in his throat, and he would dearly have liked to speak or to hear Jacob say something.

The cart moved forward.

Vick did not like the look of the old man walking behind it. The dead woman's husband, dressed in an old coat, carried his head high in an attempt to lend a little dignity to their journey.

"It's no use, Jacob," said Vick.

Jacob spat in a graceful arc into the ditch.

"I could have told you that ages ago," he said.

Is it her? Vick asked himself. What kind of hair did she have that other time? Those eyes of hers won't be looking like that anymore, then. When you died, you didn't look at anything anymore and you didn't think of anything. You were through. And you were at peace! At least, that's what people said. Why was he thinking about it? It was just plain silly to think about it. But what if she had never recovered from that blow and did die? Go on, he told himself, the blow couldn't have been as hard as all that. But did it really need to be so hard for such an emaciated body?

They reached the barrier. *Halt!* The end of the ghetto.

The cart went on, but the small procession accompanying it remained behind.

Vick and Jacob stood looking at the cart until it disappeared beyond a bend in the road. Vick thought that now they would never know whether it had been her or not. "Jacob," he said, "I guess the cart won't be back for bread anymore today."

"Well, shall we go then?"

"Yes, let's. Come on!"

"Sure, I'm coming," Jacob said, but he remained where he was.

"All right, I guess we'd better let them pass first . . . ," Vick added.

The old men were coming back. Theresienstadt was welcoming them with the damp breath of its brick and mortar lungs.

Now and again, Vick would scan the horizon. The high rock beyond the town was, after all, a ship sailing off for some other world. The summit of the rock—the ship's prow—was cleaving through limitless space, marked at the start by the hill and thicket, then by nothing at all.

Vick looked at Jacob. What would he do if they were not such good friends?

"What do you keep staring at the hills for?" Jacob asked.

Vick did not reply.

"Come on, walk faster, can't you? The wind is such a nuisance."

"We'll catch cold," thought Jacob angrily.

They went on side by side. The countryside filled Vick's soul with something strange and inaccessible, making him afraid. He put his arm around Jacob's shoulders and pressed close to him.

"I'm cold," he said.

"Well, don't think you're making me any warmer," Jacob retorted. Nevertheless, he clung to Vick, too.

At last they were in town.

They did not feel like talking. Jacob no longer sniffed the air, seeing that things turned out the way they did. They passed barracks with the high-sounding names Dresden and Hamburg—towns the two boys had never seen—and walked past the delousing station, across the square with the church (underneath it was said there were secret passages) and along by the coalyards.

It seemed to Vick that Theresienstadt was a huge town; but that was only an illusion which sprang from the fact it was so overcrowded. What made him uneasy was that things had gone wrong right from the start today. And that cart should not have gone to that house. What if it *was* the same old woman, after all? The houses, the whole town seemed to him to be swathed in dirty bandages. Even the passersby seemed to have caught the infection, and Vick tried to find out whether their clothes hid the festering blue spots of impetigo.

Jacob's ankles were purple with cold—he had exchanged his socks for two ounces of sugar. But Jacob was pleased that, because of his growth, his trousers had become too short for him. Now he was walking on, hands in his pockets, his nose a red blotch in a pallid face, and a scarf around his neck, spitting to the right and left as he went.

"Vick," he said suddenly, "maybe it won't be so horrible here in the summer, will it?"

Vick stared at him but said nothing.

"Maybe it won't, Jacob," he said, finally. "There are flowers here . . . and sometimes even fruit."

They started on a second trip around the town. Vick, in his checkered shirt, by this time was almost as cold as Jacob.

"Jacob," said Vick.

"What?"

"What do you think the woman in that house died of?" He had wanted to ask something else: Had it occurred to Jacob, too, that it might be the same old woman he had wanted to give a piece of bread to that time?

"How should I know, Vick? Nobody told me, did they?"

"I only asked."

He smiled happily. If Jacob did not know either, there was no need for him to worry about it.

"I must say, Vick, you have some crazy ideas sometimes."

Of course, said Vick to himself, Jacob had not even thought of it because those eyes had not haunted Jacob as they had haunted him. I won't think about it anymore, he promised himself.

They were climbing the steps to the Eastern Rampart.

Vick was suddenly overcome with joy. He ran, leaping over one puddle and stamping in another until the water and mud splashed into the air. He ran to a tree, then climbed it all the way to the monkey branch and even higher, up to the top.

"Don't be silly!" Jacob called out.

And now Vick caught sight of Helen, walking along the rampart with Fifka. No doubt he had bragged to her about how he killed the cat. Perhaps he had even invited her to join him in eating the meat. Vick put his fingers in his mouth and gave a sharp whistle. Then he started to swing on the branch. He felt he had been relieved of a great burden which Jacob had given him. Who else, if not Jacob, would have known whether it had been the old woman?

"Vick!" came Jacob's voice from below. "Have you gone crazy or what?"

What was Helen thinking just then? There, now she was looking his way. Vick set the whole tree swaying and clambered onto the thinnest branch of all.

It gave suddenly and violently. Vick's frail little body spun downward like a corkscrew. He hit the trunk and its branches, and the last one caught his shirt and ripped it right down to the double-stitched waistband. Then he plonked down in the wet grass.

It began to rain.

Jacob's heart gave a bound. He stood where he was, as if rooted, his shirt open at the neck and his scarf loose, feeling a contraction in his throat.

"Vick," he managed to say at last.

Vick opened his eyes.

"Am I hurt, Jacob?"

He isn't dead, it flashed across Jacob's mind. He sprang toward Vick and slowly raised him.

Fifka and Helen arrived. With all three supporting him, Vick got to his feet.

"God, you are damned lucky," Fifka said, and then to Helen, "All right, come on, he'll manage now."

"Lucky," whispered Vick.

The town was slowly becoming engulfed by the mud.

＊

Moral Education

It always took Charlie a long time to go to sleep. Before sleep finally claimed him he experienced a fleeting feeling of friendship and
of pride at the fact that he had been allowed to join the select circle
of boys in Room 16. Even in the semidormant state he could make
out the individual voices in the conglomeration of sounds and smells
that filled the room, each of them awakening admiring images in his
brain.

Room 16 buzzed with noise. It was a spacious room, filled with
three-storey bunks, some of them fat, others gaunt, with ladders at
their sides and narrow spaces between them. Charlie was lying right
at the top in the comer, without a blanket, listening.

Thomas Knapp, known for short as Handsome, called out to
Danny Hirsch:

"Hey, have you finished *The Eighteen-Carat Virgin?*"

"Not yet. But you know what? I'll buy it off you."

"Look, Danny . . ."

"You can have my lunches for a week. Here, take the coupons!"

"Look, Danny, I can get you something similar—it's by Pitigrilli,
too. . . ."

"My lunches for a week. I'll go without. Well, is it a deal?"

"Oh, all right, then."

Sitting up on his bunk, Danny again riveted all Charlie's attention to himself. How wonderful it must be to be able to make such
an offer! Danny's figure seemed to grow in front of his eyes. He
could see what an immeasurable distance separated Danny from the
others. The envy that he felt towards Danny choked him until at last
he closed his eyes and conjured up a daydream in which he saw himself in Danny's place, offering Handsome far more than a mere week
of lunches.

Handsome was lying on his stomach, supporting his small, well-combed head in the palms of his hands. He was singing under his breath:

I'm all alone . . .
Oh, come back to me
Don't let me be
All alone . . .

He was pleased with himself. He had Danny's lunches for a week. As for *The Eighteen-Carat Virgin,* he had read it through three times already, word for word (confidentially, nothing to get excited about!). And he was sure no one would find out that he had torn out all the more interesting pictures. Snore away in peace, he thought.

"Good night, guys," he said.

I'm all alone,
Waiting through the night . . .

Full of esteem and boundless admiration, which he could not have put into words but which fully consumed him in its ardor, Charlie was softly whispering his good night to the wall.

No one heard him and no one replied. Not even Snow White, the sick boy who slept in the bunk under his.

"Good night, Snow White," he said again.

". . . night."

A quiet, unhealthy voice was wafted up to Charlie, followed immediately by a bout of coughing. When his parents had packed him off from Prague to Theresienstadt, Snow White had already been suffering from a disease for which the thick air of this town could not be good. But it was only for a fraction of a second that Charlie allowed his attention to dwell on Snow White's sickly voice. His entire being clamored for some action which would give him the right to take part in these evening conversations, nonchalant and self-possessed, as though each and every one of these boys knew his own price, and on the strength of its weighed even the most insignificant word he let out into the vapor-filled air of Room 16. He felt the blood tingle in his veins with the urge to do something, anything at

all, but *something,* an act which the boys would talk about in connec-
tion with his name before they went to sleep. With these thoughts
Charlie fell asleep in the dense silence of Room 16, all its vapors and
smells floating above his and Snow White's bunk.

A piercing whistle heralded the morning. All of them were startled into wakefulness. Reveille! The prefect entered as soon as the
sound of his whistle died away.

Snow White was coughing, while the twenty-year-old prefect,
Schierl, called out:

"Get up, all of you!"

"Snow White can't—don't you see how he is coughing?" said
Tony Fetman in a low voice, casting contemptuous glances at the
prefect.

"Morning!" growled Danny.

Then they carried Snow White, still coughing, away to the infirmary.

"Not a single one of you is to remain behind, understand?" said
Schierl, looking peremptorily at his watch.

At two minutes past seven he succeeded in driving out even
Oscar Kleiner, who ambled out of the room, a flower in his button-
hole, the boys' roaring accompanying him all the way down to the
office where they were detailed to work.

Charlie did not move. He found it hard to believe that Schierl
was leaving, thinking that he was the last out of the room, and that
he, Charlie, had actually managed to evade his vigilance and remain
behind after reveille. Crouching down on his bunk, he felt a warm
glow of pleasure as the door slammed behind the prefect. But perhaps the only reason they had missed him was that he did not mean
anything around here. They did not even know about his dreams, he
thought. Still, he had cause for satisfaction; he had slipped through.

A new, slightly overcast day penetrated into the room through the
large battered windows set in green walls, veiling it in a silence that
seemed strange and unnatural. The bunks were drowned in an
unusual, all-pervading quiet; from the outside the dust-filled light
entered only as a small, timid rectangle between the bedsteads.

The door opened softly. Charlie lifted himself up cautiously on
one elbow. Fetman! What's he want here? he said to himself. Holding his head watchfully raised above the bunk, he could see every-

thing—even the small suitcase which Fetman was pulling out from underneath his bed, the neat compartments inside it, as well as its contents, shiny and glittering: a bottle of Eau de Cologne, shaving kit, and two bluish silk shirts.

Involuntarily, as though the things he was looking down at had wrung from him an ejaculation of astonishment, he gave an unintentional sigh.

Tony Fetman snapped his suitcase shut. He was not alone, it flashed through his head. In a single leap he was at Charlie's side.

"What're you doing here, you stinker?" he gasped.

"Nothing," whispered Charlie, quickly swallowing a mouthful of saliva that almost made him choke.

"You're nosing about, you scum," said Fetman.

"I'm not," replied Charlie, stuttering. "Honest, Fetty, I . . . I've stayed behind . . . that's all . . ."

"How come? Schierl cleared the place out, so don't tell me you've stayed behind just like that!"

"But I did," said Charlie. "I fooled them . . . Schierl I mean . . ."

"He hasn't set you to spy on us, has he?" said Fetman, in a milder tone of voice.

"He doesn't even know me properly," Charlie replied.

"Come on, climb down!"

Placated, Tony Fetman jumped down and returned to his bunk. If this puny, frightened punk of a Charlie had really pulled a fast one on Schierl, it was not exactly a bad show—for him, that is. On an impulse Fetman produced a packet of biscuits.

"Here," he said. "As for this suitcase that you're goggling at, that was sent to me by my aunt. You get my meaning?"

"Sure," said Charlie, somewhat offended. Then he added: "Thanks."

Full of admiration, he bit into his biscuit, gazing into Tony Fetman's mischievous blue eyes. But Fetman could not bear so much devotion.

"Look, punk," he said, "you don't have to look at me as if I'd saved you from starvation, you know."

Seeing that Charlie was taken aback by his words, he went on more kindly: "Maybe we'll take you with us one of these days."

"Will you really?" asked Charlie.

"You bet. If I say so, then you can bet your life on it."

Charlie said no more, and Fetman asked him: "Do you know where Oscar is?"

But that was more than Charlie knew. His eyes roved involuntarily under Oscar's bunk. It had been made up carelessly. Under it was a pair of carefully polished yellow shoes with decorative brass buckles which so perfectly belonged on Oscar Kleiner's feet—and this was, moreover, so widely known—that they were quite safe there.

"If you like," Fetman said, "you can come with me right now."

"Where are you going?" Charlie inquired.

"Come along and you'll find out."

"O.K. I'll just put my things on. I'll be ready in a jiffy."

"But get a move on," said Tony Fetman. "We've got to beat it out of here. And quick!"

After that he took no more notice of Charlie for a while. He was thinking of where to find Oscar Kleiner. He *must* find him; there was no question about that. With his help, he thought, it will be easier to get rid of that stuff in the suitcase. In his mind he divided off Oscar's share. Oscar was sure to want the box with the shaving tackle, although he had hardly any whiskers to speak of as yet. But that was all right—he deserved it; yesterday he had given him an inconspicuous nod. That had been his part in the business—the rest had been up to Tony himself: a swift leap, a dexterous grab, and a quick getaway. When it came to turning the booty into money, however, there was nobody like Oscar to make a neat job of it!

Charlie was ready to go.

They got out by clambering over a narrow wall. Tony went first, swinging his thin body up with the aid of the lightning-conductor wire. Now it was Charlie's turn. He managed it and stood, elated, at Fetman's side. He had the whole day to himself, to be spent with Tony Fetman, free from all supervision by Schierl or by the Valta brothers. Fetman, however, was annoyed.

"Where has that idiot got to?" he asked for the third time.

Oscar Kleiner was nowhere to be found.

They gave up at last and just walked aimlessly about the town. Tony Fetman told Charlie that every real guy in the ghetto had to have a girl—"the real thing, you know"—before he was fifteen; Charlie stared at him wide-eyed, reproaching himself for being such a poor fool. They were all far, far better than he was. With tears in his eyes he resolved to put into action, at the earliest opportunity and in every detail, all the things that Tony Fetman was telling him about.

At noon he was able to let him have his own lunch; three and a half boiled potatoes and a plateful of watery soup, the entire overture to six hours of hunger until evening, when bread would be doled out to them.

After that they managed to find Oscar Kleiner at last. He was leaning against the half-rotten beam of the house commonly known as Electricians' House. The attic, far removed from the din and bustle of the town, was the haunt of a select company between thirteen and eighteen years of age.

"Hello, Oscar!"

He did not seem surprised.

"Hello yourself, Tony," he said. "What's cookin'?"

"Have you got time?"

"That depends," Oscar said, pointing his chin in Charlie's direction. "What's this pup doing with you?"

Charlie flushed. Oscar Kleiner was standing there in front of him, spectacles on his nose, his dimpled chin still pointed at Charlie.

"I've brought him along," Tony Fetman said. "He's all right."

"Anything up?" asked Oscar Kleiner.

"Nothing much, Oscar," Tony said. "Everything went off without a hitch . . . you can have the shaving bag."

"That all?"

Tony nodded.

"O.K."

"Look, Oscar, I've got a couple of shirts, nice silk stuff. Trade them for me, will you?"

"When? Right away?"

"I've been looking for you all day," said Tony.

"You could have found me here already after lunch. I didn't want to make trouble for Schierl, so I lent a hand with the digging. He was making eyes at me as it was. Look at those rays of sunshine, Tony!"

Charlie, too, had noticed the "rays of sunshine," as Oscar called them. They were dancing to the muted strains of an accordion—at the moment with Handsome and Danny Hirsch. Diana and Liana, both of them brunettes, were the daughters of a man who until recently had bought up feathers from all over the country, reselling them in the shape of first-class pillows ("Rival" trademark) at three times the price. The candles on the beams disappeared in darkness from time to time, giving Charlie the impression that the dancers were moving about in a gloomy halflight. He was breathless with wonder. A different world, he thought. A world that was completely unknown to the other boys in Q House.

"Oscar!" said Tony Fetman challengingly. "I need it. Will you do it for me or won't you?"

"I dunno," replied Oscar calmly.

"You don't know, you say?"

Oscar Kleiner was gazing at Tony's lean face, then he glanced briefly down at Charlie. He's found someone else, Oscar thought, but when he needs something, he knows me all right.

"I'll do it for you, Tony. Sure I will," he said at last.

Tony Fetman smiled. "Don't put on airs, Oscar."

"You know where you can go," said Oscar. "Shall I take back what I said."

"All right, then. I've got them ready at home, under the mattress."

Charlie listened with bated breath.

"Want to stay for a spot of dancing?" Oscar asked. "Little Bashful here can stay, too," he added, digging Charlie in the ribs with his elbow.

Charlie gulped, unable to stop himself. He was being invited into this company. God Almighty! Could it be true? Feeling out of place, he looked around. Handsome and Danny Hirsch were standing in the corner, teasing the two girls. Who might all the others be, he wondered. They had not so much as noticed him They could not all of them be the boys from the electrical workshop, the elite of the ghetto. They were boys, Charlie meditated, whom even Schierl and the Valta brothers didn't dare mess about with!

"I can't dance," said Tony.

"Nor can I," whispered Charlie timidly.

"All right, then, beat it," said Oscar Kleiner. "I'll scram in a minute, too."

They filed out of the attic.

Charlie would have liked to turn round, but he did not do so because he was ashamed that he did not know how to speak with girls, nor with Oscar Kleiner.

"Now beat it!" Tony Fetman told him when they were outside. "I've got something to settle with Oscar."

He slunk away like a beaten dog. As he walked off, speechless, with each step he returned in his imagination to the darkened attic. That was it, he reproached himself, he did not know how to dance, nor how to utter a few nonchalant words to the girls. He whispered their names into the darkness: Liana and Diana. Phantoms of grandeur and wealth. Charlie little cared that it was a past grandeur and a vanished wealth. If only he could stand there next to them, all relaxed and unconcerned, like Handsome and Danny Hirsch! He was sick with the realization that it was not like that—and perhaps never would be. All he had to do was to leave and that was the end of it. If he were one of them, he would have tomorrow to look forward to, but as it was there was nothing, nothing at all. Nothing! Nothing! Loneliness, insignificance, futility, disenchantment. He felt as though he had been in a warm place and they had driven him out into the frost.

He wandered about the streets. Emptiness. And yet there smoldered in him a faint hope that this day need not be the last after all. The fragrant smell of the lime trees blossoming on both sides of the street, the open windows, and everything he had experienced a while ago roused a desire to get over it all somehow, to escape this emptiness and frustration, to stand up and shout: Look where I am. Here! And I'm standing pretty firm! Just you try and push me, you creeps! I won't fall!

That evening Room 16, despite its air of gloomy contemplation, seemed to him gay and lively, unostentatious, of its own accord filled with the real feats of the boys, who never talked about them until they were discovered. What a lucky fluke, he thought; had it not been for his chance getaway from Schierl that morning, he would have known nothing about the way Danny Hirsch, Handsome, and Oscar Kleiner had spent the afternoon. He would have been that much the poorer now, and he would be tomorrow and after that unless *something* happened. *Something!*

He rolled about on the bunk, listening to the noises in the room. Snow White, back from the infirmary, was coughing. They did not want him in the infirmary and he, unaccustomed to shouting and quarreling, had obediently brought his bedding back again.

A few moments later Charlie smiled as he intercepted a veiled allusion to Liana and her sister in something that Handsome said to Danny Hirsch. In a flash he forgot all about Snow White. He smiled with them, and suddenly it occurred to him that his excursion with Tony Fetman and the meeting with Oscar Kleiner and the others in the attic of Electricians' House, as well as his lucky escape from Schierl which had started it all, the present from Tony, the greater part of which he still had safely stowed away under his pillow, and a glance at Tony Fetman's suitcase ("as for this suitcase that you're goggling at, that was sent to me by my aunt!")—that all this meant the beginning of something that he himself was perhaps going to finish. The snag, however, was how—where to start, when and with whom. And a thousand other things. Nevertheless, he felt better. And when Tony Fetman threw a cigarette up to him, Charlie saw that he was *in,* and that Oscar Kleiner had succeeded in trading everything. He comprehended the satisfaction of those two down below, as if it had been he who had exchanged the shirts for cigarettes—the most stable currency in the ghetto—and as if he had a perfect right to share the proceeds. Feeling very happy about everything, Charlie turned on his side, put the cigarette, which had been thrown up to him already lit, between his lips, took a deep pull at it, and started coughing violently.

Just like Snow White, he thought. Snow White . . . shouldn't he offer him a biscuit? Or should he rather keep them all for himself? Snow White never had anything. He took another draw at his cigarette and his head swam. He felt sick. It was no use, he didn't know how to smoke. But never mind, he'd have another try. He started coughing again.

"What's the matter?" Snow White asked him in his quiet voice.

Charlie thought he was going to choke.

"Nothing, Snow White," he said. "Why should anything be the matter?"

He would give the kid that biscuit, after all, just to show him that he was somebody.

"Here, Snow White, take this and eat it."

"What is it?" Snow White asked.

"Go on, take it!" said Charlie, handing him the whole packet. Let the kid see that he knew a thing or two!

He waited for Snow White to ask where he had got them from, so as to be able to say nonchalantly: never you mind, punk!

But Snow White fell to coughing again as he had done in the morning. Nobody took any notice of him because they were all staring at Handsome, standing with his legs apart in the narrow rectangle between the bunks in the center of the room and giving an imitation of the Dutch singer, Hannibal van de Hambo, from Amsterdam, trilling up and down the scale: "Tra—la—lala—lala, tra—la—la . . ."

Danny Hirsch called out to him: "You sing so beautiful, Handsome—just like Hannibal. But I hope"— here his voice broke as he could not keep his laughter any longer—"I hope that he didn't give you private lessons!"

Charlie knew, as they all did, that on his walks through the town Hannibal van de Hambo jotted down the names of boys in his notebooks, inviting the best looking ones to his room.

"This has got to be investigated!" Oscar Kleiner shouted from his bunk.

Handsome repulsed their jibes calmly and with assurance. "Not me," he said to Danny Hirsch, "and I don't want to name any names." Then he added: "You sheep—baa-aa-aa . . ."

This was followed by shouts and catcalls from all over the room.

Handsome glanced round the bunks, taking in the storm he had aroused.

"For heaven's sake!" he said. "You are a lot of kids, that's what you are . . . Well, and what if I have been there? Baa-aa-aa . . . !"

He made horns on his head with his fingers, then he put his tongue out at them. "Baaaa . . ."

"We want to know what he takes—and what he gives," Danny said, choking with laughter.

Tony Fetman meanwhile stole up to Handsome from behind, and suddenly shouted in his ear: "Down with your pants!" Handsome turned round, startled. Another roar of laughter. Charlie could hear even Snow White laughing.

"In the first place, don't ruffle my hair," protested Handsome, smoothing his hair back as he spoke. "And then . . . well, I got a pound of oat flakes out of him."

"Gosh! I'll be knocking at his door first thing tomorrow. Honest!" shouted Tony Fetman. Then he said: "What can he want with a body like this?" and he pulled up his shirt.

"Nothing much," replied Handsome, looking him over. And then, grinning at all the boys: "He'll stroke your hair a little, as he did me . . . and, well, your bottom too . . . But nothing more, really, he doesn't want anything more."

Danny Hirsch sat up on his bunk: "But, Handsome, you were telling me only this afternoon how he begged you with tears in his eyes to unbutton your pants."

"Well, so he did," admitted Handsome. "But I didn't."

Nevertheless, they all knew that he had, and more than once.

And Charlie tried to imagine how it had all taken place, before Handsome walked away with a big packet of Dutch oat flakes which would provide him with sweet porridge for more than a week. He looked at him with a strange feeling, a mixture of admiration and disgust, of pity and envy, as well as a certain respect for having had the courage to do it. This respect he felt not only for Handsome, but for all the others, too.

Tony Fetman was dancing round the room, "playing" on his own ribs as though they were an accordion and shouting: "Let him touch my rib!"

A cool breeze was wafted in through the large window, open at the top to let out the assorted smells. Room 16 slowly went to sleep.

Pity he hadn't kept at least one biscuit, thought Charlie. He hoped that Snow White at least appreciated the fact that he had given them to him. He was sleepy. The breeze lulled him to sleep, and the idea that here somewhere there floated a ticket that would admit him to the boys' company gently stroked his forehead; all he had to do was to stretch out his hand and pick it up. This had been the finest day of his life, both the morning and the afternoon, and he would be able to think about it all day tomorrow, and later too. After this there just had to be a way somewhere, and he had to find it.

The building site to which Schierl sent him the next morning was half an hour's walk out of town.

"Take these pickaxes," the German overseer told them. "You're not in the ghetto here, and our Führer knows how to reward honest work. You work and you'll see." Then he left.

All day long Charlie worked on the half-built air-raid shelter by the German hospital, Tony Fetman next to him. Tony swore loudly at each spadeful of earth he threw up. "Like hell we'll see," he said at last. "I'm packing up." And he put his spade down and stopped working. Then they went home.

From that afternoon, remarkable only for Tony Fetman's having thrown away his spade and not budged from the brick on which he had sat down, Charlie's life ran its course, the previous day returning only in memory, a day full of fantasies and facts, the personification of an esteem in which he, too, might share.

The days passed without change. Except that the next morning, as he got up and climbed down the ladder to the floor, Snow White, always resembling a pale flower, was even paler than usual, his face motionless, as if carved out of blue and white marble.

For a long time Charlie just stood there looking at him, not daring to touch him.

"Fetman!" he said at last. "Come and take a look at him. He looks queer. Is he asleep?"

Fetman strolled over slowly, glanced at Charlie, then dropped his eyes to the floor, and very quietly, as though he were forcing himself to speak in his normal tone of voice, he said: "He's finished . . ."

"Gosh, boys," said Handsome, frightened, "you'd better call Schierl."

Fetman crossed over to his bunk, got a postcard out of his suitcase and, together with Danny Hirsch and Oscar Kleiner, put together a message for Snow White's parents, counting all the time: they already had twenty-eight words and only thirty were allowed.

Schierl arrived.

"Somebody help me carry him," he demanded.

Tony Fetman volunteered.

Charlie would have liked to help, only he was scared: Snow White was looking so queer. Like a statue. The two youths carried him out. Nobody mentioned Snow White any more. That's how it's got to be, thought Charlie. Snow White simply was and now he isn't any longer, because everybody will turn into a statue like he did one day, and in his case it was only to be expected anyway. Handsome collected Snow White's bedding.

"Look, boys," he said. "He's got some biscuits here."

But nobody took any notice—perhaps they did not want to hear. Only Charlie looked on in silence as Handsome stuffed the biscuits into his pockets.

Snow White's bunk was not to remain empty long—in a short while Schierl brought in another boy to take his place, a boy who looked happy that he had been transferred to Room 16 and did not even insist that the bunk which had been Snow White's should first be remade.

Schierl then had some things to say to various boys, telling Charlie that he was to work permanently on the air-raid shelter.

"Why permanently?" Charlie asked.

"And why not, you lazybones?" Schierl snarled at him.

And Charlie kept quiet. His fate, it now seemed to him, was definitely sealed. He'd be going out every day to dig that shelter until it happened to him as it had to Snow White. He almost wished they would find him like that in the morning, his face like blue marble with white spots.

The days dragged on.

Occasionally Oscar Kleiner or, very rarely, Danny Hirsch took Tony Fetman's place, shoveling up the earth, but none of them were there permanently, until the air-raid shelter was finished, as Charlie was. And so he was constantly under the impression that even by going out to dig the boys were following some secret plan of their own which he did not understand. There was some kind of a wall between him and some action in which he had not been invited to participate.

He made up his mind at last: he was going to earn his admission ticket to their company. He must, God Almighty, he simply *must!* Every second he thought about it was torture. On his way to and from work, all the time, with every blow of his pickax, which he could hardly hold up, he was thinking it over, trying to think of a way . . .

But how to fool Schierl as he had done that morning? Schierl was clever. By sending Charlie he was able to keep in the ghetto his favorites, who brought him his meals and probably gave him a share of what they received in their parcels, same as it was said of the Valta brothers.

He would have to invent a really good excuse not to have to go digging.

One morning he went up to Schierl and said brazenly: "The German overseer doesn't want me there anymore, Schierl. He says to send somebody who has more muscle. Otherwise he's going to raise hell, he says, and make our eyes pop out of our heads."

"How's that?" asked Schierl in surprise.

"I don't know," lied Charlie, averting his eyes and looking steadfastly at the floor because he was afraid Schierl would see from his face that he was lying.

"Ehm," said Schierl, uncertain of himself. "All right, then. I'll send you somewhere else. But don't you run away!"

Charlie stood where he was, jubilant. But what next? The action he longed for was still immeasurably distant and unreal.

He gazed out of the window. Summer was waning, the fully opened lime blossoms were falling to the ground in a green shower and the rain was washing them away. And there was autumn already to be felt in the last breath of summer, but not even autumn could waft away from the boys that certain indefinable something that caused Charlie to admire them. If anything, the contrary. Nothing changed. His visions haunted Charlie wherever he went. Only he himself was so painfully real. He had again got the better of Schierl, and again he did not know what to do. Everything depressed him. He had nothing but his tormenting dreams. And everything both inside and around him was denuded. He felt chilly.

"I can't have you lazing about here," Schierl told him downstairs in his office. "You'll go and work on the building site."

Charlie was detailed to work as a laborer on a building site in the town. It was near the town hall, fortunately in a deserted spot where only a chance passerby appeared now and then. It was on the left side of the ghetto, near the barracks that housed both the prison and the ghetto administration.

Throughout the first week Charlie maintained a special vigilance, carefully scanning his surroundings. He wondered what might be behind the bars on the top floors, as well as down here where even he could reach. And on the eighth day his great dream suddenly emerged out of the darkness, growing larger with every glance he took at the greyish-black mass of the town hall and the surrounding desolation.

In the evening Schierl was struck by Charlie's appearance: he seemed pleased as Punch about something. What was the matter with the kid? But he paid no attention to it.

I have found my admission ticket among the boys, Charlie kept repeating to himself. I have *found* it! Now he could join Handsome, Danny, and Oscar Kleiner as an equal. He had to keep it quiet, though. Be patient for a few days. But his time was coming, he thought contentedly. One evening, not too far off now, he would say: boys, come over here. I've brought this for *us*. When he thought about it, however, he could not help trembling. In the evening his thoughts swept along like an avalanche, an endless succession of images without beginning or end, in a vicious circle unrelieved by repose, heralding to him and him alone that his name carried the mark of action, that he had climbed up to the summit of recognition. And once it had happened, once everyone in Room 16 knew about it, he thought, it would never be forgotten as long as this lousy town remained a ghetto!

A restless night. Endless deliberation: with whom was he to do it? He came to a sudden decision: those two with whom he had been allowed to go that day when he first felt that he was alive, that afternoon on which he had seen the two girls in the attic of Electricians' House. Yes, that was it—Tony Fetman and Oscar Kleiner. He'd do it with them. If only it were morning!

In the morning he stopped Tony Fetman in the washroom: "Tony Fetman," he said. "I know about something. It's a cinch!"

For the first time he was able to enjoy the effect of his words on Tony's face, just as he had pictured it so many times in the past few days. If everything continued like this, he thought, it would be a great climb up the rope of his imaginings to real feats, right among the elite of Room 16, a room in which, though he lived, he did not as yet belong because he had not proved himself in action.

"On the level, Charlie?" asked Fetman.

"Look, you tell Oscar and we'll do it tonight."

It was too good to be true.

After a talk with both of them, Charlie decided to postpone it a day. That talk was almost as beautiful as what was in store for them tomorrow.

"But we'll have to get hold of a picklock to get out," Tony said with a trace of reproach in his voice.

Charlie did not feel at all remorseful. That was probably all as it should be. He could think something up, and he could also make a mistake, couldn't he. That, after all, was why three of them were going.

"Sure . . ." he said. "Only I forgot to tell you."

In the evening the boys in Room 16 fell asleep, weary, the room full of body smells.

And then the three of them plunged into the womb of advancing night, not stopping until they reached the gate near the town hall, near the house into which they would shortly steal.

The wind soughed in the limetree leaves, rain ran along the roofs. Charlie was not afraid; he had mastered his fear on the way. He was now adequately big even in his own eyes.

"Oscar!" he whispered. "Wipe your glasses and chuck a stone into the street opposite."

They backed away a little. Oscar picked up a stone and hurled it. It fell with a ringing sound on the paving stones some way ahead. But that was all, nothing moved anywhere. Charlie was satisfied.

"There's nobody around," he said.

The only policeman, standing beneath the little wooden shelter by the town hall, was asleep on his feet and, it seemed, had heard nothing. It was still raining heavily.

"Come on, boys," said Charlie.

The passage in which the storehouse lay smelled of decay.

Oscar Kleiner, somewhat excited by the thought of this raid put forward by Charlie and Tony Fetman—perhaps the biggest he had ever taken part in, breathed through his mouth so as to keep the stench out of his nostrils. He was glad he had been invited along in spite of the clamoring voices inside him which exhorted him to chuck it while there was still time, to get out of there and go home. After all, he could wait as he usually did when they went raiding with Tony Fetman. The voices were loud and insistent. All at once he felt pains in his stomach. Quickly he crouched down on his haunches on the edge of an empty laundry basket standing in a corner of the passage.

"Hell, what a stink!" said Tony Fetman.

Charlie looked at him. "Tony," he said, "you're going to climb in there alone, aren't you?"

"That's right," replied Tony.

Here we go, he thought. This was where it really started for him. Not that he was exactly enthusiastic about it, but he felt reluctant to spoil his reputation of a cold-blooded hunter who could keep his head in the thickest of troubles, which was probably how Charlie pictured him. Anyway, he told himself, what was there to fear so far? Everything was exactly as Charlie had described it. The pointed ends of the bars grinned impassably in the darkness. But for us, thought Tony, they will not be impassable! Several of them were shorter than the others and did not reach right up to the ceiling. That was the important discovery Charlie had made. The gap was just big enough to allow Tony to wriggle through. He took hold of the bars and pulled himself up.

"Don't make a sound, you two!" he said, looking down.

At the top he clamped his teeth. Better close his eyes, too, because—it flashed through his head—to get stuck here would be damned unpleasant. He'd say it would!

Then he jumped from four feet up, lithe and silent like a cat.

In the dark of the storeroom he could see tall piles of boxes containing margarine and jars of marmalade.

"Here you are, boys!" he said.

One by one he was rapidly passing the boxes through the bars, not thinking, but working in feverish haste so as to get it over with as soon as possible, like a machine that is revved up to full speed in sight of the finish.

Oscar Kleiner and Charlie piled everything into a sack they had brought with them for the purpose.

"Is it enough?" Tony Fetman pressed himself right up against the bars so that he would not have to shout and could hear their reply.

"What?" whispered Oscar Kleiner.

"Enough," said Charlie. "Come on out and we'll scram."

Carefully, moving like a machine all the time a jump, a grab with the hands, quick work with the legs—Tony Fetman climbed back over the bars, dragging under his arm another sack, which he had concealed under his shirt and which was now partly filled with small loaves of bread. He'd made it, he thought. He would prove he was no coward even on a show like this.

"Don't be stupid, leave it behind!" said Oscar Kleiner.

The sack with the loaves thudded as it fell to the ground on the other side. Tony obeyed Oscar because Oscar knew what was what. And it was no use quarreling: Tony believed it brought bad luck to the expedition.

"Hurry up!" Charlie urged him.

At last they were together again.

"Pick it up, Oscar," said Tony.

Charlie picked up one end of the sack without waiting to be told. But Oscar Kleiner was crouching on the ground again.

"You pig!" said Tony Fetman derisively. "You stink like an ape."

Nevertheless, it was all so pleasant and gay in the tense situation that Charlie felt relieved. Tony was trying to be tough, but his voice was high and thin like a child's.

"Ssssh!" hissed Charlie.

Did he imagine it or had he really heard something?

"Stand over by the wall!" he whispered.

They huddled together against the whitewashed vault. What's up, wondered Oscar Kleiner, buttoning up his trousers. Upstairs, a lamp flashed its yellow ray. Horror took hold of all three. Had someone heard them?

Charlie pulled a pair of pliers out of his pocket, heavy black-smith's pliers. Someone was coming down. There was no doubt about it now. They could hear the footsteps. A hot wave took the place of the first chill of terror. Charlie grew pale.

Oscar Kleiner was seized by stomach cramps. A moment longer and he would have to let go . . . Quickly he unbuttoned his trousers again.

It might be better to leave everything behind and clear out of here, thought Tony Fetman. But all of them knew that they must not budge, for there was the policeman outside the town hall.

Take it easy! Charlie commanded himself. Just stand still and take it easy, everything wasn't lost yet. He sweated as he gripped the pliers tighter in his fingers. What would happen now? It had not occurred to him that someone might disturb them right at the end, had it? His eyes blurred. How they would all laugh at him for having started something and then messed it up like this! And Schierl was sure to take him to task, and then they would probably lock him up, or chuck him out of Q. The action he had dreamed about was lost somewhere in the darkness which enveloped him and all that remained was derision and nothingness. So that was it—he was no good at anything. People would not talk about him and his deeds. His knees felt weak. In front of himself he saw a dark, gaping abyss. So that was how it would end. And it had started so well. Tomorrow already the boys might have been whispering about it, about what Charlie had done. He had almost managed to become one of them. He would have thrown each of them a piece of the margarine, non-chalantly, as though it were the most natural thing in the world for him to have it and to give it away. Well, he wouldn't do that now; he would do nothing. They'd all think him a fool, that was all.

Suddenly he spoke up: "Beat it! I'll cover you."

His voice was hoarse now. He took a short step to get in front of Tony Petman and Oscar Kleiner, who was rubbing his behind against the wall. The pliers in his right hand, he was ready to strike. He was going on up to the summit of the only deed life had allotted him so far.

Yes, he told himself, on the verge of tears. He had to do it. The dark figure was only a little distance away now. Charlie locked his teeth, shaking all over, and raised the hand holding the pliers.

"Charlie!" whispered Oscar Kleiner. "Not this! Don't!"

Tony was frightened by the thought of something he had never experienced before. He felt as if he were standing on the brink of a deep, stone well and at the same time as if tongues of flames were licking at him. Whatever happened, perhaps they'd still get away. He'd do it himself if necessary, he was no chicken, but not this!

The lamp approached. It was a woman with a child on her arm. Charlie could not see her as yet, hidden as she was in the shadows. He was standing by himself in the bend of the passage below the staircase. Now for the last step, and then he'd strike.

The child whimpered suddenly. They were right in front of him. Charlie closed his eyes, sprang, and hit out.

"Let's go!" he said hoarsely.

The woman leaned against the wall, swayed, but did not fall. The pliers fell to the ground, ringing with a curious sound that seemed to roll about, long and clear, in the passage, like a bronze bell.

The tongues of flame in front of Tony Fetman's eyes disappeared.

"Come here, you idiots!" he said. "Let's take it with us."

Oscar was holding his trousers up and Charlie was staring unseeingly ahead of him.

"That woman will come to in a minute, so hurry up!" Tony Fetman urged them in a sibilant whisper. "Why, she's staring at us already!"

Charlie still had his eyes fixed on nothing.

"Don't stand there gaping and come along!" Tony ordered him.

The child was crying.

Tony Fetman caught both of them by the shoulder.

"This way!"

Dragging the sack behind them, they crept out of the passage and along the low wall outside. The policeman was still dozing under his little roof at the end of the street and the rain was soaking his cap.

Not daring to stop, they hurried through the streets, the cobblestones under their feet glistening with rain. Charlie was terrified by the slightest sound. What's happened to that woman? he wondered. He had socked her good and hard, that was a fact.

Silent streets, and then, at last, Room 16. The room welcomed them fast asleep, unaware of what had taken place. Nobody was awake. They hid the sack in Charlie's bunk. "Nobody will suspect you . . ." said Tony.

He did not even protest. He felt as if he were drunk. Immensely tired, he lay down fully dressed next to the sack. As he stared dully at the wall he saw in front of him the white face of the woman and heard the child weeping and the sound of the falling pliers ringing and ringing, and all of a sudden Charlie cried out.

"Shut up!" hissed Oscar Kleiner.

Tony Fetman crept up to his bunk. "Be quiet, Charlie," he said. "D'you want to give the game away now we're back?"

Charlie moaned intermittently.

"Don't worry," whispered Tony. "The woman was standing up, you only tapped her on the nut, that's all. And people must have come right away, only they wouldn't know what it was all about. So you have nothing to be afraid of, you idiot, she's alive, sure she's alive . . . you understand . . ."

But at the same time as he was trying to convince Charlie, he was also trying to figure out how to get rid of the sack first thing in the morning.

". . . so don't be a fool, and go to sleep," he concluded, then climbed down and returned to his bunk.

But Charlie kept on sighing. He could hear the heavy breathing of Tony Fetman and Oscar Kleiner. How come they can sleep? he thought enviously. On the other hand, he was not sure that they were both really asleep. More probably not. He himself was suffocating under the weight of the ceiling, which seemed to hang so close above him, threatening to fall and squash him on his bunk. So that was it: his ticket of admission to Room 16, the boat in which he was to sail out on to the surface of their recognition, something intoxicating and enthralling, the legend of a deed, a nice little legend to warm the heart, even laced with a touch of envy as the boys would repeat it before going to sleep. A terrible disappointment nailed him to the bunk. Thus he lay until morning, conscious of nothing but this bottomless disenchantment, everything inside him stifled and numb. He wished fervently for the light of day, yet when at last it came, the darkness of the night seemed more merciful to him.

The morning found him horribly pale, with large blue rings under his eyes. He got up feeling very unsure of himself, disappointment inside him and all over him.

Oscar Kleiner lay with his back turned to Tony Fetman. He, too, was not far from fainting. No, Oscar Kleiner was not a real hunter like Tony Fetman, after all. He was better at selling things. Tony was the most cheerful of the three.

"Nothing's happened, you suckers!" he said to them by way of encouragement.

And then, as they were all three standing side by side in the washroom, drying themselves with Oscar's towel: "You'd better sell the stuff straight-away today, Oscar. And wipe your glasses!"

Oscar looked around apprehensively, afraid that someone might overhear.

"What?" he asked, adding desperately: "But where?"

"Well, what d'you think? Of course it's all up to you, pal," Fetman said, looking derisively at both of them, from Charlie to Oscar, and from Oscar to Charlie.

Oscar nodded sadly. "All right, I'll try . . ."

"You can keep my share," said Charlie in a faint voice.

"Don't talk crazy," said Tony.

"You'd get nothing out of it . . ."

"No, really, I don't want anything," Charlie repeated.

It wasn't that he was afraid, he told himself. If they were found out it would be too late, even if he did get something out of it.

Then he went to have another wash. The cold water made him feel better. I am not going to get anything out of it, he thought, and he felt as if a weight had been lifted from him, repeating it over and over to himself as he had said it aloud a while ago. The feeling that had crushed him all night long, the apprehension that he would, in the light of day, be disgusted with himself, that he would be afraid to go out into the street, that dreadful feeling had passed. He would have to look frequently at that house, he told himself. Perhaps the woman really *was* alive.

In the yard he collected a pickax and a spade, and in the same leisurely way as always—only his face showing a noticeable pallor—he quietly and without rancor greeted Schierl and walked off toward the town hall, to the building site on the left of the ghetto.

❖

Stephen and Anne

He lay there quietly.

The beam he was gazing at had a dark, nut-brown color. On it someone had scribbled the word *quarantine*. It struck him as funny that the walls here inside should be the same red color as the outside walls. He already had his bed—a narrow strip of the paving-stone floor. In the semidarkness he could make out the rounded shapes of the women, who were getting ready to lie down in the uncertain, flickering light of the candles. He had been lying here in this way for many seconds, in the grip of a fever he was not even aware of, and full of tantalizing thoughts.

Then he fell asleep. He would wake up, wild with desperation, thinking that it was almost dawn, would close his eyes again, desiring to protract the delicious darkness in which he dropped, rose and dropped anew.

He awoke early in the morning. Astonished, he looked around to find out where he was. Next to him slept a girl, covered by knapsacks and a dark blanket, on his other side an old man who snored with the exertion of sleep.

He narrowed his eyes and saw her clearly like the white summit of some snow-capped mountain. Her brow was smooth and her skin well-nigh transparent, she had loosely flowing golden hair and an equally fair nape. The violence with which her image kept returning to him frightened him.

He waited for her to wake. Her hair was like autumn leaves, her lips were pale and half-open. He felt a current pass through him, a current in which there was the light of dawn and the quiet of night.

She sat up, slightly startled. She covered her face with her long fingers.

"Good morning," he said.

"Good morning."

"Please don't be angry that I am lying here," he said. "I didn't see properly last night."

"It doesn't matter," she replied.

She looked across him to where the old man was lying.

"Are you getting up?" he asked.

"Yes, I am," she said.

"Have you been here long?"

"A week," she replied.

And then: "I was already asleep when you arrived."

"We came in the night," he said.

"Some transports do come at night," she replied.

"We don't even know each other," he said.

She smiled, and he could see both bitterness and embarrassment on her lips.

"My name is Stephen," he said.

"Mine is Anne," she replied. And she repeated it: "Anne."

An official appeared on the threshold of the wooden staircase.

"It's one of ours," she said. "He has a star."

A wave of silence swamped the attic.

"What's he want?"

"He is going to read out the names," she said.

"Our names?"

"Yes, perhaps our names, too," she replied.

The official stopped a few paces away from them. He spread out his papers like huge bank notes. Then he said that those whom he was going to read out had been selected by the Council of Elders—entrusted with this task by the German HQ—and would go and live in the ghetto.

"And the others?"

"Elsewhere," she said.

"Where?"

"Nobody knows," she replied.

And then: "In the east," she said.

The old man next to them was awake now. He was holding a wrinkled, sallow hand to his ear, so as to hear better. "My name is Adam," he said. "Adam," he mumbled.

"Haven't you been read yet?" Stephen asked her.

"No," she said.

Suddenly she felt ashamed that they had not read her yet.

"My name is Adam," murmured the old man.

Then Stephen's name was read out.

"That's you," she said. "Stephen."

"Perhaps he'll read you, too," he said.

He did not.

"Be glad," she said.

He was silent, frightened suddenly by the infinitude of leave-taking that clung to him.

"Don't cry," he said.

"I'm not crying," she replied.

The official announced that those whose names had been called were to go downstairs into the courtyard within ten minutes.

"Just those I've read out—neither more nor fewer," he said curtly.

Then he added: "I'm not making this up—it's orders from HQ."

"Adam," the old man repeated.

The official left.

"Are you thinking about it?"

"No," she answered.

"They'll read you tomorrow," he said. "Or some other time."

He could not make himself stand up, yet he knew he would have to.

He took her hand.

"Come and see me, won't you?" she said.

"I'll come," he replied.

"We have known each other so short a time," she said.

"I'll come for sure," he said again. "I'm alone here. We can be friends."

"If they leave us here," she said.

"Why?"

"I've heard things."

"What things?"

"That we are to be sent on," she said. "Maybe within a week."

He helped her with the knapsacks.

"You're lucky," she said.

He was looking at her, unable to reply.

The current rose up in him from somewhere deep inside, right to the top and back again to his finger tips with which he was touching the palm of her hand.

"Perhaps," she said quietly, "I will still be here."

"You will," he muttered.

And then he added: "Certainly you will."

"Go on, then," she said.

He looked at her, and he again felt the current, being drowned in it. Then he got up, letting her hand slip out of his, and something stopped inside him; he felt it in the contraction of his chest and the smarting of his eyes that increased with each step he drew farther away from her.

"Adam," mumbled the old man.

Then he ran along L Avenue; everything that had enveloped him like a spider's web and that alternately burned and went out inside him, driving him forward and drawing him back to the attic of the *quarantine,* turned over inside him and reverberated like the echo of those words.

He put down his knapsack on the bed assigned to him.

Then he ran back the way he had come, not caring what would become of him and his things.

He dashed inside. He saw her, so slim, on the grey pallet.

"Stephen," she said.

Then: "It's you."

And finally: "So you've come." She lowered her eyes.

"Annie," he said.

"I didn't really expect . . ." she said.

He ignored the old man, whose snoring disturbed everyone near him. He sat down at her side on the mattress, out of which the straw projected like so many arrows. He did not feel any need to say more than that one word he had said already.

"Annie," he repeated.

He embraced her shoulders and felt the current surging up from inside. The feeling that he was protecting her with the hand that touched her stifled him.

He sat silently next to her, in front of the barrier of stone that was the old man, whose glassy eyes did not take them in and whose sallow neck, resembling a human tree trunk, shielded them from view.

Suddenly his eyes met those of the old man.

"What is it?" she asked.

"Nothing," he replied.

He could feel that she was afraid. She pressed herself closer to him.

Then she saw the old man's gaze and she was frightened by what she read in it—a wild, imploring insolence and an inquisitive envy.

"My name is Adam," the old man muttered.

He kept holding his hand up to his face to catch the sound of words that did not reach him.

"Let's get away from here," said Stephen.

"Yes, let's," she said.

Then she added: "What if the official comes?"

"Why should he?"

Her eyes fell and she looked at the floor.

"Let's go, then," she said.

She did not dare to look again into the dark pools of the old man's eyes. She rose. She had on a coat of some warm, blue material.

Looking at her, the coat and everything else seemed to him to be as clear and clean as the sky.

He had to step across the old man's mattress.

He knew he would speak to him.

"Look after Anne's things," he said.

And to Anne it seemed as if only these words really woke the old man. He dropped the hand that had acted as a hearing aid. His almost-brown eyes grew wide and soft.

"Adam," he said.

Then he added: "Right! You run along, children!"

She had to lower her eyes once more.

"Is that your brother?" the old man asked.

They looked at each other. He felt the current again running through him.

"Yes," he replied for her.

They went out, and it seemed to them that everything they looked at was without shadow.

And Stephen wished that the current should pass through the tips of his fingers to Anne, that she might feel in that touch the sun, and hope, and the rosy rays of day and its light.

"Brother and sister," he said.

And then: "More than that."

They walked round the blacksmith's shop. On the other side of the slope that towered above the town they saw the rambling building of the Council of Elders.

"If only I had an uncle here," she said.

"Has he gone?" he asked.

She turned her face to his and, with her finger quite close to him, tapped her forehead.

"Silly," she said, "I was thinking of an uncle who does not exist."

"Are you alone?"

"Completely," she replied.

"Are you hungry?"

"What could you do about it?"

"Do you know where I live?"

"No," she said.

"Here," he said. "Wait a second."

He ran upstairs and pulled a piece of cake out of his knapsack; this he broke in two, leaving one of the halves to the boys who were watching him.

"For your hunger," he said when he was downstairs again.

"Thanks," she said.

Suddenly they both laughed.

"Let's go back there," she said then.

"There?" he asked.

"Yes," she said.

"Yes," he repeated.

When they were sitting down again, he said: "They'll read you tomorrow."

"Oh, I'm not thinking about it," she said.

"There are other things apart from that," he said.

"What things?"

"Other things," he repeated.

Then they went out, but they only had time to walk once round the town. The darkened trees began to merge with their own shadows, the twilight toying with the leaves.

"Come," she said. "I'll accompany you."

He gazed into her eyes, so close to his. He put his arm around her shoulders, which were frail and gentle, making him think it was up to him to protect her. The strong feeling that seemed to have a life of its own inside him and rose in waves up to his throat and farther, both the light and the dark curve of her silhouette, that which at once constricted him and released him from the shadows, holding out the promise of a sensation of freedom—all this flowed into the single word which he now uttered:

"Anne!"

"Stephen!"

He kissed her on the mouth.

"I've never . . . been like this before," she said.

It was his first kiss as well as hers. And he again felt those waves returning, clean and fragrant, and he kissed her lips and eyes, which were now filled with tears, and felt a desperate longing to never, even at the price of death, live otherwise than at this moment.

They walked a little way from the door, to the spot where a yellow, wooden fence divided off the ghetto from the HQ. They shivered with the chill of evening.

"It's not so late yet," she said.

"Annie," he said.

"Where shall we go?" she asked.

"Annie," he repeated.

"We'll have to be going," she said, and stood still. He felt the irrevocability of the hour that closes the day like a thin blade having the power to cut even the invisible current somewhere deep inside where no one can see.

He led her wordlessly round the block of houses next to Q 710. He was aware that some outside influence was disturbing that current inside him, and yet he was glad he was walking by her side and feeling her warmth, and at the same time unhappy because he knew what was coming; his throat was constricted by the same huge hoop that was encircling his chest and pressing against his eyes.

"Annie," he said.

"Yes?" she replied.

And then, after a long silence: "If you want, Stephen," she said, "come and see me in the night."

"I will," he whispered. He felt as though she had cut through ropes which had until now bound him.

"Yes, I will," he said again. "I'll come for sure."

"You can go across the courtyards," she said.

Then she added: "That's how they do it here."

"Yes," he said.

"We'll be moved soon," she said. "I feel it."

"I'll come," he repeated.

"I feel it somehow," she said.

And then, "I'm terribly afraid. It's even worse now."

"Don't worry," he said. "I'll come for sure."

"It's not far across the courtyards," she said.

"Yes," he said.

He took off his coat and threw it over her. She returned it to him.

Then, all at once, she ran off, suddenly and unexpectedly. She tore herself away from his hands, regretting that she had said what she did. She had known the laws of the ghetto a week longer than he. He heard only her steps, receding into the darkness.

A fraction of that moment was before his eyes every second that passed by, deepening the darkness, these fractional parts of the picture composing a huge mosaic which contained the current and her half-open lips and her tears.

Then the boys became quiet and went to sleep.

He knew he would stay awake. He pieced together the fragments of the night, and only when it seemed to him that the stillness was going to overwhelm him with its immense, unbearable weight did he steal from his bed.

He jumped over the knapsacks and shoes lying in the middle of the room and stood by the door. He reached out for the handle. In the instant when the cool contact poured a whole ocean into his brain, the shining brass growing dull under the imperceptible shadow of his palm, he was again conscious of the warm waves and heard the creaking of the wooden stairs that led up to the attic. At that moment he heard his heart beating, a bronze bell tolling inside him. He pressed down the handle, cautiously but firmly.

The ocean poured itself out into emptiness. The room was locked. He felt the soft blow. The earth fell away beneath him. He swallowed his tears. Now he could see the emptiness, and in it a small face and the transparent skin of her forehead, that indescribably fragile something that filled him with a feeling that there was a reason for his existence, those frightened eyes and that breath bitter like almonds.

He crept back to his bed, and then again to the door. The white square, full of an overpowering silence, gave back a mute echo of the brotherhood he felt for her, a brotherhood that from that moment elevated him above this world and at the same time flung him down to its very bottom.

He rattled the handle.

"Be quiet!" someone shouted. And added something else.

He tried to make himself believe that she could see him all the way from where she was, through the silken web of the night, that it was all one great window, and that behind it was she.

Then he lay on his back, his eyes fixed on the grey ceiling, upon which was her image, indistinct and hazy, but clear in all details— her eyes and lips. Her hair fell loosely down in the shadows and her voice sounded in the stillness.

His eyes smarted. He was aware of this only every now and again, in the intervals of his imaginings in which he heard every word a thousand times and once, as a single word, and then as one great silence.

She penetrated everything: the white door and the stillness of the night. She returned to him in his feverish visions, and he walked with her, his hand on her shoulder, and the waves rose and fell in him and filled both of them.

In the morning he ran, breathless, through the town. He flew upstairs. All he found was an empty attic. The transport to the east had left in the night.

Blue Flames

The taller of the two gendarmes frowned and repeatedly cleared his throat; he had had an uneasy feeling right from the moment when he first entered the ghetto. The two of them were just passing the bandstand of the Ghettoswingers, and the shrilling of the trumpets did not abate in the slightest. The gendarme's weary mind vaguely registered the shouts of the tanned youths, calling someone named Woodpecker and exhorting him not to slack off, but sing; he replied by saying they could all go to hell because he was on his way to the blacksmith's shop to get some exercise. Then they waggled their shoulders and yelled:

Up and down and down and up
Our ship goes rolling.

The gendarme was irritated, and felt a desire to hit the boy. It was a persistent feeling, and he could not get rid of it.

"They're crazy!" he said, bending down slightly toward his smaller companion. "In this heat."

"They're on a ship," grinned the other. "It's not so hot there."

He pushed his helmet a little to the back of his head and blew beads of perspiration off his lips.

The taller gendarme had pale, cheese-colored cheeks in a lean, pockmarked face. The collar of his service shirt stood out stiffly from his emaciated neck. As he tried to moisten his dry lips, his Adam's apple jogged up and down in his throat.

"Still," he repeated, "in this heat!"

"What do you care—here?" said the smaller one.

The taller one did not reply any more. Now and again he nodded his long horselike head sleepily, without moving his parched lips. His distrustful, green eyes scanned everyone in the street, but he said nothing and never stopped. They traversed the town with long quick strides, like a knife cutting bread.

"They say Holler is behind it all," the smaller one spoke up after a while.

"That's what I say," said the taller one wearily. To himself he swore at the heat.

"It stands to reason," he added, "that if you make such a racket, you'll only get knocked about more."

"More or less," replied the smaller one. "If you were here you wouldn't care."

The dusty smell of the chestnuts and lime trees clung to their mouths.

"Phew!" spat the tall one.

"If the commandant has allowed them to, why shouldn't they have a little fun?" muttered the smaller one with a frown.

"Even so," the taller one insisted.

Their heavy army issue boots slid along the pavement, and they listened to the clinking of their hobnails. That was an ordinary pleasant sound, but above and beneath it squawked the jazz. The youths behind their backs roared as if they were drunk.

"What's that coming?" asked the taller one suddenly, and licked his lips.

Before the other could reply, a carriage came into view and rattled towards them.

The taller one slowed his pace a little.

A piebald horse with white and grey spots scattered over his rump jutted out of the silver-polished harness. Enthroned in the purple of the now much-faded blankets which covered up the patches in the upholstery of the seat behind the coachman, sat Ignatz Marmul-staub, member of the Council of Elders.

"Will he stop?" asked the taller gendarme inquiringly.

"He might," replied the other.

"He should," the tall one corrected him. In spite of all the compassion he felt for this town because it was a Czech town, he felt pleased that here at last was something he could tackle; a job worthy of a sergeant of the gendarmerie who was already half on duty; and on the other hand the responsibility of someone who would never be freed from the obligation of accounting for himself to the gendarmes on the highway.

"Mr. Marmulstaub," the coachman said in a confidential undertone as he half-turned toward him, "the gendarmes!"

"Where?" came from his passenger. "Ah! In front of us. You'll have to go slower."

He leaned out of the coach.

"Your obedient servant, gentlemen," he said in a gruff voice. And he was going to add something about the weather and the heat.

They did not as much as raise their eyes.

"Do you think he ought to stop?" the taller one asked his companion, bending down toward him.

"He could," said the smaller one.

"Rightly speaking, he should," the taller gendarme insisted in a loud and stubborn voice.

Marmulstaub colored, thinking: too late to stop now. He had simply missed it. And then: they weren't addressing him. On the contrary, they didn't even respond to his greeting. And anyway, they didn't call him back, and they looked so uncouth in their polished helmets covered with green cloth.

"He drives around like a king," murmured the taller gendarme angrily without moving his narrow head.

"Well, that's not such a big impertinence," replied the smaller one, "considering the heat."

"Damned cheek, I call it," countered the taller one.

"They drew to the side," said the smaller one in a languid tone. "That's enough for me."

"They couldn't do less," added the tall one.

"We were in the middle of the road, and our boots are for pedestrians," the smaller one replied calmly.

"Too much mollycoddling, that's what I say," complained the taller one.

"Oh, well, it's so terribly hot, pal," the smaller one evaded a reply. He had actually meant to say it wasn't worth talking about. Now he took his helmet off. He had sparse, straw-colored hair, wet and crumpled with perspiration.

"It is that," agreed the taller one, and he too lapsed into silence.

Then he swallowed some saliva he had laboriously gathered on his tongue. The Adam's apple, which protruded like a knuckle of a fist rammed inside his throat, leaped erratically upwards and fell again.

They passed through a narrow gate in the fence which ran round the ghetto. The concert in the main square was only a barely perceptible sound now, almost inaudible. The SS man who walked up and down the other side of the fence was given a perfunctory salute and replied in the same mute way.

The smaller gendarme put on his helmet.

2

"No," Marmulstaub answered the coachman when they had reached the square. "Don't wait for me."

He had decided not to use the carriage anymore. It attracted too much attention to himself, as he could see from his encounter with the gendarmes. And others, too, were irritated by it, he could see that right now by looking at the people in the square.

"You know what?" he said. "Take the carriage away for repairs. It creaks abominably."

"It creaks all right," replied the coachman, who was just thinking the same thing, "because I have nothing to grease it with."

Just as he left, the music stopped.

"What's up?" someone asked Marmulstaub.

"Why?" he replied. "I don't know."

"Can't you hear it?"

"What should I hear?" he asked, but at that very moment he, like everyone else, heard the murmur of the car belonging to Herr von Holler, which carried through the cleft of sudden silence, the car's horn cutting across the hush of the crowd and ringing out sharply over their heads. Ignatz Marmulstaub, however, was quick to notice that Herr von Holler, the ghetto commandant, was not in the car, its only occupant a mere private of the Signals Corps.

The crowd thinned out.

"Why don't you go on playing," he said in a hoarse voice. This wretched town, he thought, hangs its tail and sits on its backside even when it doesn't have to. After all, he had turned his back on those gendarmes a while ago, and nothing had happened.

He delighted in their almost tangible astonishment. The people kept their eyes glued to his face as though they could interpret even the motions of his lips and tried to guess in advance what shape his thoughts would take.

"You can go on playing!" he repeated huskily.

He noted with pleasure that the concert was beginning anew.

At that moment he caught sight of little Liselotte.

She, too, had seen and heard him, was his first thought. In the joy that welled up in him he forgot all about the gendarmes.

"Good afternoon, miss," he greeted her, narrowing his eyes.

"Good day," she replied.

"It's a fine day today, and there's music," he said. "Quite a change, isn't it."

"But it's also advisable to keep out of sight because one can't tell what might happen. That is another change."

"What could happen?" he smiled. "After all, everything has already happened."

"I have more errands than I have leisure in any case," she said. "Even though there is music."

"Can I help you in any way?" he inquired.

"No, it's all women's stuff," she said.

"Still, I might be able to do something for you," he suggested.

"I must do it myself," she said quickly, noticing at the same time how he was looking her all over.

"Always without me, Miss Liselotte," he said reproachfully. "Always without me."

"Good-bye!"

"Yes," he muttered, more to himself than to her.

He threw his jacket over his other arm. With his right hand he now began, swiftly and impatiently, to wipe his perspiring brow, and to scratch himself on the chest and under the armpits. His face went red, for he felt that the little one had lied to him. He had accurate information about her, let her not forget that, and he knew what he knew.

He stood there jacketless, with large round shoulders, his head bowed heavily over his chest, and his shirt unbuttoned right down to the semicircle of the trousers' top. From under drawn brows he followed what went on around him, watching the youth with a conductor's baton as he carved triangles in the hot air.

Then his eyes began to rove, appraising the clusters of human bodies. Here and there his gaze would rest, and he would narrow his large, dark eyes, which then took on a deep purplish tinge as they merged with the reddish swollen pouches under his eyes and the red-colored mesh of threadlike veins in the corners.

The sun was burning hot, and the women were dressed in the lightest of dresses. His eyes traveled hungrily along the white thighs of girls, slipping right down, down their calves to the ankles and back again, up along their throats, now shining with beads of perspiration, and their red or pale lips. In each and every one of them he saw in his mind's eye something of Liselotte, her narrow waist and her breasts like small, halved apples. Eagerly he linked his imaginings with the sound of her voice and with her scent. Hot blood pulsed through his veins. Yet, despite this internal fire, his appearance was one of almost immovable tranquillity, the only sign of life, indeed, being the constant rubbing together of his extraordinarily small, delicate, and white hands.

A little way from the railing stood some small, thirteen-year-old girls from L 410. He felt them all over with his purplish gaze, saying to himself that here there were no little girls.

But he was disturbed by the glances he knew were being directed at his back.

3

For some time now Herr von Holler had been looking out for his car, which was not back yet. Then he left the window, walked slowly across the room, and reached for the telephone, studying the pinkish crescents on his fingernails and listening to the gentle whirring of the fan.

He dialed a number and waited.

"Von Holler," he said at last. "Heil Hitler! Why am I calling you? Do you want to be present this evening at Löwenbach's interrogation?"

In his mind's eye he saw the small courier in civilian clothes.

"Heil Hitler!" said a voice. "When?"

"Tonight, if you have no other program."

"Not really," rasped the voice.

"It'll be good fun," the commandant continued, trying to prolong the conversation. "The fat one is going to assist. The one you saw yesterday. I've just sent for him."

"I remember," said the voice. "You have an inexhaustible sense of humor."

"You flatter me," said Herr von Holler. "But sometimes it is necessary. Just imagine you were cleaning the dunghill and then took a hot bath."

"One day you're going to lose that Jew of yours," crackled the voice at the other end. "I hope you will not miss him."

"His time hasn't come yet," said the commandant.

"Not willing?" hooted the voice.

"For the time being," parried Herr von Holler.

"Exaggerated," came from the receiver.

"Someone has to be last. That's no advantage. Let it be him."

"You cannot do without one ugly Jew, but on the other hand you want us to bleed the ghetto and rid you of a whole half of them at a time."

"You must understand, he's my secret weapon. Apart from the knout, the bullet, and the rope. Often a single word is enough. A word from him, that is."

"In short, that rotten Jew of yours is so excellent," clanged the voice, "that he is on velvet and doesn't even know it."

"I wouldn't like to enlarge upon it over the telephone," evaded the commandant.

"One of these days we'll put him in the waxworks for you," chuckled the voice. "You and your pet Jew!"

Herr von Holler did not reply for a moment. Did that half-grown civilian nincompoop think, he said to himself, that just because he was a courier plying between Berlin and the HQ he could threaten him? Of course his, von Holler's, fortress was overpopulated. That wouldn't matter so much for its own sake, he thought, but it did matter in view of the forthcoming filming of the ghetto!

"Well then, if you want to come," von Holler said in a tone

which indicated that the conversation was at an end, "I'll give you a call."

"Accepted with thanks," came the voice. "What time?"

"At eight."

"Right!" replied the voice.

And the phone went dead.

Von Holler began to pace the room with long strides, tall and bony, proud of his noble origin and of his ability to put on a rough or genteel air, according to who his interlocutor was. If only he knew the extent and the limits of the authority vested in the man from Berlin, he would find the right tone for dealing with him, too.

He stopped by the table. Picking up some papers, he glanced through the lists of names which Marmulstaub had brought him, scanning them with curious eyes. But the weak glimmer of interest quickly vanished—they were names for a museum. They lacked the romantic touch which they had once possessed. Then his gaze was attracted by the dark brown desk diary with the von Holler coat of arms. Thursday had been ticked off for some reason. Oh, yes, he recalled, today Marmulstaub's jazz band was performing. And the fat one would most likely be there. What a pity he had not thought of telling the officer who had gone to fetch Marmulstaub.

4

Meanwhile the coachman had unharnessed the piebald outside the town gate between two slopes.

"The Council of Elders has sent me," he said. "Namely, Mr. Marmulstaub. The carriage needs a complete overhaul. It was idle for a long time."

"Mr. Marmulstaub is going to drive in it?" asked the blacksmith, doubtfully inspecting the gig.

"All the gentlemen from the Council are going to drive in it," the coachman rebuffed him.

From the blacksmith's shop came the monotonous clatter of hammers.

"Hey, boy!" the blacksmith, a lean man with clever eyes, called into the open door. "Come here a moment."

A lanky youth in a leather apron came out.

"This is Woodpecker," said the blacksmith. "We'll give him the job."

"Overjoyed," said the youth. "What's this for? A coronation?"

"Something like that. It's for the greater glory of the town," said the lean one.

"Delighted," muttered the boy angrily.

"Don't make fun of it," the coachman murmured, turning to the blacksmith. "That's neither nice nor proper."

"This is overtime work, isn't it?" complained Woodpecker. "And for what? Three kicks for lunch! And there is music in the square."

"Mr. Woodpecker," the coachman said to the boy, "we need it soon."

Then he itemized all the faults of the vehicle.

"All right, then. Tomorrow," said the blacksmith. "Suit you?"

"Suits me fine," said the coachman.

He patted the horse on the muzzle, and was annoyed to see Woodpecker offer it an empty palm, which the piebald licked rewardlessly. He walked away with the horse collar and harness over his left arm. He was an elderly man, and his burden made him bend almost double.

The boy made no move to help him. As soon as he was alone with the gig, he aimed a vicious kick at it. It was considerably dilapidated. He scratched the backs of his hands, and lost even the last vestige of inclination to start the work of repairing the carriage. The wheels seemed to him to be clocks with plump hands and transparent faces, through which he could see the Ghettoswingers playing in the square where he had left them not so long ago. Tramp and Mylord among them. And the girls from L 410.

He went off to have a wash.

"I'm going," he told the blacksmith, who was a bachelor and lived over the shop. "I know pretty well what's wrong with it now, and I've repaired a thing or two already."

"That'll do," said the blacksmith. "It's too hot today, anyway, and you still have a restless nature. You can finish it tomorrow. The toad won't croak."

5

The German automobile was coming back. Herr von Holler's dispatch rider had taken to the Council of Elders the food ration papers which were normally delivered by the Council's chairman, Löwenbach. It was actually for these papers that he went to the HQ shortly after lunch, and he had not come back. The sound of the horn, its clamor shattering the curtain of silence, was again borne above the crowd.

The eyes of the crowd sought comfort in the face of Ignatz Marmulstaub. Again as before, he felt he was the center of their attention, and he was again pleased by it. Somewhere in that crowd, he told himself, was little Liselotte. The thought that she, too, witnessed how he was looked up to took away the bitterness of the thoughts that preceded it.

Then he actually saw her.

Some tall youth behind him was shouting, with a whole gang of boys accompanying him:

Wiggle your backside,
You lazy girl!

He saw at once that it was meant for her, and he wondered that she only smiled inanely and pretended not to hear.

One of the youths began to spit, aiming at the toes of Marmulstaub's shoes.

"Good shot, Tramp!" the others yelled.

Irritated, Marmulstaub stood aside, stepping on the tall youth's foot as he did so.

"Sorry," he murmured.

"Like hell," shouted Woodpecker, bending down and nursing his foot in his hand.

Marmulstaub had turned round and thus lost the little one from sight.

"Well, wiggle that backside of yours!" hooted Woodpecker in an angry tone, but more for the benefit of his friends than of the fat man next to him. "It's big enough, anyway!"

"Go to hell," said Marmulstaub darkly. "Idiot!"

His purplish eyes investigated the crowd. He could not see her any more.

"After all, I didn't do it on purpose," he said apologetically.

And suddenly he realized that the looks which the people were now giving him were not in the least admiring. He was annoyed by their ill-concealed malice.

"Look at him," said Woodpecker. "He swears at me although he almost crushed my toes. The ugly toad!"

Marmulstaub blanched. Helplessly he stared after Woodpecker, who had easily penetrated the thick throng of people who had frustrated his efforts at finding the girl. But that did not hurt him any more. That nickname should not have been uttered. He felt sick.

He turned away from the swarming crowd and the syncopated music, accompanied by the wild shouting of the youths who performed all the town's calls and ditties.

He sought to escape from this noisy outer world into the silence of introspection. He no longer perceived the multitude around him and the din—he was quite alone. Now he could ponder the dreadful incompatibility of his own spiritual system and the surrounding world. His was an elevated spirit, the others were rabble. He had the pleasure of something that was infinitely removed from this moment and this town, not only in time or distance.

He did not hear any further derisive echoes. He only felt the cooler air brought here by the wind from the river Oder, and, automatically and without thinking, he put on his jacket. Closing his large, dark violet eyes, he listened to the music that gushed forth on strings of infinite delicacy inside him, a minute web of tones and a wave of images.

6

"Out of the way!" shouted the First Officer as he pushed through the crowd.

He returned to the square. Physical contact with people repelled him. He felt a temptation to pull out his pistol and shoot his way through the throng.

"Make way, you scum!" he yelled. "Do you hear?"

He had to find that fat pig of a Marmulstaub because the commandant had no one of lesser rank handy, and the dispatch rider had taken the car to deliver those grub papers! And, to crown it all, Marmulstaub was neither at the Council of Elders nor at his home.

"Get away from here!" he yelled. "All of you!"

Then he climbed on to the wooden rail that surrounded the Ghettoswingers.

"Shut up!" he shouted.

And he found that they obeyed him at once, even though he had not even turned round to face them.

"Marmulstaub to me!"

Marmulstaub stood a little farther off. He raised his eyes from the ground and lifted an arm. His small, white palm dangled in the air. He gathered himself together quickly. The darker green uniform, different from that worn by the gendarmes, had frightened him.

The First Officer had already seen him. So he was here, after all, he thought. Satisfied, he climbed down again, motioning the band to resume playing. They did so immediately. You had to yell at the Jews, he told himself. Then they understood.

Marmulstaub's eyes roved the crowd. Was there really only malice in the faces which he passed? Perhaps not, he thought. But he could find no sympathy anywhere. And yet, he told himself, a little while ago they had all but kissed his feet, every single one of them.

Herr von Holler's First Officer was waiting for him by the railing, and nobody knew why. Lo, Marmulstaub meditated, there was the Book of Life open in front of him. What would he read in it if it were pushed under his nose? What did the icy reserve which he felt all round him mean?

He stopped at a distance which he felt the officer would consider respectful enough and bent in a deep bow. In his head, which was approaching the dust of the pavement, he weighed everything he knew about himself against his estimate of what the others knew, those others who were watching him now. Even thus, with his forehead to the ground which he preferred to look at rather than the uniform (for, in spite of everything, a German uniform still inspired fear in him), even thus he felt his own terrible lack of security.

Yet there was consolation in the knowledge that between the lines of human thought there was always a space in which one could read differently. Marmulstaub slowly straightened himself. Not for a moment did he contemplate revenge against his Jewish town for the hostility he divined behind his back. Did those who did not find his efforts useful want to see his head roll in the dust? Did they wish this through a desire for justice? Or through envy?

He saw his two hands. Well, they were clean, he told himself with satisfaction. Clean. And yet—he thought as he resumed a completely upright posture—and yet they had hung on him an invisible reproach. That nickname . . . And when they feared trouble a while ago, they had bent their gaze on him. And none of them could deny that the well-nigh imperceptible favor shown him by Herr von Holler—so scantily shown at that—was a useful drop in the insignificant ocean of other people's actions.

"If you please," he said. "I'm at your service, Herr Kommandant Stellvertreter!"

It occurred to him that perhaps he would not even be required to go with the First Officer, in which case the humiliation would be transformed into an honor, for it would mean that this German officer had had to come and find him in order to have a word with him.

"Don't babble!" barked the officer. "Come on, you're coming with me!"

"May I ask where to, sir?"

"To the commandant's office."

"On foot?" he inquired politely.

Nevertheless he felt that he could no longer save anything in the eyes of the crowd.

"Naturally on foot, Jew!" said the officer, shaking his head slightly in astonishment and spitting disgustedly.

"*Jawohl,*" replied Marmulstaub apathetically.

"Stop your chatter and get along!"

But Marmulstaub was not thinking of the reason for this call from the commandant. To that extent at least he was calm. And, as always when anything was about to happen, his mind now fixed again on the vision from which he was forcibly torn only by the external interruption of the officer. Carpets in a long, silent corridor. Then he saw a city within a city, far removed from the hubbub of life, or rather its present travesty. A citadel of the spirit. A place surrounded by Rome.

"This way!" shouted the officer.

"At your service, sir," replied Marmulstaub.

Undisturbed, his imaginings dwelt on in that place. He was a librarian there, sorting out Judaic documents.

The echoes of distant melodies once again ceased to touch him. Let the music which he had raised for the town out of the commandant's very bones and sinews play on without him! He would remain, as hitherto, merely the initiator of everything. A hawser. A lever. Let others tug and pull, but there had to be something else, as well: a traction force, a firm point.

He found that at this moment he was quite well disposed toward that offensive nickname. Almost as though it did not belong to him.

"Terribly hot today, wasn't it?" he addressed the officer amicably. "But now it is getting a little cooler at last."

"Who asked for your opinion, you stinking Jew?" replied the officer furiously. "Get a move on! Faster!"

Marmulstaub noted with satisfaction that Herr von Holler's second-in-command continued to use the formal mode of address, and he stepped out a trifle quicker.

"I'm coming," he answered calmly, adding guilelessly: "Surely we needn't hurry so."

7

The commandant motioned him to a chair and spoke quite affably. He had immediately dismissed his deputy, so that they were alone in the office. He sensed the disquietude of the man in front of him, and he therefore began the interview more mildly than he had intended.

"The ghetto, I hear, is indulging in wild music," he said.

"In moderation, Excellency," replied Marmulstaub.

"Then that's all right," said the commandant.

"Certainly, sir," nodded Marmulstaub. He waited for what was to come. He was sure something was coming, and was prepared to disarm the commandant by prompt acquiescence to everything he might want, in order to avoid any unpleasantness. But the other uniforms he had met earlier that day had weakened him. He knew he was trembling.

"Have you seen Löwenbach?" Herr von Holler asked him.

"No, I haven't," he replied.

"That's just the point," said the commandant. "You should have paid more attention to him."

Marmulstaub's anxious eyes searched the commandant's sinewy face.

"I don't understand, Excellency," he quavered.

"Don't be frightened," added the commandant. "For the time being he is still alive and well."

He stopped speaking. Marmulstaub went on trembling.

"I gave him your lists to sign, and he refused. You know that we don't like that sort of thing. Quite apart from the fact that these are to be labor transports, and all of them are to come back to us."

"I am not frightened," whispered Marmulstaub.

"You will deputize for Löwenbach. That's why I wanted to speak to you."

"It is too great an honor, sir," said Marmulstaub, who had grown completely pale.

"Don't be so modest!" said the commandant.

"And Mr. Löwenbach?" he asked quickly. "Has anything happened?"

"I trust he will agree. For the present he is here, downstairs. Let's hope he's not too cold. However, I cannot guarantee it."

The red color which had meanwhile begun to return to Marmulstaub's fat cheeks vanished at once. He had been right in thinking that there were unpleasant things coming. He was now equally sure that this was still not the end of it. The uniform. He had known, hadn't he, that if Herr von Holler were in uniform, it would all be so much the worse. But if Löwenbach was under arrest, what then? All of a sudden he caught sight of the commandant's narrow eyes and knots of muscle, and he understood: the signature!

"I can't deputize for him," he whispered. "The gentlemen of the Council haven't approved the nomination."

"Don't talk rot! We are not Parliament!"

"I only ventured, Excellency. . . ."

"We are going downstairs now to ask Löwenbach if he agrees. I have some business there anyway. I'm only waiting for my guest to arrive." He glanced at his watch, adding: "But there's still time."

"For God's sake, no, Excellency," murmured Marmulstaub, trembling.

"What are you afraid of?"

"I . . . I am not afraid, Excellency."

He saw what was going to happen as clearly as if it were actually taking place before his eyes. The man from Berlin would incite the commandant, and vice versa. In the end, Löwenbach would agree to anything. And he, Marmulstaub, was to be present.

"A transport is being prepared on the basis of these lists, sir," he began.

"Only preparations are being made at present."

"And Mr. Löwenbach's signature . . . is that so necessary?"

"As far as I am concerned, no," said the commandant.

"I see," whispered Marmulstaub, feeling a wild, secret joy at the thought that these tendons and knots of muscle were not omnipotent. There was something that had authority over them.

"And then, it is necessary that things should be done the proper way," Herr von Holler went on. "As you know, we have a visitor here. I don't want anything to be missing."

"And may I ask if there is anything that you miss?" asked Marmulstaub cleverly. All at once he felt calmer.

"Your notes, for instance," came the crushing reply.

"I took the liberty of supposing, Excellency, that you preferred me to give you my views by word of mouth."

"How am I to interpret that?" said Herr von Holler. "As mistrust? Is that what you wish me to read into it?"

"No, sir, no! Please!"

It came to Marmulstaub for the second time that he would have to give in, or the commandant would have him dragged down to the cellar to join Löwenbach. And he saw that this blackmail would continue until he pulled out his fountain pen. His joy at the unknown authority of his imagination dissolved before the muscular and sinewy face of the commandant.

And yet he decided, in the shadow of the preceding admission of Herr von Holler, to reveal the only thing he knew.

"Excellency, Mr. Löwenbach intimated to me that perhaps not all the transports would be labor ones, and that they were not to return."

"That's why he is in the cellar!" The commandant rose abruptly to his feet.

Marmulstaub felt uneasy sitting down. Still, he said to himself, it worked. His trump card. He got up from his seat, too, now, feeling sad. After all, when it was by word of mouth he had never refused this fellow anything.

"Yes," he said quietly.

"That is nothing but swinish propaganda. We punish that here. You know how."

"Certainly, Excellency. I would myself take measures if it were to spread to the ghetto."

"That sounds better, Marmulstaub," muttered Herr von Holler. "The cellar is big and very cold. It is full of rats. I should hate to see you there, too."

"Thank you," whispered Marmulstaub.

The commandant sat down again, leaving Marmulstaub to stand.

"Prepare everything for an inspection of the town," he said. "I don't want to come across anything that is not in order."

"In what way, sir?"

"I wish to take my guest round the town. There's going to be trouble if I find anything wrong!"

Marmulstaub, however, was convinced that this was only the commandant's new ruse to get him to sign. The slight pleasure he had felt at his revelation and at the commandant's having risen from his chair—as well as at the fact that he still had not signed—was gone. At the same time he felt a sharp disappointment at the realization that Herr von Holler was not trembling under the threat that he, Marmulstaub, might tell someone in a position to investigate the matter that the transports were not coming back, while his own body trembled violently at a mere hint from the commandant that he might be put among the rats. With him it was all completely different.

"I had a short list of defects, sir, to which I have for some time been meaning to draw your attention." And Marmulstaub began to search his pockets.

"But you no longer have it," said the commandant with chilly, almost indifferent scorn.

"I must have put it somewhere . . ." said Marmulstaub defensively.

After a short pause he added: "I'll find it by tomorrow."

If only the commandant did not have his uniform on, he would be easier to talk to.

"That's all," said Herr von Holler. "Have you a pen?"

"I have," Marmulstaub whispered, "my oral consent, Excellency . . . ?"

"You can keep that!"

The scraping of the nib could be heard distinctly in the silent office.

"May I go now, Excellency?"

"Don't you want to have a word with Löwenbach?" asked the commandant, and he suddenly felt a strong urge to burst into laughter. If he did take the fat man down, he would surely fall apart, the coward. And then that dwarf from Berlin would think he wasn't fit even for the waxworks.

"I would prefer to go and look for those lists of defects," said Marmulstaub cautiously.

"Are you afraid of the rats? You fox!"

"No, sir," replied Marmulstaub. "Not of the rats."

"Löwenbach wouldn't bite you," laughed Herr von Holler. "All right, you can go." And then he added, "Is it true what your wise men say, that he who touches is touched?" and smiled again. "Oh, you always want back with the caveman, don't you?"

The blood came back into the face of the man in the black overcoat so rapidly that the commandant could not keep back an amused smile. But it was not a pleasant smile; it was just as unpleasant as his whole sinewy, muscular, and highly colored face. Better get rid of him, he thought. He was sure to shit in his pants if he was forced to attend the interrogation. And that, if you please, was his pet Jew, his exhibit! He had secured such a name for him. Had even ensured that he would be the last to go. Perhaps he had really overrated the fat man's usefulness.

Marmulstaub was filled with an immense relief. But in spite of that relief, from somewhere inside him (where his imaginings created the vision of a pair of hands—someone else's hands and yet somehow also his own—clasped together, fine, white, and unsoiled) a feeling of sadness was conveyed to his consciousness, sadness at the fact that he had signed after all. That his signature would remain for all time, and that someone might see how he had helped himself out of trouble. Still, he was happy to see that he enjoyed the commandant's confidence. And happy that he need not be present when Herr von Holler took his guest down to the cellar to Löwenbach. And that he was allowed to leave by himself.

He returned to the town. On the road he met the two gendarmes whom he had already encountered earlier that afternoon.

"Your obedient servant, gentlemen," he greeted them, and pulled out his pass.

"Well, well," said the smaller gendarme to the other, "the gentleman is on foot."

"And what about the carriage?" jeered the taller one. But he was only speaking to his companion.

They took no notice of his pass.

8

A man from Marmulstaub's office stopped him at the intersection of the main L Avenue and the highway.

"Mr. Marmulstaub," he began, "have you also heard that there will be new transports?"

"No," he replied in a friendly voice, "I haven't heard that."

He felt a sudden twinge of regret for this town. Tomorrow, perhaps, it would already begin to shake in its foundations. He had had to lay before Herr von Holler lists of people which concerned almost half of the whole town. He decided to be merciful and to keep back as much as possible. Mustn't torment them.

"They say that Mr. Löwenbach has not returned from the *Kommandatur*," the man went on. "He refused to sign something, they say."

"I know nothing about that," said Marmulstaub curtly. "Did he say anything about it before he left?"

"They say he did," said the man. "What do you think—about the transports?"

"I don't know," he repeated.

"And Löwenbach—will he come back?"

"I don't know," he muttered darkly.

"Did they put him in the cellar?"

"Man," said Marmulstaub, "are you interrogating me or what?"

"Someone said," the clerk continued remorselessly, "that they would be labor transports."

"I tell you I don't know, man, I don't know, really," Marmulstaub tried to ward off further questioning. "If I knew, I'd tell all of you in time. Everything."

"And what about our women?" the man rambled on.

"I don't know!"

"Will they come too?"

"Leave me in peace, will you!"

And he walked on, fearing all the time that he would be bothered again.

The Ghettoswingers were still playing in the square, but only a few people remained to listen. These young greenhorns, Marmulstaub thought, were always carefree. Youths like that one in the afternoon. Nothing ever happened to them. It was because they had no feeling of responsibility, he said to himself. Irresponsible in everything and always. He suddenly felt envy toward Woodpecker, whose face he now pictured in his mind, but whom he did not know, and he wished he could, by some process of reincarnation, assume the irresponsibility of that longish, semichildish face with its expression of impudent innocence and swear at people, calling them frogs and toads. Where could he possibly have put that list of defects which he had thought to remove in cooperation with the commandant's people in the interests of this very town? Could he use this to redeem himself? No, he thought, that was impossible. Löwenbach had thrown the glove too insolently and too far. He would have to pick it up. Then it crossed his mind that it was bad luck that the commandant had had to think of him, of all people. Still, his hands were clean, because Herr von Holler had to call *somebody*. It might just as easily have been someone else. If it came to anything, he would have to be forgiven. Yes, his hands were clean. He began to pity Löwenbach. He remembered the mention of the rats. Even his thoughts were unsoiled.

He felt tired. Something seemed to weigh him down and choke him. Sad and depressed, he thought of sending for little Liselotte. She had rejected him in the afternoon, but now, now he could send for her as the deputy of former chairman Löwenbach. He entered his house and called a servant.

9

Here they called Liselotte Lizzy. She was sitting in Room 20 of the youth dormitory at 710 Q Street.

When Woodpecker had called for her and told her that tomorrow they would be saying good-bye to the Fortress and that they would like to see her before they went, she put on a jacket and came with him.

"I know it already," she said. "The sparrows on the roof are chirping about it."

"Fine, Lizzy," he murmured.

"Where are we going? To number 20?"

"That's right, Lizzy," he said.

"All right then. Let's go," she replied. She had the feeling that somewhere something was about to end today. She could see no reason why she should refuse. She had refused once before today—in the square that afternoon. The fat fellow, first among those who knew how to make life pleasant for themselves even here and who, she was sure, would always manage to make life pleasant for themselves.

With the agility of a cat she climbed on to one of the top bunks, let her legs swing down, and whistled to herself as she saw the boys' eyes licking her calves. She had been here on several other occasions, but never had there been so many boys.

"Here, some pancakes for you, Lizzy," said Woodpecker. They ate, washing the food down with water which they all called rum.

"You've used too much garlic," criticized Lizzy, her mouth full.

"Not us," said Woodpecker, adding: "The social worker made them for us."

"Who's that?" asked Lizzy, and climbed up again.

"Oh, that's a woman," Woodpecker laughed, "who gives you a lot of advice, and if you have the runs, she hides your lunch—in her own stomach. Understand?"

"But she's got to be pretty ugly," interjected Mylord, "or she wouldn't take the job."

"Well, gents," cut in Tramp, "tomorrow night hardly half of us will be here. And quite possibly not a single one."

He jumped up next to Lizzy and put his arm round her shoulders.

She looked at him in surprise and threw away a toothpick she had in her hand.

But then she understood without having to ask.

"Hey, Tramp," called Mylord, the Ghettoswingers' first trumpet player, "give Lizzy our best wishes."

Then they started to talk in whispers.

Tramp pulled the blanket so that it hung down like a curtain across his bunk.

"Throw us up that rum!" he demanded.

Woodpecker threw him a bottle of water. All they saw was Tramp's hairy hand as it stretched out, caught the bottle, and vanished.

The Kid sat by himself a little apart from the others.

Having earlier distributed the contents of a parcel he had received from his parents, he was now reading a letter admonishing him to look after himself and to come home in good health.

Tramp jumped down.

Lizzy was drinking; they could all hear the water gulping in her throat.

When Mylord climbed down she began to sing.

"Not bad," commented Mylord. "Woodpecker's turn."

Woodpecker heard how they all accompanied Lizzy's singing, and he continued to hum to himself even when the others had stopped.

I'll get me a new pair of skates
or behind a nunnery's gates
unburden my heavy heart.

Then everything was just that song.

"How about a break?"

Woodpecker was back with the others.

"Don't be silly," called out Lizzy. "Later."

Woodpecker was fastening his trousers with a piece of string. The song kept sounding in his ears. There was everything in it. Something that was behind him and something a long way ahead. And also this moment. He tied a knot on the string.

One by one the boys climbed up and, after a while, clambered down again.

The Tramp bowed in front of the Kid.

"For God's sake, how many more?" said Lizzy in a thick voice.

"She's a bitch!" said Woodpecker under his breath, "but she has staying power."

"Christ's sake, Lizzy," pleaded Mylord. "You wouldn't let the Kid go away immaculate, would you?" Then he added: "He is just fourteen today!"

The Kid was terribly bashful.

"All right, then. Him and no more," said Lizzy hoarsely.

"I don't want to," said the Kid quietly.

"Don't be silly," Mylord exhorted him.

"Such an opportunity, you silly little punk," said Woodpecker loftily.

"Sure," said Tramp. "Such an opportunity!"

"But I don't want to," repeated the Kid.

And then, while he undressed and pulled himself up on to the bunk and breathed heavily, Woodpecker, Mylord, Tramp, and the others called out to him in encouragement.

And the Kid did not even notice that Lizzy had not stopped humming.

Afterwards, she went out into the corridor to have a wash.

"Don't make a noise," Woodpecker warned her.

Then they sat her in their midst, feeling very masculine as they embraced her with a proprietary air which they had just earned the right to adopt, and they sang about the nunnery and the skates.

Lizzy stroked the Kid's head.

Then she combed his hair, and no one laughed to see it.

"Shall I see you home?" asked Woodpecker. "We're going to pack." Then he added: "We got these things ready for you before you came."

And they began to fill her pockets with all sorts of things.

"We couldn't take it with us, anyway," murmured Woodpecker. "So why let someone else grab it?"

The things included towels, combs, hairbrushes, and various odds and ends such as a darning kit and jars. At first she tried to refuse, but then she took everything they gave her.

When she was downstairs, they threw a fine quilt after her.

"That's from the Kid," chuckled Woodpecker.

"Thanks!" she called.

"Bye-bye, Liz!"

"See you!" she replied.

And as she went home, loaded with the boys' gifts, she felt just as sad as she had before, when Woodpecker called for her.

10

"Well, Kid," said Woodpecker harshly, "didn't kill you, did it?"

The Kid bowed his head. Taking a pencil out of his knapsack, he began to scribble a postcard to his parents.

"You can sleep with me tonight," continued Woodpecker. "One blanket will do for us both."

"Why did you have to throw just his woolen one after Liz?" Mylord asked him.

"Well, he had to pay something, didn't he?"

"Let me alone," spoke up the Kid. "I don't mind."

He sat on the stool and wrote.

Woodpecker and Mylord left to say good-bye at L 410.

The others also disappeared, and the Kid was left all by himself.

Dear parents, he wrote, *we're leaving for somewhere, but please don't worry, I am grown up now.*

He counted the words: fourteen. Almost half the permitted number.

They call me Kid and everyone is nice to me.

That was twenty-four. Another six to go.

I'll write again as soon as possible.

He crossed out "as soon as possible," writing only "soon" instead, and signed his name.

For a time he just sat there as if carved out of wood.

Then he carried the card out into the corridor and pushed it into the mailbox.

But he did not come back.

First he stood a long while next to the mailbox, and then huddled himself in a corner against the wall, wishing it had not happened; or that he might be going somewhere else than with Woodpecker, Tramp, Mylord, and the others; that it was many, many years later; or that they were all dead; or at least that he himself were dead.

The wall was cold and grey. Someone had scratched all kinds of hieroglyphics on it. Why did they all say he was grown-up now? What was it that had changed? Was that all it was? He gazed into the bowl of the sink on the wall, the disappointment he felt darker than night. And his parents were far, far away. His mother. A cramp took hold of him. The slippery white basin fascinated him. Then he began to vomit.

II

The servant waited for Liselotte until nine. When he had returned the first time to report no success and Marmulstaub had ordered him to go back and bring her even if he had to wait till midnight, all thoughts of tasting his master's tidbit for himself left him.

"Find out immediately where she is!" said Marmulstaub angrily.

That was something his servant was unable to do. None of the women who lived in the same room with Liselotte knew where she was to be found.

"You can't wait for her here," they said. "This is a woman's dormitory."

He felt too embarrassed to put any more questions to them and he could not explain anything. Marmulstaub would never forgive him if he did that.

So he settled down in the corridor and waited. The tower clock chimed the half-hour. Half past nine.

No one appeared in the corridor all this time, only an old woman, unable to sleep, had once walked past.

"Shameless creature!" she spat at him. "Don't you know what's in store for us?"

Completely taken aback, he gasped for breath. The old woman judged him with a glassy stare.

Then all was silence. The clock chimed ten. At that moment he saw the girl.

"Where have you been all this time?" he called in a muted voice. "You're not allowed out after eight, and my master is waiting for you."

"Your master?" she asked in surprise. "Who's that?"

"Mr. Marmulstaub," he said.

"Your master can kiss my ass," she blurted out.

With a somewhat weary agility she opened the door with her elbow.

"Couldn't you lend a hand?" she suggested.

The servant held the door for her.

Liselotte threw the things she had brought with her under her bed. Relieved, she unmade the bed, not intending to go out anymore.

The servant stood in the open doorway, appraising her with his eyes.

She paid not the slightest attention to him now, and climbed into bed.

This roused him to anger.

"I'll give him your message, woman," he muttered, enraged, the first words that came into his head. "But on your own head be it!"

She made no reply. With a tired but at the same time determined gesture she pulled the blanket right up to her throat.

"Well?" whispered the servant.

"And you too!" she flung at him.

"What!" he said in a raised voice. "You vessel of impudence."

"Be quiet!" hissed someone.

"Unheard of!" added the servant as he closed the door carefully behind him.

He had seen the uselessness of his efforts already at nine o'clock. Now he walked back wondering fearfully whether it would be enough to say—if someone stopped him in the street—that he had not been out on his own behalf, but upon the order of the new deputy chairman of the Council of Elders, Ignatz Marmulstaub.

Mouselike, he crept along the house walls.

Luckily no one saw him. The ghetto was asleep.

12

"Go to bed," said Marmulstaub sleepily. "It's official business, and we'll settle it tomorrow."

But he himself could not go to sleep. Although he tried hard to direct his thoughts to Liselotte or at least to the lost list of defects, something impelled him to dwell on the events of the afternoon. There in the darkness in front of him he saw, like a pair of ghosts, the SS uniforms of Herr von Holler and his second-in-command. And then he saw Löwenbach. In his imagination he was stifled by the dungeon in the cellar. Where could he have lost that list? In his mind's eye he also saw the small queer man in civilian dress who had accompanied the commandant the day before yesterday. Why did Herr von Holler wait for him last night? Did he perhaps want to take him down to see Löwenbach? He felt his forehead. He was sure he had a temperature. His pulse was racing. And his heart. What was he afraid of, he asked himself, why was he afraid? He must not breathe so loud. The sound of his own breathing frightened him. Heavily he rolled over on the bed. With the palm of one hand he wiped his forehead and both cheeks. He swallowed with difficulty. He had pulled out his handkerchief several times during the afternoon, it occurred to him. And in the carriage he had even taken his jacket off. Yes, that was it, in the carriage! Before that tall, gangling lout threw that word in his face. He was suddenly firmly convinced that he had seen the blue envelope with the folded octavo sheets lying on the purple seat. He concentrated on this thought with a physical effort, and felt perspiration ooze out all over his body and his pulse pumping crazily. Confused, he swallowed whole mouthfuls of saliva. He mustn't give in to the fever. But the more he thought about it, the more certain he was that he really had left the list there. And since that afternoon interview with Herr von Holler forced its way to the forefront of his consciousness, he conceived the idea of linking his tour of inspection with his own intention of taking a look at the shop where they were repairing the carriage, at the faded and torn purple of the seat, or of making inquiries of whoever was repairing it. But he was unable to make that the focal point of his thoughts. Still he saw his signature, even if illegible, on the list from which the transport was to be assembled. Why had Löwenbach not signed the thing? Again he wiped the sweat off his face. He ought to have known that he could not make himself an obstacle in the path of a man such as von Holler. If for nothing else—if for nothing else!—he deserved to be punished. Fool. Why didn't he see that himself? For Marmulstaub had exonerated him in every other respect.

13

"Nobody's going anywhere," said Woodpecker at eight in the morning. "I asked downstairs. It was all a lot of talk."

His way took him past the fence, on the other side of which two gendarmes were going on duty. They looked familiar to him, but he did not realize that he had seen them the day before in the square. The taller one bent down to the other and was speaking away at him. Woodpecker did not even turn to look after them. He only saw that they entered the gate of the German *kommandatur*. What might they want there, he wondered idly, but then he forgot all about them.

So nothing had happened.

Just a panic, that was all.

But there was yesterday. Remember, how he had got out of repairing that carriage? And Lizzy and the Kid. And there had been something in the air, something that said that nothing mattered, that he need not fear anything. At least inside him, right inside. An experience, a real experience for life, as Tramp was fond of saying.

Yesterday's ditty about the skates and the nunnery came into his head. Tam-ta, tam-ta, tam . . . He could not get rid of it, its every note conjuring up for him a picture of yesterday's evening with all the details of their leave-taking at 410. But over and above all, those moments before it.

He began to imagine how next Thursday the wild melodies would again come pouring out of their trumpets. That was life. One day life was going to be just that and nothing else.

The workshop welcomed him with the grey pounding of hammers and the bluish hissing of flames above the blacksmith's bellows. He put on his leather apron, thinking disgustedly that he had in front of him an entire afternoon on that damned carriage.

"Good thing you're here," the blacksmith greeted him. "That's it, don't give way to panic. Have you heard the whispers up your way?"

"I should say so," replied Woodpecker.

"Well, it's possible, my boy," added the blacksmith, speaking more quietly, "that it's going to be said out loud. And that it will be true. But even then we won't land on our asses."

"I couldn't care less if we do go," said Woodpecker as he laid both the axles of the coach on the ground in front of him. "At least I'll get to know something new."

"That's what I say, kid. It seems to me you know a thing or two already—such as girls—or perhaps a good feed?"

"Not that," said Woodpecker, going red in the face. Did they perhaps know about Lizzy, he wondered.

"Here, take a look at this, you scamp," said the blacksmith quietly.

Woodpecker glanced at the paper the other held out to him, and in the relief which he immediately felt he almost blurted out that that was nothing, that he had the same or something very similar at home, and that it was his duty to pass it on to someone else just as the blacksmith himself was doing. And that his paper said exactly the same thing—that the Allies were giving the Germans a beating. He breathed a sigh of relief. Nothing about Lizzy then.

"What does it say?" he asked, and read perfunctorily: "Death to the Fascists . . ." Then his voice fell, with disappointment as much as relief, and he looked at the blacksmith. "I know this."

"Hide it," murmured the blacksmith, adding: "Well, I have to run along, kid. Let me know, won't you."

"Sure," Woodpecker said with a laugh, patting the pocket into which he had thrust the leaflet.

He lit the fire, and as he pumped the bellows he watched the bluish flames swell up into the air and to either side. His mind was fully occupied elsewhere—there was yesterday, and now there was this leaflet, all of it rousing in him the notion that somewhere behind a barrier there was life waiting for him and putting out its tentacles to reach at him with these events. His fantasies found form in the flickering flames.

"Well, boys," said the blacksmith when he came back a few moments later, "there's no mistake about it: the old gentleman, Mr.

Löwenbach, hasn't come back. Something's up. Maybe a transport."

And he left again immediately.

"He's going to scout round for news," muttered the other black-smith, who was usually in charge of the workshop in his absence, "until . . ."

Woodpecker waited, curious to know what the blacksmith was going to say.

But the other was silent, while Woodpecker reflected that the whole thing was probably not so terribly serious. Again he saw everything in the fire: Lizzy, pressing Mylord's hand, and the Kid, crouching on his stool and writing. Yesterday seemed to disappear in the transparent flames which now held a bluish promise of better things to come: everything would change when Russia and England with America defeated Germany and Lizzy would walk along the street with her children and nobody would stop her. And the Kid would ride a junior bicycle and his parents would wrap him up in cottonwool because they wouldn't know any better.

He raised his eyes. Rot, he thought. Nothing but dreams. Better think about getting Lizzy to come to number 20 again one of these days.

14

The doors of the blacksmith's shop flew open violently.

"Attention!" shouted the blacksmith, who was standing by the door, with great presence of mind.

Englebert von Holler, SS, and his civilian companion entered the workshop, all of whose occupants tensed expectantly.

"At ease! Carry on work!" said the commandant.

The first thing that came into Woodpecker's mind was to put his hand in his pocket and throw the leaflet in the flames. But before he could move, two other SS men and the two gendarmes, the tall one and the small one, whom he had met that morning, came into the shop. Damn, said Woodpecker to himself. What a mess!

The taller of the two gendarmes took up a position directly behind Woodpecker. He instantly recognized the loud-mouthed boy of yesterday afternoon, and again felt an urge to box his ears. Just like that, more in a fatherly fashion now than anything else. Yesterday he could not have imagined the tanned hooligan in a leather blacksmith's apron such as the one he had on now, standing there so strangely silent.

"Where's the foreman?" asked the commandant, without much interest.

"I am substituting for him," said the blacksmith. "He's working outside." Scouting round for news, that was what he was doing, he thought. And certainly a damn sight luckier than he was, even though he was so very careful about everything.

"Stop that hammering!" shouted the small man beside Herr von Holler.

The workshop grew quiet, and Woodpecker wondered how this would end. All of a sudden he saw it all as a sporting event, though, to be frank, it didn't look too good. It didn't look good at all. A real jam. Because he had that thing in his pocket and was unable to take it out and throw it away unobserved.

"Are you working on anything for us?" the commandant asked.

"Yes, Herr General," replied the blacksmith. "The fittings for the door of your Mercedes."

"I'm not a general, idiot! Don't you know the badges of rank?"

"No," stammered the blacksmith.

"What else?"

"Nothing—only the carriage . . . for Herr Marmulstaub."

"What carriage?"

"A creaking one, sir," faltered the blacksmith. But he did not mean it as a joke.

"Who is repairing it?"

"Woodpecker . . . I mean Mahler, sir."

"Stand aside! Woodpecker-Mahler to me!"

Woodpecker came up to him as slowly as he could. This is bad, he kept repeating to himself. This is bad. Although the distance separating him from the commandant was small, he shuffled along for what seemed to be a very long time. He had paled slightly, for it had occurred to him what the possible consequences might be. You are in a pretty pickle, boy, he seemed to hear the foreman say.

The small man standing beside the commandant cast a severe look at the tall gendarme behind Woodpecker. He understood at once what was expected of him, and he prodded the boy. He can take that in place of the box on the ears, he thought irritably, saying out loud:

"Get a move on!"

Herr von Holler had in the meantime turned to the small fellow.

"They're shaking like leaves in the wind. You can see for yourself. We have long ago liquidated the pigsty of tolerance here," he said with satisfaction in his voice. (Perhaps the tiny idiot had heard something about that already, he reflected.)

"Are you sure?" queried the small one.

"I think so," replied the commandant nonchalantly, thinking of the ruin that was Löwenbach last night and of the astonishment shown by the half-pint of a man at his elbow, who had after all not expected such an interrogation.

15

Woodpecker saw only the pair of eyes on a level with his face, the strangest eyes he had ever seen. They were narrow, green, all-knowing and able to look inside you. He also noticed the thin straight nose with nostrils slightly distended and overgrown with thick black hairs, as well as the ginger moustache above the compressed lips. But the muscular and sinewy face of the commandant escaped him, it seemed completely alien and incomprehensible. So this was his enemy. But he did not know as yet in what way they were to fight.

Herr von Holler held his short, silver-and-diamond-studded cane in a gloved hand. It shone, casting a dazzling aura around it.

"Mahler?" he inquired.

"Yes," nodded Woodpecker.

"Who is this brat who swaggers like this?" demanded the courier, though he saw quite clearly that the boy was far from swaggering— he was merely much taller. As soon as he heard the man's words, he bent his knees a little to make himself appear smaller.

"Would you mind lending me this?" asked the small man, pointing to the commandant's cane. Then he took it, gave a slight leap, and hit Woodpecker on the forehead.

"There, that's it," he said when Woodpecker bent farther still.

"Excuse me," said Herr von Holler, taking back his cane.

The boy's eyes wandered helplessly around the workshop. He had known this would happen, so what was he so surprised about, he reflected. He would pretend that it hurt him more than it actually did. Even so, he was in a mess. God, if Tramp or Mylord or the blacksmith could see him now! He must crouch down a bit more so as not to rile that runt of a man any more than necessary. Then they might think he was afraid and would not search his pockets. On the other hand it occurred to him, that was just the sort of thing they did. Well, he must be on his toes and wait.

The courier's eyes bored into him.

"What has he got on him?" he asked, but the question sounded as if it were addressed to the commandant.

"Do you smoke?" asked Herr von Holler, pretending not to notice the little man and looking as if the whole affair were beginning to amuse him.

"No," said Woodpecker.

"Turn your pockets out," the commandant ordered him. "It'll be too bad for you if I find the least scrap of tobacco!" And, turning to the courier, he added: "Tobacco, that's my specialty."

"You won't," said Woodpecker insolently.

"Take out everything," continued the commandant, "and turn them inside out."

So here it was, thought Woodpecker, this was it. As bad as he had imagined it would be. How was he to get out of this jam, how was he to fool them? Slowly he began to empty his pockets, turning round as he did so to prevent the commandant from seeing that he was leaving one pocket out. The fight was on. He would have to keep his wits about him if he was to get the better of those two. Or else it was going to be even worse than he had expected. Good job he had the apron on, he could at least pretend that it was difficult to get at the pockets.

"It seems that he doesn't smoke," said the commandant, amused.

"This one too!" barked the courier, and ripped the boy's apron off.

Woodpecker had kept his hand there too long. He saw now that he was losing the contest. With exaggerated slowness he pulled out his handkerchief. Or perhaps it was not so slow, after all. The whole thing seemed to him—certainly at this moment—more like a game of hide-and-seek. Then he took out his penknife and a lump of sugar he had brought for his break.

"Well . . ." said the commandant.

"He's got something there," snapped the courier.

"Let's have a look," said Herr von Holler, and put his hand in the boy's pocket.

Woodpecker went deathly pale. It struck him suddenly that this was no game, nor had it been right from the start. He was in for it now and no mistake. With everything included, and he had heard of the things they did to people. He was not likely to go home now, and, who knew, perhaps he would never go anywhere again. Perhaps, also, not even a fraction would come true of everything he had thought about such a short, and yet such a long, while ago—over the blue flames.

Herr von Holler unfolded the sheet of paper he had extracted from Woodpecker's pocket. His expression changed.

"So," he said as he passed the leaflet to the courier, "this kind of thing is being carried around here! After all my precautionary measures. Very well."

"Filth!" muttered the other after a moment, his small pig's eyes glowing with excitement.

Woodpecker now felt the eyes of all upon himself. The foreman was out. What was he to say, he wondered, when they asked him, as they were sure to do straight-away. He'd say something, but not the truth. *Just something.*

"Where did you get this?"

Here it was. They were asking already. Must he reply at once? His eyes searched the ground.

That damned fool, Marmulstaub, Herr von Holler swore to himself. Why the hell did he have to drag him here of all places?

"Well? Why don't you speak?"

"I don't know," said Woodpecker.

"How did you get hold of it?" hissed the courier. He leaped up and hit the boy in the face with his fist.

And then he was showered by blows from both of the men standing in front of him.

Suddenly it all seemed silly to him. He could not possibly tell them, surely they must see that for themselves. He just did not know. That was all the answer he could give them. They had no sense of fair play. He ducked a blow only to get another from the other side. (Now a tooth fell out.) If he acted differently, he thought, it would be a dirty thing to do. That brought him to the end of this chain of thought. There was no more to it, nothing more to be said. Perhaps they were going to beat him good and proper, he told himself, and then some more. And not only here and now. There were still the SS men and the gendarmes. But not even then could he blab. Well, could he? He could take it all right, he told himself (and swallowed a second tooth). After all, they could not beat him forever. They would get tired in time. But he would not. He could take more. Maybe he would soon stop feeling the blows even.

Then he was conscious only of the orange glow from the commandant's ring every time the fist came near his face. He was not going to blab, he thought once more, wearily. What would the foreman say if he did?

"Perhaps this would loosen your tongue," he heard Herr von Holler say menacingly.

Woodpecker saw a pistol in the commandant's hand. Well, the game was up, he told himself with finality. The game was up, and he had lost. Without being really aware of it, he clenched his teeth.

"Now will you talk, you bastard!" hissed the little man.

"Talk!" yelled Herr von Holler.

16

Marmulstaub puffed as he searched the smithy yard with his dark-purple gaze. At last he caught sight of his carriage, its wheels gone because Woodpecker had taken the axles into the workshop. With short steps he hurried to the carriage, feeling pleased both that he had brought the commandant here and that he would not have to climb up high. What was there that Herr von Holler could find amiss here? Nothing. On the contrary, Marmulstaub thought contentedly, here they were working for his garages! Clumsily he clambered up on the box. Once there, he saw the foreman on the other side, well concealed from sight and pretending to be examining the creaking springs.

"What're you doing here, man?"

"Mending your coach, dear sir," replied the blacksmith, irritated that the toad should be nosing about just here. He had seen him arrive with the commandant, but Marmulstaub had left him as the armed SS men entered the workshop. The blacksmith's anxiety about the boy in the smithy was transformed in the course of his conversation with the fat man into a blind fury. "What business is it of yours, anyway? What're you looking for? Or are you a Nazi, too?"

Marmulstaub ignored this outburst with the calmness of condescension. He did not even raise his eyes. "My carriage," he said. "All right. Didn't you by any chance find a blue envelope here?"

"No," replied the foreman, gazing questioningly into Marmulstaub's dark blue eyes.

"You are an insolent fellow," said Marmulstaub.

It suddenly struck the blacksmith that if the fat man were really looking for his envelope, this was an opportunity to call the boy out from the workshop.

"I'm sorry," he said quickly. "I'm a little nervous."

"Forget it," said Marmulstaub, and he climbed heavily to the other side. For forgetfulness, he thought, was the burying place of human folly in which all words and deeds were interred. With his small white hands he explored the purple seat right at the back.

"Somebody else was working here yesterday," said the foreman. "You can call him and ask him yourself."

The fat man suddenly seemed to change in his eyes, he seemed kind and almost gentle. And his word, thought the blacksmith, carried a lot of weight with the commandant. He implored him with a gaze.

"Who?" asked Marmulstaub. He could see that the other man was badly shaken by something.

"Ask for Woodpecker," came the eager reply. "He's there with them—in the workshop."

Marmulstaub climbed down without saying anything. He pulled his coat straight and cleaned his shoes. Then he disappeared behind the smithy door, and the foreman again hid behind the coach.

17

"Marmulstaub!" shouted the commandant as soon as the fat man entered. It was the second time that he had raised his voice. "You idiot! Where have you taken us?"

"Excellency . . ."

"Where have you brought us, you stupid ass? This is the limit! We are doing our best for you—a coffeehouse, and Catholic services on Sundays. Hostels for the children and music for the whores. And the lousy rebels' nest is not even being shelled. This is mutiny! Here, you read it!"

Marmulstaub caught the leaflet as it was thrown to him.

Then he noticed the boy; realizing in spite of his fear and confusion that it was the hooligan who had insulted him the day before. It was a wonder he had recognized him, though, seeing that the boy was bloody all over. So I haven't escaped it, thought Marmulstaub, only it is the boy instead of Löwenbach. He was still standing in front of the commandant in an extremely uncomfortable posture, bent almost double.

"I wouldn't give it to him, if I were you," said the little man in a quiet, irritated voice. "You are taking him too much into your confidence."

The commandant threw Marmulstaub an ominous look.

Marmulstaub remained as he was, undecided whether to read the leaflet or not.

The courier spat in front of him.

The fat man automatically took a step backwards. The commandant's greenish grey uniform with the silver epaulettes and the black skull and crossbones on the cap terrified him. His condition was aggravated by the sleepless night he had spent, by the suspense in which he had been until that moment of relaxation a little while ago, by the sight of the boy, and the diamonds on the commandant's cane, as well as by the pistol in his other hand.

"It is impudent," he said humbly. "I can only say, Excellency . . ."

Horrified, he looked at the boy and blinked his eyes. Why had this happened? After all, he had forgiven him that word.

"I have finished with you, Marmulstaub!" said the commandant. "The transport will leave tomorrow. You will put it together right now, from that rag you signed in place of Löwenbach." In the eyes of the fat man he saw an unspoken question. "Where to? You'll find out! Blockhead!"

"Excellency . . ."

"Don't babble! You'll go with them, you bloody fool, you idiot! You can piece Löwenbach together on the way. And tell this one to talk, or you'll be taking his corpse along tomorrow!"

"Yes, Excellency," whispered Marmulstaub.

But as he turned obediently toward the boy to urge him to speak, he saw in his eyes a glow that frightened him.

Woodpecker had suddenly begun to hate them all: the tiny man who had to spring up at him whenever he wished to hit him in the face, preferring therefore to beat him about the hips and thighs instead, and Herr von Holler, who had looked so mild at first, and the fat toad because he trembled and kept quiet. Woodpecker's hate now included even the foreman, who was the only one lucky enough to leave the smithy in time. All of a sudden the commandant lost his knotty and sinewy incomprehensibility. Everything around Woodpecker—the commandant's face and the faces of the others—merged into something bestial, something that bore only a faint and almost imperceptible resemblance to human countenances. He was seized by a desperate longing to return their blows, and his eyes sought that familiar piece of metal, the carriage axle he had been repairing.

And still Marmulstaub did not speak.

"Speak up, or I'll kill you!" threatened the commandant. "Who wrote it?"

"I did!" shouted Woodpecker wildly, his eyes having found the axle. "And the Russians and . . . ."

He jumped for the iron rod, bent down to the ground, and then straightened up again (he could not tell whether it took him long or not). He began to wave the axle furiously and thresh all around him, blindly, for he could not see for blood. At first his eyes misted only gradually, but then the scene in front of him seemed to dissolve into darkness and he saw nothing anymore. He heard a shot, then another. He closed his eyes. Opening them once more, he felt he could almost see the sharp points which penetrated his chest in countless places, and he forced himself to keep his eyes open a little longer. Grasping the axle more firmly in his hands (it was indescribably heavy now, yet at the same time without any weight at all) he struck with it where he thought he saw the commandant's cap.

Marmulstaub groaned. He had expected the second and third shots to be directed at him.

Both, however, ploughed into the body of the boy.

18

Just before eleven both the gendarmes, the tall and the small one, reported to Herr von Holler, who had a bandage on his head.

"Take both of them to the trucks!"

The cellar into which they had to descend to carry out the order was dark and filled with a heavy stench. Rats scurried about under their trouser legs.

"Out, quickly!" said the taller gendarme, and caught hold of Löwenbach's arm.

"I can't," he whispered.

"You must!" said the gendarme.

The smaller gendarme pushed his helmet to the back of his head and supported fat Ignatz Marmulstaub.

"Thank you," said Marmulstaub hoarsely.

"All right, come along!" said the small gendarme when they were outside.

In a few moments they were marching through the ghetto, a strange procession before which people stood aside, unwittingly forming a line on either side of the street.

On the left side, where Marmulstaub walked with downcast eyes, the people began to spit demonstratively, muttering among themselves in a menacing rumble. In their invective they, however, refrained from gesticulating, afraid that such gestures might be mistakenly thought by the gendarmes to be meant for them.

On the right side, where the taller gendarme half-dragged the pitiful wreck of a man, the pair was accompanied by commiserating glances.

They arrived at the "bigwigs'" house in which both of them lived. Although it was against Herr von Holler's orders, he having commanded that the two men be taken directly to the train, the gendarmes allowed them to go up to wash and change.

They waited outside, promenading up and down the pavement in front of the house.

"Hot, isn't it?" said the taller gendarme, his Adam's apple jumping wildly up and down his throat. "As bad as yesterday."

"It's been like this for almost a week now," replied the smaller gendarme. "How about going to the river this afternoon?"

Just at that moment the crowd which had gathered in the street made a dash for the house.

"Out, all of you!" shouted the tall gendarme. He managed to chase most of the intruders out.

"Have you gone crazy?" the smaller gendarme upbraided them as he waved others back from the staircase and through the passage into the street.

At last they succeeded in driving out everyone who had no business to be in the house, a small woman with a vividly painted face being the last to go. Marmulstaub was sitting on the floor, weeping and groaning.

"Come on, get up," said the taller gendarme.

"Thank you," said Marmulstaub hoarsely.

The tall gendarme nodded to his companion, indicating that it was time they were going.

Out in the street once more, he bent down to the smaller gendarme. "This infernal heat!" he said in a strangled voice.

"I don't mind it," replied the other wearily, pushing his helmet back from his forehead.

Soon they reached the railway station.

The Ghettoswingers stood assembled by the side of the train. They began to play, at a word of command from Herr von Holler, just at the moment when two SS men accompanied by the little man from Berlin were throwing Woodpecker's canvas-shrouded body into the last cattle-truck. They did not shut the truck's sliding door until David Löwenbach and Ignatz Marmulstaub had got in.

The trumpets screamed. Mylord pressed the mouthpiece to lips which were completely devoid of blood. The saxophones wailed a familiar melody:

We are becoming seasick,
An ill-fated crew are we.

Hope

Simon stopped at the foot of the stone staircase. The stairs exuded the chillness of the earth and the greyish reflection of the rainy day. Only a few moments ago he had assured himself that it was unnecessary to keep watch today, since the curfew was still in force. We're not allowed out, he kept saying to himself, and so no one will come in, either. But then he caught sight of Chana's eyes. He cast a quick, distrustful look at the figure of the old Jew from Essen, sitting there all hunched up as if to keep out the cold. And since it was his turn today, he at last picked himself up and went out.

He sat down underneath the small roof made out of old crates. His body moved every time he breathed, filling his lungs with the sharp, malodorous aftertaste of excrement and lime. His throat was constricted. He rocked automatically backwards and forwards and from side to side as though trying to extricate himself and to avoid the streaming rain. This movement told him that he was still capable of something—that he was capable of more than just sitting still. However, he was glad that nobody else knew about it: they couldn't ask more of him than of the old man from Essen. And yet, on the other hand, he longed to be able to let someone into the secret of his strength, and to have it appreciated.

Even now, when everything was deadened by the rain, the pungent smell of the courtyard seemed to him to be hostile. He must not move about so much. He counted how many more times he would have to come out here . . . three or perhaps five. But he would have to come down in any case, even if it were not for this . . . When he added together everything that seemed good to him, he again had that feeling, which he had already experienced yesterday, that he would witness something that he could not quite comprehend. He yearned for it, but at the same time he was afraid to think about it in case it vanished as soon as he got to the bottom of it.

Heedless of the rain which ran down his face, he looked up. He saw the tall buildings, overgrown with wilted ivy on walls covered with copper-colored and greenish mold. Somehow this house reminded him of the past.

Here and there a bluish crystal of light flickered through the rain. He inclined his head to one side. Soon he felt the damp even through his coat. It was too worn, it occurred to him, and he felt a constricting pity. But then he thought how lucky he was to have a coat at all—those up there, where an invisible cloud concealed everything that would probably take place tonight, or perhaps not till tomorrow, did not even have that. He crouched on his seat, watching the grey mass of cloud, which looked like dark, wet shadows. He still did not feel cold enough to have to leave. Crossing his arms over his chest, he kept his body as warm as he could.

A poster hung on the wall of the latrine:

Nicht vergessen
vor dem Essen . . .
die Hände waschen!

He stared for a moment at the black type. Then he tired of it. His eyes wandered over the glistening puddles. To anyone watching, it might have seemed that his eyesight was poor, for he suddenly started to rub his eyes with the backs of both hands. Or it might have seemed that he was crying. But Simon was not crying.

He walked away, going right through the middle of a puddle that had grown larger in the persistent downpour.

"You're back already?" Chana asked him in surprise.

"Don't worry," he replied. "Nobody's going to steal that dirty hole."

"Come and sit down," she said, adding: "Why, you're wet through, Simon. Don't you want to take your things off?"

"Aren't you cold?" she asked finally.

He was tired, and so he did not reply. He would have liked to strip everything off because the coat chilled him, but he sat down on the mattress as he was. For a moment he sat there, looking at Chana's hair. Fifty-two years ago, he reckoned in his mind, she had a small and bright black bun. That was the fashion in those days. He must not think of the cold so much, he said to himself.

"I'm not saying anything," she remarked after a while, seeing that he still did not make any reply but just sat, watching the water dripping from the tails of his coat to the floor. She was anxious in case anyone scolded him for not keeping watch outside, since it was his turn.

Simon was fully occupied with his thoughts. When he was close to Chana he always felt he was wronging her. He stroked her hair with a short, quick gesture. He felt as though he were saying goodbye. He narrowed his eyes in order to see only the dim outlines of the fantasies that were carried along, gossamer-like, on waves of thought based on his past life to somewhere in the future where no one could see. He was unable to tell her about this, yet equally unable to escape his imaginings.

He rose. "I must go down, anyway," he said at last.

And then he added: "But not for that."

"I know," she replied. But it took her some time before she understood.

Downstairs, Simon passed the wall with the poster hanging on it without looking at it. His coat was completely wet by now and it chilled him more and more.

The black and yellow colors underneath the skull and crossbones—the symbol of typhus—shattered his deliberate nonchalance. Good thing I didn't undress, he said to himself. He looked away, and stretched his hands out to the rain. Now, he thought, I am clean and safe again. But what if it stopped raining? The poster suddenly seemed to come to life—wherever Simon turned, he always saw the rain-soaked paper in front of him. He shivered. Then he turned and went in.

With considerable difficulty he withdrew his feet, wrapped in rags, from the rough, knotty clogs, which he found to be full of sticky mud. At any rate he could still stand quite a lot—he could, if need be, walk about like this for as long as an hour.

Dragging himself upstairs to Chana he breathed heavily and rapidly.

"Come and sit right by me," she said. "That'll warm you up."

"I got very wet in the rain," he remarked.

"Doesn't matter," she comforted him, and involuntarily moved a little to the side.

"Thanks," he said. "It's raining heavily today."

"It rained yesterday, too," she said. Then she took his numb hands in hers.

"Quiet there!" called out Mother Cohen, who was lying by the wall on the opposite side of the room. "We're still sleeping."

"We can talk, can't we," Simon said angrily. "I've been down twice already!"

Without saying anything he borrowed Chana's shawl and wound it round his waist. He felt a sharp twinge in the spot where his kidneys were. Never mind, he thought, something is bound to hurt when you are old. Well, in this case it was the kidneys. It was a single stab of pain each time, and it started first thing in the morning.

Simon's neighbor on the left, the desiccated Jew from Essen, who had amused himself all evening yesterday by counting the inhabitants of the house, now got up and stood by Simon's mattress, shifting from one foot to the other. But Simon did not say a word.

Suddenly the man from Essen caught sight of the puddle that had formed under the tails of Simon's coat.

"Ah!" he said. "It's raining, is it?"

Then, with a quick movement, he snatched the strong, gold-rimmed glasses from his nose and raised his arm, blinking his eyes shortsightedly as he did so.

"I'll trade them," he said excitedly, "for bread."

"But, man," Chana replied, "you won't be able to see if you do."

"And what is there for me to see, can you tell me?" the old man demanded irritably. "What should I look at? You perhaps?"

Simon started.

The man from Essen began to sob, strangely and convulsively, gazing all the while at the puddle by Simon's mattress. Then he interspersed his sobbing with disjointed, incoherent words. As he did not understand a single one of them, Simon did not think it necessary to comfort the old Jew from Essen.

"Oh, heavens," said Mother Cohen, "it's impossible to sleep in this place."

"Why do you keep grouching, then?" said Simon sarcastically. "And anyway, it's morning already."

"Men shouldn't cry," said Mother Cohen all of a sudden.

"No, they shouldn't," Simon agreed.

"I'm talking to your wife," retorted Mother Cohen.

"Simon isn't mangy," protested Chana.

"Did I say he was?" asked Mother Cohen.

"He was down for the second time a while ago," added Chana. "And he got wet through."

"But he doesn't cry," said Mother Cohen.

"Stop crying!" said Simon, turning to the Jew from Essen. They could not accustom themselves to the sound of a man crying.

"They're all like that in Germany," said Mother Cohen, "either they shoot or they cry."

Then she added: "Either you're doing some silly counting or you worry your head off."

"He isn't crying any more," said Simon.

"I wasn't crying," the man from Essen claimed.

"You were," Simon insisted.

"Leave him be," said Chana.

"Don't argue!" shouted Mother Cohen.

"What's the matter with you?" asked Chana, surprised. "What are you getting so excited about?"

"Hm," said Mother Cohen. And then: "My son arrived yesterday."

"Your son?" asked Simon. "You have a son?"

"Yes," she said.

"How old is he?"

"Forty."

"He is still young," said Simon.

"He'll still be able to find something, if he survives," added Chana.

The idea came to Simon suddenly that there were still people who had sons, and that they were in fact younger through having somebody. They, Chana and he, had no one, it occurred to him. Only he had those fantasies of his. And that, come to think of it, was perhaps even better, because Mother Cohen's son might leave or something might happen to him, whereas he could keep his fantasies, whatever happened.

"You must be glad . . ." said Chana.

"I don't know," replied Mother Cohen. "I've been expecting him."

"Well, you got your wish," said Simon.

"That's just the point," remarked Mother Cohen.

Simon understood—it should not have happened. But none of this should have happened to any of them. And he thought, "She should have told us yesterday already."

The flat-bottomed funeral cart arrived at noon. Somebody had cut off the wooden ornaments and knocked away the canopy on its slim, gilded pillars. The cart brought food and medicines.

A blond cook, about eighteen years old, exposed his bare chest to the rain, surveying everything from his frog's-eye view in the courtyard. In a white apron girded with a leather belt, his arms bare, he wordlessly filled the old men's mess-tins.

"What have you brought us?" Simon asked him. "The end of the war?"

"You don't want much, do you, Grandpa?" the cook retorted.

Simon felt that there was a great deal of contempt in those words, even after the young fellow produced an extra keg of groats. But he kept quiet for fear of not getting anything.

"You should give us the extra straightaway," he muttered.

"Why, you old so-and-so," said the cook, "I pinched this for you at my own risk. And what's more, I could keep it for myself if I felt like it." He spat in an arc over the heads of Simon and the man from Essen.

Simon walked up the stairs to Chana.

"I got some extra for you," he said.

"Groats with saccharine," remarked Mother Cohen. "Fine things they invented in Germany, I must say."

"You're a wonder, Simon," said Chana.

The man from Essen finished his meal first. "We've invented other things as well in Germany," he said. He had put his glasses on again.

He shouldn't take everything that's said about Germany so personally, thought Simon. Nobody said anything.

"We've given Germany everything we had," continued the old man from Essen. "In the war even our brains and our blood."

After a while he added: "Perhaps that was a mistake. But would you like to say that your whole life, and my life and the lives of so many other people, was a mistake? That maybe it wasn't life at all, but a sort of shadow, without form, without smell or taste, something empty and dead?"

All of a sudden Simon recalled everything he had thought about down there, when he was completely alone and reflecting on things that were far away and yet within reach.

"Anyway," he rebuffed the old man, "Hitler won't last." Strangely enough, he now felt that he had pleased him. He did not know himself what had made him say it. Even now he had to admit that this house, and the train which had brought him and Chana here, and the rails over which the train had rattled, and the gendarmes who had come to drive them out of their flat and later out of the trucks, and the wooden shack which he was to guard from daybreak to nightfall today—that all this acted as a prop for the man who was responsible for their being here on these mattresses. Was this perhaps the fruit of those interminable reflections down there, where he had tried to forget the squabbles and the idle bragging that went on within these four walls, where the frontier between fact and fantasy disappeared, and when he did not have to think all the time of the stabbing pains in his kidneys nor fear the weariness that he knew would come one day; where, on the contrary, the conviction gathered force that there was in him some power and hope that he, a human being of little account whose death, when it came, would be noticed by no one apart from Chana, still had a lot to learn. Now he looked at his rain-washed hand and started to count off on his fingers all the things he knew and all the things he did not know. And among those that he did not know there was something that was enormous and yet somehow familiar to him.

"And what if he does last?" asked the Jew from Essen. "What if he wins?"

"He won't," said Simon, thinking that perhaps he should not just leave it at that. It also occurred to him that the man from Essen considered himself more German than Jew and that injustice perpetrated by the country in which he had been born hurt him more than it did Simon and Chana.

"How could he win?" asked Mother Cohen, both anger and fear sounding in her voice. "Why do you listen to this nincompoop?" she added.

Chana was silent.

"He's fighting the whole world."

Simon, all of a sudden, had nothing to say.

"Simon," said Chana, "is your coat dry?"

"I think so," he replied.

Then they were all silent again. He could return to his thoughts of a few moments ago, the thoughts he had had yesterday and every time that there was silence in the room. He knew that he was with Chana and yet a long way away from her. Involuntarily he pressed his hand to his kidneys.

"Do you want your shawl back?" he asked.

"No, I don't," she replied.

"I'll give it back to you if you want," he repeated.

"No," she said, "I don't want it." And she thought: He is fighting the whole world—even the heavens.

Simon held her hand. She recalled snatches of conversation that ended in just such a silence. Here, she thought, in this room they had already had a morgue, a church, and a general staff.

Simon was eagerly playing with the tips of his fingers. She could not fail to notice this, as he had let go of her hand. His eyes took on a gleam that frightened her. He was counting the Allies on his fingers. And on the last he saw a country so large that he could not imagine it otherwise than as a bear. He saw it with an inner vision that was manifested outwardly only by the feverish luster of his eyes—saw it both as a small bear-cub and as an old, angry beast of prey, then as a she-bear determined to protect all her children. Automatically he clenched his hot hands into fists, giving up his count. He had only one wish—that the she-bear succeeded. Staring ahead absentmindedly, he opened his right hand and gazed at the tip of his little finger.

Chana was frightened. His eyes looked almost inflamed.

"Simon . . ." she began.

Receiving no reply, she repeated his name once more: "Simon!"

"Leave me alone," he said.

"Simon, I'm scared."

"Don't be," he said.

"But I am, and I don't know why."

"Don't be," he repeated.

"I am. For you."

"Don't be," he mumbled again.

And again there was silence.

The old man from Essen grew restless.

"Here we are waiting for supper," he said suddenly, "and they're not bringing it. That means that either they've left our house out or they're late. If they've left it out, it means that either the cook was offended because of those groats or he thinks we've had enough. Then there are again two possibilities: either he's on his way or he isn't and is taking time off at our expense. That means . . ."

"Stop it!" Mother Cohen interrupted him.

But then she added: "Come to think of it, it's true. It's pitch dark outside and supper nowhere. What time is it, actually?"

"Simon," said Chana, "I'm afraid for you."

"Perhaps he's not coming at all today," suggested Simon.

"I'm afraid for us," Chana repeated.

"After all, you've heard that nobody's allowed out today because someone was seen smoking on the ramparts," Simon went on.

"But they came at lunch-time," said the old man from Essen.

"So they did," replied Simon. He wanted badly to get back to those thoughts of his. But Chana would not leave him alone.

"Let me be," he said, "There's nothing the matter with me."

"Well, at least give me your hand."

The Jew from Essen looked their way.

"Do you think they'll let us starve to death?" he asked Simon.

"Surely not," Simon replied.

"Here?" asked Chana.

She was joined by Mother Cohen, who said: "I suppose it's possible that they won't come."

Simon was listening attentively.

"Wait a minute," he called out. "I think there's somebody in the yard."

"You should be down there, keeping a lookout," said Mother Cohen.

"It's raining," said Chana. "And it's dark already."

"Be quiet!" muttered the old Jew from Essen.

"There's nobody there," said Chana.

"Just the wind," the old man whispered. And then he went on:

'Twas just the wind on a barren plain;
The pilgrim said: "Oh, stay!

Tell me where thou flyest, brother mine,"
But the mute wind would not say . . .

"That's nonsense," said Simon.

"You figure it out for yourself," the old man replied. "It's the thirteenth today, and a Friday at that. An unlucky day."

"Nonsense!" Simon repeated irritably.

Chana started. The old man from Essen began to pray by the wall.

He let go of her hand. He was now whispering through his bloodless lips, repeating the words "they'll come," fearfully rejecting doubts which occurred to him, wondering what would happen if it did not come off. Then again, his eyes half-closed, he would think of something that was a long way ahead of him, something that he could concentrate on only if there was a silence such as this, his thoughts penetrating the darkness on wings of light. His long, bony fingers reminded him of all his fantasies, the Allies, and the last, big country shrouded in something that Simon did not understand but in which he nevertheless put all his hopes. In it were both courage and fear; it was as dark as the coming night and at the same time as light as the hope he had had that morning—as light as the remaining strength that he knew was dormant in him because he could feel it, strength sufficient to allow him to grasp all of it and hold it in his hands, which until now he had kept outstretched, and to keep it for himself. Now, as he held it out at arm's length, all he wished for was that the she-bear succeed, because now he saw her only as a mother. He hoped that the people who would come from over there would be like the mother bear of his imagination. And, in order not to wrong them, he now in his heart of hearts removed the question mark behind what had been only a short while ago still a question: whether they would really come. He had never before experienced such a feeling of absolute resignation as now took hold of him. His eyes burned.

The old man's prayer seemed to be never-ending. But Simon said to himself that it did not matter. With his aged hand he was stroking the mother she-bear, feeling her to be quite near to him now, and thinking that she had good and wise eyes.

The cart with the evening coffee did not arrive.

"I don't think they'll come," said Chana.

"They will," he replied.

"Aren't you hungry, Simon?"

"No, I'm not," he said.

He was gazing through the window into the rainy night, and through the night toward the distant mountains whose summits were biting into the sky, and farther still.

"They won't come," said Chana.

"They will," repeated Simon. He took her hand.

"I'm afraid they won't come."

"Don't be afraid," he reassured her. "They will."

"Simon," she asked, "what's the matter with you?"

She bent her head and laid it on his chest. His coat was still wet. He wiped away her tears with his hand. And then he stroked her, long and tenderly. "We shall wait, my dear," he whispered. He could not sleep that night; he was waiting.

DIAMONDS OF THE NIGHT

For Pepi and Eva

What's good in a man, expresses itself in action.

✿

The Lemon

Ervin was scowling. His feline eyes, set in a narrow skull, shifted nervously and his lips were pressed angrily into a thin blue arch. He hardly answered Chicky's greeting. Under his arm he was clutching a pair of pants rolled into a bundle.

"What'll you give me for these?" he demanded, unrolling the trousers, which were made of a thin nut-brown cloth. The seat and knees were shiny.

Chicky grinned, "Ye gods, where did you pick those up?" He inspected the cuffs and seams. "Jesus Christ himself wouldn't be caught dead in such a low-class shroud."

Ervin ignored the sneer. "I'm only interested in one thing, Chicky, and that's what I can get for them." He spoke fast.

"Listen, not even a resurrected Jesus Christ on the crummiest street in Lodz would wear a pair of pants like that," Chicky went on with the air of an expert.

He noticed the twitching in Ervin's jaw. "Well, the knees still look pretty good, though," he reconsidered. "Where did you get them?"

It was cloudy and the sun was like a big translucent ball. The barn swallows were flying low. Ervin looked up at the sky and at the swallows swooping toward unseen nests. He'd been expecting Chicky to ask that and he'd prepared himself on the way.

He displayed his rather unimpressive wares again. He knew he had to go through with it now, even if the pants were full of holes. The skin on Chicky's face was thin, almost transparent; he had a small chin and rheumy eyes.

A member of the local security force came around the corner.

"Hey, you little brats," he snapped, casting a quick glance at their skinny bodies, "go on, get out of here!"

They turned around. Fortunately, a battered yellow Jewish streetcar came along just then and diverted the security guard's attention.

"Don't tell me it's a big secret," Chicky said. "Anybody can easily see those pants belonged to some grown-up. What're you so scared of?"

"What should I be scared of?" Ervin retorted, clutching the trousers close. "I've got to cash in on them, that's all."

"They're rags."

"They're English material, they're no rags."

"Well, I might see what I can do for you," Chicky relented. "But on a fifty-fifty basis."

Ervin handed over the bundle, and Chicky took a piece of twine from his pocket and tied up the trousers to suit himself, making a fancy knot. He looked up and down the street.

The security guard was at the other end of the street with his back to the boys. They were on the corner of an alley which hadn't had a name for a long time. It was intermittently paved with cobblestones. People hurried on; Ervin and Chicky moved closer to the wall. The streetcar now took a different route. The next stop was out of sight.

Chicky, the smaller of the two, the one with the shaved head, was clutching the brown checkered pants under his arm as Ervin had done.

"But don't you go having second thoughts, Ervin. Don't let me go ahead and work my ass off and then . . . "

"My dad died," Ervin said.

"Hm . . . well," Chicky remarked. "It's taken a lot of people these last few weeks," he observed.

"Now there's only one important thing, and that's how you're going to cash in on those pants."

It occurred to Chicky that Ervin might want a bigger share of the take because the pants had been his father's.

"Who's your customer, Chicky?"

"Old Moses," Chicky lied.

"Do I know him?"

"Little short guy."

"First time I've heard of him."

"He just comes up as high as my waist. He's absolutely the biggest bastard in town. But he kind of likes me. Maybe it's because I remind him of somebody."

"He's interested in pants?"

"He's interested in absolutely everything, Ervin."

"Funny I never heard of him."

"Well, I guess I'd better be going," Chicky said.

"What do you suppose your friend would give me for these pants?" Ervin asked.

"Give *us*, you mean," Chicky corrected.

"Anyway, go on and see what you can do," said Ervin, dodging a direct answer.

"He might cough up some bread in exchange for these pants. Or a couple ounces of flour." He unrolled the trousers again. "Like I told you, the knees are still pretty good and the lining's passable. The fly isn't stained yellow like it is in old men's pants. In that respect, these trousers are in good shape and that tells you something about the person who wore them. I'll try to get as much as I can for them, Ervin." He bared his teeth in a tiger grin.

"I need a lemon, Chicky."

"What about a big hunk of nothing?"

"I'm not joking," Ervin said curtly. "All right, then half a lemon, if you can't get a whole one." The expression on Chicky's face changed.

"You know what *I* need, Ervin?" he began. "I need an uncle in Florida where the sun shines all year long and trained fish dance in the water. I need an uncle who would send me an affidavit and money for my boat ticket so I could go over there and see those fish and talk to them." He paused. "A *lemon!* Listen, Ervin, where do you get those ideas, huh, tell me, will you?"

Chicky gazed up into the sky and imagined a blue and white ocean liner and elegant fish poking their noses up out of the silver water, smiling at him, wishing him bon voyage.

Swallows, white-breasted and sharp-winged, darted across the sullen sky. Chicky whistled at them, noticing that Ervin didn't smile.

"That lemon's not for me," said Ervin.

"Where do you think you are? Where do you think Old Moses'd get a lemon? It's harder to find a lemon in this place than . . ."

But he couldn't think of a good comparison.

Chicky's expression changed to one of mute refusal. He thought to himself, Ervin is something better than I am. His father died,

Ervin took his trousers, so now he can talk big about lemons. Chicky's mouth dropped sourly.

"It's for Miriam," Ervin said flatly. "If she doesn't get a lemon, she's finished."

"What's wrong with her?"

"I'm not sure . . . "

"Just in general. I know you're no doctor."

"Some kind of vitamin deficiency, but it's real bad."

"Are her teeth falling out?"

"The doctor examined her this morning when he came to see my mother. The old man was already out in the hall. There's no point talking about it."

"It's better to be healthy, I grant you that," Chicky agreed. He rolled up the pants again. "At best, I may be able to get you a piece of bread." He tied the twine into a bow again. "If there were four of us getting a share of this rag, Ervin—your mom, your sister, and you and me—nobody would get anything out of it in the end."

"If I didn't need it, I'd keep my mouth shut," Ervin repeated.

"I can tell we won't see eye to eye, even on Judgment Day."

A Polish streetcar rattled and wheezed along behind them. The town was divided into Polish and Jewish sectors. The streetcar line always reminded Ervin that there were still people who could move around and take a streetcar ride through the ghetto, even if it was just along a corridor of barbed wire with sentries in German uniforms so nobody would get any ideas about jumping off—or on.

"It's got to be something more than that. Everybody's got a vitamin deficiency here. What if it's something contagious, Ervin, and here I am fussing around with these pants of yours?" He gulped back his words. "And I've already caught whatever it is?"

"Nobody knows *what* it is," said Ervin.

"Well, I'm going, Ervin . . . "

"When are you coming back?"

"What if we both went to see what we could do?"

"No," said Ervin quietly.

"Why not?"

Ervin knew what it was he had been carrying around inside him on his way to meet Chicky. *It was everything that had happened when he'd stripped off those trousers. His father's body had begun to stiffen and it felt strange. He kept telling himself it was all right, that it didn't matter.* Instead, he kept reciting the alphabet and jingles.

This was your father, a living person. And now he's dead. Chicky was the only one he could have talked to.

"I haven't got a dad or a mother even," Chicky said suddenly. A grin flickered. "That's my tough luck. They went up the chimney long ago."

The sky above the low rooftops was like a shallow, stagnant sea. Chicky lingered, uncertain.

It was just his body, Ervin told himself. *Maybe memory is like the earth and sky and ocean, like all the seashores and the mountains, like a fish swimming up out of the water to some island, poking out its big glassy eyes just to see how things look. Like that fish Chicky had been talking about. Nobody knows, not even the smartest rabbi in the world. And not the bad rabbis either. But while he was taking his father's trousers off, he knew what he was doing. He wasn't thinking about his father, but about an old Italian tune he used to sing and which Miriam loved. Father sang off key, but it sounded pretty. Prettier than a lot of other things. It was about love and flowers and his father had learned it during the war when he fought in the Piave campaign.*

He already had the trousers halfway off. And he knew the reasons he loved his father would never go away.

The swallows flew quietly in low, skidding arches. Ervin looked around to see how the weather was, and finally his gaze dropped. The rounded cobblestones melted away.

"All right then, I'll bring it around to your place later," Chicky said.

"By when do you think you can do it?"

"In two or three hours."

"But, Chicky . . . "

Chicky turned and disappeared around the corner as another streetcar came clanging along.

Now Ervin could think ahead, instead of going back to what had been on his mind before. He set off down the alley in the opposite direction, toward the house where he and his family had been living for two years.

The tiny shops upstairs and in the basement had been hardly more than market stalls which had been converted into apartments for several families.

He remembered how he discovered that his father no longer wore underpants. The stringy thighs. The darkened penis, the reddish pubic hair. Rigid legs. Scars on the shin bone. His father had gotten those scars when he was wounded fighting in Italy.

Then that old tune came back to him, sung off key again, the song from somewhere around Trieste that he and Miriam had liked so much.

Hell, who needed those pants more than they did? Father had probably traded in his underpants long ago. Who knows for what?

So Father died, he is no more, Ervin thought to himself.

He reached home, one of the dwarfish shops where he and his mother and sister lived.

The corrugated iron shutter over the entry had broken a spring, so it wouldn't go all the way up or down. He could see a mouse.

He squeezed through a crack in the wall. Mother was scared of mice, so he'd repaired the wall boards through which the mice came in and out. Pressing against the wall, Ervin was suddenly aware of his body, and that reminded him of his father again.

"It's me," he called out.

It had occurred to him that there was nothing to be proud of, being unable to cash in on the trousers *himself.* (Even so, his mother must have known what he had done.) He had to take a deep breath and adjust to the musty smell in the room. It was easier to get used to the difference between the light outside and the darkness inside.

Mother greeted him with a snore. She had long since lost any resemblance to the woman who had come here with him. He peered around him. He had been almost proud of having such a pretty mother. On top of everything else, her legs had swollen. She hadn't been able to. get out of bed for the past eight weeks. She'd waited on everything for Father, and now for him.

"Where've you been?" his mother asked.

"Out," he answered.

He crawled into his corner where he could turn his back on everything, including his father who lay out in the hall wrapped in a blanket. Miriam, too, was curled up next to the wall, so he couldn't see her face. He heard her coughing.

He bundled his legs into the tattered rug that used to be his father's. *He'd always had the worst covers. He didn't want to admit he was a loser, and as long as he was able to give up something for them, maybe it wasn't so obvious. The dim light made its way through the thin fabric of dust and dampness and the breath of all three of them. When he lost, he put on the smile of a beautiful woman. He was making a point of being a graceful loser. As if it made any difference to anybody except himself.*

"Did you find anything?" his mother asked.

"No . . . "

"What are we going to do?"

"Maybe this afternoon," he said, his face to the wall.

"Miriam," his mother called out to his sister. "Don't cough. It wears you out."

"Mirrie," Ervin said, "Miriam." She didn't answer.

"Can't she speak?" he asked his mother.

"It wears her out," she repeated. "You really ought to look around and see if you can't scrape up something."

"There's no point so early in the afternoon."

"You ought to try at least," his mother insisted.

That's how it used to be with Father, Ervin recalled. *She always kept sending him somewhere. But Father had gone out just as he'd done now, and, like him, he almost felt better outside; he also may have believed that just by going out he was getting back in shape, that he'd be able to do what he used to do in the beginning. Then Mother started saying things couldn't get any worse. She never went wrong about that. That's because there is no limit to what's "worse." The limit was in his father. And now Ervin had to find it, just like his father.*

"I already told you, I can't find anything just now." he said.

"You ought to go out and try, dear," his mother went on. *This was what Father had had to put up with.* "You see how Miriam looks, don't you?" his mother persisted.

"I can see her," he answered. "But I can't find anything now."

"This can't help but finish badly."

"Oh, cut it out. I'm not going anywhere," Ervin declared flatly. "I've already tried. There's nothing to be had."

"For God's sake, listen to me," his mother cried sharply. "Go on out and try. Miriam hasn't had a thing to eat today."

The stains on the plaster were close to his eyes. The room was damp, and it almost swallowed up the sound of his mother's voice and his own. The dampness didn't bother him, though. He could hear faint scratching noises in the walls.

The boards he'd put up didn't help much. He almost envied mice. Just as he'd felt envy for trees when he was outside. Ervin suddenly wished he could catch one of those little animals. Pet it, then kill it. Father had told them about the time they were besieged during the First World War and the soldiers ate mice.

To kill and caress. Or simply kill, so you're not always bothered by something or somebody. So it is—to be killed or to kill.

But if Chicky was right, a trained mouse should get along great.

"I wonder if I shouldn't air out the room a bit," he said into the silence.

"Have they been here already?" he asked after a while.

"No."

"They're taking their time about it."

Now, in her turn, his mother was silent. "Who knows how many calls they have to make today?"

"Why don't you want to go out, child?"

"I will. In a while," he answered. "It doesn't make any sense now, though."

"Ervin, child . . . "

The room was quiet, the silence broken only by Miriam's coughing.

Ervin put his head between his knees, trying to guess where the mouse was and what it was doing. He stuck his fingers in his ears. The scratching continued. *So Father's still lying out there in the hall. He doesn't have any pants and Mother doesn't even know it. He's naked, but that doesn't bother his old Piave scars. Mother could use that extra blanket now,* he thought to himself. *But he left it around his father for some reason which he didn't know himself. So I don't have the feeling that I've stolen everything from him, including our second tattered blanket,* he thought to himself. *It was lucky she couldn't get out of bed now, even if she wanted to. Her legs wouldn't support her. She'd see that Father had no pants. They'll probably take him along with the blanket. What the hell? They were certainly taking their time. They should have been here an hour ago. It was a regulation of the commanding officer and the self-government committee that corpses must be removed promptly. Everybody was scared of infection. The corpse collectors were kept busy. They probably didn't miss a chance to take anything they could get. Everybody knew they stole like bluejays.*

Miriam would probably have been afraid to sleep with a dead person in the same room, even if it was Father, Ervin decided.

"There's some rabbi here who works miracles, I heard," his mother said. "Why don't you go and see him?"

"What would I say to him?"

"Tell him that I'm your mother."

"I don't have any idea where he lives. And even if he could perform a miracle, he certainly won't put himself out to come over here. He waits for people to come to him."

"I feel weak," his mother told him.

Suddenly it occurred to him that maybe his mother would have been better off lying out in the hall beside his father. It would be better for Miriam too. Mother's gestures and the things she told him were getting more and more indecisive.

"Why don't you want to go anywhere?" Mother said.

"Because there's no point," he replied, "I'd be wearing myself out in vain. I'll find something, but not until this afternoon."

"Miriam won't last long. She can hardly talk anymore."

"Miriam?" Ervin called out.

Miriam was silent and his mother added: "You know how it was with Daddy."

"He'd been sick for a long time."

And when her son said nothing, she tried again. "Ervin . . ."

"It doesn't make any sense," he growled. "I'm not going anywhere now. Not till later."

He sat quite still for a while, staring at the blotches and shadows moving on the wall. Rabbis say your soul is in your blood, but some kids and old people say it's in your shadow. There are a lot of lies around. Who cares where your soul is? Maybe under your dirty fingernails? Maybe when you have diarrhea? He could hear mice scampering across the floor toward the mattress where Mother and Miriam were lying. Mother screeched, then Miriam.

Ervin was bored.

It might be more comfortable and pleasant to wait outside. But there was something in here that made him stay. He remembered how he and Chicky used to play poker. They always pretended there was some stake. That made it more interesting. You could bluff and pretend to have a full house when you didn't even have a pair. But there was always the chance—which they'd invented—that you might win something. He remembered how he and Miriam used to go ice-skating. She was little and her knees were wobbly. He'd drag her around the rink for a while, then take her into the restaurant where you could have a cup of tea for ten hellers. Miriam's nose would be running, and she'd stay there for an hour with her tea so he could have a good time out on the ice. Once his mother had given them money to buy two ham sandwiches. His arches always ached when he'd been skating. So did Miriam's.

If they'd come for Father—and he wished it were over with—he wouldn't have to worry that the body would start to decay or that his mother would find out he didn't have any pants on.

"Why don't you go out and see that miracle rabbi?"

"Because it doesn't make any sense."

At first, Mother only had trouble with her legs. And Miriam hadn't coughed *quite* as much.

The sentries along the streetcar line always looked comfortably well-fed, with nice round bellies, as though they had everything they needed. When these sentries passed through the ghetto, they acted as though victory was already theirs, even if they might lose this little skirmish with the Jews. *Daddy once said that this was their world, whether they won or lost.*

Ervin's stomach growled. It was like the noise the mice made. He stretched and waited for his mother to start nagging him again. But she didn't, and it was almost as though something were missing. *He didn't want to think about his father's body wrapped in that blanket out in the hall. Daddy had been sick long enough. He was certainly better off this way.*

After a while, he wasn't sure whether his stomach was making the noise or the mice. His mother groaned. He thought about a nap. Just then he heard someone banging on the iron shutter. He got up.

"Well, I'll be on my way," he said.

"Come back soon," his mother replied. "Come back safe and sound."

"Sure," he answered. As he approached the shutter, he asked, "Is that you, Chicky?"

"No," a voice replied. "It's the miracle-working rabbi with a pitcher of milk."

Ervin pushed the broken shutter and slipped through. It was easy. His body was nothing but skin and bones now. He had a long narrow skull, with bulging greenish blue eyes. He could feel his mother's eyes on him as he squeezed out. Outside in the courtyard he pulled down his shirt and his bones cracked. Chicky was waiting on the sidewalk.

"So?" asked Ervin.

"Even with those stains on the seat," Chicky started.

"What're you trying to tell me?"

"He gave me more than I expected." He smiled slyly and happily.

Chicky produced a piece of bread, carefully wrapped in a dirty scarf. He handed it to Ervin. "This is for you. I already ate my share on the way, like we agreed."

"Just this measly piece?"

"Maybe you forgot those stains on the seat of those pants."

"Such a little hunk?"

"What else did you expect, hm? Or maybe you think I ought to come back with a whole moving van full of stuff for one pair of pants?"

Chicky wiped his nose, offended.

"You just better not forget about those stains on the seat. Besides, almost everybody's selling off clothes now."

Ervin took the bread. Neither one mentioned the lemon. Ervin hesitated before crawling back into the room, half-hoping Chicky was gong to surprise him. Chicky liked to show off.

"Wait here for me," he blurted. "I'll be right back."

Ervin squinted through the dimness to where his mother lay on the mattress.

"Here, catch," he said maliciously. He threw the bread at her. It struck her face, bounced, and slid away. He could hear her groping anxiously over the blanket and across the floor. As soon as she had grabbed it, she began to wheeze loudly.

She broke the bread into three pieces in the dark.

"Here, this is for you," she said.

"I don't want it."

"Why not?" she asked. He heard something else in her voice. "Ervin?"

He stared at the cracks in the wall where the mice crawled through. He was afraid his mother was going to ask him again.

"My God, Ervin, don't you hear me?"

"I've already had mine," he said.

"How much did you take?"

"Don't worry, just my share." He felt mice paws pattering across the tops of his shoes. Again, he had the urge to catch one and throw it on the bed.

"Miriam," his mother called.

Ervin left before he could hear his sister's reply. He knew what his mother was thinking.

Chicky was waiting, his hands in his pockets, leaning against the wall. He was picking his teeth. He was looking up at the sky trying to guess which way the clouds were going. There must be wind currents that kept changing.

For a while the two boys strolled along in silence. Then just for something to say, Chicky remarked: "You know what that little crook told me? He says you can't take everything away from everybody."

Everything melted together: father, bread, mother, sister, the moment he was imagining what Chicky might bring back for them. Mice.

"He says we can *hope* without *believing*." Chicky laughed, remembering something else.

"Do you feel like bragging all day?"

"If you could see into me the way I can see into you, you could afford to talk. When my dad went up the chimney, I told myself I was still lucky to have my mother. And when I lost Mother, I told myself that at least I was lucky to have a brother left. He was weaker than a fly. And I said to myself, it's great to have your health at least."

Ervin was silent, so Chicky continued: "Still, we're pretty lucky, Ervin. Even if that's what my little businessman says too. Don't get the idea the world's going to stop turning just because one person in it is feeling miserable at this particular moment. You'd be exaggerating."

They didn't talk about it anymore. They could walk along like this together, so close their elbows or shoulders almost touched, and sometimes as they took a step together, their hips. The mice and the chameleon were gone; Chicky was really more like a barn swallow. Chicky was just slightly crooked. The thought suddenly put him in a better mood. Like when the sun came out or when he looked at a tree or the blue sky.

"He's full of wise sayings," Chicky resumed. "According to him, we have to pay for everything. And money and *things* aren't the worst way to pay."

"Aw, forget it. You're sticking as close to me as a fag."

"What about you?" Chicky's little face stretched.

"They haven't come to get him yet, the bastards."

"I can probably tell you why," Chicky declared. "Would you believe it, my granddad's beard grew for two days after he was already dead?"

"Do you ever think you might have been a swallow?"

"Say, you're really outdoing yourself today," Chicky remarked. "But if you want to know something, I *have* thought about it."

Ervin looked up into the sky again. He might have known Chicky would have ideas like that. Ervin himself sometimes had the feeling that he was up there being blown around among the raindrops when there was a thunderstorm. The sky looked like an iron shutter. Sometimes he could also imagine himself jumping through the sky, using his arms and legs to steer with.

"Ervin . . . " Chicky interrupted.

"What?"

"That old guy gave me a tremendous piece of advice."

"So be glad."

"No, Ervin, I mean it."

"Who's arguing?"

"Aren't you interested? He asked me if your old man had anything else."

"What else could he have?"

"He was just hinting."

"These have been hungry days for us. That crooked second-hand man of yours, his brains are going soft. I hope he can tell the difference between dogs and cats."

"Considering we're not their people, Ervin, what he told me wasn't just talk."

"My dad was the cleanest person in this whole dump," said Ervin.

"He didn't mean that and neither did I, Ervin."

"What's with all this suspense?"

"Just say you're not interested and we'll drop it," Chicky said.

"Come on, spill it, will you? What *did* he mean then?"

"Maybe there was a ring or something?"

"Do you really think he'd have let Mother and Miriam die right in front of his eyes if he'd had anything like a *ring*?"

"He wasn't talking only about a ring. He meant gold."

"Dad had to turn over everything he had that was even gilded."

"He hinted at it only after I tried to explain to him about the lemon."

"You know how it was. Mother doesn't have anything either."

"He only hinted at it when I told him how important it was for you to have that lemon, Ervin."

"Well, what was it he hinted, then?" Ervin noticed the expectant look on Chicky's face.

"He hinted that it wasn't impossible, but only in exchange for something made of pure gold. And that he didn't care what it was."

"Don't be a bastard," said Ervin slowly, "Forget it. My dad didn't have anything like that. Go on, get lost."

"He even indicated exactly *what* and *how*."

"Look, come on—kindly spill it," Ervin said with irritation. *Once again he saw his father lying there wrapped in the blanket. It flooded through him in a dark tide, like when his mother didn't believe that he hadn't taken more than his share of the bread. He'd known right from the start what Chicky was talking about.*

Ervin didn't say anything.

"Gold teeth, for instance. It's simply something in the mouth he doesn't need anymore, something nobody needs except maybe you and me."

Ervin remained silent.

"Well, I wasn't the one who said anything about a lemon," he concluded.

Ervin stopped and so did Chicky. Then Ervin turned and looked him up and down, eyes bulging.

"Aw, cut it out," Chicky said wearily. "Don't look at me as though I killed your dad."

Suddenly Ervin slapped him. Chicky's face was small and triangular, tapering off crookedly at the top. It was very obvious because his head was shaved. Then Ervin slapped him again and began to punch his face and chest. When his fist struck Chicky's Adam's apple, Ervin could feel how fragile everything about him was.

Again he saw himself stripping those brown checkered trousers off his father's body. The undertakers would be coming along any minute. They should have been here long ago. He thought of how he'd managed to do that before they came and how he'd probably manage to do even this if he wanted to. And he knew that he couldn't have swallowed that piece of bread even if his mother had given it to him without those second thoughts of hers. He kept pounding his fists into Chicky, and it was as if he were striking at himself and his mother. *He kept telling himself that his father was dead anyway and that it didn't matter much and that it didn't have any bearing on the future either.*

Then he felt everything slowing down. Chicky began to fight back. Ervin got in two fast punches, one on the chin, the other in the belly. Chicky hit Ervin twice before people gathered and tried to break it up, threatening to call the security guards.

Ervin picked himself up off the sidewalk as fast as he could. He shook himself like a dog and went home through the courtyard.

"Ervin?" his mother called out. "Is that you?"

"Yeah," he answered.

"Did you find anything else?"

He was shivering as he sometimes did when he was cold because he'd loaned his blanket to his mother or Miriam.

"Mirrie . . . " he tried.

He bundled himself up into the rug. He was glad Chicky had hit him back. It was hard to explain why. It was different from wanting to catch a mouse and kill it. He touched his cheek and chin, fingering the swollen places. Again he waited for his mother to say something. But she didn't. Mother only knows as much as I tell her, he said to himself. Mother's quite innocent, Ervin decided. Despite everything she's still innocent. Would she have been able to do what she had criticized him for? He wished she'd say something, give at least an echo. He thought of Miriam. For a moment he could see her, tall and slender, her breasts and blond hair.

The twilight began to melt into the dampness of the cellar. The spider webs disappeared in the darkness. He wished they'd muffle the edge of his mother's voice. He waited for Miriam's cough. The silence was like a muddy path where nobody wants to walk. *And his father was still lying out there in the hall.*

When someone dies, Ervin thought to himself, *it means not expect-*

ing, not worrying about anything, not hoping for something that turns out to be futile. It means not forcing yourself into something you don't really want, while you go on behaving as though you did. It means not being dependent on anybody or anything. It means being rid of what's bothering you. It's like when you close your eyes and see things and people in your own way.

That idea of a path leading from the dead to the living and back again is just a lot of foolishness I thought up by myself. To be dead means to expect nothing, not to expect somebody to say something, not to wait for someone's voice. Not to stare enviously after a streetcar going somewhere from somewhere else.

He looked around. Miriam had begun to cough again. She's coughing almost gently, he thought to himself. She probably doesn't have enough strength left to cough anymore.

My God, that lying, thieving, sly old man, that bastard who's fed for six thousand years on Jewish wisdom and maybe would for another half an hour—but maybe not even that long. That dirty louse, full of phony maxims and dreams as complicated as clockwork, lofty as a rose, rank as an onion, who perhaps wasn't quite as imaginary as I wanted to think he was, judging from Chicky's descriptions which made him sound as though he'd swallowed all the holy books. That slimy crook with his miserable messages, that you have to pay for everything and that money and things aren't the most precious currency. But he also said you can't take everything away from everybody, as though he wanted to confuse you by contradicting himself in the same breath. Where did he get those ideas?

"No, I don't have anything," he said suddenly, as if he knew his mother was still waiting for an answer.

He heard her sigh. From his sister's bed he heard a stifled cough. (She's probably ashamed of coughing by now.)

Nothing's plaguing Father anymore either. Not even the craving for a bowl of soup. He wasn't looking forward anymore to seeing Ervin dash out onto the field in a freshly laundered uniform and shiny football boots, which he took care of, in front of crowds of people waiting for entertainment and thrills and a chance to yell their lungs out. If they come for Father now, they'll do just what Chicky said they would. Anyway, the undertakers themselves do it to the old people. He remembered his father's smile which got on his mother's nerves.

He stared into the darkness. His mother was bandaging her swollen legs. Her eyes were very bright. She's probably feverish, he thought. She made a few inexplicable gestures. *What if the rabbis are right and there is some afterwards? Then his father must be able to see him. Where do you suppose he really is,* Ervin wondered, *and where am I? Does anybody know? Inwardly he tried to smile at his father. It would be nice if I could really smile at him. To be on the safe side,* Ervin tried smiling at his father again.

"I'm going out and take another look around," he said.

Mother ceased her strange movements. "Where do you want to go in the dark?"

"I want to have a look at something."

"Be careful, child."

He went out into the hall and the place he had avoided before, so he wouldn't have to look at the wall beside which his father's body was still lying. He was squeezing through the crack in the wall. For a short while an insurance agent had lived in the corner shop. *But this isn't your father anymore,* he told himself; *he was only until yesterday. Now there is nothing but a weight and the task of carrying it away,* he reminded himself immediately. *But I'll think of him only in good ways. And Mother and Miriam will think about him as if nothing's happened.*

He threw off the old blanket. He closed his eyes for a second. I won't be able to eat very much, he realized, as though he wanted to convince himself that this was the only difference it would make. Everything moved stiffly. He had to turn the head and open its mouth. He grabbed it by the chin and hair and that was how he managed. He couldn't remember exactly which tooth it was. He tried one after another. He was hurrying. He didn't want Chicky and the men with the coffins to catch him at it. Instead, he tried to imagine that lemon. It was like a yellow sphere at the end of the hall. Suddenly he couldn't remember where lemons came from, except that it was somewhere in the south, and whether they grew on trees or bushes. He'd never really known anyway.

He picked up a sharp stone. He had a sticky feeling as though he were robbing somebody. He tried to decide which was the best way to knock it out. He tried several times without success. Then he stopped trying to get at just that one tooth. There is no other way, he kept repeating to himself. Do it. Do it fast. The faster the better.

Finally something in the jaw loosened. Ervin could smell his own breath. He tossed the stone away. He was glad nobody had seen him. Into the palm of his hand he scooped what he'd been seeking. (He was squatting and the head dropped back to the floor.)

Ervin stood up slowly. He felt as though his body and thoughts were flowing into a dark river, and he didn't know where it came from and where it was going. He wiped his hands on his pants. The cellar was dark, like the last place a person can retreat to. For a moment he closed his eyes. He had to take it out into the light. He headed for the other end of the corridor.

He'd hardly stepped out into the street when he saw Chicky's face in the twilight. There, you see, Ervin said to himself. He was keeping watch after all. Chicky would have done what he'd just done if he'd had the chance.

"Hello, kid," Chicky began. "Hello, you Jew bastard." Then Chicky exploded: "You lousy hyena. You son of a bitch. I suppose you've come to apologize. At least I hope so."

Ervin was clutching the thing tightly in his fist. He stared at Chicky for a long time.

"But I got in two good punches, didn't I? Like Max Schmeling." Chicky sounded pleased with himself. His eyes shone.

But then he noticed that the skin under Ervin's eyes was bluer than any bruise could have made it. He noticed, too, the pale blotches on Ervin's face. And how he kept his hand in his pocket.

"No hard feelings," Chicky said.

"I have it."

"I was sure you'd manage . . . "

Ervin pulled his hand out of his pocket and Chicky's glance shifted swiftly.

"Bring me that lemon, Chicky, but the whole thing." He unclenched his fist. It lay there cupped in his palm, a rather unattractive shell of gold the color of old copper, and very dirty.

"You won't take the tiniest slice for yourself."

"If it's pure, Ervin, you're in luck," Chicky said.

When Ervin did not respond he continued: "Sometimes it's just iron or some ersatz. Then it's worn through on top. The old man warned me about that in advance. But if it isn't, then you're damned lucky, Ervin, honest."

"When will you bring me that lemon?" Ervin asked, getting to the point.

"First hand it over and let me take a look."

Impatiently, Chicky inspected the crown, acting as though he hadn't heard Ervin. He scraped away the blood that had dried around the root and removed bits of cement. He blew on it and rubbed the dull gold between his fingers, then let it rest in his palm again.

"For this, the old runt will jump like a toad."

"I hope so."

"But first, Ervin, it's fifty-fifty."

"The hell it is," he answered firmly.

"I'll only do it for half."

"If Miriam doesn't get that lemon, she won't even last out till evening."

"Why shouldn't she last out? I'm keeping half."

"You're not keeping anything," repeated Ervin. "Now get going before it's too late."

Ervin glared at him, but there was a question in his eyes. Chicky acted calm. None of his self-satisfaction had filtered through to Ervin. His throat tightened. He began to shiver. He could feel the goose pimples on his neck and arms. It wasn't the way he wanted to think it was, *that his father had died and otherwise everything was just the same as before.* And when Chicky looked at him, Ervin could read in his eyes that instead of bringing a lemon or some kind of pills that have the same effect as lemons, Chicky would probably bring another piece of bread.

Ervin heard a quiet gurgle rising in his throat. He tried thinking about that runty second-hand dealer.

"I'd be crazy to do it for nothing," said Chicky slowly. He squinted warily and his nostrils flared. He bared his teeth. There were big gaps between them.

"Either we go halves or I tell your mom how you're treating me."

"You're not such a bastard, Chicky, are you'?"

"Well, I'd have to be," replied Chicky.

"Get going," Ervin said.

"That sounds more like it."

"I'll wait at home."

"All right."

"And hurry up. Honestly, it's very important."

"Fast as a dog can do you know what," grinned Chicky.

Small and nimble, he dodged among the pedestrians. In the meantime, two men with tubs had appeared. Chicky must have passed them. The tubs were covered with tattered sheets and something bulged underneath. Everybody stepped aside as the porters passed. They knew what they were carrying.

Ervin didn't feel like going back home. He crawled into the opening of a cement culvert pipe. His long skinny head stuck out as he sat there watching the sun set behind the clouds. It dropped slowly. The barn swallows were flying lower now than they had been earlier that afternoon, flying in flocks, suddenly soaring up, then back toward earth.

It all began to melt together before his eyes: the silhouettes of the buildings and the cobblestones that had been pounded into the earth and then washed loose by long-gone rains. He watched the sky which was full of barn swallows and the sun disappeared. Rain was gathering in the clouds as their colors changed.

I ought to be like a rock, he told himself. Even harder than a rock. He forced his eyes up to the sky where the swallows were wheeling. Maybe swallows are happy, free, without guilt. He tried to swallow the distance, the wet air and the disappearing light, the flowing wind.

He kept looking up and down the alley so he wouldn't miss Chicky when he came back. And he wept, quietly and without tears, in some little crevice which was inside.

✦

The Second Round

"It's going to be me," said the boy in the middle, the one they called Marquis.

"Don't try to be a prophet," replied the second, a tall man of about forty. "Where's it say it'll be you?"

"I know what I'm talking about," Marquis growled. "Quit stalling and get started."

The third, who stood beside him, was small for his nineteen years. He had not spoken yet. He shifted his feet impatiently while the other two argued. He turned from one to the other, watching their faces as they talked.

"Maybe it'll be me," the tiny man piped up.

"We'll soon see," the tall man said. He was gaunt, the way people are who haven't had enough to eat or enough sleep for years. He was covered with scars and scratches which blurred into each other so you couldn't tell which were new and which were old.

"Listen, don't dawdle around," Marquis repeated.

"We all stand absolutely the same chance—nobody has any advantage or disadvantage when we draw lots this way," the tall man went on.

The little one looked up at him. Fear had set in. He could see in his mind's eye what the person who won (or lost?) would have to do. And what would happen if he didn't succeed. There were at least a hundred reasons why he might fail, but these were outweighed by the thing they were risking this for. The little one didn't like to hear the others fight. They'd been edgy for the last few days. At first, they'd gone a bit wild, then apathy took over, but finally they'd pulled themselves together as they always did. They were more fidgety than they used to be, though. It wasn't just because they were hungry and cold at night and wet during the daytime. It wasn't the feeling in the air, either.

From beginning to end, it was always that other possibility. It was more than food, it was hope.

The little one studied the older man's face. His skin, carved with irregular, curving furrows, looked like a map of the moon filmed from a great distance. He reddened, then turned pale again. There was doubt in the eyes of the older one, along with an indefatigable determination. The tiny one had a bellyache after six days of nothing to eat but roots and grass. You could almost see through his skin, as Marquis had told him that morning. He envied the older man for having skin that gave some protection against dampness and cold, against sunshine and bugs, skin that was as tough as the hide of an old rhinoceros.

The little one had wanted them to count him in when they drew lots, but he hoped it wouldn't fall to him. He felt a mixture of embarrassment and fear and self-reproach. He didn't want them to notice what was going on inside him. His belly started to ache again.

The tall man turned to the others. "Whoever pulls the shortest twig," he said, "is the one who's going to have to do it. Unless he chickens out at the last minute."

The little one was silent.

"O.K., now, get going, all right?" Marquis mumbled. "You expect us to listen to you make speeches all night? We've heard it a hundred times."

"I've been ready for ages," the tall one answered.

He was at least twice as old as Marquis and he had noticed that it made Marquis feel good when he could talk back to him. He could see right through him. They'd been together too long, and yet there was no one else they were closer to and they all realized that they had nobody else besides each other. This bothered Marquis, as the older man knew. He also knew that if it fell to Marquis, he'd do a better job of it than the rest of them. That was what he wanted to happen and that's why he forgave himself in advance, even though deep inside, he was resentful. Marquis must have realized it, because they knew each other inside out, without having to say a word.

So the tall man put up with Marquis's insolence. Maybe he would have been more straightforward and uncompromising too, twenty years ago. Sometimes, being that way looks like self-confidence, but the two things were quite different. He used to be a lot like Marquis.

It had evaporated over the years. Some unexpected experiences had evaporated into thin air too. Nothing is ever really lost, he told himself. Not even here. He learned how to suppress his anger and pity, and, sometimes, his defiance.

Before the war, the tall one had worked as a janitor at the Astronomy Institute. He liked to talk about it. Sometimes he'd act as though he used to be responsible for the stars and for setting things straight among the galaxies. During the winter, when he and Marquis and the little one worked on the ramp unloading coal and cement and sheet metal, they'd baptized him Big Dipper.

He'd been warming himself one day in front of an iron brazier full of hot coals. It was intended for the German sentries. He'd moved over to make a place for the two of them and that had made them feel closer. He told them about the stars as they stared into the molten coals. He was probably the first person to tell them that the Milky Way had nothing to do with milk, just as the Spanish flu, which spread all over Europe after the Great War, had nothing to do with the Iberian Peninsula.

But more important than the stars had been the warmth he'd transmitted to them within two minutes, the experience that went together with his age. His eyes mirrored a strong will, and something else which even the past few years had not been able to destroy.

Even after the sentries came and drove them all away from the brazier, they'd stuck together. Later, it was because he grew so haggard, because of that wrinkled, furrowed skin which looked like it belonged to an animal, rather than to a man. Because of all the things that happen to a man who's always a loser.

"We know you," said Marquis. "We know you too damn well. You even envy a dog by now. But do you know whether a dog envies you?"

Marquis eyed the older one with caution. Just like the little one (who was shivering), he could see the three twigs he was holding, one of them shorter than the others. Birch twigs, carefully peeled. He opened his palm so they could see them lying there—no special markings, except that one was shorter.

Now all there was to do was to decide who would draw lots first. The oldest lifted his thumb from the twigs. When he lowered it over the ends, they all looked the same. The tall man held his fist closer so Marquis and the little one could see better.

The little one could feel his whole body tense up. They were going to have to choose one of those little sticks under the dirty thumb of the oldest. It wasn't a dress rehearsal anymore. Big Dipper had shuffled the twigs with his eyes shut. He knew which was which, but even so, he couldn't foresee which twig either of the other two would pick and which would be left for him.

His hands moved nimbly, as though the twigs were cards or dice. He evened them without glancing at his hands; he didn't even open his palm. They couldn't see what he was doing and maybe they didn't want to. He shuffled the twigs again to confuse even himself. With his left thumb, he could feel that the protruding twigs were now even.

"It's going to be me, I know it already," the little one babbled softly. He tried to overcome his fears by talking.

"Shut up," grumbled Marquis, but his tone was different than when he talked to the tall one.

The oldest one said nothing. He stared up at the sky, looking for stars the others couldn't see. He wanted to convince them that this was absolutely fair—no fraud.

He wasn't thinking about the twigs. He was thinking about what a miracle it would be if they survived until spring. If they lived through it till the end. Spring was already well advanced, though, even if it didn't look like it, there by the railroad tracks in the middle of the woods. He was also thinking how lucky it was that nothing was happening just then, because everything that had happened during each of those three hundred and sixty-five days in every single one of the past three years had contained not just the seeds of other misfortunes, but the absence of what they were still looking forward to.

"Swear to God," breathed the little one.

The other two threw him a scornful glance, as though they were mutely letting him know that even if the lot fell to him, it would be better for all three if they didn't have to depend on him.

He looked like a dwarf beside the others. He'd just gotten over typhus, so he had a right to speak of the favors of fate, since he'd survived—with his frail little body. His hair had fallen out and the smooth, thin skin on his skull made him look like he'd been scalped. His lips, purplish from fever, were full of cold sores and scabs. If you only saw his lips, you might have thought he was an old man.

The little one could hardly stand on his feet. But he was quite right to think that if he allowed himself to be excluded from this lottery, he'd have to count himself out too from what was supposed to happen afterwards, regardless of all the possible obstacles. He was still very weak, even though Marquis had given him his share of beets on a few occasions and shared the water from his canteen. As long as the beets and water lasted. He wished they'd go ahead and get this over with so he could go out behind the train, unbutton his pants, and relieve himself in the bushes.

"What're you waiting for?" Marquis demanded. "Why do you want to turn this into a circus?" He faced the little one. "You wish he wouldn't stall too, don't you?"

He looks like a sick, overage baby, Marquis thought to himself. He knew that if he got anything in his stomach, it'd go right through and out his pants. Judging from the way he was shivering.

Marquis spat in the grass. But he couldn't help admiring the little one for having gotten over a bout of typhus. A lot of people had been done in by dysentery, pneumonia, or less serious diseases. The little one must have a very strong will woven among the tiny fibers inside that funny-looking skull of his. Evidently it wasn't enough just to *want* to die.

Maybe next time, he'd be knocked out by the first fever that came along. Or just by a hint of what might happen to him. The same as it had happened to other people.

Marquis looked out across the field. It was lovely, covered with last year's grass. For Marquis, it had a marvelous kind of indifference—like rocks and rivers which go on untouched by everything that happens. He'd never been able to put it into words. Then he looked up at the sky. Clouds drifted with the wind, going somewhere. It was that *somewhere,* unattainable for human beings, which almost drove him crazy sometimes.

"Look here," said the older one. "We'll start with the youngest. Or alphabetically. Although . . ." He turned to Marquis. "You fit both categories. It's your right to have first go."

When he noticed his expression, he went on, "Let's go over the whole thing one more time, right? Whoever draws the shortest twig, or whoever gets stuck with it, is the one who's going to do the job. The twig you draw is for all day. Or all night. And all day tomorrow.

In other words, for as long as we stay here and until the job gets done, right? Is that clear to everybody?"

"I've heard it a million times," Marquis interrupted. "If it's something that's written in the stars, then try reading them and tell us where the next star's going to fall. By now, I couldn't care less. You don't need to drag this thing out the way you're doing. Let's see your hand."

The wrinkled man was clever enough, he realized, to convince him he ought to begin because he was the youngest, as if it were something to be proud of. But he still didn't seem to be in a hurry. Perhaps he was doing it on purpose. He wanted to make sure everybody was quite clear about the rules, because that was the only part of the whole exercise that was fair. He noticed that the little one's chin was quivering. He was dying of anxiety, knowing that if Marquis didn't pull the shortest twig, it was going to be up to him.

"It's written in the stars," the oldest one declared. "This is fair and square, honest to God. It's the fairest way we could do it."

"Nobody's arguing with you and nobody needs to bother drawing after me," said Marquis. "Come on, let's get it over with."

He looked like he had last autumn, when the tall one had introduced him around in the fortress. There were girls there who looked after the horses and who shared themselves with everybody. Except the little one. Finally, even he got his share too.

That was when Marquis acted as if that bedraggled, much-handled, Jewish stablegirl meant something more to him than just feeling high for a few seconds, followed by ten hours of disenchantment and half a year of worry. One of them told him he was handsome. He remembered it now.

They hadn't succeeded in knocking it out of his head. There were some things he'd hung on to, things that were important to him—like hair for that poor guy centuries ago who ended up wishing for just enough strength to pull everything down around his own ears, along with the people who had first robbed him of the source of his strength and everything that was connected with it. But there was betrayal there, and Big Dipper had been careful during the past three years, so nobody could say he'd been involved.

They didn't talk about it, but Big Dipper understood what it meant for Marquis, even in such circumstances, to hold to his principles, never underestimating anybody, but not overestimating them either. Not to brag and not to let yourself be put down by every fool that comes along. It took a lot of effort.

The little one watched Marquis's lips and then he glanced at Big Dipper's hands. He could feel how hard his heart was thumping.

"All right, come on, for God's sake, I'm telling you for the third time," Marquis snapped. He took his thumb from his belt loop through which an old piece of rope was threaded to hold up his pants.

The tall one shoved his clenched fist under Marquis's nose. He glanced around quickly to see if there wasn't a guard or the *scharführer* nearby.

Marquis gave a cursory glance at the tips of the three twigs sticking out of Big Dipper's fist and made his choice, picking it out with his dirty fingers.

The oldest one's fist was like an open wound or a big, leathery hill.

One of the twigs was shorter than the others. They all saw it. Marquis felt a sudden wave of anger toward the wrinkled one. It wasn't unadulterated wrath or jealousy or impatience. It had to do with the ancient, crippled yearning he'd sensed in the tall man, like a sum of failures he'd never admitted, a stubborn effort to act like somebody who can take it as well as dish it out, someone who doesn't see betrayal everywhere, and who can still trust in his own destiny. The yearning was warped with someone who doesn't know the dimensions of reality, who doesn't recognize the obstacles, but who goes on putting up a brave front.

Everything inside Marquis was seeking a scapegoat now so he wouldn't have to apply to himself the things he held against the tall one. He looked at the tall man's toothless gums as though they were accusations of his former greediness. Or as though the very tact of his standing there were a reminder of the pit we dig for ourselves.

"I'll take this one," said Marquis.

"O.K., you take that one," echoed Big Dipper. He looked at the little one as though he were asking him to be a witness.

"Sure, you take that one," the little one repeated.

The wrinkled one relaxed his fingers, but kept a careful hold on the two remaining twigs.

Then the little one drew. "This is mine," he said, pointing to the twig at the left. He held his breath.

"All right," said the wrinkled one. "The third and last is mine. Everything that's lucky and unlucky comes in threes. Now let's compare . . . "

He opened his hand and held up his twig as though it were a scalpel or a gold coin.

The little one was the first to notice that his twig was the same length as the wrinkled one's as they lay side by side in the middle of the grubby, calloused palm. When Marquis laid his twig next to the other two, they could see at once that it was the shortest.

"You were right," said the wrinkled one. "It's up to you." He tried not to sound too relieved. But he couldn't contain the tension inside his throat. He didn't want to make Marquis angry or nervous. "It had to be somebody," he went on.

The little one couldn't even speak. He couldn't get over what he'd escaped.

"Don't worry about it," murmured Marquis. "It's as clear as day. It's me, and no sense talking about it." Then he laughed, to shake off the same fears the little one was feeling. I'm not going to slash my wrists on account of this, he told himself. It had been clear to him for a long time that when you want the best, you've got to be prepared to give the best you've got in yourself.

Marquis's smile wasn't a happy smile. For a long time he'd known what it was, that particular kind of anxiety that comes over you at times and you don't know why. It comes just before dawn, around four o'clock in the morning. Later, it starts in the middle of the day. Even when there is no immediate cause for fear.

The little one squatted down.

"I'm not complaining, am I?" Marquis demanded. "It's not such a big deal."

"The important thing is breath control," said the wrinkled one.

"You two lie down over there so nobody sees you," Marquis said. "If I can't do it on the first round, I'll try with the second, at my own risk. I don't want anyone drawing lots, all right?"

"But try to do it the first round," said the one with wrinkles. "You know why I tell you that. I don't want to scare you, but . . . "

"Well, all right, then shut up. I can't stand it when somebody nags even before you get started. You know as well as I do that I'll try my damnedest to do it on the first round. I'm not doing this for the fun of it."

"Sure you can do it," the other murmured. "I know what I'm talking about when I say that."

"I'm in good shape," Marquis went on.

"If it'd been me, I'd have tried too, but I've got a bellyache," put in the little one. "I wouldn't like for us to draw lots a second time if I failed. Like I was dead already."

"I don't take such a gloomy view of it," said Marquis.

"Nobody does," replied Big Dipper.

Marquis was silent. There was always a difference between what the little one said and what the one with wrinkles said. You could stand not eating for six days when you could drink, but if this were to go on twice as long, they'd be finished. It'd be easy for the Germans. They wouldn't need to fire a single bullet. All they'd need to do would be to allow them all to lie down at the edge of the woods on the ninth or tenth day, and after that, their worries would be over. By the time summer was over, they'd all have rotted. Anybody who found them in their rags and tattered shoes, before their flesh was entirely gone, would say "good riddance."

He looked up at the sky again as though he were trying to forecast the weather. Actually, he was. Looking at the old man's scabrous face, he felt like yelling that everybody is a crook, even if he doesn't cheat anybody but himself, and even if he swears he's honest now. He wouldn't believe anyone again.

He inspected the terrain again, although he knew it by heart now. It looked the same as before. That was good.

Postponing it would only be temporary relief. The tall one read his mind.

"Like we said—just watch your step and look out for the *scharführer*. We're pretty sure of his movements by now. I've kept my eye out. Nobody gets out of the train at this time."

The wrinkled one, Marquis, and the little fellow could all see the German in his riding boots as he passed the staff coach and the supply car, which were coupled together, but uncoupled from the locomotive and the rest of the prison transport train.

"I know what you mean," Marquis said.

The German N.C.O. finished his rounds and disappeared behind the train.

"All he'd need to do would be to stop to take a leak and then it would take longer than usual," the older man observed. "But if you keep count for yourself, you won't go wrong. Well, O.K., you know what you're supposed to do. I don't need to give you advice."

Marquis suddenly realized that Big Dipper was usually right, no matter what he said. Not just today.

There were empty fields on both sides of the train. The woods were some distance away. That was why the Germans had left the two coaches there, out in the open. Marquis's thoughts turned back to the little one. Scared little sissy. He'd probably been that way ever since he was born. It must be an awful effort for him to get through each day. Every minute must be a trial of will.

After Marquis had succeeded in dissolving within himself the rage he felt toward the older man, he could feel something like resignation flowing through him. Or calmness. Or the remnants of inner strength. He was simply concentrating now on what came next. He used to admire that kind of concentration in grown-ups.

The railroad track ran through a green meadow at the bottom of a valley between two steep hillsides that resembled two camels. There was a culvert in the middle with a concrete bridge. The ditch along the tracks wasn't deep. It was choked with mud, dead leaves, and last year's pine needles. There were woods on either side. One hill curved away as though it were leading off into some dead-end spur and ended abruptly with wooden buffers set into old cement blocks.

The tall man and the little one lay alongside the tracks. At first, they pretended to be searching for something to eat in the underbrush.

"Keep your eyes open," whispered the tall one. "Count. Keep counting just to be on the safe side."

"Quit nagging," murmured Marquis, as though he had his mind on other things now. "Don't worry. Relax. Get some rest. You're going to need it." After a pause, he went on, "Well, here I go. Wait here. A jaguar is never scared . . . " He watched the *scharführer* as he finished his round again. As soon as he turned away from the supply car, Marquis moved out, hunched forward, taking long, swift strides. Then he broke into a run. He started counting.

He couldn't see the other two anymore, but they were watching him—small, dark brown, timid eyes lost in a face which seemed to be getting smaller and smaller. Big, cautious eyes of an aging man.

The one with wrinkles put his arm around the little one's shoulders. He was shivering. They lay next to the tracks like creatures exhausted after a day of grazing and troubled by something they'd eaten. Or hadn't. Most of the other prisoners from the transport were lying next to the tracks too or along the banks of the creek. They were the ones who had made it, who hadn't been left along the wayside yet. The two men stared fixedly across the silver tracks, watching Marquis run, counting to themselves, wondering how it was going to turn out.

They knew as well as Marquis did that he had sixty seconds to get to the supply car. If there were no complications, he had eighty seconds to fumble with the tarpaulin which covered the car and with the loaves of bread inside. He had to do it so the *scharführer* wouldn't see. Then he had to run back to the tracks where the other two were waiting for him. He'd have to act as if he'd just been out for a stroll in the field.

If the *scharführer* saw him, he'd shoot. That had happened to two other prisoners the day before yesterday. A freight car full of bread was too great a temptation for people who hadn't had anything to eat for six days. No one else had tried it since then, though, so they figured the *scharführer* wasn't worried anymore.

"Take your shoes off," the tall man said.

"Yeah," Marquis answered.

"It will make you lighter and faster," the tall man said.

"Yeah."

"Think only of three speeds: fast, faster, and the fastest."

"Yeah, don't worry." He took his shoes and rags off.

"It looks good. It looks better than I thought it would," the tall man whispered.

"Yeah."

"Go."

Marquis was motionless for a split second.

"Go," repeated the wrinkled man. His voice held anger and pity and defiance.

In the next fraction of a second he aged maybe ten thousand

years. Perhaps he died in that moment. More than a man he resembled a piece of wood or some rock in the dust. His eyes were disappointed—deeper than an abyss where all the losses of men of all ages lay, all his conversations with death and defeat, the hidden site of victory and vice versa—and shiny, like a dead star, sending only a remnant of its original light. The cars behind them now belonged to the Krupp steel concern, for which they worked before they became weak and ill.

Marquis ran on. He could feel Big Dipper's eyes boring into his back like bright daggers, sharp knives. Or raw gashes in his skin. He could feel the little one watching him listlessly.

So far, so good. He was doing better than he'd expected. He had lost only a few seconds. He didn't have to worry as much as the little one or even Big Dipper, who would have a hard time if he had to make a break for it late some afternoon without having anything to eat. He'd probably pass out in the middle of a swamp some night, exhausted from hunger.

Marquis was making good time, even though this was just a brief spurt of force, powered by his fear of getting caught. It gave fleetness to his feet. He'd stick it out for two rounds. But there was that thing that had happened the day before yesterday, when the *scharführer* had subtracted two from their number. He'd shot two kids who had tried the same trick. Afterwards, he'd ordered a couple of Orthodox Poles with side curls to drag the bodies off into the woods, where they were left lying. Like dogs. Being able to lie down somewhere like a dead dog wasn't the kind of rest Marquis was interested in yet. Like every living being, he had a spark of hope inside him that he would survive simply because he was still alive.

The *scharführer* enjoyed shooting. He took particular pleasure in shooting people at close range.

Marquis certainly didn't identify himself with the two boys who'd been shot. But he could still see them, as though he had a third eye in addition to the two that were keeping a careful watch on the field and on the freight car. He could see the *scharführer* ordering them to get undressed. They were naked when he shot them. It probably gave him a bigger kick to shoot naked men. As if they were being born instead of dying. Well, it was over for those two now. Two rounds, Marquis repeated to himself. He makes two rounds and then he turns. That gives me twenty seconds. Like a one-man marathon.

He counted up to fifty as he ran and he counted fast. That made it twenty seconds instead of forty. One to forty. After that, he wouldn't need to bother counting anymore.

He jumped over the oil-smeared axle. Now he didn't have time to imagine himself naked, before they'd shoot him.

If this had been the end of the first lap in a race, people would have been crowding around, slapping him on the back and congratulating him.

He was careful not to slip on the oily axle. He held on tight to the straps of the canvas tarpaulin which was stiff as a board after the rain. Then he grabbed the tarpaulin itself and tried to fold it back, but it resisted. His feet felt solid on the six-sided grease cup in the middle of the freight car's wheel. There were rainbows in the puddle of leaked oil underneath.

He slid his right arm easily under the tarpaulin. But then he had trouble. He stuck it in up to his elbow. He couldn't reach far enough to get the bread. He couldn't even touch it. He'd been glad everything had gone so well so far—even though the tarpaulin was stiff—but now he suddenly felt let down.

The bread was farther back in the car than he'd expected. At first he thought maybe the bread was all gone, and he wished he could shinny up and see for himself to make sure there was cause for panic. Then he put himself in the place of the *scharführer* or any German N.C.O. They were going to need a lot of bread, even though they were the only ones on the whole train who had eaten any during the past six days.

Marquis had a skinny arm. He tried to reach as far as he could and then he saw there was no point, that he was simply wasting time. I have a short hand, he thought to himself. That's a stupid discovery.

It was a good thing he was as skinny as he was, but it was too bad his arms were too short. He stood on tiptoes on the slippery grease cup. He stretched as far as he could and poked into the darkness. One good thing about not having had anything to eat for such a long time was that he wasn't very fat. This little old hand of mine isn't just a hand, he told himself encouragingly. It's a crane. It's a miraculous tool made of flesh and blood and bone, a fantastically sensitive and delicate affair, a handy thing to have around when you're in a hurry.

He was in a feverish hurry now, but that didn't make any difference in the depth he had to reach. And couldn't. It's an elephant's trunk, he told himself. A monkey's paw. A pair of tweezers stitched onto my body. Seagull's claws. When a man has to, he always goes beyond his limits. But he wasn't sure that this was the case now. He'd sacrifice his left hand to extend his right. No doubt. He wouldn't hesitate for a split second.

He tried to guess how much time had gone by. A hand and fingers aren't a strong enough magnet to pull bread out of the bottom of a freight car, that was obvious. Again he felt anger, pity, and defiance, and an echo of panic.

He groped into the emptiness. My arms are too short. I've got short legs, too. Too short for a job like this, anyway. I never realized I was born with such short arms and legs. He felt that his life, too, was short. The echo of the Big Dipper's words. Everything that's lucky or unlucky comes in threes. We'll see. Let's try again. Let's go for the jackpot. He stopped counting and thinking about time. It's not good to consider everything at once. Seconds pass without me, too. Here's the pay-off. The sooner the better.

He stretched as far as he could, like one of those snake men he'd seen in a sideshow once. Aw, this thing's not going to fail just because I've got short arms, is it?

At last his nails grated against the bread and he touched it with his fingertips. It was like touching a nut he couldn't see. Or a turtle's shell. It was hard and dry. He had to stretch another inch. Finally he had a loaf of bread between his fingertips.

Once again he thought of all the things that were connected with bread. It wasn't just life, which is what the bread stood for and what life must have. There was death—extinction—which is what *not* having bread means.

The loaf slid out of his fingers. Don't panic!

He leaned over so far that his feet barely touched the grease cup over the axle. He went through the whole procedure again, almost mechanically. Whenever I move my hand that way, I waste too much strength. You can choke your arm just as easily as you can choke another person when you squeeze his neck. He felt around for better footing.

As soon as I find a place to put my foot, I'll use my other arm. He counted to twenty. He groped for the bread again. He put his weight on the other foot. Two stabs of pain shot into his left leg in quick succession, as though the muscle were being torn in two. He tried to ignore the message his leg was sending him.

I'm counting, slowly. O.K., who am I trying to kid? . . . twenty-eight, twenty-nine, thirty—a long pause—thirty-one . . . I can make it in fifty seconds even if the wind's against me.

A cramp grabbed at his left leg. He changed feet again and wasted a few seconds, trying to massage the pain away from his calf.

He got the bread in his grip again. Carefully, he drew it toward him. It dropped. He told himself that his fingers probably weren't strong enough, that he wasn't determined enough. But he knew it wasn't true. He was afraid to think about time now. He tried imagining time as an old rag, something you toss over your shoulder.

I can do this job even in forty seconds, he reassured himself. He wouldn't need to run. It wasn't a complete lie, although it wasn't completely true. The important thing wasn't the distance he'd have to run, but whether the *scharführer* would spot him.

He knew this wasn't just one of those little truths you scrape together into an alibi, and when you add them up, all you've got is just another lie.

He broke into a cold sweat, which had sometimes happened to him when he'd seen people shot down right beside him.

It was the kind of cold sweat that comes when you're trying to reassure yourself that it's all right to go on when they're just a few steps from you shooting and hanging and sending people into the showers. As long as it's not you. Nobody's as careless and selfish as a person in danger, trying to live, to survive a second, a day, two days longer. He knew that blindness, deafness, and muteness after which comes shame, but not very much. Maybe only an echo of shame. A stupid feeling of guilt without having committed any crime.

The little one sweated that way because he'd had typhus and he knew that's what it was, that he couldn't kid himself or anybody else about it.

Marquis got the crazy idea of waiting until the *scharführer* came

around again and hailing him with a friendly grin from the axle:
"Hi, there, old buddy, how're you doing today?" Something really
crazy.

But instead, he could see the *scharführer* shooting those two prisoners yesterday. Pistol shots sound different in the woods than they
do in an empty field or in the courtyard of a barracks. They probably sound different too when you're standing beside a train. The
results are the same, though.

Big Dipper was telling him what he thought of him, speaking
wordlessly, without even opening his lips, so nobody could see or
hear a thing. It wasn't just the cup of bitterness which everybody
must finally drain, whether he wants to or not, and no matter how
he rationalizes about the different ways of getting out of it. It wasn't
just the disappointment of realizing that most people expect you to
do something they can't do themselves. And prefer not to.

Then Marquis tasted the condescending scorn which would
come after. "The trip to get the bread was very short, but to me it
was a trip so long that it might have been a trip to another world,"
he said. The little one would probably put in his two cents' worth
also, to minimize his own fears. They'll thank me when I tell them
my arms were just too short. I'll be lucky if I get to tell them anything. Unfortunately, arms aren't like a length of rope you can splice
together and extend. Their anger would all boil down to one thing:
that he hadn't done what he was supposed to do.

God, isn't it disgusting how little it matters what you want and
why you want it? For whom and against whom? That your intentions don't mean a thing, no matter who they help or hurt?

When I start thinking like that, I'm beaten to begin with, he said
to himself. If I don't stop it, I'll be dead even before they shoot me.

The *scharführer* was still making his rounds, unaware of what was
going on behind his back.

Marquis told himself that he must not lose heart. He could hardly feel the pain in his left leg anymore. The thing he held between
his fingers now, easing it upwards, this was just a trifle, nothing very
important. Not worth getting upset about, he told himself. The loaf
felt very hard. It must have been pulled out of the oven quite a while
ago.

He'd seen a few people with bullet holes in their heads and it didn't take much effort to remember what they looked like. The holes looked rather innocent and harmless. As harmless as when you grab a wire, telling yourself it's not electrified, or that it won't matter.

There are some things we run after and it turns out that we run in vain. Then there are things we don't pursue, and those are the things that escape us. Marquis tried a third time. He had stopped counting or even trying to guess how much time he had left. He was staking everything on getting that loaf of bread. But he could still see the other two—the little one and the one with wrinkles. Their eyes were strained and bulging.

As long as they don't shoot you, you're still alive, he told himself. It sounded quite lucid and simple.

There isn't any loaf of bread. It's a Brazil nut, the kind we used to steal when we were kids from the grocery store in the building where I was born. Brazil nuts used to be on sale all fall until Christmas. The grocer joined the Germans in 1939. He bought his three boys Hitler-Jugend uniforms with belts and daggers. To toughen up, they wore corduroy shorts all winter and brown shirts with neckerchiefs and braided leather rings. Dressed like that, they were absolutely sure that they were more important than they actually were.

When you join such an organization, itself supported by another organization, you're no longer just an ordinary mortal. You belong to two intertwined organizations and that makes you twice as much— you're something to begin with and then you're part of something even bigger besides.

Dad hated that sort of thing. He used to make fun of it, before he went up the chimney. The ones who sent him there didn't do it them- selves, so they'd have to bear the responsibility—they did it for the orga- nization that covered or embraced them.

It was a good thing he'd had practice stealing Brazil nuts. But he'd stolen them for private reasons. He'd only been risking his own skin. It had always been that way. It had been easy as pie, snatching those nuts with five fingers. The thing he was working on now felt like the cheaper Brazil nuts, the ones that used to be kept in a bag outside the store—a burlap bag that was always rolled open like a sailor's thick, turtleneck sweater.

Hastily, he tried with the other hand. It happened again—twice, a third time. He moved slowly, so he wouldn't have to accuse himself of having been in too much of a hurry if it failed. He was furious with the bread, and yet he pleaded with it, explaining things he would have easily understood if he'd been in the place of that loaf of German bread, which was getting heavier and heavier.

Extracting the bread from the freight car would be just as glorious as not getting it would be bad. Last time, when he was sure he had it in his grasp, it slipped through his fingers just as he reached out for it with his other hand.

Now all that mattered was that nobody saw him crouched next to the train. He got his hands on the bread again. Defeat is always ugly. It's like an outcry, and reasons are only a fading echo. But wasn't it already a fading echo? Everything? What was that hidden voice in him he was listening to? Shut up. Shut up. Don't talk to yourself like some stupid former rabbi. He dug his nails into the loaf, like a weak animal clawing at a bigger, stronger one. That bread was dead, but they were still alive. But the inanimate loaf of bread probably stood a better chance than they did. Its crust cut into the flesh at the base of his nails and his cuticles. He knew it, but he paid no attention to the pain. He knew he wasn't going to drop the bread this time and he held onto it as though this were the most important thing he'd ever done. He wondered how much time he'd wasted.

Then there was no time for such thoughts, because he felt the loaf slipping from his grip again. As if his fingernails and the cramped joints and the blood which must have soaked in and softened the hard crust weren't enough to hold it.

One, two, three . . . He leaned forward as far as he could. He bent his arm up over the side of the car. He heard it crack. Once again, he stabbed his fingernails into the loaf. Something snapped.

He pulled out the loaf just when one wave of pain had erased the first. He didn't realize quite what had happened. He thought he'd dropped it again.

He shifted the bread to the other hand and jumped down. Everything seemed to be cheering him on again, as if this were just a race with time and he'd lost a couple of seconds, that was all, and he'd be able to make up for them. It's good that I don't have my shoes and rags, he thought. The tiny one will take care of them. That's all you can expect from him after his luck with typhoid. The rest of his luck depends on this loaf of bread—mine too. Come on, he spoke to the loaf. Don't make it more difficult for me. You must realize the limits of every effort, don't you? Come, he repeated, trying to convince the loaf of bread, the soul of the loaf. You are not my enemy, are you? He was ready to promise the loaf everything under the stars for now and forever.

It was one of his peculiarities that in moments of acute danger he didn't think of risk, but simply about what had to be done to get out of it.

He'd found out that thinking about the risk before it comes is worse than the danger itself. It drains something out of you.

The *scharführer* was still on the other side of the train. Marquis could hear voices. He could make out whole sentences. There was a field ahead. The wind had died down. He might be able to make it back to the others in twenty seconds. As he ran with his precious prey, he decided that he could now afford to feel at least a little bit proud of himself. Like when he'd realized that a man's best accomplishments are paid for with what belongs to him alone: his bones and blood, his sweat and shredded muscles, frayed like a blade of grass.

He didn't even need to think about it; it was the substance of the years he'd spent in camps and the years before that, as though there were really nothing more between them than a thin sort of membrane. It was all part of the same life, no matter what some people said.

Just then, he heard the *scharführer* behind him.

"Hey, what's going on! What're you doing?" he yelled. "Stop. Halt."

Marquis winced under the impact of the rough voice and dashed on, trying to move even faster. He knew he was making a mistake, but it was one of those mistakes you can't correct because it was part of everything that had happened to him before. He bent double and kept going. He had almost stumbled when the German yelled at him; it was as though he'd been grabbed by the collar.

Any second, he expected the *scharführer* to pull his pistol and shoot him in the back. That would be best. He ducked instinctively. He didn't want to get shot through the head.

"Halt," howled the *scharführer*.

Marquis scraped together all the strength he had left so he could throw the bread to where the other two lay waiting along the tracks.

In his mind's eye, he could see them and even hear them breathing heavily. He heard inaudible voices, cheering him on as they'd done the whole way: while he was running, while he was trying to get the bread out of the freight car, and now on the way back. He gritted his teeth and pressed his lips tight. His strength was waning fast, but he knew that if he went a few more yards, he wouldn't even be able to throw them the bread. And he'd probably get shot in the back first.

Their voices—the little fellow's and the wrinkled one's—came to him across the field, from the railroad tracks and out of the crescent-shaped clearing hemmed in by the forest, out of the sullen afternoon sky, from the cold earth of early spring over which he ran—from everywhere he heard them.

He closed his eyes for a second and heard them more clearly than all other sounds. It was like the hum of wind and trees, as if voices were coming out of the blades of grass.

"We drew lots and it was up to you and you didn't do it," accused Big Dipper.

"You're really a goddamned sissy," drawled the little one.

"It looks like that was just dumb luck when you got that last loaf of bread from the scharführer. It was supposed to feed ninety-two people on this transport. You know how to show off for the dead."

"The higher you fly, the harder you fall," observed the little one.

"You're like a cat that scares birds but can't catch mice," declared Big Dipper. He said it sadly, as though it came as no surprise.

"It's really ridiculous for you to get mad at us on top of everything else," the little one went on.

"We were lying here and counting," said the tall one. "Before he shot at you, you should have told him you wanted to have your school tuition refunded, because they obviously didn't teach you how to count. When you were right in the middle of it, you suddenly starting fooling around and I tried to signal you—I whistled La Cucaracha like we said, but you didn't hear it! My eyes were flashing like Sirius crossed with Proxima Centaur. And you were lucky the scharführer took eight seconds to blow his nose. And after that, he didn't walk as fast as we were counting,

because he was trying to stick his handkerchief back in his pants pocket."

He noticed that the little one wasn't sweating anymore. He didn't feel like asking them whether the only way to measure what you win is by what the other fellow loses. As if it had never stopped being true. Certainly not here and not now. He wasn't looking for justice anywhere but within himself. He was angry at himself.

"I tried. Honest," he told them. "And finally I did it. You act like we're in a courtroom. You're so smart at arithmetic, but I broke my arm in the process, you know? I'd like to see either of you do it any better with a broken arm!"

"You've always been a champion at alibis," said the tall one. "Next time, Little Red Riding Hood, maybe? Aw, come on, kid."

"I'm not a kid to you."

"For me, you're a little blue-eyed Jewish baby doll. Who was it that pitched corpses out of the train for you when you got sick to your stomach and were as white as if you had talcum powder all over your face?"

"I can't stand dead bodies, that's all," said Marquis.

"Man, there's an awful lot you can't stand. First you can't stand rats, then you can't stand dead bodies. You can't stand anti-Semites and finally you can't even stand Jews. As long as I've known you, you haven't liked Jews from Poland, but you wouldn't give two cents for a German Jew either. According to you, French Jews are degenerate and American Jews like their pocketbooks better than their poor little cousins on the battlefields of Europe. Rich people are too spoiled and poor ones are too crude. Weren't you born in the wrong century by some mistake, that you're so hypersensitive? What kind of stomach do you have? In your next life you can apply for a janitor's job at some university, maybe. Or an emcee."

"You know why I can't stand dead bodies when they're lying in big piles, looking worse than when they were alive," replied Marquis. "It's just because they remind me of my own people who went up the chimney and I don't want to remember them in such an ugly way just because that was what happened to them."

The tall one wrinkled his brow. "It's not up to me to pass judgment on your not being able to stand dead bodies, but you can't stand people, living or dead. You're awfully intolerant. With a character like yours, you better not rush into anything. Between your love and your hate there is no border. One can hardly guess what you will do next—embrace someone or kick him in the pants? Praise or thumbing your nose? You were always just a bundle of mismatched emotions, misplaced fights, and misguided ideas. As if this all would be only passing the time. So now you are showing us. Maybe you'll be an insect in your next life. Just be careful nobody tramps on you. And don't bite or sting anybody, like you're doing now, O.K.?" There wasn't even a shade of caring in his voice. It was an open sneer.

"It was written in the stars as soon as you pulled that shorter twig," observed the little one. *"Too bad you couldn't have seen yourself. You acted like a regular sleepwalker."*

"It was a chance of a lifetime," said Big Dipper. *"Don't make a face like a losing gambler. Do you still hope your tables will turn for the better? That your card will arrive? You don't have the stomach for that. There is no quick fix in your little, clumsy, and dirty hands."*

"It's not over yet," said Marquis. *"I've still got a couple seconds before he grabs me with that free hand of his—one's enough for drawing a gun."*

"You're too slow for this sort of thing," declared the tall one. *"You couldn't have run that distance even in a thousand seconds."*

"You're really bushed, aren't you?" put in the little one. *"You're as white as if somebody'd been threatening to pump your stomach and drain your veins."*

"That little twig brought you bad luck," said the Big Dipper.

"I told you you don't need to feel sorry for me," said Marquis. *"People don't call me Marquis for nothing."*

"Nobody's going to call you that anymore, unless they're weak in the head." Big Dipper grimaced knowingly. His skin looked like the hide of some animal that's been extinct for centuries and has reappeared by mistake or been dug out of a swamp or some ancient burial ground after roasting in the sun for a million years.

The little one's eyes got farther and farther away.

It was as though his eyes and the blotches on his face were distant stars, fading off into space so fast you couldn't even see them go.

"Catch," Marquis mouthed the word. The sound came out as a whistle. He couldn't squeeze enough air out of his lungs.

"Halt!" yelled the *scharführer* behind him. "Hit the dirt! Stop those skinny pipestems of yours, you little rat, before I shoot you full of holes. Stop!"

Marquis didn't bother to answer. Even if he'd had a chance to choose between making the same mistake twice or acting differently, he wouldn't have done otherwise. He gulped for breath. His ears still rang with their angry accusations.

"Halt, or I'll break your neck!" shouted the *scharführer*.

That had been another one of his silly games—letting them call him Marquis in a concentration camp or on a transport from Buchenwald to Dachau before they shoot them all. But as long as you've got the strength for it and if you're good at make-believe, it's one more proof that you're alive. You can play games even if you're hungry and thirsty and scared. But once they've killed you, you can't play anymore.

With his good arm, Marquis threw the bread as far as he could and watched it bounce and roll off the grass.

He decided to stop running. Maybe that would confuse the *scharführer*. He turned and dropped to the ground and the German almost stumbled over him.

"Give me that bread, you thief," he screamed, and then Marquis realized that the sergeant hadn't seen what he'd done.

"I don't have any bread," he replied as he got to his feet.

"What do you mean?"

"You can see for yourself."

"Aha, so you haven't got any bread, huh?" said the German.

"No."

The veins in the sergeant's temples throbbed and his face reddened. "You think you can tell me a barefaced lie, do you?"

"I'm not telling any lies."

"Take your clothes off."

Marquis began to get undressed. He stripped off his jacket and held his breath in pain, hoping the N.C.O. wouldn't notice his disabled arm. He'd shoot him just for that, without knowing how it happened.

"I see I've got to help you remember," said the *scharführer*. "I'll have to teach you how to tell the truth."

Marquis watched the sergeant draw his pistol. He did it absently, as though he had something else on his mind. Marquis stood naked in the middle of the field.

Carefully, so the *scharführer* wouldn't notice, Marquis had his eye on the little one and the tall man, who were squatting nervously to one side. Between the railroad tracks and within sight of Marquis and the other two stood three men with side curls. They still wore the long shiny coats and furry hats they'd brought with them from Poland. They'd found the bread and had instantly torn it to pieces. The loaf was filthy, smeared with axle grease, mud, and the blood from Marquis's fingers. They crouched a few paces away from the other two and began to stuff their mouths with bread.

"I'll count to three," said the *scharführer*, "so you can change your mind. Maybe you think I'm your daddy or your mommy, that you can tell me a lie straight to my face. Well, you're wrong. There aren't any more daddies and mommies here."

As soon as the three men with the side curls had torn off a mouthful of bread, they left the rest for the oldest among them, figuring that the *scharführer* was going to be busy for a while. At least as long as it took him to count to three.

Marquis wasn't blaming anybody. He was cold, though, and that made him wish he'd get it over with. The German brushed away a gnat from his clean-shaven cheek with the muzzle of his pistol. Then Marquis heard him release the safety catch.

He felt oddly at peace, but he didn't know how to explain it. Those men with the side curls were hungry and now, after six days of nothing to eat, they'd gotten their hands on a loaf of bread. He couldn't be angry with them, even though he had a right to be. It probably wasn't normal *not* to be angry. The Germans always claimed that the Jews' were unvaluable lives. Maybe. Maybe not. Who knows? Who cares? This doesn't matter now.

He looked beyond the German who was standing there, his pistol aimed right at him, and he saw the little one watching the men with the side curls, his eyes swimming with tears of rage. Marquis couldn't tell him, "Forget it, that bread doesn't belong just to us . . . " The little one swallowed back the urge to scream at the three Poles to at least leave them a couple crumbs. He knew he mustn't open his mouth. So he was crying.

"One . . . " the *scharführer* began. He eyed Marquis's scrawny body and his narrow, shaved head.

Marquis focused on the index finger, bent at the first joint and resting on the trigger. The other two were watching also. They saw the finger move, then stop.

This didn't make the men with the side curls feel any better. Or worse.

Well, I guess it's really screwed up this time, Marquis told himself.

Then he realized what the numbers on the railroad cars probably stood for. An "l" at the beginning meant load capacity or depot of origin. How can a person turn into a railroad car?

" . . . two . . . " the N.C.O. went on.

The men with the side curls were choking on that bread. Served them right. If I didn't have to stand here waiting for the *scharführer* to count to three and shoot me and get it over with, I'd go over there and slap them on their backs. They must know that once that shot rings—two shots, maybe—their banquet will be over. And they must know how it's going to end.

Do you suppose they still think it was no more than a loaf of bread? Can't they imagine what it meant for the three of us?

The men with the side curls weren't planning on running away anymore. They had nowhere to go. Marquis stared into the muzzle of the pistol, which was so close that he could see its every detail. He thought back briefly over the life he was about to lose. It really hadn't been worth much—aside from what little value it had for him. It was a very long time ago when people who'd been losing had with the last remnants of their strength still tried to put a brave face on their defeat. They knew why. To look good in defeat is the ultimate a person can want. It had something to do with the dream of a beautiful life, even though it had all evaporated. And something always happens to make you lose. It was like walking around with a veil over your eyes and when the veil is ripped away, you suddenly see what's there. This was the last second of his privilege of living. Big deal.

Too bad, he thought to himself. But, fortunately, only for him. This would be over quickly and he'd have no time for regrets. It didn't cross his mind now that a man can die a coward or full of courage. Although he'd thought about it often enough before. The familiar feelings: anger and pity and defiance again.

The explosion would crack when the German got to three.

Once, as a child, he'd found an eighteenth-century watch among his father's things. It had a hammered silver case with a tiny engraved design. Father had been proud of it, as he'd been proud of an old American victrola and the propeller of a German monoplane that fell on the Italian front during the Great War and which Mother used to scold him about because it just gathered dust.

The watch had been shaped like a pear, which surprised him because he had always thought watches were round. But that was just because he'd never seen any other kind. Father used to say that time is death. That wooden propeller blade, with its greenish bronze or copper edge, had something of death about it too. The victrola didn't work anymore; its spring was broken even before Dad got it.

Time reminds everybody of death, but who goes around day and night talking about it? Was this the source of that strange anxiety which sometimes comes over us, without our knowing why? Like some strange sister of joy, it was a tremor of fear, of ending, of all that begins and passes away. Was this the source of that odd loneliness we feel even when we aren't alone, and which is akin to stardust?

Marquis felt a special kind of sorrow, a quiet kind he'd never felt before, like telling himself that, regardless of everything, it was all right now. It was easier to adjust to the idea and accept it. Better than a lot of regrets. It's fine, it's fine, he kept telling himself.

If the *scharführer* shot him in the leg or spine, it would be worse. The pistol was two paces away, aimed at the middle of his forehead. It was funny how close it was and how clearly he could see it. His eyesight had gotten worse in camp. Fine, good, fine.

The *scharführer's* index finger pressed against the trigger at the level of Marquis's eyes and pulled it back to where it would release the spring. The bolt would strike against the lock with a metallic crack, and the shot would flash out of the barrel.

Marquis thought he could smell the fragrance of the forest, of pure air scented with resin and leaf mold where pine needles and trees and moss rot away and go on living. He stared at the man's finger, as if it were hard for him to realize what was happening. He wondered whether he ought to tell the *scharführer* that these men in the long shiny coats had the bread. He'd never done anything like that in his life, but only because he'd been afraid of cowardice and of what other people would say, even if he weren't around to hear it.

That was stronger than any other impulse. Even now. The temptation lasted only a fraction of a second.

Marquis closed his eyes. Although he had heard it so many times already and was near it and saw how it struck so many people, something new was opening up before him. He got rid of the heaviness and felt light. He wasn't responsible for anything, to anyone— not even to himself anymore. It's good. Everything's just good.

" . . . three," said the *scharführer*.

It all began to flood through him and it was different than he'd always heard it was and different than he'd imagined it would be. It came in a quiet swirling, like wind rushing across a field, a sensation of emptiness, or the sleep he'd been looking forward to that steals away consciousness, and now it was coming toward him like the wings of a honeybee or a dragonfly, whirring and hovering in one place. Or like the tugging current of a river. Or the stars Big Dipper used to talk about and which he could see in the daytime as well as at night. It was the kind of restfulness the little one had yearned for when he'd been all worn out after endlessly unloading freight cars and could finally lie down under the trains. Sometimes even under the locomotive. Just to get some rest. It's fine to feel or not to feel.

Marquis wasn't looking anymore, but even with his eyes closed, he could see that finger pressing the trigger. As if anything else could happen now. Then he blacked out. But it wasn't a pistol shot he heard, but the little one's voice.

"The bread's over here."

It was more of a wheeze, sounding very close, and choked with the bitterness and fear which timid people can never shake off.

Marquis opened his eyes and saw the little one leap in front of him, shielding the muzzle of the German's pistol, a dilapidated human wall between the bullet and his head. The kid was almost strangled by fear. Drops of cold sweat as big as rosebuds stood out on his dirty, scabby skull.

"*Scheisse*, you shit," said the *scharführer* and turned back toward the train where the Poles were huddled by the wheels. "What're you doing over there?" Then, as though he'd recovered, he demanded, "Well, what do you think I'm here for, just to keep an eye on you?"

It didn't make any sense, but all of a sudden, nothing did. The little one smelled of sweat. He was soaking wet.

"Move on." The *scharführer* prodded him with the muzzle of his gun. "You hear me?" He looked over at the freight car and at the three Poles, frozen to the spot, their mouths stuffed with bread they couldn't chew. They couldn't swallow it and they could hardly breathe.

"*Scheisse!*" repeated the *scharführer*.

Everything that came into his mind collected within the shell of that single word.

"I've only got so much patience left," the N.C.O. went on. "And nobody's going to play around with me." He fired a few shots in the direction of the Poles. It was impossible to know whether he hit anybody or not.

They didn't know that, for a moment, the *scharführer* felt that greyish urge he always got in his finger when he was holding a gun and had his sights set on a Jew. Or any prisoner, for that matter. It was like a flame that consumes, even though what it burned may have been the courage and comradeship which he knew were purely German virtues, unknown in lower, inferior races. He never had any doubt of that. It was like a brush fire, like when lightning sets fire to a field of dry grass. He had a fleeting vision of a smoldering broken rope. One, two, thousands of convicts. The day before yesterday he'd shot those two easily. No trouble at all, and thanks to that, he got rid of all complications. (As though everybody he didn't shoot would sooner or later annoy his life.)

He spat in the grass. He felt scorn and revulsion for the little one and the others, but he wondered whether there was more to it than that.

He shoved his way between the little one and Marquis, stepped over Marquis's rags, kicking them away. They watched him as he went with that strange rocking gait. He headed across the green field, watching for gopher holes or puddles, through the grass that had been flattened by the wind. He moved toward the staff car and its freight wagon, full of supplies.

He had begun his regular rounds again, once every hundred and twenty seconds.

Everything for the three of them was suddenly like many tiny flames bursting into a dazzling fire that crackled and rose higher and higher before it dropped, flickered, and swallowed itself.

Big Dipper pulled himself together. He threw himself on one of the three Poles. He started yanking from his fingers what was left of the bread. Then he pried from his mouth what he hadn't managed to swallow yet and angrily slapped him across the face.

"We drew lots, didn't we? And you got it," the little one told the middle-sized one, the boy they called Marquis. "And I felt stupid leaving you in that mess to catch hell, with nothing to show for it."

The White Rabbit

Thomas, otherwise known as Ugly, took off his glasses, then put them on again. He'd been standing there for an hour. He was waiting for Flea. She might have stuck out that little shaved head of hers by now, he thought to himself. So he wouldn't have to tramp around like this to keep warm.

They'd brought Flea here with encephalitis, the cross-eyed disease. She couldn't touch her finger to the tip of her nose.

When it was cloudy and windy, like today, the Cavalry Barracks didn't seem so big. He looked around the cobbled courtyard. Thomas was getting goose pimples.

The contagious brain disease ward was in front of him. The mental hospital was behind him. There were bars on the windows on both sides.

He was disappointed when the first patient he saw through the bars was a woman mending a stocking.

You probably couldn't escape through those bars, he decided. And even if you could, where would you go?

Red brick ramparts rose in back of the mental hospital, surrounding the star-shaped fortress town. There was a moat under the ramparts. Ammunition warehouses had been turned into stables, with crumbling loop holes in the walls. The cannons had long since disappeared. Rainwater accumulated in the gutters and storage space.

Anyway, it's all full of rats here, Thomas thought to himself.

The time Thomas had been with Flea, it had been up on the ramparts. He'd brought her a jumprope made out of string from food parcels. Girls from mixed marriages whose parents stayed in Prague were allowed to get two parcels a year. He wondered whether he could make Flea feel good by picking her a dandelion. Last year,

when the dandelions went to seed, all you had to do was kick them
or blow on them and the downy parachutes landed far away, bur-
rowing their little white feet who knows where?

He began his walk. For a change, he snapped his fingernails
against the fence in front of the mental hospital. The little folks with
the pointed heads were still inside, but it was time for their outing.
Unless the doctor thought it was too windy.

When Thomas looked through the windows into the stalls, he
could smell the old horse blankets.

He flapped his arms and jumped up and down to get his blood
circulating. Then he trotted around in a circle like a horse. When he
stopped, he looked up at the window of the hospital ward.

"You're really taking your time today," he said out loud. "What
are they doing with you there, Flea?"

With his back to the mental hospital, the barracks looked hostile.
Everything seemed hostile. He took a deep breath.

"No matter where you look, it's full of anti-Semites," he said.
Then he looked up at the window.

"I just hope you don't have to wait out in the hall," he said. "This
morning it looked like it was going to be a cold day. The sun was
like an underdone plum pie."

"Yeah," he said later.

And then, "Certainly."

"Yes," he said after a while. "Yes and no."

And then, "I think you can get away for a minute, can't you?
Have they taken leave of their senses, to keep you locked up like an
animal for days and days? Play it cool. Good heavens, what do they
think I would do with you besides take a walk?"

"It depends," he said again.

He tried touching the tip of his nose ten times in a row from a
distance of thirty centimeters. Then he tried closing his eyes and
walking a straight line as if it were a tightrope and he had to keep his
balance.

He sat down on the ledge again. He leaned back and looked up at
where Flea was supposed to appear at any minute.

I can't hang around here forever, he thought to himself. He
rubbed his ankles to warm up. To hell with them, to hell with them,
to hell with them—three times for good luck. I'm really going to

have to leave in a little while, he said to himself. During the day, he had a job stacking wood behind the house of a German major, he and an old man who took care of the major's rabbits. He looked up at the window again and then he got the idea of taking one of the rabbits and showing it to Flea.

"Just showing it to her, not pinching it," he said aloud.

He could just see those two young rabbits: the black one with chestnut brown eyes and his little white brother. What if I brought the white one for Flea? I bet she's never had anything like that in her hands in her life. He looked up. He took off his glasses with the rusty steel frames. He rubbed them clean. When he closed his eyes, he could see himself even more clearly giving Flea the little rabbit.

The glasses felt cold when he put them on again. He rubbed his nose with the back of his hand. It was so cold his eyes watered. The wind was blowing toward the mental hospital. He could just see the German major's garden with its two big Canadian spruces. The old man went to work like Bismarck. He'd been a zoology professor.

He believes life is a miracle. That cosmos is a miracle. That life—any life, even in Theresienstadt—is a miracle. So help him God. If somebody thinks the life of the commandant of Theresienstadt is a miracle, fine, or the life of Hitler is a miracle, God help him too, because he'll end up behind the wall of a mental hospital sooner instead of later. Yesterday the old man told Peter that the sheer magic of being proves it all. All what? And why? Kick in the rear. Kick in the rear, nothing else.

Thomas wrinkled his nose and forehead. The cold slipped in through his sleeves, into his shirt and up his pants' legs. If only Flea would stick out that little shorn head of hers that looks like a dingy tennis ball, he thought to himself.

He thought about the white one. About poking his finger into its mouth, between its soft lips.

"An animal doesn't trust anybody," he muttered. "Animals just keep defending themselves," he added. And he grinned to himself.

Last time, he'd asked the old man why he put the black one and the white one in a separate cage. The old fellow explained it as if he were lecturing at the University of Heidelberg. When Jews get old, nothing's ever a simple yes or no. For every "maybe," one hundred and twenty "but's" or "if's". The female had simply eaten one of her young. And now the major would eat her. His stomach rumbled.

He heard a noise behind him. The mental patients were coming out into the garden, much later than usual. They came two by two, women and men. They were holding each other's hands. They filed past the fence. Some of them were chewing something.

"I don't trust anybody either," said Thomas. "And if I didn't defend myself, then I don't know who would."

The loonies looked peaceful. They were frail. But they always reminded him of animals and he didn't know why. But they didn't look dangerous. What were they chewing? A kick in the rear to everybody, he thought to himself. Where's Flea? For ten minutes, he stared at the toes of his shoes. Then he stared at the hard-packed earth and up at the window.

"Flea," he said all of a sudden.

He raised his head, took off his glasses, wiped off the mist, and put them on again and blinked, his grin widening.

"Flea!" he whispered again. "Hi, there, Flea."

A wave of warmth washed through his body. So she came after all. A good thing I waited. It's good I didn't miss her.

He called up to the girl in the window. "Like that professor I stack wood with says, Flea, a living head finally gets the hat it's been waiting for."

He looked up at the window. "How are you? What're you doing with yourself?" He wiped his nose. "How're you feeling? I hope you're all right, Flea."

He laughed. "I knew you'd show up, Flea. How are you doing? What's new?"

On the first floor, low enough for him to see but too high to hear her answer, a skinny little girl in a white flannel nightgown stood behind the grilled window. Thomas figured the window must be eight or ten meters high.

"You're barefoot, Flea," he said. "Aren't you cold?" Then he added, "You look absolutely normal, Flea."

The girl pressed her nose to the window. The tip flattened against the glass.

"You've got a cute little nose, Flea. I've got a nose like Mount Everest."

He chuckled briefly. "You know what that old fellow told me yesterday? That maybe I'm not crazy, but I'm definitely not normal. He said life is a miracle. He speaks about the sanctity and vitality of life, about the massacre and ignorance of values, can you imagine? And he believes he is normal, can you imagine, Flea? He still thinks secretly that to play it fast and loose means to lose, not to win, this old loony. Sometimes it makes me want to laugh. I won't bug you with him more. So, Flea, it's nice to see you again. What's happening with you?" He furrowed his brow and jutted out his chin, craning his neck. It was blue with cold. He tried to understand what her lips were saying.

"Encephalitis gets every other kid now."

Again she opened her lips and said something which he couldn't understand down below.

The girl in the window pressed her nose against the glass. Its tip flattened white. "As soon as the loonies come prancing out of the stable, you've got to show up," he said. "They operate like clockwork."

He was silent for about two minutes. He smiled at her for a while, hopping from one foot to the other. Then he rubbed his hands together. And smiled again. He had the impression that she smiled back at him.

He looked around cautiously to make sure nobody was listening. The girl opened her lips again. The glass grew misty from her breath. She drew something on the windowpane with her fingertip. She watched for a while as Thomas stared up at it. She was trying to tell him something. Her lips moved. Thomas did not respond because three people were going by. He waited until they passed behind the mental hospital. Fortunately, nobody paid much attention to anybody else in the Cavalry Courtyard.

Thomas held out his empty hands to show he didn't understand what the girl wanted. She responded with a few incomprehensible gestures.

"Just try touching your nose from a distance of thirty centimeters," he said. "Like an exercise. You'll see, you can do it, Flea."

The girl looked down at the mental patients as they paraded past. Then she gazed up at the treetops and the sky.

"You can't imagine how windy it is out here," said Thomas.

Then he hugged himself to warm up. "I'm going to have to go. I'm going to have to get back to my stupid woodpile." He quickly wiped his nose. The girl didn't stir.

"What I'd like best would be for us to hibernate together, you and me," he said. He remembered crawling into his mother's bed on Sunday mornings, when she didn't have to go to work. Kick 'em all in the pants, he thought to himself.

The girl's lips moved.

"When spring comes, we'll go up on the ramparts," he said. "We'll walk over the heads of the loonies, but they won't even know it. I've investigated and found out how thick the walls are here. Can you hear me?"

But he knew she couldn't hear him. He looked up at the window.

"So long, Flea. We'll be seeing each other again."

He backed away along the fence of the mental hospital, as though he were dodging something. He watched Flea, who was still standing at the window, her nose and mouth and forehead pressed against the glass. She could cut herself, he thought to himself, and waved at her to get back from the window. When he couldn't see her anymore, he turned and dashed as fast as he could across the courtyard, through the gate and down the street. He imagined that Flea was watching him, so he ran even faster.

After a while, he felt that he was getting tired. But he kept on running because he was in a hurry and also because he knew it was one way to warm up.

He bumped into several pedestrians, but he didn't bother to excuse himself. Bumping into Jews isn't a punishable offense, he said to himself. Bumping into Jews in Theresienstadt is almost a pleasure. I'm a fine anti-Semite myself by now, he thought.

He took a short-cut across the field, hoping some dumb or short-sighted German soldier wouldn't take a shot at him.

He'd already made up his mind how to do it with the white one. The professor wouldn't even notice its absence overnight, and if he came to work a little earlier than today, he'd have plenty of time to put the rabbit back where it belonged.

Even if the old man did find out, he'd pray first that nothing would happen to anybody. As if some prayer could ever have saved anybody or anything, Thomas thought to himself. He could just see the old man taking off his shoes before going up the steps into the major's house so as not to dirty his Aryan carpet.

At night, the rabbits were locked in their cage. The padlock could be pried loose and put back. Or he could take the old man's key out of his pocket. Usually, there was only the major's terrier around the cage. He was further away from being a watchdog than the old man's prayers were from his God.

The terrier licked everybody. He was particularly fond of the flies of gentlemen's trousers. The major liked to play with the terrier in the evenings. Nobody ever heard him shout at the dog. Even when he ordered the old ladies from the Hamburg Garrison to scrub the sidewalk in front of the gates with their toothbrushes, he did it in quite a normal voice.

The rabbit was what would raise Flea's morale, he thought to himself. He was running more slowly now, still visualizing the rabbit and how he'd show it to Flea. And how she would stroke its white fur. Maybe she'd even kiss its little nose.

He slowed down to a walk, but he could just see himself and Flea, walking side by side with the white one. Flea was leading the white rabbit on a leash just as the major's wife sometimes led the fox terrier.

A few of the boys from L 218 would probably choke with envy. But they'd have to swallow it. The girls from the Home in L 408 would too. Then I'd like to see anybody dare call me Ugly.

"Don't hurt the animals," the old man reminded him.

"As if I ever did," Thomas replied. Then he said these logs were the heaviest he had ever lifted.

When the old man did not respond, he went on: "Well, so tell me what can be heavier."

"Time," the old man answered. "Time is the heaviest thing there is."

"Nobody gets the last word with you," said Thomas.

Some rumors had it that the old man's brother was a former German admiral. It was possible. There were at least three or four German generals there. Now they were only Germans, not generals, because they were Jewish. That stuck with them. That they couldn't lose. A kick in the rear for everyone, he thought to himself. How must it feel, to be an admiral and then—suddenly—not to be one? The old man's crazy. He reads and recites poems. He trades them for his weekly ration of bread or margarine. Does he really believe in miracles? He wouldn't harm anyone, not even the German major. What's he driving at? What's he hinting at? Yesterday the major told him that all characters like him are parasites and wherever they flourish, the Aryans suffer. That locking us up, guarding us or killing us is only self-defense, from their point of view. The old man just looked sad and said nothing. Sometimes you couldn't be sure if it was the major or the old man himself who thought that in that old body of his were the living ghosts of other people, and of dusty libraries and distant coffeehouses. Or maybe it was only in his mind that it seemed that way. But to travel too much, read too much, or live too long isn't healthy these days. Now the face of the old man looked like a broken pot.

"Lift that little branch there."

"Why?"

"Because I say so."

The old man eyed him suspiciously as Thomas wheezed and puffed. He was feeding the rabbits. There were just eight cages and Thomas watched him. Now he was at the pen where the two young ones were, the black and the white one.

Thomas peeked into the cage where the white one was. He knew almost every splinter by now. Its fur—the white one's—was cleaner than the old man's hands. He'd have to be careful not to break its neck. It's a very fragile animal, honest, he told himself. He tried not to think about involving the old man. They said that Jews breed like rabbits.

"I wish I knew how to tell the difference between truth and fiction the way a rooster can tell the difference between night and day," the old man said. When the old man was silent, he looked beautiful. But sometimes, he looked good even when he was talking. God knows why, Thomas thought. He looked great even when the major was beating him. It's possible that his brother was an admiral. What could his sister have been?

Thomas stacked the lighter birch logs on top with the oak on the bottom. He'd already carried the kindling to the side of the house. The major liked to burn a mixture of cherry, linden, and oak. It even smelled different from outside. The oak logs still smelled of pitch.

"We only live for ourselves, but to do even that, we need others," the old man said.

"It could be worse," Thomas responded. "We're almost finished." Sometimes it's just a waste of time to answer the old man, he thought to himself. It wouldn't be a big deal to make the old man spend his last days in anger. Was his brother really an admiral?

Rabbits are lucky, he thought to himself then. But people aren't actually so bad off either.

He was watching the rabbits. He thought about snow. Then he thought of wood and fire. He thought about the grass which would soon be hidden by the snow. About the warmth of rabbit fur.

The white one is certainly the better of the two, he thought to himself. It'd be nice if Flea could enjoy just a taste of him—just a bit. He could imagine himself walking along the ramparts with Flea and the white one: it was spring already. In the meantime, he put words together in his head, as if he were talking to Flea. "Winter's rough. It's worst for children and animals and old folks. A long winter's a killer."

He stuck his hands into his pockets. "Winter's anti-Semitic," he told the old man. And then he added, "Transports to the east are anti-Semitic, too. I hope they will forget us."

But he was thinking about walking alongside Flea with the rabbit on a leash like a dog or cat or a weasel. They could make a little coat for him out of some old rag. When it rained Flea would pick up the white one and carry it in her arms. The way girls like to pet and nuzzle things.

He looked up and noticed how the sky was darkening. The sky was low, heavy with evening. I'll be putting the old man on the spot, he thought to himself. It's only this once. He won't even find out. Why shouldn't I be anti-Semitic too, for once, he thought to himself. Why had the old man said yesterday that the evil nature of man could only be defeated in every person's struggle against himself? Was it personal? No wonder the old man caught pneumonia in winter. Suite him fine. Kick in the rear. The old man likes his special words, like "spirit" and "expiation," but on the whole he talks like a stumblebum, like a stumblebum. When he first came to town, he had red sideburns. Being so thin, he must have looked like an antelope.

It was almost dark when Thomas opened the cage. The young rabbits' paws scrabbled in terror against the back wall of the cage.

"What're you scared of?" Thomas whispered.

He pulled out one of the animals.

"You aren't white," he told it.

He took the other one. He held onto it with one hand and closed the cage with the other. Then he stuck the white one inside his shirt.

"Quit wiggling," he chided. "And don't scratch." The old man claimed they weren't far removed from rats, except in cages. He could feel its soft fur, its tiny claws, its dampness, and its smell.

At L 218, he sneaked across the courtyard and up to the room, taking the stairs two at a time. The lights had already been turned out. He slept in the corner on a three-tiered bunk, at the very top. He crawled carefully up the ladder so he wouldn't wake anybody.

He had the white one beside him. He imagined himself talking to Flea. It was as if every thought had its own wavelength which Flea could intercept and to which she responded. Or as if he were promising Flea a fire where she could warm herself and he was guarding it for her now.

Then, as if he were shivering with the cold that was really her, he whispered, "Don't worry about the nights. Look up at the trees. Maybe they know all there is to know. I don't know. Trees live a long time. Maybe they don't feel what they don't want to feel; maybe they only feel what they want to feel." He was whispering.

He couldn't sleep. He was afraid he'd smother the little beast. He touched his lips to its fur, as if he were whispering something to it, or as if he were telling Flea something.

"You're a sweet little beasty, you really are," he said to the rabbit, and he turned over on his other side, along with the rabbit, trying to find a more comfortable position on the mattress.

I'll be dead tired in the morning and so will you, but for you, it won't matter, he said to himself. The little animal trembled whenever he moved. "Quit twitching like that," he said. "And don't scratch like a cat." He'd already accepted the fact that the white one was wetting his bed.

"Illness is the worst anti-Semite," he told the rabbit. "And then the one up there probably isn't the least of the anti-Semites, either," he added.

For the rest of the night, he thought about how Flea would look when she saw the white one. So he'd be able to get at least a little sleep, he carefully stuck the rabbit into a shoe box and poked a few holes in the lid with a fork. For a while, he listened to the rabbit rummaging around inside.

Get rid of 'em all, he thought to himself. Bury 'em all six feet deep. Among the rats and bedbugs, a white rabbit is the prettiest creature. Almost as pretty as one of those leather jackets worn by pilots or some of the boys who had come here and already left for the east. He should pull himself together one day and ask the old man if his brother was really an admiral. He was nervous, but at the same time, he smiled inwardly. He could hardly wait. An admiral or not an admiral. He had a good feeling as someone who in spite of everything is in control—if not more at least from evening till morning—suddenly he couldn't breathe. He felt an unknown dizziness. A beautiful flame—harmlessly enveloping his eyes. Quiet trepidation he didn't know before. I love you, Flea. Very, very much. His lips were whispering. More than all the people in Theresienstadt. More than . . . he was at the end of his words and at the beginning of his first tears in Theresienstadt. Then he fell asleep.

In the morning, the rabbit was going wild inside the shoe box. Thomas went out with the box, wrapped in a pile of dirty laundry, saying he'd been told to report to the delousing station.

"I haven't been deloused for a week," he told the monitor.

When he got to the Cavalry Courtyard and looked up at the bars on the windows of the asylum, Thomas was reminded of the old man. He searched the windows. The cardboard box had come unstuck. He could feel the white one against his belly. If the major could see him here with the rabbit, he probably wouldn't feel much like singing. They'd treat the old man the same way.

Germans are careful about their belongings, he thought to himself. And they're just as fussy about the things that have now fallen into their possession, he thought finally. People are much nicer when they aren't too tidy. A lot of Jews are untidy. It's a lot better that way, he thought to himself.

The rabbit had gotten him thoroughly wet. It made him cold. He waited for Flea and inwardly counted the minutes. She really should have stuck out that little shaved head of hers by now, he thought to himself. His feet and knees and wrists were turning blue. The cold crept inside his neck and under his fingernails. His teeth chattered and he could feel his chin trembling.

He put the pile of laundry on the ground and kicked the shoe box aside. Where does a rabbit get so much heat, while I'm so cold? Then he thought about the old man for a minute. Maybe life is a little miracle after all. Who cares why? Who cares anyway? But maybe it isn't always so confused—everything, everywhere. There's always some second of joy. What did the old man mean by saying it's unending? He definitely couldn't be thinking of himself.

Flea always takes her time, that's for sure, he said to himself. His glasses fogged up. He took them off. He wiped them on the rabbit's fur. Then he petted the white one. He was still shivering from the cold and now he was starting to feel the urge to go to the bathroom. He peeked inside his shirt, trying to look into the white one's eyes.

"You can stand it for a little while longer, can't you?" he asked the rabbit.

He turned around, because he heard footsteps behind him. He saw the inmates from the mental hospital as they began to file out, two abreast, the men together and then the women, hand in hand.

Suddenly a small girl's head appeared in the window above. She pressed her nose and lips to the pane.

"You aren't Flea," said Thomas, disappointed. He almost choked the rabbit.

The hands on the other side of the bars and the glass made a gesture saying, no, she wasn't.

"I can see that myself. Where is she?" he asked.

The head moved, maybe giving him some signs or hints, nodded good-bye, and disappeared. The window was dirty and someone had written his or her initials in the dust in the corner.

"Wait," called Thomas. "Can you hear me or can't you? Where's Flea, I'm asking you!"

"Who are you looking for?" A woman's voice behind him.

"Me?" he echoed. "For Flea."

"Who's that?"

"A girl from L 408. She has encephalitis. She can't touch the tip of her nose."

"Hasn't she got a name?"

"She has, but I don't know it," Thomas said.

"What do you want her for?"

"I brought her something."

"In which window?" the woman asked.

"You know your way around here? There, right above us."

The woman gazed at him. "A little girl with brown hair?"

"Yeah, but they cut it off right away," said Thomas.

"Have you been waiting a long time?"

"Not very long," he replied.

"Take it back home," the woman said suddenly. "That girl isn't here anymore. Are you her brother?"

"A friend," he told her. She ought to be able to see for herself that I'm not her grandfather, he thought.

"She's someplace else," the woman said.

"Where else?" he asked.

"Elsewhere," the woman repeated and patted his head. She noticed how he jerked away, as if he didn't want her to do that.

He looked after her for a little while as she walked away, but then she turned around once more.

How am I supposed to know where? Thomas wondered. "Am I a fortune teller?" He was talking to himself out loud. "It's really enough to make you mad, that's a fact."

And Thomas, otherwise known as Ugly, thought about how Flea wouldn't be able to see the rabbit today, at least, and about how he'd tell the old man that he'd wanted to cheer her up by showing her the rabbit because she was a girl and had something wrong with her brain. And he took the rabbit back.

The Old Ones and Death

I'm going to pray," said Aaron Shapiro. And when his wife did not answer, he added, "I'll say a prayer for you, too."

From the room which served as a synagogue and whose tenants had died before winter set in came the chant, " . . . *in the beginning, God created the heavens and the earth . . .* "

"If you forgive, you'll perish," said the other old woman. "Everyone who forgives will perish."

His wife still did not respond. She stared ahead with eyes where dreams no longer swam, where thoughts no longer had any life. It was that hazy stare of old people behind which was the mysterious nothingness which was drawing nearer, the absolute end, the annihilation of everything and everybody, the awful end in helplessness, grief, grief, and the sleep of everything there is.

There was also the reminder of what was waiting for him too. It no longer contained stubborn thoughts or joy or an aching heart. He couldn't help thinking about what he couldn't help being reminded of, or what he was being warned about, and what he was being prepared for. He thought about those who were dying, about dead birds, cats, and dogs, about the fallen horses he'd seen during the First World War. But no matter how far back he looked, he'd seen nothing like this. All the sense of it had been lost.

"*In the beginning, God created the heavens and the earth . . .* "

Her quiet resignation cast a troubling shadow over him, like her extreme frailness which couldn't be blamed only on the frosts of January and February. The mind is like the body when it's tired, he decided. Like everything else. To be here or somewhere else, to live or not to live, to look out through a broken window or not to look.

"A person doesn't get much peace and quiet in this lovely and not so lovely world," said the second old woman.

He peered at his wife as though he were looking at something which reminded him of the long voyage for which we can all prepare ourselves. Long? Short? There was something miraculous. But we're never really ready to go. Like stepping into a dark, unheated room from which no one has ever come back.

From the room across the hall he could hear the words, " . . . *and the earth was without form and void, and darkness was upon the face of the deep.*"

The only thing that still amazed Aaron Shapiro was the secret thought of how easy it is to betray someone or to lie to him, even to the person closest to you. All I know is I don't want to, he kept telling himself. And at the same time he knew that was just what he was doing and that he'd go on doing it for as long as they were here.

This brought back echoes of quite different thoughts. He was tired. During the past three years, the bones that held up his spine and the muscles which would not allow him to stand up straight had transformed his body almost beyond recognition. What a surprise he would be for people who had known him before.

Subconsciously, he knew well why he didn't want to stay in the room with his wife, having to tell himself that everyone was dead long before he really died. He had learned to accept the news that someone he had known was dead. As if it had to be, as if someone always stays behind to keep looking back.

He had noticed how his wife's fever rose as darkness grew out of the light. Then he watched the moon pour across the face of the night. As long as we're young, he thought, we accept the loss of our friends as a necessary evil. Someone goes, others stay. And deep underneath it all flows the tide of complacency—that it's not *me* yet. We arm ourselves with indifference. At most, we manage to prolong the life of our best memories so we do not grieve so much, so we can hush the remnants of our conscience which resist seeing things so simply. And in the end, we're never really well enough prepared.

He looked away from the old woman. The other old woman pretended that Marketa Shapirova's fever was nothing unusual. He could imagine what it would be like when he would be left alone. Will I think back on how she lay there? No, he said to himself. We'll go back in our minds to how it was when everything was still all right. Only the most miserable are able to take comfort from the way things are. The weak believe in miracles. And the strongest accept the way things are now as if they'd never been different.

He still hung on, tooth and nail, to what he had to go back to. But it didn't comfort him. When other people's lives fall to pieces, he said to himself, and mine's been spared so far, I'd like to think I'm no exception, that the worst will avoid me.

I'm probably just an exception after all, but the other way around. When a person no longer likes his own life, he still prefers himself to anybody else. He stepped toward the gap in the damp walls where there used to be a double door. Both sides of it had been burned for firewood early in the winter. Like the floorboards, which had also kept them warm for a while. But what had been good yesterday had already evaporated. Melted away. As if it never had been. Memory preserves only the bad parts, so they can be avoided next time. Wood, fire, warmth. All that *was*. It isn't anymore.

By the time I come back from prayers, I'll be able to say that about Marketa. He tried to associate her in his mind with fire, with warmth or light. He stepped around a hole in the floor. They'd burned the doorsills in December. Nothing but ashes was left of the transom, too. December, January, February. Then spring will come. March, April, May, and June. Warm wind, mild rain. Trees will grow green. The sun will be stronger. He thought about nights in June and July. About swallows in their nests and summer birds. About forests with wild strawberries nobody was picking.

Before, the old man would pray from morning till evening, but now he would leave a lot of the prayers out. He prayed for those who will not see the sun set anymore and, when he was unable to sleep from dusk to dawn, for those who would not make it through the morning. There was a sense in his prayers which he clung to like a drowning person clutches a blade of grass, but it got lost like a memory of what used to be beautiful once, what lasted, and in which there isn't the original motive for long. Now he preferred visions of birds, trees or moss, of wild strawberries, or of the smell of grass or the firmness of rocks.

He no longer remembered when something had happened to his prayers—or when something had happened with him—as when a clock spring snaps. He didn't know whether it came the way old age comes to a man—slowly and surely when he begins to appreciate what's left, when his eyesight worsens, his hair falls out, and his teeth get rotten, when he feels like a mowed field or a cut-down forest, a muddy meadow or the falling houses of an old city. But at the same time he relishes that he is still living, a part of life. He thought about hours beyond time, beyond the movement from generation to generation, more persistent than a man. Only he sensed what happened and ground off his prayers as if he could have them accompany the old dead and the growing new dead.

Several days in a row he dreamed that all his teeth fell out. It always happened that they fell out in groups, several of them at once, from the left or right side or from the middle, until he was toothless. He would wake up sliding his tongue around his mouth to be sure that he still had those that remained. I have lived a long time, he said to himself. I have to accept that it's the end. It's not so bad. It's not good, either. Is it beyond good and bad? Beyond reward and punishment? Maybe. Somebody may know, I don't. But even if nobody fears it, I do. The words stumbled in his mind.

"I must go so I don't miss the prayers this evening," he said.

"I'll wait for you," she said almost inaudibly.

Her voice sounded different than it had last evening, than a year ago, than that morning. As if it were coming from another world, or as if that were where it was going. It sounded dry and crushed and betrayed. As though she saw something or as if she were afraid of something she couldn't put into words. As though it had to do with something for which there were no words, something that was still a part of life, but a step beyond it. Something she probably couldn't talk about to anybody else. It sounded as if she were still here, but it wasn't she anymore. Like the voice of an aged, frightened child. Or like the cry of a not-yet-born baby.

The other old woman and Aaron Shapiro were suddenly seized by fear. Something clutched at the old woman's throat and she began to weep silently. But she was strong enough to pull herself together and, when Shapiro glanced at her, to act as if nothing in particular had happened. It took her a few moments to stop crying. Her face was smudged with tears.

"Years used to seem so long to me, then days did, and now when an hour passes, I feel as if a hundred years had gone by," said Leonie

Markusova. She managed to laugh about it. Aaron Shapiro went out into the corridor.

Leonie Markusova looked over at the old woman who was lying down.

"I grant you, it's not very cheerful," she said. "Snow, wind, the way it gets dark so early. Like being in the mountains somewhere."

Marketa Shapirova stared up at the ceiling. It looked like a map of some strange country. A strand of grey hair had come undone. She hadn't combed her hair for five days.

"You've skipped quite a few meals by now," observed the other old woman. "Why do you suppose they haven't come today in particular?" she went on.

She paused. "I don't like it when things are so quiet."

It seemed to her that the old woman who was lying down had raised her thick grey eyebrows.

"A person can experience a lot, still it's only a drop in the ocean," she said. "Why can't I honor my past as I did only a few weeks ago? Did it change because I changed? Who controls our lives?" Then she said, "Isn't it funny? You live not one reality, but two, three, who knows how many? One reality is here—and it's mixed with the reality which was—as if things and images wouldn't die. It includes what will be. I never had time to think about these things. Only here I have more free time than I want."

Marketa Shapirova could see the other old woman's face as if through a fog. She knew her husband had gone. She didn't want him to resent her, the way you resent people who have nothing left to give you anymore. It takes the greatest amount of strength to get along and put up with someone you no longer love, she thought to herself. When things get difficult. At the time of death, we're cruel to each other.

A person's worst enemy isn't the one he kills, but the one whose happiness he takes away.

She hung on to two phrases the other old woman had been saying: *they came* and *they didn't come*. Both of them knew it had been a long time since anybody had come around who didn't have a specific reason for it. Not even the delousing doctor with his black net gloves had passed by within the last few months.

"There's just a handful of us." She looked up at the sky. "The world looks beautiful."

"I don't envy anybody anything," said the second old woman. "Except when they can bend over and turn around and straighten up again."

Everything and everybody was preparing them to die. Like a bottle of perfume which has evaporated, even though the bottle has been tightly corked. Something happens and the perfume isn't what it used to be. Until you've crossed the borderline of childhood, you never think of death as something which has to do with greying, thinning hair, with gaps in your teeth, tender gums and aching joints, or stiff bones and sores.

"What is it that makes everything fall apart?" whispered Marketa Shapirova. Then she realized that she was going to die without a single German soldier even having to fire a shot.

And someday the one who had caused it all to begin would be dead too. What wouldn't be dead, though, would be the urge to destroy—or the spirit behind this urge, which used to remind her of poison. How come everything people want and strive for runs aground and is wrecked?

It was a long time ago when she'd first come to grips with loneliness. She'd been ten years old and had had to play by herself. Later, it was all bound up with all the different ways in which Aaron Shapiro had been selfish. And her own selfishness, too. But it had been a long time since she'd thought of how a man is selfish. Of what he expected of her sometimes, and what did not give her as much pleasure as he thought it did. Then later, he got tired of her without even saying so. The nights he came home late.

The moment. A strange feeling, waiting for someone who might come. The way the other old woman's children's children sometimes came to visit.

She thought about bread. Then she thought of honey. She imagined a slice of bread and butter and golden drops of honey on it. A glass of cold milk. Then she visualized the way her hair had looked when she'd been young. Finally, she called back the faces of her children who were somewhere in the east. Dead. Maybe not. Is it, after all, good that they are so far? But she knew already. It was said it happened in March, twenty-four months ago. So this is *the moment,* she thought to herself. She felt very much like a tree that's rotting away. Like a river flowing into the sea and losing itself there. Like a cloud before it turns into rain, to drops of water too numerous to be counted. Are we what we are, and, at the same time, because of that, have we already stopped being it without having become anything else yet?

"Something holds firm," she whispered.

Like a fire that's burned itself out, a river when it flows away, or an extinguished star. After winter, spring comes, but not the other way around. And all of it was true, she said to herself. I was right.

"It's a long time since I've heard a rooster crow," she whispered.

Subconsciously, Marketa Shapirova began to sense that all things were either false or foolish. *The moment.* Like taking off a dress, beautiful or threadbare. I'm naked, she said to herself. And I'm alone. There was no pride that it was Friday, and there were none of the candles she used to light.

It all unwound hazily before Marketa Shapirova's eyes—life carved out of the kernel, without even the thinnest shell. Life—some ancient extinct womanhood.

Now and then she thought about her body. The body of an old person is like an icy ocean out of which large and small icebergs poke their sharp peaks. The icebergs are the pains no one knows about. Not just soul pain which takes in grief and loneliness. Real, physical pain in the joints and bones when you breathe.

Pain gives itself away at night by outcries that can't be suppressed, or groans that push their way out of the chest and through the lips, because sometimes the pain is too great or goes on too long.

Usually nobody spoke of those things anymore, so the frigid ocean and its icebergs were like an arctic sea at night, full of things which can't be seen even above the water's surface.

But sometimes there were quiet tears or a loud catch in the throat for no apparent reason. Old people know there's always a reason for such tears, though; the reasons are many.

"So it goes," she whispered. "Well, well . . ."

Colliding with such an iceberg isn't dangerous. Its sharpness and coldness are only inward. They melt on the outside, melt like smoke, reminding us only of what used to be. Not like the ship that sank so long ago, the ship with the lovely name, like the name of an ocean grave. The steamship named after a Greek god.

It was like one of those icebergs or like that ship on the ocean's floor. Better forget we've even got a body.

She wanted to think about what was most important, the thing that guided her, about what she wanted to believe in. Don't harm animals, don't harm yourself, take no one's life. That was certainly difficult, but who said it would be easy? For a long time she'd felt like a sinking ship. For too long, perhaps.

"So it's good," she whispered. "Good, good, very good."

"I thought the cat got your tongue," said the other old woman.

Marketa Shapirova half-opened her eyes and blinked. "I'm giving you an awful lot of trouble."

"Don't exaggerate," Leonie Markusova said. "When we can't do what we want, we've got to do what we can, as the saying goes. People are as smart as animals. They say when you can't go up, try going down. And when you don't know what to do, you've got to find out. They also say that whoever doesn't outlast what's evil, won't live to see things get better." After a while she went on: "I don't like the dark. I hope you're warmly dressed. The wind gets in even under the covers. Can't you feel the draft from the floor? You know what I keep dreaming about more and more these days? Bathing for hours in warm water. I fill the tub to the brim. Then I go to sleep in a nice clean bed. Hungry perhaps, but clean. Isn't that silly?"

Marketa Shapirova was thinking of how *the moment* had begun to fill with weariness. For forty years, you might say. Aaron Shapiro had forgotten about it forty years before. All that's left are rocks and ocean, he thought to herself. Light is left, and darkness. The war's like a skin you crawl inside of to keep warm. And suffocate. She tried to smile, at least inwardly.

They're gassing people in Poland. They don't even need to bother with gas here, she thought to herself. In Germany and Poland, they shoot them. It's not necessary here.

As long as there's light, Marketa Shapirova thought to herself. It creeps across the walls like bedbugs swollen with blood. The young women are complaining about how many soldiers have raped them. Nobody rapes old women.

The young people were grumbling, too, about all the dances and parties they were missing. All the schools they had to leave. The past looks lovely and important only when the present is miserable, the here and now, and when the future looks unclear or even dismal. When does a person cling to the future? When things are going right? That's why it doesn't help to remind people that they ought to forget about the past. It isn't something you can forget about when somebody tells you to, any more than you can order somebody to love. It's just one of those things. The past can be stimulation as well as prison. And it can be a third thing, too, something each of us sees in his own way.

What's important is what's in store for us, maybe far away, or hidden, secret, but it's enough to be aware of it. You can tell if someone has something to expect. Even unfulfilled promises, mismatched loves, betrayed friendships—even if only in the beginning. She was looking for courage in herself, for wisdom. *The moment*, she murmured to herself.

"I don't like this kind of weather, I'll tell you that," declared Leonie Markusova.

Marketa Shapirova opened her eyes and closed them again so she wouldn't have to talk. Trees don't ask questions when a storm is coming. They're blown over or they rot away, no matter how deep their roots go. Rocks crumble too, and lakes and rivers dry up. What was once an ocean is dry land now. There are gardens and fields where a desert used to be, and deserts in place of fields and gardens. So it goes, over and over again. And in between, there's the person and *the moment*, wandering along between the end and the beginning. Killing is the key to explaining man and life. We're born into a world where one simply kills. And, in inexplicable ways, killing brings with it the killing of those who kill. But it's not quite the same.

"I hope you don't feel too cold?" asked Leonie Markusova.

Marketa Shapirova was deep in thought. The old language came back to her, the one used in prayers. Nothing lasts forever—no one person and none of the things he's created. Not even the most finely woven dress, or the stoutest stone house, or chair and table made of oak. But we don't realize that for a long time or we don't want to know. Hope is something we can construct from nothing, just like God, and we don't even notice when hope begins to lose its probability. Nobody and nothing resembles something which hasn't been here before. Even though it looked different. And it'll all happen again.

It's what comes in between that we can influence.

At one time, it was said that either love or justice determine a man. The wise and the foolish disputed which was foremost. That wasn't all there was to it, of course. What about the other way around? We can be as modest as we like, but we're always the center of our own world.

The moment. The moment. The moment.

She knew exactly. When you abandon everything you can believe in, you're abandoning yourself. As if you've never existed. But that takes a long time. If you're no longer in control of your own life, can you at least be in control of its end? Yes? No? Why? How to stop your life becoming so small, almost invisible, smaller than the tiniest grain of dust, as the dark heart of a snowflake? She tried to imagine stunted grass, the stumbling block that made her sick. No one could move it out of her way. It kept devouring her energy.

Once again she remembered that amorphous anniversary, neither fish nor fowl . . . four times ten years. Nothing but a zero left at the end. A cancellation of everything and everybody. She could feel Leonie Markusova watching her.

When Aaron Shapiro had begun to deteriorate (and he was failing fast), he too stopped believing they'd ever get out of this. That was when he had begun to grow away from her and they never got close again. We exist, he said, we still exist, although the one whose very name I can't bring myself to utter wants nothing more than for us not to exist. Our lives mean no more to him than the existence of vermin or pests. And he's not alone. Nobody could start and accomplish all this just by himself. We've even lost what we thought we had won. He was probably already afraid at that time, concealing his fear with a smile, like when he concluded a good business deal, fearful his truth was really just a wish. He wasn't even allowed to go into a shop to buy flowers. In Nuremburg, the Great Reich had adopted laws that had made them prisoners even before they went to jail. And later they learned to understand the hazy, metaphoric language, the new meanings of old words.

Her vision took in her brother too. Artur Morgenstern. He came to their wedding forty years ago. And here they'd met again. He said the fortress town was punishment for the profligacy which had spread since the destruction of the Temple, eating into Jewish heads wherever they were to be found.

Did that profligacy afflict children and old people, though?

It'll become a burden for them when it's too late, Artur Morgenstern had said. Not really a burden, even. Just pangs of conscience, which don't leap like sparks from one fire to another. They are transmitted from one generation to another, maybe even bypassing one to flicker up in another.

The moment. Just one branch of the family is perishing, Artur Morgenstern said. The most beautiful and most steadfast. "We're good at weeping," he concluded. "Maybe it's a good thing we do it so well. Yet not entirely."

Even with her eyes closed, Marketa Shapirova could see the torn and desolate green wallpaper. But no sparks can spring out of ashes. All the wind can glean from ashes is more ashes.

"It's snowing," the other old woman said. "I like snow. It's so clean. It doesn't remind me of blood. It's not so cold when it snows."

"Yes," said Marketa Shapirova.

"It's good that it's snowing," the other now said again. "You look at the snow and you wonder. It's so clean, so fresh. It changes everything, or almost everything. It comes so slow. Not so abruptly. It transforms me too, maybe. You want to feel like another person sometimes, somebody other than you were yesterday. It has a different music, snowing." Myriads of snowflakes reminded her of myriads of reasons for their life here.

Leonie Markusova heard fragments of words from the other room where the men were praying. " . . . *And God made two great lights . . . to rule the day and the lesser light to rule the night. He made the stars also . . . and [this] was the fourth day.*"

Marketa Shapirova was remembering the sounds of the birds she'd once heard in the fields. You could hear them far and wide. Those sounds had brought to mind words like *distance, shame, afterwards . . . The moment.* One bright midday she'd even heard a skylark sing. She remembered how peaceful she'd felt, as if she herself were a wheatfield which would soon give birth to bread.

Suddenly a pain shot through her body. Like labor pains. Like the pain of her own birth. It was a good thing her mother wasn't here, that she couldn't be her own mother. From their transport, everybody's mother had been gassed last September in the east. It was a good thing, too, that her own children weren't here either. They'd been gassed somewhere in Poland two years ago last March.

The skylark's song, the fields and meadows and forest—these were some of the best things. A clear sunny day, bread and butter and salt—the joy of being alive. All that was left now was *the moment*. But it wasn't quite all. She could almost sense the bridge between the two. She remembered a dream she'd had from time immemorial, perhaps even in her mother's womb. Now she no longer needed an explanation for her inexplicable anxieties and strange fears. There was no longer any bitterness left in her.

The dream had been as white as her wedding gown, as white as the halo around the sun when you see it in the morning, before the snow drowns it in whiteness, in white flakes, like a message being sifted into her aching joints. Is *the moment* white?

She could still feel the world and life within her, but it was like wine now, in her skin and the violet blotches of impetigo.

It warmed her to recall that dream of being inside her mother's belly. Being born is a warm experience. *The moment. The moment. The moment.*

"We're like stunned fish," the second old woman remarked suddenly.

I can say that long before *the moment* came, I'd already lumped everything into my prayers, Marketa Shapirova thought to herself. There probably aren't any prayers like that anymore, prayers that cover everything—hunger, food, desolation. Darkness, frost, snow, gusts of wind, and both faces of loneliness which we take turns in welcoming and rejecting.

"It's still snowing heavily," the other woman repeated.

"It's outside, isn't it?" whispered Marketa Shapirova.

"The human body is a fortress that defends itself against thousands of enemies," Leonie Markusova said. "When it doesn't defend itself, it falls." After a while she added, "It's such a contempt for human life, what shall we do?" She thought to herself, how come all the time there are so many more lies and so much less meaning for a single life?

But Marketa Shapirova was lost in her own thoughts.

In everything there is an invisible judge and prosecutor, a secret joy, a long-gone, gentle expectation which came back to her like an echo. *The moment.*

He needn't have gone on so far ahead of me, Marketa Shapirova thought to herself. She could almost see her brother, standing there in front of her. He could have advised her now. He probably saw the world in quite a different light. For many people, we're just the clink of coins in the pocket, less than a drop of water— dirt to be swept away with brooms of fire. For only a few are we sunshine in the heart. Why haven't we ever been able to think about others in the same way as they think about us?

She could see her brother now as he had stood there when he was alive, slightly bent, as if he were looking for something on the ground, lost in the overcoat and suit which were too big for him, wearing that crumpled, wide-brimmed hat.

She could see herself, too, as she'd stood once in front of the bathroom mirror naked. It was all gone now. First it had grown old and wrinkled, then finally disappeared entirely.

The difference, which had been the cause of it all, seemed petty and ridiculous. Nobody had ever redeemed it yet. Otherwise, things would look different than they do.

Life can't be any better than the person is, after all. The whole world is like a great, clouded mirror, and underneath the part we think we know, quite different things are hidden.

Her brother's bushy eyebrows. The hat made of fox fur, the gift of a rabbi in a Warsaw suburb. Looking back, she thought admiringly of her brother. While he was alive, he submitted to all the rules and regulations of his faith as one submits to weakness or temptation. At first he thought the Germans would be afraid. The Germans weren't afraid of anything. Exactly the opposite was true: they were the ones who were afraid of the Germans.

Or was it something else the Germans feared? She herself was a practical, earthbound person, less observant than her brother. She ate everything, even if it contained blood, which holds the souls of animals. She had spoiled her stomach with soup made from extracts, with ersatz German honey and butter and meat, with gravies made from ersatz lentils, but only after Artur Morgenstern chose to starve to death rather than eat food he considered unclean.

The moment. The moment. The moment. Life. Before her closed eyes Artur Morgenstern and Aaron Shapiro began to merge into a fuzzy tangle. She could see them in a dimming, almond-tinted glow.

Where are they? My God, where is everybody, all the ones who used to be here? She remembered sitting under a pear tree in the court-yard last year while a few youngsters yanked off the unripe fruit to prove how strong they were.

In her mind's eye, Marketa Shapirova could see a treadmill with a squirrel running inside. A double wheel with silver spokes. White sunshine. The faster the wheel turned, the harder the furry little animal inside kept running. The spokes flashed by faster and faster until the difference between the spokes and the light vanished. The circle was impenetrable.

Nothing, nothing, nothing. And that includes my anniversary, too. So far, she'd still had enough strength left to save a piece of bread for Aaron Shapiro for Friday. Yesterday she'd eaten the bread herself. *The moment.* Evening, night and morning, forty years ago. Strange how all that was left of it was one single night, forty years ago. The touch of hands, face against face, dead memory of a young body.

Marketa Shapirova could hear the sound of a river flowing.

"There was an old columbarium for urns from the crematorium behind the fortress. Every six months, a special squad of Jewish or Communist or Social Democratic prisoners dumped the ashes of the recent dead into the river. A lot of ashes had flowed down to the sea by now, but the level of the ocean hadn't risen by one single millimeter," the other woman said suddenly.

Marketa Shapirova didn't answer.

Someone said the columbarium was being used now for storing potatoes. *The moment.* Books about the brave, the innocent, the honest. She heard mice. Snow slid off the roof and fell into the courtyard with a soft thud.

"Nothing can surprise me anymore, not even the snow or ice," Leonie Markusova added.

Marketa Shapirova thought about the sound of a river current. It's for all of us, sooner for some, later for others.

I'm a wave in that river, she said to herself. And this is *my moment.*

Aaron Shapiro, she called out silently, *come back. Hurry if you still want to find me here. You know how I hate mice. I'm terrified of mice* and Germans. *I'm not afraid of you anymore or even of myself. My life, Aaron Shapiro. I've never been unfaithful to you. I simply wasn't very close. But that wasn't my fault or yours. And I was only unfaithful to you in my thoughts. One time, at a party, a strange man kissed me on the lips. Sometimes I kept you waiting and held you off when you were very close to me. I didn't want you to be close and I don't know why. This is* the moment, *now. Closed doors—not those you opened for me whenever I was with you.*

Do you remember, Aaron, that German emigrant from Berlin who came to see us in our old apartment in Prague in 1936? He didn't want the charity we offered him to be more than we could afford. So we wouldn't think ours was the only well where he could quench his thirst. He didn't want us to feel toward him like rich people feel toward the poor, fearful of easing their poverty with their own money. We were simply frightened by his fear. People are frightened by other people who are unhappy. He knew nobody can understand until they accumulate first-hand experience themselves. He had blue eyes. He was so embarrassed. How many emigrants have felt embarrassed since then—as if they were the first to have had to leave someplace where they would have preferred to stay? Leaving a home, a school, a house, and finally a country. Then there were those dreams, Aaron. Do you know the ones I mean?

I watched the sun set, although my eyes were closed, Aaron. It's a circle. I've come back to the beginning. The moment. *Listen to me please, Aaron. It won't be very much more. But it's all. Listen. Listen.*

Never leave me alone in the evening anymore, Aaron Shapiro. All of you that's with me is your name. My forehead's on fire. Put your hand on me.

She groped for the thermometer. She knew she was alone now. Dimly, she put the thermometer under her arm, poking her hands through the rags in which she was dressed. She tried to guess how long two minutes lasted.

She could see a tangle of fire before her eyes. *The moment.* Fever. Mice paws. Cold. Fear. A feeling of sinfulness, of disappointment, guilt, and loneliness. *The moment. The moment.*

She tried to raise the glass tube to her eyes. She couldn't see anything but snow. Every day, she realized vaguely, there's one infinitesimal bit more of the silvery stuff. More of it meant a smaller fragment of life.

Aaron Shapiro, she called out silently. A flame had lodged inside her temples. She could hardly feel her body anymore. That is, she wasn't aware of it as pain. It was as if her body weren't hers at all, as if it had nothing to do with her. It's burning itself into me, Aaron. She felt as if she were going blind, groping with her hands, trying to catch what was escaping. Where was it? What could she do? What should we do? Was she going blind? deaf? numb?

She rolled over on her side. The thermometer slipped out of her hand. It fell and broke. She banged her head on the floor. She no longer dreamed, even secretly, of starting life all over again. She wouldn't have wanted to.

The wind blew in gusts of snow. I won't need doors anymore, she said to herself. I won't need shoes, either.

"Aaron," she whispered inaudibly.

And then, "Who's to blame for it all? At least I haven't killed anybody. If life means whether you kill or don't kill, then I was one of those who didn't."

There was the rose that Aaron Shapiro had bought for her that time; the rose he'd been unable to buy himself because the Great Reich didn't allow people like him to enter a flower shop. Cold snow and mice again. Her fingers stretched as though she were feeling around the floor for the thermometer. A gust of snowflakes touched her hand and settled in between her fingers.

"Aaron Shapiro," Leonie Markusova called into the room where the service was going on. It was musty, and since those people had died of typhus in there last year, it reeked of old disinfectant. Leonie Markusova had never been in there before.

She stood shivering in the doorway without her coat, which she had put over Marketa Shapirova. She wore only a dress with no buttons on top, and under her shawl, it was obvious she had no underwear.

She was trembling all over and her teeth were chattering.

He looked over at her. "Women aren't allowed in here, don't you know that?"

The man conducting the service came from Hamburg. Since dusk, he'd already mixed up the Friday evening prayer with the Book of Ecclesiastes and he kept repeating, " . . . *of every tree of the garden thou mayest eat freely . . .* " and "*In the beginning God created the heavens and the earth . . .* "

There was something in his eyes which was quite the opposite of what he was saying as he recited the verses about how it all began.

"I came because of your wife, for heaven's sake," said Leonie Markusova.

Aaron Shapiro stared at the floor, droning on about offerings of food, about devotion and strength, quiet nights and fruitful days, of gathering strength, of rest, of laws, of sturdiness of body and strength of soul. He tried to avoid his own shadow without knowing why.

He turned toward the cantor, muttering his prayer feverishly, feeling Leonie Markusova's eyes on him.

After a few words he went back to imagining the soups he'd been thinking about before, a catalogue of all the Swiss soups they used to buy.

"You'd better go see her," Leonie Markusova said.

"I must finish this prayer."

"It's the Sabbath," the cantor spoke up, "so we must not complain."

"All right, I'm coming," said Aaron Shapiro.

Suddenly, for the first time, he thought about the Feast of Gladness. At other times he had recalled the Feast of Lights. But now it was all eclipsed by a hungry yearning for soup, the Swiss ones he'd been thinking about or any other kind, made out of dogs or cats or mice. In his mind's eye, he saw a kettle full of piping hot soup.

"Marketa isn't any better," said the second old woman.

"Today a person's better off being a little grey mouse," the old man grumbled to himself. "The tiniest mouse there is. He makes himself as small and unobtrusive as possible so nobody even notices him."

Behind them they could hear the cantor, intoning in his raspy voice. Then he was drowned out by the wind.

"I think she's taken a turn for the worse," said Leonie Markusova.

All at once everything came back to him—the things he'd been running away from when he'd gone to the other room. He had tried to bear up, like when he'd realized there was no point in drawing far-reaching conclusions about his fate. It was only in the beginning that he'd been convinced his decline and fall paralleled the world's decline and fall. Or that the extinction of everything and everybody went along with his own extermination. It was only at first that he was sure things couldn't go on that way, that something would have to happen. That was before he discovered that nothing would.

He went out of the room, ducking his head and shielding his face from the snow. For a moment, he felt the way he used to when he was on his way home. But it didn't add anything to what he knew. At first he'd been homesick for the streets he used to walk along, for places he used to go, people he knew. That filled his days and nights. There were so many people, so many places. But gradually, like old skin, it all shriveled away and no longer seemed to be so alive . . . their apartment, the house, things. After a year of the inactivity to which he'd been condemned, even remembering seemed unreal. It had all evaporated, like a whisper.

The stony floor of the corridor was already full of snow. The snow was white, pure, and smelled of clean water, of distant rivers, of close skies. It was hard to walk fast. And it wasn't warm. The stones were cracked. The snow was reaching his ankles. I need shoes, he thought to himself. The old black English shoes with a silver buckle and impenetrable soles would come in handy. He had left them at home, in the old apartment with the white sealed doors.

It had been now a long time since they'd been forced out of their apartments, houses, and cities and lands. It took years to build a home but only a short decree and a few hours to become homeless.

Now he could hear the cantor's voice again, and it sounded as if he'd been talking to God the whole time, addressing him as if he were an unfaithful mistress. He spoke accusingly: "Look how devoted I've been to you—how we've trusted each other! All the things we've looked forward to!" That whole afternoon and evening, it sounded as though the cantor's mistress had become a whore. "I lied to life and life lied to me." It was all the crippled yearning that had broken down here.

As if it had come out of the fog, fear, and hunger, or from the apathy these had produced, for the first time in his life he asked himself a question—though he probably wasn't the first one to ask it. What had God done before he created the world and what would he do afterwards? It was just one of those things which no longer had anything to do with him. He was just as unconcerned as when the cantor said that the worst sin of all is the crime of pride. He had a hunger which consumed him the way fire feeds on itself. He shivered with cold. Hunger and cold were like two walls with no room for anything else in between but loneliness, in which a man is a stranger even to himself. The things which had been uncertain before—like prayers for his wife's recovery—were becoming even more indefinite, something like distance, fog, nothingness.

"She's in a bad way. You ought to stay with her," the old woman said.

He let her go ahead. By now my hunger couldn't even be satisfied by soup made from my own blood, he said to himself. He remembered being with Marketa once in a French restaurant and ordering veal marengo, the classic French-Italian recipe created for Napoleon, as the waiter insisted. Tender pieces of veal simmered with tomatoes, pearl onions, ripe olives, and fresh mushrooms, folded in a crepe, and served with a spinach souffle and green salad.

"We can't just leave her like this," said Leonie Markusova.

"What do you mean, 'like this'?"

The wind dashed snowflakes into his face and they clung to his beard. They were big flakes and they did not melt. The house was completely white.

The other old woman watched Aaron Shapiro sink gratefully onto his wife's mattress to rest a bit.

Aaron Shapiro saw the broken thermometer on the floor. Beads of bluish mercury and splinters of glass. The mattress was thin and worn and smelled of ammonia. The straw was old.

"Marketa," he said. "I'm here—I'm with you now."

The snow gave off enough light so he could see how swollen her eyelids were. He could imagine the swirl of visions growing dimmer and dwindling behind them. He was almost annoyed to see she wasn't dead yet, and he was ashamed of himself. That wasn't what he'd wanted. He waited to see whether his voice would get through to her.

If I were in her place, I'd try to make it easier, he thought to himself. The snow made the room look lighter and the snowflakes, as they fell, made him think for a moment that her eyelids trembled.

"Can you hear me?" he asked his wife.

He noticed the other old woman watching him.

"Raise her head a bit," she suggested. "Does she have a fever?"

"I don't know. She doesn't feel hot."

"It's a shame," she said abruptly.

"It's dark," he said. "I can't see a thing."

As the wind shifted, it brought back the cantor's quavering voice. *"In the beginning God created the heavens and the earth . . ."* It sounded like both a path and a maze, like remembering and forgetting. *"In the beginning God created the heavens and the earth . . . and God saw that it was good . . ."*

"If they do come, send them for the doctor right away."

"You think she can hear me?" he wondered.

"The nearest doctor is in the Hamburg Caserne."

"I'm afraid she can't hear me."

"Why wouldn't she hear you? Marketa Shapirova."

"What did she have to say?"

"I had a few things to say myself," the other old woman retorted. "Or do you think I have no voice left or what?"

"Maybe she hears me and doesn't feel like answering."

"Try again in a little while. That's what I did."

Aaron Shapiro looked at her. Then he tried again. "Marketa. If you can hear me, but you're too sick to answer, just nod."

Her nearness felt different than it had when he'd left her earlier that evening.

Later, the light took on a different color as it was reflected by the snow. Around ten o'clock, ersatz coffee made from acorns was brought over from the Hamburg garrison where the working women were housed. He lifted the coffee mug to his wife's lips, holding his hand under her head.

"Drink some of this," he said.

The other old woman drained her cup in a single draft while it was still hot. Aaron Shapiro spilled coffee over his wife's chest and down the front of Leonie Markusova's coat.

"There, that's right," he said.

"Is she drinking it?" the other old woman asked. She hesitated to take back her coat. Should I? Shouldn't I? She didn't. "You are not cold," she asked. "Are you?" Then she lay down.

Aaron Shapiro could hear three different kinds of doubt in her voice. He couldn't contemplate snow.

"It's still snowing," she said. It was coming down in heavy flakes. "It's snowing as if it's never going to stop." After a while, she went on. "I'm surprised they brought us the coffee. This weather would have been a good excuse not to."

When he looked over at her, he realized she was still waiting for them to come.

"She'll drink it when she feels like it," he said after a while.

"Let's hope so," said the other old woman.

"You'll drink it when you feel like it, won't you?' he said to his wife.

"Maybe she feels more like sleeping than drinking," suggested Leonie Markusova.

"That's possible," he agreed.

"It wore her out, talking."

"I can imagine."

"What time do you suppose it is?"

"I have no idea. Ten o'clock? Eleven. Two."

"Do you think it'll go on snowing all night?"

"Do you intend to wait up all night and see?"

"I can't sleep anyway."

His arms were numb and he was afraid to move. The coffee had made a puddle on the floor. It would have been fairer if they'd killed us, he thought to himself. We don't mean anything to our friends anymore, and our enemies don't even notice. He could tell the other old woman wasn't sleeping either.

"Youth is nothing but a false paradise," he said. "Look at this snow. Just snow, snow, snow. And wind." He couldn't understand how it happened that kindness turns into cruelty, the way happiness becomes unhappiness, and life turns into death. "So much snow. And what will become of it?"

"What makes you think it's so?" Leonie Markusova replied to his words about a false paradise.

"It smells terrible in here," he went on. "Do we all stink so much now?" He stretched out slowly at his wife's side.

"Be glad you can still notice it, at least," the other old woman said. Then, after a while she added, "It's a funny light, isn't it?"

"Good night," he murmured to no one in particular.

"Good night," the other old woman replied.

"Good night, Marketa," he added.

"Good night," repeated the other old woman.

For a little while, Aaron Shapiro thought the sound of the wind and the snow outside was his wife's wheezing. And Leonie Markusova's breathing. Quietly he sipped his cold coffee, leaving just a bit in the bottom of the cup.

"Good night," he said again into the white darkness, just to confuse the other old woman in case she wasn't asleep yet. He spread his topcoat over his wife. Now she had three coats besides her blanket. Because it kept snowing it wasn't the coldest night. But everything was made wet, including her blanket and all the coats.

"Is she finally asleep?" whispered the other old woman. Her voice gave her away. She was fearful she would have to spend another night like the night before.

"Can't you sleep?" Aaron Shapiro asked her.

"I don't want to," Leonie Markusova told him.

"Maybe she's dreaming about the people she was happy with," he went on.

"Where do you suppose they are? What's become of everybody?"

He felt a sharp pain in his anus, as though his whole body was forcing itself through with a hollow, searing pressure.

"What's the matter?" asked Leonie Markusova. "It's ridiculous the way it goes on snowing. What will we do? Where can we take shelter? Where can we go?"

Just as he was dozing off, he heard footsteps and voices.

"I've been waiting for you to come," the other old woman said. Her voice had a different ring to it than when she'd been complaining about the snow.

Two girls had slipped into the room.

"You came over here in all this snow?" the old woman marveled.

"It'll be over within fourteen days," the second girl said.

"You came in this weather?" the old woman murmured contentedly.

"Apparently they have some secret weapon. They won somewhere in a town between some river and the steppes. Half the world's fighting against them by now. Even Brazil."

"You know where that is?" the first girl asked.

"I think so," the other old woman replied. She had no idea. The snow was white and illuminated the girls' faces, shoulders and arms, their visible breath. For a split second a different world crept imperceptibly into the room. The snow was veiling the old wooden beams, the cracked walls, and the stones on the floor. There entered for a fraction of a second, with the white breath of the two girls, a whiff of some distant, fighting, valuable life, an echo, where no explanation was needed. It was just as light and bright—and spinechilling.

"It may be over sooner than we think. In a week or two."

"Can you stop in at the Hamburg Caserne?"

"It can wait till morning," Aaron Shapiro said.

"What for?" the old woman demanded.

"I'll tell her your news," Aaron Shapiro added.

Then they were alone again.

"People are only human," the other old woman said. "They kill and steal and lie, but sometimes they surprise you."

She was silent for a while. "It's probably going to snow forever. By morning we'll all be snowed in."

Everything smelled. Old underwear, old skin, old sweat.

Even after a few hours Aaron Shapiro could tell she hadn't fallen asleep yet. She probably had a horror of the dead. The hours dragged on. She finally dozed off toward morning. He envied her sleep. For some things, our lives are too short, for others, too long.

"Marketa," he whispered. "Marketa."

He knew he'd changed because of what he believed in and what he'd stopped believing in, and by what, through indifference, was no longer even an echo of what it used to be. But he couldn't help it that it wasn't what it used to be. But probably nothing was. He could not find a trace of relief on her face.

Then he whispered to her, "Can you hear me?"

"I'm with you," he said at last.

Inwardly he wondered why it wasn't true. He touched the dead woman's forehead as if he wanted to see if his wife was still alive.

He wondered whether he had lost the last small fragment of the heaven he dreamed about in secret.

Guiltily, he realized that above all, he was sorry for himself. I envy the living and the dead. I envy the living their life, the dead their death. I also envy the portions of my own past which have already perished. And I don't have in me the kind of shame which could reverse it.

Marketa Shapirova's body at the crack of dawn was as cold as wax. Her long grey and black hair was the only thing about her that was still alive and growing. She did not move, even when he drew as close to her as he used to. He ran his bony fingers across her face, over the fathomless wrinkles, like the crevasses of every age and every battle, feeling how rough and dry the skin was. He waited for a while. Not a single tear came.

He left her eyes open until the morning.

The dark heavy snow went on falling.

Beginning and End

Jiri had noticed it, along with everybody else, as soon as they arrived. One corner of the ceiling of the one-story building was dark and sagging, a cobweb of wire and scaly plaster. It looked as though there would soon be a hole or at least that it would leak and rust when it began to rain. Or maybe it would simply collapse.

"It probably isn't rotten," he said.

"Bacteria, gentlemen," redheaded Richard observed, "are already teeming through the space between heaven and earth." He moved into the bottom bunk ahead of Jiri. He knew where the roof was rickety, like everybody else.

"Stop that," repeated the man who'd been saying "Big deal" when they were trying to figure out the camp's standing and had ranked it among the better ones. Red tidied his bunk. No matter how often they were moved around, he always went to the trouble to make a little piece of the camp homey, even if only for one night. After all, he said, a camp is kind of a home, too. In a way.

Red changed the subject. "This guy was all right until he found a letter from his mother to her lover. *I dread his breath close to me, his penis, which revolts me as passionately as I adore yours. I dread these lies I'm living. How can I bring up children this way?* This is what I call an innocent, naive world," he said. It was one of Red's many little stories. Yesterday he spoke of demons. The day before yesterday he resurrected all the ghosts of the alleged famous members of his family in Old Prague—rabbis, alchemists and judges, horse traders, pariahs, gamblers and coffeehouse parasites. He also returned to some elegant pre-war restaurants, describing them in great detail. He must have remembered the names from top to bottom and left to right.

At Jiri's side stood a shortsighted boy who was rather round-shouldered. He couldn't see well, but he didn't wear glasses. Hardly

anyone who had come from Poland wore glasses. One experience
had been enough for him. In Birkenau, everybody who didn't take
off his glasses in time went up the chimney. And then—as Red
added—each of them rode off on his own little cloud. Like in a bus.
Sometimes Red spoke of stars instead of clouds.

Jiri studied the wires sticking out of the ceiling. The shortsighted
one peered at the wires too.

Red Richard's pants were held up by a piece of strap from a German rifle. During their move from Poland to Germany, he had worn
it right next to his body. It was made of ox hide and it had a little
pouch attached to it, which he'd mended with glue. He didn't have
to carry cyanide around in a wad of cotton in his ear anymore.

Tidily, Red removed his jacket. He took out some thumbtacks
wrapped in a piece of paper. He folded the paper and put it away
again. It was a letter he'd carried around with him for a year and a
half.

He pushed a thumbtack carefully into the foot of his bunk and
hung his jacket on it. He rolled up his pants into a pillow and placed
them at the foot of his bunk.

"From now on, this is my sovereign territory," he announced.

He smoothed his shirt. They knew how proud he was of his one
gram of poison. Almost as if his twin brother he left in Auschwitz-
Birkenau was already dead, he had his own court of regulations and
laws next to those of the Germans. Some of them changed with each
day, night, hour, and minute, but some didn't change in spite of different barracks, kapos, commandants, and guards, because they were
part of Red Richard. He was the one who decided on the exceptions.
The gram of poison was proof of the control Red wanted to keep, if
not over his life, than at least over his death.

"You're awfully elegant," said Red's neighbor, the man with the
rough voice. They all knew why he said it, too. He thought Red
would share it with him.

It was getting dark. The hillside had been a pleasant green. Pine
trees, spruce, and birch grew here. There was that strange, aloof kind
of gentleness about the place that you find in nature. And it wasn't
the first time Jiri had read into it things whose answers had been
lost. As the sun set, the hillside first turned red and then began to
darken. The shadows elongated and the field in front of the bar-

racks, the building itself, and the sky, all turned cold. This is the way the world cools off each day, before tomorrow becomes another day.

"I don't like people who make such a production of saying their prayers, as if they're telling me, 'Hey, look how good I am and how we're being wronged.' Or as if they want to insure themselves, like 'If anybody's going to survive, at least we prayed.'"

Red adjusted his shorts.

"I can see how those Hungarian and Polish Jews, who've been claiming God's a hunk of dead sweet wood, are going to try to revive him. Like those beautiful Australian swimmers giving mouth-to-mouth resuscitation when somebody drowns."

"What do you mean by that?" asked the man with the saucepan.

"I'm talking about how some people treat God like a luxury, something that only goes with good conditions. About how God'll start convalescing just as soon as the Hungarian rabbis start getting their strength back again."

Immediately he added: "Have you ever heard of those Japanese kamikaze pilots? The ones who fly those planes that are also torpedoes and time bombs? How they take off, headed right for an enemy ship or moving target, and smash themselves to smithereens, target and all?" The he said, "I saw a picture of a group of them getting ready to take off. They were receiving cherry blossoms from the nicest girls in town. Somebody threw away a copy of the papers, but before that, I got a careful look at them. They all looked feeble-minded. It took me by surprise. I expected strong-willed guys, not sissies."

"Maybe somebody else is still going to come," said the man holding an empty saucepan by the window.

In Poland someone had told him that in Germany prisoners are fed twice a day, sometimes five hundred, but at least three hundred calories. He kept one foot in his bottom bunk so nobody else could take it. Finally he placed his pan at the edge of the bunk and lay down. This wasn't the first time he'd been fooled. That can happen despite a lot of experience to the contrary, because it's always better to believe in some things than not to.

"This camp's like the planet Neptune," said redheaded Richard. "You see, Neptune was never sighted with any of the earlier telescopes, like the other stars, but somebody figured it must be there.

Some Frenchman, followed Mr. Newton's crazy theory. And then some German actually did discover it. He saw this little dot in the sky, and, lo and behold, it was Neptune. And me, in Birkenau, I used to dream about a camp like this one, where you just worked and they didn't have Cyklon B. At first I just imagined it, then I really found it. A new planet. *Meuslowitz bei Leipzig Aussenkomando Buchenwald.* My lovely little planet, where at least they don't gas people."

And then he said, "I can see already that if things go on this way, we'll leave here in a parlor car. I already know what to order for dessert with expresso coffee. Strawberry Crepe Supreme—luscious fresh strawberries, with sour cream or whipped cream, and brown sugar. Waiter, please!"

"What happened to that fellow's mother?" asked the man with the saucepan to change the topic. He was lying down too, already. He had his saucepan with him, like a lover.

"She'd tell him, 'You're stepping out on me, aren't you, darling? Come on, 'fess up!' And he'd say, 'Look, imagine two apple trees and one gardener. Which tree should he tend: the one with the sweet apples or the one whose fruit is tart and tasteless? You know what I mean?' She did. 'Except you're no gardener,' she said. 'You're a whore-chaser. And don't expect me to play along.'"

Nobody had anything to say to that. It looked as though Red Richard had finally run out of ammunition. They were in a new camp, and in addition it was in German territory. New possibilities had opened for them, all tempered by the usual uncertainties. Besides, none of the German officials had come to check, which wasn't the only thing that contributed to their uneasiness. They knew it was the silence that had set him off. Sometimes just talking was enough. A short while ago they'd heard some Polish women singing. Then there was the din of the chemical and munitions plants. There must be a kennel somewhere in the middle of the hill, now fading into darkness, because now and then, dogs barked. They knew what kind of dogs those were.

But there was the excitement of change, which was like a curtain, but you couldn't see what was behind it yet. Twice during the afternoon, enemy formations had flown over the camp. They were accompanied from the ground by two sixty-second and four fifteen-second sirens.

Until that time, they had stood out in front of the barracks, and the only thing the German guards ordered them to do was to look at the ground during the air raid, not up at the sky. Whoever looked up would be shot. During an air raid, looking at the sky was, the guard said, *"Strengstens verboten!"* The order was a threat; there above the thin clouds, the planes were a first encouraging sign, flying out of range of the local anti-aircraft fire. Red knew they were B-17's, Flying Fortresses, which could fly farther than anybody had ever dreamed was possible. It was like touching another world which was still unvanquished. And the fact that they were in Germany, and not in Poland anymore, meant something too, even though they didn't know how to evaluate it yet.

Jiri pondered the changes. He watched as darkness slowly fell. He thought about two things most. Both of them were connected with Germany. In the freight car which had brought them here, a nineteen-year-old soldier had been guarding them, and this soldier told them what was on his mind because he couldn't find anybody but prisoners to talk to. He'd been present when the transports came from Hungary, twenty-one days and nights, one after another. And now he was on his way home to his parents on leave, and he knew that if he told his mother or his father or his grandparents even a fraction of what he'd seen, they'd think he'd gone out of his mind. But the soldier was afraid it wasn't madness. And he was scared that when he had to go back, he'd really go out of his mind, or he wouldn't, which he considered to be even worse. He spoke of suicide, and Jiri told him what he'd heard from Jewish war veterans, that the best way is to stick a loaded revolver in your mouth, but to be sure, it's best to fill the barrel with water first. And then there was the lieutenant who'd brought them here and turned them over to the guards. He hadn't yelled at them once the whole way from the station.

"Hasn't it been quiet?" Red asked suddenly. "I always get suspicious when it's so quiet. I'd just as soon erase days like this from the calendar."

Red told the story he'd heard from an Argentinean Jew who'd been in the Brazilian wholesale coffee business in Prague before the war. "When God made man," he said, "he took some clay, patted it into shape, and stuck it in the oven. When he took it out, he saw he hadn't made a very good job of it; he hadn't left it in the oven long enough. So he put it back in again. When he took it out again, he saw he'd left it in there too long. So he tried a third time. Finally he succeeded. That was how he made the first Jew."

"Don't you know any better stories about ovens?" demanded the man with the saucepan.

"Just that I'm starting to get ovens mixed up with heaven," Red said.

Even those who were still standing around or saying their prayers began to get undressed. It was possible they'd forgotten that their real camp life began only in the morning. Probably.

Jiri decided to take his clothes off too. That was when Red Richard cautiously lit a candle. Red had dozens of habits which made him look like one of the chosen who had survived until now. *Now* was a candle. When Jiri was naked he could feel Red looking at him.

"Actually, you do have quite a nice white body. And that thing of yours happens to be young and white too. Women are going to enjoy doing it to you."

Jiri hung his clothes over the edge of the bunk to air out for a while. He'd worn them for the past two weeks. He looked down over his body and felt his bones, running his hands over his skin.

"Some women love to do it," Red went on. "It's just about the gentlest thing they can do with it. But you mustn't expect them to do it too often. Or just not *that* way. But every good lioness will do that for you, to the very end."

Jiri didn't say anything. It was still one of the more confusing stories he carried with him. Hunger, cold, and fear weren't so bad because they were physical pains. But Red's feelings got confused whenever he started thinking about incest and all the kinky things people are always asking from each other, always singing the praises of some strange practice, God knows what.

Red grinned. "Life's worthwhile as long as a woman can do that to me," he said. And then he said, "Now the only thing is to survive. But once I survive, then the quality of the life I lead will be important. You know what I mean?"

It was peaceful and quiet all around. It reminded them of just how short a time the ground flak had tried to hit the foreign planes. Women insurgents from Warsaw lived in the next barracks. Red had found that out.

"Isn't it strange that a lot of chess grandmasters all around the world are anti-Semitic? Sometimes even when they are Jewish themselves. Why? One world chess champion—you probably know who I mean—escaped to Berlin from Moscow and claims that Jews aren't intelligent enough to play chess decently. He should try me."

"I don't even wonder anymore," commented the man with the saucepan.

"A lot of people in charge today are pretty eccentric," Red Richard added. "It's nothing new. One French writer smoked cigars while making love to prove sex isn't the greatest pleasure on earth. My last janitor in Prague didn't like it when he made love to his wife from behind and she ate an apple at the same time."

Jiri rather enjoyed it when Red talked about women. There was a tantalizing mystery that Red was close to, here and in Poland. But even Jiri had his own two experiences, and both of them corresponded to what Red had said. When he'd worked at the dividing machine in a munitions factory, a splinter of metal had flown into his eye. The little German corporal took him to the factory doctor, a woman who refused to treat him, saying it wasn't her duty to look after the prisoners. Besides that, she told the guard, the eye was badly infected and nothing could be done without an operation anyway. To show the guard, she made him sit down on a stool and turned a bright light on Jiri's throbbing eye. The corporal put another worker on his machine and took him back to the barracks. Jiri knew what it meant to go blind in a camp. The guard stopped in front of the infirmary. There was nobody there but an untrained Russian nurse's aide. The corporal asked where she was from. She told him she had been captured when the German army approached the besieged city by Lake Ladoga. "*Ach Ja, Petersburg,*" said the corporal. She talked with the guard as if she wished her words could kill him. In the meantime, she boiled a scalpel and removed the splinter from his eye. Afterwards, they'd killed that Russian girl.

"A person ought to enjoy himself before he's exterminated," Red concluded.

And then: "Doesn't it seem almost ridiculous that they'll kill you in any case, even if you have some peaceful occupation like a traveling salesman in leather and dry goods? Or that death has so many faces; in the end, you get exterminated, whether it's in a war, by mistake, in an accident, by starvation, by a bullet, or in a train wreck, with gas or germs. But you can always count on it."

He warmed his hands in front of the candle flame for a while, and then he blew it out and pinched the wick so it wouldn't smoke.

Nobody had to answer that.

Jiri looked out the window. They were just at the edge of the hillside. Judging by their barracks and the barracks of the Polish women, this must be a new camp.

He thought of how they had been brought here from the railroad station that afternoon by a gaunt lieutenant in an SS field uniform, with the two lightning bolts and a skull emblem on his cap. The lieutenant's teeth were bared and it looked as though he were grinning, but he wasn't. His jaw was crooked and scarred; probably malaria.

On the way from the station, each of them had tried to map the route in his own memory—it might come in handy someday, you never knew.

Red sighed, as if he were forced to interrupt his monologue.

"Money's nice," he said, "but you can never feel close to it. You can't love it like you can love a woman."

Then he added: "Try caressing it and then wait for it to caress you back. Try buying something with it on a desert island."

Jiri crawled up on his bunk and stretched out. Red lay on the bottom, the nearsighted boy in the middle. Jiri tried not to notice the rotting ceiling. He was chewing on a straw. It was strange, tearing off a blade of dry grass in Poland and to be chewing it still in Germany. Sometimes, he'd bite off a little piece and grind it slowly between his teeth, as though he didn't want to part with it. He wondered how long he could make it last.

He didn't understand that SS man in the green cap with the visor who had brought them here and left immediately. He hadn't shouted at them once, all the way from the railroad station. Red was busy trying to find the most comfortable position.

"We aren't exactly satisfied with the food here either, Lieutenant. The diet is unsatisfactory. I miss zinc and iron in my blood and, of course, vitamin C. Nobody should blame me if Jewish children born after the war are shorter and skinnier." And after a deep sigh, "I was spoiled at home. Until my fifteenth birthday, my father and mother were divorced, but then they remarried each other. My uncle was famous for his high-quality smoked herring."

That reminded him of the story of his Polish uncle who fell in love with a rabbi's daughter, with whom a corporal of the Polish cavalry was also in love. The corporal challenged his uncle to a duel, while the rabbi's beautiful daughter looked on, enchanted, thrilled that because of her these two young men would suffer at least a nosebleed. "They agreed to meet on the following day at sunrise in a grove of fir trees. But that same evening, Uncle thought it over. With his pistol money, he bought steerage passage on the SS Batory and later became the smartest grocery store owner on the island of Manhattan. When I last heard of him, Colonel, he'd framed her letters in gold. She started writing to him when her corporal gave her a disease. Our people are always moving up in this country, even if otherwise there's a shortage of rope. But I'd like to point out that a few people do get very nervous when they don't have a rational home life, like some of the people I know. Some individuals would still be quite at home in the jungle, sir."

They didn't know what to expect, even though they saw for themselves what was missing. There usually weren't gas chambers in labor camps. The crematoriums were too small, too.

"Did you notice that SS man was wearing gloves all the time?" demanded the skeptic, whom the other men had nicknamed Golden Eyes.

"He probably had his hands shot up in Africa," Red Richard stated promptly. "Around Tripoli or in the Sahara. Or maybe someplace that isn't even on the map."

Nobody had anything to say, so Red decided he might as well go on talking. "We've got the right to file a lawsuit with the International Railroad Stations Court, which now occupies the building of the former League of Nations in Geneva. It's swamp fever. Every three days, tremendous attacks of fever. Imagine that impertinent protozoon moving in on your red blood corpuscles as if they were a dormitory and then destroying them."

"Yackety-yak," the rough voice spoke up. They couldn't turn Red Richard off, but maybe they didn't want to.

Jiri was only listening with half an ear now. He could see the lieutenant's gaunt face. Those green eyes he'd tried to read. What kind of person was he, what could one expect from him?

"Maybe he's a decent guy," he said.

"How can you say such a thing?" asked the man with the saucepan.

"He laughed at me," said Jiri.

"It's chills, I tell you," insisted Red.

"We have no proof and nobody ever will have," observed Golden Eyes.

"What evidence do you have?" a voice asked harshly.

"What evidence *don't* you have?" asked someone in a gentle voice.

"He'd be one of our ninety million," Richard replied.

"I wish at least somebody would behave a little better," Jiri said.

"You're still a greenhorn Jew and not just because you got stuck with the worst bunk," declared Red. "A gentleman in uniform like that can only be decent six feet under, to put it politely and objectively. Absolutely under the turf."

"He hasn't yelled at us yet," Jiri pointed out.

"He's still going to have a few opportunities, kid," said the skeptic.

"Anyway," said Jiri.

The darkness thickened. Jiri wondered what kind of person the man in the SS cap was, how he would probably behave. Not just because he hadn't yelled at them, but because that was not, after all, normal here.

Here, air raids would probably be the worst part. The order not to look up. An order like that is quite welcome.

For the first time in his life he wished he could be sure about this one person, at least, even though he was only one out of ninety million. He knew it was ridiculous, the longer he thought about it. But it would be a kind of breakthrough. He knew what it would mean if this one single person were to be the exception to an infallible truth.

"Can you sweeten with salt and salt with sugar?" Red called in his direction.

Jiri stretched out and put his hands under his head. He observed the texture of the hole in the ceiling. The cracked roof above him reminded him once more of the gaunt, sallow face of that guy with malaria.

Jiri wondered what would happen if he smiled at that malarial face. It's just high spirits, Jiri reminded himself. Things better not talked of. Better to keep quiet. But he wished somebody would help him make up his mind what kind of person the officer was and how he would treat them.

"Is it comfortable up there?" called the nearsighted boy.

"It's all right," Jiri told him.

"I wish somebody would explain to me why, of all things, a person is always inclined to impress his own enemies," mused Red.

"If you want to, you can lie down here with me," offered the nearsighted boy.

"Actually, I have nothing against fags personally," declared Red Richard. "I don't object to bald heads or flatfoots and deviants; as long as nobody is trying to rape me, I like practically everybody. Humanity would become extinct if everybody was a pansy, and quicker than Papa Himmler plans it."

They were used to Red calling Doctor Mengele "my dearest, good-hearted cousin" and Adolf Hitler "the peaceful, misinformed or misled lover of children, dogs, and toothbrushes," who had no idea how Papa Himmler and his *Unterführer* treated him with his *Einsatzgrüppen*—his top-secret special commandos—and that to comprehend all this was just a matter of having "the right Nazi *Weltanschauung*." To Red, General Heydrich of Prague was "a gentleman and close friend, a person of incredible kindness," and a mass grave was "a little German rose garden"; he called extermination camps "my favorite spas, where no one in the end is cold. That's just waiting for one's turn. It's been a marvelous experience, God knows. Hitler wants only the very best for all Germans—except he wants it from all others. No exception," he mused.

"Who needs generations of anti-Semites with you around?" said the man with the saucepan.

There was in Red some still unvanished need for an achievement, recognition or personal identity, more than a number. Remnants of his inner life which kept him getting up while falling. There was also something of the charlatan in him, with all the twists of his fate, missed family members, friends and enemies, and it was unbelievable how easily he could get more attention.

"The Nazis shouldn't be happy making me work for them," said Red. "If I would labor as a slave so effectively for myself, I wouldn't be happy at all. And then, one has to try to make every place where he is at home the most beautiful place in the world." He caressed the wood and the wall. "We have been very lucky coming to this place. So far things were very informal. A person must know how to adjust—to everything. The faster the better. There goes the wind, there goes the coat. Where are those times where plague and tuber-culosis were the greatest killers?"

"Are you talking from starvation?"

"No. I'm thinking what the Germans are going to do when they kill us all, when they'll have some time left. To kill the others is mat-ter-of-fact suicide. They would have to kill themselves. I wonder if the last man on earth will be Hitler."

"You're talking from fever."

"Maybe. I already survived here a day. And I'm thirty."

"That means you have a bigger half of your life behind you."

"Who knows at dinner that he'll live to breakfast? For sure you know only what's behind you."

It was quiet again. Jiri had never experienced this kind of silence.

"Even the best of them can only be good under two well-weighed tons of dirt," redheaded Richard voiced Jiri's thoughts.

"Our kind of people have to be smart. We've got to start thinking things over right now: what is, what was, and what will be; where did it start and where is it going? And everybody is everybody else's referee, even for ourselves."

"For me, they're dead, even if they're still alive," said the rough voice.

"I don't agree," Red answered promptly. "One thing I'm not sure about is how many of them and which ones we are going to allow to run loose around the world. Or whether I won't swiftly and diligent-ly prepare graves for all of them with nice turf cushions."

They'd all prefer to be far away from here, Jiri thought to himself. Yet he was still wondering whether he ought to risk smiling at the malarial skull-face. He liked listening to the redhead's blabber. The mysteries of how it was going to be when the war ended, of what was on their minds now. It was what they were all waiting for, but they couldn't imagine it. Somebody will come to the camp gate and grab the latch.

"Hi there, fellas! Well, it's all over. Other dances are in style now. You're lucky you lived through it. Pick up your marbles and clear out of here and make room for others. Just go, as far as your legs can carry you. We're going to raze this place to the ground."

An American Tommy or a Russian Ivan or some "rassig" Jewish face in an Allied uniform. Who knows?

The moon came out. The silhouettes of the fence, the hillside, and the watchtowers were visible. The wind carried the sound of dogs barking.

Jiri was almost glad no one replied to Red's last remark. Even though he usually waited for these replies. He just could not imagine what it could possibly be like, just as he could not imagine so many other things. Maybe I'll have to sock that malarial skull-face. But he would feel a lot better if he could be sure of what was a real smile and what was a grimace.

We are insects to them, lice, or something worse. And it's been that way for three years. But like everything else this too contained a bit of paradox.

"Somebody ought to go out and have a look around," said the rough voice.

"I agree, for a change," answered Red Richard.

"Why should we just sit and wait for nothing?" said the rough voice.

Jiri knew it upset him to think about revenge. That was the strongest yearning that was left, after the urge to eat one's fill, or take a bath. It took the edge off all the talk about women which Red and he too relished so much. But even that was only possible when they weren't getting knocked around or when they weren't absolutely famished. When hunger was bad enough, it consumed everything else. But just a mouthful was all they needed—a bit of bread or a piece of sugar beet—and then they started thinking about getting back at them again. Everybody was waging his private war with Germany. Just as Germany was waging war with every one of them. As Red put it, they were all at war, but one more so than the other, and the difference included every second, every eclipse of the sun or of the moon, every blunder or wrong number, every stone kicked aside or the other side of any second. Their loathing had a thousand faces. And it was only when a person's true thoughts fell away, that things began to fall apart. But despite everything, loathing had already killed a lot of people, Jiri thought to himself, and it would still kill a lot more. But there were also a thousand faces to letting oneself be killed, too. And, in addition to witnesses who could tell about it, there were countless other people who could no longer speak about it.

And now they were in Germany and the question was whether they were right to regard all Germans in exactly the same way. Sometimes during the night they would talk about revenge and hope they would miss the most brutal part of it, so that they would not repeat what should not be repeated. Even Red and the nearsighted boy were like little kids who think that it is sufficient to shut their eyes in order to obliterate what they cannot then see. It wasn't just cowardice that made so many of them wish it could happen without them, especially the man with the rough voice for whom "Germany had ceased to exist." He even pronounced it with a small "g." It was more like spitting than speaking the word. He said that for him, there couldn't be a less interesting country on earth than Germany. Why? Because there was no mystery to the Germans anymore; they'd lost all their secrets.

"I can go out and have a look around if you want me to," Jiri said.

"I'll go with you," offered the nearsighted boy.

"You can't see worth a damn, there's no point," Red told him.

"I can see in the dark like a wildcat, if you want to know," said the boy.

"All my earthly possessions," said Red, stroking his belt.

It was warm outside. The wind from the hillside smelled of resin and green leaves. The reek of chemicals rolled from the factory. All munitions plants stink like that, Jiri thought. They smell different when they are new.

Now they could figure out roughly the position of the camp and of the small town. The camp was concealed from the north by a gently sloping, wooded hill. The white trunks of the birch trees were thin, like famished women. There was something firm and tender in them. Outside, beside the barbed wire, there was a splintered wooden propeller, probably from some small American plane that had been shot down nearby. The propeller and the other pieces reminded them both of the afternoon's raid.

It was kind of a mirage: the thirsty man in the desert who quenches his thirst with an image of cold water. It's only a dream of water. This had been the nature of their thoughts many times before. They were like men who were finished but don't fully realize it. Knowing it makes it come sooner.

That accident with the steel splinter in the eye had happened at

Auschwitz-Birkenau, in the *Buna Werke* where he and the nearsighted kid used to work.

All I'm after is to feel what it's like to be that German, he said to himself. It's clear to me why I want to.

"Sometimes they have fighter planes with plywood sides to make them lighter," said the shortsighted boy.

From the south, you could see the town. Houses and church steeples and fences were silhouetted in the moonlight and starlight. They figured it must have a population of several tens of thousands. They were always making calculations as if everything depended on it.

The factory was working two shifts, and now and then a light flashed as if someone were adjusting blackout curtains. Then everything was drowned in darkness again.

In the moonlight, a church spire stabbed the sky. It was a handsome Catholic church with a cross on top. The name of the town was Meuslowitz. The nearest big town was Leipzig.

"We can use that propeller for firewood," said Nearsighted. "It would be a pity to leave it here," he added. There were kennels beside the powder magazine. The dogs were barking. That reminded them of hunger. Hunger made Jiri afraid and fear reminded him of something else too. It was all connected. The women's barracks were not far and they could hug its shadow. They could both stay in the shadow.

"I can see Red getting back to Prague XII and heading straight for the post office, saying, 'Mr. Postmaster, I'm back again. Isn't there some registered mail here for me?'"

Nearsighted was whispering and in his whispers there was a soft chuckle. It was a nice evening. They felt good. Jiri's tension eased. It's worth risking things for a little bit of freedom, he thought. It gets impossible otherwise.

"There'll be a lot of that after the war," whispered the shortsighted boy.

"That's still a long way off," Jiri replied.

He realized it was seething inside the boy too, ready to boil over, like in himself. The sky was clear and silent, full of stars.

"It's a beautiful evening," said the nearsighted boy.

"I don't think there's any sense in talking so much about it yet," observed Jiri.

"I think it's Friday," said Nearsighted.

"You're right, like that kid this afternoon when he said he felt God in his breast," said Jiri. "He thought it was because they hadn't yet managed to kill his conscience."

"Let's hope they won't kill it along with him," said Nearsighted.

"I think that can wait," said Jiri.

The shortsighted one didn't answer.

"Are you hungry?" Jiri asked him. "If there are Italians and Frenchmen here besides us and the women from Warsaw, we'll really have a great time in the factory."

"I hope we go to the tool room to work," said Nearsighted.

Then they noticed there was someone standing on the other side of the barbed wire.

"Do you think there's electricity in it?" asked Jiri.

"You'd better not try."

Jiri whistled softly. It was one of the Polish women. Her profile was turned to the moonlight, which made her shoulder appear to be made of silver. She was about twenty. She was dressed in a potato sack and smelled of potatoes. Nearsighted took a few steps forward.

"Good evening," he said.

"Good evening," said the woman in Polish.

It was pleasant to hear a soft woman's voice. Maybe it was just as good for her to hear his voice.

"Where do they hand out the food around here?" he asked.

She understood him well. Her hair was short, blond, and bristly. She looked at them a long time before she answered. They told her where they had come from and how many they were. They learned that there were about two thousand women in the camp and that most of them worked at the ramp unloading steel sheets for the munitions factory. They were watched by female guards with Alsatian dogs. Those Catholic songs came from the barracks where she was.

"Not in the evening anymore," she replied in Polish. "They hand it out at noon. And in the evening, it's just for the night shift so they won't get hungry at work and start stealing."

She pointed into the darkness with her forefinger. Then she said she had been in the sewers. Neither Jiri nor the nearsighted kid understood what she meant by that.

"Just once," she repeated. Then she smiled and stepped back, as though she were afraid of them after all.

The church steeple she'd been gazing at was silvery from the front and dark on the other side. The Polish girl paused a few steps away from them. She seemed to be crying. But when they looked at her, she smiled. They could see her white teeth and the gaps where her teeth were missing.

"Good night," she said.

"Good night," they answered her.

She backed away into the darkness. They passed her barracks and went back to their own.

"What did she say?" asked Red.

"It's like everywhere else. You get fed just once a day," Jiri answered.

"OK, I understand, Herr Brigadier General, one meal every twenty-four hours for a twelve-hour shift. That's less than my grandfather got while building pyramids in what's today Cairo. Progress continues—human kindness as well as technical advancement, more for the working people."

"Yeah," said the saucepan man. "In Germany they are not even consuming sugar. I haven't seen a cube of sugar now for more than two years."

"It means the years of great famine are not over yet?" said Red.

"What did you expect?"

"So there are young girls here," sighed Red. "It means a combination of work and love, and it's a perfect merging of your interests and mine, Herr Obergruppenführer. To be gallant again. Feminine forces do influence my seeing, thinking, and daydreaming. Are they as esoteric as I'm used to?"

"You know, it's nice and warm out," said the nearsighted boy.

"Was she pretty?" Red was interested.

"I couldn't see very well, but she looked all right," he replied. "She was smiling and crying."

"Women do that, it makes them beautiful."

"Well, go on and open the door then, if it's warm outside," suggested the saucepan man.

"Don't make a draft for me here," said the man by the door.

Suddenly they stopped. There was no sound, inside, outside, or anywhere else. The silence pressed in on every side, as if there were no factories here, no town, nothing but forests. They waited for Red Richard to break the silence. Red was exhausted now; he too was silent. Sometimes he imagined he was smoking cigars, and his life was a circle that looked just like the smoke rings he puffed over the top of his imagined glass of beer.

"Red?" the saucepan man called out.

"Would you believe it, I finally feel like sleeping?" Red yawned. "I can't get excited about it," he said.

"This is quite a small camp for such a big factory," Jiri observed. "With two twelve-hour shifts."

"Their barracks is as big as ours," said the nearsighted boy.

"Lieutenant, it would almost pay to have a café or canteen, with the number of people we have here," said redheaded Richard finally. "Those rebellious ladies from the east can form a choir with us. Or just a room with a few tables."

"A whorehouse, you mean?"

"No, just a couple tables and chairs where people can sit around and talk and listen to nice dance music."

"What are you going to call your new café?" asked the rough voice.

"Chez Theodor Herzl or The Leipzig Café. What's the difference? Honolulu Bar, Bar America, Dusseldorf Coffee House, Latrine Café. It doesn't matter."

"You really don't need anybody but yourself," declared the saucepan man.

"Are you jealous?"

"Yeah," said the saucepan man. "I'm dying of jealousy."

"Nobody can ever manage all by himself," Red stated sadly, as if he could see in his mind the kidnapping of a bride before the wedding night. "Here finally I feel like I'm in a tavern. Solitary but not alone."

"You never stop trying."

"My mother used to say you should be fair in your judgments of other people," said Red. "Otherwise you are going to lose an awful lot of them."

"Once when we were building air-raid shelters back in Theresien-stadt, we beat up a Jewish boy because he made it very clear to us that he was more German than anybody else," said Jiri. "We let him exercise his muscles with a shovel and pick for a couple extra hours, so he'd get it out of his system. His dad was *Oberscharführer* Kleindienst, personal chauffeur of some big wheel in General Daluege's staff in Prague. When they were taking a shower, one of his chauffeur buddies noticed that he was circumcised. So overnight, they crossed him off the list of supermen and sent him straight to *Theresienbad.*"

"I was afraid he wanted to prove something else," said Red. "If you know what I mean."

"No, I don't, to tell you the truth," Jiri admitted.

"That reminds me of a lot of things, and most of them were beautiful," said Red, and then he fell silent again.

And like a mist, the unknown, the thing they felt so intimately, still remained. The yesterday which repeats itself over and over again.

Jiri didn't know whether the present was what kept bringing back nightmares, or whether it was those old nightmares that were responsible for their presence here.

He knew that it was only among the people he was with now that he could feel less alone than he had ever felt, each of his own, as though he were approaching the moment when it would be better to touch the wires or to put an end to his own quest for himself by the kind of suicide that was offered him.

Those were the moments when many of them had wanted to die. All they wanted was for it to happen quickly and painlessly with a strong jolt of electricity into the wires, because sometimes there wasn't much. Or a good dose of Cyklon B, because sometimes the Germans were being frugal, and instead of the customary five minutes, people choked and strangled for more than half an hour. Sometimes—for children—it took as long as three hours.

It was a thick web of loneliness, fear, and apathy in which you could discern a wish not to live. As they used to dream of sunny streets where people walked free and unafraid, or of children at play, of men and women in love, these dreams were suddenly confronted now with other dreams where the most beautiful thing was to die.

But now Red and the others were silent, as though they'd grown tired of listening to their own words.

Everything Red wanted to hear was expressed again in silence.

Jiri tossed restlessly in his bunk. They could hear him rolling around in search of a better position. They all knew what for. Nobody had any idea of what time it was. The flickers of light in the factory probably meant it was only ten o'clock and the shifts were changing.

He thought about circles without even being aware of it: the circles which were the thousands of men, women, and children who dreamed of leaving the camps or of dying.

Where it begins, he thought, it also ends, and the end is where it begins. There was no feeling of time or place, no realization of the finite. Maybe no one would believe in such a place, such people, such time—maybe it's only inside me, part of my sick memory. People and places passing as if they never were, reminding me that I am still alive. Other things are repeating themselves as they continue on and on.

His nights and days. There were weeks without Mondays or Tuesdays or Saturdays. There was only light fading into dark and dark progressing back into light. Days went by unnamed; a week, a month was completed and the circle began again.

It started when they had been transported from the gypsy camp in Auschwitz-Birkenau with a big "T" on their foreheads to this small camp without gas chambers at Meuslowitz by Leipzig, not far from a German military cemetery, at the end of the town, with a group of Catholic women from Warsaw and Italian deserters who shared the barracks. The change was what had given way to his new thoughts and had brought some tiny new hope for something better, perhaps a break from the circles. At night or a moment like this he also thought about leaving all of this someday. A chain of thoughts grew, bringing him closer to the time when—perhaps—he would walk out of the gates of the camp and return to things he had known before all of this began, and to things he had never known but only heard of. It brought him images of new colors, people and smiles. Images of the wall of the German military cemetery—he never saw inside because of the huge wall. Maybe it is in nine cases out of ten a lie, and yet.

Every day—without knowing why—and every night he searched for a reason for everything. He searched for a beginning; where and why did it all begin? But the beginning of their world was just as ambiguous as its ending. There were many why's, but nobody was able to figure them out. The better or worse parts of some crippled privilege of seeing, breathing, or dreaming. Of all that makes people, things, or images strong or weak—secrets, values, measures. Something everybody wants to understand and no one understands. There was a confusion of why's, something that begins in the dust, but touches the stars. Why's—his why's. It was like a long bridge between the camps and freedom, between death and life, a long-dead miracle that couldn't disappear.

But still Jiri, like all of them, when not deadly tired, and even then, searched for an answer. He searched for a break. His one possibility lay in the neighborhood of the German military cemetery or in the face of the German lieutenant who had brought them here. He hadn't shouted at them once, and there was a chance that the grimace on his face, distorted by malaria, was a piece of a smile. Who was he? Really? What did he want? Why was Jiri persuaded to try to smile at him the next chance he had? Perhaps the lieutenant was different from all the rest. Maybe there were still some things left. It would all depend on the lieutenant's response to his smile. But what if the opportunity never came? He thought about it now, that mouth sick with malaria.

"You know what Alexander of Macedonia said when they asked him why he was crying? He'd already conquered the whole world and he was grieving because he had nothing left to conquer," red-headed Richard said.

"You must be awfully well read, Red," said Jiri.

"Not really," grunted Red Richard. It was worming its way into his brain as insistently as silence was into Jiri's skull. "I heard about it last week at Auschwitz-Birkenau when we were twelve hours out on the *appell-platz*. And, also, that he never made love to his women. They had to be up on him and make it to him. The greatest of men are doing things upside down."

Then he said, "It's a kick to look at your beauty from below. Don't forget it, kid."

"No, I won't," said Jiri.

Red had black spots before his eyes. He sighed. "You can love them, respect or despise them. All at once or a bit of everything every so often. And they still will remain an inspiring mystery, a talking sphinx. You would need three dozen brains like Charles Darwin or Albert Einstein to get it. It's the only mystique of life remaining a puzzle even after my residence in the gypsy camp in Auschwitz-Birkenau. There was, is, and will be a military hazard for every male trying to conquer all their biological and psychological fortifications."

"My ankles swell and my ears ring when I stand up for a long time," put in the man with the saucepan. "My skin feels tight, as if my chest and my legs and arms and head had all grown bigger and my skin'd shrunk, the thing that holds it all together. Like a balloon pumped full of air. And my heart thumps like I'd been running. When I have to stand too long, I see movies I've never even seen in front of my eyes. Movies I'll probably never see."

"It's all the same to me, when I've got to stand for a long time," the shortsighted boy contributed. "I couldn't care less by now."

"Does the water rush into your legs from the rest of your body?" asked the man with the saucepan.

"Actually, the last time I really felt in my element was in Birkenau," Red went on. "There was this rabbi from Transylvania, a heretic and mystic, who asked another heretic-mystic whether a chicken's still kosher after it's swallowed a pin. And how many worlds God made and discarded before he created this perfect work. They used to talk about the sperm of people that have already perished and are stored away somewhere in Switzerland. And that the story of Frankenstein was written by that English lady after a visit to Prague. Apparently, she was influenced by the story of the Golem, who was invented by Rabbi Löw. And that being too suspicious and clever for his people he never got to be the chief rabbi of Prague. They preferred his older brother. The family left for North America. (They should be merchants in the counting machine business by now.) Those two rabbis in Birkenau looked at the smoke coming out of the chimney and pondered whether it was really smoke or the difference between truth and lies. Or between right and wrong. Or, just and unjust. One of the rabbis claimed the world began as a ball which exploded and went on sputtering. That's how it's all going to end anyway, he said. The other one was imagining how they were going to blow up along with everything they were talking about. That was their last selection. They went up the chimney, along with

the story the first rabbi had told: God let it be known that the seed
that was supposed to bring forth a child to a certain Jewish woman
would turn out to be the righteous one who would fix everything as
soon as it had grown. So the devil complained that it was unfair to
him: Well, what am I going to do with them if all of them are to be
faultless? To which God replies that he shouldn't worry: that there's
another seed—of his man—in another lady. The catch is that the
second one'll look just as trustworthy as the first; so, besides the two
of them nobody else in the world will be able to tell. Good, huh?
Get it?"

"Didn't they say that man is greater than God?" asked the man
with the saucepan. "And that creation and destruction are like German food from the same pot?"

"No, they just said that two kings can't wear one crown. And that
a king's not a king until everybody recognizes him as such," Red
went on. "When they looked up at the chimney and at the smoke,
they were convinced that fire isn't what it makes of other things, but
what it is. When you throw wood on a fire, it turns black. Put a
piece of tin in the fire and it gets red. Iron whitens. It was terribly
important for them to find out for themselves that fire mainly heats.
Understand? Next to them, I had the feeling that it wasn't just the
Germans who were trying to drive us back into the caves."

"Don't you know some other joke? Even an old one," suggested
the man with the saucepan.

Jiri touched the ceiling, trying to feel where the dark stain started.
He thought about the Polish girl and about the watchtower and the
church steeple. That brought him back to the lieutenant with the
malarial jaw and the grimace which could be a portion of a smile.

He looked through the window at the stars. A lot of people will
want to go back to where they came from. The names of many
countries and many towns where people used to live before everything blew up like an overheated boiler came to mind. As if it had
had to happen sooner or later. But things would probably never be
the way they used to be, before they'd gone away. It would be nice if
it were as easy as finding the key to a door which had always been
slammed shut. Some of them would go to America, like those two
former rabbis from Prague, or to Australia, somewhere far away
where no one knew them and where they too knew nobody who

could remind them of anything else. Perhaps they would be more impatient than other people—or quite the opposite. He could imagine how it would be. They'll have had a different education than other people, but who can tell whether in the future, it will turn out to have been any worse? A few of the survivors will be somewhat deranged, although nobody will ever be able to tell. They'll be deranged in the sense that their madness will be like an invisible bridge spanning the distance between what was and what is yet to be. But maybe even those who were far away when all this happened will go mad later, Jiri thought to himself, after it's all over. They'll become a little deranged, too, because they weren't part of it and because, in a certain sense, they'll be envious. In the train the day before yesterday while coming here, Red had tried to imagine the first man who'd walk up to the gate of Auschwitz-Birkenau from outside. He would tell him, "Touch me; I'm a phantom. I was gassed and burned in the ovens of the crematorium number four." And this first person outside Auschwitz would touch him and say, "It's not true; you're alive." "Yes," Red would cry. "But it's in my head. I'm thinking of being fed Cyklon B all the time."

For almost ten minutes, he imagined how he would explain to those who fortunately hadn't been present. He looked for words and phrases and stories to tell them about it and he knew he probably wouldn't be able to find the right ones. And silence explains nothing. Maybe there would be songs about it. Legends and myths, like those at school, some forgotten, some still familiar. The saga about Red. He recalled few people who would deserve it, if anybody survived. It would be wonderful if there were to be at least one good, true song about it. A song about how the end came before the beginning, and how no one—literally no one (not even those who used to find an explanation for everything in prayer)—had known about it.

Everything pushes its way to the surface more easily at night, Jiri thought. But what he thought about most was the shaved-headed kid in uniform with his short, energetic strides and a way of looking at you which neither threatened nor made any promises. He could think about him for hours. Nobody said a word. And nobody could sleep. The air was clean and heavy, with both the smell of the factory and the scent of the forest, the strange fragrance of life, of crippled freedom, the odor of night, of closeness and of distance, and some unchained latitude, some dissonance, which was stealing their sleep and their night and their lives away. It was quiet for a long time, a heavy stillness disturbed only by the monotony of the machines in the ammunition factory that every one of them felt. They were grateful for it and at the same time scared, but nobody talked— maybe because they were scared. It was that invisible borderline where man stands with one foot inside and the other foot outside, as if one half of him were animal and the other half man, with ten thousand years of fear and ten thousand years of hope in his temples, in his limbs, in his nails and teeth and in his wakefulness.

Suddenly there was a roaring noise in the darkness. At first it was faint, no more than a strong wind. Then it resembled a breeze running along the tops of the tall grass, like breath before it becomes a voice.

They knew what was happening before anyone said a word. It sounded different from the two afternoon air raids. The silence was like a time bomb. Murmurs ran through the room. You could hear the men shifting around in their bunks. The little one and his people were suddenly praying. There were no sirens to be heard. It was as if the flak were crouching with them in the darkness. They were B-17's. Hundreds or thousands of motors at an inaccessible altitude. To Jiri, they meant something between what was and what will be.

Then the voice of the engines began to sound like the sea or a sandstorm; then came a crashing of rocks and a soft buzz like when a mosquito flies into your ear. But this was just the beginning.

The aircraft came from unknown bases. They had crossed the ocean, a continent perhaps, and certainly many cities. They'd passed beyond German anti-aircraft stations, that torn net of defense. The activity of thousands and thousands of unknown people lay behind this raid. It was like a gift which brings destruction, as if their destruction could be a gift. And it was a gift.

As I've observed the best death is the quickest one, Jiri said to himself, as if he were building a bulwark of words between himself and the engines above. He was ashamed of his fear but proud to be on the side of those unknown men above flying the machines, in spite of the fact that these men made it more dangerous from everyone, including them, on the ground. He felt a mixture of fear and gratitude and dread and admiration—something between an urge to cry out and choking, between triumph and defeat, between grandeur and anxiety. There was no relief in knowing that the nearsighted kid and the redhead and those who were praying all felt the same.

He was still afraid, like an animal driven into a trap, although the knowledge that the trap will be destroyed along with him mingled with the satisfaction of feeling that there was somebody stronger than the Germans. Well, this was Germany—the third air raid in one day.

"Let them," Red said again. And then in a voice that almost seemed to crouch, he added: "I think we ought to attract them somehow. Maybe people have a kind of magnet inside. Or else they transmit a secret code on unknown wave lengths. Maybe we're all like time bombs that haven't gone off yet and nobody in the world knows what makes them tick, not even us. But inside, something goes on ticking away even if you can't always hear it."

"Aw, you're just talking," said the man with the saucepan.

"You've got to figure it out for yourself," Red insisted. "Now they're going to start rolling it out like when my mother used to roll out the dough to make apple strudel."

Sirens began to scream in the town below, along with the bark of anti-aircraft guns. Something had obviously gone wrong on the ground. The factory sirens joined in the chorus at short intervals. The top emergency alarm.

"Where do you suppose they're going to?" wondered the short-sighted boy.

"Just you wait. As soon as things quiet down, I'll phone the General Staff," Red answered. "Quite enjoyable night life you have, Lieutenant," he rambled on. "I'm beginning to like it here so much I'll recommend it to the others."

There was silence for a while before he added: "The Germans, the Jews. It's not dead. It'll never be dead. It'll only look like it's dead. But maybe it will be dead one day, like a dried sea bed or a crumbled rock formation. But as long as there's some sort of half-naked man, with a coat or skirt of bulrushes or grass, it won't be dead."

"Wouldn't you rather keep your mouth shut now?" said the rough voice nervously.

"Why now?"

"Because somebody might suddenly come in here and understand you," the rough voice explained.

"Yeah, the lieutenant intends to visit us at just this moment," said Red.

"Don't worry," said Jiri. "If a bomb fell in here, we wouldn't even have time to run to the latrine."

He was driving out everything that had been accumulating inside him with the roaring of engines, with the flash of searchlights that began to comb the sky. Every bomb that falls here will solve a lot of things, he thought, including the mystery of the guy in the green cap and the leer that looked like a smile. He reminded himself that this was not the first time. Everyone of them died like this every day. Many times a day, every night.

"Maybe they're just flying over," suggested the nearsighted boy.

"There's a powder magazine on the other side of the hill," said the saucepan man. "I noticed it along the way."

"The Germans are really strange and funny people," Red observed. "Some of their great leader's girlfriends apparently committed suicide. He liked to have them pee on his head. It's OK with me. Everybody has his own inclinations, isn't that right?" Sometimes he talked about the great leader's peculiar desires and tastes where women were concerned. It turned their stomachs.

"We seem to be near a solution," said Red. "Of course, Herr Field Marshal. But it has to fall through."

"Don't worry," said the man with the saucepan. "And kindly shut up for a change."

"I don't see them," said Red. "I wish above all to be like them every second from start to finish with clean hands." And finally, "I had always longed for cozy camp quarters in a good neighborhood with the best reputation. A good name of a place—wide and far—is a jewel."

"Only a madman can enjoy night, a place, and situations like this," said the skeptic.

The roaring was right above their heads now. It filled the room with a force they could only perceive, not alter.

The roaring grew so loud that it seemed to be packing itself solidly into all the space that was left between the planes and the ground.

"The German sky has become English or American," said the shortsighted kid.

"It'd have been worse if the American or English sky were German," said Red. "But maybe not for us yet."

Then the roaring grew, as though the center of the formation of planes had drawn into a tight tense circle. It would have been like an eclipse of the sun, if it hadn't been night.

"I'd like to be far enough along to be able to tell jokes about gas chambers," Red remarked. "I'd like to be with the people who'll be telling them. For instance: 'That amusing figure skating double pirouette, the Bergen-Belsen. Or the triple Freiberg-Mauthausen-Buchenwald.'"

No one laughed. "The Germans must guard so many prisoners that by now it makes them prisoners as well," added Red.

And then he added: "It's just those bastards who wish every day was a pile of shit they could flush down the toilet. No excitement, no inspiration, a grey existence. No rewards or punishment. For them, people without blue eyes and blond hair and the one right and permissible Nazi *Weltanschauung* are an infectious disease, incapable of appreciating or creating something beautiful. Who else would want to do what they do, spend their time flushing everything down the john, one day after another in darkness, cold, and boredom? One night after another, their whole life."

"Directly over us," whispered the shortsighted boy.

"Just imagine if you'd been born a few parallels west, you'd be flying up there now, a kind of cousin of mine," said Red. "Good night, Papa Himmler. Good night, my dear Hitler. Festung Europa, jawohl, for the next thousand years, with German military families who've already been serving you since the twelfth century—like, for example, Herr Richer's family. It's really annoying that the Americans have Jewish generals, isn't it? How can they dare to disturb you? What kind of pyjamas do you have today? Have some fun with us, *viel spass*. Best regards from the universe." Then he said, "Take it easy. We shouldn't exaggerate the size of our enemy forces. When the wolf howls the echo rings, isn't it so everywhere, for everyone?" And finally, "I look up at the sky and I really love what I hear. So it's true, that what went up will come down again."

"What happened with that fellow when he found out his mother had been unfaithful to his dad?" Golden Eyes asked nervously.

"She discovered he was cheating on her because, all of a sudden, he started wearing clean underwear every day," Red replied in an altered tone.

"But maybe the boy just read it somewhere."

The redhead tried to recollect what she had written: "'*Then in the morning we'd make love, but it will never happen. It would be too wonderful. You would be the mechanic of my trembling.*' And her son read that letter."

"You didn't happen to be that boy?" asked the man with the saucepan.

There were thousands and thousands of planes. The heavens thundered. It was as though somebody were rolling thousands of oil drums across the sky. Even the earth was rumbling, making it seem as if it were about to open up and swallow itself. It was like an earthquake, bigger than the whole earth, yet hidden inside its own nucleus and just as inexplicable.

"They've been right above us for too long," put in the nearsighted boy. "There are too many of them."

"A lot more things are still good," said Red Richard quietly. "Internal combustion engines were perfected back in 1926. Light metals and alloys. George Gershwin, who was born in 1898, just like my mother. Some ideas, but there are plenty of those; the problem is that they never materialize."

He had hardly finished his sentence when the first explosion came. The window shattered. Everything collapsed along with it. It must have struck very close. The wood and walls mingled with earth. The roaring of the planes filled the void of sound as the noise of the explosion and falling debris diminished, and then it too began to fade away. The earth was again enveloped in the now muffled sound of bombs falling in the distance.

"What happened?" asked the nearsighted boy.

"That was close," said the man with the saucepan.

"It fell around here," said Golden Eyes.

"As long as you can hear it, it hasn't hit you," said the skeptic.

"It exploded in the woods," said the nearsighted boy.

"There'll be a nice crater left," observed the man with the rough voice.

"They're flying away," said the nearsighted boy.

"After the war they can use that crater as a garbage dump for the ones who move in here after us," suggested the rough voice.

"Jiri?" asked the nearsighted boy looking up at the ceiling. "Are you still alive?"

"More or less," Jiri answered. "It's over."

"Does anybody have a match?" Red called out finally.

"If *you* don't have something, nobody has," Golden Eyes replied. It was obvious he was thinking of something else.

"I had some in my jacket pocket," said the nearsighted boy. "Does anybody know where my jacket is?"

"I don't know anything. I'm almost dead," Red said. His voice sounded strange.

Jiri touched the ceiling. The roaring had lessened, like a huge net somewhere in the distance, drawn high above them. Jiri felt around cautiously to determine how far he could move. Then he checked to make sure that he still had all his limbs and that he could still sit up. He ran his hand through the web of wires in the roof. They were still intact.

He looked up at the plaster that clung to the wires. The wooden walls hadn't survived the explosion. Where the ceiling ceased to offer any protection, the starry sky began. The tongues of the searchlights were no longer there. Anti-aircraft fire rained up from earth, as though gunners wanted at least to use up the prescribed amount of ammunition.

"My leg's broken," groaned Red Richard.

"Where are you anyway?" asked Jiri.

"It took me along with my bunk," Red said.

"That's unlikely because I'm right above you."

"It's no joke," said Red.

"How can you tell?"

"I swear."

"Where are you?"

"Jump down, but not on top of me."

"I can't," said Jiri.

"There's a plank digging into my leg, come on, don't be a bastard," said Richard. Then he added: "I've got a letter in there with an address to write to." And at the end: "Pass me the belt, at least."

Jiri lowered himself from his bunk. Then he saw what had happened. The bunks were held together by bits of wood and wire and were wedged among the broken floorboards and debris. Red lay on the ground. Jiri understood that the thing Red had in the little pouch on his belt was better than being sent away, supposedly to the hospital.

"I can't lift it by myself," said Jiri after a moment. "It's heavy. The whole building's lying on you."

"That's me all over," Red grunted. "The whole damn house has to fall on me." It didn't sound funny, but Red was trying.

He touched Jiri's elbow. It was so dark that the shortsighted boy had to bend low to see where Richard was and where the beam was that lay on his leg.

"Grab it in the middle," Jiri told the nearsighted boy. "We've got to raise it about half a meter, that is above the knee. Then we'll take two steps to the left. Put it down when I tell you, right?"

"Hurry up," Red urged.

Finally they lifted the beam. When the walls collapsed, the room had been cut in two. The men were separated now and could communicate only by shouting. Outside, they could hear the Polish women singing in their barracks. It was one of those sweet Polish hymns. Suddenly it stopped. Then they heard the dogs barking and whining.

"At last," Richard groaned. "My leg's crushed."

"It's not over yet," the saucepan man declared.

"I'm going to lose that leg," Richard went on softly. "I've been in good health for too long, considering we're in Germany. It's not a good country for me. Why did they drag me in?"

"You'll survive," the saucepan man reassured him.

"I knew it as soon as we got here," Richard went on. His voice was discouraged, but he tried not to show it. He looked worried and tired. His morals hadn't gotten him anywhere. He lapsed into silence, and in his case, that was the equivalent of quitting.

"Don't you have the feeling those planes are coming back?" the shortsighted kid asked.

"They're going to wipe out Leipzig," Richard said. "Then they'll wipe us out. I'll be through with it."

Four searchlights were switched on above the camp. Suddenly they could see everything in bluish clarity— the woods, the little town, the church, the factory, where the camp was and where the factory building started. The searchlights came nearer. They were like trees on fire, burning and falling slowly to earth, as if attached to small parachutes. They looked like branches of fir trees on fire, their ashy needles falling.

One squadron left the invisible formation far above them and, seeing things as easily as if it were bright daylight, eight of them bombed everything that up until a few minutes ago had been a new munitions factory producing artillery and ammunition for machine guns. They crashed the prisoners' barracks, destroying the thick flat rings of wires and walls around the factory, a sort of protection separating the Polish women from the Italian and Jewish men. It only lasted a few seconds. The waves stormed over and overpowered the noise of the engines. The winds rearranged the ruins. The roaring of both levels of planes and the bombs at the ground merged and deafened them. And then it subsided.

The explosion ceased. The planes began to disappear again into the night. Suddenly it was all quiet again. Nobody said a word. But it was a different kind of stillness from the quiet of a few minutes ago. There was some suppressed ignorance of the presence of everything that went wrong in life, of life's brutality.

"That's the end," Jiri said.

"They did a good job," said the man with the saucepan.

"I'm dying," said Red.

The sirens now changed their volume and rhythm. The air raid was over. They could imagine how things looked outside. They heard the ambulances and fire trucks rushing around. The air was torn with the barking of the German police dogs. The night was filled with sound. Everything was still functioning. There seemed to be a lot going on outside. They felt a part of all that activity and at the same time isolated from it.

"Some of their planes are supposed to have wooden bodies so they can fly with a load of the biggest bombs there are and not get hit," said the nearsighted boy. "Wooden bodies and Rolls Royce engines."

"Nobody has it," said Red. "Please don't trample me, at least." He needed to hear himself. Maybe he was testing at least some of his faculties.

Jiri handed Red his jacket and pants, but not the belt. That he kept. To be on the safe side, Jiri carefully clambered up on his bunk.

"I'll lie down beside you for a little while," said the nearsighted boy.

"If you want to," Jiri moved over.

"It's cold at night," said the boy.

"What time is it?"

"What does it matter?"

"Is it warmer like that?"

"Absolutely."

Jiri thought about Red Richard who didn't want to bother them with his pain, and how he'd taken away even the mouthful that could have helped him, that capsule hidden in his belt. They'll know what to do in the morning. Keeping your pain to yourself means a lot more than sharing your joy, Jiri decided. He thought of Red Richard, of what awaited him after the night passed, at the first crack of dawn. He thought about the things Red would never do or say. Then, once more, he thought of the man with the leering face.

The nearsighted boy pressed closer to him. They lay there under the stained square of ceiling which was the only thing that had resisted the air pressure, thanks to the web of wires. And who knows what else?

Briefly, Jiri recalled the kennels where a Nazi flag was flying when they'd arrived that afternoon. He could still see the officer who'd brought them here without yelling at them once. Then, as he chewed his straw, it seemed that the stalk of grass contained more than some distant peace.

"What do you think's wrong with your leg?" asked the rough voice.

"It's a nasty fracture, but the splintering is probably the worst part of it."

"Could you manage to stand on the other leg in the morning?" They all understood what he meant.

"I'd rather stay seated as long as I can," Richard replied.

He howled like a dog during the night several times and asked the others to forgive him.

"Don't apologize," said Jiri.

"I hope it'll be morning soon," whispered Red. "Excuse me for having been born."

But there was still a long time until dawn. The night was full of feverish, distant voices. There was just a hint of light, a smudge of haze in the distance. Jiri was waiting for the sun to come up. He tried to estimate how much energy he could use until then without being utterly exhausted in the morning. He could not sleep because he kept thinking of all the things which, as Red Richard said, happen only once . . . things you can't lose twice. The only thing beyond confusion. The distorted privilege of breathing was the last value he had, the last revealed secret, which might not be a secret at all. With his voice hiding a signal of distress, his disreputable, robust voice sounding uprooted now, full of dislike for himself. He pressed his hands to his belly. For an answer to everything, Jiri looked toward where dawn was promising to appear. But even there, he knew there was no answer.

Suddenly he heard Richard trying to sit up.

"Stand up!" he said in a tense, cracked whisper.

Jiri saw the gleam of flashlights and a sheen of helmets. He jumped down from his bunk, the nearsighted boy after him.

"Do you have any dead or wounded here?" asked an SS officer.

"I've got a broken leg," Richard told him quietly. At the bottom of his worries was shame, and at the bottom of his shame was the knowledge of what would happen now. The question was not could he stand up, but could he afford not to stand up. He knew Germany too well not to recognize that. Knowing it, he tried to present himself as matter-of-factly as possible, hiding what his voice might show of the disorder of his mind, and what he feared might make a weakling of him. "Looks pretty unpleasant," he added. Those were the last three words anybody heard from Red Richard.

"We need one man quick," said the officer. Richard looked down.

"Well then, who?" the officer in the helmet asked more sharply. He spilled a semicircle of weak light over them.

"Me," Jiri replied. He stepped forward because he didn't want the man in the helmet to get any other ideas.

"Don't you want to get dressed?" asked the officer.

"I'm dressed already, it's all right," said Jiri.

The officer didn't ask more.

They moved to the place where the door had been before and went through the grove of trees along the hillside. The bombs had ripped open the second circle of wire fences and destroyed the watchtowers.

The grass was wet with dew. The woods were thin. The bark of the birch trees was peeling and the beeches looked old and solid, though not as supple. But they still looked like trees in the morning, fragile, but strong. Hazelnut and blackberry bushes grew close to the earth and there were cranberry and huckleberry plants among the moss. The taller trees cast shadows. The approaching dawn was invisible as they crawled up the hillside because the woods had grown thicker. Jiri hadn't been in a forest for three years.

The tall officer was silent the whole way. He took long strides and glanced back now and then to see if Jiri was keeping up with him. Higher up there were clearings in the woods with patches of last year's heather.

"You're going to collect our dead," the tall officer said finally.

"All right," Jiri replied.

"Take a swig of this first," said the officer and handed him a field flask of rum.

"Thanks," said Jiri. He pretended to take a drink, but he just wet his tongue, holding it so the liquid wouldn't trickle down his throat.

"We're only people, made of skin and bones," said the officer. Jiri wiped his eyes.

"Start at this end," said the officer. He adjusted his helmet as if it were a cap, up from his face. "Fifty paces north from here." He gestured toward the hilltop with his hand and chin. "My men are digging pits there. Drag over everything you find."

Again, he indicated the direction with his extinguished flashlight and took back the flask.

"Then you can go back to your barracks by yourself."

"OK."

"Then you'll get your reward."

"I understand."

"I hope you've got good nerves and a strong stomach."

For safety's sake, Jiri simply nodded.

"This is Germany. I keep my word," said the officer.

It was only after the officer had gone that Jiri realized what he was supposed to do. He watched him leave. He didn't even turn around. It was difficult to concentrate on the task ahead of him and not to think of his barracks where Red Richard, the nearsighted kid, and even the praying guys had probably crossed him off their list.

Jiri tried to collect the bodies without looking at them or thinking about what it was he was collecting or even about the fact that this was maybe the last thing he'd do in his life. These woods had been the retreat, then, for those voices they'd heard shouting, people who couldn't find room in the concrete bunkers built into the hillside further down the slope. And it's probably a nice big bunker, Jiri figured. But only for those who got there in time. For prisoners there were no bunkers or shelters, of course.

He could taste the rum on the roof of his mouth. The rim and the neck of the tin flask. The place Red was talking about, where elephants go to die, he said to himself. Trees turned upside down in the bottom of a snake pit. Red's broken and crushed leg. That gram of cyanide which, if he had only had it on him, he could have dropped into the officer's rum.

The bomb had fallen into these woods just missing their barracks with the reinforced concrete ceiling. The things nobody can ever predict. The trees loomed into the morning sky, broken and charred. Some lay flat.

He could hear birds singing, but when he looked around, he saw none. Suddenly he was glad it wasn't quite daylight yet. As for all those many German promises, rarely kept even when officers made them, he did not feel like thinking of them. But regardless of his preferences, wishes, and fears, daybreak was coming. The light was growing stronger and brighter.

There was a kind of emptiness around him once the officer had left him, and Jiri started the job. He told himself each time that it was only a boot or a button or a glove, a cap, a sleeve, just *something*. He went from tree to tree, from bush to bush, from trunk to trunk. He stumbled into the lair of some animal which wasn't there anymore.

He kept telling himself that this was an *it*. He didn't allow himself to admit what he knew, that these were parts of something which might have looked the way he looked himself. Then he stopped bothering about being all covered with blood. He tried to dig up in himself a revulsion for the people who had been killed here and lay around now, ripped apart and scattered into pieces which nobody could ever put together again. As if they hadn't been alive just last night. The other side of their existence was very far and very near at the same time. He told himself repeatedly that this was *their* business, that he just landed in it the way people like him had been landing in such situations during the past few years. It was not just that no one had ever asked his opinion about anything. He had nothing to do with it except that he was supposed to clean up. *Because this wasn't his fault.*

The more he thought about Red, the more thoughts came into his head. In Birkenau, Red had escorted his twin brothers to the showers because he couldn't stand the idea of German doctors performing experiments on them. It wasn't hard to imagine what they'd have to look forward to afterwards. He didn't want them to be castrated. But at the same time he didn't share his one gram of cyanide, because he never knew when he'd need it for himself. Even the most generous and unselfish people in Birkenau were still pretty selfish when it was a question of how to die fast and painlessly.

"Do you think I am crazy?" asked red-headed Richard.

"To go to the chamber and to choke kindly for thirty-five or forty minutes only because some Nazi *feldwebel* is thrifty with Cyklon B?" So day after day, he talked to them, convincing them that going into the showers wasn't really the worst thing that could happen to them. He was afraid the Germans would maim them. So he thought that convincing them to go voluntarily was the best thing he could do for them. All they knew was that when he came to Birkenau and found the two of them still alive, he'd asked them where their parents were. Smiling, they told him they'd "gone up the chimney." They probably smiled because they didn't think he'd believe them at first. They also knew why it was sometimes better to go up the chimney than to stay in Birkenau. And maybe they smiled because they were still alive. Maybe mad already a little, but still alive. Or—and everyone who had spent even just a few hours in Auschwitz-Birkenau knew this— that yesterday's sanity was today's insanity. Perhaps it's good to be insane, to consider whatever happens as normal, current, and familiar, as Red claimed. Maybe Red was crushed and at the same time fascinated by the wild game his family's life turned into.

And if it had been the other way around, they would have gone with Red, just as afterwards he went with them to the selection— because a person simply couldn't win at every selection. They would have given him advice, as he did with them, to be careful about cold water, so he wouldn't catch a cold when he went outside afterwards and get pneumonia. As if all three of them didn't know that in Birkenau there was no "after the showers." This shower game and all the talk about *afterwards* was something they had played even with themselves. Everybody knew why. For three days afterwards, Red wouldn't speak to anybody.

What he said next carved itself into Jiri's memory. He understood why Red was so afraid they'd maim him. That letter he always carried around with him represented the past, vanished like a phantom, and Red was scared he'd never be able to piece it back together with his future. But it was all part of the game which Red played with himself, that there still *was* some kind of a future. And that, as long as he still lived, it was one link in an unending chain. It was for the other side of his hope that he kept that gram of poison. He had the feeling that Red was the other side of the forest. The thing he was collecting. It was only later that he realized that he too was part of the other side—on this side.

There was always something else, this *something else*, the way they lived and which was part of the inscription on the gates which read: *Eine Laus dein Tod. Jedem das seine.*

His back, arms, and head began to ache. The forest smelled of blood, of flesh and bones, and of wet rags.

He didn't even want to think about whether he was glad this had happened to those around him because that reminded him of Red Richard's wounded leg and what that was bound to lead to.

He did what the officer told him. He couldn't measure time. He knew that whatever reward he might get (it was real rum he'd been offered) he'd give to the nearsighted kid. All of it. Or to Red Richard. Let them divide it up. And they cleared away the witnesses, tough luck. He couldn't stop thinking of Red Richard.

Suddenly he stopped. He straightened slowly. And he knew clearly then what had happened and what was to be.

He'd been feeling chilly, but now he began to shiver and the chills grew worse. Goose pimples broke out. Again he realized that there were things which would never be the way he wanted them to be—those two layers of which existence is composed, according to Red Richard.

He focused his eyes on a birch tree draped with rags. He looked at the lonely, slender trees at the edge of the clearing. All he saw were branches, jagged and swollen by the splinters of the bomb, and then *those things.*

Those things which still looked clean and tidy. The green collar of a coat and silver tabs, a scrap of sleeve, a pants leg, and all of it full of *what* had been there before. At the level of his face, a cap swayed in the early morning breeze. A cap with a dark visor and underneath it, *something* he recognized though he'd seen the lieutenant only once and briefly. He knew he couldn't be mistaken. *That* was *it*. It belonged to the skinny fellow who had escorted them from the station. There it was, with *its* crippled malarial jaw, the immobile, convulsive fragment of a smile.

And Jiri suddenly realized that it wasn't a smile and it wasn't a grimace of grief; it wasn't anything at all. He knew now that he'd never discover what was behind that face with twisted mouth, what kind of man he'd been. Whether he would have slapped him back if he had smiled.

At the same time, he knew it wasn't just *that*. And also that he probably never would do what he'd been planning to do sometime in the future. Richard the Redhead had said in the train that, sometimes when danger has passed, an enemy is something different. But not even Richard was always right about everything. He knew that nobody should ever do it unless he's sure of what that grimacing face in the cap was really like. Or *wasn't*.

It was just another motionless circle. The past, present, and future, which remain unknown—unreachable. Every one of them with his little drop of what he is, or only will be, alive or dead, healthy or crippled, from outside or within, every one of them, with their identification marks, memories, illusions of origin, honors, losses and defeats or hopes. Or no more? What if it disappears tomorrow? What will be left? It occurred to him how many German soldiers from the local garrison wear their warm green coats improved by the hair of the Jewish dead along with the wool. He wasn't sorry that when it comes to that not even his skin will be left. A little piece of soap with which German children will wash themselves like the Redhead used to say, when they came from school, because the most important of all, for the local children, is order, obedience, and cleanliness.

There was silence all around, except for a murmuring like trees sighing in the wind now and then, as though a squirrel were running from one tree trunk to another. The trees were swaying in the wind, fresh, peaceful, and alive. That was a different kind of life, and the man was envious. On the other side of the hill, the sound of German voices rose, the men, women, and children who hadn't made it into the shelter that had been built just for them.

The ones who kill and the ones who are killed, thought Jiri. It makes a difference, being able to die only once, but only afterwards.

He began wondering how long he'd have to stay there. Picking up corpses and bits of human beings and flesh and clothing was all a part of warfare, just like working in a munitions factory or on the ramps. Like the women in the clean-up crews in Birkenau. After new transports arrived from Holland, Denmark, Hungary, or from the Czech and Moravian Protectorate, they had to wash down the walls to get rid of the remains of babies whom soldiers had dashed against the walls like tennis balls. The guard never waited for the rain to do it. There is always near you a fellow who wants things worse than the guy before him—the worse the better, as Red used to say.

It was strange that the Germans weren't interested in baby clothes, even though they were quality woolen stuff—red, pink, and blue swaddling clothes, pillows, and quilts.

The women swept out the boxcars, picking up the tasseled caps and pacifiers, the rattles and toys.

These babies, the ones smashed to a pulp against the walls of the crematorium, or even here in the sweetsmelling forest, weren't the only things Jiri thought about. When he did a job like this, he always thought about the living. The living were the ones who had to bear it. Inside the living, images were accumulating which you'd prefer to erase, if you only could. But there was a difference in that.

He tried to think about wild strawberries growing in the woods, and blackberries, and about how you can squeeze them to make juice that's redder than blood. He'd rather envied the trees and moss. It too was something a bit different.

And suddenly he realized he wasn't afraid of blood or of smearing his hands and clothes and soul with blood. Suddenly he knew that he wasn't frightened anymore, that life would never be the way it was before all this. And this disturbed him, rather than encouraged him. As if he knew that everything, literally everything that happens to a person, can never be wiped away again as if it had never happened.

He tried to find out from the movements of the trees and from their soft voices what it was that made them, alive or dead, different from human beings. He looked up, as if searching for justice in the crowns of the trees, as if it could be somewhere, even when everyone had been killed.

The secret of the lives of trees lay in circles, too. It seemed that nowhere will anyone find an answer, or a reason, or a difference between the beginning and the end. Perhaps there will be some memories that are not erased, and later they will recur in their own never-ending circle. Things that happened and died—what was.

He heard the birds again. They were singing, but he couldn't see them. He heard human voices, arguing in German.

Jiri leaned against a tree, five paces away, his back turned to the last birch tree. He rubbed his lips against the bark that hung in moist, thin strips from the shattered edges of the broken trunk. It was smooth and mute and almost clean.

The sun drank up the remnants of the night.

Michael and the Other Boy with the Dagger

I

The ammunition factory surrounded the camp like a giant bulwark. Behind the plant there was only one high wall with barbed wire and a dry moat because the prisoners had stopped running away since they had no place to run to. Also, because slosh and mud brought flies spreading typhoid and other diseases and the Germans were as afraid of these diseases as of the inferior races—Jewish, Polish, or Italian prisoners. When the officer stood in front of the column of prisoners, the guards in watchtowers, higher than the first floor of the plant, were reminded of a triangle at the highest point of which he would stand and to which he would return even if he walked as though inspecting a parade unit. A single German officer, and five rows of fifty people each, and yet no one ever raised as much as a finger against him. The guards had slackened in their vigilance long ago, and the prisoners were too weak. Most of all, they desired peace, some bread and water if they did not indulge in any prison tricks and, mainly, if they did not sabotage production.

2

Whenever Michael had to stand there, he looked angry. He was vaguely conscious of the old man's hoarse voice. He could tell he had it in for him again. Michael was standing in line with forty-five other prisoners, and there were five more rows of men behind them—two hundred and twenty-five hairless heads covered with crumpled cloth caps. He kept his hands in his pockets and shuffled his feet. He'd found a pigeon feather that morning. He was careful with it and wedged it into his pocket so it wouldn't fall through the hole.

"Pull yourself together," the old man said.

Michael didn't budge. *On the reservation, the last scions of Vinnetou, the Red-skinned Gentlemen, recall the vanished glories of bygone days. Four hunters on white horses with red and white lances and bows and arrows and guns. The first man said, "Life is like the rainbow, a complete circle, the other half belongs to the next world." The second man added, "Wrinkles come with wisdom, for the lines of years store knowledge." And the third man said, "Seek for a vision for there lies your direction." A man on a fourth horse said, "The sun has given you the color you deserve."*

"Michael, did you hear what I'm telling you?"

Michael didn't bother to reply. The old man's voice sounded like earth moldering away, old soil drying up and crumbling into dust.

"Do you think you might be able to stand up just a little straighter? And take your hands out of your pockets?"

"You want me to freeze?"

"For God's sake," said the old man.

Michael knew he wasn't lined up right. He knew the old man didn't dare pick on anybody else. He couldn't pick on anybody else. He couldn't pick on anybody. *The vanished glories of bygone days. Furs you can lie on, other hides and furs to walk on and still others to cover yourself with. Light shines on those who trust the Creator, giver of life. Rising with the sun promises a life with a new awakening. An Indian only wishes to live with the earth, the white man wishes to conquer it. A great people is a friend of the eagle for they are common. Courage brings strength to those who seek it alone.*

Michael took a deep breath. He closed his eyes.

The number four is a sacred number for the Apache people. It represents four directions and four colors. When the Apaches give thanks to the Creator, they thank him for these directions and colors. To the east, the black color represents the sun which provides us with warmth and light. Without the sun it would be dark and black. To the south, the blue color represents the water provided for the plants, animals, and humans. To the west, the color yellow means mother earth which provides us with all the necessities of life. To the north, the white color means the air we breathe. Thank you, Great Spirit, for these things.

Michael suddenly bared his stained rodent teeth at the old man and wiped his nose with the back of his hand. When he managed to get under the old man's skin, he felt alive again, as though he weren't a total flop.

"Have you decided you want to be tonight's scapegoat?" asked the old man.

Michael calmly licked the index finger of his right hand, the one with the broken nail. His tongue probed the wound. Everything is starting to fester for me. He'd cut himself on a wire. He was lucky. There wasn't enough electric current—they needed it for the ammunition factory. You need luck every second, thought Michael. Every fraction of a second. In the wintertime, when there was a snowfall, even the crows got electrocuted.

Michael swallowed. But something merged with the sweet taste, the yellow stuff mingled with blood that he sucked out of his finger, and it wasn't only because of crow's meat roasted on a shovel over the coals in the barracks stove. He'd hung a foot wrapping over a wire to dry.

"Nobody ever makes us a present of this rubble," said the old man. "We'd always be within easy reach."

That morning Manitou had watched the assembly line of the factory go off to the happy hunting grounds, along with the night-shift crew and dozens of Italian black ants and German white ants who hadn't made it to the shelters in time. And the Jewish red ants who weren't allowed into the shelters under any circumstances. You will lie with your head on a stone instead of a pillow. To hear the roaring of earth when the white man approaches to rob and to kill you. The earth and the stone will save your life.

By afternoon they'd have a rough idea of how many white, blond ants were left in the rubble, how many ants dressed in green and brown uniforms and how many black and red ants. Then the *hajot*. Black ants weren't allowed in until the very last minute, and then only if there was enough room. When the bombs started dropping between heaven and earth, the red ants could sizzle in their own juice right on the spot so they wouldn't get any idea of rejoicing over an air raid.

The old man's voice broke into his thoughts again. Michael raised his little bird face, covered with mud and freckles.

3

"Attention!" bawled the old man. "*Mützen ab!*"

Michael whipped off his cap. The count came to two hundred and twenty-five men. The old man began with the words "dirty Jew," as if it were a title. Then instead of a name, a number tattooed on the forearm. "Two hundred and twenty-five dirty Jews, sir," he concluded.

"Precisely," said the officer.

The officer looked around and stopped some five paces from the old man, who turned away so he wouldn't have to face him directly.

So *Herr Standartenführer* hasn't gotten it in the neck yet, Michael thought to himself. He's skinned through this time too.

"Two-hundred and twenty-five men plus one," repeated the old man.

The colonel drew a sheet of paper from the wide cuff of his coat-sleeve. He compared the figure with the roll call. One of his eyes was made of green glass. That was why they called him Eyeball. Some people never have enough of anything. When they are sent to Prague, they want to see Moscow, and then even that isn't enough, because it's only at a distance—they need to see Paris, Brussels, Amsterdam. And who knows where they'll stop? They're losing, along the way, not only their shoelaces and soles, but also their hands, legs, eyes. It suits them. Just more, thicker. The colonel was shaven, clean and well dressed. He looked at them. Did he see what they saw? Did any of them see his need to achieve, to satisfy his visions? The white, the pupil, and the iris of each eye was different, but you could never be sure which eye was which. Michael wanted to find out which eye was living and which was dead.

"At ease," said the colonel.

"*Mützen auf,*" the old man ordered.

All two hundred and twenty-five men—along with the old man—put on their caps.

"You're going to have to clean up this rubble," announced the colonel. "No more shifts. Everybody has to work. You'll get additional help on the spot."

"Yes, sir."

"The quicker you get the job done, the sooner you go back to one

shift. The better you work, the more willing I'll be to consider letting the Italian deserters help you unload the cement and rolled steel
from the trains."

"Yes, sir."

"Trains can't wait."

"No, sir."

"And nobody should fuss around too much with rubble."

"Yes, *Herr Standartenführer.*"

The colonel surveyed them with his live eye.

"Attention!"

"*Mützen ab!*" shrilled the old man.

One could see that before the old man got thin he had weighed as
much as a bull, even though he was only skin and bone now. His skin
was turning to dust and swelling up, full of blisters and rashes as
though he had not washed for a long time. His face was pale and grey
at the same time and the skin on his neck and chest was shriveled and
unclean. Perhaps, judging from his expression, he had already forgotten his name. It had already been a long time and they all had only
numbers tattooed on their left forearms or foreheads. Probably no
one had asked his name in years. Here, people had not been registered by names, maybe they were not even registered at the German
headquarters. Some transports of Italian deserters and Polish Catholic
women came with shaved heads and foreheads imprinted with a large
"T" for transport in red or violet letters. Later they too would be tattooed. The old man's ears stood out. They drooped like sagging sails.
Like the ears of an old lying dog who doesn't hear anymore. He was
of medium height and when he tried to stand upright just his ears fell
forward; his shoulder blades protruded from his back. At moments it
seemed his skeleton was not held together by skin but by the rags in
which he stood before the column facing the officer.

The camp was located in the middle of the factory, as if the Nazis
wanted to protect the munitions plant from air raids or someone
held to the notion that it is darkest under the candle. The prison
barracks rose on the place where a soccer field, a garden, and a pool
for the workers stood before the war. New huts were added with the
influx of fresh prisoners. The pool was first made into an air-raid
shelter and then reconstructed by prisoners into a latrine. All the
construction was arranged in a large square. A row of prisoners' bar-

racks in stone formed the lower end while the rest was filled with transportable wooden huts. Most of the space formerly taken up by the soccer field, the stands, and the track now served as a platform for roll calls.

"*Scheisse!*" Eyeball bellowed suddenly. "If what I'm telling you strikes somebody as funny, well . . ." But he didn't finish the sentence. He walked rapidly along the front row.

The old man gulped. He turned white. His skin shriveled and his eyes narrowed. He stared fixedly at the *Standartenführer*.

"He who laughs last, laughs in German," declared the colonel. "I hope you haven't forgotten that. You can ask your Jahve to remind you, if you need to. Maybe he doesn't begin anywhere, but he definitely ends here."

"Yes, *Herr Standartenführer*."

"How long have you been here?" the officer demanded.

"Five years, *Herr Standartenführer*."

Michael didn't move a muscle. Nobody did. *The vanished glories of bygone days.* Our *Führer* needn't have done us this honor, Michael thought to himself. He wasn't the only one who was thinking the same thing. He wouldn't ask for more than a pair of wooden clogs. He had to wrap up his left foot in rags each morning to replace the shoe he'd lost.

"How many are there of you?" asked the officer.

"Including children, sir?"

"Do you multiply overnight, perhaps? Am I supposed to think you give birth through this hole?" Eyeball pointed to his buttocks. "What I want from you is work, work, and more work. How many of you are unable to work?"

"We're all quite able, *Herr Standartenführer*."

"Take your shovels with you then. At ease!"

"Yes, sir. But we haven't got any shovels, sir. *Mützen auf!*" the old man said.

He knew he'd made a mistake immediately.

"We never got any shovels, *Herr Standartenführer*. They don't give us shovels, sir. We've never had any picks or shovels or things like that here, *Herr Standartenführer*."

"Come here!" Eyeball ordered. "So you haven't got any shovels, you say?"

"We've never been allowed to take shovels into the camp, *Herr Standartenführer*. Things like that aren't allowed here, sir."

The old man bowed his head and took off his cap although he hadn't been told to.

"Come here!" Eyeball repeated. "Right over here, where I'm pointing."

The old man stepped up to the spot where the colonel was pointing.

"Do you want to get undressed?"

"Sir," stumbled the old man.

"You should be able to see beyond today."

"Yes, sir."

"I wonder where you find your reasons to think so well of yourself," said the colonel. "Where did you get the idea that my patience is limitless?"

Three shots rang out in quick succession. The old man tottered forward, as though he couldn't believe it. He staggered backwards as if he wanted to run away but couldn't, so he crumpled to the ground with shock and wonder in his eyes.

Michael could feel the other two hundred and twenty-four men freeze. He stared squarely into the colonel's eyes, trying to figure out which of them was real. The old man lay there on the ground. They ought to put something under his head at least, Michael thought to himself. Or cover him with something. He wished Eyeball would appoint somebody to substitute for the old man. The irises of both eyes looked exactly the same now.

That brought him back to wondering what he always wondered when they killed somebody. Each person has more than one life in him. You've simply got to split your life into little pieces. Each piece. The little pieces never come together entirely so that they can all be destroyed together. The old man took a long time to die. Poor guy, Michael kept saying to himself. Poor old thing.

"You there, at the end," cried Eyeball. "Take him away. Throw him into the latrine. I'm not going to ask for favors much longer. You there, the one at the end of the row. I hope you understand me?"

Michael was the first to step forward.

"Can you carry him by yourself?"

"I've carried lots of people already," Michael said.

"Where?"

"To the infirmary block and to the crematorium. I've carried even heavier people. He isn't so heavy."

Michael focused on the thought that each of us has three lives: childhood, maturity, and old age. First you're scared that you won't get something, then that you'll lose what you've already got. Poor old guy. Poor little old fellow.

He wished he could find a way to make the old man more comfortable. As if it mattered. Fear was always what had annoyed him most about the old man. Just because he was scared, the old man would infect him with it, too. The old man was good, but he didn't have courage. He was committed, but didn't trust himself. He was in charge but it didn't make him stronger. He thought he couldn't depend on those weaker than him, because that would make him even weaker than they were. He saw it coming. But not so fast, maybe. It was quick, but maybe it was better that way. Oh shit, God. Why did it have to happen to him today, after he'd survived the raids?

"I hope you haven't strained yourself," said Eyeball in a jocular tone. "Are they making smaller sacks these days? How far?"

"Yesterday it was between fifty and eighty meters."

Michael waited for Eyeball's orders to approach the old man before he died. It wasn't over yet. The old man wasn't dead yet. Michael began to be nervous. He was afraid the officer would notice how nervous he was.

"Why are you gaping at me like that? Haven't you ever seen a *Standartenführer?* Well, what are you waiting for? You expect him to fart in his pants or what? I'm too good a shot for that. It all depends on you, whether or not we stay friends."

"He's still alive," he lied to the colonel.

"Where's he hit?"

"In the shoulder. One bullet went in just above the heart. The third at the side. You can see for yourself," Michael went on lying.

He spoke humbly, in the way the colonel disliked and yet expected. For a few seconds, Michael thought he heard soft, snoring sounds coming from the old man's gullet.

"Move aside," ordered the colonel. "Let's put a little bit of life into this dying."

He squinted. The colonel kicked him. Michael ducked, then tumbled backwards, legs in the air. He rolled over so he could spring to his feet before the colonel started shooting. The German fired four shots, deafening Michael. He could count them, so he hadn't been hit. So it wasn't true, Michael thought, the rumor that only soldiers and N.C.O.s—*Unterführers, Scharführers, Oberscharführers*— beat or shoot the prisoners, but that *Standartenführers, Hauptsturmführers* and *Oberführers* don't. They all did it. They always know how to kill, fast, very, very fast, well, very, very, very well.

"Take him over to the latrine," commanded the *Standartenführer*. "On the double!"

Michael stood up. He watched the colonel reload his pistol and stick it back in its holster. Looking like a scared bird, Michael reached into his pocket, took out the pigeon feather and dropped it on the old man's body.

Two prisoners at the end of the row and two others behind them picked up the old man's body. The colonel watched them with his good eye. They carried him to a wooden shed with a tarpaper roof at the edge of the camp, opposite the infirmary and next to the laundry. With his good eye the German was looking for someone else to do roll call.

The colonel was satisfied with himself. He had demonstrated the worthlessness of this little bunch superbly, these two hundred and twenty-five men. A flock of ants. The rubble, the bomb debris rose up into the heights, while the prisoners bearing the body of the old man with the hoarse voice and the rest of them sank back into the muck.

"In the meantime, get undressed," Eyeball said. "You've got twenty-five seconds. Put on your caps!"

They stood, facing the officer with his hands in his pockets, and with their caps on they were even more naked.

4

Later in the afternoon, chilled to the bone, they were told to get dressed again. They were given forty-five seconds, but they did it in twenty.

A pudgy little man in civilian clothes appeared at the camp gate. With a big round swastika badge stuck like a cookie in his lapel.

It was a log gate. Even before the little man led them off to the bomb site, Michael was trying to forget the ditch full of quicklime under the wooden roof.

He thought about the moment when Eyeball was reloading his pistol. The thought shaped itself into a wish that, instead of the hoarse old man, it had been the colonel with the green eye lying there next to the latrine wall. He'd ordered all five lines of forty-five men to go in there. It would be great to see all the *Standartenführers*, *Gruppenführers* and *Obergruppenführers* there. But it was only the old man in the ditch.

The pudgy man tried to avoid looking at the factory, saying, "A great deal of damage has been done. There are considerable human and material casualties. Our common effort to help is what counts."

From behind the walls and ruins came a slow melody, maybe a funeral march. It came very mildly and became almost loud in a moment, before it started receding and disappeared.

The back of the factory tract had been hit hardest. Broken pipes and twisted wires, chunks of cement and shattered machinery were piled as high as the second floor. The bombs ripped the facade of two administrative buildings away. Wet smoke kept coming from there.

Now I've begun my life in these ruins, Michael said to himself.

The pudgy little man was saying, "I don't care what your origin is or where you come from. All I care about is how you work. That's the way we'll understand each other."

"Divide up into groups of fives and tens," he went on. "The last five will work singly. Some of the bombs are timed and some haven't exploded yet, but they will as soon as we start cleaning up. Call our people. The ones in the green field jackets are the sappers and that's what they're here for."

He eyed Michael. "You skip up there," he told him, pointing to what was left of the big long hall on the second floor. A steel ladder with its rungs dangling loose led up to it. "Stack up the bricks there. You don't need to go all the way up to where the roof's caved in."

White, blond and blue-eyed ants are the most peculiar ants there are, Michael decided. A cold wind was blowing, full of dust and debris. "One more thing," the pudgy man said. "To touch German property—death."

Michael looked around, wondering what he could strip from the first German corpse. The lathes looked like shattered cannons. The big gears resembled great burnt-out clocks.

For a while Michael watched the swarms of Italian black ants and Jewish red ants. The white ants would soon pull themselves together. They will rebuild the factory in a couple of days. That's what those white ants expect of us. He'd have them lying in the bottom of the latrine, too, next to the Old Man number 60363. Then he'd shovel quicklime over them. It would eat out their lungs and their eyes and their ears and their livers and they'd stink too, the way the latrines stink. And for a couple seconds before they drowned in the stinking filth, he'd hope they were conscious.

He didn't touch a brick for the first twenty minutes. He already knew how fast the rebuilding went. He had worked for six weeks on the railroad repair crew, and even after the most damaging air raids, which sometimes lasted seven and a half hours, the holes were filled and the twisted nails were replaced with new ones stolen from Bohemia, Moravia, Romania, and Norway; the work was finished in hours, in a single afternoon.

Two *Wehrmacht* soldiers were chatting under the fire escape that had been torn loose by the force of the explosion. They were swapping stories about how, during air raids, the burned, wounded old folks, mothers, and children would jump from the flaming upper stories of their homes. And about what panic and chaos make people do. The last time, they brought in red Dalmatians to sniff under the rubble after an all-day and all-night British and American terrorist air raid. There aren't enough red Dalmatian dogs in Germany these days. Too bad. We'll have to get along without them. Or with fewer, he corrected himself.

The first one was talking about how he'd circumnavigated the globe in a submarine and who the captain was and who he was related to. They sailed so far out into the Atlantic that he thought they were going to attack North America. When they wanted to submerge off Crete, they went down a critical five centimeters and almost didn't come up again. The only country he ever really saw was Albania. Suddenly they stopped talking.

A wind had risen. It whistled among the bricks and rubble and broken steel and iron, mingling with other voices. It's a world of my ants and their ants. Most of the ants are inside a fence with numbers. It's an accident, what sort of ant you're born among. Every one of us has three lives.

5

It wasn't until about five o'clock that Michael finally started stacking bricks. He was cold. He had to have something to show for the time.

Michael kept thinking this raid hadn't amounted to very much if they were just stacking bricks and rubble instead of people. He made three piles of debris. The bits that were less than half a brick he threw away. Suddenly he stopped dead. What he had pulled out looked like a sock. It was a dirty, dusty old sock. He wondered if there weren't a leg under all those bricks. Or a piece of a leg. Or maybe there was a locker around somewhere, like in the dressing room where the workers changed their clothes. He shook it out.

It was a woolen sock. And here I've been wearing a tattered burlap rag around my foot, he thought to himself. Suddenly he forgot everything else. Like an echo, he could hear himself reassuring the officer with the green glass eye and the pudgy little man with the swastika that he had no intention of stealing anything.

He could see the green glass eye in front of him. That strange, inanimate eye with its exaggerated white, looking as if it were made of some algaelike substance. The sock felt good. Suddenly everything felt quiet and empty.

The sock had taken his breath away. He brushed off the dirt. He sat down on a pile of bricks and took off his clog. Nobody must see me, that's the main thing. And who's going to bother climbing that broken ladder, through all this mess?

Carefully he unwrapped the bit of burlap. The fabric was ready to fall apart.

He rejoiced at having found the sock and everything that went with it. He was reminded of the Italian workers—the black ants—who had found some German flannel shirts and sweaters in a bombed-out warehouse last winter after an air raid and had brought everything back to the barracks with them. They wore the stuff beneath their prison undershirts until spring came, and then they took it all off and burned it.

Michael pulled the sock up as far as it would go. It was a grown man's sock. He stood up and slipped his foot back into the clog. The sock had a hidden smoothness. He admired the way his foot looked. He stood on one leg like a stork.

He forgot all about the old man and what he'd wanted to do. Suddenly he was once more part of the world where people wear socks, where they put underwear on clean bodies and socks on their feet before they put their shoes on. He didn't even notice the cold wind anymore or the whirling dust that stung the cheeks and feet and hands. Everything that was left bare.

He could see himself walking down the street on a windy, winter day and as he walked along beside his father, his hands were stuck deep into the warm pockets of his winter coat. Father asked if he wanted roasted chestnuts.

Then they went home. Mother was angry because they were late. Steam rose from serving dishes on the table. Father had planned a surprise for later that evening, a magic lantern show. They pulled down the window shades.

When Michael shut his eyes, it seemed almost as dark now as it had been that Sunday when they had seen the lantern slides. He'd known this kind of darkness one other time. It was in Poland on the night of October twenty-eighth. Or twenty-ninth. The night was thick with smoke.

Something else came to him from somewhere. It was his mother's voice. She'd been carefully hidden the whole time. I didn't go up the chimney at all, she said. She smiled at him. Are you hungry, child? How about a good cabbage soup? How about standing next to the oven with me for a while, boy? Don't I look pretty to you? Don't we have a good life? Home, bread, decent clothing? One has to be lucky. I see you're one of those lucky ones. Good, my child. Very, very good.

He let her wear the sock for a while. She was just as tall as he was. Afterwards, they all sat down to supper around the kitchen table.

I'll keep the sock on as long as I'm stacking bricks. But only to find the other sock.

6

There was a loud crack and a rattle of plaster. Suddenly he saw a German boy from the Hitler Youth clean-up squad sliding down the rubble that had been heaped up under the caved-in roof. There was nothing to break his fall to the ground floor. Michael knew nothing could keep the boy's body from sliding down the avalanche of plaster. And if he weren't killed by the time he hit the cement floor, he'd be impaled on the sharp blades of the machines.

The slide of broken plaster reached Michael first. He braced himself so the hurtling body wouldn't drag him along with it. Jagged bricks and the edge of something metallic struck his shin.

Michael held out his arms as if he were trying to get his balance. Then he felt the impact of another body against his chest. Instinctively, the other body molded itself to him. They slipped and fell and chunks of plaster showered down with them.

The German boy scrambled up and spat. He rubbed his green eyes and ears and nose. He had a dagger stuck in his belt and he was wearing a dirty shirt and torn black corduroy pants.

"Look what they've done, the filthy swine!"

His forehead and knees and elbows were bleeding.

"What are you doing here?" he demanded.

"What do you think?" Michael replied.

"Where do you belong? What division are you from? This is our section."

"I'm from the Jewish group. Your *Führer* assigned today's little chores to us."

"I saw you from up there. You've been looting."

The *hajot* looked at Michael's hands and pocket and then at the way he stood there in his rags, covered with the dust he'd raised in his fall. He wasn't used to hearing people like Michael talk; for him, until this moment, they were dumb like dogs or butterflies or lice. His words sounded like the result of the touch of the pure as it approaches the impure. "Come with me," he said.

"I only take orders from one kind of person," Michael refused.

It had only taken a second for him to clutch that strange body so he wouldn't be killed.

"It's going to take your people a hundred years to put things back together again," Michael said. "You can tell your father that. Or your mother."

But that wasn't what he wanted to say. What he did want to say was beyond words. He had no words for it inside of him. He felt he had been hit with an invisible bolt of lightning. Like a human being or a rabbit paralyzed with a cobra's stare a long time before being bitten. It was not the kind of muteness he faked when he wanted to tease the old man 60363 and which he stopped doing when he realized the old man wouldn't wonder if he lost his speech at all. There was a man with them in Birkenau who became mute on the same ramp, the way one gets a hiccup. He went to the chimney with it, mute till the end.

He started to get nervous. He knew exactly when he began to get that nervous. "You'll also drop dead. You're as close to being a corpse as I am." Finally it was out. But even that wasn't all he wanted to say. He still felt tongue-tied, even though he had spoken.

There'd been no point in telling the officer they'd never had any shovels, Michael decided. He spat, as if he were saying good-bye to his second and third lives. As if they were feeding themselves with shovels. He realized that the words he would need were not born in him yet, and this made him feel mute or doublecrossed because they remained inside, never getting to his throat, let alone his tongue. It all seemed to him as if he had run away from words which dodged him: the whole factory, the *hajot*, he himself and the entire world beyond the walls, barbed wire, and dried-out moat in which Germans now grew hotbed field mushrooms. Whenever he opened his mouth, it seemed as though he was gasping for breath. It was a world beyond the words he had once learned to use.

Their eyes met and held fast. It lasted longer than it took for the *hajot*'s division to come and go.

"I hope you don't think you scared me with your crazy talk," the *hajot* said.

Without saying it or being able to say it, they felt that death— whomever it would call upon—would catch up with them all. Knowledge or a sense of the forbidden attracted them to one another like a magnet. It joined, divided, and joined them again.

"It doesn't matter as long as it's just talk," Michael answered slowly. "Unless they've killed all your folks—father, mother, sister. Everybody."

He had reconciled himself already that talking was as good as not talking. Not only because it was better to say nothing than to call punishment upon yourself by using words. And yet. Yet. There was some need, some attraction that drew him closer to the German boy whose life he'd save, just to lose his own. But it was life that connected them, because it was death at the same time. It couldn't be put into words, it was intangible, but it was as complete as everything in life is; it was what connected birds and people or a grain of dust and the stars. It was strong because it was so weak and weak because it was so strong. He felt dizzy. In a dusty moment they stood there looking at each other. For a split second the boy looked at Michael as if he were a rat, a bunch of rats, devouring the granaries of Germany, as he had seen in one of the movies not long ago. Michael felt it. He was looking into the wolf-green eyes of the *hajot* and realized he couldn't understand him anyway. He waited for the *hajot* to blow the whistle he wore on his black leather string. When the *hajot* saw the column walk with their leader downstairs, he put the whistle close to his mouth with the same speed at which those downstairs were coming. They both knew what it meant to blow it. *Hajot* breathed in. Now his wolf-green eyes lowered themselves toward the dump underneath. A shout rose from the edge of the munitions plant, someone turned the loudspeaker on for music, a limber military marching song as though nothing had happened and everything was going as usual, and then switching it off again to make silence, to hear whether there were some sights or cries of the still-living in the ruins. A three-men German unit unleashed two dalmatians and a three-year-old black labrador to search the rubble for whoever might still be breathing. Michael was only waiting. There was nothing more he could do, except to start running toward the German boy with fair, dusted hair and shirt, knock him off the edge of the floor stumps, and fall down with him, knowing at least that way it would be behind both of them. The edge was just two steps. He estimated he was standing at a disadvantage, with his back toward the edge. It occurred to him too that he could do it alone. One step. And at the same time he saw that the boy let the whistle drop from his lips. He did not blow it. Wonderment filled Michael for a second. He looked into the light green eyes of the *hajot*, red from dust, at his dry, cracked lips. He had no time to explain it. The German boy turned and limped to the ladder.

To begin with, Michael took off the sock. He began to wrap the piece of burlap rag around his foot and ankle again. He shivered.

The German boy stood in the middle of the rubble.

"Hey . . . " he said suddenly.

"What?" Michael said back. He started to get nervous again. He was cold, like when they didn't let him sleep. He sounded the same as when he was speaking to the old man 60363.

The German boy limped over to the ladder. Michael glanced down at his foot now wrapped in burlap again. The sock lay on a pile of bricks. There must be a corpse around here somewhere still wearing the other sock. Maybe it was a female corpse. But that was unimportant. Feet and hands. Fingers and lips. Breasts. Ears and fingers. He was thinking about the circumstances under which all people are equal, different languages the same, just as different faces and measures of time or existence. No one is superior and no one is subordinate to someone else. He began to feel the ultimate equality of all people. It was only a fraction of a second, as fleeting or as basic as eternity, before he returned to this time, to this land, this place, where the ground was melting under his feet like the moving sands of a desert, and yet allowing him to stand here. For a split second, he felt the world was a place for all people, before the feeling evaporated again into the cold air, together with his white breath.

Michael didn't see the German boy start down the ladder. He didn't see him fall.

He could hear the noise as it echoed from the other side of the shattered hall, but he couldn't see anything. It was a long way down and the ladder collapsed quickly. He could piece it all together from the sounds. All three dogs started running and barking. It took only a few seconds.

7

Darkness came quickly. The signals began again. Whistles—three long and three short. The people down there looked like ants. The rubble had been tidied up.

The sun was setting. It was a winter sunset above the outlines of the shattered assembly plant in the munitions factory, above the crippled town. The sunset was like a dying bird looking for its nest. It was the way some days die, as if there were blood and heartbeats and a strange anxiety in every splinter and shard of time, everything we have inside us and which we look for in each other.

The purplish color that came with twilight drowned the space between the sky and earth. It drowned the invisible ranges of hills below the sea level where the white, blond, blue-eyed ants and the funny little black ants and the starved, watchful, always sleepy red ants lived their three lives or uninterrupted, though short and insecure, single life. They looked like they were one single species, washed in that watery light.

It was that invisible water; it has a weight which made it impossible to pull away. They were all there, shoulder to shoulder, including the old man with the hoarse voice. And suddenly, *right in front of him, lay the land transformed by age-old dreams. He wrapped the warm white fur around him and walked across the other skins and hides and lay down on another robe of fur.*

It hardly mattered to him anymore that he wasn't going to find the other sock.

Who knows what will happen tonight or tomorrow morning? Before more freight trains start coming and going. It was cold. The scream of German ambulances cut through the last of the short sirens, signaling that it was time to go back to the camp. Michael went slowly.

The tall grass rippled across the broad prairie. The wind whispered and chanted and made no threats. Life was like the rainbow, a complete circle, the first half in this life and the other half belonging to the next world. Wrinkles came with wisdom, for the lines of the years stored knowledge.

Michael had a pearl-handled rifle in his holster and, under his saddle, a strong white horse. He was seeking for a vision for there lay his direction. The sun years and moon years that the hoarse old man with ears big as soles used to talk about. The sun has given them the color they deserved. His horse was strong and spirited. His name was Michael. Only the earth knew how to heal for we were made by the same substances. The land, where there was sun and warmth and people lived as most of them had lived before, lay in front of him. The next world was awaiting those who have befriended nature. Light shined on those who trust the giver of life. Rising with the sun were promises and life with a new awakening. A great people were friends of the eagle for they were common. Courage brought strength to those who were seeking it alone. He was ready to lie down with his head on a stone instead of a pillow. To hear the roaring of earth when the white man approaches to rob and to kill. The earth and stone will save his life.

A cloud of dust rose silently in the distance and settled slowly. And the wind brought with it from afar the promise of a wonderful life.

The Last Day of the Fire

I

Chick was sitting on a three-legged cobbler's stool daubed with dried resin. He was looking at the old man. So this is my granddad Emil. And I'm his grandson. My mother was his daughter, he's his mother's son and so on, back into the inscrutable past. Mother Sonya, Grandmother Theresa.

"It's late," the old man said.

"What makes you say that?" Chick asked.

He could never quite understand why older people look back so much, as if the world had begun elsewhere, before they came along. By now, though, he could imagine why they didn't want to look ahead.

"You want my shirt?" asked the old man.

"Mine's enough, thanks."

"The sewers must be swarming with rats."

"I hope you don't feel like talking about rats. Sure, the sewers are full of them. But the Germans don't go down there. They're more scared of the sewers than of fire and contagious diseases. It'd be stupid for them to go into the sewers. But they're dumb if they don't."

He looked over at the old man who couldn't see him. We belong to each other, he thought. But I can see him, while he can only hear me.

"Frame houses are the worst, the kinds with wooden floors and rafters and attics," Chick said. "Or those old dirt floor shacks made out of homemade bricks. Most of them are held together with wooden laths or poles. Sometimes I can imagine a forest on fire."

Now and then he thought about food and about water. Once, someone had told him about a meal of several courses, starting with

323

soup and big chunks of roast beef that covered a whole plate and boiled potatoes with melted butter.

"I wish people would burn as easily as trees do," the old man replied.

Chick made up his mind not to answer.

"The hope killed them," said the old man. "It killed the very best of them. And hopelessness straightened out the very best of us."

Well then, so my mother, Sonya, was his daughter, Chick reminded himself. Mother wasn't with them anymore. They'd picked her up on the street last year and shipped her to Treblinka. They thought there were factories there. Like here. Father went after her in February. By that time they knew where he was going. Father was a barber. Maybe it gave him a few extra days. In some camps the barbers were better off. The Germans had a lot of uses for the hair—mattresses, coats, insulation. Some barbers slept softly on the floor full of hair. And it misled the prisoners as well, to get a quick haircut like in a military camp. At one time everyone wanted to be a barber. Then an electrician. Finally an upholsterer to process the hair. Only to work in the kitchen was better. But in a short time many people hated barbers. There's no sense in asking why. Before his father left he took care of Chick's hair. Did he manage to meet mother? Maybe. What kind of haircut did he give her? And where was that hair now?

The word even got back here about which camps were the end stations—like Treblinka, not from here, or Kulmhof-Chelmno, east of Poznan, or Belzec, which was some hundred kilometers from Lublin, or Majdanek on the outskirts of Lublin and Sobibor, forty kilometers south of Brest Litovsk.

Chick was cleaning his fingernails with a stick. The old man wrinkled his nose as he sniffed the smell of the singed streets and houses. When he inhaled, it sounded like someone raking leaves. Occasionally he turned his head toward the high wall which divided them from the city outside. The old man's nostrils, thick with hair, distended.

"We lived a decent and beautiful life," the old man said. "Maybe it's our innocence that irritates those who hate us so much and makes them kill us and burn us and hang us. It was a magnificent life because we lived in peace with ourselves. But we were always in the minority."

"Where's the difference?"

"It cheered us and encouraged us that we knew how to live so we could survive. We have a splendid history. Every one of us. The dead and the living. But the spirit of those who have already died has passed into the lives of those who aren't born yet. But this is the end of the road now, at least for us."

"You mean for both of us?" Chick teased him.

"Who knows whether somebody will ever find out what became of us? Who knows whether somebody will still be left to weep for us?"

God forbid I should look like him someday, Chick said to himself, observing the skin of the old man's neck and face and forehead. But, fortunately, this is not my biggest problem.

There were grey hairs on his chest. The backs of his hands and his neck were like a crocodile's skin. His shirt was open. His untrimmed hair, the hair of an old man, was thinning at the temples and lay limply across his scalp, like old twine. When he wasn't talking, his lips made the boy think of a broken safety pin. At the beginning the old man had prayed. His prayers were mild and angry both, modest and full of pathos, and sometimes, without his realizing it, they sounded funny and majestic just as he did when he was at his best. But now he hadn't prayed for twenty days.

2

"The fire's been burning for twenty-one days," the old man declared.

"I'm surprised you still bother to keep count."

"Since the day he was born."

"Hitler, you mean?"

"I don't want to say the name."

"You're going off your rocker," said Chick.

Chick had already seen plenty of old people burned alive. Instead of extinguishing the fire, the wind made it burn even brighter. Whenever anybody tried to put it out by dousing it with whatever water was still left, he went up in flames like kindling.

Women and children burned fastest. That was odd, because they were all nothing but skin and bones, men and old folks just as much as the women and children.

Chick spat. People are as different when they're dead as when they're alive. Except for the ways in which death doesn't differentiate. But some people are lucky when they're alive and some are lucky too in the way the fire catches up with them. Or a bullet. You could adjust to it, even when nobody wanted to. Sometimes when the patrols picked up somebody, they simply backed him against the flames and shot him so he'd burn on the spot, as soon as he fell.

He spat again. He only wanted the best for the old man. And the best was what was fastest. Or whatever was his own decision. He doesn't expect me to do it for him, does he?

"I've never seen the ocean," said Chick. He imagined water. It was pleasant and unreal, imagining. "A pond would be enough," he added. "Or a river. Or at least rain."

The old man lifted his head, and Chick suddenly wondered how he was going to die.

"I'd never have thought that someone who teaches people how to sing would have had the chance to see so much of the world," added Chick, getting off the subject of water. He didn't want to annoy the old man anymore, although he used to enjoy teasing and annoying him. Father also took care of the old man's hair, but no magic could help. Father used to say he was only a barber, not a magician, as people expected.

The old man's lips tightened, then they parted as if he wanted to say something. From his expression you could never tell whether he was smiling or just the opposite.

"I taught others and that's how I taught myself," he said.

His mouth looks like a flytrap, Chick thought. But all he can catch are ashes.

"Your mother was a beautiful woman," the old man stated suddenly.

Chick raised his head. They were back where the old man wanted to be—with the Levy-Cohen clan. The old man kept going back to something which had perhaps been the beginning of it all, as if it were evaporating in front of his eyes.

"She had eyes like pearls. And she walked like a dancer. When your mother was nineteen years old and went to a party, the boys got dizzy."

"She had short legs and was grey all over. Even her skin turned grey. She said you'd beaten her when she was a little girl. Maybe she was pretty like you say when she was young."

"I remember your father on his wedding day—he was the happiest man that walked the earth."

"I wish I had your worries," said Chick.

"He was the happiest man that ever walked this earth the day he got married and that morning when you were born. Wherever you looked there were vases of roses. It was in the spring."

Chick realized the old man's memory was failing. For a long time he hadn't known when he was born and when certain things had happened. Sometimes he couldn't remember the days of the week and he'd have to start counting from the first day of the Uprising. Sometimes he had a hard time remembering his wife's name and his children's names. But there was a lot he did remember. He knew the names of all the days of the week since the fire started.

Again Chick wondered how the old man was going to die. Where did everything come from and where was it going? Chick wriggled uncomfortably, like somebody with an itch. He wondered what had made the old man think about his mother.

"What's wrong?"

"Fleas," Chick answered. "The last time I washed my shirt was the day before yesterday."

"Roses," said the old man. He scratched his shoulders. The hair on his temples was a yellowish white. Ashes lay among the hairs.

Chick was silent.

It was as if the old man were already saying good-bye. Or as if he could no longer believe that it had missed them again.

He thought about how the best of them, who at that very minute were being driven out of the bunkers by gas and fire, had perhaps already written themselves off in their own minds. It was over.

"We all wanted the same thing," the old man went on. "To have a good job and know that somebody and something would go on here after we'd gone."

"You're getting soft in the head, that's all," said Chick. "If you're so anxious to leave something behind, why didn't you plant some trees? Trees always live longer than people do."

"Come over here and let me pat your head."

"Big thrill . . . " said Chick.

He was thinking how sometimes women carried grenades under their skirts and, when a patrol caught them, they'd blow everything up, including themselves. He didn't make any move toward the old man. He said it to the old man.

"I just want to hold your hand."

"I'm OK where I am. Want something?"

"Just to have you a little closer."

"We both stink to high heaven." Chick chuckled. He made a point of laughing a little bit too long and too loud before the moment slipped away.

"You're from a priestly clan. The Levy-Cohens. Your mother Sonya and I and my father Leo and my grandfather Ferdinand and great-grandfather Joseph. Far, far back."

"I am happy with a father who's a barber."

Chick stopped scratching. From the window to the south, he looked across one bombsight to another, an almost levelled field of ruins which were still smoldering. In the distance an infantryman was spreading fire with a flamethrower. The old man couldn't see it. But he felt its hot gasp. It occurred to him that he hadn't heard the old man sing for a long time, although usually, not so long ago, the worse things got, the more he sang.

3

That afternoon, heat and ash fell in waves over the whole city. Firemen and special divisions of the Polish police, armed with manual and engine-driven firehoses, drove the fire and ashes back inside the wall. Nobody had ever seen anything like it.

Steam rolled out of the sewers like the smoke from the factories behind the ghetto. The thickest smoke rolled from those factories which had been directly hit.

After lunch it rained for a little while. The fire brigades outside the wall took a rest.

But it didn't rain enough to put out any fires, or even for them to quench their thirst. It was just a few drops, enough so you could hold out your hand and lick them off.

"Lots of people drown in the sewers," Chick said.

It was the rats he was thinking of. Rats grew fat on the freshly drowned bodies, although they didn't turn up their noses at those who had been drowned or strangled by the smoke some time ago. It's almost easier to defend yourself against people than against rats. But rats never meant any of things Chick had been thinking about earlier, and despite the revulsion he felt, the sewers represented both the world of rats and the world of people—people who allowed themselves (or were forced) to be herded into the sewers to join the rats or those who did the herding. They were acting on behalf of the rats. The rats were doing fine. For them, the more, the merrier. But he never told the old man about the rats and he was uncomfortable whenever the subject was brought up.

"Don't you ever pray anymore?" asked Chick.

"We're fighting back now," the old man said. "Self-defense is man's first and last responsibility. Defending yourself is more important than praying."

Some of the rats in the sewer must be as big as little rabbits by now, Chick thought. The fire never went into the sewers. On the outside, where the sewers opened, German patrols had set up booby traps so that, while the eye might glimpse the sky or the river or a field, the hand or foot would trip an automatic switch. These German inventions were reliable. But *their* inventions were almost as reliable.

Sometimes young people sent the older ones ahead to clear the way for them, and, other times, the oldest ones went voluntarily to face the booby traps.

Chick watched the fire. In its own peculiar way, it jumped from house to house, sometimes from one window to another or from one roof to the next. It skipped over certain streets or houses and kept coming back to others. For a while it disappeared entirely, then leaped up once more. One fire flared as another died down. Others merged into one and then split up into smaller blazes. Again he tried to imagine the burning forest.

He could never figure out why, except that it was because of the wind and whatever material was burning. Most of the houses caught fire and burned down during the night. Fires got worse then. Some of the fires only began to smolder as day was breaking.

"Is it true there's a lot of stealing going on?" the old man asked.

"Not everywhere. Usually it's only where everything's already burned down."

Chick noted a few isolated explosions. He knew that if the shells fell on them, it would be over quickly. Looters from the Polish side were interested in the gold teeth of the corpses and such things.

Only the best people can survive, Chick decided. And the luckiest and strongest rats.

"Must think they'll find gold here," the old man said. "Without gold, you can live. Without bread and water, it's worse."

"Mother sewed this velveteen patch on the knee of my pants," Chick mused. "Corduroy wears better than velveteen, though."

He looked out at the fire and wondered what to do about the old man. The walls of the room were sweating with the heat. The plaster cracked and flaked like the crust on freshly baked bread. But he didn't want to think of food right now. He licked his parched lips. To kill the old man meant destroying everything that made him suffer too, together with how much worse that suffering might be when Chick was gone. Under the circumstances, killing the old man was the kindest thing he could do for him. He cleaned his eyes and nose with the rag of his jacket.

Heaps of rubble were all there was left of some blocks. The devastated streets were full of echoes. He was quite aware that he mustn't leave the old man here at the mercy of the fire. And that he mustn't let him fall into the hands of the Germans. All he had to do was figure out what to do about it.

He thought of his mother and father. It was a good thing his parents weren't there anymore. If the hope that they were going from worse to better hadn't killed them, being *here* would have. Although getting killed here meant not letting yourself be killed. The old man was right. Hope can be a damned messy business, he thought to himself. There's nothing worse than false hopes. A person can let himself be lured into hell that way. Hopelessness is much better. Hopelessness puts a stone in your hand, at least, if not a dagger or a bomb. When someone has nothing left to hope for, then at least he is sure of it. If somebody doesn't like it, let him take a running jump. And I'd be the first one to jump, I guess. Because I don't like it.

4

"Is there anything that could still save us?" asked the old man. "To save you?"

"It's hard to tell which one of us is dirtier. We stink. Just like the Germans say we do. I've almost got more dirt and fleas than skin."

"Do you have lice, too?"

"And you?"

"Don't doubt it."

"What time is it, probably?"

"Rain would save and drown us too. I wouldn't mind a cloudburst and some floods."

"Can you eat that? Can you stick your hands inside and warm them when it's cold and rainy? Can you shoot it out of a gun?"

"Their burns don't hurt me," the old man continued.

"I'll put the keg outside to catch a bit of water in case it starts to rain after I leave." When the old man said nothing he went on. "Rain would foul up their plans for them."

He reached up and prodded at the ceiling with his stick, inspecting it. Then he absent-mindedly kicked the keg of dirty rain water they'd used for washing up until the second week after the fire started. The wooden sides were dry and shrunken and it smelled musty, which took away your thirst.

He looked up at the ceiling again, then at the old man. He saw it wouldn't be difficult to make it fall. Once and for all. He calculated the thickness of the ceiling. The old man wouldn't suffer long under a load like that. He knew right away it was a good idea. I'll make a neat job of it, he said to himself.

The old man was silent. Chick was concentrating on the ceiling. He looked for the reinforcements embedded in the plaster.

"Remember how sometimes I used to crawl in bed with Mother on Sunday mornings?" Chick asked suddenly.

"I remember in Prague how the women used to sing in the synagogue," the old man answered. "I can remember everything."

"When a person remembers something that's happened to him once, is it like living it over a second time?"

"As much as saying you exist twice when you look at yourself in a mirror," the old man told him.

"Or like when people remember something that's happened, it becomes eternal?"

"Only as long as you know *how* to remember," the old man said.

"That's what I wanted to know," Chick said.

"What's the matter with you?"

"Something's been biting me. Something bites me all the time, even though I've washed my shirt and pants. My shoes are full of mud. I feel sticky all over."

"Rome burned down when Nero was emperor. It was a big city, too. He went crazy and set fire to all the houses and then he watched the ashes fly. Herostratus burned down the Temple of Diana in Ephesus so nobody would ever forget his name. It never was our world. It was always theirs. We had nothing to do with it."

"Maybe we're small fry, too, in comparison with those who went before us. But I wish just once we could be in the shoes of the people who think up and organize such lovely spectacles. Not just always in the spectators' seats. I guess lots of people are going to remember this major general, too."

"Are the bites bad?"

"I probably have sweet blood."

Chick looked up at the ceiling. He could picture Rome, a strange city full of temples and water streaming off blazing roofs. Then he pictured a carafe of clear, cool water on a table full of all the food the old man had talked about before.

"Are you still here?" demanded the old man.

"Can't you hear me?"

"I hear you when you talk, but not when you don't."

"I've been thinking about old Blumentritt who used to live here before we moved in. Too many of those jumpers were in a hurry. You don't have to worry though. I won't let that happen to you."

The old man stiffened in surprise.

"It's just as bad to let them kill you as it is to burn."

"The worst is that first second, before the flames swallow you up. You don't even know about the rest of it. Apparently it's like when an airplane crashes. I'm telling you," Chick reassured him, "you don't have to be scared."

"I wish I knew where you're going," the old man said suddenly.

His cheeks dropped over toothless jaws. "Don't come back for me," he added.

Nervously, Chick spat.

"Mila Street's burnt down and Nizka's gone. It's as though the city's on a grill, the way they used to roast mutton. It's starving to death and dying of thirst. It won't last much longer. Not as long as it's taken already." The old man's voice came in a sizzling hiss, as though it were already on fire.

"Go down into the sewers," he said. "Don't come back for me. Go east or west. Leave me here. I've learned how to guess what's going on around me. If worse comes to worst, I'll jump."

"Forget it," said Chick wearily. But it occurred to him that in many ways he really was a lot like the old man. It was a silly idea, but it sustained him for a while. He couldn't keep on torturing himself with thoughts of water and food. The old man was not so crazy. He was right. To jump is not a big deal. It would take just a little bit longer. But he's so slim. He might fly off like a green butterfly. And what then?

The roof above their heads held up what was left of the upper stories of the house and the roof.

"Babies aren't being born anymore, wells are poisoned, bakers' ovens have turned cold. Even the rainbow is on fire. It's disabled, just like me. Its eyes have been burned out, too. And it's deaf because its ears have been clogged with ashes." The old man coughed for a long time, as if the ashes were choking him.

"A sick horse couldn't have said it any better," Chick observed.

"The wind's turning against us," the old man said. "Only those who fight ought to eat."

"Eat *what?*"

"Things will never be what they used to be. Those were the best times—when we were all together. There's only one place where we'll still be together, but that'd be a shame for you. I won't mind one bit, staying here by myself for a couple of hours or a couple of days."

The first thing he'd have to do was put the old man and his chair under the middle rafter which held up what was left of the roof. Then drag the water keg closer.

"After a while I'll go out and look around for something to eat and drink," Chick said.

If he climbed up and stamped his foot hard, the rafter and the whole floor would fall right on top of the old man. But then he'd fall, too. The rafter was enough.

"Before you go, I'd like to hear a few of those things that were in the first declaration." the old man said.

"The part about how we'll all go down in defeat, but the Nazis won't get a single drop of our blood for nothing? Or how it tells you to take a knife in your hands or an ax or a piece of metal?"

"Yes. *No more defenselessness! Barricade your homes! Be sly and deceitful, don't be afraid of using any trick! Let them try to take us! Let every mother turn into a lioness to defend her young! Away with panic and doubt! Away with the spirit of slavery! Whoever fights for his life can save it!*"

He remembered a lot of it, but he didn't remember it absolutely accurately; and maybe he didn't remember all of it. He had that instead of prayers.

If the old man's lucky, the rafter and the floor will fall at the same time, Chick thought to himself.

"Yes," said the old man. "And then the part where they say we've been like sheep, but it was no sin to be that way, and now it's more of an art to stay alive, when people are trying to take your life away from you—or that way!"

"Yeah, you have an excellent memory," Chick lied.

"Or how, if we're supposed to perish, then let's do it with firm and avenging hands on the triggers of our guns and the handles of our daggers—so they will not tremble even with our last thoughts."

Chick drew in a deep breath.

"And now we must destroy the enemy by attacking him at the gates, out of the ruins, from the underground labyrinths, from the gutted buildings, making him pay with a sea of blood," said the old man.

Chick knew exactly what the old man wanted to hear. Some things are hard to remember, other things even harder to forget.

"As we move down the road to our death, we must be like blazing torches, destroying as many of our enemies as we can on the way, serving as a signal that rivers of our blood will mingle and stain the rivers of their blood."

"Yeah."

He'd read it all to the old man dozens of times during the last twenty-one days. And Germans only lied.

"I hear a siren," the old man said.

"I'll make it as easy as I can for you," said Chick. "I'll drag your chair into the middle of the room. You'll have that big rafter right above your head. It looks like a jagged splinter. It still holds but if somebody pulled at it—even a little bit—it would fall. Then the whole roof will probably cave in."

"I get the idea," the old man said after a while. "Now?"

"No, not now."

"Yes."

"Now I'll just move you a little bit, because I've got to go out," Chick repeated. "You decide for yourself about the rest of it. But only after I've gone. And only— you know, don't you?"

"Yes, I'll be able to use it."

Chick leaned against the chair. The old man was hunched over, propped on the scorched arm of the old chair. Its crimson upholstery was ripped. It must have been a handsome Italian chair once.

"I get the idea," the old man repeated after he'd moved into the middle of the room.

"I don't quite get it myself," Chick said.

"You'll be blessed, child."

"Who's going to bless me? You've already cursed everything and everybody."

A cloud of dust and ashes floated down around the chair. It reminded the old man of how one kills horses beyond help.

"If you don't want to, just sit right here and nothing will happen to you," Chick said.

"Fine," the old man agreed, "You're leaving now?"

Then he felt the friction of skin against skin. Chick always did that when he went out. It was as if the grandson were brushing dust or mud off his face or his breast.

"I'll give it a try," the old man said.

"Be careful, though. As long as you're sitting down nothing can happen."

"Don't come back again," the old man told him as he eased himself back into the armchair.

The old man had big ears, like floppy, wrinkled telephone receivers.

"Everything OK?"

"Yes," the old man answered.

"Fine."

"Yes."

"So I'm going."

"Go."

It was good, Chick thought to himself—no shaking hands, no embrace. Everything has its limits. It's an advantage to leave this way. But then he got second thoughts, so he shook hands with the old man and embraced him briefly.

Then Chick left without a word.

5

Suddenly the old man felt alone. Like a rickety ship deserted on the open sea, encircled by darkness and waves and swirling water he couldn't see.

An idea had been going around in the old man's head during the past few days about people long extinct, people he'd only read about, like the light of dead stars, of all the people whose glory had grown as great as the shadow they cast when they faced the sun, who thought they were greater than the sun itself. And they had perished, despite their glory, because they hadn't understood the message that had been born one day.

He and his people would perish, too, because they had understood. To kill and be killed. A bullet for a bullet. A knife for a knife.

Among the strange sounds which came from far and near, a voice that had seemed remote when he was alone drew closer.

He could feel bits of ashes settling on his skin. He sniffed to get the ashes out of his nose.

He thought of how he had lived through the twenty-one days of the fire, ever since the day, on the birthday of the one who was master of the life of every Jew, a band of forty thousand plucked up the courage to fight back after three times a hundred thousand of his Jewish brethren had been slaughtered in Treblinka, not far from here, in the midst of woods the old man knew very well. A great silence was coming back from those woods. A stillness full of cries and sweat; a quiet enveloping the forest, this town, this room, the whole world, creating an impregnable barrier between the earth and heaven. He felt this stillness just as before he had felt songs or prayers, or water or food. It isolated him from everything and everyone, so that he felt like the last Jew on earth, like the last man still alive under the stars.

He wondered what it would be like when everyone was dead. Was it all a mistake somebody had committed ages ago, or was it part of a single destiny which began somewhere and would end, as everything human must end? Would all this be forgotten like all failures punished by defeat? Is it a defeat? It's not a victory, no.

How far would it reach? How long would the children of today's children remember this? Will there ever be children in the world anymore?

He kept very quiet so the patrol wouldn't know he was there. Before nightfall he heard isolated screams and shouting. But he couldn't tell whether they were battle cries or calls of the dying. He could imagine men and women, their bodies on fire, running like burning torches toward the German soldiers to stab them with their knives or pieces of sharp metal, unless they were stopped first by German bayonets or bullets or flamethrowers.

He tried to figure out what it was that had breathed strength into the weak and revealed the weakness of the strong. He wished he knew where his grandson Joseph was, the boy known as Chick Levy-Cohen.

His throat tightened at the feeling of brotherhood there would be once this war was over—if anybody survived. He wished he could reach out and touch all the tailors and slave laborers from the munitions dumps and war plants, the brushmakers and tinkers, bakers and streetpavers, all those who had banded together to tell the rest of the world, *Look at how we died when we found out who was against us.*

He knew at that moment what it was he used to depend on, the way he was depending on the rafter now. It had once been the best of what he felt. And it had retreated before the dependability of the rafter.

He thought about the device his grandson had rigged up for him. His eyes stared opaquely into space. He could not see things that were to be seen, but he saw other things which were invisible. He could hear the walls of houses as they cracked, buckled, and crumbled. It happened slowly and you could hear it happening. Some of the houses survived when a shell struck them, even though their inhabitants didn't. But a few hours later, the house suddenly collapsed, although nothing had touched it since. It was as if it wanted to bury its dead under its rubble twice, a hundred times, on into infinity.

A shell whistled, fell, and exploded some five houses down the street. He breathed in the sudden, hot smell of explosives, the brain and body of the bombs, the dust from broken stones and wood and wool. He clutched at the arms of the chair and groped along the floor with the soles of his shoes to get his bearings in case he decided to stand up.

He knew that if he took a careless step he might fall into the very depths of the house. Come and go, fall deep or wait for a touch overhead. Among all the different sounds, he could distinguish between the ones that were important and those which weren't. The second shell didn't come. He felt a bond between all the living and dead and with those twenty-one days he had survived.

6

"I see the rafter's shifted just a little," Chick said when he returned. "Things have been pretty lively here, I see."

"You shouldn't have come back."

"A shell, was it?"

"One, about a block away," the old man answered.

"We're still lucky."

"Aren't you tired?"

"Not really."

"You've got a good nature," said the old man. "You were born with it."

Chick dragged the old man and his armchair back to the wall again. There were new burns on his face and hands, along with the old ones.

It was almost dark. The only light that came in was from the fires, and this light had its own peculiar strength and weakness. The sky was clear again, as it had been for several days. Maybe the world on the other side of those walls is lovely now, Chick thought. Maybe the fog doesn't cover everything. Maybe it's been melted by the fire.

The reflections of the fire lit up the sky as if there were a carnival going on somewhere, far away and very near. Somewhere they could never go, though.

Maybe the soldiers are celebrating something, he thought.

From under his shirt, Chick pulled a small loaf of Polish bread. The old man fingered it.

"Bread," he said.

"Without water."

"Where've you been?"

"Go ahead and eat."

"Can't you tell me where you've been?"

You could hear the old man's jaws crack as he bit off the bread and mashed it between his gums. He looked terrifying, covered with soot and ashes, starving and wild with thirst, weak, but still strong enough to eat. Chick started to eat, too. He kicked the side of the barrel, and he rubbed his singed left eyelid. He had no eyebrows or eyelashes anymore. Mother would probably have been glad if she could have seen the two of us here together eating bread, he thought.

"Are you going to sleep now?" the old man asked him.

The Junkers flew over in the middle of the night. They dropped two loads of bombs on the burning desert of rock and debris. The night turned bright with new fires, old ones swelled, and those which had been smoldering revived. The old man couldn't see it. His extinguished eyes were fixed on the place where Chick lay, next to the wall. He couldn't sleep.

The boy didn't even wake up during the raid.

The old man listened to the night noises after the planes departed. He turned his face to the wind that was blowing through the window. He couldn't see the bright lights of the airplanes that didn't have to worry about anti-aircraft fire here. He didn't even see the radar lights blinking on the Junker's underbellies and wings and rudders. Like red-eyed fish.

The old man listened to the silence and to his grandson's breathing.

Chick woke up at daybreak, tired after his night's sleep.

"You should have waked me up a long time ago." He rubbed his eyes.

During the last few days, he'd been having awful dreams. But some lovely ones, too. Sometimes he dreamed about great, strong, beautiful ships which would take him and the old man far away from here. One of the ships was called the *Majestic*. It was as if those ships were living beings. They talked to him about their voyages and ports of call and about the stars, just the way he talked to them. Sometimes they talked about lands where there was no war going on. He imagined a country like that and how people lived there, even when he was awake. But it wasn't painful for him. He knew the old man's memories were painful and he wanted to avoid that for himself. But as long as he was awake, those dreams seemed sillier and sillier. Those were strange night-secrets, that the dreams which seemed beautiful in the dark still felt that way at daybreak. Or else he dreamed he heard a lovely song. The song was he, the old man himself, and all the people he'd ever known and who were no more. He also dreamed of victory, the day when each one of them would take on a thousand Germans—not like it was in reality. Just the opposite.

"You were tossing around and yelling something about getting another bottle. Were you thirsty?" the old man asked. "What are you going to do now?"

Chick was smearing red paint over his eyelids and forehead, throat, and chest. He wound an old hiking sock around his head. He looked as though he'd been wounded.

"Toward morning you were mumbling something about tigers and bottles," the old man told him. "Ah, my little boy."

"Don't call me boy. It makes me feel like a sissy."

Chick touched the sock-bandage to make sure it held fast. "You haven't slept for twenty-two nights. Where does that get you? You going soft in the head or what?"

The boy's skin was thin, almost translucent. The paint protected him against the wind, but it didn't let his skin breathe, either. Coats of old paint were covered by a coat of new.

"What good is it to anybody when you don't sleep, I'd like to know? You're not helping me. Or yourself, either."

"You looked like a little baby girl when you were born."

"A Levy-Cohen. Don't start in on that again."

"Will you move me over into the middle of the room again?"

"Sure."

"I know where you go when you go out. How many of them have you taken care of by now?"

Surprised, Chick looked quickly into the old man's blank eyes.

"Two," he said.

"They'll raise monuments to you for every one of them you get."

"Aw, skip it."

"Are those the bottles full of kerosene, like the ones Fink, the shoemaker, was talking about?"

"Why do you ask when you already know?"

"I know as well as you do that before they could begin, they had to get rid of whoever was old and corrupt. Even a blind man finally sees everything, if he lives long enough, as the saying goes. How do you do it?"

"I lie on the sidewalk like a corpse, my head limp, my eyes blank. When a tank comes along, I wait until it passes; then I jump up, lift the cover of the turret, set a match to the bottle, and throw it in. A Molotov cocktail. The hydraulics are in the turret."

"Hydraulics," the old man murmured. Like he was talking about a dream or a lovely song which can never be forgotten.

Chick wiped his nose on his sleeve. Then he pulled the old man and the armchair into the middle of the room.

"Is it true that somebody who believes but behaves like a beast goes to hell, and somebody who *doesn't* believe but behaves decently goes to heaven?" asked Chick.

"I know what's *not* true," the old man replied. "I know what hasn't even been written down yet."

"Don't panic," Chick said once more.

"I'll wait," the old man said. "I'll stay here as long as I can. I'll stay right here until I die. Even if everything gets covered with ashes and all the buildings and streets disappear, I'll stay here along with everything that disappears."

7

On his way to the sewers Chick tried to imagine how the German commander must look. He recalled the old resentment he used to feel toward the old man. It wasn't hate anymore, although it wasn't love yet. Who knows what it was? He'd been right when he said that with time, everything changes—the big things get smaller and the smaller things disappear entirely. It doesn't take long to get used to new things and to forget how it used to be. Although you probably never forget entirely.

He went down into the sewer between Svatojirska and Bonifraterska Streets, which were Aryan. He was looking for bottles. He figured that overhead, Saska Gardens or Krashinsky Park were smoldering. There were still signs in the sewers indicating street intersections. He was scared of rats, large or small, skinny or fat. They were grey and fleet and looked like cats or like squirrels sometimes. The worst was when one of them ran across his hand or foot or even brushed against his face when the tunnel narrowed and he had to crawl on his belly.

Two hours later, he was glad when an old man, who was guarding one of the exits, showed him how to get out.

Killing is a kind of pleasure, too. When you kill, you don't allow somebody else to get the jump on you by killing you first. He never thought he could kill somebody as casually as tying his shoes. For Chick, killing had begun to mean what light meant. They'd learned within the last three weeks.

He felt the granite cobblestones under his feet. He began to tense up as he always did before he was getting ready to go into action.

He could hear the difference between the noise the motor made and the rumble of the treads. It loomed in front of him so suddenly that it took his breath away, choking him with the dust it raised.

He saw the tongue of flame as it leaped out from the other side of the tank, licking up the sidewalk and the street and the houses as high as the third floor.

Even before the air began to shudder, he could hear the hiss and sizzle and see the shimmering orange glare.

A blue violet flame ruffled into orange and the fire shot out at him before he knew what was happening. First it touched him with its molten fingers, then it blinded him, taking his breath and voice away and stopping his heart. It was only afterwards that the flames caught and consumed him. All there was on the sidewalk was the smear of soot and ashes left from his body.

8

The old man called Emil Cohen—a member of the Levy-Cohen clan on his mother's and his father's side—waited. By now, we've lost our ambition to prove something to ourselves. We have nothing to prove anymore. Nobody knows we exist. Nobody knows anything. And nobody asks anybody how it all could have happened.

The sun turned pale. He couldn't see, but he could feel it sinking into a grey and crimson trench of mist, torn by the wind and veiled by soot and ashes. For a few seconds, he thought he knew the very moment when the sun went out. He was cold. But at the same time, he felt like singing, as if the thing he had captured inside him were more than just a sudden throb. It was like a mother giving birth to a child, like when that miraculous, lovely spark strikes between a man and a woman. His lips quivered as if he were praying. But he wasn't. "They're dying and burning," he whispered. "They're dying and burning. There's no more water, no more food. Only fires. Ashes. We have no ammunition. No guns. How long does it take to die of thirst?" He wanted to call out to someone, "Come, before we all perish and burn. Come, before it's too late for the very last of us and for you too. Do you hear me? Can anybody hear me?" But he knew, of course, that no one could hear him. "In a few hours, maybe, we'll be dead. We'll all be burned and dead."

Everybody who lives on his knees sooner or later dies, but everybody who dies fighting will at least be remembered, he thought. Still, even if none of them were remembered, it was better to die fighting.

To die in dignity was more difficult than the dying itself. It was a shadow devouring—just as the flames—itself. All limits were canceled—of every law—of reality—in the shadow, in flames, in ashes. "My" is only a whisper in an all-embracing voice of all fighting people, he thought. He didn't think only of himself. He thought about those who would be once free. Suddenly he could imagine birds in the air under the blue sky and golden sun, the world.

But he no longer asked himself which was more important, forgiving or hope, and which to choose. We're dying, just like we've always died, only with small interludes of peace and quiet. Why are things that way? Dying, dying, dying, and yet that long echo of past life. What price must a person pay just to survive?

But he knew he'd never get an answer. Nobody ever had. There were just those moments of tranquillity, those happy interludes between one catastrophe and the next, when people didn't have to look into themselves so profoundly and ask questions to which there had never been any answers and perhaps never would be.

Yet at the same time, he knew that such an answer does exist inside every person, even if it dies with him, and that, in a way, it never dies.

The old man inhaled deeply and smelled the acrid streets and houses. He could feel the fire on his leathery old hide and in his nostrils as clearly as if he were seeing it with his own eyes. The song he whispered had no words. It was just a voice. It rang with the fate he shared with so many others. He didn't worry any longer about attracting the attention of the German patrols. In his whispering there were the voices of all the people who had lost possessions, families, and finally life. And there were also the fears for all who wondered what would be, what would happen to them where the transports went, where they would go, how the war would end, and what would happen to the world.

Would the world go on turning from the sun toward the sea and from the sea toward night, from night toward mountains, and from the mountains toward people, regardless of how many people died? He didn't know how many there were. Just that there were a lot. And that there were going to be more. A lot more.

The old man couldn't weep because he had no eyes. He knew his grandson Joseph would not come back this time—the last of the Levy-Cohen clan, the kid called Chick. He could feel that to live and to die meant an eternity made up of people who were and the people who are yet to be, that eternity which is only *now* joining life with everything beyond life. He knew now what it was. The dead are the best in what they give to the world at this moment. Because nothing is worth more than life. It's all over. This is the end. For us, it's all over now.

His song made no sound and his voice was like the wind blowing one dying flame into two, then four, and so on, kindling infinite fires. At the same time, it sounded like water being poured over the fires, putting them out. Like a breath before it becomes a voice. The old man forgot he was over eighty. For a few seconds, he had the impression that the whole world was rocking under his feet. But he could see that nothing had changed. Nothing had happened that hadn't happened before.

He could feel the strongest desire of all—the yearning to survive—seeping out of him. It had once been strong enough to get them this far. He was trying to alter in his mind the greatest thing he believed in, as if he'd come to a point beyond which it was easy to understand in what conditions the opposite of life is more than life itself.

He felt the flames and thought of water, of which there was none. In his mind he saw widespread abandoned wilderness, the ocean floor, and dry, empty riverbeds from which the water had left. The sea, betrayed by its shores. All that was left was a dried-out bottom, now different from what it once had been, the ocean which would never again be as it was before or which would no longer exist. He thought about destiny the same way he thought about the sea: shiny, like when the surface reflects the sun during the day, and the moon and the stars at night.

Then he thought he felt the first tongues of flame licking at the wall on the side where a window used to be. It was like stepping into a swiftly flowing stream. His coat began to burn. He could still imagine where Zamenhof Street was located, and Nizka Avenue.

Then he lifted his arms and took a step forward. And he touched the rafter above his head, gripping it firmly with both hands.

Black Lion

A tattered red flag hung over the doorway of the house on the corner. The right wing of the old town hall had been hit by tank shells about four o'clock the afternoon before. Smoke was still rolling from its tower.

The German-owned watch shop in the building on the corner of Parizska Boulevard had been looted.

The boy called Black Lion only needed to glance at the bullet-pocked plaster of the house and at the shop to know where they'd *been*. When his eyes slid down the shattered face of the building and fixed on the two men from the Revolutionary Guard, he knew where they still *were*. He hitched up his pants.

"Come on," he nodded to the two boys who were with him and looked back to make sure they were coming.

"What's in there?" asked the first.

They ducked inside behind Black Lion, the boy with the shaggy mane. It was chilly in the hallway. The walls were paneled shoulder high with shiny brown marble and white cherubs.

The shorter of the two guards looked around. "Get out of here," he told them sharply.

"These two kids just came back from a concentration camp," explained the shaggy one. "They'd like to see a little action too."

"Go on, scram," the man with the Revolutionary Guard armband repeated. "This isn't a theater performance. It's not for little kids."

He looked back. His taller companion didn't even notice as they all rushed up the stairs together.

"Aw, let's forget it," said the smaller of the two youngsters, the one called Tiny.

"Are you sure it's going to be worth it?" asked the second, the one called Curly (although his head was shaved).

346

"This'll be a sight to see," said Black Lion. "I wouldn't miss it for the world. It may turn out to be a real spectacle."

When he got to the landing between the second and third floors, the shorter man, whose RG armband had slipped to his wrist, looked back and saw Black Lion dashing up the stairs.

"Get out of here," he bellowed. "How many times do you have to be told?"

"We'll keep an eye on things for you here on the stairs," Black Lion volunteered. Tiny and Curly slowed down, hesitating.

The two men from the Revolutionary Guard stopped in front of a double door painted grey green and covered with stickers. Two curved serpents with flashing green tongues coiled on each side of the door.

The name plate had been removed from under the doorbell. The tall RG pressed the button. He pushed it twice, then twice more quickly.

Cautiously, Black Lion moved up to the next floor.

"What're you still hanging around here for?" growled the smaller of the two guards. "Get out of here or else." He ran his hand over his pistol. Both men were carrying revolvers with wide German Army straps made of pale cowhide.

"These two boys are from a concentration camp," Black Lion repeated. "They'd like to see a little action too. That's only fair."

The tall one eyed him sharply. The bushy-haired boy's eyes were sunken and his face was gaunt.

Both armed men had equipment seized from Afrika Korps stocks during the first few days of the Uprising. The shorter of the two spat into a corner, next to the door that led to the attic.

"What're we going to do here, anyway?" whispered Tiny.

"Maybe you'll get a chance to give them a kick in the ass," Black Lion told him.

He spoke softly. They looked up at the door of the apartment. Some of Black Lion's tension had rubbed off on them. The building had a familiar, musty smell, the kind old buildings have.

"Maybe we can squeeze some food out of them," suggested Curly.

The smaller guard overheard. "Are you hungry?"

"I told you where they came from," said Black Lion. "They've been staying in our house. They escaped on the way from Buchen-

wald to Dachau. My dad's hidden them in the laundry of our building for four weeks. They've been on the run for over two months."

Curly grinned at the smaller guard. "We're not exactly hungry,"
he explained. "You might say we've got an appetite."

"Justice comes first," Black Lion said.

The tall one kicked the door. "All right, come on, how about it?" he
yelled. It echoed through the building. "Are you going to open up?"

Black Lion tensed. He peered at the door, waiting to see what he
expected to see, what he wanted to show the other two boys. He
wished he could get through that grey green wood. He drew a deep
breath.

The door made a hollow sound when it was kicked. Tiny looked
down to see how deep the elevator shaft was.

Standing behind the Revolutionary Guards, Curly noticed how
well-dressed and well-equipped they were.

"Justice," murmured Black Lion. "We're in luck."

"Come on," echoed the shorter RG. He looked around at the two
boys who were watching curiously and at the shaggy-maned youngster who was mumbling something about justice.

"They ought to have opened the door by now, that's for sure,"
Tiny observed.

Then he turned to the shaggy one. "When somebody hammered
on the door like that at the camp barracks and if we were at the
other end, they usually didn't give us this much time," he explained.
"We really had to move."

"Kick the ventilator, why don't you?" Curly suggested.

The tall one turned around. "Keep your good advice to yourselves. We'll handle this."

"I'll look after things," Black Lion spoke up promptly. "Leave it
to me." He went over to the door and kicked it without a word, then
put his shoulder against it to see how strong it was. The hinges split.
Something cracked inside the lock. Black Lion felt pain shoot
through his toes and shoulder.

The tall one moved his right hand away from the door. In his left,
he held a German Army pistol. Just then, the door opened.

A woman in an apron stood in the doorway. She looked frightened.
She was pale with big dark rings under her eyes as if she hadn't slept or
eaten or had any fresh air for at least a week. She was trembling.

"What is it you want?" she asked in broken Czech.

"Grellova?" the tall one demanded curtly.

The woman nodded. The tall man pushed her aside, holding his pistol. The two men with the RG armbands stepped inside. The tall one gestured to the woman with the muzzle of his gun.

They both looked to see if there was anybody behind the woman, and it was almost as if they were trying to shield her. The short one tried to close the door. Black Lion quickly stuck in his foot. The shorter guard didn't do anything. He wanted to see what the tall one was doing.

Black Lion wheeled around. "Quit dragging your feet," he snapped at Tiny. "Come on. Quick." The hall of the apartment was dark and stuffy and full of junk—rolled-up carpets, a stepladder, sandbags.

"Where's your husband?" the tall one asked the woman.

"In bed," she answered.

"What's the matter with him?" the short one asked.

"He's had an attack—bad heart," replied the woman.

Tiny lingered in the doorway so he wouldn't have far to go in case he needed to make a quick getaway. Black Lion propped the door open with a coal scuttle. Curly tried to see through the glass-paned door that led into the kitchen from the hall. It was frosted glass. The tall one stepped forward and elbowed his way through the door into the next room.

A gaunt man in striped pajamas lay there in bed.

The shorter Revolutionary Guard shoved the woman ahead of him.

"Why did it take you so long to open the door?" barked the tall one.

The short one nudged his gun into the woman's back. "Well?"

"I wasn't sure whether . . . " she answered.

"Were you expecting someone else?"

"No."

"I suppose you don't like it when people come around without letting you know," the tall one said.

Paintings had been removed from the walls. All that was left were faded spots. There was only one, a Madonna, hanging on one of the side walls. It was a spacious room with old German furniture and two windows overlooking the street.

Black Lion sensed something he couldn't put into words, something that was part of what he meant by justice. He was quite sure that what was going to happen next would be the kind of a scene he'd dreamed about. He had no doubt that until yesterday this German woman named Grellova, who was practically wetting her pants in fear now, had been yelling, "Heil, Hitler!" and saluting until her arm ached. He didn't feel sorry for her because her face was so white, as white as if someone had slapped her. Or for the hunched way she was standing. He wasn't sorry for her at all.

The tall one yanked off the quilt. With his pistol, the shorter one motioned the woman toward the bed. The man who lay in bed was unarmed. The tall man lowered his left hand.

Black Lion turned to the two boys. "Nazis," he said. "They'll get what's coming to them now. They're scared shitless. But up until yesterday, they were still shooting at us. Up until then, they were ready to gouge out both my eyes. Just yesterday, they'd have gladly tied you like a calf to the turret of a tank and lugged you through the streets until you were full of bullet holes. Sometimes, when they caught one of the rebels, they cut off their . . . "

"Hmm," mused Tiny.

"They're scared shitless now," Curly agreed.

Tiny figured that, for a German, the woman's voice should have sounded steadier and that the fellow in the bed shouldn't have been trembling so much. He couldn't compare them to the other Germans he'd known. But it occurred to him that the man's pajamas were striped, like prisoners' uniforms. His were probably made out of better material, though.

The shorter guard felt the quilt. "It's cold, you bastard," he yelled. "Get up."

The man scrambled out of bed. He had sharp grey eyes and stubbly chin and cheeks. He hadn't shaved for at least three days. He stood next to the woman. They looked like prisoners of war, which was probably what they wanted to look like. The man was barefoot and he kept shifting from one foot to the other. But he didn't move, and even though his bedroom slippers were within reach, he didn't attempt to put them on.

"Have you got any guns?" demanded the tall one.

"Don't lie," barked the shorter. "Or else . . ."

"We haven't got any," the woman said quickly. "We've never had any weapons here."

The man's chin trembled. He couldn't speak.

He looked like someone with an industrious life behind him, like a busy military clerk in the appointment of the railroads or a logistic who'd spend years and most of his energy working limitless hours, days, and nights, pale as an office rat, never or seldom asking questions. From both his light green eyes looked choked wishes, missed intentions, unmet needs; problems and conflicts and disgusts; but at the same time futile orders that had not been and won't be executed. Every inch of his skin was sweating. He shifted his weight from the left leg to the right one and back. In his green pupils the short RG could read unfulfilled solutions, sitting there like a hiding fish. The man had something also hiding on his lips that he didn't say.

"What did you do with them?" asked the tall one.

"We never had any weapons," the woman insisted.

"We . . . " the man began.

There were two gas mask cases on the china cupboard. There were sandbags and fire axes in the corners of the room.

Black Lion watched the faces of the man and woman. She looked even more drained and tired than she had at first. It was a different kind of weariness than the kind that goes with sleeplessness. It was one of the many varieties of fear which they were tasting now—fear of force, fear of helplessness, fear of injustice, as well as of justice and of what they all had in common.

The woman stood beside the man, as if she longed to lean on him. The fellow looked ready to collapse. But he probably hadn't looked like that yesterday, or the day before. There had been shooting on Tuesday from this building, out onto the street. Into the square, too.

The windows were perfect for shooting in any direction.

"Let's see your identity cards," ordered the tall one.

Cautiously, the woman edged to the wardrobe. "We keep them in here," she said and took out her purse and their documents. Her face was the color of ash. Her fingers shook as she turned the key in the wardrobe lock.

The tall one pointed to the door with the frosted glass panes. "What's in there?" he said.

"The kitchen," the woman answered. Her words seemed to be sending signals, as if by saying "kitchen" she meant "please."

"They're really scared," murmured Tiny.

"We know that feeling," Curly added, just as quietly.

"But it's different when *they're* the ones who're scared," Tiny added, and he sounded almost puzzled.

"This is a new one on me," Curly said. "Honest to God, I thought they really *were* stronger than you and me, I honestly did."

The tall one inspected their identity cards as if he were looking for something. He leafed through them from beginning to end and back again.

"Grellova?" he repeated.

"Yes," declared the woman.

"Heinrich Grell?" The man nodded.

"Grell, Heinrich."

The shorter RG kicked open the door into the kitchen. Out rolled the hot stench of scorched wool.

The tall one stuck the I.D. cards into his pocket.

"Something's burning in there," said Black Lion.

"Go take a look," said the tall guard.

"Go on," urged the shorter.

Black Lion reached the kitchen range in three strides. With his shaggy hair and flattened nose, he did indeed look like a lion in profile.

Tiny and Curly followed. They weren't in such a hurry, though. When Black Lion opened the oven door, smoke poured out into the kitchen. He took a poker and raked out what was left of a German Army uniform. The tarnished silver buttons were still there, and warped epaulets.

"Take a look at this," announced Black Lion.

Curly looked into a wooden bin. "Coal," he said.

"It's a uniform," Black Lion said.

"Let's see. SS?" demanded Curly.

"Green wool," Tiny observed knowingly. "He wasn't in the air corps, then. It doesn't look like Luftwaffe stuff."

"A big wheel," Curly noted.

"He probably was high-ranking," Black Lion agreed. "The rats!" he went on. "Rats! Rats!" Then he closed the door of the oven.

"Should I run water or something?" Tiny asked.

Black Lion kicked the oven door shut again as the short RG had done. He looked from one to the other. He knew this must be making a big impression on the two boys.

The oven door fell open again. The back of the grate was full of soot from the burned woolen trousers. Scraps of paper lay along the sides. Black Lion wondered what it was they'd been trying to burn. An hour later, they'd have cleaned out the stove and there'd have been nothing left.

"They miscalculated," he said out loud. "Put out what's left of the fire." He picked up the remnants of the uniform and carried it back into the living room on the poker.

"It doesn't say in your I.D. that you're an officer," the tall one remarked.

"I was in the reserves," the man replied.

"Are you or are you not an officer?"

"No . . . yes, I was, but I'm retired now," the man stuttered. His eyes blinked rapidly.

"Put up your hands."

The man raised his hands. The tall one inspected his arm below the elbow. He was looking for the distinguishing tattoo of the SS.

"He had to," said the woman.

"Shut up!" the short guard ordered.

"He had to," she whispered.

"I told you to shut up," the short one snapped. He turned to the man. "Were you a member of the National Socialist Party?"

"We had to be," replied the man, his chin quivering.

"Rank?"

"Colonel."

"*Standartenführer?*"

"Yes, sir."

"You must have been well informed, I guess."

"Not so well, sir. Not always. Communications have been disrupted for several days already. Not today or yesterday, sir. We were totally isolated here, sir."

"Yes," said the shorter RG. "I know. Can you remember how to write your own name? Barely, what? Yeah, it's just a technical matter, like always, I'm sure."

Neither the man nor the woman knew what he meant.

"I was in an organizational unit; there was no shooting or fight-ing," the man said. If he was talking to the woman, she didn't react. "We're not the people you're looking for," the man said quietly.

The short RG was looking at him as at a man who'd walked a long distance in a short time. The man was defending himself as if he were trying to postpone something which had come so abruptly.

"You think well of yourself, don't you? *Standartenführer*," repeat-ed the short RG.

"Yes, sir."

"What branch?"

"I was just an accountant."

"Let him lie down," the woman said.

"That bed was empty a minute ago," said the short one. Then he turned to the man. "Is this your wife?"

"Yes," answered the man.

"Any children?"

"No," the man replied.

"Is there anything you have to tell us?" queried the short one.

"What do you want to know?" the woman asked.

"You just figure out what might interest us."

"I don't know what would interest you," the woman murmured.

The man's chin kept trembling. His eyes shifted from the linoleum on the floor to the Revolutionary Guards, to the three boys, and back to the bed, but he never once looked at his wife.

"Why did you want to burn your uniform?" asked the tall one.

"The war's over," the woman said.

"I'm asking him."

"The war's over and we lost," the man said finally. "It's over. We don't want to have anything to do with it anymore."

"Somebody was shooting from your windows," burst out the tall guard.

"Not from ours," the man said slowly.

"From this very window, and from that one over there." The tall one pointed.

The shorter RG kept eyeing the windows, then the smoldering wool of the uniform, then glancing back at the man and woman. As if he were looking for something and he didn't know what.

"Who was shooting from here?" the tall one demanded once again.

"It wasn't us," the man retorted promptly.

"He's a sick man," the woman said.

"You can trust us," the man declared.

"He's got a heart condition."

"I've been sick for years," he said.

"We're human beings just like everybody else," pleaded the woman.

"We're innocent," said the man.

"God knows what you're trying to blame us for," the woman went on.

"Sure, we were probably the ones who were doing the shooting from your windows. At our own people," said the tall one.

"It wasn't us," the man with the quivering chin insisted. His pajamas were too big for him.

"Do you have a medical certificate?" asked the short one.

"No. We burned it," said the man.

The woman kept staring at the picture of the Madonna in its old cracked frame, as if it were a mirror.

That was the first time the man glanced at the woman, and then he noticed what she was looking at.

"So who was it, then, that was doing the shooting?" the tall one demanded, as if he already knew the answer. Or as if he wanted to make sure of something else. "I only ask a question once," he went on. "I don't have to remind you that what you don't tell us, we'll easily find out for ourselves."

"We're not the ones you're looking for," the woman said.

"Who, then?" the short one bellowed suddenly.

"The general's bodyguards," whispered the man in pajamas.

"Are you one of them?" asked the tall one.

The short RG looked up sharply.

"No," the man answered immediately. "They've already gone. They left yesterday. They came here without asking. They just took over our apartment on orders from above. They didn't even ask us. We couldn't have refused. It was still dark when they went away."

"Who do you think you are?" the tall one demanded. "Who do you think you are?"

"Well?" yelled the short one. "Don't you hear what we asked you?"

"We had nothing to do with them," said the man in pajamas.

"Otherwise we wouldn't have stayed on here," the woman added.

"Why did you burn your medical certificate?" the small one demanded.

"We wanted to start a new life," the woman said.

"We had nothing to do with them and we were glad when they left," the man insisted.

"That's the truth, we didn't have anything to do with them," the woman said.

"Like with that cold bed, hm, you bastard."

"We've got some money we put aside for our trip," the woman said.

"A little extra, more than we need . . ." The man did not finish his sentence.

"What do you mean by that?" asked the shorter Revolutionary Guard.

"A few family jewels," said the man.

"Don't even talk to them," the tall guard told the shorter.

"How many wedding rings do you have? How many gold molars?"

"We haven't got any wedding rings," the man said.

"It's just our personal jewelry," the women went on.

"Don't talk about it with them," the tall one told the other.

"It's our own jewelry, a little bit of gold," the woman repeated.

"Gold from somebody's molars," the short RG persisted.

"Skip it," the tall one told him.

"Things like that don't mean anything to us anymore," the man continued.

"Why did they come to your place in particular? Why did they leave you here?" the tall one asked the man.

He shrugged his shoulders. "I don't know."

"How should we know?" the woman asked softly.

"When did they come?" asked the taller guard.

"I don't remember exactly," replied the man.

"So much has happened during the last forty-eight hours," the woman said.

Black Lion was surprised by the flat, curt tone of the conversation. So this is justice, he said to himself. *Justice,* walking into an apartment where somebody's tracks are being covered up, papers and a uniform burned, a place from whose windows somebody had been shooting. In whose rooms a German general's bodyguards had spent the night. And yet this justice was wrapped in fog—ignorant, brutal, and loose. Nothing was for sure, everything was in the air, drifting away and then called back again. It was a brief interrogation and it could only go one way. He could imagine where it would lead. How come they were now so weak when up until yesterday they'd been so strong and strict? Now nothing can help them—not even the voices of the "heart, strength, blood, and land" they counted on for so long. Justice is when somebody gets what he deserves, not what he thinks he deserves.

There was only one kind of justice everywhere during his childhood—at school, in the street, on the radio. It was the only kind he'd been introduced to, and he couldn't imagine any other. It was the avenging justice, the kind that hit and humiliated first, before the rest. It fascinated him. He knew it could never happen again. He felt initiated into this justice in its raw brutal likeness. The man and the woman now looked like twin eggs.

There were mattresses on the floor behind the drawn window drapes. Like all the other German-occupied apartments, this one had been used until yesterday as a gun emplacement. The muzzles of machine guns and bazookas had poked out between those mattresses and sandbags. They'd had plenty of everything, including rifles and pistols.

"Get over against the wall," snapped the tall one.

It was the wall where the picture hung, next to the window. The man and woman stood side by side, hugging the wall.

"You might as well enjoy yourselves and take it out on them," Black Lion said to Tiny. "If you feel like taking it out on somebody. And help yourselves to whatever you think you've got coming to you."

Tiny just looked at him.

"I don't give a shit," he said. All he was thinking about was that they didn't need to stay until it was all over.

The uniform was still smoldering. They noticed that the floor was scarred from when the furniture had been shoved around.

"Face the window," the tall one ordered.

The man broke into a sweat. Large drops stood out on his neck and forehead.

"You boys go out in the kitchen for a minute," said the smaller of the Revolutionary Guards.

Black Lion went first.

"And close the door behind you."

"Turn to the window!"

The woman was sweating too. She was as white as a sheet.

Black Lion was the last to leave the room. When, out of the corner of his eye, he saw the man and woman facing the window, he suddenly realized what was going to happen. The three of them stepped over the scraps of uniform. Black Lion left the kitchen door slightly ajar. Cold sweat broke out on his forehead, like on the man's and woman's. He felt a buzzing in his head. Justice. *Justice.* Like climbing a hill. Justice, he said to himself. *Justice.*

So these are Nazis. They'd been members of the Party. And even if they said they *had* to be, they were probably glad they'd *had* to be. Now that would serve them as a shield. And just yesterday, and the day before, they'd been shooting at the insurgents on Parizska Boulevard from both windows. Who knows whom they'd shot before? Nobody *has* to do anything unless he's willing to take the responsibility for it—today, yesterday, and tomorrow. Otherwise, he's a rag and he shouldn't expect to be treated with kid gloves.

He wondered how far it was from the windowsill down to the sidewalk. In his mind's eye, a picture composed itself of cobblestones dug out of the street, of burned fragments and treads from a Nazi tank. All that was left of it was a pile of scrap iron and, beside it, the stains which are all that's left of people. Until the rain washes them away. There had been people who were hit and who then bled to death before anybody could help them, simply because they were in the firing line of these windows. Although it was the last day of the war. Maybe the last hour.

The kitchen window opened on the courtyard. It was the same distance from the ground as the other windows in front. The pavement was all that was different.

"Tiny," he whispered.

"What?"

"Curly?"

"Yeah?"

"They're going to put them on trial in there. The interrogation is over. They know what they wanted to know. Got it? No delays, no lingering. They won't torture them for long. It's justice—to do it quickly. Just to say what they should do, and they'll do it. On the spot and fast. And all that goes with it."

"They'll probably go on lying for a while and try to wiggle out of it," said Tiny. "If I were in their shoes, I'd squirm like a worm."

"I hope you two got the message," concluded Black Lion.

"You're white as a sheet," said Curly. "Is there something wrong with you?"

"No."

"Now you're red in the face all of a sudden," Curly went on, peering closely at Black Lion. "What's the matter?"

"Nothing," said the shaggy one. He watched as the two boys rummaged around in the kitchen. What were they looking for?

Just thinking about it made him feel feverish. *Justice.* That was what was happening in there. During a bright day. In his presence. The boys surprised him a little. They behaved more like they were going through a storage bin than conducting a revolutionary trial. What were they looking for?

"Justice," Black Lion muttered again, staring at the boys as if he were trying to remind himself of why they were there.

"Hey, look, we found some food," said Tiny.

"A jar of apricots," Curly announced. "It hasn't even been opened yet. You want some?"

Black Lion felt a kind of surprise bordering on disappointment. There you go, he thought to himself, gorging yourselves now of all times. But along with disappointment, he also felt a shade of admiration because of the way they'd simply shrugged their shoulders in the laundry room when his father had asked them about where they'd come from, where they'd been, and how they'd got here. Were they really in camps for three years? So what? Who cares?

He turned toward the door which was half-open. He could see what was going on in the other room. The two men with the arm-bands were standing side by side now, feet apart, blocking the door-way in case the man and woman decided to try to make a dash for the stairs. Both their pistols were aimed at the hearts of the man and the woman.

But the man and woman didn't move. They faced the window, their backs to the Revolutionary Guards.

"What do you see when you look down out the window?" asked the taller.

When they did not reply, the smaller yelled, "Well, what d'you see? What do you see down there? Don't act like you're blind."

"Nothing," the man in pajamas answered humbly. "Houses," he offered. "The street. People. People. Otherwise nothing in particular. It's all over now. For you, this is peacetime already."

"What do you see down there on the sidewalk?" pressed the taller guard.

"Just let us say our prayers," the woman whispered.

"Speak up—what do you see from the window when you look down at the sidewalk?" the taller one went on, as if everything depended on what they saw.

"What do you see there on the pavement?" He lowered his voice menacingly.

"Don't act like you're deaf, dumb, and blind," shouted the smaller guard. "Don't act like it's peacetime for us and hell for you! Who's it hell for? Who? You think we're crazy, that it's something that can be forgotten? Forgive and forget? Go ahead, talk—tell us what you see down there, or else."

He moved his gun closer to the woman's back, but he didn't touch her.

"Let us say our prayers," she repeated.

"Do you think we can't prove it?" yelled the smaller guard.

"Wait," the tall one told him.

"We're people just the same as you are," the woman murmured softly. "We're just people. War was bad for all of us."

"See that fellow with the bandaged head standing there by the lamppost? What did he do to you?" asked the taller guard. "Answer my question first, then you." He stepped closer and motioned at the man with his gun, then at the woman.

"What more do you want?" asked the man.

"Answer what I asked you." Now the tall one began to shout too.

"What do we need their answer for?" whispered the smaller

guard. "What for? What good does it do? What difference does it make to what's past?"

"Wait," the tall one repeated.

"I never saw that person before," the man in pajamas said.

"We don't know anybody around here," the woman added.

"You shot at him!" the tall one said.

"Make them look at those bloodstains on the sidewalk," urged the smaller one. "Tell them that since we're being so patient, they ought to be good enough to at least look at those bloodstains on the sidewalk."

"We had nothing to do with it," said the man.

"We had nothing to do with it," the woman echoed.

"No, we didn't," the man went on.

"No," the woman added.

"I want you to look at those bloodstains," the small one insisted.

"So you don't see anything in particular when you look out the window?" said the tall one.

"Nothing that would have anything to do with me," the woman said.

"You call *that* nothing?" yelled the smaller.

"People," the woman went on.

"For how many days were you shooting up here?" demanded the tall one coldly.

"We didn't do any shooting at all, on my honor as an officer," the man said quietly. "I don't shoot civilians. We're not bandits."

It was clear that talking, any kind of words were better for the man and woman, since they bought time. But it was bad for them too, because the shorter RG was getting restless.

"Yeah, the war was bad for both sides," he said, accepting it both as the truth and a lie.

"Does this rag belong to you?" asked the tall one, pointing to what was left of the uniform.

"Yes," the man admitted.

"Where's your pistol?"

"The general's bodyguards disarmed us," said the man.

"What've you been doing?" the tall one asked the woman.

"I was a nurse on the Eastern Front, then in the West. Afterwards I joined my husband who was stationed here." She leaned her hand against the wall and touched the picture of the Madonna, making it crooked.

"We're your prisoners and we expect you to hand us over to the authorities according to the laws which are valid in every civilized country."

"We aren't enough of an authority to suit you?" the smaller guard barked.

"Step over to the window," the tall one said. "One step, no more, no less."

"We didn't shoot at all," the woman insisted softly. "We never did any shooting."

"Did you keep your windows open all during the uprising?" the small one asked.

"Open the window wide," the tall one ordered the man in pajamas.

"Open the window over on your side too," the small one told the woman.

"One step more," repeated the tall one. "All right." He paused. "Now move a little closer. Right to the window. So your legs are up against the frame. That's it."

"What is it you want?" the woman asked.

"What are you going to do to us?" the man asked.

Black Lion clutched Tiny's shoulder. He leaned against Curly. He felt hilarious and confused, happy, completely surprised, red in his face right up to his deeply open shirt, with goose pimples all over his arms and legs.

"They're going to have to jump," he said. "Justice. In one minute they're going to have to jump."

"We want you to take a good look at what's down there," said the tall one.

"We want you to see it so close that you get spots in front of your eyes," the shorter one added.

"They'll have to jump," Black Lion went on. "And they'll be squashed like bedbugs. This is justice." He swallowed saliva. It suits them well. I swear. I swear.

His eyes were glued to their backs. He watched every move the man and woman made and heard every word the Revolutionary Guards said to them. The windows framed the four of them.

"I demand to be put on trial," said the man in pajamas. "I request a regular court to which I can transmit all my information and all my property."

"Hand us over to your authorities," the woman pleaded.

"Tell them we'll hand them over the quickest way," the smaller Revolutionary Guard said to his companion.

"We'll hand you over all right," the tall one said. "Nobody will be handed over so swiftly and surely."

"We didn't do anything," the woman repeated. "We didn't do anything to anybody. You have no right to do something to us which we haven't deserved."

Then her lips parted as though she'd intended to say something else. But she didn't say it. Her lips contradicted what was in her eyes, which were still watchful and filled with fear. Was the decision of both Revolutionary Guards already fixed? Was it as irreversible as it sounded to her? Both she and the man looked as servile as they could look.

"We found this uniform here—there was shooting from your window—you haven't answered a single one of our questions: how long you've been here and what went on while your general's body-guards were here. You even refuse to look at those bloodstains. That blood didn't come from one single person. Just what you can see ought to give even the two of you an idea of what you've been hand-ing out to everybody else so generously. You have one minute. I'll count to sixty."

"I'll count," offered the smaller one.

"Look down there," said the tall one.

The shorter Revolutionary Guard had begun to count and he was already at eight.

The man and woman said nothing.

"Lean out the window and look," the tall one said.

Then, when the smaller one had gotten to twenty, he said, "What color is the pavement?"

"Lean out a little farther," the tall one ordered.

"Oh, my God," the woman choked.

"No," muttered the man.

The back of his pajamas were soaking wet. So was the back of the woman's dress.

"But we haven't done anything," she murmured. When her husband did not say a word, she went on: "But we didn't do any shooting."

There was sweat in her words, and tears too, but all dried up. No more mumbling, no more choked back screams in the woman's voice. She listened to the counting of the smaller Revolutionary Guard. Sixteen, seventeen, eighteen . . .

When she stopped talking, her husband's wheezy breathing became audible. His breath came in sharp jerks. As though he were praying. Or talking to himself, saying the same thing over and over. He no longer looked at his wife, although her eyes clung to him. Both of them stood there, frozen to the spot.

The two, the man and woman, kept staring down at the pavement, at the bloodstains to which the Revolutionary Guards had wanted to draw their attention.

The tall guard let the safety catch click on his pistol. The smaller one did the same. They did it calmly, not rushing. The smaller Revolutionary Guard now counted up from forty. Forty-one, forty-two, forty-three . . .

Black Lion was sweating like the man and woman by the window. From the street came the sounds of people and cars and bells ringing in the distance, fragments of shouts and laughter. Justice was at work now. It had a face of its own, a voice, words, and numbers, forty-four, forty-five, breath, silence, time. It was something you couldn't hold in your hand and yet it could fill a room like some invisible substance, thick enough to cut with a knife. Like not having enough air—or too much. Like the energy everything is full of. Or like fumes when somebody strikes a match. Forty-six, forty-seven, forty-eight . . .

It was a strange kind of pressure that had to be released. The counting was coming to an end.

"They'll get it, they'll get it, even if they hadn't told all the lies they've told already, or if they'd kept their mouths shut even tighter than they have," he said.

And then he whispered, "They're going to have to jump. They'll probably do it together. They're going to have to jump."

He'd been watching the two boys as they opened a jar of apricots. They ruined a fork and spoon doing it.

The man took the woman's hand and held it tight and the woman clung to him. They didn't say anything for a few seconds. Fear distorted their faces. The corners of their mouths fell. Also the crotch and legs of the man's pajamas became yellowishly drenched. Their clasped hands cramped and intelligence evaporated from their eyes. The smaller Revolutionary Guard was at the number fifty. Fifty-one, fifty-two, fifty-three . . .

Their eyes resembled those of fish accustomed to the surface of a pool where everything was bright and transparent, but which suddenly swim into the depth, and under the unexpected pressure of unknown and heavy waters, in the dark, are unable to orient themselves, plunging deeper and deeper to the very bottom, without a motion. The woman was weeping. Suddenly she was not the woman who had opened the door. She looked at her husband. They embraced each other. Their look was deeper than the space between the fourth floor and the pavement with bloodstains in the middle. At that moment they looked so tired and exhausted that the awareness left their faces as if they already ceased to exist. Fifty-eight, fifty-nine, sixty, counted the smaller Revolutionary Guard.

"I'll tell you when it's over," Black Lion whispered.

A hollow thud came from the next room as the woman fainted and collapsed to the floor.

"She passed out," said Black Lion disappointedly.

The man in pajamas bent over her.

"You forgot your bad heart," the tall one said.

The man looked away.

"Don't take one more step," the tall one commanded. He glanced at the smaller guard, who stared back at him.

"In a while they'll come and take you away," he said. "In the meantime, we'll look around. Give me the key to everything that's locked up and show me everything that can be opened. Don't try to put anything over on us or conceal some hiding place."

The man shuffled slowly over to the wardrobe where he'd hung his civilian clothes before he'd jumped into bed. He pulled some keys out of a pocket of his pajamas and handed them to the tall guard.

Then he walked over to the picture of the Madonna and took it down. There was a lock set in the wall. In it he had money, Reichsmarks, and jewels in a wooden Japanese box.

"See if you can bring her around," the tall one told the man. "Get some water," he said to the smaller one.

Then the smaller RG opened the wardrobe. He took his time. Besides the civilian suits and shirts and underwear, there were two big suitcases, a man's and a woman's, both packed and ready to go.

"Where are those two concentration camp kids?" the tall one called.

Black Lion stepped into the room from the kitchen. "Here," he said, pointing through the open door at the two boys.

They stopped eating the apricots.

"Help yourselves to anything you need," the tall one told them.

The wooden rack in the wardrobe sagged with clothes that smelled of mothballs because nobody had worn them for years. There were almost a dozen suits and coats. Tiny bent down carefully, because behind the two suitcases in the bottom of the wardrobe where the shoes were, he saw a knobby sack made out of white linen.

"What's in it?" demanded Curly, who was standing right behind him.

"Sugar," Tiny replied. "Lump sugar."

"How do you know?" wondered Curly.

"Take what you need," the tall one repeated. "And then get the hell out of here."

Tiny took the sack of sugar and straightened up. "This," he said. Curly made a face. "Grub," he said.

The taller Revolutionary Guard broke into a laugh. "Scram," he said, but in quite a different tone.

The shorter guard grinned.

Black Lion picked up the case with the gas masks and watched the two boys leave ahead of him. They paid no attention to the man and woman. He looked over at the open window. The light was bright. It was twelve P.M., noon. The sun grew warm. White clouds swam high and the skies were deep blue. The streets were now full of people, of noises. Some men down on the pavement started singing songs forbidden until just yesterday. From the top window in the building across the avenue flew a new blue-white-and-red flag, held by two people—a man and a woman, smiling.

When the boys got downstairs and out on the sidewalk, they kicked around all the bits of brick and broken plaster they wanted to. After that, just as obliviously, they passed the dark stain on the sidewalk next to the corner where the sewer was. The man with the bandaged head wasn't standing there anymore. The street was full of people different than the ones who had been there before, and in a little while, others would take their place too.

Then, with an unflagging sense of pride, Black Lion took Tiny and Curly home with him. He had an unquestionable feeling that what he had just experienced had been *justice*. No remorse. But he'd had a different feeling about it when they'd gone into the building than when they'd come out. And suddenly he felt satisfaction that those two people, whom he'd seen for the first time in his life, and probably for the last, hadn't jumped. That they didn't have to jump. So what? Who cares?

"Come on," he said to the little kid. "Let me give you a hand with that sugar."

Early in the Morning

D on't you worry about me," the boy said sharply. "The excitement's all over, if you had the notion anybody's still jumping," the fat man told him.

He knew who he was right away, from his clothes and his face and eyes. He could tell immediately. He'd seen the boy yesterday, tripping over the corpses beside the overturned German machine gun. He was still wearing the same silly, wrinkled blue knickers, an army shirt, and white shoes with big gold buckles.

"Where did you get this splendid wardrobe? The Red Cross? The Salvation Army? Some early prey?"

He cleaned his nose with a huge red handkerchief.

"You should have been here last night if you wanted to see them jump," the fat man added. The boy must have hurried. Just as he'd hurried yesterday beside that German machine gun.

It was the boy's eyes that were strange—squinting, almost adult eyes whose lashes had been scorched. His eyebrows were singed too, as if a bullet had whizzed past his head. Or as if he'd gotten too close to a fire.

He's really got funny eyes, the man thought to himself. Even the pupils were narrow, as if he regarded everything he saw with suspicion. Those eyes didn't match his delicate, childlike complexion and rosy lips. It was as if someone had carved them out with a knife and left two sharp splinters of steel behind.

"I told you they're not jumping anymore. It looks like it's all over. Now they're just moving along like wind-up toys. Or robots. As if each one of them is somebody else now. Times have changed."

The boy had two long scars on his forehead, as though his skull were coming apart beneath the skin. Or as if someone had beaten him.

"How come you're so handsome?" the fat man said.

Like those kids who, for five or six days, had been going around killing and stealing whatever there was to kill and steal. A fuzz of golden hair showed from under his cloth cap.

"No death-defying leaps today," the fat man continued. "You haven't missed anything."

The boy just eyed him narrowly.

"All the fun and games ended last night," the fat man assured him. "That's all I can tell you. And now nobody else has any business here on this bridge. You might get hurt. Somebody else might get hurt too. I don't want to argue with you."

"I'll stand over here by the guardrail," the boy said.

"You're not standing anywhere, that's what I'm telling you. You got your share yesterday, I can see that."

The boy said nothing.

"All of this—these two bridges, from one end to the other— they're military territory now, see?" The fat man strode off slowly, slapping his gun. It was a new 1944 German machine gun. Reserve cartridges stuck out of his pocket. The gun was slung across his chest, but he was so fat that it hung high.

"I bet I can read your mind," he said. Something warned him he ought to get rid of the boy before there was trouble. "It's your tough luck if you don't believe me when I tell you nobody's jumping anymore. It's all over with."

He peered at the boy suspiciously. "If you're looking for somebody, you picked the wrong bridge. Forget it. Can't you see they're finished, even without your help?"

A brisk morning breeze was blowing. The river was dirty. Next to the suspension bridge, which had been destroyed before the war ended, a temporary wooden bridge had been built, later reinforced with a few extra pillars to support trucks and streetcars. Tanks only risked it when the bridge was empty.

The bridges looked like sisters, side by side.

"Just don't tell me you came here to admire the old bridge or see how much this wooden one can carry," the fat man said. "I wasn't born yesterday."

"Yeah, well, I didn't have to throw up last night the way some people did," the boy recalled.

Yesterday, while the shooting was still going on, the youngster had been standing on the corner of Parizska Boulevard and Jachymova Street, where the barber shop and the beauty parlor were, across the street from the bank and the Sherry Bar. They'd closed the bar on Saturday as soon as the shooting started. Somebody had boarded up the glass doors.

The youngster watched the shooting at close range. It was almost as if he *wanted* a bullet to nick him, if not hit him directly. Or as if he wanted to see whether he was invulnerable. He stayed there until it was all over. As if he were looking for something or somebody. Or as if he found it immensely entertaining.

The rebels finally succeeded in killing a German machine gun crew. The boy was the first to rush forward.

Everybody expected he was going to rob the soldiers or take their guns. But all he did was pick up a glinting cartridge case which lay on the ground beside the empty ammunition belt. He didn't touch the dead German soldiers. It must have been something else he was looking for. What? The sheer satisfaction of the war ending that way and not another one? All the why's he was looking for rose up in his blue eyes.

The energy in his movements made his walking look more like running. He had clever, quick eyes, lit and burned by some flame inside him. There was something playful but grave in those eyes. He looked at the dead soldiers as if they'd all suddenly suffered a stroke and he was checking to see if they were really beyond recovery. I have more patience than he does, the fat man decided.

The fact he hadn't robbed them was what saved his life, because as he moved on to give others a chance, a tank standing next to the Law School had opened fire and killed a woman who had been running over to tear the clothes off the gunners.

It blew her into pieces. It tore off her arms and legs as if she'd been a tousled rag doll, and all that was left of her were a few wet scraps of flesh and bone and cloth and shoe leather.

The barber got a piece of shrapnel in his thigh. Half of the bystanders were shot and half were kept as hostages by the Germans. That was when the fat man got sick to his stomach.

Later, for a change, the Sherry Bar had been turned into a prison for captured German soldiers and officers and civilians because there wasn't enough room for them in the textile shop or the anti-aircraft shelter in the building where the funeral parlor was.

The captive German soldiers streaming down the street from the stockyards and across the wooden bridge didn't seem in such bad shape.

A defeated army never looks scary. The rows of men came and went with a disordered kind of regularity, with uneven gaps between, the way water flows from a far-off spring. That was how the Revolutionary Guard dispatched them from the freight depot and the other railroad stations and highway check points toward a single staging area. According to the fat man's calculations, there must be at least one whole division.

"They have a lot of miles in their soles—half of Europe and Africa. They were running from the east to the west, but the uprising put a barrier in their path and spoiled it for Papa Schorner," said the fat man. "The war started here and ends here. It's as simple as one and one."

He had to admit that even now, when he saw them as helpless as they were, a shiver ran up his spine—like when he'd gotten sick to his stomach the day before. He could imagine how he'd feel if those soldiers marching along here now were marching in a different way. Fortunately . . . .

He couldn't even say whether they were moving in a more orderly formation than they had been earlier that morning. He hadn't seen the ones who had come through during the night. He'd reported for duty at five o'clock that morning. He hadn't had much sleep during the past five days, so he was a little edgy and, at the same time, proud of himself for his endurance. Anyway, he wanted to be left alone and he didn't want the youngster hanging around.

He could find no trace of softness or humility in that kid's face.

"There's a tavern at the other end of the wooden bridge," he said. "It's called the Fatted Calf and half the town's in there. They'll give you free beer and something to eat. Why don't you go on over?"

He remembered an SS guard who trained in Dachau near Munich and later in Mauthausen in Austria, among other places. He learned every-thing expected of an SS guard in the concentration camps. They sent the worst criminals to Mauthausen, which was known to be a camp of the third category, and punished them with the hardest work. The precise order was: no one was ever meant to return. He saw how they treated prisoners, including heftlings, who were labeled as especially undesirable.

There were 146 steps in the quarry up which the prisoners carried heavy boulders. An SS member waited at the top and when the spirit moved him he pushed the man on the last step who had made it that far with the remnants of his strength, and the prisoner, with the heavy boulder on his shoulder, wooden clogs slipping on the rocks, lost his balance. As he fell, he dragged down the other prisoners behind him; they toppled like dominoes. They fell one after another, the heavy boulders they'd been carrying on their shoulders on top of them. Bloodied and broken-boned, they prayed that they would get a mercy bullet. Most of them were just left to be dragged up by the next group of prisoners.

The prisoners, including a Russian general who the Germans particularly hated, stood naked in an open space in front of the barracks. They poured cold water over the General's body in the freezing Alpine air, several degrees below zero, so he'd slowly freeze. The SS guard had seen this frozen man with his own eyes and he was reminded of him whenever a new group of prisoners, soldiers or officers was brought to Auschwitz-Birkenau; he enjoyed recounting the story to them.

Sometimes the SS members amused themselves by giving a prisoner at the top of the quarry (about thirty-five meters up) an umbrella and telling him to jump. The pit into which they wanted him to jump was filled with blood. The Germans and the Austrians gave a new dimension to the words good, evil, *and* brutality.

After the occupation of the Netherlands, when dockworkers protested the treatment of the Jewish population, a hundred of them were sent to Mauthausen to show how much they could carry. Within one month of their arrival the Gestapo sent ashes back to their families in Amsterdam. The prisoners all perished, down to the last one of them.

As far as carrying rocks back and forth in each concentration camp where the SS guard was stationed, he considered himself charitable to let the prisoners carry rocks smaller than the ones he'd seen them transporting at Mauthausen—back and forth, senselessly—just to keep them occupied to exhaustion, and so they would see just how little meaning their existence had.

Once, he'd looked at the rock he was carrying on his stomach, his fin-

gers laced together: *was it a sliver of rock from those which had formed the earth? He, like many other Germans, was mesmerized by the thought.*

The prisoners were straggling along in a more disorderly fashion than at first. The disorder annoyed the fat man for a while, but then he got used to it. With the sloppy way whole units straggled by, drifting apart and intermingling—flyers and engineers, cannoneers and infantry, motorized artillery and flamethrowers. The fear, which each of these soldiers, individually, had inspired only yesterday, evaporated.

Even to look at, a defeated army is a mean and pitiful sight.

To the fat man, there was justice to it and, at the same time, it was unfair. Each soldier was carrying a fragment of shattered prestige which had been trodden into the dust—a bit of the former glory of an army, now defeated, which had come here intending to stay for a thousand years. They were leaving now, so thoroughly despised that it wasn't worth the trouble to do more than prod, look, or pity.

Yet there was something about them, a captured army, that filled the victors, and those who had helped them to victory, with satisfaction, even though it hadn't been a battlefield surrender. We'll deal with that later, when we have time, and we'll have lots of time, he thought. The killers were caught. What once was will now be corrected. The fat man felt all the dimensions. It's irrefutable now, but still there's something baffling. Yesterday they lost the few crucial hours they would have needed to reach the right exit roads and pass through the new security. Except that maybe they could have gotten out by air or rail; they still had a lot of armored trains in the country. It's hard to be unbiased, he thought, and looked at the long columns of delayed soldiers and then at the boy. The boy was breathing quickly, as if it was difficult to exhale fully after each breath. He looked like someone with heart pains, or muscle cramps in his legs or arms.

In some lines, members of almost every branch of the armed forces marched side by side, most of them without belts and some of them barefoot. Some soldiers only had on underwear beneath their coats.

As the morning wore on, it got tedious. The fat man saw that words wouldn't get rid of the youngster. It wasn't hard to imagine what was going on inside his head. It wouldn't be difficult to grab one of the soldiers once they got beyond the stockyards and to take away his belt or coat or trousers.

"I wouldn't mind if they were still jumping, but they aren't," he repeated.

He could think of other possibilities when he looked at the prisoners and at the youngster.

"By now, you can see for yourself they're not jumping. You've been hanging around here long enough already. If you thought they were, you see with your own eyes they're not."

There are some kids like that who don't miss a thing, the fat man decided. They can sniff out everything. Not like hyenas or vultures. Like beasts of prey, they want to catch their prey alive. Yet look at him—those blue eyes and fair hair, that delicate skin. Maybe part of it's curiosity. But that isn't all.

Why? There could be a thousand becauses—or none at all. So many explanations that they were all mixed up with everything else. The boy bothered him, and that feeling grew stronger every minute. These boys hadn't even been to school, or if they had, it wasn't for long. They'd learned their own rules for all their days and nights, and all the hours in between. They were drunk with freedom—too independent, too self-confident. They were Mom's pretty brats. They aren't all alike, but somehow they always manager. They don't have to learn from books.

"Should be a nice day today," the fat man said. He had blue childlike guileless eyes.

On the first day of the uprising, on Saturday at noon the fat man recalled, two youngsters like this one came up to a German soldier who figured they wanted to trade some food for his gun and ammunition. But instead, they tossed a coal sack over his head, and one of them started hitting him with a beer bottle, the other with an iron pipe. The soldier groped around as if he were playing blindman's buff, while the youngsters talked to him through the sack. They didn't even bother to drag him off into a hallway and finish him up in there. The fat man saw it when all that was left of the beer bottle were splinters of glass.

A woman had screamed as if the soldier were somebody she knew.

"You want to kill him?" Then she ran away yelling, "They want to kill him, they want to kill him."

Nobody stopped them. Nobody called from a window in the next apartment house. Nobody else ran away like the woman did. Nobody told them to stop, that enough was enough.

The boy watched the lines. Each row of prisoners disappeared from sight as the street turned behind the stockyards and ran along the river, so at a distance it looked as though they were marching right into the water. The fat man had it figured out by now how long it took for one column to reach the bridge he was guarding. The boy was still trying to work it out. There must have been at least ten thousand prisoners. Maybe two, three thousands more.

"Now you've seen them in all their tarnished glory, so why don't you go on over to the Fatted Calf, how about it?" the fat man suggested. "Why not have a little fun and relaxation?" he asked after a long pause.

As the first soldiers of the new column approached, he stepped forward to keep a closer eye on things. He had no time to worry about the kid now. If any prisoner got too close to the side of the bridge, he only had to yell at him to move into the middle of the roadway.

"Look, we've gotten acquainted now and there's nothing more to say," declared the fat man. "But right now, this is military territory, pure and simple, and I have my orders and my responsibility is not to allow anybody to loiter here."

"I've got as much business here as you have," the boy said.

"What'd you mean, you've got as much business here as me? Are you a member of the Revolutionary Guard? Are you sixteen years old, at least? Where'd you come from, anyway? Why do you keep sticking your hand in the fire? You want to lose it at the very last minute? How come they let you through on the other side? It doesn't look as though you got much sleep last night. All right, look around. You've seen all there is to see, nothing else is going to happen, so get moving, huh, why don't you? I've got just so much patience. If you thought they were jumping, now you've had a chance to see for yourself they're not. It was different last night."

"That isn't why I came. I'm here, though, and I'm staying for a little while. No regulations apply to me."

"I've got to keep a close eye on everything and I don't want any distractions that might cause trouble."

"I'm not in your way, am I?"

"I'm not saying whether you're in my way or not. I'm only telling you I have to have a free hand here, just in case. Don't try to aggravate me, or there'll be trouble."

"I didn't come here to argue. I came to look around. I want to see them go."

"Didn't you?"

"Not enough."

"Not enough? How many more do you need?"

"Ha," said the boy.

"You'll really make me mad if you don't believe me when I tell you they're not jumping and if you try to kid me into believing you're just interested in seeing them go. You can see better from the other side."

"I want to see them up close, that's all," the boy insisted.

"But not for an eternity." The fat man cleaned his nose again with his huge red handkerchief. It was so big it might have been a flag. He was just perceptive enough to know that the boy didn't fear him at all. He stood on a dusty sidewalk, his small skull high and narrow, as if he were touching the skies with his shaved head. Was he waiting for a miracle? Was he trying to figure out something the fat man didn't see, hear, or feel? The fat man wished the boy would spell it out, right out loud. He'd be glad of that, but he had his doubts about the boy's wisdom anyway. There was probably just something the boy wanted to have his way—or both his ways.

Every fifty meters or so, the column of prisoners was escorted by two or three members of the Revolutionary Guard. When the fat man saw them, he just winked or nodded or wagged a finger so it wouldn't look as though they didn't know how to run things in an orderly way.

As far as you could see—toward the stockyards or in the other direction, where the Prime Minister's offices used to be—no more than three guards were to be seen. The soldiers seemed to be marching into captivity all by themselves. As though their last drop of discipline had trickled into this final act of obedience, which resembled the dregs of something else—or its total collapse. Had they softened up or was it just exhaustion? It was as though they were going voluntarily, trying to avoid something they were still afraid of. And as if they were using their helplessness like a shield, for the admiration of their guards, protecting themselves by the fact that there were so many of them going together.

"They're going now like the Jews went before," the fat man remarked.

The youngster didn't react. After a second or two, the boy grew red in the face. His look was strange—a mixture of embarrassment and mourning, suspicion, defiant anger, and fear. Some barrier rose in his eyes, built of dust, doubts, misunderstood sentiments, different measures and different values. Again he gave the fat man the impression he was having difficulty with his breathing—as if he might have a sudden respiratory attack, or heart failure, as if the weight of the age was on his shoulders. There was bitterness in his eyes. That was when the fat man understood why the boy had come here.

"Did you ever hear the old story about the fellow who played his pipe and all these rats followed him and behind the rats, there were people from some country where they'd never been able to make good? So they followed the fellow with the pipe into another country where even greater disappointments waited in store for them. And that was the end of the line for them."

"This isn't quite the same thing," said the youngster.

"They look a little more human when they've been beaten," the fat man said.

"How many are there?"

"What do you care? Lots. Half of Schorner's army." The fat man had a big belly, drawn in by a wide German belt from Afrika Korps stocks. Most of his clothing was of German origin.

"Who are you?" he demanded suddenly, in his eyes anger and concern. "Who are you, anyway?" Then, as if he wanted to give the boy time to answer or to prepare himself in case he got no answer, he went on: "If anybody told you they're still jumping, well, it isn't true, see? They haven't for quite a while, I can tell you that. The last one who jumped did it at daybreak." He eyed the youngster curiously. "I'd like to know who you are." He supposed the boy was Jewish. He figured it out even though the boy didn't look Jewish, with his gold hair, straight nose, and blue eyes. In part he figured it out just because the boy was here, which seemed to mean he'd been there. The anger receded from his look and left just the concern. Suddenly he thought he saw in the boy's face frozen rivers or bone-drilling winds, desolate forests or rugged mountains. That raised a question about the boy's stamina, strength, and experience. The boy's hands were dangling.

The boy took off his cap. It was an Italian-style cloth cap, but the fat man knew caps like that were worn in places other than the army.

When he did it, it was obvious that his head had been shaved recently. Then he rolled his sleeve back over his elbow and proudly showed the fat man the tattooed numerals and two letters. A capital C and a small one.

Suddenly the fat man's eyes turned from the numbers on the boy's forearm.

"Hey, what the hell . . . " he said. "What's going on?"

"Don't you want to shoot him?" the youngster suggested quickly.

The two of them watched as one of the prisoners stepped out of line when his column passed the wooden railing on the other side of the bridge. The man dashed toward them with outstretched arms, jacket flapping and head lowered, as if he were charging them like a bull. The fat man grabbed his machine gun and aimed it at the prisoner.

The man was about twenty paces away. That would have given the fat man time enough to raise the gun muzzle to the level of his chest and to pull the trigger before he got much closer.

"Let me worry about it," snapped the fat man. "I'll deal with it. If I do something wrong, you can correct me."

When he was only a few steps away, the prisoner swerved suddenly, scrambling over the railing, and jumping into the water. He just missed one of the cables that dangled from the other bridge. As if he'd wanted to catch it, but failed.

There was a loud splash, as though a bale of cotton had hit the water.

"Well, I guess they're still jumping after all," murmured the fat man.

"Are you going to leave him there in the water?" the youngster asked.

"Is that any of your business?"

"So for God's sake, shoot," the youngster said. "Or give me your gun. Don't you want to let him have it before he gets away?"

"Son of a bitch, so they're still jumping," mused the fat man.

The circles in the river's surface widened and floated off with the current under the suspension bridge.

"Are you going to let him get away? You're going to let him swim for it?" the boy demanded.

"The ones who jumped last night had a chance, but that guy doesn't."

"Don't you want to kill him and get it over with?"

"Most of the ones who jumped last night just swam away."

"I might've known."

"Where do you suppose you can swim to from here?"

He looked quickly in the direction of the column.

"Kill him before he gets too far!"

"He'll be under suspicion the whole way, and maybe even later. Don't get discouraged. I'm not quitting. I'll show him. He didn't get anywhere. He must be tired by now. I told you not to get mixed up in this. It's none of your business. Don't you worry."

He raised the machine gun so he could shoot over the railing. He had to pull the strap over his head because his belly got in the way when he tried to aim down over the railing.

"I thought these little performances were over," he said. He readied his gun.

The boy looked on impatiently. None of the other prisoners had moved out of line in the meantime. The columns of men plodded along as though that one prisoner were an exception which had nothing to do with them. Within a few seconds, the unit, to which the prisoner who had just jumped off the bridge belonged, had passed by. Everybody looked straight ahead and kept on going.

"You can't believe everything you hear," the fat man continued. "They're still jumping."

The wind whistled through the steel cables of the suspension bridge and you could hear the water lapping against the riverbank and the heavy tread of the prisoners who had shoes and the creaking of the new timbers in the temporary bridge.

"So they're still doing it. But this is the first one since I've been on duty."

"So what? Who cares?"

"You keep your nose out of this," the fat man told him.

"Just don't let him get away," the youngster urged.

"You know how much rat poison he has to drink?"

After a little while, the prisoner surfaced. He had tried to swim under the bridge under water, against the current, and that had slowed him down. Then, when nobody could see him, he was going to turn and float down with the current until he reached a safety ladder further down the quay.

"What if everybody decided to do the same thing?" said the fat man.

From the bridge, the fat man was carrying on a long-distance conversation with the prisoner. "Why do you want to make me bloodthirsty? Up until yesterday, I was. But today I'm not anymore. I didn't want to be bloodthirsty today."

"Shoot him," said the boy.

The fat man turned as though he hadn't heard. "Well, he didn't intend to drown himself, anyway. He just felt like jumping. We're all glad we're alive on this earth, you, me, him, aren't we after all?"

"Kill him," the boy repeated.

"You're kind of impatient."

"Why did they put you here?"

"You're not very forgiving either, are you?"

"Kill him," the boy said. "The faster the better."

"Wouldn't that be good for him? Let him swallow some rat poison first."

"Why?"

"For the fun of it," the fat man said. "It's cold, isn't it?" The fat man was talking to the prisoner again. "It's a lot colder than it looks from the road or when the sun's shining like now. It's easy to jump in. It's harder to get out."

He watched as the prisoner struggled to take off the water-logged coat that was dragging him down. He was trying to get his shoes off too. The fat man was thinking about what could complicate the prisoner's stay in the water. Maybe a sudden heart attack. Or maybe his heart would rupture, coloring the water around it. Or maybe just that slow sinking and drinking. "It can't last more than a few minutes. You're too heavy."

"So you're my first jumper," the fat man told the prisoner in an almost kindly tone. He aimed the gun awkwardly, shifting it to follow the man's movements in the water. He gave him a chance to start swimming. Then the point of the gun's muzzle halted somewhere about the prisoner's leg. He probably didn't realize he wasn't very deeply submerged as he plunged under the water's surface. Or he got tired and floated up into the current.

"Yesterday, I'd have told you that a smart general would rather lose a battle than lose a war. But today, I'm not so sure."

The fat man shot at the prisoner's thigh. He fired two rounds. The first one was short, as though he were only practicing. The second was longer. The bullets cut through the water as though somebody had underscored a line with two projections. Those were the man's legs in the water now. The echo of the shots filled the hollowness under the bridge, but there were other sounds too.

"He doesn't have anything to escape with now," the fat man said. "Even if he swam to where there are none of our patrols."

"All he can do is swim with his arms now," he went on. "The current'll help him, though. But for how long? He'll drink his fill of these waters. I wish I knew why they jump. What gets into them? Why is it always bridges they jump off of?"

The fat man looked over at the youngster. "Somebody must have told you they're still jumping." He grinned. "Even if he makes it to shore, he won't have anything to crawl out with and to walk on. I got him in the legs good and proper. He can only make it if he's in the water. Not on shore. Unless one of our soft-hearted folks helps him. Well, now what do you have to say?"

The youngster swallowed hard. To the fat man his eyes seemed full of a hidden language without words—or even empty. Without knowing why, the fat man had the impression of a small boat bouncing on submerged rocks. He smiled. "Isn't it cozy? Did you ever see something like that? I bet not." He looked into the boy's eyes.

At that moment, the boy was visualizing those people from Budapest, the man from the Sonderkommando *whose son was sent into the ovens and who was allowed to accompany him as far as the door to the shower room. But when he wanted to go in too, the guard said no.*

Afterwards, the man knelt in the earth. It was muddy after the long

October rains. He stayed there for twelve hours, raking the mud with his fingernails, as if he wanted to pull something out by the roots.

That evening, the other prisoners urged him to come to the barracks before he got shot. He wanted to be shot. But when they came a second time to coax him in, he made them promise to gather up stones to defend themselves. He pleaded with them to break at least the few German skulls that happened to be around.

They formed a circle around him, like a wall, so the German guards wouldn't overhear what he was saying. One of the prisoners slapped his face to silence him. For his own good.

The one who slapped him was the one the guard shot first. Then he fired a path through to the man who was kneeling in the mud.

"Are you saying your prayers for your son or yourself or what?"

The man on his knees was silent.

"I'll shoot you too. I'm only human. I'm only flesh and blood too. I don't have as much patience as you think I have. Nobody's going to play around with me."

So he shot him and asked no more questions. Behind his back, the guard could hear the other prisoners slipping off to the barracks.

"Have you got so little ammunition that you just shot his legs?" the boy asked, instead of answering the questions he'd been asked.

That evening at the Revolutionary first-aid shelter—at the former Wilson Railroad Station—he'd met several men who had ended up in Prague after escaping from the death transports and were in hiding here, some for thirteen weeks already, and others for just a few days or a night. Next they were heading in all directions of the compass. One had wanted before the war to sell liquor in Warsaw or America; another to pray in Jerusalem. The latter told him he looked like his younger brother. What was his name, he wanted to know? Could he show up here? No, the man said.

The man's name was Meilech. Means the "king" in Hebrew, he said. He worked in the Sonderkommando *in Auschwitz-Birkenau eight months in 1943 and listened daily to the men of the SS telling the newcomers to undress, not to worry, just to hurry, they were only taking showers. The arrows pointed "To Disinfection." The SS told them they'd be working; Germany needed workers.* Arbeit Macht Frei. *Then the SS*

would take off their caps and collect wedding rings from the poor, jewels
from those better off, and watches from everyone. One Monday, the man
said, he heard his name in the washroom. He saw his younger brother
Joseph begging for water and asking him what was to come. He couldn't
tell him. He ran to the SS guard on duty and told him that his little
brother was to be gassed and cremated in five minutes. Could he give
him a little bit of water before he went in? He got permission to take a
small cup from the Jewish cook in the SS kitchen, but his brother was
already in the gas chamber when he returned, so he handed the water to
the nearest man and asked him to pass it on to his brother. He yelled to
Joseph that the same fate awaited him, too, and all of them. Who knows
if his brother heard? So. Now he was headed with it to Jerusalem.

"You're awfully bloodthirsty. You'd have killed him, wouldn't you?"

"What're you saving your bullets for?"

"That's none of your business," the fat man replied. He shoved a
new round of ammunition into the gun. His eyes were ingenious
but not excited, in balance with the world; he did everything matter-
of-factly. His belly revealed what he was able to consume and what
kept his huge body moving. At this moment, his blue eyes were not
as kind as his voice. From time to time he looked as if he were driving a truck, his big hands holding the machine gun as if it were the
wheel of a truck or bulldozer. His eyebrows were thick and fair. But
he was more solicitous than frightening, both admiring and despis-
ing his enemies.

"Don't make me nervous," he went on. "I don't know why they
were still jumping. It's not a question of saving ammunition. We've
got plenty of ammunition."

He chuckled disbelievingly. "Who'd have thought it? That they'd
still be jumping. And in broad daylight. Is it possible that they collected so much about them, each one, that at the very bottom of it
all, it turns against them? It's a pretty lousy pack."

The river was dirty as it flowed through the middle of the town.
The sun was shining and a breeze blew. A yellow suitcase was floating
upside down in the middle of the river. The lid was open and it acted
like a rudder, so it turned slowly about its own axis as it drifted along.

Long straps floated out from one side, and from the other, shorter ones with buckles.

The prisoner waited to grab the side of the suitcase. He clutched at the lid. The suitcase didn't hold him and it began to sink.

"That's what he gets for jumping," said the fat man. "Look at this parade. Tough luck. Don't get excited."

At last the prisoner realized he couldn't put his whole weight on the suitcase and maneuvered himself around so it would just keep him above water and he could float downstream with it.

This time, the fat man fixed his sights on the shoulder of the man in the water.

"They still jump," he murmured, taking aim.

"Kill him," said the boy. "You should finish him, not this."

"There we go," the fat man said. "You wish him a fast end? And a fast life for the two of us? You must have a big guileless soul, I can tell."

The steel cables of the bridge sang in the wind. The columns of prisoners went on their way, going in the opposite direction of the current of the river. After a few seconds, the captives who came onto the wooden bridge had no idea what had just happened.

"At least a hundred of them saw him jump, but it's never more than one that does it. Even at night, there's never more than one."

The fat man slung his machine gun over his head again and held it against his belly. "You're making a mistake if you think I don't know how to handle things," he said. "What is it that gets into their heads, that they keep on jumping? How come they behave as if I were only air here?" At the bottom of his blue eyes there was now something else. "Everybody wants his reward. Everybody should get paid. Does he think I'm just a piece of flesh here?"

The boy looked over to the other side of the river where there was a pile of sand and stones heaped into a gigantic pyramid, ready to reinforce the riverbank. People were dragging the prisoner out of the water with hooks and poles.

Suddenly, a stake was raised in the middle of a heap of stones. Like a mast or flagpole. After a while, sooty smoke began to curl around it. As if wet wood were burning. Then there was a scream.

"They jump in here and then they pull them out over there on the other side. And burn them like rats. I told you, it reminds me of that story about the fellow who played the pipe."

He kept looking back and forth from the columns of men, to the stake on the other side of the river.

"They can't do anything anymore. Not a thing. They're frozen to the bone. All they do is jump like crazy hoptoads. Like a flyer who jumps even when he knows he doesn't have a parachute. I wouldn't be able to do it. I have a fear of depths. I can't even look down from a hill and not get dizzy. Good thing this isn't the highest bridge in Prague. Oh, my . . . Who'd want to fry like a rat with its tail burned off?"

The boy turned away from the stake which had finally caught fire. There was something in his blue eyes he couldn't share with the fat man. Maybe it was the one thing he really had to share with anyone, but so what? Who cares?

For one split second, he could still see the red brick wall where the showers were and the chambers and the oven. Seven days a week and seven nights, no intermission, the smoke rose into the sky and for miles around, the air reeked of burning hair and fingernails and bones, skin and grease. Or as if they were manufacturing glue. Or soap. He was making himself ready for it. That was the first Tuesday in October of 1944.

That was where he'd been when they picked out his little sister and sent her on the wrong side. By that time, his mother and father and sixty people who had once comprised his family had long since gone up the chimney.

He'd been quiet as a mouse. He was afraid it had gotten inside him, like those worms which work their way inside a person's skin and you can never get rid of them unless you cut them out, skin and all.

It was as if he'd caught some infectious disease which he couldn't give back to those who had infected him.

He'd been in that same camp for twenty-eight days. Every one of those twenty-eight days, he felt as though ashes were falling on him. The chimney was a football field's length away from his barracks. He got used to the sight of the red brick building. It became part of the daily landscape; there was nothing to wonder about.

His sister was in every flake of ash that fell. But she was never alone. That Tuesday in October he convinced himself that it was better for his sister and maybe for him too. He also convinced himself that dying is the best way of living when it comes to such a Tuesday noon, just as the Germans convinced themselves.

And now, in that split second, which was like a ripple in the river, like a single pulsing of one single ripple, he thought how it would be if now—at this very moment—he could share that half a loaf of bread he had with his sister, the dab of margarine and half a jar of jam. Unless somebody had stolen it from his room in the YWCA in the meantime. And why is it he can do nothing of what he thinks about, to tell it as if it has made him numb, if only in one direction.

"Isn't this more fun than yesterday?" asked the fat man. "Well, some of them still go on jumping." And he added, "Wednesday was always one of my favorite days. Wednesday, Saturday, and Sunday."

The prisoners slouched. These were an older batch. They hardly noticed the burning stake on the other side of the river, but the ones behind them glanced over now and then.

"Look out," cried the boy.

"Well, what do you know, they're still doing it!" murmured the fat man. This time he began to shoot as soon as he got his gun strap over his head. And this time his eyes didn't seem so guileless. He did it partly as a concession to the boy. Jews were, are, and will be that insistent, he thought.

The prisoner sank several times and then bobbed up again. From above, he looked like somebody in a diving suit with too much air inside. Or like a frog. His head and arms and legs groped about like feelers.

"He probably felt light as air when he jumped. Now look how heavy he is," said the fat man. "Look how his coat's soaking up the water. Look."

The water around the coat was turning red. The fat man put in another round of ammunition. The row of prisoners was denser now, coming along one after another. They weren't walking any faster, though.

The stake collapsed with a resounding crash. The wind carried the sound of it across the river. The boy drifted over to a pile of cobblestones at the end of the wooden bridge.

"I'm surprised you've still got the urge," said the fat man. "It's different when they jump."

The boy looked at the cobblestones, at the prisoners, and down into the water. He heard the creak of the cables in the wind. He turned his eyes away as the water turned red around the man, mingling with the current and swirling into the mud and the sediment.

He went back in his mind to the friend he'd had in Poland. They'd belonged to the same fishing commando. His name was Arthur Cohen, and he went out with the German boats to gather gulls' eggs on the islands.

The birds on the water were as white as winter stars. They were shy of people. They fed on fish which, in turn, fed on ashes. Then it turned out that there were other things besides ashes they fed on too.

People worked up to their waists in water and sometimes even up to their necks, cutting reeds and catching carp under the eye of Waffen SS guards. Women prisoners carried away the reeds they'd cut, and when the reeds dried, they were used at the front for camouflaging planes and tanks and panzers.

One Thursday afternoon, they'd heard someone singing across the water. This was strange, because hardly anybody ever sang in those days.

It was a Greek girl, from a company of Balkan women who'd arrived from Rhodes a few days before.

From that day on, she sang for seven days, and they all looked forward to hearing her. It was beautiful. As if something very far away had suddenly moved closer, bringing with it a sweet and gentle touch.

The song she sang was in a foreign tongue they couldn't understand, but there was none of the coldness in it which they felt around them, none of the dampness which was destroying them as they worked in water from morning till evening. None of the hunger, either, which forced some of them to eat raw fish.

The Greek girl's voice had sunshine in it, like a warm breeze on a summer's night, because there was hope in it and a feeling of the future unspoiled by the present.

The song the Greek girl sang may have had a loving sound to it and maybe that was why they looked forward to it for those seven days. As if it were more than just a song.

The eighth day was a Thursday again. Just as the girl began to sing, the German guards set their police dogs on her. The dogs tore her apart before her song broke into a scream and before both merged into a single sound. From then on, he always considered Thursday the worst day in the week.

After that, all they could hear was the water's voice. But now there was always something about the water which contained the song of the dead Greek girl.

One day later, they transferred Arthur Cohen from the fishing squad to another where he was given the job of dragging out and burning the corpses which had been submerged in the mud and suddenly bobbed up above the surface, so there seemed to be more dead bodies than there was mud to cover them.

They were a strange sight, those corpses smeared with mud that water could never wash away.

The guards were annoyed by the stench which the wind blew toward the German barracks.

The ashes of the corpses which had been fished out of the mud and burned were loaded on small boats and taken out into the middle of the pond and dumped in, until finally all the protruding corpses had been converted into ashes.

Cohen was told he'd done a good job and that a similar assignment was waiting for him at another camp. There were rivers around; they never saw Cohen after that. Every commando involved in the burying and burning disappeared within three months at most. Usually it was six weeks.

He had stayed with the fishing commando, so he was lucky. Sometimes he would stare into the water and listen, as though he were waiting to hear the Greek girl's song, which never came.

He gathered gulls' eggs for a guard's wife whose name was Hilda. He had a nice little rowboat. They'd bring back a basketful in the evening if they'd gone out in the morning, or in the morning if they'd worked at night.

And he knew he'd live—at least as long as there were eggs to be found in the gulls' nests. He liked looking into water. Even there, in the camp, he liked to listen to the hidden language of water. He liked to pose his questions to the shiny surface: What will be? What will happen to him now, and later? What other river, lake, or pond will he see one day, or is this the last bit of water he'll ever look at?

"Where'd you get those golf knickers?" asked the fat man.

"Across the street from the Hotel Graf, where the repatriation station is now," the boy replied.

With a practiced eye, the fat man studied the youngster and the pile of cobblestones and the column of older soldiers.

"You're living it up these days if you're staying in a hotel," the fat man said. "Some people really know how to manage." He was waiting to see what the boy would do with the stones.

"What'd you say there was in the hotel now?"

"There's a sterilizer and a delousing station," the boy said. "And a first-aid station and dormitories for people who didn't get into the YWCA or YMCA. That's where they hand out repatriation I.D. cards too."

"So that's where you heard they were still jumping? The word gets around fast, huh?"

The boy didn't answer. He kept looking over to the other side of the river. He felt a change in the attitude of the fat man, but it wasn't enough of a change to make him want to confide in the guy. There was too big a difference between them; they couldn't be friends. And yet his attitude had changed too, a little. It wasn't so much the difference in their ages, and he didn't think about nationality or language. He didn't want to look at Fatso. For a second he shut his eyes against the morning sun.

On the opposite shore, not far from the heap of sand and stones, a Russian soldier was sponging off his horse. It was a grey horse and it gleamed like a statue in the sunshine.

He could still see those eight captive Russian officers in Auschwitz-Birke-nau, in the former gypsy camp in October of 1944, when ten or fourteen thousand German gypsies had in three months already gone up the chimney. The Germans told them to undress and bathe, like the other new arrivals. The officers wanted to be turned over to their counterparts—to German officers. Their spokesman was a huge man, big as a mountain. Finally the guard went off to find the commander.

"What is it you want?" the commander demanded.

The giant took one step forward. The others stood in a rigid line, chins high.

"We are officers and we request that we be treated according to international laws and norms."

"As far as we know, Russians never adhered to the Geneva Convention."

"We expect to be handed over to military authorities."

"Ach," chuckled the German. "It's not our interpretation." He

slapped his riding crop against the palm of his hand. He carried a pistol in a holster at his side, but he didn't touch it.

"So you really suppose you won't obey a German guard because he's not an officer?" Again he laughed. "So you really want to be handed over to an officer?"

"That's exactly what we're asking and we insist on it," the giant said.

"Gentlemen, I'm truly sorry. Truly sorry. We have very few officers in this installation here. So we're forced to use rank-and-file guards."

He laughed a third time. Suddenly he struck the giant across the face with his riding crop. Then he began to shout at them, telling them to realize where they were. And he strode off down the line, striking each of the other seven Russian officers across the face with his riding crop, just as hard as he'd struck the giant.

Blood-swollen bruises rose on the cheeks of the startled Russians. They were unable to defend themselves. The behavior of the German commander had shattered them. Blood trickled over the giant's chin and into his mouth, along his lips and onto his neck and collar.

The commander knew what blood does. He turned away, but even then he didn't draw his pistol or look back. It was as if he were walking away from a dog he'd thrashed. Or as if they were only installations, on inventory here, like wires, or poles. Or as if nothing, nobody could move the rules even slightly. There were a few seconds of stillness. The Russian officers didn't move a muscle.

At one word from the guard, the Russians stripped, folded their uniforms and piled them, with their underwear and shoes, in front of them. Then, at the guard's command, they turned and marched into the showers.

"You didn't think you were better than Jews, did you?" asked the guard. "Everybody here's a Jew—Russian or American, French or English. Whoever's a foreigner in Germany is a Jew, and Jews have to obey orders." Then he said, "Who needs formalities? It's enough to agree."

When they'd been gassed, the commander observed, "For us, everybody is inferior, just like the Jews are, and so they end up like Jews. I'm the one who decides who's a Jew."

"What's your name, anyway?" the fat man persisted.

"What's yours?"

"Hey, just for fun, show me that repatriation card of yours, will you?" The boy took off his cap again. The card was stuck inside the band. It was a two-page identity card listing the places he'd been during the war, his present residence, and how much money he'd been given to start with by the Revolutionary National Committee for Prague II.

He handed the card to the fat man and dug the toe of his white shoe into the pile of cobblestones.

"Theresienstadt, Auschwitz-Birkenau, Neugamme. Neugamme —that's the first time I heard of that one. Buchenwald—I've heard about that. Dachau too," the fat one said. "How can you have lived through something like that, kid?"

The boy stepped back and picked up a cobblestone. It was a cube of granite, blue and white.

"Listen, kid, it's different when it's me doing the shooting," the fat man drawled. "I'm not talking about yesterday and last night. That was different. I guess you probably had your share too."

The boy held on to the cobblestone.

"Neugamme, Neugamme," murmured the fat man. He handed back the I.D. card.

"I'd put that stone down if I were you," he went on. "Or just watch if it makes you feel better, but forget the other thing. Unless somebody else decides to jump. If they do, then I'll lend you my gun." He waited for the boy to show him some gratitude, but wasn't surprised when it wasn't expressed. It must make him proud, those camps—a special experience. Still he couldn't have treated him better, from the very beginning. Where was his mind? Far? Near? Nowhere? With whom? Where are his people? Are they coming back? When? How?

In his thoughts, the boy was back with the children who had come to Theresienstadt from Poland in the middle of the war. They'd raised an awful fuss at the delousing station and nobody could understand why they were so scared of taking a shower.

Terror overcame them in the boiler room and when the bathhouse personnel asked the nurses and doctors to help undress them, the children bit and scratched and fought as if their lives were at stake.

The boilers were heated with coal, the toothbrushes and soap and towels were real and the place was really meant for baths, but these children had other visions.

"Gas! Gas!" they screamed.

In Poland six months later, some of those same Theresienstadt doctors and nurses and bathhouse personnel understood when they were told, "Go and bathe. Don't lose your soap and towel. Remember your clothes hook and where you've put your things. We want you spick and span."

"Did you ever imagine they'd jump this way?" the fat man asked, wondering what the youngster was going to do with the cobblestone. "Did you ever imagine that someday, in just one single city in Europe, you'd see more than one whole division of the German Army going along like a herd of sheep? And that you'd be standing here watching, you and me?"

"As a matter of fact, we used to talk about it," said the boy.

"I'll bet you did."

"We talked about it a lot."

"Did they give you enough time to talk?"

"The older people, the ones who were around thirty or forty, didn't seem to want to talk about anything else finally."

"Whether they were going to jump like this?"

"No. Whether we ought to kill them and burn them or not—and whether we would."

"I can close my eyes for a minute, if you want me to."

The boy was silent.

"You can just pretend I'm not here for a few seconds, if you'd rather," the fat man went on.

The boy turned his back to the lines of men.

"I didn't think they'd jump either, although now it makes sense," the fat one said.

"Some of the people with us couldn't get it out of their heads," the boy recalled.

"You're talking about yourself now?"

"I'm talking about the ones who were obsessed with the idea, but they aren't anymore. They aren't, period."

"For a minute—just while I shut my eyes—it's all yours, if you want."

"There's no point talking about it."

"About what?"

"So."

"Isn't life an interesting privilege? A strong chance? Isn't it fun? Everything's going our way, boy."

"What?"

"Is that why you came? I hope, in the meantime, they won't drink up all the beer over at the Fatted Calf."

The fat man crossed to the other bridge railing, as if the box weren't there. The youngster peered intently at the rows of soldiers as they streamed by, tightly bunched and moving faster. The fat man seemed to be indicating that he was turning things over to the youngster now.

"Just for a minute, though," he called.

The boy's sharp little eyes were fixed fast on the fat man's back, then on the column of prisoners. He squinted because he hadn't had much sleep and his eyes were bloodshot.

His gaze stopped on the face of a soldier in a blue uniform. He was trudging listlessly, with no idea that the boy was watching him. He was listless because that made it easier to go—and to face the fact of where he was going.

But in his thoughts, the boy was back at the Demartinka streetcar barns where the Revolutionary Guards had herded all the Germans from the neighborhood.

They were people who had been captured on the other side of the river, which the German commanders had been unable to evacuate. Most of the German civilians had been trying to reach the American lines.

There were three old streetcars in the car barn into which they tossed their belongings—suitcases and clothes and small possessions. Things they wanted to take with them. One flat-bottomed repair car was already heaped with their belongings.

After they'd been registered, the captive Germans had to run the gauntlet through the crowd in front of the car barns. Each got his share.

The people screamed at them and beat them and spat in their faces. They couldn't seem to get enough of it. Only once were they silent, when a woman with a baby in her arms passed through. They pressed so close, she must have felt their breath on her skin. Then a pistol shot rang out. Someone fell across the streetcar tracks about ten meters in front of the woman with the infant. Five shots were fired.

"Look," somebody screamed. "She's the one who fired those shots! The woman."

She had a 6.35 pistol wrapped in the baby's blanket and she managed to fire four more shots into the crowd. The narrow corridor of people broke up. All there was to see was the baby's blanket exploding into the air.

"So your name's Robert," said the fat man from the other side of the bridge. "That's a nice name. I won't even ask if you were named after your dad."

The boy looked away from the soldier and the fat man knew he wouldn't throw the stone now.

"No, not after Dad," he told the man.

"Well, at least you saw them jump," the fat man said. "You've got a real nice name, kid. Girls'll like to say it. But you're still young for that sort of thing. Not too young for some things, but for others, yes. For messing around in the moonlight and so on. Hey, tell me, what's on your mind all the time?"

"I'm just watching them go," replied the boy. It was true, but it wasn't the complete truth, though it wasn't a lie.

Back in northern Bohemia, in the Little Fortress, next to Theresienstadt, he could still see the superintendent who, before the war, had been a sexton somewhere in the Austrian Alps. He had clear blue eyes, flaxen hair, and a milky skin. He made his rounds through the fortress, impeccably dressed, scrubbed, and neatly combed. Nobody ever saw him hurry or heard him shout. On Sundays, he strolled with a prayer book in his left hand and a pistol in his right. He looked like Jesus Christ. Or the way people sometimes said Christ might have looked.

From every group or transport, the superintendent would pick out a father and son. First, he had them put in separate cells. For one week, they were given nothing to eat or drink. On the eighth day, they were fed, but at different times. Then the superintendent told them they were going to appear in a bullfight, but without the bulls. Then they'd have a chance to show how smart they were.

On Sunday, the pair were brought out to a dry moat between the ramparts. It looked like an arena in good weather, but it was a soggy sort of stadium when it rained, the turf heavy and slippery with mud. After a bath, the father and son were led before a podium where the superintendent stood, flanked by trained police dogs on one side and, on the other, the noncommissioned officers. Facing them were the prisoners: men, women and children (if there were any in the fortress at the time). The superintendent laid his Bible on the rail in front of him and, on top of it, his Parabella 9 mm pistol and, alongside these, a pair of kid gloves.

The father and son were told to strip naked. Then they were each given a club heavy enough to kill a man.

At a signal from the sexton and one of the Waffen SS, they were to start fighting and one of them had to win. To win meant that the other had to die.

There were sons who killed their fathers without a word, and fathers who killed their sons. People had been brought together in the fortress from villages and ghettos and prison camps—anybody who was able to work in the nearby quarries or in the underground munitions factories burrowed deep under Kamyk Mountain.

The superintendent watched as if he were seeing something he'd seen before. He'd seen Jewish fathers and sons fighting and Gypsy fathers and sons, people of all persuasions, heroes of resistance movements, people for whom courage had never been a thing that's put to the test, until they discovered that all human qualities have their limits. But they weren't the ones who set the new limits.

Maybe what he saw took him back to ancient times, when sons were a father's property to the last extreme. Perhaps it made him feel like he was returning to some ancient heritage, customs or beliefs, as though he had carved out of reality a new way to compensate for some remote, forgotten lawlessness.

Sometimes the victims just stood there motionless, waiting to be shot. Then he'd set the dogs on them to tear them to pieces and he fired his pistol only when one of his dogs was in danger. The father and son had clubs, after all, and sometimes they would turn on the dogs.

Occasionally, the victims wept and embraced each other. Or prayed. Sometimes they rushed forward to dash themselves against the ramparts, but the moat was too deep.

Sometimes the father and son agreed among themselves to strike a blow at the very same time, to kill each other simultaneously. But there were other stories. Only someone who had been there could understand how such things were possible. For as long as he lived, anyone who wasn't there could only try to imagine how it was.

The superintendent beamed on the victorious son or father, as though he had suddenly brought him back to reality. He studied him with his pale blue eyes while he ran his hand lovingly over the ramparts, as though he were caressing a human being.

The victim was allowed to watch the next performance. To see himself in a living mirror, so to speak.

The superintendent either shot the father for having killed his son or the son for patricide. Nobody ever survived these combats. As patiently as a mother waits for her child, the superintendent would look forward to new arrivals from the ghetto or the transports which came from the occupied countries in Europe.

Afterwards, he would chat with the prisoners who had been ordered to take the corpses off to the crematorium. He would comment on the blueness of the sky, what nice weather it was, about the grass which grew particularly green under the four gallows. He rattled on about how bricks were made in the days when the Spanish Empire reached from setting sun to rising sun (which was how it was going to be with Germany someday) and when the Spanish had built fortresses all over the world, just like this one in north Bohemia. It was called the Small Fortress, but it was small only in comparison with the one in the ghetto at Theresienstadt, a few miles to the southeast.

He used to like to watch the flocks of migrating birds as they flew south each autumn and came back in spring. He used to talk to them, as though he were seeking the real meaning of the words he spoke. "We're on the scent," he said, "but the beast has eluded us again. For stupid animals, a clever trap. They mustn't escape again."

Some of the fathers and sons knew from the start what was going to happen when they were singled out. But no one was ever sure, until he was led into the moat and told to strip naked and was given a club, to kill or be killed.

In the wintertime, the superintendent watched the snow fall for hours and when springtime came, he raised chrysanthemums in the moat.

"For people who've never seen it, you can talk till you're blue in the face about how they jump," the fat man said. "You can explain how we were right here when it happened. You've got some money, don't you? You need some more?"

"I don't need more than what I've got."

"Never refuse money. Only loonies turn down money."

"I don't need any," the boy told him. "Whatever I need, I can get for myself." It wasn't just money, advice, or love he didn't accept from anyone he didn't totally approve of. Was it something he learned in the camps? It was beyond laws and rules, like a secret code. He made each decision in his mind case by case, person by person. Then too he was a little superstitious. He had to approve every giver before he accepted any gift. Why? Never mind. So. Yes, no, or yes and no as well.

He was thinking too about that woman on Rytirska Street on Saturday noon when the uprising in Prague started, five days ago. A German policeman was hanging from a lamppost in his burned uniform, just as they'd dragged him out of the police station.

"So we're the same kind of beasts as they were," the woman yelled.

"Why? You feel sorry for him? They wanted to pave Wenceslaw Square with our skulls. Or were you in another country during the war, maybe?" a big-breasted blonde screamed at her, the veins throbbing in her neck and forehead. "You want to keep him company?"

"We'll put that bitch on trial too," somebody shouted from the back of the crowd.

Only yesterday, on Thursday, people had needed somebody to tear apart, to burn or trample. At the YWCA, a rumor spread that the Germans had poisoned the water. That they will destroy Prague before leaving. Women took jugs of water around to the centers where Germans were being held, to make them drink the water first, although they had no way of knowing whether it had been poisoned or not.

"I told you, I don't want any," the boy repeated. He was still holding on to the stone, the fat man noticed. He was terribly nervous. Why? The longer they were together, the more distracted the boy became. Even today it's not fun to be Jewish, the fat man thought. I'd better not ask why.

"Hey, look at this beautiful mermaid I have on my chest," he said, unbuttoning his shirt. "And the handsome American cowboy beside her." On his belly and chest, he had a naked woman who looked like a worm except for the luxurious bosom where a name was tattooed at heart level: Rosalie.

"That's made the same way as those little numbers and letters on your arm," the fat man said.

The boy glanced briefly at the designs.

"You know what I mean? That's what you can have done with those tattoos of yours. Have them done over. Find a girl with a fine name and go ahead. You've gotten your name back. That counts, doesn't it?"

The fat man kept his eye on the boy's hand with the paving stone.

"Look, Robert, go on home and tie a knot in your handkerchief, if you've got a handkerchief, and if you don't, you'd better get yourself one and tie a knot in it so you don't forget. These guys aren't jumping anymore." He jerked his head toward the prisoners. "So tie a knot in your hankie. Do one for me while you're at it and one for yourself—for what you *didn't* do."

"What time is it?" asked the youngster.

"About ten o'clock. Things have been pretty lively in the little while you've been here, Robert. Come on, let's have a nice, big smile, Robert, O.K.? You won't say no, will you? Throw away that stone and give me a smile. Aw, come on! Look, Robert, you're still awfully young for throwing stones, even if you do have a nice, long list of places in that red I.D. card of yours. I'll grant you that. But you don't have to go around with such a chip on your shoulder, do you? Nobody's going to bite you. You can have those numbers and letters changed into a very pretty little design, you just wait and see."

And he thought, it's better to be Jewish than German—that's for sure. Things are pretty topsy-turvy. Times have changed, hopefully for a long time to come. The war was like a long illness and knowledge together. What the war taught them transcends the forgotten, knowledge and illness together. The boy himself had put the bitterness in his blue eyes, and there was distance and closeness in them at the same time. They also held confusion and decisiveness, along with unknown measures and hidden, private values. In his eyes you could see the essence of all these things, and maybe also a conviction that he'd been chosen for some strange privilege, the fat man thought. Yes. In these eyes you could see understanding and misunderstanding together, in equal proportions.

The boy stared at the fat man, but he was really seeing those people at the railroad station yesterday. They didn't say a word and when he came, they put their fingers to their lips, signaling him to silence. From his shaven head and cap, they recognized him as one of theirs even before he rolled up his sleeves and identified himself by the tattoo.

That same morning, a Revolutionary Guard had shot one of them because he'd said something in German before he could explain himself.

Those people weren't Germans, though. They spoke German and Yiddish among themselves because that was the only way they could understand each other. They hadn't wanted to stay in Germany. They'd wanted to cross the Channel, but the English refused to let them in as if the noun "promise" and the verb "to keep" had nothing to do with each other in some countries before, during, or the first days after the war. One of their elders explained all this in a whisper. They didn't get papers and were too discouraged even to wait and try again.

The old man told him that the brother of the one who had been shot had gone to some station to talk to the head of the Revolutionary Guard.

Actually, he wasn't talking to anybody. He was at an emergency first-aid station after having had a heart attack, but nobody had told the old man because they didn't want to upset him even more.

The people just stood there in silence until late that evening when their train pulled in and the brother of the one who had been shot was well enough to board it with them.

They had nothing to eat and didn't want anything, to the amazement of the railroad workers who kept offering them food. All they would accept was water. The worker said to someone that even then, they sprinkled it first on their hands, as if they were washing them. Only afterwards would they drink it.

"Well, how about it?" the fat one pressed. "Don't things look better now—for us, anyway?"

"Sure," the boy said and he actually smiled at the fat man. It wasn't much more than a flicker, though.

The fat man shoved his machine gun to the side.

"They're not jumping anymore." He took out a cigarette case and offered it to the boy. "You smoke?"

"Sometimes," the boy replied and helped himself.

"You want me to light it for you too? But you'll smoke it for yourself, I hope."

"I can light yours for you too, if you want me to."

The youngster tossed away the cobblestone. He threw it into the river after a helmet which was floating down the middle of the stream, half-full of water.

"You've got a pretty good arm, Robert," said the fat man. "My name's Tony."

"Sometimes," the boy replied, peering beyond the fat one at the columns of men.

Last evening, at the first-aid station, he'd met also a man who had returned from Germany. He was waiting now for the first train back to Krakow. He wanted to go to Auschwitz-Birkenau. So he could be near his people, he said. He was dreaming of a house near the river Sola, close to the former Frauen Konzentration Lager. *He had difficulty breathing. Nerves twitched in his wrists and his nails. In his eyes the impressions of people he'd lost there—his wife and two daughters—began to form like ghosts, vaporous shapes growing slowly more solid. As he walked his body was bent, cramped, as if from fatigue or lack of oxygen in the blood.*

The train he was waiting for came from Vienna and it was going to Warsaw. A lot of prisoners from Mauthausen got off in Prague.

The man told him he could feel at home only where his own people were. He spoke about the sad miracle of being alive.

"They aren't jumping, but you can never be one hundred percent sure. Lots of people go quietly out of their minds and they're the only ones who know it, as long as they don't decide out of the blue to make a jump for it. At night, sure, but in the daytime? Does that make sense? I just wonder how many more people are still going to go off their rockers."

When the youngster didn't answer, he went on. "Keep your eyes open, Robert. Look over there—I can see the wall of the slaughterhouse because I've got good eyes and I can almost see the end of the line. And it's still morning. Not even noon yet. Doesn't it look to you as though that's the end of them?"

"It looks like the end," the boy agreed.

Yesterday, at the Powder Tower, when he was walking with Red and the little sister Red had brought back, they'd run into a father and mother who were looking for their son who was supposed to be coming home. His name was Milan. Theirs was a mixed marriage. They'd been questioning so many returnees, they already recognized who had come from where.

Red used to play soccer with Milan at the Hagibor sports club. He could barely remember what Milan had said about his parents, but he told his little sister to go over and stand in the sunshine next to the Tower while they talked.

He obviously didn't want her to hear things she didn't have to hear.

He spoke obliquely, in brief, transparent phrases, but Milan's parents wanted to know more than he wanted to tell.

Red and Milan had been together until early March. When the Germans started to retreat, they loaded the prisoners into freight cars in Gleiwitz and put on an engine only after they themselves were moving out of the camp on another track. They couldn't have had better hostages. The prisoner's train shielded the trainload of soldiers.

The mother wanted to know details. At first, the father did too, but after a while he didn't.

Red tried to sound vague. He went on and on about how long everything took, how their train moved as if it were dragging its feet. And how they got stuck in some little town and how their engine was always the last one to get water, how long it takes for somebody to reach Prague—when he's lucky and doesn't have to walk the whole way, if he finds better connections.

Although he'd been lucky himself, Red said, it had taken him since the fifth of March to get back. Imagine that. And he'd had his little sister with him too.

Since early March, Milan had had no legs. They'd been amputated below the knees because they were frozen. But Red didn't tell them that, of course. He just described what a hard winter it had been in Gleiwitz. More than thirty below. And that time they hadn't had anything to eat for three weeks, so they'd eaten anything—literally.

Red glanced over at his little sister and smiled at her.

Two Jewish and German first-aid helpers carried Milan into one of the camouflaged freight cars. The camp was being evacuated and the Germans wanted to leave things nice and tidy with nobody left behind to tell some scrubbed American or Australian about what had gone on here.

They even took the dead with them.

Again, he looked over at his sister and smiled, as if he were telling her to be patient, that he'd soon be finished and they'd be on their way.

Red had been observing Milan's parents and realized they couldn't take it. He also realized that this wasn't the best way to start his new life—by giving somebody false hopes. His little sister leaned against the Tower, basking in the sunshine.

Suddenly Red had enough when the mother said something to indicate that she didn't think he was telling them the truth.

"If the two of you had been together for such a long time, how come he didn't come back with you, when you even managed to bring your little sister?" she demanded. "You were together for two years, you say. So where is he? Where can he be? What did they do to him? Where did you see him last? You said you were together almost all the time. So how come you got here and he hasn't come back yet? Where is he, for God's sake, where is he?"

"They cut off his legs," Red said abruptly.

The mother closed her eyes and cold sweat beaded the father's forehead.

Red glanced quickly and apologetically at his little sister. He hadn't meant to blurt it out that way. It just slipped out. Like when Milan's mother said it seemed to her that an awful lot of people were coming back. Red knew how many were coming and how.

"Oh, God," the mother whispered. "Is he alive?"

"He was in the same camouflaged freight car I was in, right at the bottom," Red replied.

And he smiled briefly again at his sister and took her back to the YWCA dormitory where they were living. They were a tiny pair with fair fuzz on their heads instead of hair. It had just begun to grow in again. They looked like children. Red had obviously been trying to make a part in his hair, but it wasn't long enough for that and he had scratched his scalp with the comb. He put his arm around his sister's shoulders as they walked along Na Prikope Avenue like two young lovers.

The mother bit her lips until the blood ran. The father wanted to take her home, telling her he'd give her some ointment for her lips.

Then it was Robert's turn to be questioned. The parents appealed to him and the mother kept saying his name over and over, as if she were identifying him with Milan, beseeching him, skinning herself alive at the same time. She touched the boy's hands and face and shoulders, as if she wanted to make sure he was real.

"Robert?" she said. "Before Milan left, he told us he knew somebody named Robert. You worked together, didn't you?"

"At the beginning of the war, we made pouches for stamps for German soldiers out of white patent leather," he told them.

"And you were together afterwards too?"

"Just until the beginning of 1944."

"What happened then?" the parents asked.

"We got separated. We were both working on a construction site."

The mother's eyes beseeched a lie, and when the father looked at him, it was a silent plea for lies. That would certainly have been better than what little Red had told them.

"We're trying to find somebody who's seen Milan since that little fellow we were just talking to—Red."

"What do you suppose could have happened to him?" the mother demanded.

The Germans had done other things besides amputating frostbitten arms and legs. It would probably have been impossible to tell them what they'd eaten in those days, when they'd been given no food for three weeks, day after day—twenty-one days. It was better not to talk about that.

He had been in the same camps with Red and Milan. First in Theresienstadt, then in Birkenau. In the Gypsy camp at Birkenau, they went through the reception procedure, passing under a rope stretched some 5 feet 8 inches high. Anybody shorter than that went up the chimney. The second qualification was carrying heavy stones. And third was simply who could stick it out the longest, according to the slogan, "Every man for himself."

Anybody who tried to escape was hung by the Germans with the aid of helpers from among the prisoners in the Gypsy camp. They were hung on a thin string, so it took a long time. But it was an entertaining spectacle.

The orchestra played a popular French dance tune, "J'attendriai." In German, it had a special significance: Komm zurück, ich warte auf dich, den du bist mein Glück . . .

Milan and Red had wheeled the victims to the execution ground in a wagon with a little roof. Its wheels squeaked. Come back, I am waiting for you, for you are my happiness.

Three Revolutionary Guards on German horses came along behind the last column of prisoners of war. All three horses were grey and their bodies reeked sweetly, their smell mingling with that of the captives' bodies and the river and the springtime air. The third Guard was leading a white, saddled horse with no rider.

"That horse's for me," the fat man said. "I'm going to leave you now and go on with them. You can take over here if you want to."

He paused, "Well, Robert, I'm glad to see they're not jumping anymore. Hey, look, that horse has an English saddle—the one that's for me. Well, so long Robert. Look on the bright side of things. This isn't military territory anymore. All it is is one temporary wooden bridge and one broken-down suspension bridge."

The fat man shifted his machine gun onto his hip so it wouldn't get in his way. Gingerly, he kept the muzzle pointed at the ground. He approached the horse.

"How about another nice big smile, Robert, hm?" he said. "And if you still have the idea they're jumping, well, it's not true. The big war is over. The biggest ever, as a matter of fact. You'll spoil this beautiful day for me if you don't give me one more smile."

He'd always waited for this moment—when it would be all over. He'd imagined the date when it would be—the hour, the place, the witnesses, the kind of weather, every circumstance about it. He thought how the Germans would suddenly disappear and nobody would know what became of them. As if they'd never even existed.

Whenever he imagined this moment, he could see a judge in a black robe. He came to him in his dreams three nights in a row, asking what verdict he proposed for the guilty Germans.

"Murder for murder?"

"No," he replied to the judge. "No, I don't think murder will do."

Then the judge shoved back the black cap so he could look into his eyes.

"They killed your mother and father, your little sister, so you have the right to kill them too. You can torture them if you want to."

"But I don't want to kill anybody anymore, and I don't want anybody to torture anybody else either."

On the second night, the judge appeared in a red robe.

"The moment of retribution has come and justice requires you to kill those who wanted to kill you."

"They didn't kill me," he said.

"But a thousand kinds of death were prepared for you—by lead, rope, gas, electricity, cold, hunger, whips, thirst, and humiliation."

On the third night, the judge appeared, wearing a white robe.

"It's all over," he said. "From this moment on, there will be no more killing. But you can still do it. You have the right. In your case, killing means defending yourself. That won't stain your conscience."

"No, I don't think I want to. I don't need it."

He didn't. He really didn't want to. After that, the judge never appeared to him in his dreams again. He never told him anymore that if he didn't kill one of those who had taken from him everything a person has only once, he'd reproach himself for as long as he'd live. Everything urged him to kill. He simply wished he could wipe Germany out of his mind, at least until it all wore off, the way a stone wears smooth in a swift river. He had to be responsible for that to himself, including finding an answer to the question of when a person has the right and the duty to defend himself and when the two coincide. The Sola never floated the dream away.

The fat man clambered awkwardly onto the horse's back. He pulled the saddle crooked and the girth slipped back and forth over the white horse's belly. The other Guard, who was riding along after the prisoners, looked back and laughed. Finally, the fat man made it. He perched like a jockey on the horse's back. His blue eyes were smiling. He tried to wipe his forehead with his huge red handkerchief.

"Well, now, you know what I want to say, Robert, but just don't tell me you came down here to watch them jump." It occurred to him that the boy, Robert, watched the soldiers go to assure himself that they were really going. He thought that the boy, after all, had to see with his own eyes that they were leaving in order to believe it. Also, watching them go—humbly—like the Jews or the Gypsies had gone to the railroad station and from the ramp at the end station in the East to the showers and the gas, he saw that in a similar situation they really were no better than the others. All at once the boy's eyes seemed to him innocent, without the shadow as if irritated by ashes which was there a while ago.

The white horse's hooves danced along the cobblestones. The fat man had a hard time keeping in the saddle. The horse began to move on.

"I hope you'll find whatever it is you're looking for, Robert," he called back to give himself courage. "You won't have trouble at school, don't worry. You'll find a lot of new friends. They'll like you, I'm sure. You'll adjust easily. Send me a note—nothing nit-picking, just a few words. And then . . . don't look back, Robert." He turned his head back to the left. For safety's sake, he kept his eyes ahead. "They're not interesting anymore. They lost all their mystery, their secrets," he said. "You want some more smokes?" He managed to toss the boy a pack of cigarettes.

"Thanks," the boy called.

He pulled out a cigarette and stuck it between his rosy lips and the rest he put in his pocket before lighting up.

"Didn't I tell you, Robert?" the fat one called. "They aren't jumping anymore."

Horseshoes rang on the cobblestones. The sound merged with the tread of the last column of infantry. The wind sang through the cables of the bridge. The wood creaked. Below, the water flowed on and on, just as dirty as it had been that morning. It carried with it odds and ends of army uniforms and equipment, human bodies, rags, sewage, pots and pans, logs and planks, blood and oil, and it all rolled on the waves. A cold mist rose from the river. But its surface glittered in the sunshine. It was nearing noon.

Then the boy went back to the other end of the bridge toward Revolucni Street. He wasn't so nervous anymore. He moseyed along in his blue golf knickers and white shoes with the gold buckles, a cigarette in one hand and the empty machine gun shell in the other. He flicked the cigarette into the river in a long arc. He watched it soar, then land on the surface of the water, and go out.

As he walked on, he whistled into the golden shell casing.

DARKNESS CASTS NO SHADOW

For my Mother

I would like to thank Ed Kessler, Myra Sklarew, and Henry Taylor for their valuable aid in the preparation of the manuscript. Above all, I want to thank Jeanne Němcová for her noble and elegant contribution.

Darkness Casts No Shadow

I

Is everything lost in the darkness?

"He's started shooting," said the first boy, whose name was Danny.

"The crazy fool," the second replied uneasily. He looked up into the shredded clouds. "He probably thinks we're soldiers."

There had been no peace in the sky since the plane appeared. The flatcar tossed from side to side and the wind lashed them, blowing soot into their eyes. The pilot had evidently decided that the train below was now in the right place. But first he'd give them a demonstration of dive-bombing techniques complete with acrobatic tricks.

"If he intends to blow up the locomotive," the first boy said, "he'll have to do it before we get to the tunnel."

It was an American plane, lumbering along above the train.

The second boy, whose name was Manny, swallowed an answer.

"Either that or we're goners," the first went on: "We don't have much time for arguing, Manny."

His mouth dropped as he looked up at the plane and then at his companion, then at the back of the freight car they were riding on. "Will you jump after me? Or do you want to go first?"

The pilot set his sights on the train again. Manny wanted to wait and see whether he'd realize his mistake—that the train wasn't an army transport, even though there were guards with rifles in every freight car.

The train was moving faster now through a wide ravine that ran between two steep wooded hills. It whistled, long and plaintively. The German engineer either wanted to unnerve the pilot or make him understand it was a prisoner train. On the other side of the tunnel, the hill was covered with fallen trees. A stream flowed through the meadow to the right, bubbling into white foam over the stones. The weather had been good, with showers in the morning. The sky was a bluish-grey above the scraps of clouds.

The noise of the airplane was coming from a different angle. The pilot was gaining altitude again. Now he flew at the train in two big S-shaped arcs. He was confident they couldn't get away. As the pilot headed straight toward the railroad tracks, there was a knocking noise through the roar of his motor as though he were running out of gas or as if one cylinder had failed.

"What about Frank?" asked Manny, who had a freckled face. His ears stuck out; they were very obvious because his head was shaved. His cheekbones were covered by thin bluish skin, as delicate as a girl's.

Frank Bondy was a man of about forty. He was in the left corner of the freight car close to the engine, sitting on several blankets, next to a German soldier with corporal's insignia.

Instead of answering, the first boy began to unbutton his over-coat. It reached almost to his ankles, and the back was scribbled with black and white paint so everybody would recognize him if he tried to escape. They all had *KL (Konzentration Lager)* painted on their backs in white paint too.

His dirty fingers, stiff with cold, tugged at the buttons. He kept watching the plane.

He stretched out his arms to keep from falling as the train lurched on.

The older boy also began to unbutton his coat. "He could go a little faster," he said.

The second boy was watching Frank, too. The plane's machine gun fired and it didn't stop. The bullets whistled past the engineer's cab and the coal tender. The passengers in the first coach must be chopped up into little pieces by now. The pilot banked, as though he wanted to slice his wings right through the middle of the train. The approaching rattle of the machine gun mingled with the noise of the engine and of the wheels racketing along the tracks.

"Don't you want to ask Frank one more time?" asked the second boy.

The locomotive rushed toward the tunnel with a loud whistle and the train bounced and clanged from side to side. The valley had a slight downhill slope. We're in the tenth car, the first boy thought to himself. It'll be our turn when he comes round the third time. He could see the plane's underbelly, grey as a fish. The pilot's maneuvers were precise and elegant. He had plenty of time.

"That guy up there can give us a great military funeral," the second said.

Frank hasn't been the same since his last birthday, the second boy thought to himself. It hadn't taken long for him to lose his spark.

The first boy wondered whether there was an anti-aircraft emplacement on the tunnel, and, if there was, whether whoever was manning it was going to let the pilot shoot up every soul on the train before bringing down the plane. Afterwards, they'd give the pilot a funeral.

The plane would look like a smoldering pile of tin. They'd already seen plenty of piles of tin along the tracks.

"We've got nice weather," said the first boy. "It's not raining, so we won't skid."

"There's a lot of wind," the other boy said.

"It's early yet."

"That's good."

On his second pass, the pilot came in from a hair-raisingly steep, banked curve and the machine gun began to bark, breaking into the regular clatter of the wheels over the seams in the tracks. The roar and whistle of the motor above them, running at top speed, came in spurts. There were bursts of vapor a few feet from the ground.

Something flickered in Manny's eyes, as though the pilot, the train, six days without food, and the events of the last three years were shadows out of which he was about to step.

The boys' overcoats were water-soaked and they reeked. The second boy had narrow shoulders. He shifted from one foot to the other, testing his legs and muscles to make sure they were still functioning, as if wondering whether he'd be able to run after they jumped out. And how far he could get. Not being able to run more than a short way was as bad as not jumping out at all. It was a waste of time, thinking about it. They'd been waiting for this chance for eight months. Before that, they'd waited two years and four months. They'd even thought about it earlier, but that was in Prague and they still didn't know what was in store for them.

"He's not going to dive," the first boy said. "Maybe just once."

Finally Frank raised his eyebrows. He always did that when he didn't know what to do next, but the boys didn't know it.

"Frank doesn't want to," the first boy said. "He's scared."

"The engineer's putting on the brakes," observed the second boy.

"Nobody can fool me anymore. O.K., let him stay behind and get killed."

"He can't stop this train now. He ought to let off steam, or it'll kill him. I guess he wants to jump overboard, too."

The plane was ahead of the locomotive again, nose to nose.

The guard, who was sitting at the back of the car beside Frank, was from somewhere in Transylvania. The boys watched him raise his gun and aim at the plane.

The hill ahead looked like a sugarloaf. Fallen pine trees lay at the bottom. There were patches of snow on the rocky northern slope.

The dark mouth of the tunnel was suddenly illuminated. It looked like a stone horseshoe against the hill. The tunnel was obviously too short to shelter more than the engine, if the engineer managed to stop in time.

The brakes caught briefly, then slipped again. The wheels screeched and sparks flew.

The two boys grabbed each other to keep from falling. The older man watched them calmly.

Looking at the tunnel, Manny was reminded of something Frank had said when they'd been in the old camp. He'd watched them building the crematorium and the gas chambers. "It's not gas, it's a tunnel and people come out on the other side," he said.

The plane began to climb again, making a whistling noise. It seemed to be tethered to the sky with an invisible cable. When it reached five hundred meters, the plane bounced as if there were a hill in the clouds, and turned its nose back toward the earth, ready to finish what it had started so leisurely.

The line, marked out by gun and cannon, shortened the distance between the pilot and the boiler of the engine, wiping out the dotted line of bullets. The thing that made noises like a missing cylinder suddenly perforated the boiler in many places. Steam began to escape in hissing jets from holes the size of peas. The brakes screamed.

The fireman and the engineer jumped off the train and ran along the bank of the stream, trying to reach the tunnel.

"Now, Manny!" said the first. He tore off his coat and dropped it on the floor of the railroad car. Frank must have noticed even though he was watching the tail of the plane as it passed over the end of the train. He stared at the second boy, who slowly began to take off his coat.

"He'll come back and shoot this train up like a field mouse," said the first boy.

Frank was glaring at them angrily now and at the same time, pleadingly.

The engineer and the fireman melted into the shadowy stone walls of the tunnel.

"I'll go first," said the second boy. Then he jumped over the side.

As soon as the roaring plane was farther away and when the train had almost stopped, screams could be heard from the first coach, which had gotten a dose of machine gun bullets by mistake. That coach was filled with women, prisoners who had taken part in the Warsaw uprising and were caught a year ago while hiding in the sewers. It looked as though the wind was sucking the plane back into the sky.

The second boy closed his eyes when he jumped. He had no idea how long it took—maybe two or three seconds. He turned his head. He felt a few sharp jerks. The train had come to a stop. It was the fastest he had moved in six days, during which he'd had nothing to eat but grass, roots, and a piece of turnip Danny had grabbed out of a freight train going in the opposite direction. There was light all around him, but it was like darkness. He waited to feel the impact of the earth. He knew he mustn't fall back against the train or forward into the creek. He must know *how* to fall; he mustn't sprain anything. Or land on a rock.

He realized he didn't have the best shoes for this kind of exercise. They were no more than remnants of shoes, tied together with rags. He'd given his shoes to Danny in exchange for the piece of turnip.

He wished he could skip these next few seconds or the next hundred years. Just so he'd be somewhere else, far away from here. At that moment he hit the ground. Danny was right beside him.

"Let's go!" said Danny. "Come on, Manny!"

The first boy plunged into the creek. His knees gave way, but then he pulled himself together and dashed on, a few paces ahead of the second boy. The water was ice-cold.

The plane was above them again, spilling its golden bullets in double streams of fire into the rest of the train. It was easier to run without coats.

In those first few seconds, everything was erased that had happened to them during the past three years. And the three years before that. Like the meadow they were running through, which brought them closer to the first fallen pines. The feeble early springtime sun was shining on the other side.

Seen at close hand, the hill was bell-shaped. It rose gradually at first, then got steeper.

The pilot had turned away again. The summit of the hill, when they looked up at it, was like the wall of a precipice. Woods began on the other side.

The Transylvanian had just jumped off the train, hampered by his gun.

At first, the second boy thought the guard wanted to hide behind the train, away from the plane. But then he saw that he was shooting at them.

People were jumping out of the freight car the boys had been in. And out of the others, too. But not many, because the other guards had also started shooting.

The boys were halfway up the hill. They'd have shot us anyway, the second boy thought. He looked over at the first boy as he ran. That encouraged him, but it scared him, too. It never occurred to them to stop.

The pilot was firing at the train, which kept the soldiers from chasing the boys. He fired into the supply car and the caboose.

"Faster, Manny!" the first boy panted.

The other boy breathed heavily. He dropped his chin on his chest. The climb was worse than he'd expected. The bullets whizzed all around. The Transylvanian was aiming right at him. He'll get me first, straight in the back.

Both of them had to slow their pace. Manny clawed at the earth to keep from slipping. The earth grew softer as they neared the top. Twice, the second boy had to bend double before he could take another step. He tried not to slip backward.

"Faster!" called the first boy.

The second boy lifted his head. He saw what used to be his old shoes on the feet of the boy ahead of him. In that split second, he remembered the turnip and the way it had tasted. Like the way a cow's breath smells.

He slogged through the mud up to his ankles. He told himself to run. He wasn't thinking about the Transylvanian guard and his gun anymore.

The clear sky was curtained by the hillside and nothing was left of it but a thin sliver of light.

The hillside rose toward the tree trunks, but they thinned out again near the summit. The boys leaned against the trees and then pushed on again. Some of the stumps were rotten and some logs, caught in creases of earth, rolled away when they leaned against them.

The second boy crawled on all fours. He was panting. They were a little less than three-quarters of the way up the hill. He could feel a searing pain in his chest. He knew he couldn't stop it as long as he kept running, and he knew he mustn't stop. Both sides of his lungs felt torn. His heart was beating wildly.

After a few seconds, he felt the first stabbing pain in his kidneys. He knew he hadn't been hit by a bullet. He clutched at his side. He couldn't inhale or exhale anymore; all he could do was gulp for air. He tried to leave more time between inhaling and exhaling. Then he decided that of all the people who had ever mattered to him, Danny was the only one who was still alive. He tried to imagine what would happen to him if he lay down, caught his breath, and rested until the pain loosened its grip on his body. The goal on which he fixed his sights was no longer the top of the hill and the sky, but the first boy's back. It kept getting farther and farther away as the space between them widened.

The second boy plodded on in the footsteps of the first.

As they plunged through the mud and underbrush, the bullets reminded him of the train. He was wrapped in pain, the way the darkness was wrapped in light and the stones in water.

A bullet from the Transylvanian's gun whizzed between his legs. Instead of the American plane, he briefly imagined a fish swimming at great depth. It was the same color as mud and as this hill. He looked up at Danny's feet.

Fleetingly, he thought it might really be quite pleasant if the Transylvanian would shoot him. Not just in the leg or spine. Or the pilot could hit him.

For a moment the second boy paused. He tried to straighten. Quickly, he doubled over. He took a step and the pain stabbed again. He tried to walk, bent over. He felt like a clock that breaks down because somebody has wound it too tight.

His legs felt as if they were made of wood. He was no longer looking forward to running down the other side of the hill. Having the mountain between themselves and the guards' guns suddenly didn't seem so important anymore.

Step by step, they were nearing the top of the hill. The first boy turned off at an angle so the climb wouldn't be quite so steep.

The second boy pleaded with himself to hang on, to crawl the rest of the way to the top, if he had to. He pleaded with his chest, with the pain in his side, with his muscles and legs. With his eyes and with his fate.

Then he stumbled and fell and knew he couldn't get up again. He knocked a fist against his forehead. Then he simply writhed on the ground, trying to ease the pain, telling himself that keeping down made it harder for the snipers below.

"Manny!" The first boy turned.

He was crawling on his hands and knees, clutching at roots to keep from slipping.

"Manny!" He urged. "Come on . . . just a little bit more. A few steps." There was mud in his eyebrows and tears streamed from his bloodshot eyes, as though they were trying to wash away the dirt.

"Just a little farther, Manny." He looked up, then turned away. "We're almost there!"

A wind was blowing along the ridge of the hill. It made the words sound ragged.

"What's wrong with you?" asked the first.

The second boy was startled by the sound of his own voice. He lay in a muddy furrow between two stumps. He had watched Danny climb, bit by bit, until he turned and saw him lying there.

"Get up!" Danny called over his shoulder. "Get up!" And he plunged on.

2

The plane was just above them. The second boy rested his closed eyelids on the earth. The pilot circled the valley, the train and the hill. Maybe he's taking pictures of us, Manny thought. Then two rows of shells spattered alongside him like heavy rainfall in water and were swallowed by the sticky mud. More shells lashed into the earth above his head. He didn't even bother to open his eyes. The pilot probably thought the red cross on the staff coach was just another German trick.

I couldn't care less, the boy said to himself.

The pain had eased a bit.

The pilot wasn't shooting anymore. He could still hear shooting down in the valley. The stump had protected him. They didn't know how to shoot. Bad marksmen. A lot of them who had been good marksmen weren't shooting anymore.

Suddenly Manny was flooded by an awful loneliness. Only occasionally did he think he could escape it, which is what he thought when he jumped off the train. It always came back. It was a loneliness which felt the way mud looks; it was the roar of the airplane overhead and the shooting down below and it was Danny's footsteps getting farther away.

Maybe Frank Bondy will live through it. I'm all by myself, too, like Bondy down there. Like Danny is, somewhere up ahead. How often have I been so lonely?

In front of his eyes, Manny saw the whole thing. That crushing loneliness had come back again.

That September afternoon in 1944, a heavy fog rolled in over the bare plains of Poland. It rolled in waves, over people's bodies and into their souls. A thin, translucent fog. Through it he could see the stumpy brick chimney above the square building where the ovens were. Flames were licking out of it, smelling of burning bones and grease, purple and russet-colored flames, which congealed into a black cloud of soot from which ashes fell like rain. Everybody wished for wind or for the earth to rotate in the opposite direction. The ashes had a bitter taste. They were strange ashes, different from those left by burnt wood or coal, old rags or paper. They contained within themselves fire or human breath, even though they were as cold and dead as each ash is. They were people who shrank away, repelled, yet they held their hands out to catch the ashes as they fell. Then they looked at them or closed their eyes.

A song from Strauss's Die Fledermaus *kept running through his head. He and his family had gone to see it in the clandestine cabaret in Theresienstadt a few days before they were sent to Auschwitz-Birkenau. That was shortly before Father was made into soap. The purplish black smoke came later, after the roaring of the invisible ovens had ceased, and after that, there were waves of whiteness out of which fine ashes swam. That song and the fog melted together for him, spreading out over the length and breadth of the plain, a curve of melody and a web of words, saying you'll be happy if you just forget what can't be changed.*

He'd felt terribly alone. He couldn't understand it. He stood by a cement pillar and sang. The soldiers, the SS, the kapos, and the prisoners all thought he'd gone out of his head. Everything was done to make a person feel alone; some called it maturity or being grown-up, and it had two sides, like a slice of bread, because when a person feels deserted and alone, he is no longer bothered by anything, so he's no bother to anybody, not even to himself. That's why no one passed up a single portion of bread, even though they probably didn't eat it with the same appetite as yesterday or as they would tomorrow. They had just come back from watching the hanging of some prisoners who had mutinied. They may have been innocent or guilty, but they had insulted the guards, so now they were swinging in the wind and the ashes, rain and snow came sifting down on them.

Sometimes it went so far that he felt no responsibility even for a part of his own mind or body. He was unable to tell his left hand from his right, his feet from his hands, and one hair from the other, as though they were branches of a distant tree. Yesterday's rain and tomorrow's decay.

He'd seen a few people who had been turned into absolute strangers to their own families.

That lonely feeling had come back to him at Auschwitz-Birkenau, which was as big as hundreds of military outposts, or thousands of villages put together. A planet of the night, but of different nights than he had ever known.

That evening, he stood close to the wire, looking at the tufts of grass and envying every blade. He envied the grass for the touch of the sun and wind. He wished he were a blade of grass, feeling whatever a blade of grass could feel.

Beyond the wire there was a no-man's-land between the men's and women's camps. He saw a herd of women, most of them naked, carrying something under their arms. Shoes, probably. You couldn't tell. Their heads were shaved. The last twenty women were wearing flimsy shirts. They were barefoot. The wind was cold. This was another planet, too, Frauen Konzentration Lager (FKL), the women's camp, rows of barracks, but one within sight, almost in reach of his hand.

He couldn't shake off the idea that since all that was left of Father was that song, the purple smoke, and a few ashes, it might have been better if it had happened to Mother, too. He prayed he wouldn't see her among those frail, naked, barefoot women, picking their way through the October mud and stones and snow. He didn't want to be like those men who wave good-bye to their mothers as they go into the gas, or those who closed their eyes so they wouldn't see their wives filing into the showers. He looked carefully. He was glad when the naked ones had almost passed and his mother wasn't among them. There were just two more left. The next to last woman was his mother.

He was glad she hadn't seen him. He was sorry she hadn't gone straight to the gas chamber like the other women of her age, that the doctor had sent her off among the living, even though her hair was grey. He couldn't call out to her. He wasn't sure if it would be a good idea. The relief he had begun to feel left, like an ebbing wave, like a shadow of something which had no face, no shape.

He felt drawn toward the high tension wires. That was the easiest way out. He could imagine what lay in store for his mother. He waited until he couldn't see her anymore, until she was swathed in fog. He tried to push away the thought of where his mother was going or where she was coming from and how long she could hold out when she got to wherever it was she was going. Sometimes the women were forced to take showers when it was below zero. Those who lived through it were assigned to work.

The next day, he felt almost reassured that Mother must have frozen to death before she got to wherever they were going. It was a day of rain and snow. The women's wooden barracks were too far away for him to be sure of anything. And then he'd buried his mother, too, with that song, even though she was still perhaps alive. He could almost put himself in the skin of those women at the FKL who, after October fourth, had to watch their sisters and mothers being hanged because they'd helped carry out fuse cords from the Buna Werke. It was with their help *that the* Sonderkommando *blew up Oven Number 4 and then let themselves be shot because nobody had joined with them. Had Mother found that younger sister there, standing under the gallows, watching her older sister's body sway? He felt himself in the skin of both sisters and of his mother, but he didn't know anything for sure, and he was afraid to know, yet at the same time terrified of not knowing. He thought about her every second of the day, and he stayed awake all night thinking of her. It was as if something had been torn out of him. It was as if they'd torn off his legs or arms, but the gaping holes looked different than when people have no legs or arms.*

It was a raw and melancholy sort of loneliness. It was wishing you weren't alive, feeling that the best thing in the world would be not *to be. Feeling you're in your own way, just by being alive. "That's how it goes here," a Hungarian rabbi had said once. "You don't have to accept the idea that everyone lives and dies alone," he said. It was like a huge sinking ship, where no one cries out any longer, but each hears the same old refrain, "Every man for himself." That was before his bread ration was stolen. But even that's not fatal.*

There were plenty of people who adjusted to it. They wanted to be ready for the moment when being alone wasn't the worst thing that could happen to them.

Manny dug his fingers into the earth and opened his eyes. His fingers were bleeding. He wondered how long the sticky, crumbling earth would hold him.

The circle the plane was making above the hilltop reminded him of something, but he couldn't think what it was. It was one of those things he'd rather forget, but he managed to think about it, now and then. The thoughts came and went of their own free will. He was now hidden from the plane's guns by the stumps.

He'd often thought how differently people die when they're condemned to it, but before that noon, he thought about it in another way. Secretly he had hoped that, when his time came, he'd be able to die like that blond fellow from Copenhagen.

He remembered the blond, blue-eyed Jew from a Danish transport who was stopped by an SS officer in front of the gate of the Little Fortress in Theresienstadt. That was where people were sent who had committed some offense against ghetto regulations. "Take off your hat, you dirty Jew!" ordered the officer. The blond fellow slapped him so hard he fell down. He even managed to hit his adjutant, who drew his pistol before the officer got to his feet again and emptied his gun into him. Then Manny watched them literally trample that blond man into the mud.

He heard the plane screech as it circled, doing aerial acrobatics for the entertainment of everybody on the ground who was still alive. Including the two boys. That's good, he thought to himself. The second boy's eyes were fixed on his friend's back.

Danny was struggling, helping himself with his hands. The plane's machine gun blazed a trail of bullets near him. He had about eight steps left to take—Manny had thirteen. The gap had widened.

Something darkened before his eyes. But what he saw when the darkness lifted wasn't Danny's back anymore, but his belly. He wasn't going in the opposite direction, he was coming toward him.

"Give me your hand!" he wheezed. "Hurry up!"

It was hard to hear him above the noise of the plane and its gun. The pilot was aiming his cannon at the locomotive.

"We have to run or we're done for," shouted Danny. "Get going!" He gasped for breath. "Do you want me to kick you? I'll kick you! Get up! Give me your hand! Manny!"

Danny seized the boy's hot, wet and bleeding hand. There was mud between his fingers. It felt like dough. Manny felt himself being jerked to his feet. But he couldn't get up.

The needles that had been stabbing Manny's lungs and kidneys had changed into Danny's hand.

"Come on," said Danny. "Just thirteen steps," he went on. "We're almost there." He waited. "You don't want me to drag you the rest of the way, do you?"

Below, they heard the shattered locomotive groaning and wheezing, and, above them, the plane. Vapor rose from its cannon.

"Just a few inches more, Manny," said the first boy.

He heard many different undertones in his voice—the steely groan of a ship's propeller scraping a rocky bottom . . .

We've made it, Manny told himself. There was a forest on the other side of the hill. From the sound, several guns were still firing together. The pilot circled toward the hills and the train in an ever-widening radius. For us, it's over. The pressure of Danny's hand suddenly relaxed. For a second, Manny was afraid they'd killed him.

3

They were in a small rough clearing, covered with tree stumps. Empty tin cans were neatly piled beside the remnants of a campfire full of wet ashes, tree bark, and dead leaves.

Danny rolled his head away and rested it against the rim of the campfire. Tears streamed from his eyes. His empty stomach turned inside out. Then he coughed and it sounded as though he was gagging. He didn't even bother to swallow his saliva or wipe his mouth.

The treetops tossed in the wind on the other side of the hill. The air smelled green. Here the sky looked bigger, pale blue as it stretched off into the distance.

Danny kept on trying to vomit. He rubbed his mouth against the stones encircling the campfire and tasted the ashes, ashes mixed with wet snow.

Manny lay on his back and closed his eyes. The sky felt close enough to touch if he'd just reach out. But he didn't want to. He couldn't. There was a deep furrow between the stumps of the trees which had been chopped down and those blown down by heavy winds. It was a shallow bowl of earth and it had a bottom, sloping sides, trees, the surface of the earth and its center, rainwater and rain which had not fallen yet. His eyes watered. He inhaled the scent of the wet grass. It didn't matter that his mouth and ears and eyes and nose were full of sticky, shapeless clay. He had a bitter taste in his mouth, but it was different from the way the ashes had tasted in Poland. There was blood on his lips; it had a sweet taste. He tried not to notice how Danny was coughing and gagging. Then, briefly, he thought back to that autumn afternoon.

The sky was overcast. In the fog, you couldn't see the ropes from which gaunt, rag-clad women's bodies swayed. You couldn't even see the eyes peering out through the cracks in the KFL barracks at the swaying bundles of rags the fog rolled in. Afterward, it had rained for days. In the mornings and at night, it snowed. In between, there were ashes, drummed into the earth along with the rain. In the afternoon, there was fog. He could hear slow, languorous music. Like that last evening when they'd been with Father at the secret cabaret in Theresienstadt.

But now, looking back, it seemed almost pleasant. It proved people were right who had feared the transports without knowing why. There are things a person fears without knowing why.

When they'd ordered Father off the ramp and straight into the gas, Manny had felt more alone than ever. It was the twenty-eighth or twenty-ninth of September; he couldn't remember exactly.

There had been madness in his grief, sometimes loud, sometimes quiet as a whisper, like ashes drifting to earth. This loneliness suddenly had a face and a voice which it hadn't had before.

He couldn't understand why they'd killed his father, just because he wore glasses and was fifty-two years old.

He stood next to the concrete pillar and stared at the flames. He wanted to inhale as much smoke as possible into his lungs. He saw a low chimney. It was the crematorium. Red bricks. The pillar was new. On the other side of the crematorium were the factories where mattresses, candles, and soap were made. He was afraid they might order him there. He kept looking that way as if the door might open and Father step out, fair-haired and blue-eyed, looking like the director of a bank, as the Aryan Gazette *once wrote about him. The last of the fenceposts looked quite small in the distance. A song—the one they sang in the cabaret—* "Glücklich ist, wer vergisst, was doch nicht zum ändern ist." *A silly little song can outlive so many people.*

He took a deep breath of the burned bones. He could taste them. He held up his hands to catch the ashes. But all he caught was rain or snow or fog.

"Be glad things are the way they are," said Danny. "You know what would have been even worse for him and for my father."

Danny never talked about it. Both of them knew how much worse things could be.

But there was still to be added to it the violet skin on Mother's fragile body. He could hear her voice. Like when she used to read prayers to him when he was a little boy. Her voice was lovelier to listen to than the prayers, and when she prayed, Father always smiled.

He had never been able to figure out that smile. He was afraid to

look a woman in the face, fearful it was Mother. Or was it because of
something else?

The Hungarian rabbi used to tell Danny: "We're all on our own . . .
alone . . . nobody has anybody. Other people only get in your way."

Danny was still coughing; but he wasn't gagging anymore.

The ridge of the hill was covered with grass flattened by wind and
wet fog. There were tufts of earth and low bushes. Manny inspected
it, along with the white, sweat-stained face of his friend.

Everything seemed different inside the woods. Nobody could
find them now, even if any of the guards from the train came up
looking for them. The boys lay side by side. There was no need yet
to decide how long they could stay there resting.

Manny looked across the stretch of grass ahead and focused on
the furrow of stillness beside the deserted army campfire. When he
took a breath and felt no pain, it was like the lifting of a weight
which had pinned him to the ground.

He looked around. He touched the grass and stones, breathing in
the silence that blanketed the forest and the silence which was in
between them and the train.

"Everything's all wet," he said.

"It's soft," replied the first.

Danny finally stopped coughing. Manny touched his chest and
felt how thin the skin was.

"Frank stayed behind," said Manny.

"He shouldn't have," replied the first boy. "It's his own fault."

"They all stayed."

"It'll be better down below. It isn't so windy in the woods."

Manny rubbed his ankles.

"That pilot massacred them," said Danny.

The wind pushed low clouds across the sky.

"Manny?" said the first. "It's behind us now."

Danny watched the clouds and the sky, the hill, the valley and the
long stretch of forest.

"Everyone has to get out of it however he can," he said.

"I had an awful pain in my side. Both sides. That never happened
before."

"It was awfully steep."

"It was a good thing it wasn't so steep at the beginning." Manny paused. "That was a funny plane. Close up, it looked awful small. I thought they had faster machines."

"I don't think about it anymore."

Danny brushed his hands through his hair, then rubbed his eyes. "I don't want the mud to cake," he explained.

After having run so fast and having lain in the grass so long, Manny was cold. He began to shiver and moved closer to Danny. When he touched him, his entire body began to tremble.

I wasn't alone then, like I was back there on the hill, Manny said to himself.

He remembered being with Danny in Auschwitz-Birkenau when he got dysentery; Danny got it, too, because he'd fed him with his own spoon in order to show him that it wasn't contagious. They worked in the Auto-Union car factory and then in DAW, Deutsche Ausrüstungwerke, a German munitions factory. They got something to eat only once every twenty-four hours—salty soup, to make them thirsty. The only water was in the washrooms, where there was a big sign, "Warning: Not suitable for drinking."

Every morning and evening during the epidemic, the older boys from the Gypsy barracks dragged Manny and Danny out to the appell-platz for roll call. One thing became evident: you didn't have to be the strongest or the smartest in order to be able to help others. The Scharführer from Waffen SS led the weakest to the car which took them to the gas chamber and said, "We're all only people." And: "To err is human."

You could trust Danny. Except for the time he let Danny collect his soup ration while he was carrying rocks . . .

It's awfully easy to let somebody die.

"I wish the past were as dead for me as it is far you," Manny said.

Danny was watching the silent dot which was the plane as it disappeared between the treetops and the hill, into the curving horizon.

"Crazy fool," he said sadly.

"He probably doesn't have enough gas or ammunition left. Those bullets looked like gold. Now he's going to fly back to some base and brag about what he did. I hope he took pictures. I'd like to see his face when they're developed and he takes a look at them."

He watched the plane with undisguised envy as it flew away.

"It's not important anymore. Anyway, we really had to run for it."

"I'm cold," Manny repeated.

Danny looked back to where he had first seen the dot of the plane in the sky. He put his arm around his shoulder.

"You *pipl,*" he grinned.

"*Pipl,*" replied Manny.

Nobody, except Frank Bondy, bothered debating about whether it was an innate affliction or an acquired inclination. It simply *was.* And there was a lot of it. *Pipls* were the comeliest little cherubs. Who knows where the name came from? Maybe it was derived from the German word for spigot or little pipe or hose. Maybe somebody just made it up. Nobody ever bothered to think about it.

Pipl was part of the vocabulary at Auschwitz-Birkenau; it was like saying "organize" when you meant "steal." But linguistics, Frank always said, was on the bottom rung of his ladder of interests.

"It doesn't matter anymore," the first boy said. "It's over and done with now."

The *pipls* were a caste. Often they were the smallest and weakest boys, but also the attractive ones who had the power. Most boys would have liked to become *pipls,* just as fifteen-year-old girls dreamed of becoming fashion models, or prostitutes in Paris or Istanbul or Belgrade.

Some youngsters dreamed of becoming *pipls,* the way some grown-ups dreamed of belonging to the Gestapo or being German army officers because of the advantages and status it brought. Plenty of food and clothes, a roof over their heads, and not having to be scared you'll be gassed as soon as you get too skinny.

At Auschwitz-Birkenau, the materials from which dreams were woven changed, but the dreams themselves remained unchanged. Being a pretty little Jewish child took on a new value.

Some parents even wished their children would be chosen as somebody's *pipl.* There were hundreds of reasons, but the main ones always overlapped.

Sometimes the parents, or one of them, wished it for their child's sake; other times, it was for their own good, or so they thought.

When they used to lie so close together in the same bunk, just keeping warm, Danny was always scared somebody would get the wrong idea.

Danny was thinking how wonderful it was, everything that lay ahead, and how it buried what they had left behind, including those last few minutes when they'd been clawing their way up the hill.

"Hey, little Jew bastard," he said. "What are you thinking about?"

"About the girl Frank used to ask me about."

Danny wondered whether he hadn't just invented her. It wouldn't have been the first thing Manny had dreamed up.

"And about the forest," he went on. "And those weapons we helped to make. They probably killed a lot of people."

"I lost my cap," said Danny.

"Maybe Frank never really figured on coming with us at all," said the second.

He glanced at Manny and wiped the mud off his lips. The plane had been out of sight for a long time.

4

For several hours they had been walking over the same kind of hill as they'd crossed yesterday. They'd stopped arguing about how far the next town was. They didn't know exactly where they were. According to Frank, the train had been headed from Buchenwald to the camp at Dachau. In southern Germany, in other words. They were headed eastward. East was where the sun rose.

Talking had exhausted them. They plodded on through forests that had no end. Now and then, the pine trees stopped and fir and hemlock started.

"It isn't so damp," said the first. "Maybe it didn't rain here that much."

They were cold. Low sharp branches scratched their necks and cheeks and could have put out their eyes. For hours, they heard crows.

The first boy turned around. "You ought to walk faster, Manny."

The second boy understood. He tried to imagine sounds other than the cawing of the crows.

"We're really alone here," he said.

They hadn't been alone that morning. It was lucky they hadn't fallen into the clutches of the man in a green uniform carrying a rifle.

"So far, so good," said the first boy. "We're doing all right."

It was another hour before they spoke again. The ground was level, but the woods were full of fallen trees, marshy places and holes. Sometimes they had to wade for several yards.

The crows were flying very high.

"We didn't get far this morning," said the second boy.

"We were lucky, though," remarked the first.

Manny looked ahead, noticing the different kinds of bark on the tree trunks.

When he heard the crows, he could never think of pleasant things. They started cawing in the middle of the night and woke the boys, who got up and continued on their way.

It's a good thing I'm not a soldier, he thought. He tried to keep the same distance behind Danny.

He wondered if he could catch some animal with his bare hands. He thought how people hunt down animals. Then he turned it around and thought about how animals hunt down people. The first boy was thinking about food, too, but in a different way. The crows made him hungry, but the idea of eating one turned his stomach. It wasn't just because they would have had no way to cook it. Sometimes he broke off a twig, chewed on it for a while, then spat it out.

Frank was the only one they'd told what the people in the camp in Glei-witz in Germany had eaten after the tenth day or so. At the beginning it had only been the dead. Later, it was the sick, too.

That was the day Frank handed over all his rations to them. He said it was a good thing to fast once a year and that pious people knew what they were talking about. But the boys knew it was just an excuse. Frank said it wasn't hard for him to imagine the three of them in Gleiwitz. For several days they felt very close to those people from Gleiwitz. Or whatever it was called.

They came to a stream. Danny, who was in front, stumbled and almost fell into the water.

The other boy lay down on his belly on the bank. Side by side, the two boys washed their faces and doused their heads. They drank deeply. The first lapped the water like a cat, and the second scooped it into his palms. Then they just let the water flow over them, as though they'd fallen asleep.

The water was clean and cold, full of melted snow from the mountains. The stones on the bottom were wreathed with moss which made the water look green. Ribbons of moss clung and waved from the bigger rocks, but the current could not pull it away.

About three hours later, the boys crossed the same creek again. It was evidently a long, meandering stream. They drank again.

"It's easier in the daylight," said the first boy.

He waded awhile in the stream. He looked down at his pants. They were soaking wet. They'll cool me, he thought to himself.

The first boy looked at the second. His freckles stood out clearly.

Manny let Danny lead. He shielded his face with his hands, as though he weren't only pushing aside the branches, but trying to let in the light. Sometimes he even closed his eyes and groped along. He was tired and yearned to go to sleep, but he knew that as long as Danny had enough strength to keep going he mustn't hold him back. His pants were wet up to the knees.

Suddenly he said, "Once when we were in the train and I was standing in the middle of those who had already died, and the wind was blowing around me and the sun was shining, and everything seemed beautiful."

He looked at the first boy's back. Danny turned around.

"What'd you say?"

"I said, if you brush it all off and think about yourself, things always look pretty good."

The first boy did not reply. It was always like that. Danny only answered when it was something he understood and something that had an answer. But sometimes he had the kind of expression he had now, before he turned away to look ahead.

He was tired and he felt like sitting down and going to sleep. Or lying down and sleeping. Even just lying down. He knew that as long as the first boy had strength enough to keep on going, they'd keep going and he knew that to keep going was the right thing to do. There was no point in holding him back. It was as if he was letting himself be dragged along.

He looked at the first boy's back. Danny turned around.

For a moment he thought they'd reached their goal. When his eyes were closed, he dreamed of clean suits; he imagined them waiting for a train going somewhere, where nobody would ask for a ticket or money. All you had to do was get aboard, sit down by the window and look out at the countryside.

Sometimes Frank Bondy succeeded in doing something only a few others did—making people envy him and his memories, even though ninety-nine percent were fairy tales. But one percent was true. It was the one percent that mattered. "For some people, it's a house or maybe a window that's important. Or a beautiful fur coat, an armchair or antique or pretty dresses and shoes in the closet," he said. "For some, a chair's enough in front of a table with a loaf of bread on it and a bottle of wine or a bowl of fruit—a few pears and apples. And a view through the window of a snow-covered garden. My ideal was a house with a garden and a pond, to be able to sit in the kitchen and catch fish through the window. But it would be enough for something to snap in my brain, and I'd be scurrying off to the train station to buy a ticket to Monte Carlo. Some people know they'll live until spring and that's all they need to be happy. When I was feeling good, I just let the sun go down, knowing I'd see it again next morning. When I felt worse, and it didn't matter for what reasons, every sunset seemed to me like the end of the world. Maybe it's true, that the world dies every day at evening and it's born again in the morning. But not always for everybody."

"Just remember, boys, every person in the world always lives at least two lives. In one, he plays with an open hand of cards so that everybody can see, and in the other, he's the only one who knows what he's got. I hope you know what I mean."

He claimed that everybody had the right to happiness, but nobody could show him where to find it or how to get it.

Then Frank had added: "I hope you know what I'm trying to say." But there were a lot of things he never explained. "For some people, it's a girl with white skin and a nice belly," Frank went on. "Everybody has his forbidden tree, the tree he's forgotten, and there's always a serpent. Maybe they taught you boys something else in your religion classes, but it's the same old story. Food, drink, houses, nice clothes, shoes, and a drop of good fun, a job which fits a person to a T. For some, yes; for others, no. Nobody ever has everything."

If Frank was telling the truth, he'd lost his money in the most gorgeous and exotic places in the world. By combining his talents and personality with others', he had multiplied his money so he was as rich as a king. He had played roulette in Paris and Monte Carlo and entertained some of the loveliest leeches in the bars and nightclubs of Rome and London and Bucharest. When he talked of happiness, he smiled as though he was looking through a veil of sadness. He looked like he was a thousand years old. Or as though he only halfway believed some of the things he said. But he never said he had stopped believing in them. He described restaurants which served things an ordinary person had never heard of. Caviar and pâté and spiced sausages were the least of those delicacies; there were many others. He used to say there was nothing a person couldn't get along without, but it was nice to try all those goodies just to see what they were like. Frank never entirely admitted that it was all over.

Danny turned around. He scratched himself on a branch. He looked battered and bruised. His legs were covered with mud and pine needles and dead leaves. Manny was right behind him.

He wasn't thinking about Frank anymore, just that Danny had probably been careless and that was why he was so scratched and banged up.

"Don't you want to go a little faster?" Danny asked.

"I still feel knocked out," said Manny.

"Me, too."

"It's as if somebody had pumped everything out of me."

Maybe he's thinking about Frank Bondy, too, Manny decided. It was funny how close he felt to Danny. In the camps, he'd met a few people who'd been like brothers. Like Danny. He wasn't exactly stubborn. But he was very determined. He didn't stick his nose into things that were none of his business.

Danny stopped and leaned against a tree. He waited for the other boy to catch up with him. "A lot of people would give everything for a chance like this. Everything, Manny."

"Yeah," said the second. His thoughts were elsewhere.

He was careful about the slashing branches. He came to the tree where Danny was resting.

"Why don't you look where you're going?" demanded the first boy.

"I'm looking straight ahead."

"I thought you had your eyes closed," said the first boy.

"If anybody else escaped after us, they were probably from Kohen's bunch," said the second boy.

"You think they made a run for it, too?"

"I don't know."

"Why do you ask?"

The second boy wondered why Frank hadn't liked Kohen and his people. According to Frank, they had grandiose dreams and sacrificed the fate of other people without asking them. People in Kohen's bunch had been talking about it for years. Especially since last winter. According to Frank, it was only a question of the frying pan or the fire.

Frank didn't like Transcarpathian Jews either. They never wanted to say "kill," believing that killing one man meant killing the whole world. After all they'd seen!

"Maybe they all got shot," said Danny. "They certainly would have called a meeting before they jumped over the side."

"I can still hear those shots when he hit the engine boiler."

"I'm thirsty again," said Manny. His eyes were bloodshot. The cuts and scratches stung.

"We'd better get going," said the first boy. As he turned, he bumped his head on a tree branch. Manny waited. The first boy rubbed his forehead and kept right on going.

Manny followed. We started on Friday the thirteenth, he thought to himself, if the calendar in Frank Bondy's memory was correct. Like that "13" on the rudder of the American plane. Those Polish Transcarpathians, who never shaved their sideburns, thought very highly of the number. If we make it, I'm going to have plenty of reason to believe in thirteen, too.

Kohen's people believed in something else. So did the Transcarpathian Jews. Danny believed in himself. He was a walking prayer addressed to himself. Frank believed in the past. His version of it, at least, because they had no way of checking on him. They didn't even want to. Perhaps believing in something is our last chance. Or being strong enough to still remember. That can make the bad things a little better.

The woods were thicker now, the path choked with underbrush. Roots and rocks protruded through the moss and pine needles.

The sky glimmered through the trees. It was cloudy. You could hear pine cones falling and the screech of a startled bird as it flew from one branch to another.

The Chassidim from Ruthenia, in the Transcarpathians, were just as persistent in their belief in a fun-loving God as were the people from Kohen's group in expelling Him from their skulls and installing the Revolution in His place.

Frank watched them in amusement when they argued.

I'm going to believe in myself, too, in what's best and strongest in me and in what isn't good or strong either. When we get where we're going, I'm going to buy a number thirteen in gold and wear it on a chain strong enough to hang a chair on. Manny felt drained, hardly strong enough to lift his feet.

He thought about the house in Prague where he used to live and all the houses nobody would ever return to, and even if they did, there would be nobody to wait for them. Doorbells nobody will ring.

Danny was six trees ahead.

Manny held one hand in front of his face and pushed back the branches with the other. He wondered what time it was. They'd started out at daybreak, about four o'clock in the morning. He'd never been so cold in the month of March.

He looked around. It would soon begin to rain.

All he could see were Danny's shoes. The leather had darkened and grown stiff.

He'd been watching Danny's shoes for almost an hour. It still hadn't begun to rain.

An hour later, he realized what it was about Danny's shoes that bothered him. In the train, it hadn't seemed like such a bad deal, trading a pair of shoes for a piece of turnip. Maybe Danny hadn't been so hungry.

The first boy turned. "Don't lag, Manny," he said.

He had been keeping the same speed. He wondered when it would start raining. He thought about Frank. *That winter, they'd been talking about what the chances were for escaping. "Boys," he'd said, "when you turn hope into a tower so high you lose your perspective, you can't help but fall."* Sometimes he treated hope of escape like a rag doll tearing it apart at the seams, spilling out its sawdust or rag guts, turning it into hopelessness.

Manny's stomach growled. That was nothing new. If I don't get cramps, I'll be all right, he said to himself. *There was the German officer in Auschwitz-Birkenau who talked of the advantages of regular meals. A good number of people lost their stomach ulcers in camp. Along with a lot of other things. Sometimes the officer would order them to kneel in front of a trough, pour in highly salted fish soup and tell them to lap it up. No spoon. He expected people to eat like dogs.*

The officer had never regretted the time it took him to explain to the prisoners that they'd been born inferior and that was why they weren't given spoons, how they ought to be glad to lap up their soup from chamber pots. He had a medal from the winter battle in the East, 1941–42, the "Winterschlacht im Osten," the so-called Frozen Meat Order.

He wondered whether, in a way, that officer hadn't been right.

He went back to thinking about Manya Cernovska. Danny's lucky. He doesn't think of anything. Except maybe that they were on their way. It made the time pass more pleasantly.

Manny had a fever. He knew it without even touching his skin.

Maybe Frank Bondy needed to have them listen to him talk. Maybe it provided some continuity between the world he used to live in and the world the two boys knew. It was nice to hear Frank Bondy explain that a gentleman always flushes the toilet when he's visiting and even at home. Or what kind of socks a well-bred man should wear with a plain blue necktie.

Frank could go on for hours, telling how he'd drunk absinthe in Paris. It didn't taste good, Frank said, but it built bridges and transformed your life.

The Transcarpathians whiled away time by telling how, the tougher things got, the more joy their rabbis knew how to extract. They knew thousands of anecdotes.

It was boring to hear them pray, and they prayed a lot. Some believed the important thing wasn't who or what you pray to or for, but just the fact of praying. Frank denied that.

There was compassion and understanding in his eyes, but he didn't like Polish Jews and Hungarian Jews and he couldn't stand German Jews. Now and then he'd accept French or Italian or Danish Jews. He'd worked out a scale and he himself was always right at the top.

Frank said that some German Jews, somewhere in the depths of their souls, were proud of German victories and would mourn German defeats, as if both were not the first things that buried them. It was as if they had two souls. The first regretted their not being German, and the second condemned their not being German.

"The whores on the street were three times as smart as they were," said Frank Bondy.

He was a bit like the Germans, too, because he never told the whole truth. But as far as this escape was concerned, he'd disappointed them many times. After eight months, a few transparent lies emerged from Frank Bondy's maxims.

He had a fiancée in Prague whose address he'd given to Danny. This was one of his maxims: "Truth is the best lie." And: "You must not tell a lie, but you're not bound to tell the truth either." Or, "You can blow up a dream to be bigger than the night." Last time he said: "Haste is good only for catching fleas, boys." The girl's address was right. But he hadn't come with them.

Manny decided it wasn't really so hard to thumb his nose at Frank. They'd had to do it to a lot of people.

It's not so hard to thumb your nose. Sometimes you remember it later, but not usually. Eat, he said to himself. Everything boiled down to food.

They watched the crows in the treetops, cawing and honking and flapping their wings. He tried to get his mind off the noise the birds made by thinking about the number thirteen. Eat, eat, he told himself, as though it could bring food closer; eat, eat, eat.

Spruce and fir branches hung low. The light changed among the upper branches where it was green and bluish. The crows looked very black against the dark grey sky and the clouds were like waterfalls or castles or ships tossing in a rough sea.

The second boy looked down again, focusing on Danny's shoes.

"Manny," said the first.

"I'm hungry," said the second.

"Don't lose patience, Manny."

"Can you hear those lousy birds, Danny?"

He remembered sitting in the middle of the woods as a child, eating bread and butter and roasted peanuts.

"Heather's pretty, but when I was little, I was afraid of it."

His fevered eyes slipped over the back of the boy stumbling in front of him.

The first boy cast a bloodshot glance at Manny's eyes.

Suddenly something stabbed into his heel.

His knees gave way, then slowly he straightened.

5

By noon they were both too exhausted to talk anymore. Not even the wind refreshed them. Now and then it stopped, the humming ceased in the treetops and the silence was so complete, it drowned out the crows.

It was raining somewhere. There was a drawn-out dark sound in the air as the rain drew nearer.

"It turns my stomach, the way those birds caw," the second boy said. "Do you suppose they're following us?"

"They're always in the woods," replied the first. "They're harmless."

Manny saw how badly the first limped and Danny knew he'd noticed. He put most of his weight on his right foot to ease the pressure on the left.

"Is it bad?" asked the second.

"Why are you afraid of heather?"

"It makes me sad. I don't know why."

"Heather's beautiful."

"Does your foot hurt bad?"

"Not really," replied the other.

"Do you want me to go first?"

"It doesn't matter."

"Do you want to stop for a while? Do we have to keep going uphill? We've been walking uphill for two hours."

"We're going the right way," replied the first.

"You're just wearing yourself out."

"Don't you think it's too much uphill, Danny?"

"It's going to rain."

"Let it rain," the second boy said. "Don't be so sure I can still make it, Danny. If there's one thing about those crows that bothers me, aside from the awful racket they make, it's that they are always too high to kick. I kicked one once when I was wearing those shoes you have on now, Danny. That bird's not flying anymore."

They walked side by side. The second boy didn't need to raise his voice anymore. Maybe the first would have liked to ask where Manny had kicked the crow, but the pain in his foot was sharper now.

"Snow is sometimes beautiful, too," said the first. "When it's white. Heather and snow."

"Yeah," said the other.

"I'm not slowing down because of you."

It's probably a nail, he decided. He could feel it. He should have known. It had worked its way out slowly, but now it was jabbing into his heel.

The wind tossed the branches and the air was full of cawing crows. Maybe Manny was right; those birds might call attention to them.

"Probably nobody pays attention to crows," he said. "Forget them, can't you, for God's sake?"

Danny stopped and leaned back against the tree, feeling like Bondy, relaxing outside a hacienda in Latin America, one foot crossed casually over the other, arms folded and head tilted back, watching the sun set over the Pacific Ocean. Or the Atlantic?

The second boy leaned against another tree.

The first boy wondered whether he shouldn't try to hammer out the nail with a stone. He looked around in the moss. He knew that if the pain got worse, it would slow them down more than Manny's lingering. He grinned wearily.

The second boy grinned, too. He didn't want to be the first to sit down.

The second boy was chewing pine needles. He did it on and off. They had a bitter taste and you couldn't swallow them, but they were all right to chew for a while. He tried a pinecone. One kind had seeds inside and you could eat them.

"You're like a squirrel," the first boy said.

"We could make a good meal out of one of these," the second boy said.

The first boy was silent.

"Of course, it'd be lowering our standards," said the second. He paused. "I'd slow down, if I were you, Danny."

"Shut up, Manny."

The second stared at the moss. You'd have to swallow a lot of worms if you tried to eat a piece of moss, he thought to himself. He knew the other boy couldn't stand the idea of eating anything raw. Not just because of what they said about those people who'd been in Gleiwitz. In camp, they'd tried it with a cat. He wondered about squirrels. But it was just a thought. A squirrel's too quick to get caught. Except a dead squirrel. There are other creatures in the forest that eat dead squirrels, though.

Until a person goes a little crazy, like in Gleiwitz, the thought's repulsive, he said to himself. A fever is just one step from the madness, he thought, but it's still repulsive.

"We're still picky about what we eat, aren't we?"

The first boy pushed off from the tree and started walking. It went all right. He didn't want Manny to sit down. That would mean the end of today's hike. He didn't want to hear any more about all the things that can be eaten raw, either.

Manny tramped on after the first boy, listening to the crows as they flapped away or settled back in the treetops with the drawling, ambiguous "Kraaa."

That foot must be giving Danny a lot of pain, the second boy thought. The first boy was thinking how unfair it was that crows can fly wherever they want to and that they always have enough to eat.

"We're taking a step and a quarter for every meter," the first boy said. "We're doing fine. I can feel it in my bones, Manny. We're making good time."

The other boy was silent. For almost an hour, Manny had been thinking about a man in Theresienstadt who had caught and eaten crows. He was a basket-maker whom the major had kept around until, out of spite and envy, the other SS men had sent him off to Auschwitz-Birkenau in the major's absence. Everybody in a railroad car with a W on it was shot immediately on his arrival at the final station. The man had believed that crows had a peculiar strength because they lived a hundred and fifty years, feeding on the finest prey in the fields and forests.

It was already late in the afternoon. He wondered why Danny didn't want to take off his left shoe.

"We've left the rain behind. According to that, we can figure out how far we've come already," Danny remarked.

"I wish you could calculate it forwards instead of backwards, Danny."

"Once we get there, it won't matter."

"Have you any idea at all where we are? I hope we'll know by evening, Manny."

"This is still better than being shot at or gassed, isn't it, Manny?"

It sounded as though he was afraid the second boy wouldn't be able to keep up the pace.

"Does it hurt?" Manny looked down at the first boy's foot.

"You already asked me once, Manny. It hurt before, didn't it? Don't worry about it. I won't either."

The second eyed him quizzically.

The first boy stopped again and leaned against a tree. A globule of sap trickled onto his forehead from an upper branch.

The nail in his shoe made a difference.

"If I were you, I'd be careful," the second boy said.

"What for? I'm like an animal."

"Of the nail. Or whatever it is."

"You know what it is?"

"I can imagine. I'm not blind, Danny. If it's a nail, you could develop blood poisoning."

"I'll get there even with blood poisoning."

"Like hell you'll get there with blood poisoning!"

"I don't know what's inside the shoe," the first boy said.

"Well, have a look, Danny. Look, while it's still light."

"I don't need light for that."

"How far do you suppose we've come today?"

"We got a pretty late start."

"It was four o'clock in the morning."

"It's hard to judge distances. And there's no other way we can go except through the woods."

"Frank probably knew why he stayed behind."

"There's no use getting mad at him."

"I'm not pouring out my anger; I'm tired, Danny."

"He's just a son of a bitch, Manny, he's no prophet."

"Yeah."

"When somebody's a bastard, I don't care if he croaks."

"Every bastard *ought* to croak so he doesn't make things difficult for people who aren't bastards."

"Maybe he knew."

"Frank would never have made it this far. He hasn't got it in him. That's why he stayed behind, Manny."

The first boy's voice sounded tired and heavy.

The second boy spoke feverishly. "Don't you really want to sit down for a second, Danny?"

"Frank wouldn't have been able to keep going long without food, Manny. He wouldn't have been able to get through that swamp and underbrush. He couldn't have stood the cold at night. He'd have been eaten up by fever and exhaustion. He couldn't cover this distance, always keeping on the move like you and me."

"Maybe they sent back a new engine and a hospital coach so the rest of them could go on to wherever it was they were going. Maybe they'll be able to escape in a better place, closer to the border."

"I wouldn't believe Frank now, even if he told me what time it was, Manny."

"What if that Transylvanian tipped him off and they came to an agreement or something? Frank could have convinced him that he'd help hide him after the war."

"More than likely they shot them all. And even if they sent a new locomotive and took them somewhere else, all they'd do would be to shoot them."

He paused. "Manny, have you got a fever?"

"Frank couldn't stand not eating or sleeping. He couldn't take it, freezing cold and keeping on the go without rest, could he?"

"I didn't hear such a lot of shooting. Except at us."

"There was that hill in between."

"That sure was a bitch of a hill," affirmed the second.

"They wouldn't have starved those prisoners till they went crazy, Manny," the first said. "Look at what they did with us. They probably shot the rest as soon as we jumped out and made for the woods," the first boy continued. "So they wouldn't follow our example." After a moment's thought he added, "If not, then Frank certainly managed to trade his watch for something to eat."

"For what?"

"Something for *himself.* I bet you anything they shot the rest of them. Germans are scared of other people more than of anything else. Getting sick comes second. They're mostly scared of people they've done something to. They can't stand the idea of witnesses.

They're afraid of infection, too. They wouldn't want those prisoners on their necks, hungry and wild-eyed."

"If they want to keep that track open, Danny, they've surely sent for another locomotive and a repair crew."

"Maybe they don't have that many locomotives. And the sky's full of Americans."

"I guess you wouldn't make very good soap."

"You wouldn't either!"

"So far, they've had enough of what it takes to exterminate almost all of us."

"They used to, Manny. Things are different now. You and I know that."

They walked along, the first boy still in front, putting his weight on his toes, and he didn't object when the second boy caught up with him. Danny was limping badly.

"You can always tell which way is north, depending on which side of a tree trunk the moss grows. The woods are thick here and we're well hidden."

"I'm almost ready to call it quits for today, Manny."

"Prague is to the east. I just wish I knew how *far* east. We discussed three possible border crossings with Frank. I talked about it once with the people from Kohen's group, too. After that, it'll be easy."

"I don't care what Frank said. It's about one hundred and fifty kilometers, I figure."

"How far is that, in comparison to what we've done already?"

"About three days and into the night, I guess. At this pace, we're covering about twenty kilometers or a little bit less in one day and night. But not much more. We don't have any timetable, Manny. Most of it's hills and woods, and that's always confusing. Even when we go downhill, the land around us slopes upwards. That means we're coming to a pass, but it's still pretty far. After that, it's all downhill."

"Yeah," the second said. "All I know, Danny, is that you promised we'd be back in civilization today."

"Tomorrow, Manny. You can depend on it. We're heading the right way." After a while, he went on.

"We'll find something to eat this evening, Manny. Or tomorrow."

"Where, if we stick to the woods?"

Danny changed the subject. "Something must have happened back there. I'm glad we weren't there. It must have been nasty."

Both of them knew that it wasn't just the fate of people on the train that troubled them. But the farther they went, the more their thoughts were drawn back to the train. They had known how to behave then and what to do. It was something that *existed*, not something which was yet to come, which they must cope with.

"Do you really think they shot them?" the second boy asked.

"They've got peace and quiet now, that's all I know, but I'm not saying what *kind* of peace and quiet," replied the first.

"I hope that pilot made a hole in the skull of the guy from Transylvania."

"It's a wonder he didn't hit us."

"You know that Transylvanian bastard claimed he had a mother? He used to talk to me like I was already dead. For hours, he would tell me in his stupid German that if anybody took the trouble of making a chemical analysis of me, I'd hardly be worth two and a half Deutschemarks. Even if I lived to be nineteen. That greedy pig had it all figured out, even in Czech crowns. As a corpse, I'd be worth twenty-five crowns. He knew it in Swiss francs, in American dollars and English pounds. Money was all he had on his mind. He enlisted in the army because he wanted money and he knew how to calculate. According to him, the greater part of your body and mine is water. That's useful in making soap and candles. There's enough iron in us to make one nail."

"There's probably not enough in him to make even the trigger of a gun," the first boy said. That word, "nail," stuck in his mind.

"I don't have enough lime in me to whitewash the ceiling of a German outhouse," said the second. "Or enough sulphur to gas a kitten or a squirrel. You could make twenty-four matches from the phosphorus in me. But three and a half kilos of soap just from grease and water."

"That's why they made soap out of my dad, because they wanted to make a profit," Manny went on. "They liked his overcoat, too. His watch and his wedding ring and necktie. They wanted his underpants, too, and his socks and clean handkerchiefs. So they made soap out of him and they got our apartment in Prague with all the furniture and stuff and Dad's Italian mandolin, his fur-lined gloves and three thousand crowns he'd saved over twenty years for a rainy day."

"You got a fever, Manny."

"Aw, forget it, Danny."

"Honest, you look flushed."

"I told you, forget it. And carbon, Danny . . . that Transylvanian figured out how many pencil fillers I'd make. They made lamp shades out of Milanek Oppenheimer and Zdenek Pick because they had such nice, delicate, young skin. That guard probably never went to school back in Rumania. He didn't really know how to shoot, either. All he could do was load a gun and pull the trigger. We were lucky that it was their dumbest, meanest soldiers who came with us. Don't think they didn't *want* to hit us. How is it possible that so many dumb hicks got as far as they did?"

Manny must be running a very high fever, the first boy figured. What would happen to them, to him and Manny? His eyes glistened under an opaque film, and although it was cool in the forest, sweat beaded his forehead.

"Old Transylvania wasn't ashamed of washing his face with soap made out of little Jewish girls. The German warehouses are full of it. Twenty years' supply of soap. If people could drink blood like wine, Danny, they'd fill barrels and bottles with it and export it all over Europe and to the rest of the world, wherever any Germans live."

He almost whispered it.

"Listen, quit pretending you don't have a fever when you do. There's no sense fooling each other. We'll rest awhile before we go on, or if you'd rather, we can call it a day already. Or do you want to keep going till it gets dark, Manny?"

"They'd export your blood and mine like wine as far as Australia and New Zealand. Or North America."

"It's all the same to me if it goes to Tierra del Fuego, Manny. As long as I'm here in these woods, nobody's going to export my blood anywhere."

"They don't give a damn for our blood in Tierra del Fuego, Danny. The only ones who give a damn are you and me." He spoke quietly.

"If I'd known three or five years ago what I know now, I'd have taken an ax and cracked the skull of the first German who stuck his nose in our door," said the second. "They taught me a lesson," he whispered.

The wind blew into their faces.

"I'm scared, Manny, because they've had it now," said the first. "They'll kill anyone who can't escape or defend himself. They won't even have time to make them into soap."

The first boy took one step forward and then his knees gave way. He clutched at a tree.

The second boy swallowed his question. He was just about to ask how his little sister could have defended herself or escaped. Or whether Danny was putting Frank Bondy and little girls like his sister into the same category.

"Do you want to wear my cap for a while, Danny?" he asked. He glanced down at his shoes.

He was remembering Leonard. He could already piece together what had happened.

Leonard was Mother's youngest brother, born in 1900. Karel, her older brother, had been stoned to death in Moravska Trebova by the Nazis right after they moved into the Sudetenland. Because he owned a carpentry shop with a lathe.

Leonard was a sinewy machine operator and a bachelor, engaged for a long time to a Miss Gusta Glossova, who later gave her favors to the Germans after stealing Leonard's belongings, his watch and ring. That was before it was legal to steal.

In Birkenau, Leonard was saved by his raven-black hair, his tall, strong body, and by the fact that he knew how to work. He had the swarthy skin of a North African Jew, a prominent Jewish nose, and he could easily have passed for being fifteen years younger.

When Manny found Leonard in Auschwitz-Birkenau, his swarthy skin was wrinkled and his eyes were as sad as if he were already dead. His hands were like big shovels.

Once, during a blizzard which paralyzed the whole area, the foremen ordered the lights over the machines to be extinguished to save electric power. Leonard operated two lathes that made grenade heads. The blades were dull and needed changing. He lost a lot of time, honing the blades, so he had to hurry. He was careless and that was how he had got the splinter of steel in his finger.

He had sucked at it. The blood was mixed with machine oil. By evening, he'd forgotten about it.

Uncle Leonard had never been one of Manny's favorite relatives.

When he'd lived with them, he locked up his belongings, and Manny's father never liked to see anybody locking things in his home. Tools were something Leonard was particularly careful about. He never left them lying around and didn't like to lend them.

Once, when Manny and his little sister had wished him a happy birthday, Leonard gave a silver five-crown piece to the sister because Manny had been naughty. He promised he'd get one, too, when he learned how to behave.

But when they met in Birkenau, Leonard said blood is thicker than water, that they should stick together.

Three days later, Leonard's finger began to bother him. Within ten days, his whole right arm was infected, and he was taken to the infirmary.

His hand festered so fast, you could see it happen. The medical student-aide said it was gangrene and gave him a corner bed, but not much hope.

"When it turns black that way, you're at the end of your rope. Unless you let me amputate that arm of yours."

Leonard was in no position to know that the young man had never done an amputation before. Actually, he had, but never successfully.

The medic asked Leonard where he'd gotten his fine shoes. He was a handsome Polish youth with a pleasant little face that looked like it was made out of cottage cheese. He amputated whenever he had a chance. He was obsessed with knives. He cut off fingers, arms, and legs at every opportunity—and there were many. He cured everything with a file and a scalpel. He drank the alcohol he got from the German doctors, so he was usually drunk.

Leonard was left to lie in bed for several days until it was obvious what the Polish medic was after. Leonard's arm grew black from the fingertips up into the armpit. Then the medic knew the shoes were his.

The bandaged thing lying alongside Leonard was no longer his own hand. It stank so badly that Manny could hardly stand it when he visited his uncle's bedside. A boy from Ruthenia lay in the next bed, and the medic used to squeeze ounces of pus from his wounds every three hours, telling him he looked just like Jesus Christ. He would examine his hands as if he wanted to nail him on the wall of the infirmary like a symbol.

The Ruthenian boy couldn't stand the smell of Leonard's arm either, so he had to vomit over the other side of his bed.

The medic hated to bandage Leonard's rotting arm, so he didn't even bother. But Leonard didn't die. He fought with that blackened scrap of meat and bone as if he were really fighting with something else.

That was when the little blond Pole stopped giving Leonard his food rations. He'd already stopped giving them to the Ruthenian boy. So Leonard sent for Manny. He and Danny brought the old man some potato salad.

"Take my shoes," said Uncle Leonard. His voice sounded different than when he'd refused to give him the silver coin years ago.

"What would I do with your shoes?" said Manny. "I don't need two pairs of shoes."

"I'm not even going to need one pair."

"Didn't you hear the latest news? The war isn't supposed to last more than three months."

"Three months? Well, maybe. For you, it's morning. For me, it's midnight."

"Don't exaggerate." Manny tried not to breathe.

The boy from Ruthenia had died. Manny didn't want to look at him, so he had to look at Leonard. He didn't want to look too hungrily at his shoes, either. They were certainly good shoes.

"What'll you wear when you get up out of bed?" he asked his uncle. "You'll be feeling better when springtime comes." He swallowed hard. "They switched on the loudspeaker in the factory today. There's going to be a thaw. When they talk about the weather, they never tell lies."

"Springtime . . . ," murmured Leonard. It cost him an effort to speak.

"If you don't take the shoes, that son of a bitch is going to take them," Leonard went on. "You know, he hasn't given me anything to eat for three days?"

Manny knew that taking Leonard's shoes was like taking away the last pinch of life left in him. He didn't want to let him die before his last shadow of hope flickered out.

"I could have died this morning," Leonard whispered. "I didn't do it because I wanted you to come for the shoes."

"Aw, come on," said Manny. "I'll make sure they give you your food." The smell was turning his stomach, so he got up and went out to look for the blond medical student-amputator. He left the shoes standing next to Leonard's bed.

He found him going out the door, taking some food over to the women's camp. Manny told him what he thought of him and ordered him to give Leonard everything he had coming to him and said if he didn't do it, Manny wouldn't be responsible for the consequences.

The medic-amputator looked frail. Instead of answering, the little whey-face drove his fist, carnelian ring and all, into Manny's eye and knocked him down.

Leonard had told someone: "Life is a river. A river with electric current."

Before the twelve-hour shifts changed, somebody dragged the old man out of the infirmary to the wire fence. Leonard had asked for this. He succeeded on the third try, when it began to rain. It was enough to extinguish his almond eyes and the gangrene, too.

Those infirmary patients who could walk came to tell Manny what had happened. They told him, too, that the Polish medic was wearing Leonard's shoes. That night, Manny killed a man for the first time, even though he did it only in his mind. He killed him a hundred times that night. That was when he realized that a man is either born to kill or to let himself be killed. That was when he stopped living in the dream that the things which were happening were an exception.

He waited for daybreak. He lay on the roof with a stone in his hand and waited for the medical student to appear, for the door to creak. It was raining. He could almost hear the crunch of the young man's skull. He'd done it in his mind a thousand times.

But in the end, he didn't do it alone. It was raining, and they dragged the young Polish medic out into the rain. They didn't tell him what they were going to do. They took off his shoes and clothes and then threw him against the wire fence. He bounced back as if it were a net, so they had to push him back three times. He could have screamed but he didn't. He simply kept mumbling his name. His chin clamped down on the wire, which he clutched with his delicate hands.

The medical student died in the same place as Uncle Leonard had several hours before. They let him lie there. It looked like suicide. They collected his things and gave Leonard's shoes to Manny.

It was like a funeral for Uncle Leonard—the carrying out of vengeance and the execution of Leonard's last wish.

"Are you sure you don't want my cap?" Manny repeated.

"Forget it, Manny. . . ."

"My belly's swollen."

"Ahh. . . ."

"It feels heavy, like I've got a load of stones inside."

It began to rain, gently at first, and they soon got used to it. The first boy found a stick to lean on as he walked.

They went on through the rain, side by side, for almost an hour. They stopped when it came down so hard that they could barely see and stood under a tall pine tree with a thick trunk, a dense crown, and patches of moss around the roots. It protected them for a while, but then the wind shifted, and the rain came in at a slant. Afterward the wind turned again, but the branches still dripped.

They faced into the tree trunk. The water washed their faces and felt refreshing, running through their hair and over their necks and backs and bellies, inside their pants and into their shoes. It rinsed the wound on Danny's heel.

It felt as if somebody had turned a hose on them. They pressed closer to the tree trunk. The second boy covered his face with his hands and the other bowed his head until his chin touched the top of his chest.

The second boy took off his cap, because it didn't do any good. They were soaked to the skin. Defiantly, Manny turned his face into the rain. The first boy stood on one leg to relieve the pain, resting his knee against the tree trunk.

The second knelt, his forehead pressed to the bark. His neck glistened with water and his ragged clothing stuck to his body.

Finally the first boy slipped to his knees, too, and for a while he seemed to fall asleep. But it was raining too hard, pounding against the branches and into the earth, making a strange sound, as though this were a different world than the one they knew, part of some strange life where there was neither happiness nor unhappiness. A world without sun.

The rain came down heavier and heavier, lashing at them. Sometimes Manny opened his mouth like a fish, gulping air between the raindrops. Then he pressed his hands against his face and huddled against the tree again. The first boy clutched at the tree trunk as though he were embracing it.

Neither spoke. All you could hear was rain. It rained for almost two hours. Suddenly it stopped and the clouds began to shred apart. The sun came out. The sun lit up the forest. Its rays touched the tops of the fir trees and the branches of the bushes; they clung to the leaves and moss and old stumps. Everything looked different. A golden light lay over the shades of green, on the pine needles and stones, on the grass and tree bark, on the protruding roots—a light like crystals and bubbles. The pine needles and twigs swam in channels between the stones. Everything had changed. High in the sky, a rainbow reached like a bridge between a thousand islands of trees.

"I feel like fighting," said the second boy.

"I feel like drowning," answered the first.

"I wish Frank was here."

The birds began to sing. The sun didn't give off much warmth yet, but the water streamed down the tree trunks, finding channels, floating off the fallen twigs and leaves, flowing along the roots around the fallen log, soaking into the moss and earth.

"Yeah," said the first boy.

The air was steamy. Mist formed in the treetops, too, and the rainbow faded. Now and then a breeze ruffled the crowns of the trees, setting off brief showers below. The branches and bark glistened like snakeskin.

"It's early in the afternoon," said the second.

The first opened his lips but didn't speak. Maybe he's talking to the water, thought the second.

The woods surrounded them with something that couldn't be disturbed. The first boy scanned the sky.

"Do you think we'll be dry by evening?" asked the second. "Don't you want to wring your clothes out?"

The first boy slowly began to take off his wet clothes. His naked body was so skinny that his bones stuck out. He took off his shoes and unwound the rags he wore on his feet.

Suddenly the foamy silence of the forest was full of cawing crows and when the wind stopped for a while, you could hear the silence. The two boys were alone in the woods.

6

Toward evening they found a clearing with tall, thick grass, not far from where the rain had overtaken them. The crows seemed to be following them. They could hear them in the branches overhead, but they couldn't see them.

The first boy acted as if there was really nothing the matter with his foot. Manny figured he didn't want to look at it until they got to wherever they were going. He felt like water boiling away. It wasn't much different from what the Transylvanian guard had predicted.

It was a small clearing, shielded on all sides by trees and low bushes. At the edges lay uprooted pines and about a dozen stumps, overgrown with moss and toadstools. New saplings had sprouted between the roots and stalks of wildflowers, long since wilted.

At first, the sun set slowly, but then it sank fast, the way the rain had started and ended. The moon appeared in the darkening sky. But for a moment the night did not fall.

A dilapidated feeding shed stood in the grass at the other side of the clearing, opposite the stumps. Manny wondered what kind of animals came to feed here.

"Here," said the first boy.

"We can sleep over there." The second boy pointed to the shed. He sat down beside it and tried to extract some seeds from pine cones he found in the manger. They'd probably been put there for squirrels. But the squirrels had gotten there ahead of him, so all he got was a mouthful of pine needles which he couldn't manage to spit out.

The first boy sat down on the other side of the shed. He took off his right shoe first. He felt the other boy watching him. He ran his fingers through his toes, slowly removing all the pine needles and sand and mud. He groaned softly.

This is what he was scared of, thought Manny, lying with his head on a tuft of moss.

The first boy squinted into the shoe. It wasn't a very big tack. Actually, a lot smaller than he'd thought. He could hardly feel it with his thumb.

"Son of a bitch," he said.

"How big is it?"

"Too short to hammer out."

Manny said nothing.

"My foot's going to be infected by morning," Danny went on.

"So hammer it out!"

"Why didn't *you* do it?"

"You think I'd walk on a nail? Or maybe you think I knew it was there?"

"I've lived through everything else so far, so I'll live through a tack, no?"

Danny stretched out, too. For an hour, they were silent. Manny kept thinking that the first boy was probably convinced that he'd known there was a tack in there when he'd given him the shoes. Maybe it had been there, but Manny didn't know about it. It had probably worked its way out while they were walking. After all, Danny was taller and heavier than he was.

Maybe these shoes were good once, but they've brought bad luck to a lot of people since then, he said to himself.

"Remember how Frank Bondy used to say, 'Boys, you're still young, you believe what people tell you'?"

"It's almost better if you remember only what your Mama told you, Danny."

"She said, 'Eat, shit, drink water and you'll grow up to be a rich boy.'"

"I can't believe that anymore either."

The stars shone until midnight and then they disappeared. It was cold. They couldn't sleep. In the night, the trees looked like ghosts.

"Aren't you asleep?" asked the second boy.

"I'll hammer it out in the morning," said the first boy.

"Come closer."

"I'm cold, too."

"Can't you lie or sit closer to me?"

"I'll scrounge us up something to eat tomorrow," the first boy promised.

"I feel like I'm in a dream," said Manny. "I *am* and, at the same time, I'm not. Or as if I'm somebody else."

"You're running a fever, that's it."

"I am still awful cold."

"We're like two foxes. You look like a little fox, all curled up."

"It's as though I'm just visiting myself. It's funny. As if half of everything has nothing to do with me."

"Aw, shut up."

"I can see so many things, and all there is are these trees here, Danny—places, people, things that happened. Things I thought I'd forgotten about. Things I thought I hadn't even noticed."

"What things?"

"The kitchen at home, Danny. Freshly laundered shirts my moth-

er put away in the cupboard so I could help myself whenever I wanted to. An evening in December when she made biscuits. It smelled
so good, all through the house. Biscuits and a cup of milk, Danny."

"It makes my stomach ache, Manny."

". . . thousands of beautiful things and people, but they always
boil down to a few—biscuits, a cup of milk, clean shirts . . ."

Danny moved closer. "It's always spooky in the woods at night."

He leaned back against the shed. If it began to rain, the roof
wouldn't give much protection. The moon had shifted, covered by
scraps of cloud.

"It's a good thing it isn't raining," said the first boy. "The east
ought to be over in that direction."

"Yeah."

"In the morning, I'll find us something to eat."

"O.K."

"Now we've got to concentrate on food." He paused. "Are you
still having those visions of places and people, Manny?"

"Yeah."

"Maybe we can make fifteen or twenty miles. It's easier with this
stick." He paused. "It's a pretty good stick, but in the morning, I'll
take that other one over there by the shed. It's an oak branch."

"I'm so damned cold!"

"When we get to Prague, I'll buy us a stove, Manny, and we'll get
a good hot fire going inside . . . "

"My granddad used to sell stoves. Both my grandmothers had
tremendous imaginations. They could imagine practically anything."

"You probably take after them, Manny."

"I'm cold from underneath," the second boy said.

"The ground's still pretty cold."

"It has no end, just a hundred beginnings."

"It can't last much longer, Manny."

"Remember how Leonard used to look forward to the springtime?"

"I think you were the one that was looking forward. Sometimes
it's the opposite of what you really want. Like me, before I wised up
to that Hungarian rabbi. I couldn't get used to the idea that a rabbi
could look like he looked. But I was really trying to talk myself into

it. Actually, it wasn't the rabbi that mattered so much. It was me. I wanted to figure him out."

The second boy shifted around to find a more comfortable position. He stared at his fingers. That made him think of those people from Gleiwitz. They'd eaten their own fingers to start with—that was what Frank Bondy said, anyway.

The night melted into the wind and fog. You could hear the rustling of trees and grass and wild animals.

"I just noticed some branches over there by that stump, Danny."

"What good are branches, Manny?"

"We can cover ourselves with them."

"All right, drag them over. But I'm not getting up on account of a few dumb tree branches. You can't get any warmth out of cold wood."

The second boy dragged over a few that lay closest and piled them on top. The first boy could feel him shivering. They lay close, side by side, hidden under the branches. The forest made rushing noises, like waves.

The second boy was remembering when they had finished their first shift at the munitions factory. They were in the camp at Meuslowitz in southern Germany then, and they were allowed to take their first hot shower.

There was a mystery in bodies which made itself felt at certain times—moments they hadn't learned to anticipate. The mystery had to do with women, even if they were nowhere near, and also with each other. If they hadn't been so exhausted.

It was all the same, whether it was two boys' bodies or one, or if they were alone. All they had to do was think about a girl. One dark night, they were hiding in the barracks after their shower, and suddenly the darkness seemed even darker than usual. They held each other tight to keep warm. They were freshly bathed, and there was no need to shrink away from each other. For a few moments, something raged inside them both, a realization of what their bodies meant—beyond what they meant on the job or beyond the simple fact that they existed, the things they toyed with and didn't understand.

Danny had reached out his hand and touched Manny. Then he drew himself up in a ball. They were both naked. Manny lay there, curious to know what Danny would do next. Then Danny touched him with his mouth, as though he wanted to overpower all that darkness by meeting it halfway.

It was instinct which had darkened their minds, as though nothing else mattered. It was a combination of fear and hunger and desire.

By now they were exhausted. They were cold. Yet something had stirred inside him, reminding him fleetingly of that other time. They had slept afterward, a light sleep, like forgetfulness, only it was half forgetting and half remembering. In the morning, before they left for the factory, they acted as though it had all disappeared with the daylight. That was so they wouldn't have to be ashamed of themselves.

"Try to get some sleep, Manny, or we won't be worth a damn in the morning," the first boy said.

"My teeth are chattering." the other said.

"Forget it."

"You don't have as many teeth as I have, so they don't make so much noise."

"Forget it and go to sleep."

"I ache and itch all over."

"Don't be such a sissy."

"Danny, do you really think I knew about that tack?"

"Shut up, Manny, honest! Otherwise we won't be able to move in the morning. Forget it or we'll just exhaust ourselves and we'll die. If you start arguing about that tack, we can argue about a thousand other things."

"Are you scared?"

"Not of the dark or of the trees the way you are, Manny."

The first boy could feel how feverish he was. He warmed himself from the other boy's feverish body. He was drenched with sweat.

Manny tried imagining what it would be like if he set fire to the branches he'd piled on top of them. Or if somebody else did it, without even knowing they were hidden underneath.

"Do you think anybody'll survive this, Danny? Do you think anybody'll live to see the summer?"

"You and I will, Manny."

The woods at night, the sky and tree branching overhead, and the frost and mud below looked strange and beautiful and unreal. It was as if it had nothing to do with them. But it did. This was where they were. They were there alone, the way animals are alone and lost birds and trees and frost and stars. For a while he listened again to the sounds the woods made.

"Remember that German foreman who had three sons in the Luftwaffe and lost them all? He told me one time that I reminded him of the son who was killed over London. He'd gotten a diamond-studded ribbon for bravery. He crashed his Stuka into some cathedral."

"One of those jelly sandwiches he used to bring in his lunch bucket would taste pretty good right now," the first boy said.

"Sometimes he'd bring two sandwiches instead of one, remember?"

Manny got up to get another branch, but then he threw it away. "Sometimes I remember some of those Germans who made things easier for us than they would have been otherwise. Jews and Germans are really pretty close, when you come right down to it. Probably because we've spent such a lot of time together. Sometimes I really feel encouraged that there are some Germans who don't go along with all this. They run as many risks as Jews do."

"You said something different this morning."

"It always cuts both ways, Danny." He tried to relax his stiff muscles and find a more comfortable position.

He thought about all the food he and Danny had scrounged and shared. And the food they hadn't shared. He thought of all the people who were hiding out tonight in other forests, somewhere else. Under the clouds and other stars, where the moon had a different shape. That brought his mind back to Frank Bondy.

"Sometimes I feel I am robbing and stripping other people when I think about them. You know what I mean?"

"Once we get there, I'm going to forget everything that's happened, Danny. And I'll kick anybody in the pants if they try to remind me."

"I'll remind you then. I'll sing you some Nazi songs."

"Things could be worse, Danny. The two of us know things could be a damned sight worse."

"You get over everything in time. You know what time does, as Frank used to say."

"For God's sake, aren't you going to sleep?"

"I don't know. I can't."

"Don't think about anything. Not even about Frank, Manny. I've already crossed Frank Bondy off my list for good. You've got a fever, but you'll be over it by morning. You're like a cat. We both are."

"I wouldn't even mind lying under a locomotive. I tried it once, Danny, at the ramp in Meuslowitz. The worst part is the leaking steam."

"We'll start on our way as soon as the sun comes up, Manny."

Lying under a locomotive is better than dragging around rolls of sheet metal in the wintertime, Manny was thinking. Somebody always had to help him with the loads he couldn't manage.

"Do you remember that redheaded *pipl*, Manny?"

"Vaguely." He knew what Danny was going to say now.

"Remember when that little cherub asked me for some vaseline? He heard the people from the Czech transports might have some and he asked me to get some for him, said he'd give me as much bread and salami as I wanted the next Thursday."

"He just had a high opinion of Czech Jews, Danny. And he was pretty sure you still didn't know the difference between not having anything for supper *before* supper and afterward. I also recall that you never saw any sign of that salami."

"And I went to a lot of trouble getting him that vaseline. At that time I didn't know there was practically *nothing* you couldn't get there. Like in any big seaport. I saw things I'd never seen or even heard of."

"Frank was the one who gave you the vaseline, I remember that much."

"He gave it to me because otherwise I'd have pinched it anyway."

"Skip it, Danny. Forget it."

"That kid wanted me to get him some more boys. He wanted me to do it, too. He wanted me to do his recruiting. He had it all figured out. He was a smart little cookie. Later, Frank took him under his wing. He said it was nothing to be proud of, but that you shouldn't kick a man when he's down."

"Hell, Danny, I'm so cold I can't fall asleep!"

"That redheaded kid was always so hungry, remember, Manny? Just like us, only different. He couldn't believe he'd last as long as the other *pipls*. He didn't have parents anymore. But while they were alive, they were glad he was a *pipl*. He was jealous of other boys. He was always worried about losing his looks, that he wasn't as cute and plump as when that German kapo picked him out. The kapo was in Birkenau on a murder charge. He'd been in jail before that, but since December 1933 he'd been kept in camps. He only kept his *pipls* until they were fifteen years old. When they reached puberty, he got rid of them. He couldn't stand hearing their voices crack. But that red-headed kid acted as if he didn't know that he and the rest of his kapo's harem were eating up our food rations. He brought other boys around as substitutes."

"Don't tell me you're feeling sorry for him, Danny?"

"Not one bit. I'm just saying that I can still remember how scared he was of getting skinny and ugly, being all skin and bones, or else getting too fat, that his ass would get too round or else it'd shrivel up. Then he was sure his old convict lover would let him go up the chimney one fine day at selection time."

"I hope that's what finally happened to him. How would that kid have gotten along in normal life?"

"He wanted to be irreplaceable. He wanted to be wanted. But he knew he wouldn't be if he went around sticking out his cute little fanny all the time or his sweet little mouth for that old convict, day after day."

"I know why he wanted to recruit other boys, and I know why you're telling me about it, too. You don't have to remind me there are worse places to be than a cold, windy forest at night."

"Better or worse," the first boy went on. "At first I thought the same rules applied everywhere."

"The two of us are different. You and me. We're better."

"Maybe. Sometimes."

"Maybe he really wasn't a faggot, Danny."

"He got sent to camp just like you and me. The only way he ever saw a girl was on the other side of the barbed wire. The kapo wangled him out of the showers after the first selection, when his parents got reprieved. He went into the gas chamber, but because he was such a little kid and people were squeezed in so tight, the cyklon gas didn't filter down to him. That was when the kapo noticed him. They were clouting the little kids who didn't get gassed, so they could shove in another batch of people. That kid was lucky. He used to like to tell me about it. Maybe he wanted me to feel sorry for him. Maybe he was just bragging, though."

"We were older when they took us, and we were lucky we were as strong as we were and that we were trained machinists. And that the kapo had a weakness for little red-haired boys."

"The kid told me what he needed that vaseline for. Apparently it doesn't hurt as much that way. But I never got one bite of salami from him. So I told him he was getting fat, that he was eating too much, just to worry him."

The second boy knew what was coming next. "You already told me how you hit him, Danny."

"Afterward, I was scared to go back to the barracks for fear that kapo of his would come looking for me to get even."

"You already told me about it, but not in such detail. I thought the past was dead for you."

"It's not as dead as I wish it were. A lot of things are, though. I probably wanted to get this off my chest, and that's why it keeps coming back." He stopped. "The kid went to the gas ovens on account of me."

"He had it coming to him, Danny."

"He wasn't so cute-looking with no teeth. He knocked out my three front teeth after I'd already knocked out his. But looking back, I still feel responsible. "

"You don't have many teeth either."

"But I'll have a new set made, Manny."

"That little redhead didn't have to be a *pipl*. And he should have given you that salami when he promised it. I don't think you need to feel responsible, Danny."

"I'm not too proud of myself."

"And you say *I'm* finicky."

"I have a feeling a lot of those little *pipls* won't live through this."

"Forget it," advised the second boy. "The more you talk about it, the deeper into it you sink."

The forest around them smelled of the coming spring. It was the smell of pitch which had been penetrated by resin. It still bore the marks of winter and the touch of the sun around noon. Life was returning to the still sleeping forest. In several days and nights, the forest will change, it will no longer be so damp, so cold.

"I think that heel of mine's begun to fester," the first boy said.

"If you let it alone, it'll clear up by morning."

"We're lucky nobody ever took it into his head to make us *pipls*, Manny."

"If I wasn't so cold and hungry, I probably wouldn't feel so bad right now."

7

They huddled close. It seemed as though the branches under which they lay were drawing off their body warmth.

"Frank used to remember things that never happened," the second boy remarked.

"I can remember forwards as well as backwards."

"Remember me telling you how my dad was in the Italian Dolomites during the First World War? He said the days were beautiful, too, but that it was freezing cold at night. Now I can believe him. There are a lot of things I believe only now, Danny, when people who told me about them are dead and gone. My dad brought back a mandolin from Italy. He paid a few pennies for it. The Germans took it."

"I often think about that little Hungarian rabbi. He lost twenty-five pounds in two weeks. His clothes were so big for him he was scared they'd send him into the gas chamber. One time, while they were busy shooting Russians, they shoved us all in the barracks, pushing us right into the corners. The rabbi held on to me as if I was his own son. Then he started preaching to me."

"Danny, you know you were just talking when you told me everything's gone dead inside you."

"No, I wasn't just talking."

"So if it's dead, bury it all. At least on such a damn cold night. I'm dead tired."

"You were at the Buna Werke when that happened. I was with the little rabbi day and night. He used to tell me that God is the killer of little children. He wanted me to believe there's no God, that they'd done plastic surgery on him, that he's really the devil or a lunatic, at least, that it's all a fraud. He made me watch German soldiers selecting people to go into the gas chambers. Or watch at the family camp where parents would push their children ahead and where you saw sons hiding behind their fathers or a daughter behind her mother. Just so they wouldn't be the ones that got picked out. The rabbi wanted me to see how God splits one person away from another, making people into strangers, making them hate each other. But God does it so that it looks like people do it of their own accord. God's testing us, he said, and we can resist. The worst part was that that little rabbi reminded me of my father after he went up the chimney. Like a smudge of soot. Then, Manny, that rabbi stole my bread ration!"

"If it wasn't so cold you'd never have thought about it. If you were feeling better, you wouldn't think about all those things. When that little rabbi stole your bread, he wasn't a rabbi anymore, he was just another madman."

The worst night was that time in September when his father went up the chimney. He was alone. He dreamed of Allied aircraft which would drop their bombs right into his bunk so that it would be clear, as clear as the clearest things: the alternation of day and night, the blowing wind, ice and snow. It was almost beautiful to imagine how a person would perish in a hundredth of a second, under the glowing core of the bomb.

"I used to know a couple of gay cafés and baths in Prague. Do you suppose they're still there?"

"When we get that far and we're on our own, we can take the same name, Danny, what do you say? Like brothers. I'd like to be a pilot or drive a racing car. How about you? You said you would, too."

The first boy pressed closer. They listened to the rustling of the forest. It came in waves, enfolding the night and the two of them and everything else that was left over and other things which weren't there anymore.

"Remember that other German guard in the train when we hadn't had anything to eat for three days? And how he told us a person is what he eats? He didn't just invent that, either."

"A person is everything. Also what he doesn't eat," Manny said.

He realized that the two of them probably looked like a pair of crippled birds by now. And that the simplest thing of all would be to give themselves up. It was both good and bad that they were so alone, on the very fringe of existence, torn loose from everything else, so they could concentrate not only on their fight against exhaustion, but also against fear.

"It's dark here," Manny said after a little while. But he was thinking about something else.

They'd always be able to remember what it felt like to be cold and thirsty and hungry and scared. What warmth means and a roof over your head. A bed. A cup and plate and spoon. What it means, not being afraid of people or animals. Or the fact that we're all born of different mothers. For him, right now, looking backward was a way of looking forward.

He was walking Manya Cernovska home. She looked almost the same as she had three years ago. She told him how his parents' apartment had been confiscated as soon as they'd left. With everything in it. "They worked out a marvelous technique for taking over Jewish property," she told him. "For instance, after you left, they authorized dances to be held, but for Jewish young people only. Apparently that was so nobody abroad could claim there was something wrong going on here. Then the Germans would come to these dances, with their wives and girlfriends, just so they could pick out whatever they liked that the Jewish boys and girls were wearing. It was like a fashion show. You can be sure your girls put on their best clothes, and those German cows took their pick, even if they didn't usually confiscate the stuff immediately. Unless they were very impatient. They waited until the next day, and then they did it according to a list that had all the necessary rubber stamps. That's how orderly the Germans are—scarves, brooches, rings or coats, evening skirts, blouses, elbow-length gloves—the kind you wear to dancing school—slippers, the sort of thing a girl is proud of, that makes her feel feminine."

"So they stole everything, then." He smiled and shrugged, as if there was no use talking about it.

"They used different words," she explained. "They said 'requisition' instead of 'steal.' Like turning your silk stockings inside out at night to air them."

"They stole away the meaning words used to have. It's like learning a whole new language in a strange new world. As if you can teach people

to get used to anything—that you are and at the same time, you aren't; that you exist, and, at the same time, you don't; that you're lying and telling the truth all together. I feel like I've come back from some other planet."

"If it were up to me I'd put them in a zoo, instead of all the vultures and hyenas," Cernovska said.

Afterward, they spoke of pleasanter things. "That camel's-hair jacket with the darts at the side is very becoming on you, Manny," she told him. "We ought to go out together more often. Can you imagine how lonely I used to be at the pool without you? Manny, listen, what happened to your mother?"

He smiled gently, "Don't ask me that."

"And your dad? And your little sister Anna?"

"They killed them."

"It's a miracle they didn't kill you, too, Manny. Sometimes I wonder why you didn't kill them back. So that every one of your people that got killed would take at least one of them along with him."

"I don't know the answer. Maybe because nobody taught my little sister in time how to kill somebody when you don't want them to kill you back. It's different with grown-ups. The best of us did fight back. Some of them are engraved in my memory. They considered it their first right to defend themselves and their consciences, too. Conscience is like your heart—you can't carve off a piece and expect the rest to function like before. For every one dead German, the Nazis killed not ten, not a hundred, not a thousand, not even ten thousand, but a hundred thousand of our people. Old folks, men, women, and children. Once the final bill is added up, and when you take into account all the extenuating circumstances—and they won't be flattering for all the Nazis' friends or enemies—there are going to be a lot of folks who will have paid back what they got or who will have hung onto what was taken from them. I'm not just referring to those scarves and brooches, either."

"That jacket really looks good on you, Manny. Look, let's talk about something else, O.K.?"

"There was a lot I didn't know before, Manny. That's understandable. But there's a lot that can't be explained. I got to know some wonderful people. Better than I am, but not as lucky as me and Danny and Frank Bondy. The people who stuck it out the best were the ones who never really believed in anything that might have just confused them. The kind of people who take things as they come."

He'd forgotten how Frank used to say that things happened the way they did because there were such a lot of fools among us.

"Do you think anybody could come along now and say, 'Hey, Manny, take off that camel's-hair jacket!' Do you think you could ever go back to camp? Very few people believed you'd ever come back. Some of them didn't even want you to. Not because they wished anything bad for you, but because, if you did come back, their conscience would bother them."

"Danny, remember that morning in Poland before they put us on the transport for Germany?"

"Sure."

"We'd been in Auschwitz-Birkenau for almost a month."

"Yeah, well, so what?"

"We practically didn't know a thing about what was going on. In some ways it's good not to know. The more you know, the worse it is. You know what I mean? It was a beautiful sunny day. Nice and warm. That was the twenty-sixth day of the twenty-eight we spent there. We left on the twenty-eighth, remember? That was a beautiful day, too. The days that were most important for us were always beautiful."

"I remember what the weather was like, but I don't remember much about the rest of it. I already told you that."

"It was on the twenty-sixth that the uprising started in the *Sonderkommando* in Crematorium Number 4."

"Well, I remember that, because all that day they shot at anybody who stepped out on the *appell-platz*. A lot more people got killed than just those Germans the folks in the *Sonderkommando* managed to kill."

"They blew up Oven Number 4. That was tremendous. Nobody got burned in that oven anymore. Remember how tremendous it was? They even wrecked part of Oven 2 and Oven 3, according to what those Slovak prisoners told us afterwards. Apparently they'd mined it quite awhile before. They got the dynamite and fuse rope from those women in the FKL who were finally hanged. They were waiting for the signal for some general mutiny. But nobody from the rest joined in the *Sonderkommando*. Everybody staged his own individual uprising. They were scared it would turn into a massacre. But if the people had joined in the *Sonderkommando*, the two of us probably wouldn't have left and we wouldn't be here. It's funny, isn't it, how everything is connected with everything else? And how a chance accident that kills one person can save your life?"

"I'm surprised you feel like talking about it."

"I do because it lasted such a short time. And because it was so wonderful. I simply couldn't believe it was possible for somebody to do something like that. They stretched wires charged with electricity so as many people as possible could escape. But they were caught by the barbed wire and were shot like rag dolls. In the crossfire of three machine guns."

"They knew they'd be transferred the next day and be killed."

"Anyway . . . "

"It only took eleven minutes in Treblinka, according to what Frank found out from those Polish prisoners. And they'd been preparing it for years. Some uprisings only lasted a matter of minutes. It must be beautiful, a minute like that."

"The thing that Danish Jew did in the Little Fortress at Theresienstadt probably didn't take more than half a minute."

"I remember him. That was beautiful, too."

"Depends on what you mean by beautiful."

"It isn't just a matter of time. But time does play a certain role." What got you started on that?"

"Because we've been on our way for such a long time."

"It hasn't been such a long time, Manny."

"The fact that we've been on our way for so long on our own must mean something. Know what I have in mind?"

"I couldn't care less."

"You don't know what I'm trying to say?"

"No."

"It'd be good if tomorrow turned out to be a nice sunny day."

"Maybe it will."

The second boy said no more. He knew he wouldn't get warm by morning.

They warmed themselves some nights, when they were working on the coal commando in Auschwitz-Birkenau, at the far wall of the crematorium.

The wall they worked beside was almost constantly warm. They could warm themselves by it only at night and, at most, for just a few minutes. Sometimes Manny pressed his cheek against the wall, then his chest, his thighs, belly, his whole body. Behind the wall the fire roared, sounding as if some dead sun were burning there. Sometimes the two boys stood side by side, keeping warm. That was really the only benefit they gained from being in the coal commando—warm red bricks. They didn't have to speak. It was as if they had stolen the warmth. They knew they would be sorry if the wall got cold. And they knew there was only one reason why it never grew cold.

"If I had a few matches, I'd light up this whole forest," he whispered.

"Then I'm glad you haven't got any," replied the first. "Who wants to get burned?"

"To warm up," said the second.

"We'll warm up once we start walking."

"All the same, I'd like to light a match to it."

"Don't be crazy."

"For five minutes."

"Please, would you talk about something else?"

"Do you remember the last selection?"

He thought about that father and his two sons. They stayed together for three weeks. And then when the first son started to get so horribly skinny, the father told him suddenly that they might not be staying together. He felt it in his bones, that because the Germans were going to be making a third selection, the three of them should separate. At least for a few days, until the first son got through it. "You want me to go to the ovens?" the son asked. And the father in reply asked, "Do you want us all to go there?" So they remained alone. Many people were separated by fear. People were afraid to be together.

Then they had nothing more to lean on. The first and last—children, mother, father could change from being a support into a dead weight.

"Are you trying to make me mad?" demanded the first boy.

The second one was silent. *Suddenly, inside his head, he heard the bombs start falling. The sun, in eclipse, cast a silver, aluminum light. The roaring of the B-17's was everywhere, like an echo. Like the time when he and Danny had been working in that munitions plant outside Dresden.*

The woods retreated. He was imagining what would come. He was picking through it as one picks through peas or weeds or removes the bones from a cooked fish. Yesterday—at least some yesterdays—and tomorrow—any tomorrow filled in and discarded words. The force with which he imagined that—discounting his legs, hands and fingers, eyes, ears and caution—was his last strength. It occurred to him that memory was a better companion than Danny; also, than quiet, distance, dampness, than the forest at night with its soggy, sticky earth and sharp branches. Some yesterdays are still alive, at least a piece of them, even though forgetfulness—hunger or fear—have gobbled them up. Perhaps even this—now—will be yesterday. He played with the words tomorrow—yesterday. A step, another step. Tomorrow yesterday. A step. Yesterday, a step, tomorrow.

The first thing he and Danny did when the air raid started, was to open the foreman's locker and swipe two pairs of overalls, one clean, the other ready to be sent to the laundry.

The assistant foreman wore a black coat with a swastika on the lapels and he saw them do it. They knew he carried a pistol under his coat, even before he reached for it.

Danny had learned to judge people. Like an animal in the jungle who can recognize what's dangerous and what isn't.

He was holding a revolver, but Danny was already running with the overalls and Danny behind him. They ran into the next building as the sixty-second sirens started, signalling a top emergency air raid. An enemy squadron had been spotted over Leipzig-Dresden, and the assistant foreman had other things to do than to chase two pairs of stolen overalls.

The earth and air were filled with the noise of explosions. The factory was directly hit. There was earth and water and air and people—everything was filled with fear. People and houses and streets were aflame and even the Elbe River was on fire. Hardly any place was safe. Nevertheless, people stampeded toward the river, and so did the two of them.

Besides bombs, the planes had dropped some kind of incendiary stuff which couldn't be extinguished. Nobody had ever seen anything like it. It made even asphalt and water burn. Houses burst into flame from top to bottom. Phosphorescent fires could be put out with sand, but the Germans would have needed a whole Sahara, plus twelve million more prisoners, to put out all those fires.

They watched rabbit hutches floating down the Elbe, sinking slowly, full of live rabbits.

There were thousands of people and there were probably ten times that many huddled in the fields along the riverbank. Then the aluminum bombers started to come back.

Now, in the darkness of the forest, he could still see those rabbits with their little pink eyes, drowning in the Elbe. The beautiful explosions began again, and then melted into the rustling of the forest.

Frank Bondy said he guessed the Germans had learned their lesson now. Some things are like hospitals: as long as you don't need them, you couldn't care less, but just as soon as you did, anxiety grabbed you. "Like that famous novelist always writes about," Frank recalled. "You know the one I mean, boys."

They didn't, just as they didn't know what he was talking about when he said, "The Jews will lose as long as they're acrobats, the way they've always been so far, capable of turning a defeat into its opposite, making a virtue of necessity instead of wiping out their enemies for a change. Victory is just as much of a long-term thing as defeat. You've got to cultivate both for at least three hundred years—like an English lawn or all the tears that flowed in Bohemia after the battle of the White Mountain."

"You know when I was one hundred percent wrong, boys?" Frank went on. "When I said I was done with making do, with what's just temporary."

The people from Kohen's bunch, said Frank, didn't make much sense. He was locked into an invisible circle made up of all his memories of past sins and satisfactions, which improved in retrospect. In jest, he once said that under normal circumstances a baker making buns in Prague is just as useful as a businessman in New York City with all his stocks and bonds. "What do you suppose makes the biggest fools out of people?" he demanded. "You can have three guesses." He never gave the answer. That was one of many things he only hinted at.

Then a lot of children, women, and men also burned to ashes— though never as many as in Auschwitz—and Frank counted himself among those who had wished it on them. Maybe it looked different,

*watching it from behind camp wires, than from Berlin or from the
bombers. Maybe it looked more elegant from above. But only those who
were risking their necks by flying here really knew whether it was just
and fair or not—and those who were behind the camp wires and who,
every day and every second for the past three years, had been in the shoes
of the people who were on fire down there. Maybe the ones who had
started it all and who were now on fire, too, ought to have known to
begin with what was fair and what wasn't.*

Bombs, Frank's maxims, the flaming river, and the drowning rabbits
with their pink eyes—they all floated up through the murmuring
treetops.

8

He felt like he was lying on a wet anthill. He didn't know whether
he'd been asleep or not. Danny was holding onto him with two
hands, the way a baby clings to its mother, breathing close against
his cheek. His left leg was bent.

"What time do you suppose it is?" whispered the second boy.

"I don't know. It's not morning yet," the first boy mumbled
drowsily. "You can't see the stars."

"You said we'd get an early start, Danny."

"We'd bump into trees when it's as dark as this. We'd just get lost."

"I rested a little bit."

"Yesterday really did us in. It's cold. And awfully damp."

"When it's dark I have all sorts of funny visions."

Slowly the sky turned grey as day began. The first boy pushed
aside the branches they were covered with.

"The visions have gone. I saw them all, though, real close this
time."

"How's the fever, Manny?"

"All I need to do is lie down and close my eyes and I see them. I
can cope with it better in daytime. If I lie down, it all passes in front
of my eyes."

"It's not just your imagination, Manny. That's normal. That's the
way it is. You can bet your neck on that."

"Or my feet."

"But not both. Someday you're bound to strike it lucky."

"It's getting light."

"It doesn't look as if it's going to rain."

"How come I never see you cry, Danny? Don't you ever cry?"

"Do you really want to know, Manny?" He paused. "When we went to the transport, my dad was working on a Jewish construction team, building barracks for the SS in Prague. My mother and sister and I had to go on ahead to Theresienstadt. They promised they weren't going to split up families. That was the first time I ever saw my dad cry. He was scared he'd never see us again. And it was too late to do anything about it. Except we could have all gone into the kitchen and turned on the gas. He told Mother to look after us, then he hugged her and kissed us kids. He stayed on in our old apartment. Some of the lady neighbors were probably pleased he was by himself. Then the apartment was confiscated. We were finally reunited, but then they separated us again. it would have been better if he hadn't cried that time."

"People remember some things for a long time."

"Dad was like a god to me for years. Then he just watched us go away, and suddenly it stopped for me. I was surprised he could let us go like that."

Frank wanted them to fetch a blanket or a piece of canvas from the factory for that Polish girl, so he could give it to her and she could protect herself against the winter. They told him it was out of the question. He told them that basically it all boils down to wanting to enough. He had four rules: First, you fight because you want to win. Second, you realize you can't win, but you keep on fighting anyway because it's important not to give in. Third, you fight from habit, because you've been taught to; you're used to it and it's expected of you. Fourth, if you don't put up a fight, you're lost.

Finally they found him an old burlap bag which he presented to her as if he were holding a bridal train.

"Those Transcarpathians felt sorry for Frank. As if they knew he'd cave in before it was all over."

"They thought they were immortal, just like Frank did, because they all believed in the same things. But if Frank died along with them, maybe they really *are* immortal now, huh, Danny?"

"The guards probably shot them fast and didn't even bother to haul them off to make soap out of."

The second boy said nothing.

"Sometimes Frank acted like a little god. Like my dad. I was just waiting for him to crack up, though. With all those superstitions of his."

Now the second boy didn't even answer. As if the attack on Frank Bondy had actually been directed against him. He could imagine why, and yet, at the same time, he couldn't imagine everything. More than anything else, Danny always depended on his own strength, his own will, and his own luck. When one of these failed him—in the night, in the wound in his heel—he wanted to patch things up with Frank before they started going again, even though Frank might already be dead.

"He was like a submarine. When a possibility emerged, he came to the surface to show what he knew. If the goal faded, he went down under the water, again, but never for very long. He just waited for another chance."

Danny paused. "His hopes were like a submarine, too. He thought some miracle would happen, and in the end everything would be O.K."

The second boy didn't answer.

He and Danny had been hauling coal for the kitchen. All six crematoria were processing the transports from Galicia and Transylvania. So the pressure on the rest of the camp had eased up for a few months.

A high-ranking commissar from Berlin had come to visit the camp commander. Twice a day, he made his welcoming speech: "Go take a bath, Jews. I know how you feel, I know what you've missed most on your way here. After all, we're only human, too. I promise you the water will be nice and warm. We don't want to deprive you of comforts you're accustomed to. Undress quickly. You're among soldiers here, this is not a health resort. We expect all of you to work. You can't wage a war without discipline, and we want to win. We'll be able to get along with anybody who understands that. But we also know what to do with anybody who refuses to understand. Save water. Turn on the water, soap up, stop the water again and only then rinse yourself off. Someone else's turn will come after yours and they want to get just what you did. Now then: women separately to my right, men to my left. Children under fourteen and men and women over forty remain in the middle. Each person is to hang his belongings on one single hook. Shoes and whatever you have in your pockets are to be neatly arranged under your clothes hook so there will be no mix-up when you come back. Today, as an exception, towels will be handed out after you finish bathing. Also, the delivery of soap has not arrived yet. Therefore you're getting one bar of soap for every four people. I apologize for that. But the water's nice and warm. The boilers are heated up. Now then, you have two minutes. . . . "

Everything ran smoothly. Mothers and fathers, their children, and other groups urged on each other. The dressing rooms were separated by a high lattice.

A tall commissar and his escort stepped over to the round window that was set in the open door of the shower rooms, like a porthole on a boat. In front of him was a devout man from the East, with his wife and seven children.

"That man is the epitome of everything Jews like that believe in."

The tall commissar merely nodded.

"It's part of their belief, which apparently cannot be extinguished by gas or burned away by fire," the commander added. "They believe smoke comes out of his nose and flames from his mouth. Actually, they might be right in a few minutes."

The devout man had three black-haired sons and four red-haired daughters. They were shaven now. The man's beard had not been cut off. Otherwise, all of them were naked and shorn. The youngest held the soap in his hands and looked it over as if he had never held such a porous cake of soap in his life, with UVA-DU and a number stamped distinctly on it.

The old folks behind them were their parents and grandparents. They looked down because they were ashamed.

The bearded man was silent. Then he uttered a single word. It was inaudible from the outside.

"The thing they fear most about gassing," the commander went on, "is that we'll separate them from the members of their families. And so in most cases, we leave them together. They think if they remain together, things won't go to extremes. As long as they remain together, the notion of a final solution simply escapes them. And then, when it dawns on *some of them, they're glad that at least they're all together and that the final solution is fairly shared among them. Every family unit is like a ship that's going to the bottom and, to start with, everybody on board encourages everybody else that they won't necessarily drown, and even if they do, at least they'll all perish. As though that really made things any easier."*

The commander was sharing his observations with the tall commissar without knowing he could be heard on the other side of the wall.

"With transports of whole families, the liquidation process moves much quicker than with transports composed of more heterogeneous units. They probably believe families have some special protective powers. It's enough to keep them together, and they're in no condition to believe that this is the last stage in the final solution. It's enough, a day or two before the final solution, to give them—at the expense of the ones who are still living—an extra slice of bread or salami, a change of underwear, to let them sleep a little longer, or to order the medic to give them some vitamin C, and they see this as a total confirmation of their belief that they'll soon be going back to where they came from. They never believe we want to kill them. They aren't capable of understanding this. Finally, they don't even believe what gets whispered around within their own ranks. And every day, every hour we let them live, every slice of bread, every bowl of porridge, every shoelace and stitch of underwear we give them induces them to believe something other than what is really waiting for them. They come here like sheep, with only a few exceptions. A kind word does more than army units whose weapons we can make better use of on other fronts."

Now both of them started into the chambers. Some of them inside were praying. The smallest were clamoring that they didn't want to die, as though they were confronting the final solution for the first time. It looked ridiculous from the outside, the foolish way they clung to life, from the youngest to the oldest.

For five minutes, the first boy tried to hammer out the tack with a stone. Then he inspected his festering heel. Finally he stretched. Both boys were stiff after lying all night on the hard ground under the rough branches.

"I feel like I haven't slept more than a second," Manny said.

9

The first boy got up slowly. He could feel a sticky pain in his foot which he had not felt when he was lying down, and it was worse than the day before.

Snow still lay in the sheltered parts of the woods. That afternoon they didn't say a word about the weather. After a few hours, the tip of the tack had worked itself through again. Perhaps the heel was so worn down, or the leather so soft, that the tack would come through again and again.

Danny was playing hide and seek with the pain in his foot. The pain had shades.

The stick he'd picked up in the feeding shelter helped him. The woods looked different in the silence, without the rain. He leaned on both sticks.

And then the other said, "Remember that strong Slovak from the *Sonderkommando* and how that friend of his told him they were going to send his mother to the gas the next day, and couldn't he do something for her? And how he told him, 'We all have mothers'? In other words, he was telling him everybody had a mother, not only him. And the other guy just kept looking at him, so the strong Slovak said, 'If you look at me that way one more time, I'm going to take a piece of iron and hit you over the head with it so you won't ever look at anybody that way again. Where do you think we are? What do you think I can do? I wasn't able to do anything even for my own mother, and the only thing my friends did for me was to put me on the second shift. And lock me up in the storeroom. Do you want me to do that to you? When are they taking her?' And that friend of his told him the selection was supposed to be the next morning. Finally the Slovak offered to do the only thing he could think of for his friend. 'Do you want me to get you into the showers along with her? That's really all I can do for you.' And he was surprised to discover that he probably would have been glad if anybody had made him that offer when his own mother had been gassed."

"The strangest things always stick in your mind, Manny."

"What's strange about it?"

"Why do you keep looking back? Why do you always keep turning around and looking back, Manny? A person'd think you don't believe in where we're going."

"That's just it, I do believe in it. When I turn around and look back, it's like I'm saying to everything, 'so long, everything—now I know about you, but in a couple days or in a week from now, I'm starting a new life and I'm going to want to start it without you.'"

"I don't suppose those things you're talking about could care less."

"But it's a fact, all kinds of stuff keeps coming into my head, things that are perverted and normal all at the same time."

"I'm thinking about the clothes I'm going to buy when we get to Prague, Manny. And the shoes."

"I like thinking about that too, Danny."

"I've got an imagination like a girl, Manny."

"Me too. I know a couple shops in the Sterba Arcade. And on Perlova Street. I know just where they sell all kinds of good-looking clothes."

"Don't forget to get deloused before you try on all those good-looking clothes."

"I never knew how many times a person had to get deloused," the second boy said.

He was so tired by now that he didn't feel like thinking over all the reasons the other boy didn't talk about the pain in his foot.

He remembered something Frank had said once, when they had caught him telling some little white lie that nobody even minded anymore. "What are we supposed to do," he said, "when we live in a world where even our best friends lie because everybody lies and lying is part of a person's character, just as it was once the thing to do to tell the truth?" And he'd smiled gently and sadly and at least his lies didn't seem so crude. Like when people knew what was going to happen to somebody, but they told him, "Hi, how are you?" or "We'll see you this evening," even when they all knew they'd never see each other again. And it wasn't only in front of the shower room or on the ramp at the station or on the way from one camp to another.

They'd learned it in the German camps but, as Frank said, there had been some important prerequisites for it even before. It was the same thing with cowardice as it was with lying and with a whole lot of other things.

Danny acted as if the cards were rigged, so he simply wasn't going to play the game, even though a lot of other people were playing and maybe that was why they all used to stick up for Danny before. Manny remembered that there was a time when they'd stick up for him, too, a little, for the same reason. Was that why Frank had befriended the two of them?

Then they finally learned that the best thing was to adjust to whatever it is that pains you because there were always other sides to it, like everything else.

So Danny simply didn't talk about the nail in his shoe, as if talking about it and about the wound in his heel might kill him.

Most of the way was downhill. Yesterday, it had been uphill. The second stick was an encumbrance, so Danny tossed it away and leaned on the other, using it like a crutch.

Occasionally the second boy would look up into the treetops. He was thinking about birds' nests and eggs. March is too early for birds' eggs.

There were old cobwebs hanging from the lower branches of the trees, ragged from the rain and snow and wind. Dead cobwebs.

Later that afternoon, a fox ran across their path. The sky grew overcast. The edge of the forest kept disappearing before them. The goal they had set for themselves got farther away the closer they got.

"I can't see the sun anymore," the second boy said.

"We're headed east. West is over there."

"We'd save ourselves a lot of detours if we were on a road."

"That depends on where we are, Manny. We're still deep inside German territory."

"This slows us down, having to climb all the time."

"Look, I can assure you that I'm not exactly in love with these woods either."

"If we were on a road, we could hitch a ride on a wagon that was going in our direction."

"You're beginning to smell pretty bad," the first boy said, changing the subject.

"Prague . . . " the second boy mused. "How far away do you think it is?"

"As my mother used to say, ask me no questions, I'll tell you no lies."

"Do you want to keep going till it gets dark, Danny?"

"We'll go just a little farther."

"How far? It's dark already."

"At least to the top of the hill in front of us, Manny, O.K.?"

They plodded grimly on, side by side. The first boy was limping badly.

"Don't you feel well?" asked the second boy.

He was obviously afraid of an answer; yet he expected it.

"No," the first boy replied.

"Are you sure moss grows on the north side of the tree trunks?"

"The wind whistles like a tea kettle, huh, Manny?"

"I've got belly cramps."

"I had the same thing yesterday."

"My eyes are swelling up."

"Just this one last hill and that's it for today, Manny."

"The sun's set already. There's no sense going on."

"Those are hunger cramps. It's nothing serious."

"You mean I'm being a sissy?"

"Among other things."

"How far have we come today?"

"I didn't keep count."

"What were you counting, then?"

"Steps."

"You want to keep going in the dark, Danny? I'm one big bruise."

"You and me both, Manny."

"You should have taken off that shoe as soon as it started to hurt."

"And go barefoot?"

"How far shall we go?"

"I saw a clearing on the far side of the hill. Right at the top."

"Hold on to me, Danny."

"Nobody could have thought up a forest that goes on as long as this one."

"I'll see if I can find some water. So you can wash up, at least."

"Where are you going to find water in the dark?"

"I wish I knew where we were."

"We're over the worst, that's for sure. Things already start to look familiar."

"Yeah, now just tell me you want to do this all over again when the war's over."

The first clung to the second boy's arm. They were both limping. Manny was remembering how many times he'd been lucky. And thinking how nothing lasts forever. Like Frank used to say: "Life gives happiness only to some folks, and it's never for keeps. Like stations where you change trains for somewhere else."

"Just this last stretch, then you can tell me to go to hell if you want to, Manny."

It was not quite dark when they came to the edge of the clearing. Then the moon broke through the clouds.

"This is what Frank was talking about," said the second.

The first slumped beside the feeding shed, as though he couldn't believe his eyes. Before he sat down, he put his stick where he'd found it that morning.

"This makes me sick," said the second.

"It was the sun that got me mixed up," the first said softly. "That lousy, fucking sun, Manny." After a while, he went on. "And those hills that zigzagged back and forth. We were hardly able to take more than a couple of steps in a straight line, right, Manny?"

"Aw, it's O.K., Danny."

The second lay down on the branches beside the shed, which were just where they'd left them that morning.

The first boy was thinking how the sun had fooled him, along with the mountains and his own feet and their bellies. He felt as if he'd been hit over the head with a blunt instrument. But he hardly had enough strength to put it into words.

The second boy lay staring off into the forest. In the dusk, the space between the trees looked like tunnels; they reminded him of the sewers the Polish women at Meuslowitz had told them about— the tunnels where they'd been captured. For the first time it occurred to him that they weren't going to make it. He didn't have strength enough to blame it on Danny. And yet inside, he did. He shivered and tried hugging himself and curling up in a ball. He wasn't listening to what Danny was trying to say about the sun. You can't get all the way to the end. Woods are even worse. They don't just go in one direction, either. The stench of sewers and stagnant water was in his nostrils. And mucky puddles. The breath of old grass and earth. A sharp reek. For a moment the woods were as red as blood.

Like the first boy, he ached all over. They were going to die here by this game shelter. They would soon be eaten up by insects and mice and foxes and wolves. The squirrels would nibble at them. Before they rotted away. Danny's skeleton. . . . In his tired brain, red went white. Bones were white.

He lay there inert, as though even his tongue was powerless. He could see and hear every move and every friction of Danny's bones. He didn't even feel like trying to move his tongue to see if it would work.

He tried to lift his eyes to the treetops, to see whether he had any willpower. He strained his ears in a conscious effort to hear the sounds of the forest. Those other sounds that accompanied his visions had come back. Things he'd heard. His bones. The sewers turned back into trees again.

The wind had uprooted all the trees and piled them where the two boys lay. He breathed heavily. They were not in some new, strange part of the forest—they had merely come back to where they had been before. He pulled over a branch and covered his head with it. He lay in almost the same trough his body had made the night before. The place was crawling with insects, red and white and translucent. He wished they'd go away.

The first boy waited until the second fell asleep and then he took off his shoe, hissing with pain.

But the second boy wasn't really asleep. He wondered why Danny hated Frank so much. When people start hating someone, it was because they were a lot alike.

He could see tree branches above him. He could see them even when he closed his eyes. The trees seemed to be falling on his head.

He could hear them crashing down on him. Silver, black and pungent, heavy trees, illuminated and magnified by the moonlight. They fell slowly like a man trying to escape something and not being able to.

As they fell, the trees stirred up a tempest of sound, like a glider coming in for a landing. They whispered as they fell on his head, like before the war when workers brought bundles of Christmas trees into town and tossed them onto the pavements.

He watched three trees fall on him after he opened his eyes. He couldn't dodge them, and he didn't have the strength to warn Danny.

"We've got to go in the other direction tomorrow," the first boy said.

The sun was high. The air was clean, biting. The earth was damp. They walked side by side. The first boy leaned on the other's shoulder and on his stick. They looked like two sick, skinny wolves. Their eyes were bloodshot and the corners of their eyes and mouths were caked with white. There were sticky patches of resin on their clothes and both were scratched and bloodied by the underbrush.

"We've got to get out of these woods," the first boy said. When the second boy did not answer, he went on, "Don't be a bastard, Manny." No response. "I bet they'd trade places with us if they could. I hope you're not planning to put on that act again when we are almost at the top of the hill."

The second boy didn't even look up. The first was worried about him. Manny stopped and leaned against a tree.

"I've seen where the woods end," the first said. "All right, Manny, if that's the way you want to be, I can be just as much of a skunk as you can." He waited. "As long as I can remember, you've always wanted to die like that Danish Jew. Remember, Manny?"

The second boy looked off toward a clearing, but it wasn't where the forest ended. It was just a stony place where no trees grew and beyond it the woods began again. His eyes were gummy.

Danny's lips barely moved when he spoke. "So far, you've never let yourself get tramped on, Manny. All we have to do is get across this patch of stones." He leaned on his stick.

"How long has it been since we've had anything to eat?" asked the second boy.

"There's no sense keeping count all the time."

"I'm staying right here."

"I'll scrape something up today. The woods are different here. I swear, Manny."

"You said the woods ended here."

"It's a different kind of forest, Manny. It's not the same anymore."

"You won't find us anything to eat," said the second boy.

With the aid of his stick, the first boy began to pick his way across the patch of rocks. He looked back occasionally, but most of the time, he peered around for a place to put his stick. He floundered over the stones, step by step, assuming Manny would follow him.

The second boy finally moved away from the tree where he'd been leaning.

"There must be a cave around here," Manny said dully.

"Inside your belly, maybe," replied the first boy.

They floundered on. The first boy knew what it would mean if he were to fall now. If that medic-amputator were still alive, he would have gleefully volunteered to cut off his festered foot and then he'd be able to hobble along on one leg, with the aid of his faithful stick.

Achingly, he wished they would make it. He turned around. "Manny!"

The second boy had fallen and lay face down on the stones. Danny went back to help him, but he had to be careful not to fall, too.

"All right, go on, just lie there and let yourself get shot at. That's your best chance," he whispered.

Blood trickled from the cut on Manny's forehead. He had fallen against a sharp stone. The wind rose and brought with it the first drops of rain. Danny brushed away the pine needles from his face.

The second boy turned his head. The stone was cool against his cheek. The blood felt warm and sticky.

He could hear Danny talking to him and, vaguely, he thought about all the people he had disappointed—Frank and his mother and himself. All of the people he'd ever known.

It began to rain and the rain washed the blood off his forehead and off the stone. The first boy stood there looking back at him. Manny was vaguely aware of his own exhaustion.

He looked past Danny, between the trees and beyond the patch of rocks. He could see branches and cobwebs that looked like streaming rope ladders which had been ripped apart by the wind and mended. He was sure there must be spiders there, waiting for bugs to come along. And he was the bug they were waiting for. He hoped they wouldn't gnaw his eyes out. The rain drummed against his head, bouncing off the stones and into his eyes.

Danny hobbled back and poked him with his stick.

"Sit down," the second boy said.

"I wouldn't be able to get up again," replied the first.

"It's full of bugs down here."

"You're bleeding a little," the first boy said. "You must have hit your head on a sharp stone."

"Wait, Danny."

Finally, leaning against each other, they tottered arm in arm across the rocky patch.

10

"Horses have been this way," said the first boy when they came to a path in the forest.

"A year ago, it looks like," replied the second. His hair was matted.

"What's wrong with your eye?"

"It feels swollen. When I close it, it's like going to the movies."

"What are they playing today, Manny?"

"I can see a naked woman made out of stone. She's sitting up above the fountain at the top of Wenceslas Square. When you stand below and look between her legs, you can see street cars."

"You and Frank must have been related."

"I can't remember how I fell and cracked my head," the second boy said.

He was remembering the time in Meuslowitz when Frank Bondy had invited him and Danny to his kapo room. He asked them to sit down, as if they knew what he had on his mind. They'd been planning an escape, and Frank said it would be a milestone in his life.

It was enough to listen to his deep and pleasant voice. It made you feel it was a privilege just to be with Frank Bondy. He told them about his past, so they'd realize what an honor it was to escape with him.

For instance, the three chairs which Frank had found somewhere so that he could invite both of them to sit down.

Speaking of their escape plan, Frank said their first duty was to get the key to the gate leading into the women's section. He explained it so it made sense, saying the electrified barbed wire in the women's camp was strung high where it ran through boggy land.

"I'd be happy if only this once the devil would work for us," he smiled. It looked as though anybody would drown if he tried to crawl under the wire. But nobody had ever tried.

There was no guard beside the bog. The muck was deterrent enough.

That evening, the boys took an imprint of the keyhole with a piece of soap Frank had given them. Danny stole some old keys in the factory. He filed down one of them from the imprint. On the fourth day, they tried it. It fit. They gave it to Frank.

A few days later, they found out that with the/help of their key, Bondy was going to see his Polish girlfriend, whose name was Wanda. She worked in the kitchen. She'd gone through the sewer experience like most of the Polish women in camp and, like most of them, was a devout Catholic. Almost all of them had been raped by German soldiers when the prison train had stopped on the way to camp.

Frank Bondy had his mouth full of apologies the next day, but each new day was an accusation, too, and so was every word they used to try to convince him to forget the Polish bitch. They were jealous of that poor Polish girl who'd fallen head over heels in love with Frank. She gave him food, anxious to erase through him everything that had happened to her.

It was Wanda, often raped, shorn-headed, who seemed to be the main obstacle to their escape.

That was when Frank gave the boys the address of his fiancée in Prague in case anything happened to him while they were making their escape. Danny was to have his watch, and his money was to go to Manny.

Frank had remembered his fiancée in Prague even when he was with Wanda. He wrote letters to her, telling her how much she meant to him, and he told the same thing to the Polish girl. He wasn't lying to either one. He used to say, "Each story has three versions. The first one you tell me. The second one I tell you, and the third one no one knows."

"Bondy-boy was just a fancy fake," said the second boy.

"Why do you keep thinking about him all the time?"

"I don't. I'm just thinking in general. How do you suppose he got along with his girlfriend in Prague?"

"Probably like a cat and a rat," replied the first. "I've dethroned Frank Bondy long ago. Like I did with my dad when the Germans came. Even though it wasn't *his* fault."

Frank Bondy told them about Russian roulette and other games in which people wager their own lives—for nothing, only because of the strange itching in their souls. Once at night, he told them about his collection of old pistols which, of course, the Germans confiscated when they came into Prague. He remembered the date, the day and the afternoon, March 1, 1940, when he came to turn in his valuables for safekeeping in the bank and then was never allowed to enter the area of the Prague produce exchange. They dreamed, then, at night, about the pistols which they would turn not against their temples, but on one of the *Sonderführers* and *Scharführers* or on some of the women *Aufseherin*. It sounded like a song with no end. Frank Bondy didn't escape from camp—he was never able to do it—but he was not able to run away from his yesterday, even though his tomorrow had become an empty box, just as when he left Prague and left a house, bedroom, kitchen and staircase which he still remembered like one of his thirty suits and thirty pairs of shoes. He left Prague on June 1, 1942, when the Germans prohibited house pets, with the exception of aquarium fish, from being kept in Jewish apartments, and forbade all non-Aryans to subscribe to German newspapers. The worst of all prohibitions, as Frank Bondy once said, was, for him, the injunction against the use of dining and sleeping cars, the prohibition against riding express trains and steamboats.

"The grass is slippery."

"Hold on tight!"

"As long as you don't eat my fingers when I grab you."

Suddenly the path led out into a field. They stopped by a tall thicket. A man was pushing a plow blade into the earth as his horse plodded across the field.

Hidden in the thicket, they watched the plowman lead the bay horse where the land sloped toward a cluster of houses from which a woman had just come. She was bringing the man his lunch.

"We'll have to kill that woman," the first boy said. "Otherwise she'll turn us in."

The man was unshaven. He wore a motley collection of clothing topped with a ragged, high-collared army overcoat.

The woman waited for the man to eat his lunch. The woman was pretty. The man must have been at least a generation older than she. She wore a woolen cap, woolen stockings and a pair of high laced man's shoes.

While the man ate, the woman watched the horse and the sky and the drifting clouds. He bit and chewed and swallowed, watching the woman.

She turned away.

"How'll we kill her?" whispered the second boy.

"With a rock or with my stick," replied the first.

"Who's going to do it?"

The man had the horse's bridle in one hand and a slice of bread in the other.

The boys watched and swallowed hard. When the man had finished eating, he bent down for the jug. It was full of milk. It trickled along his chin to his neck and down his chest.

The woman stood there, staring dreamily into space. Her black hair was combed back smoothly under a flowered kerchief. When the man had finished eating and drinking, he smiled at her and the woman picked up the jug, wrapped it in a kerchief and slipped it into her bag.

Slowly, she walked back the way she had come. She took long strides, holding herself erect, as though she knew the path by heart.

Up on the hillside, the man went back to plowing the spring earth. The woman did not look back. The unshaven plowman worked slowly, his steps following the lazy plodding of the horse. As he turned the heavy, soft earth, it cast its reflection back against his face, muddy and black.

The woman came to the edge of the village and went into a house with a red roof. This was just a little cluster of houses; the main part of the village was on the other side of the hill. There was a shed built onto the house, a hay rick and an outhouse.

A German shepherd with a long chain rushed out of its doghouse, welcoming the woman with wild barking. For the first time, the woman smiled. Somewhere beyond the village, somebody's bitch barked in response, a long wailing bark.

After a while, the woman opened the door and went into the yard. She was wearing a black dress and apron. She scattered grain to the hens. The dog barked and the woman smiled again, at the dog, at the hens and to herself.

"It looks like she's alone," the first boy said.

"How do you want to do it?" asked the second.

"Just one of us is going to have to do it, Manny."

"Which one?"

"We'll draw lots," the first said. "Choose a number from one to twenty, Manny. But hurry!"

"Fifteen," the second said. His eyes glittered. "Start with me."

The first boy counted off. "It's you, Manny," he said. His breath was hot and rank. "You've got to kill her."

"O.K., I will."

"If you don't do it to her, they'll do it to us."

"Yeah. Lend me that stick. I'll kill her as soon as she gives me something to eat."

"But before you do, make her tell you where we are and how far we've got to go."

When the woman finished feeding her chickens, she took a lump of sugar from her apron pocket. She let the dog jump around her for a while. Finally she tossed him the sugar. The dog jumped high, snapped at the sugar and gulped it down.

The air was fragrant with the smells of the forest, the meadows, of early spring and the warm cowshed. The second boy narrowed his eyes and pressed his lips tight, trying not to think about food. The door to the shed was open. It wasn't possible to see inside. It was a clear darkness, underscored by the light after the rain.

A bell in the village began to toll noon. Pigeons flapped from one rainspout to another. A rooster crowed in the chicken coop. The first boy looked at the open door of the shed.

"How about burning the whole place down to be sure?" suggested the first.

"It would be a lot of work. I'm not strong enough. Anyway, how? Why? Do you suppose that would keep her busy until we could get away?"

The first boy kept looking at the shed.

"If you can run fast."

"I can't run."

"O.K."

"I wouldn't leave you in that fix," said the first boy at once. The second boy didn't reply.

The woman went into the cowshed and when she reappeared, she had that same musing smile they couldn't make out. She didn't close the door to the shed.

"Get her to tell you how far it is to the nearest town," repeated the first. "I'll wait here."

"Wait by the woodshed."

"Don't take too long, Manny."

"You can wash your foot at the pump there, Danny."

"Most important, get rid of her."

"Don't worry, I will kill her."

"No matter what, Manny."

"Yeah."

The second strode off alongside the woodshed, holding the first boy's stick to keep the dog away. He'd forgotten how long it had been since he and Danny had had anything to eat.

Suddenly he stopped and turned his head. "I don't know what it is, but I'm not hungry anymore."

The woman was standing by the dishpan. She looked up startled when the boy entered the room with the stick in his hand. Horror flickered in her eyes.

The boy glanced swiftly around the room. A two-year-old child was under the table. The woman had a cool, pretty face and tidy hair. The child crawled out from under the table and clutched the mother's hand. The hand was trembling.

The boy was surprised by the impression he had made. He knew he must look frightful and that he'd be scared, too, if he could have seen himself. He raised the stick and approached the woman, who almost fainted. She was unable to utter a single sound. Even if she could have, she probably would have been afraid to scream, because then it would just happen faster.

But her fear was not transmitted to the child. "She can think anything she wants to," the second boy said to himself. He closed the door behind him, but otherwise he did not move.

He saw the fear of death in her eyes, and the satisfaction he felt was different from what he had expected.

He knew he only needed to take three or four steps with his lifted stick and it would be all over. He simply hadn't been prepared for the child. The idea of killing the woman had come simply; it had been much easier than when he had tried to understand why the Germans were killing his people, who hadn't harmed them in any way.

I'll take three and a half steps. I'll hit her over the head as hard as I can. When she falls, I'll hit her a few times more. What'll I do when the kid starts bawling?

Just as he knew he had the right to kill the woman, he knew he shouldn't kill the child and that he wasn't going to. But he couldn't put the two things together. He wondered what to do about the child. He could tie her to the table and lock the door. He saw a kitchen cupboard similar to what they had at home, with grey pottery cups. The chairbacks had angular carvings.

A blue tin bread box stood on the table next to the dishpan. His eyes shifted to it for a split second and the woman's followed.

Beside the bread box lay a long butcher knife. It was within the woman's reach. The second boy figured he could bar her way if she took one step. But meanwhile he had to lean his back against the door so he did not fall.

The table beside which the woman and the little girl were standing was covered with an old-fashioned, fringed white cloth with another of red linen on top of that. There was a sofa against the wall with an embroidered sampler showing a cook with a forest warden and some German proverb.

On the cupboard stood a kerosene lamp with a white shade. Beside the sink hung a porcelain coffee mill with a wooden handle. Opposite the cupboard there stood an antique clock with the signs of the zodiac, gilded Roman numerals, and hands of blue tin. The clock ticked loudly. It was a quarter past two. The woman carefully turned off the spigot, stopping the water that had been running into the dishpan, now almost overflowing. The room was silent.

The woman turned to shield the child. She still couldn't move because of fear. He looked around the room as if it were an island. The place was very clean.

So this is how people live, he thought to himself. With all this stuff. God, it's impossible! They have everything even in the midst of war.

"What do you want?" the woman finally asked in German.

"Something to eat," he replied.

The woman moved aside in that same, careful, dreamy way. Pulling her hand out of the child's grasp, she opened the bread box and took out half a loaf of fresh bread. Holding it against her breast, she picked up the knife and cut three slices. Then she put the bread back.

The second boy could smell the bread and the room. He watched her lay the slices of bread on the table so he could take them. He was dizzy. He narrowed his eyes, and the woman saw murder in them.

He imagined himself taking three swift steps forward, hitting her over the head, then finishing the job as she lay on the floor, her skirt twisted so he could see her garters.

He had to fight back the dizziness. He leaned against the kitchen door. He stood facing the clean, neatly dressed German woman and her blond, blue-eyed German child in the room to which the plowman returned each day when his work was done—was he her husband or her father? Blood rushed to his head and flooded his eyes.

He reached out and took the bread. The woman put her hands on the child's head. He raised the stick. It was his bloodshot eyes she noticed most.

"I have nothing more to give you," the woman told him.

The second boy was silent.

"No lard, no margarine," added the woman.

The second boy moved into the doorway, holding the bread against his chest. The woman was petrified with fear. Although he knew he wasn't going to do anything to her. Within him roared the words "thank you," just as a flaming sea would roar. But he didn't say a single word. Beneath the dirt, his face was flushed with blood.

The first boy was waiting for him by the woodshed, his shoes untied.

"Well, did you hit her?" he asked.

"She had a little kid with her."

The second boy gave two slices of bread to the first boy. He had carried them inside his shirt. Then he handed back the stick.

There was the time in Meuslowitz when Frank Bondy had shared with them the first bread they had in Germany. It was army issue, half rye flour, half sawdust. But then they thought they'd never eaten anything as good. That was when Frank had declared that he and Danny were his temporary helpers. They almost felt like pipls. Luckily Frank wasn't interested in pipls. They really were his assistants.

Danny was sure he saw one person in the bread line collect his ration twice. The person flushed, but Danny couldn't prove it. In the camp from which they had come, people had strangled each other for a loaf of bread. But for this, when somebody went through the bread line twice, you could find many willing hands. Or it was arranged for the block leader to send him to the "sauna," another expression for the ovens.

Justice must have really existed once upon a time, but it had gotten lost somewhere, like a speck of dust that's trampled into the earth and then one day perhaps found again.

The person from the bread line, whom nobody listened to anymore, mumbled something about false accusations. To be someone's "assistant" in the camp was like a slice of bread—there were always two sides to it.

"So you didn't hit her."

"Go ahead and eat."

"If you didn't kill her, she'll let them kill us."

"Yes," replied the second.

"You should have killed her, Manny."

The first boy raised the slice of bread to his mouth. The second watched him as he took a bite. His jaw tightened. He grimaced as though someone had run a grater across his tongue and palate and down into his throat.

He spat out the bread into the palm of his hand. "What's the matter?" asked the second boy.

"I can't eat it."

"Why not?"

The first boy opened his mouth. It was full of blood.

"It's too rough."

But it was fresh. The second boy stared at the slice of bread in his hand and cautiously bit off a piece. He spat it out immediately. The bread had also turned red with blood. He could feel the inside of his mouth swelling up.

"It's been a long time since we've eaten anything," the first boy said.

"She's got to give me some milk," the second boy replied.

"Get some for me, too," added the first.

"This time I'll kill her if she doesn't."

"She could send half the village after us, Manny."

The second boy left without a word. The first opened his shoe. His whole heel had festered. He stared at it for a while, then poked around inside the shoe with a stick. Afterward, he leaned his head against the woodshed and closed his eyes. The German shepherd began to bark again; yet he felt a feverish quiet. The leg was swollen. The wound on his heel was full of dirt and pus. He didn't want to look at two clouds which seemed close enough to touch. He played with a few pebbles as if they were dominoes, shoving them back and forth, studying them closely. He wished everything that was still alive in his body and inside his mouth would shrivel up and die. He grinned like a madman. The clouds were like hummingbird eggs. He looked over at the chicken coop. But he didn't bother to get up and go in.

Then he looked through the open door to the shed, to that dark oblong in the light, to the dark aperture behind which he imagined there was some kind of peaceful animal. He couldn't see inside.

He stared at the pebbles and at the bread they couldn't even eat. He could just imagine Manny sticking out his tongue at the German woman to show her what had happened to the inside of his mouth. Then he'd hit her.

The first boy closed his eyes again. He couldn't understand what a woman with black hair was doing, living in a German village like this, while he and Manny, blond and blue-eyed both of them (before their heads were shaved and the hair collected for mattress stuffing and for overalls for commandos from the German submarines), were considered aliens. He wondered whether the other villagers were all blond and blue-eyed, with nice straight noses, members of a race that gets purer the farther north you go. Which meant the very purest of all were probably the polar bears. That's what his father used to say when he was feeling good and predicting that the Third Reich would collapse within five months.

The purest race are icebergs. The boy sat there, listening abstractedly to the frantic barking of a dog. He waited for Manny to come back from the farmhouse.

The woman watched them from the window. She could see them dropping the empty mugs into the bushes behind the woodshed when they'd finished off the warm, ersatz coffee she'd poured for them. She could see them cradling in their hands the potatoes she'd taken from the earthenware mixing bowl where she had intended to make dough.

She watched the smaller boy help the bigger one to get to his feet. He handed the heavy stick to his companion. The tall boy was between fifteen and sixteen, she guessed.

With the smaller boy leading the way, they trudged off toward the woods. The smaller boy had a cut on his forehead. He must have fallen on a rock or bumped into something. The taller one limped.

She looked after them like a fish which inhabits the depths of silence. Her face mirrored the revulsion she felt but could not understand. It was obvious they hadn't had a thing to eat for a long time. They were dirty and they stank. Along with the fear which, now that it was all over, had turned into curiosity and the comforting knowledge that nothing had really happened, the woman was amazed and bewildered that something like this could have happened on German soil. No foreigners ever came here.

There was something else . . . red curtains were drawn back across the shutters. Seeing the curtain and the reflection of her face in the window, the woman was reminded of when she had been a young girl, before she had married and had a baby. She picked up the child and watched the two boys as they made their way into the woods. It was like watching animals.

The sun shone in through the window, bringing the two boys into sharp perspective as they neared the edge of the forest. With one hand, she touched the buttons on her dress as if to make sure they were all fastened.

The smaller boy looked back at the farmhouse.

After she lost sight of them, she stood at the window as if puzzling what to do. But she'd already made up her mind. She put the little girl down and took her cape. Then she tied her kerchief under her chin, and her hand slipped down over her breast. Her lips were pressed tight, her eyes sharp and strict, and her face calm. The fear was gone, but an echo of anger was still there because she'd been so badly frightened. She went out and got the cups and rinsed them carefully. It was like some awful disease—she was repelled and fascinated at the same time. Inside, a satanic scheme vied with a tug of mercy. Had anybody seen them coming here? Were they Jews? Is that how Jews look? Like those boys? Even her dog had been afraid of them. She remembered all those things she'd heard over the radio.

"They're swine," she said to herself, and brushed her skirt. "Pigs!" she repeated.

The little girl's eyes were fixed on the lips of her mother.

Wolves, the woman told herself. If that's how Jews look now, the world's better off without them. No need to feel sorry for them if they go around scaring the wits out of people. She had never seen real live Jews before, though, so she couldn't be sure. But it was true that they bring decadence and chaos and all sorts of unpleasantness. They disturb the peace and quiet for which people work so hard. There was something about them that others could certainly do without. The boys merged into the misty forest.

She had the feeling that, in them, the war had finally come home to her. She glanced over at the bed.

"I've behaved myself for too long," she said.

They're nothing but tramps, the woman went on to herself. Who knows where they escaped from? Who knows how many people they've robbed and killed? They'll never change.

She touched her kerchief to make sure it was properly tied. Then she set out for the village. She walked toward the mayor's office.

II

"I can walk better now," lied the first boy.

"We're going downhill," replied the second.

"This is hilly country, Manny."

"The main thing is, we're on our way again."

"Are you cold?"

From the top of the wooded hill, the whole countryside seemed to be sloping downhill. Judging from the terrain, they were in the border region.

"When somebody has so much that they don't even think about how much they used to have, they don't deserve to have it."

The first boy's foot was no help to him at all; it was just an appendage, like part of his trousers.

"I know I can make it now," he said.

Manny was recalling something that had happened on the train. They'd been on their way for three days. Another prisoner, Tommy Kosta, lay there, pale and bloodless and yellow as a lemon.

It was painful to see how waxy he looked around the nose and mouth and ears. When Kosta closed his eyes, nobody knew whether he was still alive or not. Frank tried to joke about it, saying Tom reminded him of an Egyptian princess he had seen in a museum. "The only reason she held together was because she'd been embalmed and stuck inside a mummy case for three thousand years, dressed in the finest silks and wrapped with bands of satin as thin and tough as the finest goat or calf skin. It's a wonder nobody stripped her of her finery during those three thousand years."

Kosta looked three thousand years older than he really was. He was skinnier than the day he was born. Frank knew he was still alive; he could tell by the way his body shook in rhythm with the train.

"By now, practically everybody's pretending he's almost ready to kick the bucket," Frank observed.

But Kosta was really dying. He was dying slowly, wrapped up in his blanket. The only reason nobody stole it from him was because of lice. On the third day, he began to smell, and a few people wondered whether they ought not to shove his body out of the train during the night. The guards would have been the last to object, except that they were on German territory now and lice carry typhus. Kosta had been lucky nobody wanted to touch his blanket.

When anybody wanted to relieve himself during the night, they'd step on Kosta's chest or shoulders or even on his head. That made it easier for them to pee over the side. So Kosta stank of ammonia, too.

Tom Kosta had gotten a bad name among certain people, because in Theresienstadt he'd complained to the Jewish community authorities about "those rich, spoiled youngsters who ought to be given something to do."

The train tossed Tom's skeletal body around, draped in its rags and consumed by the biggest collection of fleas, lice, and assorted vermin ever seen on one person.

In the morning, Danny watched how everybody was tramping over Tom. He made it clear that if anybody stepped on Kosta one more time in order to pee over the side, he'd catch hell from him.

It was a slow, lethargic dying. Danny practically had to kick him to bring him to in the morning. Then, like Jesus, he started picking the lice off Tom. He threw them over the side of the train. Danny had no objection to infecting all of southern Germany.

That was when Frank Bondy moved next to the Transylvanian guard, acting as though he was responsible for the other prisoners. Actually, it was just to get away from Kosta.

"Just imagine if we were girls," remarked the second boy suddenly.

"I'd rather not," murmured the first.

The second boy dragged Danny and his helpless leg through an anthill. The trees were getting sparser.

"The sun will keep on rising and setting, boys," Frank kept telling them. "It'll rain and the earth will dry out again. I doubt there have been many changes at the casino or in the clubrooms down in Monte Carlo. Aside from blackout curtains on the windows."

He used to talk about how "all symbols pale with time," how, at that very moment, people were at the seashore and in the mountains, swimming and skiing, playing tennis and soccer, enjoying their hobbies, making babies or not making them. Getting married and getting divorced. Women had their eyes on men, and men were on the lookout for women. "And what does it prove?" he concluded.

The first boy seemed to have lost all his strength except for what little it took to hobble along on one leg.

"Can you still make it?"

"Like my mother used to say, Manny—'If you want to live, you'll live. If you don't, you won't.' That's how nature's arranged it."

"We're going uphill again, Danny."

"A lot of it is just cowardice," the first boy whispered.

Both of them were off in separate worlds that were the same, but different, too. Sunbeams skidded over the rocks.

Manny thought about why he hadn't killed that woman with the child. He was tired, so he thought about it slowly, and it was as though the thought brought with it something unexpected, something he hadn't counted on. It carried inside it many other things. There used to be a lot of mystery about killing that wasn't really worth it. By now, all the mystery had been stripped away, and it was naked, just as naked as they were.

Even in retrospect, he got a bit of satisfaction from every German who got killed, as long as he and Danny were still living. Just as every German probably rejoiced over every Jewish woman, man, or child who got killed. There was an edge of vengeance to it, taken by someone else on his behalf, and gratification that it was possible at all, because it looked so impossible.

This was what it all boiled down to finally. There was a strange kind of strength in killing, even if you could recognize and control it. He knew the exact moment when he began to get tired of thinking about killing. He knew precisely when the change happened. And what this change might have meant if it had happened while he'd been in the woman's kitchen.

It was like a rubber band which pulled you back toward it with the same strength as you pulled against it. It was not just ambiguous. It had many layers of meaning, like everything he'd ever encountered and pulled over afterward.

He couldn't explain it to himself yet, but he sensed what it did to a person when he could kill. It also had something to do with the fact that he didn't. It had to do with himself, somewhere in the future, when he might perhaps ask himself a question—and be able to answer it.

To kill or not to kill had gotten into man like the blood in his heart or the air he inhales and exhales. Alongside the will to live, there was the multiplied determination to kill. It was always stronger than you were, but as long as you lived, you could try to resist it.

Maybe he'd answer the same way now. And then answer something else. There were two kinds of people, the kind who were lucky and the others who weren't.

Once again, he thought about Frank, who had somehow known that there was a difference between murdering someone and killing somebody because he wanted to kill you or make a slave of you, as if you weren't even alive or were simply vegetating in his shadow, for whatever reason—between killing somebody because you wanted something that belongs to him, because you despised him without even knowing who he was, and killing somebody because you hated him, because you knew exactly what he'd done to you and to other people. Because you were there and you'd seen it happen. The difference probably got blurred, but never entirely. It was never completely erased as long as you thought about it, even if you were very tired and your thoughts were tired, too.

He could have killed that Polish medic who amputated people's legs and hands and fingers when it wasn't necessary. He could have killed him even now because he hated him and he knew he had a right to feel that way. But even then, he'd been glad it had been somebody else who killed him. He knew lots of people (and the things they'd done) whom he could have killed without the least regret.

But he could remember situations when he'd thought it would almost be better to be killed himself than to kill.

It was different with that woman, too, because somewhere deep inside he could still say to himself that he hadn't committed any of those great, important acts he shouldn't have. It was that old feeling he'd thought had been extinguished inside him. Like when Danny said the past was dead and nonexistent for him, that you really might prefer to let yourself be killed, rather than killing somebody yourself.

He hadn't killed that woman because he would have felt guilty. The thing he was feeling right now was the same he'd felt while he was standing in her kitchen . . . the same instinct which told him things he didn't know or things he would learn much later. Or never. There was a strange kind of power which existed inside him, in addition to the real, predictable strength of his muscles, his legs and arms, the strength he needed to keep his eyes open, that strange strength hidden away inside a man that he preferred not to draw upon, as if it weren't even there if he didn't think about it. It had two sides to it too—the ability to strike someone down and kill him and the ability not to do it. A resistance to killing, the strength not to kill.

Some people were lucky and didn't have to kill, even during wartime when killing was part of daily bread, along with cold and hunger and lots of other things people didn't otherwise face. Then there were the others who weren't so lucky, and they got killed.

He thought about the child. Then, all of a sudden, it passed out of his mind. He forgot about it. He simply tried to overcome his tiredness. He knew in the marrow of his bones that this was now the most important thing in the world. Whenever he didn't overcome his tiredness—at least partially—he lost his sense of danger, and though that was both good and bad, it could be the very worst. A sense of danger was always the first thing that saved him.

It had been a sense of danger which had saved Danny and made him jump out of the train at the right moment. Then when the Transylvanian guard was shooting at them. And later when the

American pilot had fired at them by mistake. But now Danny was so tired, he didn't even think of safety or danger. It was like when they were back there on the hillside. This sense was weightless, but you felt lighter without it, as though a heavy weight had fallen away.

As they walked on through the woods, he tried to put his weight on his foot so he wouldn't make it harder for Danny. But sometimes he forgot.

Danny trudged along blindly at his side. As if he's dead, he added inwardly. Maybe he's saving his strength for wherever it is we're going.

The first boy probably sensed that the other was worried about him.

"All I'm going to do is eat, Manny, once we get there," he said softly. "I'm going to eat the whole, livelong day. Then I'll loll around in a bathtub full of hot water and eat and eat and eat some more."

He said it as though he knew it wasn't true anymore, either.

Birds sang in the treetops. It was a long, slow climb. The second boy again felt that half-forgotten heat inside him, the thing Bondy called the height of madness.

Exhaustion blotted out a lot of their initial fears. They moved like sleepwalkers, clinging to each other so they wouldn't get lost.

"Stop!" It was the rasping voice of an old man.

They both stiffened. Manny turned, but they still kept moving. They didn't have the slightest intention of stopping. Everything inside them had begun to function again. About a dozen old men were moving toward them through the trees, armed with shotguns.

"Werewolves," choked the first boy.

"They caught up with us," breathed the second. "Come on!"

They both assessed the old men and could see that they were a feeble handful of veterans who wouldn't have enough wind to keep going much longer, just as the two of them wouldn't either. But the old men were still fresh, while the boys were tired.

The only thing to do was run away, to get across the hill and disappear on the other side before the old men could catch up with them. Shadows—or echoes—of Frank Bondy melted into the forest. There was no time for him now. The old man who had called to the boys wore a civil defense arm band.

A shot broke into the stillness of the forest. They ran through the woods as fast as they could, but the faster they tried to run, the slower they went.

"Come on!" hissed the second boy.

"I can't!" breathed the first.

The second didn't answer. He saw how the first boy was gasping for breath.

"Come on!" he said.

"It's impossible."

"Do you want to just drop dead?"

"I can't."

"You must."

More shots began to crack among the trees. They counted to twelve, and the shooting began all over again. The men couldn't shoot in unison. It was hard work.

They swarmed forward, firing their rifles as they came. Some of them were wearing uniforms, or parts of them. The leader, with a hunter's cap and boar's bristle in the band, was the only one dressed like an officer, but with no insignia of rank.

"I can't make it," repeated the first boy as the second tried to drag him on.

"You can," gasped the second.

Bullets burrowed into the tree trunks and moss and earth and burst through some of the protruding roots.

The birds took fright and were silent. The best marksman was the leader, but even he wasn't much good. It was hard to get a good aim going uphill.

One old man was pushing a bicycle. Some of them used their gun stocks like canes to help themselves along.

The old man in front stopped, took aim, then yelled at the boys to halt. When they didn't, he ordered the others to fire. The woods were filled again with the noise of gunshots.

"Come on!" urged the second boy, tugging at Danny's sleeve.

"Go on!" he breathed. "Run! I'll catch up with you in a minute."

They could hear: *"Ich kann nich mehr."* And, *"Scheisse, los!"* And, *"Ich habe nicht geladen. Jetzt is die reihe an Dich! Mir tut die Hand weh; Ich habe revma."*

The voices were old. *"Ich krieg Ihm! Entweder Du oder Ich! Män-*

ner, Vervärts!" It was like an echo. But they knew it was not an echo; it was the only reality, just like their breath, the trees, yesterday, tomorrow, and who knows what piece of today, of here and now. Even the silence was different now. And they both knew that yesterday, a year ago, an hour ago was better than this, with the only exception that they were still on the run.

The first boy pulled his arm away, and the second took a few steps before he turned around. He refused to even think of surrendering to these old men. Danny lay on the ground, unable to take one more step, and the old men kept shooting. Their leader had run out of ammunition, so he borrowed a gun from another man.

"Leave me alone," groaned the first boy. "Leave me here."

The second boy was sure their only chance was to get to the top of the hill before the old men shot them. Or before they became infuriated at not being able to hit them. He didn't want to think about what would happen if Danny didn't make it, if they captured him alive.

"Don't be stupid," wheezed the first boy.

The second almost cursed. Then he grabbed the first boy and started dragging him up the hill. It was the heaviest thing he'd ever carried.

The first boy struggled to his feet. He still held on to his stick.

The second boy didn't want to think about how Danny must feel.

"Why don't you want to leave me here?" groaned Danny.

"I don't want to be alone," replied the second boy.

They came to a clump of bushes which lashed at their faces. They groped along, kicking up a pair of rabbits which disappeared into the underbrush. The boys' faces were scratched and blood-streaked.

"Halt!" yelled the first old man, reloading his gun. The magazine clicked. More single shots were fired.

The second boy couldn't catch his breath. Two German words rang in his ears, *"Halt!"* and *"Nieder!"* He felt a familiar lump scorching his chest and he waited for it to stab at his side.

The old men were crawling up the steepest part of the hill, moving a bit slower than the boys. They leaned against trees to shoot now, taking a longer time to aim. They advanced in a row, the old men with more bullets than teeth, like trees with a few feet between them.

The first boy was almost unconscious. He let himself he dragged along, helping with his good leg as much as he could. Just when Manny lost his footing, the old man in front took careful aim. As the bullet left the muzzle of his gun, it whizzed through the trees and, in the split second before it hit, several things happened all at once, only two of which were really important or perceptible. The bareheaded boy had been tugging the taller one in one direction, while the other was trying to break loose and duck into the under-brush. That was when Manny tripped over the root. That was when the bullet which, a second before, would have shattered his spine kept right on going. It merely ripped off a piece of his sleeve. It didn't even graze his flesh. It simply whistled out into a tuft of moss and pine needles.

The first boy, unsuccessfully, tried to get up. You could smell scorched cloth. The second boy grabbed Danny's collar and pulled him like an animal.

"Come on!" gasped Manny.

The first boy said nothing. "Let me be," he whispered after awhile. It was as if he were crying.

"Shut up!"

He dragged the taller boy as if he were a piece of his own body which had been torn loose. Maybe the reason the first boy didn't speak was because he was crying. The bushes and underbrush were thickest in this part of the forest. They were so exhausted that they were ready to stop and lie down and die even before the old men reached them and shot them. The top of the hill lay just beyond a thin patch of green grass, and they crawled the whole way on their hands and knees.

"Just a little farther," sniffled the smaller boy. "We're almost there, Danny." His whisper was scarcely audible. "Just a few more inches. Roll over, Danny. Roll over with me."

They had reached the top. They put their arms around each other and rolled until they were on the other side. The second boy retched. He didn't even turn his face or move away. He retched again.

Another volley of shots tore through the trees. Then everything was silent again, and the birds began to sing.

The second boy wiped his mouth on a tuft of moss. By now, they were too tired to think that maybe the old men had been too scared to follow them over the hill. How were they to know whether the boys had guns or not?

"You should have killed her," the first boy said after a while.

"It's all downhill now, Danny."

"She sent those bastards after us," the first boy went on. "Are you sick?"

"No."

"You're white as a sheet."

Wind stirred in the trees. Birds were singing. The trees waved and tossed as though they were going back to where they'd been before. The earth had a smell of early springtime. The woods sloped into a deep valley.

"How come you don't even notice when somebody wants to kill you, Manny? By now, I can tell," the first boy said.

They were tired and sleepy. They'd wanted to sleep so badly during the past three years—to sleep like they'd never slept before.

"It's great to be able to speak again," said the second boy.

He had a bitter taste of vomit in his mouth. He had nothing left in his stomach of what the woman had given them to eat. Looking at Danny, all he saw was a pair of rheumy, bloodshot eyes. "I feel like I'm all beat up," Manny said at last.

The first boy said nothing. Pain stabbed at his heel. A sharp stone, probably.

"If it had lasted a little longer, I'd have started feeling sorry for myself," the second boy went on. "When I was a kid, I went to kindergarten with a little German girl."

"If it'd been me that went into that farmhouse, I'd have killed her," said Danny. They trudged on for a while in silence. "Are you still thinking about that little girl, Manny?" the first boy asked at last.

Suddenly, in the middle of the forest, they came to an asphalt highway. The woods, the moss, the sky seemed like logs floating down a stream, and the stream itself and everything around them was afloat, one layer of water on top of another. The boys sat down by the roadside and for several hours watched trucks drive by. An army orderly roared by on a motorcycle. The noise of the motors did not seem as unreal as the sounds the forest and the wind made.

"This is the best place to wait, huh?"

"On a curve," the second boy said.

"Which way do we want to go? What do you think?"

"I'd say we ought to go downhill and to the right, Danny."

"I feel like my blood's run out. Like I'm all dried up."

They slid into a ditch by the roadside, crouched so nobody could see them from either side. An hour later, they heard the sound of a motor. It came slowly.

"Sounds like a truck, doesn't it, Danny?"

"Yeah, it's a truck," the first boy confirmed.

"Maybe we ought to get closer to the road."

"It's not going fast," the first boy said.

They lay down on their bellies. The truck was a small, three-ton model. The back was empty. The motor grumbled in the curves, and the two boys decided this would probably be their best chance.

As the truck passed, the second boy dragged the first down the bank and made two running strides toward the truck. He caught hold of the side of the truck body. Danny was two hops behind. He had to put his weight on his bad foot.

The second boy held onto the side and pulled hard. Danny felt a stabbing pain in his foot as he tried to boost himself in, but his knee gave way and he fell. The second boy tugged his arm for a little longer, then let go and jumped off the truck himself.

The first boy was lying on the highway with his stick beside him. Manny rushed back and began to shake him, telling him to get up, that they could still catch the truck. He shook him by the sleeve as if he were beating him. Or beating himself. Or the whole world. He didn't even look after the truck anymore.

It drove off slowly.

12

The room the boys were taken to as prisoners was across the hall from the mayor's office. It was in the same building as the village tavern.

The village was quiet and clean. Everything was tidy, the houses, gardens and paths, fields, trees and bushes, ready for spring, far from the war. Beyond the end of the village was a small cemetery enclosed within high white walls on which there was not one mark except for the light discoloration caused by the rain. The fields were partially plowed already. In the sheds and against the outer walls of the houses firewood was stacked. On the crests of the shingled red roofs pigeons cooed. They sat in pairs, white, grey, and black and grey. Once in a while one would fly off to take a seat on another roof. They heard two dogs barking. Another joined in. Then all three dogs became silent. At the other end of the village, where three linden trees with giant crowns were growing, a rooster crowed. The windows in the inn were clean. The village behind seemed inexplicably strange because it was so calm and tidy, everything had its own place where it had been for so long, long before the fathers and grandfathers of today's villagers had been born.

They were told to strip naked and, when it was discovered that they were not armed, were allowed to get dressed again. Their clothes stank.

You could see into the taproom when the door was open.

This must have been a school before they turned it into a tavern, Manny thought to himself. Tables and chairs were stacked in one corner.

These were the same old men who had hunted them down and shot at them in the woods. All they'd done was go around to where the highway cut through the forest. They had suddenly emerged out of the woods below the road, and there they were, right in front of the boys, surrounding them, with shotguns aimed. The mayor had a Luger. He warned them that if they made a false move, they'd be shot.

Then they had been brought here. An old man in a prewar Czech army uniform whispered something in German to the mayor. They had had to keep their hands up all the way from the road where they'd been captured, although Danny was allowed to keep his stick, because without it he wouldn't have been able to walk or even get up off the ground.

They were given permission to sit down on a bench. It was warm in the room.

They'll probably have this bench scoured after we leave, Manny said to himself. They had stood for two hours with their hands up until finally Danny collapsed. Manny was alarmed by the red blotches on Danny's face. He was terribly thirsty and sorry he hadn't taken a drink from the puddle in the ditch along the roadside.

When he shut his eyes, he could still see the hill he and Danny had crossed when they made their escape. But this time, all two thousand prisoners were behind them and Frank Bondy was there, too. He saw them clamber out over the sides of the freight car, as though jumping out of trains was some contagious new kind of Jewish disease. The women rebels from Warsaw jumped faster than anybody else.

He was glad the vision didn't come back this time—watching all those two thousand people sent straight from the train into the gas chamber.

The American pilot had been circling the hill. He wasn't shooting anymore. He simply flew above the train like an aluminum star, wings tilted so they could get a good look at him. He took a few shots at the locomotive so they would realize his guns were loaded and that he had plenty of ammunition. He hit his target every time.

The hill was strewn with people. Like a teeming anthill. They lay sprawled across each other, tripping and stumbling onward as the black anthill moved slowly up the hill. The guards stayed beside the train. Bracing themselves, they shot the fugitives as though they were shooting rabbits. Almost without bothering to aim. They hit a lot of their targets. After a while, the hill was black with people who were still running. They had to tread over bodies which just lay there and bodies that still crawled or writhed.

Among those who were hit was Wanda, the pretty Polish girl who had been dragged out of the sewer. She liked to talk about mercy and humility and nobility. She had shown Frank the scars on her breasts and thighs where she had been bitten by trained German police dogs.

He saw Danny among them. And then there was something else. There was probably a lot the two boys never told each other.

Maybe Danny had such hallucinations, too. Maybe he saw Manny going into the gas chamber.

The more tired I get, the more people I see going to be gassed, he realized.

Finally, it wasn't just Jews and German invalids on whom the Germans used their gas chambers. There were French and English, Americans and Canadians and, of course, Russians and Poles. The whole world went into the gas chambers in alphabetical order, and everybody took his towel and soap as if he really believed it. Manny blinked to shut out the sight of it.

Danny stopped to speak to the Polish girl as she lay on the hillside. "You should have killed that woman," she told him. "We would have killed her—and the child too."

Danny started running. Frank Bondy was beside the Polish girl. She had been shot through the spine.

Frank dashed forward with two blankets, one under each arm, and knelt beside her, rolling one blanket under her head and the other under her spine. Wanda told him not to lose time, that he should run. "Not many people will make it," she said.

Frank Bondy looked down at her, and the wickedness faded from his eyes. There was something else in its place. He stayed with her. As he knelt there beside the Polish girl, bullets flew above his head. Wanda had had her share, even if she had been destined to survive. Frank Bondy tried to comfort her. He told her about Blanka, his fiancée in Prague, who would help make her well again. Blanka had studied medicine for three and a half years before the Germans came and closed down the university. So she had some knowledge to build on.

Frank had a thousand and one faces. Some of them were quite likable. But there were others that weren't. They were despicable.

The pilot circled over the anthill as it thickened and thinned, then suddenly he disappeared, taking with him the whistling sound his motor made.

The sky was empty again.

Noisily, the old men came back from the tavern. They brought with them their mugs of beer from the keg that had just been tapped. The youngest among them set up a table and enough chairs so everybody could sit down.

They began to unpack the food they'd brought along. They kept their shotguns by their sides—old army guns, as old as the men themselves.

The men ate and drank and sang old German songs. Like the one about the little brother who liked to drink and leave his troubles at home. They sang another one about an imperturbable sailor, howling the refrain in unison: *"Keine Angst, keine Angst, Rosemarie. . . . "*

After a few beers, they began to go back and forth to the toilet, buttoning their pants as they passed by the boys. There were no women in the tavern.

One man, who carried his gun over his shoulder like a game warden, began to dance. Somebody wound up an old victrola, and they all sang along so that the tavern rang with their merrymaking.

A white-bearded old man unwrapped a roast chicken from a piece of newspaper and offered some to anybody who was hungry. In a few moments it was torn to bits.

Then more old men started dancing. One of them was dancing with his shotgun while he gnawed a drumstick.

The boys were being guarded by an old man with a shiny Mannlicher on his lap. He cocked it, showing he was prepared to shoot if necessary. He wore a brown oilcloth coat that was supposed to look like leather. He was eating blood sausage, but he had no teeth, so he had to mush it up with his gums, along with chunks of bread. Laboriously, he pushed each mouthful out of its sausage casing and into his mouth. Then he carefully folded the paper in which the food had been wrapped.

If there was water, the second boy thought to himself, I'd jump up and drink it out of that paper on his lap.

The first boy felt drowsy. His foot was throbbing. It was so hot in the room that he dozed off. The pain soon woke him. It was as though his foot had taken on a life of its own.

"Danny . . . , " the second boy murmured.

"No talking!" barked the old man immediately. Then he said it again: *"Nicht sprechen!"* His mouth was full. *"Kein Wort!"*

The mayor called them in. The old man with the Mannlicher stood behind them. The mayor sat behind his desk in his belted leather coat. There was a framed picture of a young soldier on the wall. There was a black band across the corner of the picture.

Danny understood German better than Manny. He had just one answer when the mayor questioned them about where they came from, who they were, and what they were doing. He told the mayor they were from Dresden. Their papers had been burned during the February nineteenth air raids, and they hadn't been able to get new ones from Prague yet. They'd walked because they didn't want to be a strain on the Reich's railroads.

"We haven't harmed anybody," put in the second boy.

He told the mayor he could phone the Prague police and check. They'd tell him that he and Danny had lived at Jungmann Square 4, across the street from the newspaper stand and the Italian ice-cream parlor. Unless there'd been some changes made in their absence.

They claimed they'd lost their papers and personal belongings in Dresden, where they'd been sent to work in a war plant.

"*Total einsatz,*" Manny volunteered.

The mayor didn't believe a word of it. At first, Manny had claimed he didn't know any German, and now it gushed out of him like blood. The mayor made notes on a scratch pad, then finally he told them to take their clothes off.

"Every stitch," he ordered and snickered like a billygoat while they undressed.

He held his nose.

"All right, get dressed," he laughed knowingly. "On the double."

"We haven't done anything to anybody," the second boy insisted.

"We didn't have a permit, so we couldn't take a train," the first boy said.

"We don't even know where we are," put in the second.

"You're in Rottau," said the mayor.

"I'm not circumcised, and they did it to Danny on account of an infection," said the second boy.

"It looks like they did it with a kitchen knife," said the mayor. "So that's how they maim you, hmm? So you have nowhere to hide. And then you go around maiming other people—here!" he pointed to his head. "And here!" he pointed to his pocket.

"We haven't maimed anybody," objected Manny.

"You've got just one minute to get your clothes on," said the mayor.

Danny's fingers were so clumsy, he had difficulty buttoning his pants.

"The motor patrol is coming for you at seven o'clock. They're going to take you to Karlsbad, where you will be brought before a court-martial. They'll decide what to do with you," the mayor told them.

"Get moving," ordered the old man with the Mannlicher.

The boys sat down on the bench again.

"We'll grab the sentry, Danny. . . ."

"Humph," replied the first boy.

"Don't forget to hang onto your stick!"

"*Ruhe!*" bawled the old man.

"Sit on the right hand side so you can jump out, Danny."

"I told you to keep quiet!" the old man repeated.

"I have something I want to tell the mayor," spoke up Manny.

"It's no use," the old man told him.

"They did it to Danny because of an infection. That's what I want to tell him."

So *Karlsbad*—Karlovy Vary—was that near! We must have been wandering around in circles. This was all Czech territory: Karlovy Vary—*Karlsbad, Rottau*—Rotava. Home, as Frank used to say, is a country where you're at home without having to take anybody else's home away from him. Frank had understood German better than they did. He knew Spanish, too, and English and Portuguese and Yiddish. His French was as good as if he'd been born in Monte Carlo. Yet with all those advantages, he'd stayed behind in the train that was supposed to be going to Dachau.

Frank had said, "There's no sense keeping count of those who do knuckle under. There are too many." We didn't knuckle under, Danny and I, the second boy told himself. The worse the circumstances, the less is forgiven.

The mayor went on about how, even though the war was almost over, they must not and would not be allowed to rule this country. The mayor feels at home here, too, he thought.

The mayor had a snout like a cucumber and a leathery face. He told them they mustn't be surprised if they were shot, considering that they had viciously attacked a German peasant woman and stolen bread, potatoes, milk, and coffee from her, not to mention all the other things they probably had on their consciences. On top of that, they hadn't obeyed orders to halt given by a German civil defense unit. Did they suppose they could fool them by taking several hours to walk a few hundred meters through the woods?

It was almost seven o'clock. There were antitank traps along the road, which had probably delayed the patrol.

The second boy looked down at Danny's feet. Those used to be his shoes. Before that, they'd belonged to Leonard. Danny smelled. He held his cap in his hands. The muscles and angles of his face had gone slack and his shoulders sagged. It was a slackness the second boy had seen before and it frightened him.

If I had Frank's watch now, I might sell it to one of those guys, Manny thought. A clock hung on the wall beside the old man, its brass pendulum swinging back and forth. It struck the half hours with a mellow, hollow tone.

Before his eyes, the second boy could see a door with a brass name-plate. The plate was bare. He placed his finger on the doorbell and pushed it. This was the place he always came back to, fearful that nobody would be there.

"Danny," he whispered.

"There's no point to it," the first boy replied at last.

The sun was sinking. The clock struck seven. It had a grand sound, as though it were summing up everything that had ever been and ever would be. The second boy listened to the clock strike, and he knew it would go on ticking for many years to come. Seven' o'clock would pass and eight o'clock, and in between the clock would chime to mark their passing. The clock had a mild tone. The bench they were sitting on was polished smooth as glass by thousands of backsides of farmers who would go forth at daybreak tomorrow to plough and sow and hunt and shoot and milk the cows, trying to make a paltry living and have a little fun. They'll say their prayers and have babies and fertilize the fields, building houses and killing game. The clock would go on telling time and striking the hours and half-hours—a hundred times, a thousand times— until the works break down and somebody buys another clock.

The pendulum swung back and forth. The sky darkened slowly. It was one of those lovely, fragrant evenings in early spring, layered with meaning. The darkness wrapped around it like some delicate fabric.

Now he was remembering the German hospital in Theresienstadt where he and Danny and Frank Bondy had worked, digging trenches for the anti-aircraft shelters.

At noon, Frank brought over a jug of soup from the ghetto. It was thin slop, but it was better than nothing, since they were only fed once every twenty-four hours and it was hard work.

He had been standing in line one time when Frank was dishing out the soup. He had pushed in front of somebody else and Frank gently motioned him to the end of the line. Frank's hands were elegant and immaculately clean in those days. With a kindly smile he went on ladling out the soup conscientiously, taking his time so everybody got a fair share from the bottom.

At last, there were only the two of them in front of the vat. Frank poured a ladle full of soup into Manny's canteen. When he stepped back, Frank touched his elbow with his elegant, clean hand. Because of his upbringing, experience, and principles, there were probably very few germs on Frank's hands. Then he quickly gave Manny another helping of soup, as brimming as the first.

Something had broken. The beautiful confidence in how things would be someday—because there were still people in the world who thought it was important—had silently crumbled, falling apart like a house of cards.

Nobody knew. Frank should have been proud of himself and pleased. Nobody had even noticed that second helping. Frank peered into the kettle to see how much he had left.

The construction of a pure, just human being, convinced that the way things are right now is simply a temporary phenomenon, was poured out with that second ladleful of soup, with Manny's second helping.

Frank smiled paternally, as if to say, "Don't play dumb." And he sent him away.

It was as though he was bragging that, if you were even slightly clever, you could save more than anybody could imagine from the servings you gave to twelve ditch diggers.

Everything evaporated, turning into muck and filth which was choking the world and from which you could never escape as long as you lived. He stank of that filthy world himself.

The mayor came out of his office. He passed by them without a glance. Danny was asleep. He looked as if he were already dead. But he hadn't died. Now and then, his body twitched and his legs would jerk, like a dead fish. The mayor said something to the older men in the tavern. They laughed and then, for some reason, applauded.

"*Herr Bürgermeister* wants to talk to me," announced the old man with the Mannlicher.

The second boy nudged the first.

"We'll grab the guard, right?"

"Sure."

"Swear you will, Danny?"

"I swear," he promised in a flat voice.

The second boy was thinking that maybe if they looked sufficiently miserable, the guards might not tie their hands. The clock struck the half-hour. This must be that same beautiful feeling that comes over you when you're going to die, Manny decided. Danny was ready to die right now, he told himself.

He could hear the mayor talking. "Take them out in front of the building at seven sharp," he was saying.

"*Zum Befehl, Herr Bürgermeister,*" said the man in the old officer's uniform.

"You know what to do."

"*Jawohl, Herr Bürgermeister.*"

13

Now it flashed through the second boy's mind that no patrol was coming, that the old men were going to finish the job by themselves. Briefly, he could see an image of the two of them lying on the road in their rags, between the woods and the tavern. They'd been shot.

The old men also looked like crippled, helpless birds. But at the same time, in comparison with the two boys, they still had some strength left, despite their feebleness. But it was a good thing they didn't beat or kick or mistreat the boys in all the ways they knew only too well. But they were going to shoot them. They would probably shoot them together. They were still capable of shooting them both at the same time. If it had to be, it'd be good if it happened fast, at least, and at the same time.

Suddenly he had a vision of that evening in Meuslowitz when the Germans had started shooting people, and everyone else had to watch.

Frank Bondy said that there was nothing new in what was happening. He whispered as though he were going back to the pyramids, to some ancient canals full of sand, as though the camps were one with the pyramids and those canals, their bottoms covered with the muck of flesh and blood of people who no longer lived and who were yet to come, as if the killings were simply part of a single current—what was, what is, and what is yet to be.

A woman walked through the hall into the tavern. She had blond hair, blue eyes, and pale skin. She wore a black kerchief over her head.

She reminded Manny of the woman who had given them the bread, the woman they didn't kill. Danny stared at his ailing foot.

The woman was wearing a leather coat like the mayor's. She was probably his wife.

She attracted him in the same sort of way that Frank Bondy had been attracted by the Polish girl who had been gang-raped. That lovely thing that's only found in women.

In his mind's eye, he could see the double bunks in Theresienstadt, and he remembered the first time he had gone there with a girl. It had formerly been stables, what the Germans called Jägerkaserne. Men brought girls with bellies big as leeches there.

The girl he went with later did anything men wanted, but she wouldn't allow them to go inside her. That was because she was scared of getting pregnant. She made an exception with him, though, and later with Zdenek Pick and little Milan Oppenheimer. Actually, it had been his father who had pushed him into it. He kept asking a little too often whether he'd ever had a woman for himself.

Maybe Father had known that something like this was going to happen, that the clock would strike and the order would be given to take them out in front of the building, just as the sun was setting.

Maybe he had known that when the clock finished striking, the signal would be given for the German rifles to be cocked, ready to fire.

The clear chime of the clock reminded him of the best things in his life. Or of the things he'd wanted to do someday. The things Father had known.

The girl had been kind. She put her hand between his legs and caressed him so sweetly that he forgot his embarrassment and apprehen-

sion that he'd be incapable. She led him on, the way you lead a child into a forest he's been frightened of at first but later comes to enjoy.

He wasn't the first boy who had been with her that afternoon, and he noticed how moist she was to start with.

"It has a sweet taste," she told him. "It smells like fresh-cut grass in the evening." She went on: "You're like a young horse. You'll have luck with girls."

Nevertheless, the boy who came out from behind the curtain was different from the one who had gone in. He didn't remember everything that had happened. He didn't even wait for Pick and Oppenheimer. There were a lot worse things you could get in exchange for an ounce of margarine.

Right afterward, the whole world felt like one big moist, juicy, furry crotch.

When he left her, he went into the toilets where everybody else went when they wanted to weep. Then, later that night, he did it by himself, and it was almost better than the first time.

The stars had shone brightly that night. He was just as alone as everybody else was on this planet out in the middle of the universe and, even if they aren't alone, they feel as if they are.

Next day, he'd met his father walking down the main street of the ghetto with the same girl and another man. Dad introduced him as her husband.

After a while, the woman came out of the tavern. She had the calm expression of someone who has had plenty of sleep.

Her eyes reminded him of two brown almonds.

I've seen eyes like that before, Manny thought to himself. Leonard had that kind of eyes. So did Zdenek Pick. And little Milan Oppenheimer. And Frank Bondy had eyes like that.

And then he realized that they weren't eyes at all—they were the crows that had followed them through the forest. He was almost glad they wouldn't have to go back to the woods anymore, even though it had been a refuge. He could feel the woman's eyes on him, and he almost expected them to peck his own eyes out.

There was somebody else who had eyes like that. My God, Mother! For a second, everything went black. He couldn't move. Not even his little finger. He'd never felt so helpless in his life. Then he opened his eyes and moved one finger.

That was when the clock began to strike the hour of seven—six deep-throated clangs and then the seventh, which would tip the balance of their lives toward the other side.

The mayor stepped out on the porch in front of his office. The woman moved next to him. His face looked as though it had been molded out of an old leather belt.

"Stand up!" said the man in the old officer's uniform and the hunter's hat with the bristle.

The second boy helped the first to his feet.

"Take off your clothes. Just leave your shoes. Fold your things and take them under your arms."

When they were naked, the taller boy in his shoes and the smaller with his feet wrapped in rags, they just stood there. Danny held onto his stick, and the second boy's arm was around his neck.

"Take them out in front," the mayor told the old man.

"*Gehen sie,*" ordered the old man.

The mayor and his wife stared at the two naked boys. Outside, the sun was setting. It grew dark slowly. Another wave rushed in on Manny, and Danny was in it, too. He knew he'd stick it out this time. He was glad he was with Danny.

The woman looked at their bodies as though she were searching for something she couldn't find.

Both of them paused when they got to the front of the building. The second boy gripped the first boy's arm more tightly so he wouldn't trip and fall.

We've said all there is to say by now, Manny decided. Maybe Danny will be the first, because he can't walk by himself. Danny couldn't even stand alone.

The rest of the old men stood in front of the building in a horseshoe formation, their rifles lowered.

"Take them into the woods," said the mayor. The woman was smiling slightly.

"Prepare to fire," commanded the old man.

There was the familiar clicking and clatter as the guns were cocked.

Manny limped forward, keeping one arm around Danny's shoulder. But by now he was so tired that it was all the same to him. He clutched their clothes under his other arm. He waited quite calmly to find out which one of them would be shot first. He didn't look around. Danny didn't either.

This is where it ought to happen, the second boy thought to himself. One last order. Then those cracking noises. We'll only hear the first ones.

"It's good," he said. "This way, it's good."

Manny could feel the earth under his feet, the moss and rocks and stones. He gazed off into the woods, and he saw Danny out of the corner of his eye. He was waiting to hear the crack, multiplied by as many as there were old men. That noise would contain everything inside it that had ever happened—the forest, their footsteps, other sounds. Tension, drowned in tiredness, was like walking while half-asleep.

Nobody would be able to follow them from now on. Beyond the shadows of the forest where it was already night, morning would come only with the sun. They did not look back, but stared straight ahead, above the treetops. They were alone.

"Danny . . . , " whispered the second boy.

The first boy raised his eyes and looked at him.

"Everything's all right," he whispered. That was the last thing he said.

Still nothing happened. The second boy had no idea what time it was. He had no more visions of things that had happened to him before. Nothing. All that was left was the thought of what might happen—where would those two bullets go? And then what would not be here anymore? The fear of what will happen and, at the same time, the desire for freedom. The foreboding with which one senses his life or oncoming death like an extended hand—only to take hold of and press—or a word, a whisper or breath, a wink of the eye—the hope for the unknown, distant happiness—within reach—in front of one, within one's self.

They were about twenty steps away from the building now. The second boy pressed the first boy closer. Danny squeezed Manny's shoulder, too. Both boys were bareheaded. A wave of resignation passed between them and a shared realization of where they were going, of the awesomeness of what they were walking into.

They were two small, naked bodies in shoes and rags, one tall, one smaller, hanging on tightly to each other.

But they still heard nothing.

It only came later, when the stars were shining high above their heads, after they had disappeared into the darkness under the trees at the edge of the forest. They pushed deeper into the tangle of low branches, and it was as though it had begun all over again and would always end the way it was ending now—once, twice, a hundred times. As often as they tried. In the moldy smell among the roots and bushes and stones and moss and pine needles and, even if they turned around, the mayor's brick house and the tavern wouldn't be there anymore. That was where the path stopped, where the woods grew dense again.

They faded into the night, like a slim double shadow. The stillness was not silenced.

✿

Jewish Lives

IDA FINK
A Scrap of Time and Other Stories

LISA FITTKO
Solidarity and Treason: Resistance and Exile, 1933–1940

RICHARD GLAZAR
Trap with a Green Fence: Survival in Treblinka

ARNOŠT LUSTIG
Children of the Holocaust